LIBRARY OF SOUTHERN CIVILIZATION

Lewis P. Simpson, Editor

Beulah

Beulah

AUGUSTA JANE EVANS

Edited, with an Introduction, by
ELIZABETH FOX-GENOVESE

LOUISIANA STATE UNIVERSITY PRESS
BATON ROUGE AND LONDON

Manufactured in the United States of America
First printing
01 00 99 98 97 96 95 94 93 92 5 4 3 2 1

Designer: Laura Roubique Gleason
Typeface: Garamond #3
Typesetter: G&S Typesetters, Inc.
Printer and binder: Thomson-Shore, Inc.

Library of Congress Cataloging-in-Publication Data
Evans, Augusta J. (Augusta Jane), 1835–1909.
Beulah / Augusta Jane Evans ; edited with an introduction by Elizabeth Fox-Genovese.
p. cm. — (Library of Southern civilization)
ISBN 0-8071-1749-8 (alk. paper). ISBN 0-8071-1750-1 (pbk.: alk. paper).
I. Fox-Genovese, Elizabeth, 1941– II. Title. III. Series.
PS3332.B48 1992
813′3—dc20 91-44959
CIP

The paper in this book meets the guidelines for permanence and durability of the Committee on Production Guidelines for Book Longevity of the Council on Library Resources. ∞

CONTENTS

A Note on Augusta Jane Evans / ix

Introduction / xi

Beulah / 1

A NOTE ON AUGUSTA JANE EVANS

Augusta Jane Evans was born on May 8, 1835, in Columbus, Georgia, slightly a year after the marriage of Matt Evans and Sarah Howard, who came from two old and respected southern families. She began life in affluent surroundings, but by 1839 an economic depression, combined with her father's improvidence, had forced the family into bankruptcy. During the spring of 1845, the Evanses, who now had five children, set out for Texas. San Antonio, where they settled, offered more danger than profit, and in 1849 they moved to Alabama, settling in Mobile, where Augusta was to spend much of the remainder of her life.

Upon the family's move to Mobile, Augusta was briefly enrolled in a private school, but soon withdrew because of ill health. Throughout her early childhood she was educated primarily by her mother, who now had eight children to contend with. Sarah Howard Evans apparently instilled a deep love of intellectual life in her oldest daughter, who, thanks to enthusiasm and a photographic memory, read widely and voraciously throughout her youth. According to family legend, at age fifteen Evans wrote her first novel, *Inez, a Tale of the Alamo,* which drew upon her own experiences of reversed fortunes, migration, and life in Texas, and she presented *Inez* as a surprise to her father on Christmas Day of 1854. The following year it was published, but neither sold widely nor earned the young author critical acclaim.

Beulah, published in 1859, did both. Its extensive sales established Evans as a wealthy woman, and its flattering reception secured her reputation as a woman of letters. On the eve of the Civil War, she was contemplating a trip to Europe and an engagement to James Reed Spaulding, an editor of the New York *Courier and Enquirer,* who had been so taken with *Beulah* that he had persevered in meeting its author. The outbreak of war cut short these and other plans, and Evans, an ardent southern nationalist, served as a nurse in a hospital in Mobile. She also pursued an extensive correspondence that included letters to statesmen and military men, notably J. L. M. Curry and General P. G. T. Beauregard, from whom she requested advice on her work and to whom she in turn offered advice on politics and warfare. And, in 1864, she published *Macaria; or, Altars of Sacrifice,* in which she simultaneously defended female independence and the southern cause.

After the war, Evans returned to the style and themes that had earned *Beulah* its success and, in 1867, published *St. Elmo,* the most popular of all of her novels. In December of 1868, shortly after the death of her father, she married a sixty-year-old widower, Lorenzo Madison Wilson. At the time of the marriage, he ranked among the wealthier men in Mobile, an officer and director of the city's principal bank, a director of the Mobile and Montgomery Railroad, and a leading stockholder of an important streetcar line. His wealth, together with her own, ensured Evans an extremely comfortable life and the ability to help others. Although she continued to produce a novel almost every decade until her death on March 9, 1909, she devoted much of her time to family, close friends, and favorite charities.

Little marks Evans' life as especially dramatic or eventful. Like the lives of other mid-nineteenth-century women novelists, hers primarily consisted in a web of personal relations with family and close friends. Although she never had children of her own, she was ever interested in her nieces and nephews. She nurtured an abiding love for flowers, evidenced in the descriptions of nature that run through her novels, and during her marriage devoted considerable time to her luxurious gardens. But throughout her life runs a passionate concern with religion, politics, and the life of the mind.

All evidence suggests that from her earliest years she read enthusiastically and thoughtfully, engaging the ideas she encountered in books, testing her mind against the most distinguished of her age. Rarely, if ever, did she question her own ability, as a woman, to match intelligence and wits with the brightest and the best. But that commitment to women's capacity for intellectual brilliance and accomplishment always coexisted with a no less passionate commitment to social and political conservatism. A southern nationalist to her core, she defended southern values as the embodiment of a healthy social conservatism that alone could contain the dangers of modern skepticism and materialism. And, notwithstanding her considerable personal ambition as a female intellectual and successful writer, she insisted that social stability required that women accept their prescribed domestic roles.

INTRODUCTION

"Thou shalt not more be termed Forsaken; neither shall thy land any more be termed Desolate: but thou shalt be called Hephzibah and thy land Beulah: for the Lord delighteth in thee, and thy land shall be married." Early in Augusta Jane Evans' novel *Beulah,* the thirteen-year-old orphaned protagonist, Beulah Benton, responds to the bemused query about her name from Dr. Guy Hartwell, whom she has just met over the sickbed of an infant she is tending: "You need not tell me it is unsuitable; I know it; I feel it. Beulah! Beulah! Oh my father! I have neither sunshine nor flowers, nor hear the singing of birds, nor the voice of the turtle. You ought to have called me MARAH."[1] Hartwell responds, searching her face, "You have read the 'Pilgrim's Progress' then?" (35). Since Beulah does not answer him, we never know for sure, although we do know that Evans had read it. But there can be no doubt that Beulah has read her Bible and knows not merely the reference to Beulah in Isaiah but also the references to Marah. In Exodus 15, she would have read of how the children of Israel, under the leadership of Moses, celebrated their successful crossing of the Red Sea, singing of their Lord's strength, of how he "*is* a man of war" and how he "hath dashed in pieces the enemy." But then the Israelites went into the wilderness, where for three days they found no water. "And when they came to Marah, they could not drink of the waters of Marah, for they *were* bitter: therefore the name of it was called Marah." Beulah would also have known the passage in Ruth in

1. Isa. 62:4; Augusta J. Evans, *Beulah: A Novel,* 35 herein. All references are to the current edition, which is based on the 1900 edition published by the Federal Book Company in New York. See note 33.

which Naomi tells the people of Bethlehem, "Call me not Naomi, call me Mara: for the Almighty hath dealt very bitterly with me."[2]

Beulah's name governs the action and meaning of a novel that chronicles the anxious and conflicted coming-of-age of a young southern woman in the late 1850s. The external action remains as circumscribed as a typical southern woman's life, primarily moving through various domestic interiors in a single southern city. But the internal action concerns all of the great theological, moral, and intellectual questions of the mid-nineteenth century. And to the conventional woman's drama of the appropriate claims of duty and ambition, independence and submission, it joins the framing drama of science and faith. Evans thus boldly and unapologetically locates the principal moral and intellectual struggles of her day in the mind of a woman. *Beulah* is a classic *Bildungsroman*—the narrative of a young woman's education and successful search for identity and a place in the world. But it should also be read as an allegory of Evans' own reflections on the role of women and the future of the South.

The publication of *Beulah* in 1859 fell at the end of the tumultuous decade of political disintegration that followed the Compromise of 1850. That mounting national confrontation over slavery and states' rights coincided with a coming-of-age of American women's fiction that itself manifested increasingly strong sectional and ideological allegiances.[3] In particular, southern women writers took the publication of *Uncle Tom's Cabin* as a personal affront. While fathers and brothers struggled over Kansas and Nebraska, women turned their pens to the defense of southern culture and the women who represented it.[4] Caroline Gilman, Mary Eastman, Marion Har-

2. Exod. 15:23; Ruth 1:20.

3. See Mary Kelly, *Private Woman, Public Stage: Literary Domesticity in Nineteenth-Century America* (New York, 1984); Jane Tompkins, *Sensational Designs: The Cultural Work of American Fiction, 1790–1860* (New York, 1985). See also Helen Waite Papashvily, *All the Happy Endings: A Study of the Domestic Novel in America, the Women Who Wrote It, the Women Who Read It, in the Nineteenth Century* (New York, 1956); Ann Douglas, *The Feminization of American Culture* (New York, 1977); Nina Baym, *Woman's Fiction: A Guide to Novels by and About Women in America, 1820–1870* (Ithaca, N.Y., 1978); Joyce W. Warren, *The American Narcissus: Individualism and Women in Nineteenth-Century American Fiction* (New Brunswick, N.J., 1989); Fred Lewis Pattee, *The Feminine Fifties* (New York, 1940); Alexander Cowie, *The Rise of the American Novel* (New York, 1948); Herbert Ross Brown, *The Sentimental Novel in America, 1789–1860* (Durham, 1940); E. Douglas Branch, *The Sentimental Years, 1836–1860* (New York, 1934).

4. See especially L.S.M. [Louisa S. McCord], "Uncle Tom's Cabin," *Southern Quarterly Review*, XXIII (January, 1853), 81–120. On Louisa McCord and on southern women's re-

land, Caroline Lee Hentz, Louisa S. McCord, and Mrs. Henry R. Schoolcraft rose enthusiastically to what they perceived as Harriet Beecher Stowe's wanton assault on everything they respected and held dear.[5] Notwithstanding considerable variation in specifics of plot and character, all focused on demonstrating that slavery as a social system represented a form of social organization superior to the system of free labor. Thus Marion Harland, in *Alone,* insisted that the "slave lies down at night, every want supplied, his family as well cared for as himself; not a thought of to-morrow! He is secure of a home and maintenance, without disturbing himself as to the manner in which it is to be obtained. Can the same be said of the menial classes in any other country under the sun?"[6] A distinct tradition of southern women's domestic fiction was developing apace with rising sectional tensions.

Augusta Jane Evans belonged to that tradition and, arguably, took second place to none as a southern polemicist. Yet, with the notable exception of *Macaria; or, Altars of Sacrifice,* her novels barely mention slavery, and even *Macaria* does not so much focus on slavery as on southern political values.[7] The few slaves who figure in *Beulah* play minor roles at best, appearing as necessary but unremarkable features of southern society. For Evans, the de-

---

sponse to *Uncle Tom's Cabin* in general, see my books *Within the Plantation Household: Black and White Women of the Old South* (Chapel Hill, 1988) and *Ghosts and Memories: Fictions of Black and White Southern Women* (Charlottesville, 1992). On the various women writers of the South, see, among many, Kelly, *Private Woman, Public Stage;* Robert LeRoy Hilldrup, "Cold War Against the Yankees in the Antebellum Literature of Southern Women," *North Carolina Historical Review,* XXXI (July, 1954), 370–84; Jeannette Reid Tandy, "Pro-Slavery Propaganda in American Fiction of the Fifties," *South Atlantic Quarterly,* XXI (January, 1922), 41–50, (April, 1922), 170–78; Elizabeth Moss, *Domestic Novelists in the Old South: Defenders of Southern Culture* (Baton Rouge, 1992); Amy Thompson McCandless, "Concepts of Patriarchy in the Popular Novels of Antebellum Southern Women," *Studies in Popular Culture,* II, No. 2 (1987), 1–15. Anne Goodwyn Jones, in *Tomorrow Is Another Day: The Woman Writer in the South, 1859–1936* (Baton Rouge, 1981), discusses Augusta Jane Evans but not the antebellum tradition as a whole.

5. See, among many, Caroline Gilman, *Recollections of a Southern Matron* (New York, 1858), 107; Mrs. Mary E. Eastman, *Aunt Phyllis' Cabin; or, Southern Life as It Is* (1852; rpr. New York, 1968), 93; Marion Harland, *Alone* (Richmond, 1854) and *Moss-side* (New York, 1857); Caroline Lee Hentz, *The Planter's Northern Bride* (1854; rpr. Chapel Hill, 1970); Mrs. Henry R. Schoolcraft, *The Black Gauntlet: A Tale of Plantation Life in South Carolina,* in *Plantation Life: The Narratives of Mrs. Henry Rowe Schoolcraft* (1852–60; rpr. New York, 1969).

6. Harland, *Alone,* 116.

7. See Drew Gilpin Faust's introduction to the new edition of *Macaria; or, Altars of Sacrifice* (Baton Rouge, 1992).

fense of southern values transcended a narrow defense of slavery, the beneficent effects of which even she occasionally doubted.[8]

In *Beulah,* Evans infuses the southern domestic tradition with a new concern with the inner lives of female characters, apparently reflecting the influence of Charlotte Brontë as well as her own Methodism. *Beulah* became a near best seller, with 22,000 copies printed in the first nine months, and won widespread critical acclaim. It probably owed much of its success to the growing taste for the "psychological" or "subjective" novel. In June of 1855, a reviewer in the *Southern Literary Messenger* had noted that "the most successful novels of the present day have been those in which the trials and sorrows, the love and despondency, the reverses and triumphs of this life, as they are experienced by women, are thrown in an autobiographical form before a sympathizing world." According to this reviewer, Charlotte Brontë had initiated the form but had since had many successors.[9]

Evans had probably read the review in the *Southern Literary Messenger.* She had certainly read Charlotte Brontë. Indeed, one of her few openly hostile reviewers in 1859 dismissed *Beulah* as a "'very humble and feeble and intellectually unremunerative' imitation of *Jane Eyre.*" The male reviewer for the Baltimore *Daily Exchange* had a special reason to be annoyed, for according to John Derby, *Beulah*'s publisher and Evans' friend, he had read the novel in manuscript and advised Appleton's against publication.[10] Other reviewers responded more favorably, and overall, the response was remarkably appreciative, especially in view of the long pages devoted to difficult philosophical speculation.

In a brief notice, the reviewer for *De Bow's Review,* a journal devoted more to political economy than belles lettres, warmly praised both novelist and novel. Evans, identified as a charming young lady of Mobile, was commended for "sprightliness," "depth of intellect," "a wide and varied range of information," and "much boldness in the discussion of social and philosophi-

8. See, for example, Augusta J. Evans to Hon. J. L. M. Curry, July 13, 1863, in J. L. M. Curry Papers, Library of Congress. Evans entertained the idea that slavery might have a deleterious effect on the character of southern women because the constant attendance of servants deprived them of exercise.

9. Nina Baym, *Novels, Readers, and Reviewers: Responses to Fiction in Antebellum America* (Ithaca, 1984), 94; William Fidler, *Augusta Evans Wilson: A Biography* (University, Ala., 1951), 79; Jones, *Tomorrow Is Another Day,* 61; *Southern Literary Messenger* review, quoted in Baym, *Novels, Readers, and Reviewers,* 94–95.

10. Baltimore *Daily Exchange* review, quoted in Fidler, *Augusta Evans Wilson,* 79; J. C. Derby, *Fifty Years Among Authors, Books, and Publishers* (New York, 1884), 390.

cal subjects." *Beulah,* he wrote, "may be considered one of the best American novels." It details the interesting history "of a very gifted and ambitious woman . . . who earnestly strove to discharge the duties of her position, and consecrated her talents to the service of the Good, the True, and the beautiful." In another brief review, the *Methodist Quarterly Review* compared *Beulah* favorably to George Eliot's *Adam Bede,* which Evans herself disliked, and praised it for exposing "the baseless and unsatisfying character of rationalism—the exaggerated subjective religion of some of our 'great thinkers'—as a substitute for the truth as it is in Jesus."[11]

The *Southern Literary Messenger* devoted seven pages to *Beulah* and praised it highly, especially for its contribution to a distinct southern literature. The literature of the North, the reviewer contemptuously noted, reveals in "its threadbare character" the "region of its birth," which "speaks rather from the head than from the heart." The South, in contrast, was beginning to produce a literature that within a few years was "destined to startle the world." Calling *Beulah* "brilliant," this reviewer commended it for its characters, "elegant diction, refined sentiment, and lofty philosophy." But he also criticized it for being too much a "modern novel" and especially for "its want of geographical location." Admittedly, it is set "in the Southern portion of our country, and those knowing the history of the writer have but little difficulty in determining the State and the city, but these nowhere appear in the book." Less ambiguously, Marion Harland pronounced *Beulah* "the best work of fiction ever published by a Southern writer," indeed the best by any American woman writer. And James Spaulding, who reviewed *Beulah* enthusiastically for the New York *Courier and Enquirer,* was so taken with it that he called upon the author. He told Derby that Evans obviously "knew what she was writing about."[12] Evans and Spaulding soon became engaged, although after Lincoln's election they broke off the engagement because of irreconcilable political views.

Evans' willingness to sacrifice personal happiness to her political commitments testifies to the depths of her allegiance to the South. In 1860, following Spaulding's visit to Mobile and the end of their engagement, she wrote

11. "Editorial Miscellany," *De Bow's Review,* XVII (October, 1859), 491; "*Beulah,*" *Methodist Quarterly Review,* XX (January, 1860), 112.

12. "*Beulah,*" *Southern Literary Messenger,* XXXI (October, 1860), 241, 242–43, 243–44; Marion Harland, publisher's advertisement of *Beulah* in New York *World,* June 14, 1860, quoted in Fidler, *Augusta Evans Wilson,* 80; James Spaulding, New York *Courier and Enquirer* review, quoted in Derby, *Fifty Years,* 392. It seems likely that Evans subsequently used an adapted account of her meeting with Spaulding in *St. Elmo.*

with a "*very sad heart*" and considerable outrage to her aunt, Mary Howard Jones, in Milledgeville, Georgia, protesting the rumors that were circulating (presumably as a result of her aunt's indiscretion) about her purported engagement to Mr. Spaulding, a "Black Republican." She had told her aunt in strictest confidence of a tentative engagement and could not bear to have it publicly known in Milledgeville that she might marry "such a creature." And by early 1861, with her political passions at white heat, she wrote to Mrs. L. Virginia French angrily refusing to have her name appended to the antisecessionist memorial that Mrs. French was circulating among southern women for presentation to the Georgia legislature. Unlike Mrs. French, who had "espoused the *Union* cause," Evans wrote, "I am an earnest and most uncompromising Secessionist" who believed "prompt and separate state action . . . to be the *only* door of escape from the worse than Egyptian bondage of Black Republicanism."[13]

Evans' interest in politics had apparently developed early. Her first novel, *Inez, a Tale of the Alamo,* published when she was twenty but mostly written, according to family lore, when she was fifteen, focused on the confrontation between Texans and Mexicans on the eve of annexation. Even then Evans covertly engaged in a defense of southern values, improbably likening the aggression of the Mexicans against the Texans to that of the North against the South. Her gothic portrayal of a villainous Jesuit priest's sinister campaign to gain control of the souls and fortunes of unsuspecting Protestants was intended obliquely to represent the intentions of fanatical abolitionists upon southern values. Even the most sympathetic critics have dismissed *Inez* as at the best an interesting youthful effort, but amidst its melodramatic excesses lay the themes that would preoccupy Evans throughout her career: women's identities and roles, southern values, and religion.

Between the publication of *Inez* in 1855 and that of *Beulah* in 1859, Evans found the focus and voice that would, in one way or another, characterize all of her subsequent novels.[14] During those decisive years, she experienced a searing crisis of faith from which, with the help of a young minister, William Harriss, she emerged the devout Methodist that she remained

13. Augusta Jane Evans to Mary Howard Jones, November 26, December 4, 1860, in Benning/Jones Collection, Chattahoochee Valley Local & Oral History Archives, Columbus College Library, Columbus, Georgia; Augusta Jane Evans to Mrs. V. French, January 13, 1861, *ibid.*

14. *Macaria; or, Altars of Sacrifice* (1864), *St. Elmo* (1866), *Vashti* (1869), *Infelice* (1875), *At the Mercy of Tiberius* (1887), *A Speckled Bird* (1902), and *Devota* (1907), which was a brief novella but published as an independent book at her publisher's insistence.

throughout her life.[15] A youthful confrontation with Catholicism did much to provoke the crisis, but so, doubtless, did her extensive reading in literature and philosophy. *Beulah* provides a fictional account of her experience from the safe remove of her own dearly won religious conviction.

Beulah's central plot follows the familiar conventions of domestic fiction, which Alexander Cowie has teasingly, although not unsympathetically, summarized: "First, take a young and not-too-pretty child about ten years old. Boys are possible, but girls are to be preferred, for the author and the increasing majority of women readers will be more at home in the detail. Make sure that the child is, or shortly will be, an orphan." If by chance the child's mother is living, she must be gently put to death. Her father will, of course, already have perished, and if not must now be married to a shallow, fashionable woman. The heroine, accordingly, falls to the untender mercies of a stepmother or a cruel housekeeper but benefits from the tempering influence of some other worthy woman, who "is destined to die about two-thirds of the way through the book of badly-diagnosed tuberculosis." The story can end after the mentor's edifying death but is better carried on "in order that the heroine may be menaced and morosely loved by a proud, handsome, moody, Rochester-like man aged about thirty who has traveled and sinned (very vaguely) in the Orient." Shocked by the heroine's refusal of his hand in marriage, the tempestuous hero again departs for foreign parts, preferably the Orient, whence he returns chastened, wealthy, and maybe even a minister. Meanwhile, the heroine has shed "her fantastic notions of female independence" and come to recognize that "a woman's greatest glory is in wifely submission."[16]

In conformity with this model, *Beulah* traces the formative decade in the life of a young woman, opening with Beulah Benton's entrance into adolescence at not quite fourteen and concluding with her marriage at twenty-four. At the outset, Beulah is indeed living in an orphanage, from which she is rapidly sent forth to take up uncongenial duties as a nursemaid. In quick succession fate deprives her of her last remaining relative, her beloved younger sister, Lilly, and provides her with the occasion to meet the wealthy, morose, and unmarried Guy Hartwell, who takes her into his home as a

15. We have little specific information about her life and thoughts during these years. The main evidence of her crisis of faith is presented by her biographer, William Fidler, who read the letters between Evans and the Reverend Mr. Harriss. Those letters have since disappeared from circulation, and I was unable to consult them.

16. Cowie, *Rise of the American Novel,* 413, 414.

protégé. But as she matures, Beulah embarks on the path of skepticism and determines to establish her independence from Hartwell by becoming a self-supporting teacher and writer. Only after years of lonely wrestling with doubt does she finally regain her faith, discover that she loves Hartwell, and decide that, if he returns safely from the Orient, to which he had fled following her repeated rejections of his attentions and gifts, she will marry him. He does, and the novel concludes with her resolution to convert him to her faith.

The formal similarities to *Jane Eyre* are striking: Beulah, like Jane, begins as an orphan who is taken into the home of the older man she will ultimately marry; Hartwell bears a strong resemblance to Edward Rochester; Beulah, like Jane, addresses her suitor as "sir," and he addresses her as "child"; Beulah, like Jane, is courted by an apparently suitable man, whom she rejects even though she has already rejected Hartwell. Both orphaned heroines struggle to earn their living, cope with the arrogant dismissals of fashionable society, and experience a difficult coming-of-age, including a search for personal independence. Evans also followed Charlotte Brontë in exploring the dynamics of female strength and independence without overtly challenging the social structures that hedged women in. But Evans was much less conflicted than Brontë seems to have been about the value of those structures and the dangers of individualism.

Most likely, Evans took *Jane Eyre* as a model, not least because, for both financial and personal reasons, she sought to appeal to a broad female readership. But she departed from *Jane Eyre* in primarily focusing on her protagonist's spiritual crisis. The success of *Beulah* is all the more remarkable because of the stringent intellectual demands that it makes upon its readers. Long passages in the novel more closely resemble an intellectual tract than a domestic fiction, and Evans' quasi-exhibitionist displays of erudition led some uncharitable critics to complain that she simply collected facts from an encyclopedia. Even Mary Forrest, who admired Evans' work, admitted that "Beulah Benton and Guy Hartwell are much more familiar with Carlyle's 'Herr Teufelsdrockh' than with Ovid's 'Art of Love.' They make a grim pair of lovers enough, and throw into spasms of impatience all who are wading through 'ontology,' 'psychology,' 'eclecticism,' etc. . . . but they . . . are in keeping with the austere, determinate character of the book." That austerity, Forrest insisted, derived from the most worthy of purposes, namely Evans' determination to wage war against skepticism, "the Upas tree of the age."[17]

17. Derby, *Fifty Years,* 396–97; Mary Forrest, *Women of the South Distinguished in Literature* (New York, 1861), 331–32.

Throughout the novel, Beulah's story intertwines with the stories of an array of other characters to illuminate her own struggles and temptations. But the central dynamic remains Beulah's personal journey through doubt into faith—through the thickets of nineteenth-century science and skepticism finally to end upon the rock of Methodist conviction. Since Beulah's ultimate victory over doubt results in her apparent acceptance of subordination within marriage, some modern feminist critics read the novel as a narrative of thwarted female independence. Thus Anne Goodwyn Jones, one of the most thoughtful critics of southern women's writing, concludes that in *Beulah* "the prescription (for individual female growth) does turn to protest and finally, depressingly, to capitulation." [18] For Jones, Evans' commitment to the southern social order and to woman's allotted role within it should be understood as a mask. In this perspective, the true life of the novel lies in Beulah's assertion of her independence, and her renunciation of it must be seen as a betrayal.

Evans' contemporaries read it differently. Many readers responded with as much enthusiasm as Fannie Page Hume, who noted in her diary, "I devoured 'BEULAH' this morning till it was time to dress for Mr. Smith's." [19] Countless other women who, like Hume, were struggling to understand their specific vocation as women, found Beulah's struggle inspiring. Few, if any, of Evans' late-adolescent, nineteenth-century women readers, especially those in the South, would have found anything objectionable either in her interest in personal conversion or in her choice of marriage as a woman's appropriate calling. It nonetheless remains difficult to determine how many even of her most devoted women readers enjoyed—or even followed—the erudition and philosophical speculation that lie at the center of the novel. But the better educated surely did.

There is every reason to believe that many aspects of *Beulah* conform closely to Evans' personal experience, notably the crisis of faith. Obviously the experience of being an orphan does not; nor, significantly, does the marriage. Evans herself never taught as Beulah does. But in other important respects *Beulah* embodies concerns that lay close to Evans' own experience and, probably, to those of many of her readers. Since much of Evans' correspondence for the years between the publication of *Inez* and that of *Beulah* has disappeared, the evidence necessarily remains indirect, but some of it bears directly on the novel.

18. Jones, *Tomorrow Is Another Day,* 91.

19. Fannie Page Hume Diary, March 1, 1860 (MS in Southern Historical Collection, University of North Carolina, Chapel Hill).

During the years that immediately preceded the publication of *Beulah,* Evans was living in Mobile with her parents and siblings in straitened financial circumstances. As a young woman in her early twenties, she would normally have expected to be preparing for marriage. We will probably never know whether her failure to become engaged during those years resulted from her singular intellectual accomplishments and desire for independence or from her father's economic reversals. Both of Evans' parents came from well-to-do slaveholding families, her mother from the socially and politically prominent Howard family of Virginia, South Carolina, and Georgia. But if her father's economic difficulties prevented her from engaging in the social life of the slaveholding elite, her background would doubtless have led her to recoil from anything less prestigious.

Notwithstanding the carping of the *Messenger*'s reviewer that Evans did not explicitly identify the city in which *Beulah* was set, her descriptions of it in the novel hewed very close to reality. During the late 1850s Evans was living with her family in a rented house on Government Street in Mobile. She had become a member of the board of the Protestant Orphanage, which she and her mother had been instrumental in rebuilding. As recently as the 1930s, many older residents of Mobile remembered the pine grove behind the brick orphanage building that figures prominently in *Beulah*'s opening chapter. Evans, who had lived through the worst yellow fever epidemic in Mobile's history, graphically describes it in *Beulah.* Although Mobile had no public library, it did have two rental libraries and a Franklin Society. The accounts of Beulah's trotting around town borrowing and returning books probably depict Evans' own experience. Even the names of her characters come directly from the Mobile of the 1850s: Hammonds, Hartwells, Graysons, Martins, and Asburys may all be found in the city directory for 1858–59. And many of the homes in which they are said to have lived can be identified.[20] Even to the description of views from houses of the waves breaking in the Mobile River, *Beulah* is as faithful to Evans' immediate environment as any travelogue.

William Fidler, the literary historian and critic who read Evans' letters to the Reverend Mr. Harriss, confirms that Beulah's crisis of faith has much in common with Evans' own. Evans' letters to her friends, notably Rachel Lyons, during the year following *Beulah*'s publication further suggest how deeply she had been thinking about the issues of the novel. At the end of

20. Sidney C. Phillips, "The Life and Works of Augusta Evans Wilson" (Ph.D. dissertation, Alabama Polytechnic Institute, 1937), 27–31. My warmest thanks to Leah Atkins for calling this dissertation to my attention.

July, 1860, Evans wrote Lyons to encourage her to take up writing as a way out of the depression from which she was apparently suffering. She especially advises Lyons, a Jew, to write a Jewish tale "and make it a substratum on which to embroider your views of life, men, women, Art, Literature." She acknowledges that women writers suffer greater trials than the world imagines, but nonetheless insists that they also enjoy special pleasures. "I speak now not of mere *gratified ambition;* I point you to the nobler aim of doing *God's work*." Evans herself had thought much on these topics and concluded that "while literary women as a class, are *not as* happy, as women who have Husbands and Children to engage their attention and monopolize their affections; yet in the faithful employment of their talents, they experience a deep peace and satisfaction, and are crowned with a glory such as marriage never gave." Yes, she does mean that literature and marriage are antagonistic. "No loving wife and mother can sit down and serve two masters, Fame and Love—. It is almost impossible—." If Lyons were married, as she apparently wished, Evans would say, "God bless." But so long as she was not, "I wish you would *write*."[21]

In August and November, Evans wrote again, underscoring her conviction that work and more work provided the best antidote to depression and, presumably, to being unmarried. The letters also contain advice on how to write a novel, suggesting that Evans had thought carefully about her own writing. Lyons should not be obsessed with "the mere accumulation of information; for after all, it is an author's own deep, original thoughts, which are remembered, and prized; and not the rehashing of classical or medieval sentiments." She should start with the plot, which must be clearly traced to the very end before a line is written. Then she would find no difficulty in embroidering and polishing. She must also be sure to "*select* the *very highest types* of character for the standard has sadly deteriorated of late in works of fiction." Many novelists had fallen into a "too-close imitation of Nature" and, worse, into "the error of patronizing coarseness, vulgarity, and ignorance." Evans remarks that in *Adam Bede* George Eliot especially errs in this regard. "The world needs *elevating,* and it is the peculiar province of the Novelist to present the very highest *noble types* of human nature."[22]

In these letters, Evans arrestingly combines her theories of novel writing

21. Augusta Jane Evans to Rachel Lyons, July 30, 1860, in possession of William Fidler, Tuscaloosa, Alabama. I wish to express my deep thanks to Mr. Fidler for sharing this letter and others of Augusta Jane Evans with me.

22. Augusta Jane Evans to Rachel Lyons, August 28, November 13, 1860, in possession of William Fidler.

with her thoughts about the situation of women like Lyons and herself. The intermixture confirms the profound importance of women's narratives to women's identities. Novels—good novels—do offer models of being and thinking; they are taxonomies of the soul and road maps for the difficult journey toward becoming a self. For Evans, this aspect of women's fictions could not be separated from the development of literature in general. In the fall of 1859, she wrote a series of articles for the Mobile *Daily Advertiser* in which she vigorously defended a distinct southern literature. Northern publishers, she argued, are subjugating southern writers and repressing the development of their genius in an attempt to ensure that the South remain inferior to the North in the worlds of national and international letters.[23] In Evens' view this gambit was of a piece with the northern attempt to undermine southern institutions, notably slavery. In northern literature, "the low sensual African is dragged up from his normal position and violently thrust into an importance which the Creator has denied him by indications as strong as physical inferiority and mental incapacity could make them." If literature failed to respect the differences between whites and blacks, she insisted, the nation would begin to ignore them as well—thereby jeopardizing "national harmony."[24]

In these articles Evans forcefully condemns the tendency to "render all classes of society dissatisfied with their normal condition." Such literature was drawing the North into chaos. In contrast, the South enjoyed the stability promoted by its own institutions. "Next to the British aristocrat, we know of no position in the world more desirable than that of the Southern planter," who belongs to the "most enlightened" class of any country. The entire nation should look to the "sons of our planters" for the "talents, learning and statesmanship" so sorely lacking in contemporary politics. In combating this persecution, southern writers should aspire to rise above special pleading and write for the most enlightened and discriminating readers throughout the English-speaking world. Evans expresses the desire that southern writers be read "wherever the English language is spoken and read" and that their works "be written in language whose style will fall under the most severe rules of literary taste."[25]

23. Mobile *Daily Advertiser,* November 6, 1859. The articles were unsigned, but William Fidler has identified their writer as Evans. See his "Augusta Evans Wilson as Confederate Propagandist," *Alabama Review,* II (1949), 32–44. See also the thoughtful discussion of these articles in Moss, *Domestic Novelists in the Old South,* Chap. 5.

24. Mobile *Daily Advertiser,* October 10, 1859.

25. *Ibid.,* October 30, November 6, 1859. For my own views on the complex role of

The *Daily Advertiser* articles unmistakably corroborate Evans' passionate identification with proslavery southern politics, but also help to explain why she did not follow other southern women novelists in endowing her novel with an overtly proslavery cast. She aspired to follow the advice she had given Lyons—to write about what she knew, but to present it in a language that would meet the most discriminating tastes throughout the English-speaking world. She ought to produce a southern literature that, although firmly grounded in the life and values of her region, would engage the human condition. The resemblances between *Beulah* and *Jane Eyre* may be taken as evidence of Evans' determination to model her work on that of the most prestigious and influential British novelist, but they do not fully account for the specific content of *Beulah,* notably its preoccupation with the struggle between skepticism and faith. On this matter, Evans was more deeply influenced by Samuel Taylor Coleridge, Thomas Carlyle, and William Hamilton than by even the most accomplished women writers.[26]

If *Beulah* follows *Jane Eyre* in plot and aspects of its rhetoric, it less obviously, but no less closely, follows "The Rime of the Ancient Mariner." At one point, Evans has Beulah herself make the correspondence explicit. Reginald Lindsey, who wishes to marry Beulah and has just loaned her his copy of Sir William Hamilton's *Philosophy of the Conditioned* to help her through her spiritual crisis, reminds her that those with a solid Christian faith know that on earth "'we see through a glass darkly.' Better this than the starless night in which you grope, without a promise of the dawn of eternity, where all mystery shall be explained. Are you not weary of fruitless, mocking speculation?" (367). She replies, "Ah, yes; weary as the lonely mariner, tempest-tossed on some pathless ocean, without chart or compass. In my sky, even the star of hope is shrouded. Weary? Yes, in body and mind" (367).

In many respects the similarities between the plot and the philosophy of *Beulah* and those of "The Ancient Mariner" are striking. Beulah, like the Mariner, has a story that must be told and retold, as a cautionary tale for listeners and as a sign of salvation for the teller. For Beulah, too, that story

---

proslavery thought in antebellum southern literature, see my article "The Fettered Mind: Time, Place, and the Literary Imagination of the Old South," *Georgia Historical Quarterly,* LXXVI (Winter, 1990), 622–50.

26. On the general problem of faith and unbelief in nineteenth-century American culture, see James Turner, *Without God, Without Creed: The Origins of Unbelief in America* (Baltimore, 1985).

progresses from a dangerous voyage to the appearance of an Albatross to the killing of the Albatross to the utter abandonment of solitude upon the "rotting sea" to the recovered ability to pray, and from thence to return to the world of the living. Coleridge's lines perfectly capture the frozen state of Beulah's heart after the death of her sister Lilly:

> Nor shapes of men nor beasts we ken—
> The ice was all between.
> The ice was here, the ice was there,
> The ice was all around.[27]

The appearance of Guy Hartwell may be likened to the appearance of the Albatross, and Beulah's rejection of his love to the Mariner's slaying of the Albatross. After Hartwell's departure, Beulah feels, like the Mariner, "Alone, alone, all, all alone, / Alone on a wide wide sea!" (ll. 232–33). Also like the Mariner, she

> looked to heaven, and tried to pray;
> But or ever a prayer had gusht,
> A wicked whisper came, and made
> My heart as dry as dust.
> (ll. 244–47)

And for both only when "A spring of love gushed from my heart" did prayer finally become possible and, with prayer, release from the carcass of the Albatross (l. 284). Thus could Beulah second the Mariner's final sentiments:

> He prayeth well, who loveth well
> Both man and bird and beast.
> He prayeth best, who loveth best
> All things both great and small.
> (ll. 612–15)

But unlike the Mariner, Beulah gets a second chance to love the love that she had sought to kill.

The similarities between *Beulah* and "The Rime of the Ancient Mariner" confirm that for Evans the central problem concerned a loss and repossession

27. Samuel Taylor Coleridge, "The Rime of the Ancient Mariner," Ernest Hartley Coleridge, ed., in *Coleridge Poetical Works* (New York, 1988), ll. 57–60. Subsequent line references will appear in the text. I am indebted to James Turner for thoughtful discussions about the relation between *Beulah* and "The Rime of the Ancient Mariner."

of faith. In October, 1859, she attempted to explain Beulah's struggle with doubt to Rachel Lyons, who felt that "Beulah's speculative doubts were not satisfactorily answered." The truth of the matter, Evans replied, "lies in a nut shell[:] Our religious states are determined by *Faith, not Reason.*" Beulah, Evans insisted, erred in constituting "her Reason the sole criterion of truth." But she kept encountering "insolvable mysteries—found that unaided by that Revelation which her reason had ignored, that she was utterly incapable of ever arriving at any belief." Evans explained that "the object of the book was to prove the fallacy of all human, philosophical systems, the limited nature of human faculties, the total insufficiency of our reason to grapple with the vital questions which are propounded by every earnest mind." So long as Beulah "trusted to Rationalism, she was wretched and sceptical; but when she put *faith* in the word of the Living God, she *found 'the ways of pleasantness and the paths of peace.'*"[28]

Whatever Evans' intentions, she represented the progress of Beulah's loss of faith as something more than an infatuation with the power of human reason. On Evans' own showing, Beulah's doubts sink their roots in the losses of her childhood and adolescence: How can she continue to pray to a God who manifestly disregards her prayers? Who strips her successively of mother, father, and sister? Almost from the outset, cheerfulness comes hard to Beulah, who has lost everything that she held dear. Significantly, her mother's death, which occurred very early in her life, receives almost no attention, either as an event or as a cause of Beulah's doubts. Even her father's death, which resulted in her removal to the orphanage, had not initially shaken her trust in God, to whom she had continued to look "for relief and reward. But the reward came not in the expected way. Hope died; faith fainted; and bitterness and despair reigned in that once loving and gentle soul. Her father had not been spared in answer to her frantic prayers. Lilly had been taken" (59). She had put her trust in the Lord, "and He has forgotten me" (60).

But if Beulah's doubts have their source in personal despair, their development is fed by extensive reading in philosophy and literature, especially nineteenth-century skeptical thought. Even when she is still in the orphanage, her paleness is attributed to her reading too much (9). Given free access to her guardian's library, she begins a determined course of intellectual exploration. Edgar Allan Poe, in particular, "was the portal through which she

28. Augusta Jane Evans to Rachel Lyons, October 17, 1859, in possession of William Fidler.

entered the vast Pantheon of Speculation" (121). Hartwell had warned her against Poe, "but the book was often in his own hand, and yielding to the matchless ease and rapidity of his diction, she found herself wandering in a wilderness of baffling suggestions" (121).

From Poe, Beulah moves to Thomas De Quincey's "Analects from Richter" and on to Jean Paul. When Hartwell questions her about the solidity of her faith, she replies. "Of course, of course! What could shake a faith which years should strengthen?" (129). Watching her, Hartwell recognizes the progress of doubt: "Do you want to be like me? If not, keep your hands off of my books" (129). But her obsession with books steadily grows. "The Ancient Mariner" is to her "the most thrilling poem in the English language" (158). Books, she tells her friend Clara, "are to me what family, and friends, and society, are to other people" (161). She reads Carlyle's works for hours without fatigue, but when midnight forces her to lay the book aside, "the myriad conjectures and inquiries which I am conscious of, as arising from those same pages, weary me beyond all degrees of endurance" (199). As she ever more frenetically reads, she becomes visibly thinner and more drawn; her normally white skin becomes whiter, her eyes strained, her hands almost transparent. Her speculations, Clara sadly reproaches her, have brought her to doubt the Bible. Her speculations, Evans firmly reminds us, are inexorably leading her to a skepticism that sees creation and creator as one. "Unluckily for her, there was no one to direct or assist her" (209).

In the absence of guidance, Beulah is no longer studying for the sake of learning alone. The riddles with which she is grappling "involved all that she prized in Time and Eternity, and she grasped books of every description with the eagerness of a famishing nature" (209). From German speculation she plunges into ethnology and then geology. "Finally, she learned that she was the crowning intelligence in the vast progression; that she would ultimately become part of the Deity" (210). And in the dark of night she fumbles along, following "that most anomalous of all guides, 'Herr Teufelsdrockh'" (210). Kneeling in despair, she tries to pray but no longer knows to whom she should pray: to nature? to heroes? "She could not pray . . . 'Sartor' had effectually blindfolded her, and she threw herself down to sleep with a shivering dread, as of a young child separated from its mother, and wailing in some starless desert" (211).

Evans especially explores the consequences of Beulah's reading through long interchanges between Beulah and her friends Clara and Cornelia. The haughty Cornelia engages Beulah in a searching discussion of Emerson, in which Beulah remonstrates with her that surely Cornelia is not an Emersonian. To Beulah, his writings are "like heaps of broken glass, beautiful in the individual crystal, sparkling, and often dazzling, but gather them up, and try to fit them into a whole, and the jagged edges refuse to unite" (229). She had long sought a creed in Emerson but had come to recognize him as the very prince of Pyrrhonists. She can accept his law of compensation "as regards mere social position; wealth, penury, even the endowments of genius. But further than this, I do not accept it" (230). Beulah cannot relinquish the idea of an immortal soul and continues to "desire something more than an immutability, or continued existence hereafter, in the form of an abstract idea of truth, justice, love or humility" (230). Cornelia, who is dying and hopes only for an unbroken and eternal sleep, feels like "that miserable, doomed prisoner of Poe's 'Pit and Pendulum,' who saw the pendulum, slowly but surely, sweeping down upon him" (231).

Cornelia's death is extraordinary, if not unique, in mid-nineteenth-century women's fiction. Evans' willingness to explore the possibility that a good woman—and even evil women were normally represented as converting on their deathbeds—might die without a shred of religious feeling demonstrates her refusal to limit the capacities of women's minds. Kneeling beside the bed of her friend who has died bereft of faith, Beulah agonizes about the meaning of that death, wonders what philosophy has to say about such grim hours of struggle and separation: "Was she to see her sister no more? Was a moldering mass of dust all that remained of the darling dead—the beautiful angel, Lily, whom she had so idolized? Oh! was life, then, a great mockery, and the soul, with its noble aims and impulses, but a delicate machine of matter? Her brain was in a wild, maddening whirl; she could not weep; her eyes were dry and burning" (319).

She asks herself, was that death? "Oh, my God, save me from such a death!" (321). At Cornelia's funeral, she writhes in the nadir of despair. "What availed all her inquiries, and longings, and defiant cries? She died, no nearer the truth than when she began. She died without hope and without knowledge" (321). But could a loving God refuse to save her? And how different was Beulah's own situation? How different would her death be? Even the terrifying lesson of Cornelia's death does not immediately save Beulah from her ceaseless questioning, although later that year, exhausted by her struggles, she reembraces faith.

The turning point comes when Beulah recognizes that her suitor, Reginald Lindsey, believes she has rejected his proposal because of her love for

Guy Hartwell: "Then, for the first time, his meaning flashed upon her mind. He believed she loved her guardian" (368). As the thought seeps into Beulah's consciousness, her normally pale face is suffused with a burning flush. "Oh! how unworthy I am of such love as his? how utterly undeserving!" (368). Evans does not clarify the referent of *his.* Logically, it should be Lindsey; psychologically, it must be Hartwell; metaphorically, it is God. Later that evening, Beulah reads the book that Lindsey had brought her, Hamilton's *Philosophy of the Conditioned,* and reviews the progress of her own skepticism, her proud and fruitless search for truth: "A Godless world; a Godless woman" (370). She recognizes that "philosophy! thou hast mocked my hungry soul; thy gilded fruits have crumbled to ashes in my grasp" (371). At that moment, Evans informs us, Beulah's "proud intellect was humbled, and falling on her knees, for the first time in many months, a sobbing prayer went up to the throne of the living God" (371).

Time and again, Evans insists that Beulah's struggle with Christianity derives primarily from the evils of individualism and the temptation to believe that the human mind can encompass all knowledge. She assumed that her readers would be familiar with Hamilton's argument, which was widely discussed in religious circles in the late 1850s. In fact, in July of 1859, about the time that *Beulah* appeared, the *Southern Literary Messenger* ran an article on *Philosophy of the Conditioned.* Hamilton was best known for his dictum, "The first act of philosophy is to doubt our knowledge, and the last act of it is to be certain of our ignorance." Directly engaging the problems of faith and reason that bedeviled Beulah, Hamilton argued that the purpose of philosophy "is to establish the theory of human ignorance and to determine the boundaries of human thought." The proliferating concern with the power of reason, he believed, had led to the proliferation of infidelity—the contempt for sacred truths and the undermining of morals. Under such conditions, the task of philosophy is to "show the insufficiency of logic as the invariable standard of truth; to demonstrate the limits of human understanding." To this end, Hamilton divided knowledge between the conditioned and the unconditioned, identifying the former as finite ideas, which we can know positively, and the latter as infinite ideas, which we can know only negatively. "The Infinite, the absolute, the one, the identical, the abstract, the substantial, the noumenal, the pure, the necessary, are unconditioned." Knowledge of the conditioned leaves a broad field for human reason, but beyond it we cannot positively go.[29]

29. "Sir William Hamilton's Philosophy," *Southern Literary Messenger,* XXIX (July, 1859), 3, 6.

Evans doubtless appreciated Hamilton's position as possible grounds from which to salvage religious faith from the greatest presumptions of secular knowledge. No human being can aspire to be God; the attempt to grasp the ultimate mysteries of life, death, and eternity is doomed to failure—and, worse, is presumptuous. In considering the great nineteenth-century struggles between faith and reason, Evans drew upon Hamilton to argue that faith and reason are of different orders. But in accepting faith as a knowledge of the heart rather than of the head, she did not repudiate the pleasures and challenges of intellectual inquiry. She simply insisted that they unfold within their allotted sphere and serve, rather than challenge, divine truth. In this respect, *Beulah* closely follows Carlyle's *Sartor Resartus* in simultaneously exploring the myriad intellectual temptations of the age and elaborating a pattern of conversion.[30]

The power of *Beulah* largely derives from Evans' ability to ground demanding intellectual debates in the psyche of a young woman. Beulah's main drama, her struggle for faith, lies at the core of her identity. Evans' depiction of Beulah emphasizes the ways in which emotional and intellectual development intertwine. And for Beulah, as for Evans herself, the problems of female identity have much to do with the acceptance or rejection of woman's ascribed sphere and role. Significantly, during her period of gravest doubts, Beulah becomes an author, first anonymously, then under her own name. Hartwell attributes her rejection of his proposal of marriage directly to her quest for literary fame. Evans herself associates Beulah's literary career with an interest in woman's independence. Beulah's valedictory address upon graduation had been devoted to "Female Heroism"; her writings had touched upon the possible benefits of a woman's remaining single as well as upon questions of philosophy and faith. But Evans does not condemn Beulah for writing or for publishing: She condemns her for her pursuit of unlimited individualism and for the infidelity to which it must lead. And she does, to the disgust of subsequent feminist critics, insist that infidelity is even worse in a woman than in a man.

Beulah manifests a relentless determination to establish and defend her independence—to impose her will and to realize her self-appointed duty, notably by earning her own living. It humbles her to hear a "woman bemoaning the weakness of her sex, instead of showing that she has a soul and mind of her own, inferior to none" (116). Haughtily, she reproaches Clara for preferring to be cared for: "You are less a woman than I thought you, if

30. On this aspect of Carlyle, see Walter L. Reed, "The Pattern of Conversion in *Sartor Resartus*," *English Literary History*, XXXVIII (September, 1971), 411–31.

you would be willing to live on the bounty of others when a little activity would enable you to support yourself" (115). Clara counters that the issue is not merely "the bread you eat or the clothes that you wear; it is sympathy and kindness, love and watchfulness" (115). Those, truly, are the things a woman needs. Can "grammars and geographies, and copy books" fill a woman's heart? (115). Can the conviction that "you are independent and doing your duty" satisfy all other longings? (115–16). Beulah will have none of it. "What was my will given to me for, if to remain passive and suffer others to minister to its needs? Don't talk to me about woman's clinging, dependent nature. You are opening your lips to repeat that senseless simile of oaks and vines; I don't want to hear it; there are no creeping tendencies about me" (116).

Hartwell yet more impatiently condemns Beulah's quest for independence. Attributing her refusal of his offers of support and his gifts to her literary ambition, he reproves her, "Ambition such as yours, which aims at literary fame, is the deadliest foe to happiness" (328–29). To a woman's heart, ambition is a tempting fiend, the siren call of fame but an illusion (329). And he chastises Beulah: "You are a proud, ambitious woman, solicitous only to secure eminence as an authoress. I asked your heart; you have now none to give" (330). Beulah does not yield but, heartsick, returns to her desk to complete an article "designed to prove that woman's happiness was not necessarily dependent on marriage. That a single life might be more useful, more tranquil, more unselfish" (331).

Throughout the novel, Beulah insists that in the behavior that others, notably Hartwell, view as willful she is merely following her duty. Thus when Hartwell tells her that her "rash obstinacy" has tortured him beyond expression, she retorts, "I have but done my duty" (167). Similarly, when Pauline, Hartwell's niece and Beulah's friend, asks what possessed her to forsake comfort in order to teach "little ragged, dirty children their A,B,Cs," Beulah responds, "duty" (249). And when Mrs. Williams, the matron of the Asylum whom Beulah deeply loves, reproaches her with having abandoned her faith, Beulah tells her, "I am trying to do my duty just as conscientiously as though I went to church" (314). But, Mrs. Williams counters, "If you cease to pray and read your Bible how are you to know what your duty is?" Mrs. Williams' question cuts to the heart of the problem. It is all very well for Beulah to claim that she is following the path of duty, but perhaps she is merely confusing duty with her own recalcitrant pride. How is she to know?

Evans leaves little doubt that Beulah risks self-delusion. She represents

Beulah, during an especially dark period after Cornelia's death, as sitting by a window of a Sunday morning, thinking of her childhood practice of going to church. Now, Evans tells us, "she felt doubly orphaned. In her intellectual pride, she frequently asserted that she was 'the star of her own destiny';" but this morning she cannot shake the memories of her own previous faith (253). In her unhappiness, Beulah picks up her Bible, which falls open to the thirty-eighth chapter of Job. There the Lord speaks to Job out of a whirlwind, asking him, "Who is this that darkens counsel by words without knowledge?" After reading the chapter with its unrelenting condemnation of the perils of intellectual arrogance, Beulah departs for church to hear Ernest Mortimer's sermon on the text of two verses from the first and last chapters of Ecclesiastes: "For in much wisdom is much grief; and he that increaseth knowledge, increaseth sorrow," and "Of making many books there is no end, and much study is a weariness of the flesh."[31] Mortimer insists that the only certainty lies in fearing God and keeping his commandments, "for this is the whole duty of man" (254).

Beulah spends many lonely months thereafter wrestling with her angel, insisting upon her independent ability to find the truth. Never does she forsake her quest for an absolute, never does she succumb to total skepticism, which she views with fear and loathing. Throughout her journey, she insists upon the words of the Christian tradition—especially "duty"—but she persists in that most horrendous of sins, pride. In a moment of despair, she poignantly tells Hartwell: "There is a truth for the earnest seeker somewhere—somewhere! If I live a thousand years, I will toil after it till I find it" (264). What else, she implores, is life for? Merely to sleep and eat? That she refuses to accept. "No, no. My name bids me press on; there is a land of Beulah somewhere for my troubled spirit" (264). And she promises to persist in her studies "unguided, unassisted even as I have begun" (264).

Evans' correspondence with Rachel Lyons demonstrates that she, like her heroine, had thought about the respective rewards of a literary and a married life. By the time that she had completed *Beulah,* she was able to write with calm assurance on the matter to her friend. By then, she was also enjoying the considerable financial rewards of her work, which permitted her to buy a house for her parents and to think of traveling to Europe. But we know less about her feelings before and while she wrote the novel. No doubt the ability to earn her living appealed to the young woman whose family was

31. Job 38:1; Eccles. 1:18, 12:12.

experiencing financial difficulties. No doubt the idea of literary success appealed to the young woman who may have harbored doubts about whether she would ever have the opportunity to marry according to her station. Evans had, in short, her own good reasons to understand the appeal of female independence.

Yet many have read *Beulah* as a blanket condemnation of female independence. That interpretation results from Evans' merciless exposure of the ways in which Beulah's struggle to establish her independence derives from a stubborn, willful pride and from her confusion of the fulfillment of her duty with the mere assertion of her will. In the novel, Evans chooses not to depict the attractions of "single blessedness," although she does have Beulah enjoy a brief period of single tranquility. By that time, however, she has recovered her faith and recognized that she loves Hartwell. Throughout most of the novel, Evans portrays Beulah's determination to establish her independence as frenetic. She invites the reader to see Beulah's interest in economic independence as primarily motivated by—indeed inseparable from—the arrogance that assumes that she can, by reason alone, comprehend the mysteries of the universe.

If Evans does not approve Beulah's presumption, she does treat it with great compassion, implicitly inviting identification with Beulah's struggles. The mainspring of that identification, even for readers who do not share Beulah's intellectual passion, lies in the subtext of Beulah's emotional and psychological development. As Beulah herself insists to Hartwell, her restless search sinks its roots in her childhood, for, she tells him, the questions that trouble her "are older than my acquaintance with so-called philosophic works. They have troubled me from my childhood" (261). But even Beulah does not entirely recognize their deep personal roots. As an orphan, Beulah lacked the formative love of parents and, at the onset of adolescence, saw those she held most dear snatched from her. Tellingly, throughout most of the novel she insists that she has no home—that Hartwell may offer her a house, but never a home. Yet more tellingly, she rarely mentions her childhood and almost never her mother. When Clara asks her why, she replies that it was "all dark and barren as a rainy sea" (213). And when Clara presses for particulars, Beulah responds that she loves her father's memory. "Ah! it is enshrined in my heart's holiest sanctuary. He was a noble, loving man, and my affection for him bordered on idolatry" (213). But of her mother, she says only that she "knew little of her. She died before I was old enough to remember much about her" (213).

Evans describes Beulah's face after this interchange as "full of bitter recollections" and her eyes as if "wandering through some storehouse of sorrows" (213). *Beulah* figures as a protracted account of melancholia, of pathological and self-destructive mourning. Shortly after Lilly's death, when Eugene, the companion of her childhood in the Asylum and the object of her devotion, is about to depart, she tells him, "When you are gone, everything will be dark—dark!" (42). The image of darkness recurs throughout the novel, invariably signaling Beulah's progressive emotional detachment from the world. At the nadir, the bleak Christmas of her extended conversations with Clara and Cornelia, Beulah is depicted as "a young child separated from its mother, and wailing in some starless desert" (211). Only after Beulah has recovered the unconscious and denied roots of her loss—the loss of the mother she claims not even to remember—can she finally begin to accept the love of those who wish her well, and then a husband. Evans thus links Beulah's loss of faith to the psychological depression that derives from the loss of all of those she loved. She also links Beulah's recovery of faith to her feelings for Hartwell. The depths of her unconscious struggles emerge from her refusal to be indebted to him for material goods, her refusal to call his house her home, her refusal, above all, to recognize that he loves her. In the end, Evans, by linking Beulah's recognition that Hartwell loves her to her recognition that she can love God, invites some confusion. Does she intend, as Anne Goodwyn Jones has argued, to suggest that Beulah ultimately loves God in Hartwell?[32]

The evidence that Evans intends no such thing is strong, notwithstanding contrary intimations that she might. Jones's argument depends upon the assumption that in consigning Beulah to the role of devoted wife, Evans is consigning her to defeat. Jones thus assumes that Beulah's struggles to realize her own individualism and independence were positive. Evans gives scant reason to think that she would concur. For Evans, conversion and faith represented the highest human accomplishment, the surest foundation for identity and peace. She valued women's strength and independence but mistrusted unbridled individualism for women or men. In her view, Beulah's struggles for independence could not be divorced from that intellectual presumption that destroys faith—the true threat of individualism as a systematic creed. In *Beulah,* Evans is celebrating not Beulah's defeat but her triumph. She does, to be sure, accept and celebrate the ordained differences

32. Jones, *Tomorrow Is Another Day, e.g.,* 76, 84, 88.

between men and women, but in having Beulah willingly accept her highest destiny as a woman she is not celebrating Beulah's subordination to Guy Hartwell: She is celebrating Beulah's subordination to God. And in the novel's concluding lines she entrusts Hartwell's salvation to Beulah.

Beulah's tragedy lies in her frozen heart—her inability to recognize and accept love. Her heart, Evans insists, is a woman's heart. But Evans never endorses the view that Beulah had scornfully rejected of woman's nature as dependent and clinging. She simply insists that woman's nature, like man's, requires divine assistance in order to recognize the path of duty. To determine duty for the self is to assume the place of God, to accept the pernicious Emersonian view that creation and creator are one. In this respect, Evans was articulating the distinct southern view of identity as grounded in particular stations—a view that women must accept their natures and their proper social roles. But she was not endorsing the view that women depend on men for their salvation. Women, like men, must accept their guidance direct from God. Women, like men, are capable of rejecting true duty and forfeiting salvation.

Evans clearly intends Beulah's name to figure as a primary sign in the novel. In the third chapter, a brash girl, daughter of the parvenu woman whom Beulah is serving as nurse, snidely comments, "Beulah—it's about as pretty as her face" (26). By this time the reader knows that Beulah is not beautiful, that she can even be seen as downright ugly, and that her lack of conventional female prettiness has caused her to be sent to work as a servant. But only after the occurrence of these material misfortunes, succeeded by the tragedy of losing her beautiful younger sister and idol to adoption by a fashionable couple, does her name become an issue. The name thus presides over the main plot of the novel: Beulah's progress from the predictable woes of unfortunate humanity through the seemingly inescapable slough of despond to renewed faith and ultimately marriage.

Critics have frequently emphasized the meaning of Beulah's name as "married woman" but have generally paid less attention to its meaning as "(married) land," thus ignoring the possibility that Evans intended her novel to double as an allegory of the South as a whole. Beulah's struggle with religion, Evans carefully demonstrates, is also tied to her disgust with "fashionable" religion. The novel abounds with examples of women who attend the correctly fashionable church while disregarding the true claims of religion: the lady managers of the orphanage, May Chilton, the Graysons. Materialism has invaded the very fabric of belief, reducing it to nothing more than a complacent, self-serving practice for the wealthy. That shallow observance of the forms of faith, with no regard for its substance, is as threatening to the fabric of southern society as the skepticism that bedevils Beulah. But Evans also demonstrates, in the persons of Clara, Mrs. Williams, and Mrs. Asbury, that true faith, like true charity, remains possible. Materialism and hypocrisy may rightfully disgust the serious believer but cannot alone account for loss of faith, although they can testify to a radical deterioration in society as a whole.

In this respect, the novel may be read as an allegory of the crisis of southern society in the 1850s, with Beulah's struggles taken as signs of the struggles of the southern people. Certainly, as early as the 1850s, the great southern divines were beginning to launch those appeals for self-reformation that would reach a crescendo during the dark years of the Civil War. The virtues that they were urging upon their fellow southerners stongly resembled those that Evans urges upon her heroine, notably the virtue of a deep, trusting faith that puts aside the graven images of materialism and, especially, unbridled individualism. The good of the self can only be found in the good of the whole, in hewing to the lines that God has laid down.

For generations after its publication, *Beulah* spoke to countless women—and no few men. For these readers, it embodied a geat human drama, which it resolved in the appropriate manner with a return to a reinvigorated faith. In so doing, it insisted that the struggles of a young orphan girl mattered, not simply as an object of charity but as a mirror and enactment of social values in general. *Beulah* conveys a forceful sense of the power and significance of women's intellectual and spiritual lives.

Beulah's undoubted appeal is all the more remarkable because of the learning, even pedantry, with which it abounds. Evans' endorsement of a distinct woman's role should not be confused with an endorsement of women as frail, clinging creatures, much less as a rejection of women's intellectual capacity. Whatever *Beulah*'s weaknesses, it testifies to Evans' possession of a powerful and wide-ranging intellect. Since Evans enjoyed exercising and displaying that intellect, *Beulah* contains innumerable explicit and implicit allusions, ranging from the Bible to classical myths to German philosophers. Many of these references will seem obscure to modern readers, as they did to many of Evans' contemporaries. Some probably reflect a mild exhibitionism, for Evans delighted in what she knew. Most are integral to the main narrative—a running commentary on the referents of Beulah's consciousness and identity.

The final chapter presents the marriage of Beulah Benton and Guy Hartwell. Marriage, Evans reminds her readers, is not the end of a life, but the beginning of a new course of duties through which she cannot follow Beulah. Evans does allow Beulah one final reflection on her past, which, she tells Hartwell, "can never die" (418). She frequently ponders the past, and the recollection of her struggles and her search for a "true philosophy" keeps her humble. "I was so proud of my intellect; put so much faith in my own powers; it was no wonder I was so benighted" (418). And in the final pages, Beulah explains her mature views on science and religion to her husband. Science, she insists, can accomplish wonders, and its powers and scope will continue to advance with the progress of human knowledge. Faith remains a matter of divine mystery: "Truly, 'a God comprehended is no God at all!'" (419). Christian rules of life and duty are clear as crystal.[33] Whatever else, the ending confirms the paramount importance Evans attached to her heroine's thought—to her grasp of and interest in the greatest problems of her age. And she represents Hartwell as respectfully and deferentially attending to Beulah's views.

33. There are a few slight alterations in this final chapter in the 1887 edition, published by Martin & Hoyt Co. in Atlanta. The significance of the changes does not seem great, although they include the dropping of Evans' paean to those who toil in laboratories and chart the frontiers of scientific discovery. Since the 1900 edition (reproduced here) is identical with the original, New York edition of 1859, it is possible that the changes simply resulted from an inadvertent omission. It is also possible that they reflected deference to what were assumed to be post-Reconstruction southern sensibilities.

Beulah

BEULAH

BY

AUGUSTA J. EVANS

NEW YORK
THE FEDERAL BOOK COMPANY
PUBLISHERS

Facsimile of 1900 Title Page

TO MY AUNT

Mrs. Seaborn Jones,

OF GEORGIA,

I DEDICATE THIS BOOK

AS A FEEBLE TRIBUTE OF AFFECTION AND GRATITUDE.

CHAPTER I.

A January sun had passed the zenith, and the slanting rays flamed over the window-panes of a large brick building, bearing on its front in golden letters the inscription, "Orphan Asylum." The structure was commodious, and surrounded by wide galleries, while the situation offered a silent tribute to the discretion and good sense of the board of managers, who selected the suburbs instead of the more densely populated portion of the city. The white-washed palings inclosed, as a front yard or lawn, rather more than an acre of ground, sown in grass and studded with trees, among which the shelled walks meandered gracefully. A long avenue of elms and poplars extended from the gate to the principal entrance, and imparted to the Asylum an imposing and venerable aspect. There was very little shrubbery, but here and there orange boughs bent beneath their load of golden fruitage, while the glossy foliage, stirred by the wind, trembled and glistened in the sunshine. Beyond the inclosure stretched the common, dotted with occasional clumps of pine and leafless oaks, through which glimpses of the city might be had. Building and grounds wore a quiet, peaceful, inviting look, singularly appropriate for the purpose designated by the inscription, "Orphan Asylum," a haven for the desolate and miserable. The front door was closed, but upon the broad granite steps, where the sunlight lay warm and tempting, sat a trio of the inmates. In the foreground was a slight fairy form, "a wee winsome thing," with coral lips, and large, soft blue eyes, set in a frame of short, clustering golden curls. She looked about six years old, and was clad, like her companions, in canary-colored flannel dress, and blue check apron. Lillian was the pet of the Asylum, and now her rosy cheek rested upon her tiny white palm, as though she wearied of the picture-book which lay at her feet. The figure beside her, was one whose marvelous beauty riveted the gaze of all who chanced to see her. The child could have been but a few months older than Lillian, yet the brilliant black eyes, the peculiar curve of the dimpled mouth, and long, dark ringlets, gave to the oval face a maturer and more piquant loveliness. The cast of Claudia's countenance bespoke her foreign parentage, and told of the warm, fierce Italian blood that glowed in her cheeks. There was fascinating grace in every movement, even in the easy indolence of her position, as she bent on one knee to curl Lillian's locks over her finger. On the upper step, in the rear of these two, sat a girl whose age could not have been very accurately guessed from her countenance, and whose features contrasted strangely with those of her companions. At a first casual glance, one thought her rather homely, nay, decidedly ugly; yet, to the curious physiognomist, this face presented greater attractions than either of the others. Reader, I here paint you the portrait of that quiet little figure, whose history is contained in the following pages. A pair of large gray eyes set beneath an overhanging forehead, a boldly-projecting forehead, broad and smooth; a rather large but finely cut mouth, an irreproachable nose, of the order furthest removed from aquiline, and heavy black eyebrows, which, instead of arching, stretched straight across and nearly met. There was not a vestige of color in her cheeks; face, neck, and hands wore a sickly pallor, and a mass of rippling, jetty hair, drawn smoothly over the temples, rendered this marble-like whiteness more apparent. Unlike the younger children, Beulah was busily sewing upon what seemed the counterpart of their aprons; and the sad expression of the countenance, the lips firmly compressed, as if to prevent the utterance of complaint showed that she had become acquainted with cares and sorrows of which they were yet happily ignorant. Her eyes were bent down in her work, and the long, black lashes nearly touched her cold cheeks.

"Sister Beulah, ought Claudy to say that?" cried Lillian turning round and laying her hand upon the piece of sewing.

"Say what, Lilly? I was not listening to you."

"She said she hoped that largest robin redbreast would get drunk, and tumble down. He would be sure to bump some of his pretty bright feathers out, if he rolled over the shells two or three times," answered Lilly, pointing to a China-tree near, where a flock of robins were eagerly chirping over the feast of berries.

"Why, Claudy! how can you wish the poor little fellow such bad luck?" The dark, thoughtful eyes, full of deep meaning, rested on Claudia's radiant face.

"Oh! you need not think I am a bear, or a hawk, ready to swallow the darling little beauty alive! I would not have him lose a feather for the world; but I should like the fun of seeing him stagger and wheel over and over, and tumble off the limb, so that I might run and catch him in my apron. Do you think *I* would give him to our matron to make a pie? No, you might take off my fingers first!" and the little elf snapped them emphatically in Beulah's face.

"Make a pie of robies, indeed! I would starve before I would eat a piece of it," chimed in Lilly, with childish horror at the thought.

Claudia laughed with mingled mischief and chagrin. "You say you would not eat a bit of roby-pie to save your life? Well, you did it last week, anyhow."

"Oh, Claudy, I didn't!"

"Oh, but you did! Don't you remember Susan picked up a bird last week that fell out of this very tree, and gave it to our matron? Well, didn't we have bird-pie for dinner?"

"Yes, but one poor little fellow would not make a pie."

"They had some birds already that came from the market, and I heard Mrs. Williams tell Susan to put it in with the others. So, you see, you did eat roby-pie, and I didn't, for I knew what was in it. I saw its head wrung off!"

"Well, I hope I did not get any of roby: I won't eat any more pie till they have all gone," was Lilly's consolatory reflection. Chancing to glance toward the gate, she exclaimed:

"There is a carriage."

"What is to-day? let me see, Wednesday; yes, this is the evening for the ladies to meet here. Lil, is my face right clean? because that red-headed Miss Dorothy always takes particular pains to look at it. She rubbed her pocket-handkerchief over it the other day. I do hate her, don't you?" cried Claudia, springing up and buttoning the band of her apron sleeve, which had become unfastened.

"Why, Claudy, I am astonished to hear you talk so: Miss Dorothy helps to buy food and clothes for us, and you ought to be ashamed to speak of her as you do." As she delivered this reprimand, Beulah snatched up a small volume and hid it in her work-basket.

"I don't believe she gives us much. I do hate her, and I can't help it, she is so ugly, and cross, and vinegar-faced. I should not like her to look at my mug of milk. You don't love her either, any more than I do, only you won't say anything about her. But kiss me, and I promise I will be good, and not make faces at her in my apron." Beulah stooped down and warmly kissed the suppliant, then took her little sister's hand and led her into the house, just as the carriage reached the door. The children presented a pleasant spectacle as they entered the long dining-room, and ranged themselves for inspection. Twenty-eight heirs of orphanage, varying in years, from one crawling infant, to well-nigh grown girls, all neatly clad, and with smiling, contented faces, if we except one grave countenance, which might have been remarked by the close observer. The weekly visiting committee consisted of four of the lady managers, but to-day the number was swelled to six. A glance at the inspectors sufficed to inform Beulah that something of more than ordinary interest had convened them on the present occasion, and she was passing on to her accustomed place, when her eyes fell upon a familiar face, partially concealed by a straw bonnet. It was her Sabbath school teacher; a sudden glad light flashed over the girl's countenance, and the pale lips disclosed a set of faultlessly beautiful teeth, as she smiled and hastened to her friend.

"How do you do, Mrs. Mason? I am so glad to see you!"

"Thank you, Beulah, I have been promising myself this pleasure a great while. I saw Eugene this morning, and told him I was coming out. He sent you a book and a message. Here is the book. You are to mark the passages you like particularly, and study them well until he comes. When did you see him last?"

Mrs. Mason put the volume in her hand as she spoke.

"It has been more than a week since he was here, and I was afraid he was sick. He is very kind and good to remember the book he promised me, and I thank you very much, Mrs. Mason, for bringing it." The face was radiant with new-born joy, but it all died out when Miss Dorothea White (little Claudia's particular aversion) fixed her pale blue eyes upon her, and asked, in a sharp, discontented tone:

"What ails that girl, Mrs. Williams? she does not work enough, or she would have some blood in her cheeks. Has she been sick?"

"No, madam, she has not been sick exactly, but somehow she never looks strong and hearty like the others. She works well enough. There is not a better or more industrious girl in the asylum, but I rather think she studies too much. She will sit up and read of nights, when the others are all sound asleep; and very often, when Kate and I put out the hall lamp, we find her with her book alone in the cold. I can't get my consent to forbid her reading, especially as it never interferes with her regular work, and she is so fond of it." As the kind-hearted matron uttered these words she glanced at the child and sighed involuntarily.

"You are too indulgent, Mrs. Williams; we cannot afford to feed and clothe girls of her age, to wear themselves out reading trash all night. We are very much in arrears at best, and I think some plan should be adopted to make these large girls, who have been on hand so long, more useful. What do you say, ladies?" Miss Dorothea looked around for some encouragement and support in her move.

"Well, for my part, Miss White, I think that child is not strong enough to do much hard work; she always has looked delicate and pale," said Mrs. Taylor, an amiable looking woman, who had taken one of the youngest orphans on her knee.

"My dear friend that is the very reason: she does not exercise sufficiently to make her robust. Just look at her face and hands, as bloodless as a turnip."

"Beulah, do ask her to give you some of her beautiful color; she looks exactly like a cake of tallow, with two glass beads in the middle—"

"Hush!" and Beulah's hand was pressed firmly over Claudia's crimson lips, lest the whisper of the indignant little brunette should reach ears for which it was not intended.

As no one essayed to answer Miss White, the matron ventured to suggest a darling scheme of her own.

"I have always hoped the managers would conclude to educate her for a teacher. She is so studious, I know she would learn very rapidly."

"My dear madam, you do not in the least understand what you are talking about. It would require at least five years' careful training to fit her to teach, and our finances do not admit of any such expenditure. As the best thing for her, I should move to bind her out to a mantua-maker or milliner, but she could not stand the confinement. She would go off with consumption in less than a year. There is the trouble with these delicate children."

"How is the babe that was brought here last week?" asked Mrs. Taylor.

"Oh, he is doing beautifully. Bring him round the table, Susan," and the rosy, smiling infant was handed about for closer inspection. A few general inquiries followed, and then Beulah was not surprised to hear the order given for the children to retire, as the managers had some especial business with their matron. The orphan band defiled into the hall, and dispersed to their various occupations, but Beulah approached the matron, and whispered something, to which the reply was:

"No: if you have finished that other apron, you shall sew no more to-day. You can pump a fresh bucket of water, and then run out into the yard for some air."

She performed the duty assigned to her, and then hastened to the dormitory, whither Lillian and Claudia had preceded her. The latter was standing on a chair, mimicking Miss Dorothea, and haranguing her sole auditor, in a nasal twang, which she contrived to force from her beautiful curling lips. At sight of Beulah, she sprang toward her, exclaiming:

"You shall be a teacher if you want to, shan't you, Beulah?"

"I am afraid not, Claudy. But don't say any more about her; she is not as kind as our dear matron, or some of the managers, but she thinks she is right. Remember, she made these pretty blue curtains round your and Lilly's bed."

"I don't care if she did. All the ladies were making them, and she did no more than the rest. Never mind: I shall be a young lady some of these days; our matron says I will be beautiful enough to marry the President, and then I will see whether Miss Dorothy Red-head comes meddling and bothering you any more." The brilliant eyes dilated with pleasure, at the thought of the protection which the future lady-President would afford her protégée.

Beulah smiled, and asked almost gaily:

"Claudy, how much will you pay me a month, to dress you, and keep your hair in order, when you get into the White House at Washington?"

"Oh, you dear darling! you shall have everything you want, and do nothing but read." The impulsive child threw her arms around Beulah's neck, and kissed her repeatedly, while the latter bent down over her basket.

"Lilly, here are some chincapins for you and Claudy. I am going out into the yard, and you may both go and play hull-gull."

In the debating room of the visiting committee, Miss White again had the floor. She was no less important a personage than vice-president of the board of managers, and felt authorized to investigate closely, and redress all grievances.

"Who did you say sent that book here, Mrs. Mason?"

"Eugene Rutland, who was once a member of Mrs. Williams' orphan charge in this asylum. Mr. Graham adopted him, and he is now known as Eugene Graham. He is very much attached to Beulah, though I believe they are not at all related."

"He left the asylum before I entered the board. What sort of boy is he? I have seen him several times, and do not particularly fancy him."

"Oh, madam, he is a noble boy! It was a great trial to me to part with him three years ago. He is much older than Beulah, and loves her as well as if she were his sister," said the matron, more hastily than was her custom, when answering any of the managers.

"I suppose he has put this notion of being a teacher into her head; well, she must get it out, that is all. I know of an excellent situation, where a lady is willing to pay six dollars a month for a girl of her age to attend to an infant, and I think we must secure it for her."

"Oh, Miss White! she is not able to carry a heavy child always in her arms," expostulated Mrs. Williams.

"Yes, she is. I will venture to say she looks all the better for it at the month's end."

The last sentence, fraught with interest to herself, fell upon Beulah's ear, as she passed through the hall, and an unerring intuition told her "you are the one." She put her hands over hear ears to shut out Miss Dorothea's sharp tones, and hurried away, with a dim foreboding of coming evil, which pressed heavily upon her young heart.

CHAPTER II.

The following day, in obedience to the proclamation of the mayor of the city, was celebrated as a season of special thanksgiving, and the inmates of the asylum were taken to church to morning service. After an early dinner, the matron gave them permission to amuse themselves the remainder of the day as their various inclinations prompted. There was an immediate dispersion of the assemblage, and only Beulah lingered beside the matron's chair.

"Mrs. Williams, may I take Lilly with me, and go out into the woods at the back of the Asylum?"

"I want you at home this evening, but I dislike very much to refuse you."

"Oh! never mind, if you wish me to do anything," answered the girl cheerfully.

Tears rolled over the matron's face, and hastily averting her head, she wiped them away with the corner of her apron.

"Can I do anything to help you? What is the matter?"

"Never mind, Beulah; do you get your bonnet and go to the edge of the woods—not too far, remember; and if I must have you, why I will send for you."

"I would rather not go if it will be any trouble."

"No, dear, it's no trouble. I want you to go," answered the matron, turning hastily away. Beulah felt very strongly inclined to follow, and inquire what was in store for her; but the weight on her heart pressed more heavily, and murmuring to herself, "it will come time enough, time enough," she passed on.

"May I come with you and Lilly?" entreated little Claudia, running down the walk at full speed, and putting her curly head through the palings to make the request.

"Yes, come on. You and Lilly can pick up some nice smooth burs to make baskets of. But where is your bonnet?"

"I forgot it;" she ran up, almost out of breath, and seized Beulah's hand.

"You forgot it, indeed! You little witch, you will burn as black as a gipsy."

"I don't care if I do. I hate bonnets."

"Take care, Claudy; the President won't have you all freckled and tanned."

"Won't he?" queried the child, with a saucy sparkle in her black eyes.

"That he won't; here, tie on my hood, and the next time you come running after me, bareheaded, I will make you go back; do you hear?"

"Yes, I hear. I wonder why Miss Dorothy don't bleach off her freckles; she looks just like a—"

"Hush about her, and run on ahead."

"Do pray let me get my breath first; which way are we going?"

"To the piney woods yonder," cried Lilly, clapping her hands in childish glee; "won't we have fun, rolling and sliding on the straw?" The two little ones walked on in advance.

The path along which their feet pattered so carelessly led to a hollow or ravine, and the ground on the opposite side rose into small hillocks, thickly wooded with pines. Beulah sat down upon a mound of moss and leaves; while Claudia and Lillian, throwing off their hoods, commenced the glorious game of sliding. The pine straw presented an almost glassy surface, and starting from the top of a hillock, they slid down, often stumbling and rolling together to the bottom. Many a peal of laughter rang out, and echoed far back in the forest, and two blackbirds could not have kept up a more continuous chatter. Apart from all this sat Beulah; she had remembered the matron's words, and stopped just at the verge of the woods, whence she could see the white palings of the Asylum. Above her the winter breeze moaned and roared in the pine tops; it was the sad but dearly loved forest music that she so often stole out to listen to. Every breath which sighed through the emerald boughs seemed to sweep a sympathetic chord in her soul, and she raised her arms toward the trees as though she longed to clasp the mighty musical box of nature to her heart. The far-off blue of a cloudless sky looked in upon her, like a watchful guardian; the sunlight fell slantingly, now mellowing the brown leaves and knotted trunks, and now seeming to shun the darker spots and recesses, where shadows lurked. For a time, the girl forgot all, but the quiet majestic beauty of the scene. She loved nature as only those can whose sources of pleasure have been sadly curtailed, and her heart went out, so to speak, after birds, and trees, and flowers, sunshine, and stars, and the voices of sweeping winds. An open volume lay on her lap; it was Longfellow's Poems, the book Eugene had sent her, and leaves were turned down at "Excelsior," and the "Psalm of Life." The changing countenance indexed very accurately the emotions which were excited by this communion with Nature. There was an uplifted look, a brave, glad, hopeful light in the gray eyes, generally so troubled in their expression. A sacred song rose on the evening air, a solemn but beautiful hymn. She sang the words of the great strength-giving poet, the "Psalm of Life."

"Tell me not in mournful numbers,
Life is but an empty dream;
For the soul is dead that slumbers,
And things are not what they seem."

It was wonderful what power and sweetness there was in her voice; burst after burst of rich melody fell from her trembling lips. Her soul echoed the sentiments of the immortal bard, and she repeated again and again the fifth verse:

"In the world's broad field of battle,
In the bivouac of life;
Be not like dumb driven cattle,
Be a hero in the strife."

Intuitively she seemed to feel that an hour of great trial was at hand, and this was a girding for the combat. With the shield of a warm, hopeful heart, and the sword of a strong, unfaltering will, she awaited the shock; but as she concluded her song, the head bowed itself upon her arms, the shadow of the unknown, lowering future had fallen upon her face, and only the Great Shepherd knew what passed the pale lips of the young orphan. She was startled by the sharp bark of a dog, and looking up, saw a gentleman leaning against a neighboring tree, and regarding her very earnestly. He came forward as she perceived him, and said with a pleasant smile:

"You need not be afraid of my dog. Like his master, he would not disturb you till you finished your song. Down, Carlo; be quiet, sir. My little friend, tell me who taught you to sing."

She had hastily risen, and a slight glow tinged her cheek at his question. Though naturally reserved and timid, there was a self-possession about her, unusual in children of her age, and she answered in a low voice, "I have never had a teacher, sir; but I listen to the choir on Sabbath, and sing our Sunday-school hymns at church."

"Do you know who wrote those words you sang just now? I was not aware they had been set to music?"

"I found them in this book yesterday, and liked them so much that I tried to sing them by one of our hymn tunes." She held up the volume as she spoke.

He glanced at the title, and then looked curiously at her. Beulah chanced just them to turn toward the Asylum, and saw one of the oldest girls running across the common. The shadow on her face deepened, and she looked around for Claudia and Lillian. They had tired of sliding, and were busily engaged picking up pine burs at some little distance in the rear.

"Come, Claudy—Lilly—our matron has sent for us; come, make haste."

"Do you belong to the Asylum?" asked the gentleman, shaking the ashes from his cigar.

"Yes, sir," answered she, and as the children came up she bowed and turned homeward.

"Wait a moment, those are not your sisters, certainly?" His eyes rested with unfeigned admiration on their beautiful faces.

"This one is, sir, that is not." As she spoke she laid her hand on Lillian's head. Claudia looked shyly at the stranger, and then seizing Beulah's dress, exclaimed:

"Oh, Beulah, don't let us go just yet. I left such a nice, splendid pile of burs."

"Yes, we must go, yonder comes Katy for us. Good evening, sir."

"Good evening, my little friend; some of these days I shall come to the Asylum to see you all, and have you sing that song again."

She made no reply, but catching her sister's hand, walked rapidly homeward. Katy delivered Mrs. Williams' message, and assured Beulah she must make haste, for Miss Dorothy was displeased that the children were absent.

"What! is she there again, the hateful—"

Beulah's hand was over Claudia's mouth, and prevented the remainder of the sentence. That short walk was painful, and conflicting hopes and fears chased each other in the sister's heart, as she tightened her hold on Lilly's hand.

"Oh, what a beautiful carriage!" cried Claudia, as they approached the door, and descried an elegant carriage, glittering with silver mountings, and drawn by a pair of spirited black horses.

"Yes, that it is, and there is a lady and gentleman here who must be very rich, judging from their looks. They brought Miss White."

"What do they want, Katy?" asked Claudia.

"I don't know for certain, though I have my own thoughts," answered the girl, with a knowing laugh that grated on Beulah's ears.

"Here, Beulah, bring them to the dormitory," said Mrs. Williams, meeting them at the door, and hurrying them upstairs. She hastily washed Claudia's face and recurled her hair, while the same offices were performed for Lillian by her sister.

"Don't rub my hand so hard, you hurt," cried out Claudia, sharply, as in perfect silence, and with an anxious countenance, the kind matron dressed her.

"I only want to get it white and clean, beauty," was the conciliatory reply.

"Well, I tell you that won't come off, because it's turpentine," retorted the self-willed little elf.

"Come, Beulah, bring Lilly along. Miss White is out of patience."

"What does all this mean?" said Beulah, taking her sister's hand.

"Don't ask me, poor child." As she spoke, the good woman ushered the trio into the reception-room. None of the other children were present; Beulah noted this circumstance, and drawing a long breath, looked around.

Miss White was eagerly talking to a richly-dressed and very pretty woman, while a gentleman stood beside them, impatiently twirling his seal and watch-key.

All looked up, and Miss White exclaimed:

"Here they are: now, my dear Mrs. Grayson, I rather think you can be suited. Come here, little ones." She drew Claudia to her side, while Lilly clung closer to her sister.

"Oh, what beauties! Only look at them, Alfred!" Mrs. Grayson glanced eagerly from one to the other.

"Very pretty children, indeed, my dear. Extremely pretty; particularly the black-eyed one," answered her husband, with far less ecstasy.

"I don't know; I believe I admire the golden-haired one most. She is a perfect fairy. Come here, my love, and let me talk to you," continued she, addressing Lilly. The child clasped her sister's fingers more firmly, and did not advance an inch.

"Do not hold her, Beulah. Come to the lady, Lillian," said Miss White.

As Beulah gently disengaged her hand, she felt as if the anchor of hope had been torn from her hold, but stooping down, she whispered:

"Go to the lady, Lilly darling; I will not leave you."

Thus encouraged, the little figure moved slowly forward, and paused in front of the stranger. Mrs. Grayson took her small white hands tenderly, and pressing a warm kiss on her lips, said in a kind, winning tone:

"What is your name, my dear?"

"Lillian, ma'am, but sister calls me Lilly."

"Who is 'sister'—little Claudia here?"

"Oh, no; sister Beulah." And the soft blue eyes turned lovingly toward that gentle sister.

"Good heavens, Alfred, how totally unlike! This is one of the most beautiful children I have ever seen, and that girl yonder is ugly," said the lady, in an undertone to her husband, who was talking to Claudia. It was said in a low voice, but Beulah heard every syllable, and a glow of shame for an instant bathed her brow. Claudia heard it too, and springing from Mr. Grayson's knee, she exclaimed angrily:

"She isn't ugly any such thing; she is the smartest girl in the Asylum, and I love her better than anybody in the world."

"No, Beulah is not pretty, but she is good, and that is far better," said the matron, laying her trembling hand on Beulah's shoulder. A bitter smile curled the girl's lips, but she did not move her eyes from Lillian's face.

"Fanny, if you select that plain-spoken little one, you will have some temper to curb," suggested Mr. Grayson, somewhat amused by Claudia's burst of indignation.

"Oh, my dear husband, I must have them both: only fancy how lovely they will be, dressed exactly alike. My little Lilly, and you Claudia, will you come and be my daughters? I shall love you very much, and that gentleman will be your papa. He is very kind. You shall have big wax dolls, as high as your heads, and doll-houses, and tea-sets, and beautiful blue and pink silk dresses, and every evening I shall take you out to ride in my carriage. Each of you shall have a white hat, with long, curling feathers. Will you come and live with me, and let me be your mamma?"

Beulah's face assumed an ashen hue, as she listened to these coaxing words. She had not thought of separation; the evil had never presented itself in this form, and staggering forward, she clutched the matron's dress, saying hoarsely:

"Oh, don't separate us! Don't let them take Lilly from me! I will do anything on earth, I will work my hands off; oh, do anything, but please, oh please, don't give Lilly up. My own darling Lilly." Claudia here interrupted:

"I should like to go well enough, if you will take Beulah too. Lil, are you going?"

"No, no." Lillian broke away from the stranger's clasping arm, and rushed toward her sister; but Miss White sat between them, and catching the child, she firmly, though very gently, held her back. Lilly was very much afraid of her, and bursting into tears, she cried imploringly:

"Oh, sister! take me, take me!"

Beulah sprang to her side and said almost fiercely: "Give her to me: she is mine, and you have no right to part us." She extended her arms towards the little form, struggling to reach her.

"The managers have decided that it is for the child's good that Mrs. Grayson should adopt her. We dislike very much to separate sisters, but it cannot be avoided; whole families can't be adopted by one person, and you must not interfere. She will soon be perfectly satisfied away from you, and instead of encouraging her to be rebellious, you ought to coax her to behave, and go peaceably," replied Miss White, still keeping Beulah at arm's length.

"You let go Lilly: you hateful, ugly, old thing you! She shan't go if she don't want to! She does belong to Beulah," cried Claudia, striding up and laying her hand on Lilly's arm.

"You spoiled, insolent little wretch!" muttered Miss White, crimsoning to the roots of her fiery hair.

"I am afraid they will not consent to go. Fanny, suppose you take Claudia; the other seems too reluctant," said Mr. Grayson, looking at his watch.

"But I do so want that little blue-eyed angel. Cannot the matron influence her?" She turned to her as she spoke. Thus appealed to, Mrs. Williams took the child in her arms, and caressed her tenderly.

"My dear little Lilly, you must not cry and struggle so. Why will you not go with this kind lady? she will love you very much."

"Oh, I don't want to!" sobbed she, pressing her wet cheeks against the matron's shoulder.

"But, Lilly love, you shall have everything you want. Kiss me like a sweet girl, and say you will go to my beautiful home. I will give you a cage full of the prettiest canary birds you ever looked at. Don't you love to ride? My carriage is waiting at the door. You and Claudia will have such a nice time." Mrs. Grayson knelt beside her, and kissed her tenderly; still she clung closer to the matron.

Beulah had covered her face with her hands, and stood trembling like a weed bowed before the rushing gale. She knew that neither expostulation nor entreaty would avail now, and she resolved to bear with fortitude what she could not avert. Lifting her head, she said slowly:

"If I must give up my sister, let me do so as quietly as possible. Give her to me, then perhaps she will go more willingly. Do not force her away! Oh, do not force her!"

As she uttered these words, her lips were white and cold, and the agonized expression of her face made Mrs. Grayson shiver.

"Lilly, my darling! My own precious darling!" She bent over her sister, and the little arms clasped her neck tightly, as she lifted and bore her back to the dormitory.

"You may get their clothes ready, Mrs. Williams. Rest assured, my dear Mrs. Grayson, they will go now without any further difficulty. Of course we dislike to separate sisters, but it can't be helped sometimes. If you like, I will show you over the Asylum while the children are prepared." Miss White led the way to the schoolroom.

"I am very dubious about that little one; Fanny, how will you ever manage two such dispositions—one all tears, and the other all fire and tow!" said Mr. Grayson.

"A truce to your fears, Alfred. We shall get on charmingly after the first few days. How proud I shall be with such jewels."

Beulah sat down on the edge of the blue-curtained bed, and drew her idol close to her heart. She kissed the beautiful face, and smoothed the golden curls she had so long and so lovingly arranged, and as the child returned her kisses, she felt as if rude hands were tearing her heartstrings loose. But she knew she must give her up. There was no effort within her power, which could avail to keep her treasure, and that brave spirit nerved itself. Not a tear dimmed her eye, not a sob broke from her colorless lips.

"Lilly, my own little sister, you must not cry any more. Let me wash your face; you will make your head ache if you cry so."

"Oh, Beulah! I don't want to go away from you."

"My darling, I know you don't; but you will have a great many things to make you happy, and I shall come to see you as often as I can. I can't bear to have you go, either, but I cannot help it, and I want you to go quietly, and be so good that the lady will love you."

"But to-night, when I go to bed, you will not be there to hear me say my prayers. Oh, sister! why can't you go?"

"They do not want me, my dear Lilly, but you can kneel down and say your prayers, and God will hear you just as well as if you were here with me, and I will ask Him to love you all the more, and take care of you—"

Here a little arm stole round poor Beulah's neck, and Claudia whispered with a sob:

"Will you ask him to love me too?"

"Yes, Claudy, I will."

"We will try to be good. Oh, Beulah—I love you so much, so very much!" The affectionate child pressed her lips repeatedly to Beulah's bloodless cheek.

"Claudy, if you love me, you must be kind to my little Lilly. When you see that she is sad, and crying for me, you must coax her to be as contented as possible, and always speak gently to her. Will you do this for Beulah?"

"Yes, that I will! I promise you I will, and what is more, I will fight for her! I boxed that spiteful Charley's ears the other day, for vexing her, and I will scratch anybody's eyes out that dares to scold her. This very morning I pinched Maggie black and blue, for bothering her, and I tell you I shall not let anybody impose on her." The tears dried in her brilliant eyes, and she clinched her little fist with an exalted opinion of her protective powers.

"Claudy, I do not ask you to fight for her; I want you to love her. Oh, love her! always be kind to her," murmured Beulah.

"I do love her better than anything in the world, don't I, Lilly dear?" she softly kissed one of the child's hands.

At this moment the matron entered, with a large bundle neatly wrapped. Her eyes were red, and there were traces of tears on her cheek; looking tenderly down upon the trio, she said very gently:

"Come, my pets, they will not wait any longer for you. I hope you will try to be good, and love each other, and Beulah shall come to see you." She took Claudia's hand and led her down the steps. Beulah lifted her sister, and carried her in her arms, as she had done from her birth, and at every step kissed her lips and brow.

Mr. and Mrs. Grayson were standing at the front door; they both looked pleased, as Lilly had ceased crying, and the carriage door was opened to admit them.

"Ah! my dears, now for a nice ride; Claudia, jump in," said Mr. Grayson, extending his hand to assist her. She paused, kissed her kind matron, and then approached Beulah. She could not bear to leave her, and as she threw her arms around her, sobbed out:

"Good-by, dear, good Beulah. I *will* take care of Lilly. Please love me, and ask God for me too." She was lifted into the carriage with tears streaming over her face.

Beulah drew near to Mrs. Grayson, and said in a low, but imploring tone:

"Oh, madam, love my sister, and always speak affectionately to her, then she will be good and obedient. I may come to see her often, may I not?"

"Certainly," replied the lady, in a tone which chilled poor Beulah's heart. She swallowed a groan of agony, and straining the loved one to her bosom, pressed her lips to Lilly's.

"God bless my little sister, my darling, my all!" She put the child in Mr. Grayson's extended arms, and only saw that her sister looked back appealingly to her. Miss White came up and said something which she did not hear, and, turning hastily away, she went up to the dormitory, and seated herself on Lilly's vacant bed. The child knew not how the hours passed; she sat with her face buried in her hands, until the light of a candle flashed into the darkened chamber, and the kind voice of the matron fell on her ear.

"Beulah, will you try to eat some supper? Do, dear."

"No, thank you, I don't want anything."

"Poor child, I would have saved you all this had it been in my power; but, when once decided by the managers, you know I could not interfere. They disliked to separate you and Lilly, but thought, that under the circumstances, it was the best arrangement they could make. Beulah, I want to tell you something, if you will listen to me." She seated herself on the edge of the bed, and took one of the girl's hands between both hers.

"The managers think it is best that you should go out and take a situation. I am sorry I am forced to give you up, very sorry, for you have always been a good girl, and I love you dearly; but these things cannot be avoided, and I hope all will turn out for the best. There is a place engaged for you, and Miss White wishes you to go to-morrow. I trust you will not have a hard time. You are to take care of an infant, and they will give you six dollars a month besides your board and clothes. Try to do your duty, child, and perhaps something may happen which will enable you to turn teacher."

"Well, I will do the best I can. I do not mind work, but then Lilly—" Her head went down on her arms once more.

"Yes, dear, I know it is very hard for you to part with her; but remember, it is for her good. Mr. Grayson is very wealthy, and of course Lilly and Claudy will have—"

"And what is money to my—" Again she paused abruptly.

"Ah, child, you do not begin to know! Money is everything in this world to some people, and more than the next to other poor souls. Well, well, I hope it will prove for the best as far as you are concerned. It is early yet, but maybe you had better go to bed, as you are obliged to leave in the morning."

"I could not sleep."

"God will help you, dear child, if you try to do your duty. All of us have sorrows, and if yours have begun early, they may not last long. Poor little thing, I shall always remember you in my prayers." She kissed her gently, and left her, hoping that solitude would soothe her spirits. Miss White's words rang in the girl's ears like a knell. "She will soon be perfectly satisfied away from you."

Would she? Could that idolized sister learn to do without her, and love her new friends as fondly as the untiring one who had cradled her in her arms for six long years? A foreboding dread hissed continually, "Do you suppose the wealthy and fashionable Mrs. Grayson, who lives in that elegant house on———Street, will suffer her adopted daughter to associate intimately with a hired nurse?"

Again the light streamed into the room. She buried her face deeper in her apron.

"Beulah," said a troubled, anxious voice.

"Oh, Eugene!" She sprang up with a dry sob, and threw herself into his arms.

"I know it all, dear Beulah; but come down to Mrs. Williams' room, there is a bright fire there, and your hands are as cold as ice. You will make yourself sick sitting her without even a shawl around you." He led her downstairs to the room occupied by the matron, who kindly took her work to the dining-room, and left them to talk unrestrainedly.

"Sit down in this rocking-chair and warm your hands."

He seated himself near her, and as the firelight glowed on the faces of both, they contrasted strangely. One was classical and full of youthful beauty, the other wan, haggard, and sorrow-stained. He looked about sixteen, and promised to become a strikingly handsome man, while the proportions of his polished brow indicated more than ordinary intellectual endowments. He watched his companion earnestly, sadly, and, leaning forward, took one of her hands.

"Beulah, I see from your face that you have not shed a single tear. I wish you would not keep your sorrow so pent up in your heart. It grieves me to see you look as you do now."

"Oh! I can't help it. If it were not for you I believe I should die, I am so very miserable. Eugene, if you could have seen our Lilly cling to me, even to the last moment. It seems to me my heart will break." She sank her weary head on his shoulder.

"Yes, darling, I know you are suffering very much; but remember that 'all things work together for good to them that love God.' Perhaps He sees it is best that you should give her up for awhile, and if so, will you not try to bear it cheerfully, instead of making yourself sick with useless grief?" He gently smoothed the hair from her brow as he spoke. She did not reply. He did not expect that she would, and continued in the same kind tone.

"I am much more troubled about your taking this situation. If I had known it earlier I would have endeavored to prevent it, but I suppose it cannot be helped now, for awhile at least. As soon as possible I am determined you shall go to school; and remember, dear Beulah, I am just as much grieved at your sorrows as you are. In a few years I shall have a home of my own, and you shall be the first to come to it. Never mind these dark, stormy days. Do you remember what our minister said in his sermon last Sunday? 'The darkest hour is just before daybreak.' Already I begin to see the 'silver lining' of clouds that a few years, or even months ago, seemed heavy and cheerless. I have heard a great deal about the ills and trials of this world, but I think a brave, hopeful spirit, will do much toward remedying the evil. For my part, I look forward to the time when you and I shall have a home of our own, and Lilly and Claudy can be with us. I was talking to Mrs. Mason about it yesterday; she loves you very much. I dare say all will be right, so cheer up, Beulah, and do look on the bright side."

"Eugene, you are the only bright side I have to look on. Sometimes I think you will get tired of me, and if you ever do, I shall want to die. Oh, how could I bear to know you did not love me." She raised her head and looked earnestly at his noble face.

Eugene laughingly repeated her words.

"Get tired of you, indeed—not I, little sister."

"Oh, I forgot to thank you for your book: I like it better than anything I ever read; some parts are so beautiful—so very grand. I keep it in my basket, and read every moment I can spare."

"I knew you would like it, particularly 'Excelsior.' Beulah, I have written *excelsior* on my banner, and I intend, like that noble youth, to press forward over every obstacle, mounting at every step, until I, too, stand on the highest pinnacle, and plant my banner where its glorious motto shall float over the world. That poem stirs my very soul like martial music, and I feel as if I should like to see Mr. Longfellow, to tell him how I thank him for having written it. I want you to mark the passages you like best; and now I think of it, here is a pencil I cut for you to-day."

He drew it from his pocket and put it into her hand, while his face glowed with enthusiasm.

"Thank you, thank you." Grateful tears sprang to her eyes; tears which acute suffering could not wring from her. He saw the gathering drops, and said gaily:

"If that is the way you intend to thank me, I shall bring you no more pencils. But you look very pale, and ought to be asleep, for I have no doubt to-morrow will be a trying day for you. Do exert yourself to be brave, and bear it all for a little while; I know it will not be very long, and I shall come and see you just as often as possible."

He rose as he spoke.

"Are you obliged to go so soon? Can't you stay with me a little longer?" pleaded Beulah.

The boy's eyes filled as he looked at the beseeching, haggard face, and he answered hastily:

"Not to-night, Beulah; you must go to sleep—you need it sadly."

"You will be cold walking home. Let me get you a shawl."

"No, I left my overcoat in the hall—here it is."

She followed him out to the door, as he drew it on and put on his cap. The moonlight shone over the threshold, and he thought she looked ghostly as it fell upon her face. He took her hand, pressed it gently, and said—

"Good night, dear Beulah."

"Good-by, Eugene. Do come and see me again soon."

"Yes, I will. Don't get low-spirited as soon as I am out of sight, do you hear?"

"Yes, I hear, I will try not to complain. Walk fast and keep warm."

She pressed his hand affectionately, watched his receding form as long as she could trace its outline, and then went slowly back to the dormitory. Falling on her knees by the side of Lilly's empty couch, she besought God, in trembling accents, to bless her, "darling little sister and Claudy," and to give her strength to perform all her duties contentedly and cheerfully.

CHAPTER III.

Beulah stood waiting on the steps of the large mansion, to which she had been directed by Miss Dorothea White. Her heart throbbed painfully, and her hand trembled as she rang the bell. The door was opened by a negro waiter, who merely glanced at her, and asked, carelessly—

"Well, little miss, what do you want?"

"Is Mrs. Martin at home?"

"Yes, miss; come, walk in. There is but a poor fire in the front parlor—suppose you sit down in the back room. Mrs. Martin will be down in a minute."

The first object which arrested Beulah's attention was a center table covered with books. "Perhaps," thought she, "they will permit me to read some of them." While she sat looking over the titles, the rustle of silk caused her to glance around, and she saw Mrs. Martin quite near her.

"Good morning," said the lady, with a searching look, which made the little figure tremble.

"Good morning, madam."

"You are the girl Miss White promised to send from the Asylum, are you not?"

"Yes, madam."

"Do you think you can take good care of my baby?"

"Oh, I will try."

"You don't look strong and healthy—have you been sick?"

"No, I am very well, thank you."

"I may want you to sew some, occasionally, when the baby is asleep. Can you hem and stitch neatly?"

"I believe I sew very well, madam—our matron says so."

"What is your name? Miss White told me, but I have forgotten it."

"Beulah Benton."

"Well, Beulah, I think you will suit me very well, if you are only careful, and attend to my directions. I am just going out shopping, but you can come up-stairs and take charge of Johnny. Where are your clothes?"

"Our matron will send them to-day."

Beulah followed Mrs. Martin up the steps, somewhat reassured by her kind reception. The room was in utter confusion, the toilet-table covered with powder, hairpins, bows of different colored ribbon, and various bits of jewelry; the hearth unswept, the work-stand groaning beneath the superincumbent mass of sewing, finished and unfinished garments, working materials, and, to crown the whole, the lady's winter hat. A girl, apparently about thirteen years of age, was seated by the fire, busily embroidering a lamp-mat; another, some six years younger, was dressing a doll; while an infant, five or six months old, crawled about the carpet, eagerly picking up pins, needles, and every other objectionable article his little purple fingers could grasp.

"Take him, Beulah," said the mother.

She stooped to comply, and was surprised that the little fellow testified no fear of her. She raised him in her arms, and kissed his rosy cheeks, as he looked wonderingly at her.

"Ma, is that Johnny's new nurse? What is her name?" said the youngest girl, laying down her doll and carefully surveying the stranger.

"Yes, Annie; and her name is Beulah," replied the mother, adjusting his bonnet.

"Beulah—it's about as pretty as her face. Yes, just about," continued Annie, in an audible whisper to her sister. The latter gave Beulah a condescending stare, curled her lips disdainfully and with a polite "Mind your own business, Annie," returned to her embroidery.

"Keep the baby by the fire; and if he frets, you must feed him. Laura, show her where to find his cup of arrowroot, and you and Annie stay here, till I come home."

"No, indeed, ma, I can't, for I must go down, and practise my music lesson," answered the eldest daughter, decisively.

"Well, then, Annie, stay in my room."

"I am going to make some sugar-candy, 'ma. *She*" (pointing to Beulah) "can take care of Johnny. I thought that was what you hired her for."

"You will make no sugar-candy till I come home, Miss Annie; do you hear that? Now, mind what I said to you."

Mrs. Martin rustled out of the room, leaving Annie to scowl ominously at the new nurse, and vent her spleen by boxing her doll, because the inanimate little lady would not keep her blue-bead eyes open. Beulah loved children, and Johnny forcibly reminded her of earlier days, when she had carried Lilly about in her arms. For some time after the departure of Mrs. Martin and Laura, the little fellow seemed perfectly satisfied, but finally grew fretful, and Beulah surmised he might be hungry.

"Will you please give me the baby's arrowroot?"

"I don't know anything about it; ask Harrison."

"Who is Harrison?"

"Why, the cook."

Glancing around the room, she found the arrowroot; the boy was fed, and soon fell asleep. Beulah sat in a low rocking-chair, by the hearth, holding the infant, and watching the little figure opposite. Annie was trying to fit a new silk waist to her doll, but it was too broad one way and too narrow another. She twisted and jerked it divers ways, but all in vain; and at last, disgusted by the experiment, she tore it off and aimed it at the fire, with an impatient cry.

"The plagued, bothering, ugly thing! My Lucia never shall wear such a fit."

Beulah caught the discarded waist, and said, quietly:

"You can very easily make it fit, by taking up this seam and cutting it out in the neck."

"I don't believe it."

"Then, hand me the doll and the scissors and I will show you."

"Her name is Miss Lucia-di-Lammermoor. Mr. Green named her: don't say '*doll*,' call her by her proper name," answered the spoiled child, handing over the unfortunate waxen representative of a not less unfortunate heroine.

"Well, then, Miss Lucia-di-Lammermoor," said Beulah, smiling. A few alterations reduced the dress to the proper dimensions, and Annie arrayed her favorite in it, with no slight degree of satisfaction. The obliging manner of the new nurse won her heart, and she began to chat pleasantly enough. About two o'clock Mrs. Martin returned, inquired after Johnny, and again absented herself to "see about dinner." Beulah was very weary of the close, disordered room, and as the babe amused himself with his ivory rattle, she swept the floor, dusted the furniture, and arranged the chairs. The loud ringing of a bell startled her, and she conjectured dinner was ready. Some time elapsed before any of the family returned, and then Laura entered, looking very sullen. She took charge of the babe, and rather ungraciously desired the nurse to get her dinner.

"I do not wish any," answered Beulah.

At this stage of the conversation the door opened, and a boy, seemingly about Eugene's age, entered the room. He looked curiously at Beulah, inclined his head slightly, and joined his sister at the fire.

"How do you like her, Laura?" he asked, in a distinct under tone.

"Oh! I suppose she will do well enough; but she is horribly ugly," replied Laura, in a similar key.

"I don't know, sis. It is what Dr. Patton, the lecturer on physiognomy, would call a 'striking' face."

"Yes, strikingly ugly, Dick. Her forehead juts over, like the eaves of the kitchen, and her eyebrows—"

"Hush! she will hear you. Come down and play that new waltz for me, like a good sister." The two left the room. Beulah had heard every word; she could not avoid it, and as she recalled Mrs. Grayson's remark concerning her appearance on the previous day, her countenance reflected her intense mortification. She pressed her face against the window-pane and stared vacantly out. The elevated position commanded a fine view of the town, and on the eastern horizon the blue waters of the harbor glittered with "silvery sheen." At any other time, and with different emotions, Beulah's love of the beautiful would have been particularly gratified by this extended prospect; but now the whole possessed no charms for her darkened spirit. For the moment, earth was black-hued to her gaze; she only saw "horribly ugly," inscribed on sky and water. Her soul seemed to leap forward and view nearer the myriad motes that floated in the haze of the future. She leaned over the vast whirring lottery wheel of life, and saw a blank come up, with her name stamped upon it. But the grim smile faded from her lips, and brave endurance looked out from the large sad eyes, as she murmured,

"Be not like dumb, driven cattle;
Be a hero in the strife."

"If I am ugly, God made me so, and I know 'He doeth all things well.' I will not let it bother me; I will try not to think of it. But, oh! I am so glad, I thank God, that he made my Lilly beautiful. She will never have to suffer, as I do now. My own darling Lilly!" Large drops glistened in her eyes; she rarely wept; but though the tears did not fall, they gathered often in the gray depths. The evening passed very quietly; Mr. Martin was absent in a distant State, whither, as traveling agent for a mercantile house, he was often called. After tea, when little Johnny had been put to sleep in his crib, Mrs. Martin directed Annie to show the nurse her own room. Taking a candle, the child complied, and her mother ordered one of the servants to carry up the trunk containing Beulah's clothes. Up, up, two weary, winding flights of steps, the little Annie toiled, and pausing at the landing of the second, pointed to a low attic-chamber, lighted by dormer windows on the east and west. The floor was uncovered; the furniture consisted of a narrow trundle-bed, wash-stand, a cracked looking-glass suspended from a nail, a small deal table, and a couple of chairs. There were, also, some hooks driven into the wall, to hang clothes upon.

"You need not be afraid to sleep here, because the boarders occupy the rooms on the floor below this; and besides, you know robbers never get up to the garret," said Annie, glancing around the apartment, and shivering with an undefined dread, rather than with cold, though her nose and fingers were purple, and this garret-chamber possessed neither stove nor chimney.

"I am not afraid; but this is only one garret-room, are the others occupied?"

"Yes, by carpets in summer, and rats in winter," laughed Annie.

"I suppose I may have a candle?" said Beulah, as the porter deposited her trunk and withdrew.

"Yes, this one is for you. Ma is always uneasy about fire, so don't set anything in a blaze to keep yourself warm. Here, hold the light at the top of the steps till I get down to the next floor, then there is a hall-lamp. Good night."

"Good night." Beulah bolted the door, and surveyed her new apartment. Certainly it was sufficiently cheerless, but its isolated position presented to her a redeeming feature. Thought she, "I can sit up here, and read just as late as I please. Oh! I shall have so much time to myself these long, long nights." Unpacking her trunk, she hung her dresses on the hooks, placed the books Mrs. Mason and Eugene had given her on the table, and settling the candle beside them, smiled in anticipation of the many treats in store for her. She read several chapters in her Bible, and then, as her head ached and her eyes grew heavy, she sank upon her knees. Ah! what an earnest, touching petition ascended to the throne of the Father; prayers, first for Lilly and Claudia, and lastly for herself.

"Help me, oh Lord! not to be troubled and angry when I hear that I am so ugly; and make me remember that I am your child." Such was her final request, and she soon slept soundly, regardless of the fact that she was now thrown upon the wide though not altogether cold or unloving world.

CHAPTER IV.

Day after day passed monotonously, and except a visit from Eugene, there was no link added to the chain which bound Beulah to the past. That brief visit encouraged and cheered the lonely heart, yearning for affectionate sympathy, yet striving to hush the hungry cry and grow contented with its lot. During the second week of her stay, little Johnny was taken sick, and he had become so fond of his new attendant, that no one else was permitted to hold him. Often she paced the chamber floor for hours, lulling the fretful babe with softly sung tunes of other days, and the close observer, who could have peered at such times into the down-cast eyes, might have easily traced in the misty depths memories that nestled in her heart's sanctuary. The infant soon recovered, and one warm, sunny afternoon, when Mrs. Martin directed Beulah to draw him in his wicker carriage up and down the pavement before the door, she could no longer repress the request, which had trembled on her lips more than once, and asked permission to take her little charge to Mrs. Grayson's. A rather reluctant assent was given, and soon the carriage was drawn in the direction of Mr. Grayson's elegant city residence. A marvelous change came over the wan face of the nurse as she paused at the marble steps, guarded on either side by sculptured lions. "To see Lilly!" The blood sprang to her cheeks, and an eager look of delight crept into the eyes. The door was partially opened by an insolent-looking footman, whose hasty glance led him to suppose her one of the numerous supplicants for charity, who generally left that princely mansion as empty-handed as they came. He was about to close the door; but undaunted by this reception, she hastily asked to see Mrs. Grayson, and Lillian Benton.

"Mrs. Grayson is engaged, and there is no such person here as Lillian

Benton. Miss Lilly Grayson is my young mistress' name; but I can tell you, her mamma don't suffer her to see the like of you; so be off."

"Lilly is my sister, and I must see her. Tell Mrs. Grayson Beulah Benton wishes to see her sister; and ask her also if Claudia may not see me."

She dropped the tongue of the carriage, and the thin hands clutched each other in an agony of dread, lest her petition should be refused. The succeeding five minutes seemed an eternity to her, and as the door opened again, she leaned forward, and held her breath, like one whose fate was in the balance. Costly silk and dazzling diamonds met her gaze. The settled lines of Mrs. Grayson's pretty mouth indicated that she had a disagreeable duty to perform, yet had resolved to do it at once, and set the matter forever at rest.

"You are Mrs. Martin's nurse I believe, and the girl I saw at the Asylum?" said she, frigidly.

"Yes, madam, I am Lilly's sister; you said I might come and see her. Oh, if you only knew how miserable I have been since we were parted, you would not look so coldly at me! Do, please, let me see her. Oh, don't deny me."

These words were uttered in a tone of imploring agony.

"I am very sorry you happen to be her sister, and I assure you, child, it pains me to refuse you; but when you remember the circumstances, you ought not to expect to associate with her as you used to do. She will be educated to move in a circle very far above you, and you ought to be more than willing to give her up, when you know how lucky she has been in securing a home of wealth. Besides, she is getting over the separation very nicely indeed, and if she were to see you even once, it would make matters almost as bad as ever. I dare say you are a good girl, and will not trouble me any further. My husband and I are unwilling that you should see Lilly again; and though I am very sorry I am forced to disappoint you, I feel that I am doing right."

The petitioner fell on her knees, and extending her arms, said huskily:

"Oh, madam! are we to be parted forever? I pray you, in the name of God, let me see her! let me see her!"

Mrs. Grayson was not a cruel woman, far from it, but she was strangely weak and worldly. The idea of a hired nurse associating familiarly with her adopted daughter was repulsive to her aristocratic pride, and therefore she hushed the tones of true womanly sympathy, and answered resolutely:

"It pains me to refuse you; but I have given good reasons, and cannot think of changing my determination. I hope you will not annoy me by any future efforts to enter my house. There is a present for you. Good evening."

She tossed a five-dollar gold piece toward the kneeling figure, and closing the door, locked it on the inside. The money rolled ringingly down the steps, and the grating sound of the key, as it was hurriedly turned, seemed typical of the unyielding lock which now forever barred the child's hopes. The look of utter despair gave place to an expression of indescribable bitterness. Springing from her suppliant posture, she muttered with terrible emphasis:

"A curse on that woman and her husband! May God answer their prayers as she has answered mine!"

Picking up the coin which lay glittering on the sidewalk, she threw it forcibly against the door, and as it rebounded into the street, took the carriage tongue, and slowly retraced her steps. It was not surprising that passers-by gazed curiously at the stony face, with its large eyes, brimful of burning hate, as the injured orphan walked mechanically on, unconscious that her lips were crushed till purple drops oozed over them. The setting sun flashed his ruddy beams caressingly over her brow, and whispering winds lifted tenderly the clustering folds of jetty hair; but nature's pure-hearted darling had stood over the noxious tarn, whence the poisonous breath of a corrupt humanity rolled upward, and the once sinless child inhaled the vapor until her soul was a great boiling Marah. Ah, truly

"There are swift hours in life—strong, rushing hours—
That do the work of tempests in their might."

Peaceful valleys, green and flowery, sleeping in loveliness, have been upheaved, and piled in somber, jagged masses, against the sky, by the fingering of an earthquake; and gentle, loving, trusting hearts, over whose altars brooded the white-winged messengers of God's peace, have been as suddenly transformed by a manifestation of selfishness and injustice, into gloomy haunts of misanthropy. Had Mrs. Grayson been arraigned for cruelty, or hard-heartedness, before a tribunal of her equals (*i.e.* fashionable friends), the charge would have been scornfully repelled, and unanimous would have been her acquittal. "Hard-hearted! oh no, she was only prudent and wise." Who could expect her to suffer her pampered, inert darling to meet and acknowledge as an equal, the far-less-daintily-fed and elegantly clad sister, whom God called to labor for her frugal meals? Ah, this fine-ladyism, this ignoring of labor, to which, in accordance with the divine decree, all should be subjected; this false-effeminacy, and miserable affectation of refinement, which characterizes the age, is the unyielding lock on the wheels of social reform and advancement.

Beulah took her charge home, and when dusk came on, rocked him to sleep, and snugly folded the covering of his crib over the little throbbing heart, whose hours of trial were yet veiled by the impenetrable curtain of futurity. Mrs. Martin and her elder children had gone to a concert, and, of course, the nurse was to remain with Johnny until his mother's return. Standing beside the crib, and gazing down at the rosy cheeks and curling locks, nestled against the pillow, Beulah's thoughts winged along the tear-stained past, to the hour when Lilly had been placed in her arms, by emaciated hands stiffening in death. For six years she had held, and hushed, and caressed her dying father's last charge, and now strange ruthless fingers had torn the clinging heart-strings from the idol. There were no sobs, nor groans, to voice the anguish of the desolate orphan. The glittering eyes were tearless, but the brow was darkly furrowed, the ashy lips writhed, and the folded hands were purple from compression. Turning from the crib, she threw up the sash, and seated herself on the window-sill. Below lay the city, with its countless lamps gleaming in every direction and stretching away on the principal streets like long processions; in the distance the dark waters of the river, over which steamboat-lights flashed now and then like ignes-fatui; and above her arched the dome of sky, with its fiery fret-work. Never before had she looked up at the starry groups, without an emotion of exulting joy, of awful adoration. To her worshiping gaze they had seemed glimpses of the spirit's home: nay, loving eyes shining down upon her thorny pathway. But now, the twinkling rays fell unheeded, impotent to pierce the sable clouds of grief. She sat looking out into the night, with strained eyes that seemed fastened upon a corpse. An hour passed thus, and as the clang of the town clock died away, the shrill voice of the watchman rang through the air:

"Nine o'clock; and all's well!"

Beulah lifted her head and listened. "ALL'S WELL!" The mockery maddened her, and she muttered audibly:

"That is the sort of sympathy I shall have through life. I am to hear that '*all is well*' when my heart is dying, nay, dead within me! Oh, if I could only die! What a calm, calm time I should have in my coffin! Nobody to taunt me with my poverty and ugliness! Oh, what did God make me for? The few years of my life have been full of misery; I cannot remember one single day of pure happiness, for there was always something to spoil what little joy I ever knew. When I was born, why did not I die at once? And why did not God take me instead of my dear, dear father? He should have been left with Lilly, for people love the beautiful, but nobody will ever care for me. I am of no use to anything, and so ugly, that I hate myself. O, Lord, I don't want to live another day! I am sick of my life—take me, take me!" But a feeble ray of comfort stole into her shivering heart, as she bowed her head upon her hands; Eugene Graham loved her: and the bleeding tendrils of affection henceforth clasped him as their only support. She was aroused from her painful reverie by a movement in the crib, and, hastening to her charge, was startled by the appearance of the babe. The soft blue eyes were rolled up and set, the face of a purplish hue, and the delicate limbs convulsed. During her residence at the Asylum she had more than once assisted the matron in nursing children similarly affected; and now, calling instantly for a tub of water, she soon immersed the rigid limbs in a warm bath, while one of the waiters was despatched for the family physician. When Dr. Hartwell entered, he found her standing, with the infant clasped tightly in her arms, and as his eyes rested curiously upon her face, she forgot that he was a stranger, and springing to meet him, exclaimed:

"Oh, sir, will he die?"

With his fingers on the bounding pulse, he answered:

"He is very ill. Where is his mother? Who are you?"

"His mother is at a concert, and I am his nurse."

The spasms had ceased, but the twitching limbs told that they might return any moment, and the physician immediately administered a potion.

"How long will Mrs. Martin be absent?"

"It is uncertain. When shall I give the medicine again?"

"I shall remain until she comes home."

Beulah was pacing up and down the floor, with Johnny in her arms; Dr. Hartwell stood on the hearth, leaning his elbow on the mantelpiece, and watching the slight form as it stole softly to and fro. Gradually the child became quiet, but his nurse kept up her walk. Dr. Hartwell said abruptly:

"Sit down, girl! you will walk yourself into a shadow."

She lifted her head, shook it in reply, and resumed her measured tread.

"What is your name?"

"Beulah Benton."

"Beulah!" repeated the doctor, while a smile flitted over his mustached lip. She observed it, and exclaimed, with bitter emphasis:

"You need not tell me it is unsuitable; I know it; I feel it. Beulah! Beulah! Oh my father! I have neither sunshine nor flowers, nor hear the singing of birds, nor the voice of the turtle. You ought to have called me MARAH."

"You have read the 'Pilgrim's Progress' then?" said he, with a searching glance.

Either she did not hear him, or was too entirely engrossed by painful reflection to frame an answer. The despairing expression settled upon her face, and the broken threads of memory wove on again.

"Beulah! how came you here in the capacity of nurse?"

"I was driven here by necessity."

"Where are your parents and friends?"

"I have none. I am alone in the world."

"How long have you been so dependent?"

She raised her hand deprecatingly, nay commandingly, as though she had said:

"No more. You have not the right to question, nor I the will to answer."

He marked the look of unconquerable grief, and understanding her gesture, made no more inquiries.

Soon after, Mrs. Martin returned, and having briefly stated what had occurred, and given directions for the child's treatment, he withdrew. His low "good night," gently spoken to the nurse, was only acknowledged by a slight inclination of the head, as he passed her. Little Johnny was restless, and constantly threatened with a return of the convulsions. His mother held him on her knee, and telling Beulah she "had been a good, sensible girl, to bathe him so promptly," gave her permission to retire.

"I am not at all sleepy, and would rather stay here and nurse him. He does not moan so much when I walk with him. Give him back to me."

"But you will be tired out."

"I shall not mind it." Stooping down, she lifted the restless boy, and wrapping his cloak about him, commenced the same noiseless tread. Thus the night waned; occasionally Mrs. Martin rose and felt her babe's pulse, and assisted in giving the hourly potions, then reseated herself, and allowed the hireling to walk on. Once she offered to relieve her, but the arms refused to yield their burden. A little after four, the mother slept soundly in her chair. Gradually the stars grew dim, and the long, undulating chain of clouds that girded the eastern horizon kindled into a pale orange, that transformed them into mountains of topaz. Pausing by the window, and gazing vacantly out, Beulah's eyes were suddenly riveted on the gorgeous pageant, which untiring nature daily renews, and she stood watching the masses of vapor painted by coming sunlight, and floating slowly before the wind, until the "King of Day" flashed up and dazzled her. Mrs. Martin was awakened by the entrance of one of the servants, and starting up, exclaimed:

"Bless me! I have been asleep. Beulah, how is Johnny? You must be tired to death."

"He is sleeping now very quietly; I think he is better; his fever is not so high. I will take care of him, and you had better take another nap before breakfast."

Mrs. Martin obeyed the nurse's injunction, and it was two hours later when she took her child, and directed Beulah to get her breakfast. But the weary girl felt no desire for the meal, and retiring to her attic room, bathed her eyes, and replaited her hair. Kneeling beside her bed, she tried to pray, but the words died on her lips; and too miserable to frame a petition, she returned to the chamber where, in sad vigils, she had spent the night. Dr. Hartwell bowed as she entered, but the head was bent down, and without glancing at him, she took the fretful, suffering child, and walked to the window. While she stood there, her eyes fell upon the loved face of her best friend. Eugene Graham was crossing the street. For an instant the burning blood surged over her wan, sickly cheeks, and the pale lips parted in a smile of delight, as she leaned forward to see whether he was coming in. The door bell rang, and she sprang from the window, unconscious of the piercing eyes fastened upon her. Hastily laying little Johnny on his mother's lap, she merely said:

"I will be back soon," and, darting down the steps, met Eugene at the entrance, throwing her arms around his neck and hiding her face on his shoulder.

"What is the matter, Beulah? Do tell me," said he, anxiously.

Briefly she related her fruitless attempt to see Lilly, and pointed out the nature of the barrier which must forever separate them. Eugene listened with flashing eyes, and several times the word "brutal" escaped his lips. He endeavored to comfort her by holding out hopes of brighter days, but her eyes were fixed on shadows, and his cheering words failed to call up a smile. They stood in the hall near the front door, and here Dr. Hartwell found them, when he left the sick-room. Eugene looked up as he approached them, and stepped forward with a smile of recognition to shake the extended hand. Beulah's countenance became instantly repellent, and she was turning away when the doctor addressed her:

"You must feel very much fatigued from being up all night. I know from your looks that you did not close your eyes."

"I am no worse looking than usual, thank you," she replied, icily, drawing back as she spoke, behind Eugene. The doctor left them, and as his buggy rolled from the door, Beulah seemed to breathe freely again. Poor child; her sensitive nature had so often been deeply wounded by the thoughtless remarks of strangers, that she began to shrink from all observation, as the surest mode of escaping pain. Eugene noticed her manner, and biting his lips with vexation, said reprovingly:

"Beulah, you were very rude to Dr. Hartwell. Politeness costs nothing, and you might at least have answered his question with ordinary civility."

Her eyelids drooped, and a tremor passed over her mouth, as she answered meekly:

"I did not intend to be rude; but I dread to have people look at, or speak to me."

"Why, pray?"

"Because I am so ugly, and they are sure to show me that they see it."

He drew his arm protectingly around her, and said gently:

"Poor child; it is cruel to make you suffer so. But rest assured Dr. Hartwell will never wound your feelings. I have heard that he was a very stern and eccentric man, though a remarkably learned one, yet I confess there is something in his manner which fascinates me, and if you will only be like yourself he will always speak kindly to you. But I am staying too long. Don't look so forlorn and ghostly. Positively I hate to come to see you, for somehow your wretched face haunts me. Here is a book I have just finished; perhaps it will serve to divert your mind." He put a copy of "Irving's Sketch Book" in her hand, and drew on his gloves.

"Oh, Eugene, can't you stay a little longer; just a little longer? It seems such a great while since you were here." She looked up wistfully into the handsome, boyish face.

Drawing out an elegant new watch, he held it before her eyes and answered hurriedly:

"See there; it is ten o'clock, and I am behind my appointment at the lecture-room. Good-by; try to be cheerful. 'What can't be cured must be endured,' you know, so do not despond, dear Beulah." Shaking her hand cordially, he ran down the steps. The orphan pressed her hands tightly over her brow, as if to stay some sudden, painful thought, and slowly remounted the stairs.

CHAPTER V.

Little Johnny's illness proved long and serious, and for many days and nights he seemed on the verge of the tomb. His wailings were never hushed except in Beulah's arms, and as might be supposed, constant watching soon converted her into a mere shadow of her former self. Dr. Hartwell often advised rest and fresh air for her, but the silent shake of her head proved how reckless she was of her own welfare. Thus several weeks elapsed, and gradually the sick child grew stronger. One afternoon Beulah sat holding him on her knee; he had fallen asleep, with one tiny hand clasping hers, and while he slept she read. Absorbed in the volume Eugene had given her, her thoughts wandered on with the author, amid the moldering monuments of Westminster Abbey, and finally the sketch was concluded by that solemn paragraph: "Thus man passes away; his name perishes from record and recollection; his history is as a tale that is told, and his very monument becomes a ruin." Again she read this sad comment on the vanity of earth, and its ephemeral hosts, and her mind was filled with weird images, that looked out from her earnest eyes. Dr. Hartwell entered unperceived, and stood for some moments at the back of her chair, glancing over her shoulder at the last page. At length she closed the book, and passing her hand wearily over her eyes, said audibly:

"Ah! if we could only have sat down together in that gloomy garret, and had a long talk! It would have helped us both. Poor Chatterton! I know just how you felt, when you locked your door and lay down on your truckle-bed, and swallowed your last draught!"

"There is not a word about Chatterton in that sketch," said the doctor.

She started, looked up, and answered slowly:

"No, not a word, not a word. He was buried among paupers, you know."

"What made you think of him?"

"I thought that instead of resting in the Abbey, under sculptured marble, his bones were scattered, nobody knows where. I often think of him."

"Why?"

"Because he was so miserable and uncared-for; because sometimes I feel exactly as he did." As she uttered these words, she compressed her lips in a manner which plainly said, "There! I have no more to say, so do not question me."

He had learned to read her countenance, and as he felt the infant's pulse, pointed to the crib, saying:

"You must lay him down now; he seems fast asleep."

"No, I may as well hold him."

"Girl, will you follow my directions?" said he, sharply.

Beulah looked up at him for a moment, then rose and placed the boy in his crib, while a sort of grim smile distorted her features. The doctor mixed some medicine, and setting the glass on the table, put both hands in his pockets and walked up to the nurse. Her head was averted.

"Beulah, will you be good enough to look at me?" She fixed her eyes proudly on his, and her beautiful teeth gleamed through the parted lips.

"Do you know that Eugene is going away very soon, to be absent at least five years?"

An incredulous smile flitted over her face, but the ashen hue of death settled there.

"I am in earnest. He leaves for Europe next week, to be gone a long time."

She extended her hands pleadingly, and said in a hoarse whisper:

"Are you sure?"

"Quite sure; his passage is already engaged in a packet that will sail early next week. What will become of you in his absence?"

The strained eyes met his, vacantly; the icy hands dropped, and she fell forward against him.

Guy Hartwell placed the slight attenuated form on the sofa, and stood with folded arms looking down at the colorless face. His high white brow clouded, and a fierce light kindled in his piercing, dark eyes, as through closed teeth came the rather indistinct words:

"It is madness to indulge the thought; I was a fool to dream of it. She would prove heartless, like all of her sex, and repay me with black ingratitude. Let her fight the battle of life unaided."

He sprinkled a handful of water in the upturned face, and in a few minutes saw the eyelids tremble, and knew from the look of suffering, that with returning consciousness came the keen pangs of grief. She covered her face with her hands, and after a little while, asked:

"Shall I ever see him again?"

"He will come here to-night to tell you about his trip. But what will become of you in his absence?—answer me that!"

"God only knows!"

Dr. Hartwell wrote the directions for Johnny's medicine, and placing the slip of paper on the glass, took his hat and left the room. Beulah sat with her head pressed against the foot of the crib—stunned, taking no note of the lapse of time.

———"Twilight gray,
Had in her sober livery all things clad."

The room had grown dark, save where a mellow ray stole through the western window. Beulah rose mechanically, lighted the lamp, and shaded it so as to shield the eyes of the sleeping boy. The door was open, and glancing up, she saw Eugene on the threshold. Her arms were thrown around him, with a low cry of mingled joy and grief.

"Oh, Eugene! please don't leave me! Whom have I in the world but you?"

"Beulah, dear, I must go. Only think of the privilege of being at a German University! I never dreamed of such a piece of good luck. Don't cry so; I shall come back some of these days, such an erudite, such an elegant young man, you will hardly know me. Only five years. I am almost seventeen now; time passes very quickly, and you will scarcely miss me before I shall be at home again."

He lifted up her face, and laughed gaily as he spoke.

"When are you to go?"

"The vessel sails Wednesday—three days from now. I shall be very busy until then. Beulah, what glorious letters I shall write you from the old world! I am to see all Europe before I return; that is, my father says I shall. He is coming on, in two or three years, with Cornelia, and we are all to travel together. Won't it be glorious?"

"Yes, for you. But, Eugene, my heart seems to die when I think of those coming five years. How shall I live without you? Oh, what shall I do?"

"There, Beulah! do not look so wretched. You will have a thousand things to divert your mind. My father says he will see that you are sent to the public school. You know the tuition is free, and he thinks he can find some good, kind family, where you will be taken care of till your education is finished. Your studies will occupy you closely, and you will have quite enough to think of, without troubling yourself about my absence. Of course, you will write to me constantly, and each letter will be like having a nice, quiet chat together. Oh, dear! can't you get up a smile, and look less forlorn? You never would look on the bright side."

"Because I never had any to look on, except you and Lilly; and when you are gone, everything will be dark—dark!" she groaned, and covered her face with her hands.

"Not unless you determine to make it so. If I did not know that my father would attend to your education, I should not be so delighted to go. Certainly, Beulah, in improving yourself, you will have very little leisure to sit down and repine that your lot is not among the brightest. Do try to hope that things may change for the better. If they do not, why, I shall not spend eternity in Europe; and when I come home, of course, I shall take care of you myself."

She stood with one hand resting on his arm, and while he talked on, carelessly, of her future, she fixed her eyes on his countenance, thinking of the desolate hours in store for her, when the mighty Atlantic billows surged between her and the noble classic face she loved so devotedly. A shadowy panorama of coming years glided before her, and trailing clouds seemed gathered about the path her little feet must tread. A vague foreboding discovered to her the cheerlessness, and she shivered in anticipating the dreariness that awaited her. But there was time enough for the raging of the storm; why rush so eagerly to meet it? She closed her eyes to shut out the grim vision, and listened resolutely to the plans suggested for her approval. When Eugene rose to say "good night," it was touching to note the efforts she made to appear hopeful; the sob swallowed, lest it should displease him; the trembling lips forced into a smile, and the heavy eyelids lifted bravely to meet his glance. When the door closed after his retreating form, the hands were clasped convulsively, and the white, tearless face, mutely revealed the desolation which that loving heart locked in its darkened chambers.

CHAPTER VI.

Several tedious weeks had rolled away since Eugene Graham left his sunny southern home, to seek learning in the venerable universities of the old world. Blue-eyed May, the carnival month of the year, had clothed the earth with verdure, and enameled it with flowers of every hue, scattering her treasures before the rushing car of summer. During the winter, scarlet fever had hovered threateningly over the city, but as the spring advanced, hopes were entertained that all danger had passed. Consequently, when it was announced that the disease had made its appearance in a very malignant form, in the house adjoining Mrs. Martin's, she determined to send her children immediately out of town. A relative living at some distance up the river, happened to be visiting her at the time, and as she intended returning home the following day, kindly offered to take charge of the children, until all traces of the disease had vanished. To this plan, Beulah made no resistance, though the memory of her little sister haunted her hourly. What could she do? Make one last attempt to see her, and if again refused, then it mattered not whither she went. When the preparations for their journey had been completed, and Johnny slept soundly in his crib, Beulah put on her old straw-bonnet, and set out for Mr. Grayson's residence. The sun was low in the sky, and the evening breeze rippling the waters of the bay, stirred the luxuriant foliage of the ancient china-trees that bordered the pavements. The orphan's heart was heavy with undefined dread; such a dread as had oppressed her the day of her separation from her sister.

"Coming events cast their shadows before."

And she was conscious that the sunset glow could not dispel the spectral gloom which enveloped her. She walked on, with her head bowed, like one stooping from an impending blow, and when at last the crouching lions confronted her, she felt as if her heart had suddenly frozen. There stood the doctor's buggy. She sprang up the steps, and stretched out her hand for the bolt of the door. Long streamers of crape floated through her fingers. She stood still a moment, then threw open the door and rushed in. The hall floor was covered to muffle the tread; not a sound reached her, save the stirring of the china-trees outside. Her hand was on the balustrade to ascend the steps, but her eyes fell upon a piece of crape fastened to the parlor door, and pushing it ajar she looked in. The furniture was draped; even the mirrors, and pictures, and on a small oblong table in the centre of the room, lay a shrouded form. An overpowering perfume of crushed flowers filled the air, and Beulah stood on the threshold, with her hands extended, and her eyes fixed upon the table. There were two children; Lilly might yet live, and an unvoiced prayer went up to God, that the dead might be Claudia. Then like scathing lightning came the recollection of her curse: "May God answer their prayers, as they answered mine." With rigid limbs she tottered to the table, and laid her hand on the velvet pall; with closed eyes she drew it down, then held her breath and looked. There lay her idol, in the marble arms of death. Ah! how matchlessly beautiful, wrapped in her last sleep! The bright golden curls glittered around the snowy brow, and floated like wandering sunlight over the arms and shoulders. The tiny waxen fingers clasped each other as in life, and the delicately chiseled lips were just parted, as though the sleeper whispered. Beulah's gaze dwelt upon this mocking loveliness, then the arms were thrown wildly up, and with a long, wailing cry, her head sunk heavily on the velvet cushion, beside the cold face of her dead darling. How long it rested there, she never knew. Earth seemed to pass away; darkness closed over her, and for a time she had no pain, no sorrow; she and Lilly were together. All was black, and she had no feeling. Then she was lifted and the motion aroused her torpid faculties; she moaned and opened her eyes. Dr. Hartwell was placing her on a sofa, and Mrs. Grayson stood by the table with a handkerchief over her eyes. With returning consciousness came a raving despair; Beulah sprang from the strong arm that strove to detain her, and laying one clinched hand on the folded fingers of the dead, raised the other fiercely toward Mrs. Grayson and exclaimed almost frantically:

"You have murdered her! I knew it would be so, when you took my darling from my arms, and refused my prayer! Aye! my prayer! I knelt and prayed you in the name of God, to let me see her once more; to let me hold her to my heart, and kiss her lips, and forehead, and little slender hands.

You scorned a poor girl's prayer; you taunted me with my poverty, and locked me away from my darling, my Lilly! my all! Oh, woman! you drove me wild, and I cursed you and your husband. Ha! has your wealth and splendor saved her? God have mercy upon me; I feel as if I could curse you eternally. Could you not have sent for me before she died? Oh, if I could only have taken her in my arms, and seen her soft angel eyes looking up to me, and felt her little arms around my neck, and heard her say 'sister' for the last time! Would it have taken a dime from your purse, or made you less fashionable, to have sent for me before she died? 'Such measure as ye mete, shall be meted to you again.' May you live to have your heart trampled and crushed, even as you have trampled mine!"

Her arm sank to her side, and once more the blazing eyes were fastened on the young sleeper; while Mrs. Grayson, cowering, like a frightened child, left the room. Beulah fell on her knees, and crossing her arms on the table, bowed her head; now and then, broken, wailing tones passed the white lips. Doctor Hartwell stood in a recess of the window, with folded arms and tightly compressed mouth, watching the young mourner. Once he moved toward her, then drew back, and a derisive smile distorted his features, as though he scorned himself for the momentary weakness. He turned suddenly away, and reached the door, but paused to look back. The old straw bonnet, with its faded pink ribbon, had fallen off, and heavy folds of black hair veiled the bowed face. He noted the slight, quivering form, and the thin hands, and a look of remorseful agony swept over his countenance. A deadly pallor settled on cheek and brow, as, with an expression of iron resolve, he retraced his steps, and putting his hand on the orphan's shoulder, said gently:

"Beulah, this is no place for you. Come with me, child."

She shrank from his touch, and put up one hand, waving him off.

"Your sister died with the scarlet fever, and Claudia is now very ill with it.—If you stay here you will certainly take it yourself."

"I hope I shall take it."

He laid his fingers on the pale, high brow, and softly drawing back the thick hair, said earnestly: "Beulah, come home with me. Be my child: my daughter."

Again her hand was raised to put him aside.

"No; you too would hate me for my ugliness. Let me hide it in the grave with Lilly. They cannot separate us there." He lifted her head; and, looking down into the haggard face, answered kindly—

"I promise you I will not think you ugly. I will make you happy. Come to me, child." She shook her head with a moan. Passing his arm around her, he raised her from the carpet, and leaned her head against him.

"Poor little sufferer! they have made you drink, prematurely, earth's bitter draughts. They have disenchanted your childhood of its fairy-like future. Beulah, you are ill now. Do not struggle so. You must come with me, my child." He took her in his strong arms, and bore her out of the house of death. His buggy stood at the door, and, seating himself in it, he directed the boy who accompanied him to "drive home." Beulah offered no resistance; she hid her face in her hands, and sat quite still, scarcely conscious of what passed. She knew that a firm arm held her securely, and, save her wretchedness, knew nothing else. Soon she was lifted out of the buggy, carried up a flight of steps, and then a flood of light flashed through the fingers, upon her closed eyelids. Doctor Hartwell placed his charge on a sofa, and rang the bell. The summons was promptly answered by a negro woman of middle age. She stood at the door awaiting the order, but his eyes were bent on the floor, and his brows knitted.

"Master, did you ring?"

"Yes, tell my sister to come to me."

He took a turn across the floor, and paused by the open window. As the night air rustled the brown locks on his temples, he sighed deeply. The door opened, and a tall, slender woman, of perhaps thirty-five years, entered the room. She was pale and handsome, with a profusion of short chestnut curls about her face. With her hand resting on the door, she said, in a calm, clear tone:

"Well, Guy."

He started, and, turning from the window, approached her.

"May, I want a room arranged for this child as soon as possible. Will you see that a hot foot-bath is provided. When it is ready, send Harriet for her."

His sister's lips curled as she looked searchingly at the figure on the sofa, and said coldly:

"What freak now, Guy?"

For a moment their eyes met steadily, and he smiled grimly.

"I intend to adopt that poor little orphan; that is all!"

"Where did you pick her up, at the hospital?" said she, sneeringly.

"No, she has been hired as a nurse, at a boarding-house." He folded his arms, and again they looked at each other.

"I thought you had had quite enough of protégés." She nervously clasped and unclasped her jet bracelet.

"Take care, May Chilton! Mark me. Lift the pall from the past once more, and you and Pauline must find another home, another protector. Now, will you see that a room is prepared as I directed?" He was very pale, and his eyes burned fiercely, yet his tone was calm and subdued. Mrs. Chilton bit her lips, and withdrew. Doctor Hartwell walked up and down the room for a while, now and then looking sadly at the young stranger. She sat just as he had placed her, with her hands over her face. Kindly he bent down and whispered:

"Will you trust me, Beulah?"

She made no answer, but he saw her brow wrinkle, and knew that she shuddered. The servant came in to say that the room had been arranged, as he had directed. However surprised she might have been at this sudden advent of the simply clad orphan in her master's study, there was not the faintest indication of it in her impenetrable countenance. Not even the raising of an eyebrow.

"Harriet, see that her feet are well bathed; and, when she is in bed, come for some medicine."

Then, drawing the hands from her eyes, he said to Beulah,

"Go with her, my child. I am glad I have you safe under my own roof, where no more cruel injustice can assail you."

He pressed her hand kindly, and, rising mechanically, Beulah accompanied Harriet, who considerately supported the drooping form. The room to which she was conducted was richly furnished, and lighted by an elegant colored lamp, suspended from the ceiling. Mrs. Chilton stood near an armchair, looking moody and abstracted. Harriet carefully undressed the poor mourner, and wrapping a shawl about her, placed her in the chair, and bathed her feet. Mrs. Chilton watched her with ill-concealed impatience. When the little dripping feet were dried, Harriet lifted her, as if she had been an infant, and placed her in bed, then brought the medicine from the study, and administered a spoonful of the mixture. Placing her finger on the girl's wrist, she counted the rapid pulse, and, turning unconcernedly toward Mrs. Chilton, said:

"Miss May, master says you need not trouble about the medicine. I am to sleep in the room and take care of this little girl."

"Very well. See that she is properly attended to, as my brother directed. My head aches miserably, or I should remain myself."

She glanced at the bed, and left the room. Harriet leaned over the pillow and examined the orphan's countenance. The eyes were closed, but scalding tears rolled swiftly over the cheeks, and the hands were clasped over the brow, as if to still its throbbings. Harriet's face softened, and she said, kindly:

"Poor thing! what ails you? What makes you cry so?"

Beulah pressed her head closer to the pillow, and murmured:

"I am so miserable! I want to die, and God will not take me."

"Don't say that, till you see whether you've got the scarlet fever. If you have, you are likely to be taken pretty soon, I can tell you; and if you haven't, why, it's all for the best. It is a bad plan to fly in the Almighty's face, that way, and tell Him what He shall do, and what He shan't."

This philosophic response fell unheeded on poor Beulah's ears, and Harriet was about to inquire more minutely into the cause of her grief, but she perceived her master standing beside her, and immediately moved away from the bed. Drawing out his watch, he counted the pulse several times. The result seemed to trouble him, and he stood for some minutes watching the motionless form.

"Harriet, bring me a glass of ice-water."

Laying his cool hand on the hot forehead of the suffering girl, he said, tenderly:

"My child, try not to cry any more to-night. It is very bitter, I know; but remember, that though Lilly has been taken from you, from this day you have a friend, a home, a guardian."

Harriet proffered the glass of water. He took it, raised the head, and put the sparkling draught to Beulah's parched lips. Without unclosing her eyes, she drank the last crystal drop, and laying the head back on the pillow, he drew an armchair before the window at the further end of the room, and seated himself.

CHAPTER VII.

Through quiet, woody dells roamed Beulah's spirit, and, hand in hand, she and Lilly trod flowery paths and rested beside clear, laughing brooks. Life, with its grim realities, seemed but a flying mist. The orphan hovered on the confines of eternity's ocean, and its silent waves almost laved the feet of the weary child. The room was darkened, and the summer wind stole through the blinds stealthily, as if awed by the solitude of the sick-chamber. Dr. Hartwell sat by the low French bedstead, holding one emaciated hand in his, counting the pulse which bounded so fiercely in the blue veins. A fold of white linen containing crushed ice lay on her forehead, and the hollow cheeks and thin lips were flushed to vermilion hue. It was not scarlet, but brain-fever, and this was the fifth day that the sleeper had lain in a heavy stupor. Dr. Hartwell put back the hand he held, and stooping over, looked long and anxiously at the flushed face. The breathing was deep and labored, and turning away, he slowly and noiselessly walked up and down the floor. To have looked at him then, in his purple silk *robe de chambre*, one would have scarcely believed that thirty years had passed over his head. He was tall and broad-chested, his head massive and well formed, his face a curious study. The brow was expansive and almost transparent in its purity, the dark, hazel eyes were singularly brilliant, while the contour of lips and chin was partially concealed by a heavy mustache and beard. The first glance at his face impressed strangers by its extreme pallor, but in a second look they were fascinated by the misty splendor of the eyes. In truth those were strange eyes of Guy Hartwell. At times, searching and glittering like polished steel; occasionally lighting up with a dazzling radiance, and then as suddenly growing gentle, hazy, yet luminous; resembling the clouded aspect of a star seen through a thin veil of mist. His brown, curling hair was thrown back from the face, and exposed the outline of the ample forehead. Perhaps utilitarians would have carped at the feminine delicacy of the hands, and certainly the fingers were slender and marvelously white. On one hand he wore an antique ring, composed of a cameo snake-head set round with diamonds. A proud, gifted and miserable man was Guy Hartwell, and his characteristic expression of stern sadness might easily have been mistaken by casual observers for bitter misanthropy.

I have said he was about thirty, and though the handsome face was repellently cold and grave, it was difficult to believe that that smooth, fair brow, had been for so many years uplifted for the handwriting of time. He looked just what he was, a baffling, fascinating mystery. You felt that his countenance was a volume of hieroglyphics, which, could you decipher, would unfold the history of a checkered and painful career. Yet the calm, frigid smile which sat on his lip, and looked out defiantly from his deep-set eyes, seemed to dare you to an investigation. Mere physical beauty cannot impart the indescribable charm which his countenance possessed. Regularity of features is a valuable auxiliary, but we look on sculptured marble, perfect in its chiseled proportions, and feel that, after all, the potent spell is in the raying out of the soul, that imprisoned radiance which, in some instances, makes man indeed but "little lower than the angels." He paused in his echoless tread, and sat down once more beside his protégée. She had not changed her position, and the long lashes lay heavily on the crimson cheeks. The parched lips were parted, and, as he watched her, she murmured aloud:

"It is so sweet, Lilly; we will stay here always." A shadowy smile crossed her face, and then a great agony seemed to possess her, for she moaned long and bitterly. He tried to arouse her, and, for the first time since the night she entered the house, she opened her eyes and gazed vacantly at him.

"Are you in pain, Beulah? Why do you moan so?"

"Eugene, I knew it would be so, when you left me."

"Don't you know me, Beulah?" He put his face close to hers. "They killed her, Eugene! I told you they would; they are going to bury her soon. But the grave can't hide her; I am going down with her into the darkness—she would be frightened, you know." Making a great effort, she sat upright. Dr. Hartwell put a glass containing medicine to her lips; she shrank back and shuddered, then raised her hand for the glass, and looking fixedly at him, said: "Did Mrs. Grayson say I must take it? Is it poison that kills quickly? There: don't frown, Eugene, I will drink it all for you." She swallowed the draught with a shiver. He laid her back on her pillow and renewed the iced-cloth on her forehead; she did not move her burning eyes from his face, and the refreshing coolness recalled the sad smile. "Are we on the Alps, Eugene? I feel dizzy, don't let me fall. There is a great chasm yonder. Oh, I know now; I am not afraid; Lilly is down there—come on." Her arms drooped to her side, and she slept again. Evening shadows crept on; soon the room was dark. Harriet entered with a shaded lamp, but her master motioned her out, and throwing open the blinds, suffered the pure moonlight to enter freely. The window looked out on the flower-garden, and the mingled fragrance of roses, jasmines, honeysuckles, and dew-laden four-o'clocks, enveloped him as in a cloud of incense. A balmy moonlight June night in our beautiful sunny South—who shall adequately paint its witchery? Dr. Hartwell leaned his head against the window, and glanced down at the parterre he had so fondly fostered. The golden moonlight mellowed every object, and not the gorgeous pictures of Persian poets surpassed the quiet scene that greeted the master. The shelled serpentine walks were bordered with low, closely-clipped cassina hedges; clusters of white and rose oleander, scarlet geraniums, roses of countless variety, beds of verbena of every hue, and patches of brilliant annuals, all looked up smilingly at him. Just beneath the window, the clasping tendrils of a clematis were wound about the pedestal of a marble Flora, and a cluster of the delicate purple blossoms peeped through the fingers of the goddess. Further off, a fountain flashed in the moonlight, murmuring musically in and out of its reservoir, while the diamond spray bathed the sculpted limbs of a Venus. The sea breeze sang its lullaby through the boughs of a luxuriant orange-tree near, and silence seemed guardian spirit of the beautiful spot when a whippoorwill whirred through the air, and perching on the snowy brow of the Aphrodite, began his plaintive night-hymn. In childhood, Guy Hartwell had been taught by his nurse to regard the melancholy chant as ominous of evil; but as years threw their shadows over his heart, darkening the hopes of his boyhood, the sad notes of the lonely bird became gradually soothing, and now in the prime of life, he loved to listen to the shy visitor, and ceased to remember that it boded ill. With an ardent love for the beautiful, in all its Protean phases, he enjoyed communion with nature as only an imaginative, esthetical temperament can. This keen appreciation of beauty had been fostered by travel and study. Over the vast studio of nature he had eagerly roamed; midnight had seen him gazing enraptured on the loveliness of Italian scenery, and found him watching the march of constellations from the lonely heights of the Hartz; while the thunder tones of awful Niagara had often hushed the tumults of his passionate heart, and bowed his proud head in humble adoration. He had searched the storehouses of art, and collected treasures that kindled divine aspirations in his soul, and wooed him for a time from the cemetery of memory. With a nature so intensely esthetical, and taste so thoroughly cultivated, he had, in a great measure, assimilated his home to the artistic *beau ideal*. Now as he stood inhaling the perfumed air, he forgot the little sufferer a few yards off—forgot that Azrail stood on the threshold, beckoning her to brave the dark floods; and as his whole nature became permeated (so to speak) by the intoxicating beauty that surrounded him, he extended his arms, and exclaimed triumphantly:

"Truly thou art my mother, dear old earth! I feel that I am indeed nearly allied to thy divine beauty! Starry nights, and whispering winds, and fragrant flowers! yea, and even the breath of the tempest! all, all are parts of my being."

"Guy, there is a messenger waiting at the door to see you. Some patient requires prompt attendance." Mrs. Chilton stood near the window, and the moonlight flashed over her handsome face. Her brother frowned and motioned her away, but, smiling quietly, she put her beautifully molded hand on his shoulder, and said:

"I am sorry I disturb your meditations, but if you will practise—"

"Who sent for me?"

"I really don't know."

"Will you be good enough to inquire?"

"Certainly." She glided gracefully from the room.

The whippoorwill flew from his marble perch, and as the mournful tones died away, the master sighed, and returned to the bedside of his charge. He renewed the ice on her brow, and soon after his sister reentered.

"Mr. Vincent is very sick, and you are wanted immediately."

"Very well." He crossed the room and rang the bell.

"Guy, are you sure that girl has not scarlet-fever?"

"May, I have answered that question at least twice a day for nearly a week."

"But you should sympathize with a mother's anxiety. I dread to expose Pauline to danger."

"Then let her remain where she is."

"But I prefer having her come home, if I could feel assured that girl has only brain-fever."

"Then, once for all, there is no scarlet fever in the house."

He took a vial from his pocket, and poured a portion of its contents into the glass, which he placed on a stand by Beulah's bed; then turning to Harriet, who had obeyed his summons, he directed her to administer the medicine hourly.

"Guy, you may give your directions to me, for I shall stay with the child to-night." As she spoke, she seated herself at the foot of the bed.

"Harriet, hand me the candle in the hall." She did so; and as her master took it from her hand, he said abruptly:

"Tell Hal to bring my buggy round, and then you may go to bed. I will ring if you are wanted." He waited until she was out of hearing, and, walking up to his sister, held the candle so that the light fell full upon her face.

"May, can I trust you?"

"Brother, you are cruelly unjust." She covered her face with her lace handkerchief.

"Am I, indeed?"

"Yes, you wrong me hourly, with miserable suspicions. Guy, remember that I have your blood in my veins, and it will not always tamely bear insult, even from you." She removed the handkerchief, and shook back her glossy curls, while her face grew still paler than was its wont.

"Insult! May, can the unvarnished truth be such?"

They eyed each other steadily, and it was apparent that each iron will was mated.

"Guy, you shall repent this."

"Perhaps so. You have made me repent many things."

"Do you mean to say, that—"

"I mean to say that since you have at last offered to assist in nursing that unconscious child, I wish you to give the medicine hourly. The last potion was at eight o'clock." He placed the candle so as to shade the light from the sick girl, and left the room. Mrs. Chilton sat for some time as he had left her, with her head leaning on her hand, her thoughts evidently perplexed and bitter. At length she rose and stood close to Beulah, looking earnestly at her emaciated face. She put her fingers on the burning temples and wrist, and counted accurately the pulsations of the lava tide, then bent her queenly head, and listened to the heavily-drawn breathing. A haughty smile lit her fine features as she said, complacently: "A mere tempest in a tea-cup. Pshaw, this girl will not mar my projects long. By noon to-morrow she will be in eternity. I thought, the first time I saw her ghostly face, she would trouble me but a short season. What paradoxes men are. What on earth possessed

Guy, with his fastidious taste, to bring to his home such an ugly, wasted, sallow little wretch? I verily believe, as a family, we are beset by evil angels." Drawing out her watch, she saw that the hand had passed nine. Raising the glass to her lips, she drank the quantity prescribed for the sufferer, and was replacing it on the stand, when Beulah's large, eloquent eyes startled her.

"Well, child, what do you want?" said she, trembling, despite her assumed indifference. Beulah looked at her vacantly, then threw her arms restlessly over the pillow, and slept again. Mrs. Chilton drew up a chair, seated herself, and sank into a reverie of some length. Ultimately she was aroused by perceiving her brother beside her, and said hastily:

"How is Mr. Vincent? Not dangerously ill, I hope?"

"To-morrow will decide that. It is now ten minutes past ten; how many potions have you given?"

"Two," answered she, firmly.

"Thank you, May. I will relieve you now. Good night."

"But you are worn out, and I am not. Let me sit up. I will wake you if any change occurs."

"Thank you, I prefer watching to-night. Take that candle, and leave it on the table in the hall. I need nothing but moonlight. Leave the door open." As the flickering light vanished, he threw himself into the chair beside the bed.

CHAPTER VIII.

It was in the gray light of dawning day that Beulah awoke to consciousness. For some moments after unclosing her eyes, they wandered inquiringly about the room, and finally rested on the tall form of the watcher, as he stood at the open window. Gradually, memory gathered up its scattered links, and all the incidents of that hour of anguish rushed vividly before her. The little table, with its marble sleeper; then a dim recollection of having been carried to a friendly shelter. Was it only yesterday evening, and had she slept? The utter prostration which prevented her raising her head, and the emaciated appearance of her hands, told her "no." Too feeble even to think, she moaned audibly. Dr. Hartwell turned and looked at her. The room was still in shadow, though the eastern sky was flushed, and he stepped to the bedside. The fever had died out, the cheeks were very pale, and the unnaturally large, sunken eyes lusterless. She looked at him steadily, yet with perfect indifference. He leaned over, and said, eagerly:

"Beulah, do you know me?"

"Yes, I know you."

"How do you feel this morning?"

"I am very weak, and my head seems confused. How long have I been here?"

"No matter, child, if you are better." He took out his watch, and, after counting her pulse, prepared some medicine, and gave her a potion. Her features twitched, and she asked tremblingly, as if afraid of her own question:

"Have they buried her?"

"Yes, a week ago."

She closed her eyes with a groan, and her face became convulsed; then she lay quite still, with a wrinkled brow. Doctor Hartwell sat down by her, and, taking one of her wasted little hands in his, said gently:

"Beulah, you have been very ill. I scarcely thought you would recover; and now, though much better, you must not agitate yourself, for you are far too weak to bear it."

"Why didn't you let me die? Oh, it would have been a mercy!" She put her hand over her eyes, and a low cry wailed through the room.

"Because I wanted you to get well, and live here, and be my little friend, my child. Now, Beulah, I have saved you, and you belong to me. When you are stronger, we will talk about all you want to know; but to-day you must keep quiet, and not think of what distresses you. Will you try?"

The strong, stern man shuddered, as she looked up at him with an expression of hopeless desolation, and said slowly:

"I have nothing but misery to think of."

"Have you forgotten Eugene so soon?"

For an instant the eyes lighted up, then the long lashes swept her cheeks, and she murmured:

"Eugene; he has left me too; something will happen to him also; I never loved anything but trouble came upon it."

Dr. Hartwell smiled grimly, as though unconsciously she had turned to view some page in the history of his own life.

"Beulah, you must not despond; Eugene will come back an elegant young man before you are fairly out of short dresses. There, do not talk any more, and don't cry. Try to sleep, and remember, child, you are homeless and friendless no longer." He pressed her hand kindly, and turned toward the door. It opened, and Mrs. Chilton entered.

"Good morning, Guy; how is your patient?" said she, blandly.

"Good morning, May; my little patient is much better. She has been talking to me, and I am going to send her some breakfast." He put both hands on his sister's shoulders, and looked down into her beautiful eyes. She did not flinch, but he saw a grayish hue settle around her lips.

"Ah! I thought last night there was little hope of her recovery. You are a wonderful doctor, Guy; almost equal to raising the dead." Her voice was even, and, like his own, marvelously sweet.

"More wonderful still, May; I can read the living." His mustached lip curled, as a scornful smile passed over his face.

"Read the living? then you can understand and appreciate my pleasure at this good news. Doubly good, because it secures Pauline's return to-day. Dear child, I long to have her at home again." An expression of anxious maternal solicitude crossed her features. Her brother kept his hand on her shoulder, and as his eye fell on her glossy auburn curls, he said, half musingly:

"Time touches you daintily, May; there is not one silver footprint on your hair."

"He has dealt quite as leniently with you. But how could I feel the inroads of time, shielded as I have been by your kindness? Cares and sorrows bleach the locks oftener than accumulated years; and you, Guy, have most kindly guarded your poor widowed sister."

"Have I, indeed, May?"

"Ah! what would become of my Pauline and me, but for your generosity, your—"

"Enough! Then, once for all, be kind to yonder sick child; if not for her sake, for your own. You and Pauline can aid me in making her happy, if you will. And if not, remember, May, you know my nature. Do not disturb Beulah now; come down and let her be quiet." He led her down the steps, and then throwing open a glass door, stepped out upon a terrace covered with Bermuda grass, and sparkling like a tiara in the early sunlight. Mrs. Chilton watched him descend the two white marble steps leading down to the flower beds, and leaning against the wall, she muttered:

"It cannot be possible that that miserable beggar is to come between Pauline and his property! Is he mad to dream of making that little outcast his heiress? Yet he meant it; I saw it in his eye; the lurking devil that has slumbered since that evening, and that I hoped would never gleam out at me again. Oh! we are a precious family. Set the will of one against another, and all Pandemonium can't crush either! Ten to one Pauline will lose her wits too, and be as hard to manage as Guy." Moody and perplexed, she walked on to the dining-room. Beulah had fallen into a heavy slumber of exhaustion, and it was late in the day when she again unclosed her eyes. Harriet sat sewing near her, but soon perceived that she was awake, and immediately put aside her work.

"Aha! so you have come to your senses again, have you? How are you, child?"

"I am weak."

"Which isn't strange, seeing that you haven't eat a teaspoonful in more than a week. Now, look here, little one; I am ordered to nurse and take charge of you, till you are strong enough to look out for yourself. So you must not object to anything I tell you to do." Without further parley, she washed and wiped Beulah's face and hands, shook up the pillows, and placed her comfortably on them. To the orphan, accustomed all her life to wait upon others, there was something singularly novel in being thus carefully handled; and nestling her head close to the pillows, she shut her eyes, lest the tears that were gathering should become visible. Harriet quitted the room for a short time, and returned with a salver containing some refreshments.

"I can't eat anything. Thank you; but take it away." Beulah put her hands over her face, but Harriet resolutely seated herself on the side of the bed, lifted her up, and put a cup of tea to the quivering lips.

"It is no use talking; master said you had to eat, and you might just as well do it at once. Poor thing! you are hiding your eyes to cry. Well, drink this tea and eat a little; you must, for folks can't live forever without eating." There was no alternative, and Beulah swallowed what was given her. Harriet praised her obedient spirit, and busied herself about the room for some time. Finally, stooping over the bed, she said abruptly:

"Honey, are you crying?"

There was no reply, and kneeling down, she said cautiously:

"If you knew as much about this family as I do, you would cry, sure enough, for something. My master says he has adopted you, and since he has said it, everything will work for good to you. But, child, there will come times when you need a friend besides master, and be sure you come to me when you do. I won't say any more now, but remember what I tell you when you get into trouble. Miss Pauline has come, and if she happens to take a fancy to you (which I think she won't), she will stand by you till the stars fall; and if she don't, she will hate you worse than Satan himself for—" Harriet did not complete the sentence, for she detected her master's step in the passage, and resumed her work.

"How is she?"

"She did not eat much, sir, and seems so downhearted."

"That will do. I will ring when you are needed."

Dr. Hartwell seated himself on the edge of the bed, and lifting the child's head to his bosom, drew away the hands that shaded her face.

"Beulah, are you following my directions?"

"Oh, sir, you are very kind, but I am too wretched, too miserable, even to thank you."

"I do not wish you to thank me. All I desire is, that you will keep quiet for a few days, till you grow strong, and not lie here sobbing yourself into another fever. I know you have had a bitter lot in life so far, and memories are all painful with you, but it is better not to dwell upon the past. Ah, child! it is well to live only in the present, looking into the future. I promise you I will guard you, and care for you as tenderly as a father; and now, Beulah, I think you owe it to me, to try to be cheerful."

He passed his fingers softly over her forehead, and put back the tangled masses of jetty hair, which long neglect had piled about her face. The touch of his cool hand, the low musical tones of his voice, were very soothing to the weary sufferer, and with a great effort she looked up into the deep, dark eyes, saying brokenly:

"Oh, sir, how good you are!—I am—very grateful—to you—indeed, I—"

"There, my child, do not try to talk, only trust me and be cheerful. It is a pleasure to me to have you here, and know that you will always remain in my house."

How long he sat there, she never knew, for soon she slept, and when hours after she waked, the lamp was burning dimly, and only Harriet was in the room. A week passed, and the girl saw no one except the nurse and physician. One sunny afternoon, she looped back the white curtains, and sat down before the open window. Harriet had dressed her in a blue calico wrapper, which made the wan face still more ghastly, and the folds of black hair, which the gentle fingers of the kind nurse had disentangled, lay thick about her forehead, like an ebon wreath on the brow of a statue. Her elbows rested on the arms of the easy-chair, and the weary head leaned upon the hands. Before her lay the flower-garden, brilliant and fragrant, further on, a row of Lombardy poplars bounded the yard, and beyond the street, stretched the west common. In the distance rose a venerable brick building, set, as it were, in an emerald lawn, and Beulah looked only once, and knew it was the Asylum. It was the first time she had seen it since her exodus, and the long sealed fountain could no longer be restrained. Great hot tears fell over the bent face, and the frail form trembled violently. For nearly fourteen years that brave spirit had battled, and borne, and tried to hope for better things. With more than ordinary fortitude she had resigned herself to the sorrows that came thick and fast upon her, and trusting in the eternal love and goodness of God, had looked to Him for relief and reward. But the reward came not in the expected way. Hope died; faith fainted; and bitterness and despair reigned in that once loving and gentle soul. Her father had not been spared in answer to her frantic prayers. Lilly had been taken, without even the sad comfort of a farewell, and now, with the present full of anguish, and the future shrouded in dark forebodings, she sobbed aloud.

"All alone! All alone! O, father! O, Lilly, Lilly!"

"Do pray, chile, don't take on so; you will fret yourself sick again," said Harriet, compassionately patting the drooped head.

"Don't talk to me—don't speak to me!" cried Beulah, passionately.

"Yes, but I was told not to let you grieve yourself to death, and you are doing your best. Why don't you put your trust in the Lord?"

"I did, and He has forgotten me."

"No, chile. He forgets not even the little snow-birds. I expect you want to lay down the law for Him, and are not willing to wait until He sees fit to bless you. Isn't it so?"

"He never can give me back my dead."

"But He can raise up other friends for you, and He has. It is a blessed thing to have my master for a friend, and a protector. Think of living always in a place like this, with plenty of money, and nothing to wish for. Chile, you don't know how lucky—"

She paused, startled by ringing peals of laughter, which seemed to come from the adjoining passage. Sounds of mirth fell torturingly upon Beulah's bleeding spirit, and she pressed her fingers tightly over her ears. Just opposite to her sat the old trunk, which, a fortnight before, she had packed for her journey up the river. The leathern face seemed to sympathize with her woe, and kneeling down on the floor, she wound her arms caressingly over it.

"Bless the girl! she hugs that ugly old-fashioned thing, as if it were kin to her," said Harriet, who sat sewing at one of the windows.

Beulah raised the lid, and there lay her clothes, the books Eugene had given her; two or three faded, worn-out garments of Lilly, and an old Bible. The tears froze in her eyes, as she took out the last, and opened it at the ribbon mark. These words greeted her: "*Whom the Lord loveth, he chasteneth.*" Again and again she read them, and the crushed tendrils of trust feebly twined once more about the promise. As she sat there, wondering why suffering and sorrow always fell on those whom the Bible calls "blessed," and trying to explain the paradox, the door was thrown rudely open, and a girl about her own age sprang into the room, quickly followed by Mrs. Chilton.

"Let me alone, mother. I tell you I mean to see her, and then you are welcome to me as long as you please. Ah, is that her?"

The speaker paused in the center of the apartment, and gazed curiously at the figure seated before the old trunk. Involuntarily, Beulah raised her eyes, and met the searching look fixed upon her. The intruder was richly dressed, and her very posture bespoke the lawless independence of a wilful, petted child. The figure was faultlessly symmetrical, and her face radiantly beautiful. The features were clearly cut, and regular, the eyes of deep, dark violet hue, shaded by curling brown lashes. Her chestnut hair was thrown back with a silver comb, and fell in thick curls below the waist; her complexion was of alabaster clearness, and cheeks and lips wore the coral bloom of health. As they confronted each other, one looked a Hebe, the other a ghostly visitant from spirit realms. Beulah shrank from the eager scrutiny, and put up her hands to shield her face. The other advanced a few steps, and stood beside her. The expression of curiosity faded, and something like compassion swept over the stranger's features, as she noted the thin drooping form of the invalid. Her lips parted, and she put out her hand, as if to address Beulah, when Mrs. Chilton exclaimed impatiently:

"Pauline, come down this instant! Your uncle positively forbade your entering this room until he gave you permission. There is his buggy this minute! Come out, I say!" She laid her hand in no gentle manner on her daughter's arm.

"Oh, sink the buggy! What do I care if he does catch me here? I shall stay till I make up my mind whether that little thing is a ghost or not. So, mother, let me alone." She shook off the clasping hand that sought to drag her away, and again fixed her attention on Beulah.

"Wilful girl! you will ruin everything yet. Pauline, follow me instantly, I command you!" She was white with rage, but the daughter gave no intimation of having heard the words, and throwing her arm about the girl's waist, Mrs. Chilton dragged her to the door. There was a brief struggle at the threshold, and then both stood quiet before the master of the house.

"What is all this confusion about? I ordered this portion of the house kept silent, did I not?"

"Yes, Guy; and I hope you will forgive Pauline's thoughtlessness. She blundered in here, and I have just been scolding her for disobeying your injunctions."

"Uncle Guy, it was not thoughtlessness, at all; I came on purpose. For a week, I have been nearly dying with curiosity to see that little skeleton you have shut up here, and I ran up to get a glimpse of her. I don't see the harm of it; I haven't hurt her." Pauline looked fearlessly up in her uncle's face, and planted herself firmly in the door, as if resolved not to be ejected.

"Does this house belong to you, or to me, Pauline?"

"To you, now; to me, some of these days, when you give it to me for a bridal present."

His brow cleared, he looked kindly down into the frank, truthful countenance, and said, with a half smile:

"Do not repeat your voyage of discovery, or perhaps your bridal anticipations may prove an egregious failure. Do you understand me?"

"I have not finished the first. Mother played pirate, and carried me off before I was half satisfied. Uncle Guy, take me under your flag, do! I will not worry the little thing—I promise you I will not. Can't I stay here a while?" He smiled, and put his hand on her head, saying—

"I am inclined to try you. May, you can leave her here. I will send her to you after a little." As he spoke, he drew her up to the orphan. Beulah looked at them an instant, then averted her head.

"Beulah, this is my niece, Pauline Chilton; and Pauline, this is my adopted child, Beulah Benton. You are about the same age, and can make each other happy, if you will. Beulah shake hands with my niece." She put up her pale, slender fingers, and they were promptly clasped in Pauline's plump palm.

"Do stop crying, and look at me. I want to see you," said the latter.

"I am not crying."

"Then, what are you hiding your face for?"

"Because it is so ugly," answered the orphan, sadly.

Pauline stooped down, took the head in her hands, and turned the features to view. She gave them a searching examination, and then, looking up at her uncle, said bluntly:

"She is not pretty, that is a fact; but, somehow, I rather like her. If she did not look so doleful, and had some blood in her lips, she would pass well enough, don't you think so?"

Dr. Hartwell did not reply; but raising Beulah from the floor, placed her in the chair she had vacated some time before. She did, indeed, look "doleful," as Pauline expressed it, and the beaming, lovely face of the latter rendered her wan aspect more apparent.

"What have you been doing all day?" said the doctor, kindly.

She pointed to the Asylum, and answered in a low subdued tone:

"Thinking about my past life—all my misfortunes."

"You promised you would do so no more."

"Ah, sir! how can I help it?"

"Why, think of something pleasant, of course," interrupted Pauline.

"You never had any sorrows; you know nothing of suffering," replied Beulah, allowing her eyes to dwell on the fine open countenance before her; a mirthful, sunny face, where waves of grief had never rippled.

"How came you so wise? I have troubles sometimes, just like everybody else." Beulah shook her head dubiously.

"Pauline, will you try to cheer this sad little stranger? will you be always kind in your manner, and remember that her life has not been as happy as yours? Can't you love her?" She shrugged her shoulders, and answered evasively.

"I dare say we will get on well enough, if she will only quit looking so dismal and graveyardish. I don't know about loving her; we shall see."

"You can go down to your mother now," said he, gravely.

"That means you are tired of me, Uncle Guy," cried she, saucily shaking her curls over her face.

"Yes, heartily tired of you; take yourself off."

"Good-by, shadow; I shall come to see you again to-morrow." She reached the door, but looked back.

"Uncle, have you seen Charon since you came home?"

"No."

"Well, he will die if you don't do something for him. It is a shame to forget him as you do!" said she, indignantly.

"Attend to your own affairs, and do not interfere with mine."

"It is high time somebody interfered. Poor Charon! If Hal doesn't take better care of him, I will make his mother box his ears; see if I don't."

She bounded down the steps, leaving her uncle to smooth his brow at leisure. Turning to Beulah, he took her hand, and said very kindly:

"This large room does not suit you. Come, and I will show you your own little room—one I have had arranged for you." She silently complied, and leading her through several passages, he opened the door of the apartment assigned her. The walls were covered with blue and silver paper; the window-curtains of white, faced with blue, matched it well, and every article of furniture bespoke lavish and tasteful expenditure. There was a small writing-desk near a handsome case of books, and a little work-table with a rocking-chair drawn up to it. He seated Beulah, and stood watching her, as her eyes wandered curiously and admiringly around the room. They rested on a painting suspended over the desk, and rapt in contemplating the design, she forgot for a moment all her sorrows. It represented an angelic figure winging its way over a valley beclouded and dismal, and pointing, with a radiant countenance, to the gilded summit of a distant steep. Below, bands of pilgrims, weary and worn, toiled on; some fainting by the wayside, some seated in sullen despair, some in the attitude of prayer, some pressing forward with strained gaze, and pale, haggard faces.

"Do you like it?" said Doctor Hartwell.

Perhaps she did not hear him; certainly she did not need the question, and taking a seat near one of the windows, he regarded her earnestly. Her eyes were fastened on the picture, and raising her hands toward it, she said in broken, indistinct tones:

"I am dying down in the dark valley; oh, come, help me to toil on to the resting-place."

Her head sank upon her bosom, and bitter waves lashed her heart once more.

Gradually, evening shadows crept on, and at length a soft hand lifted her face, and a musical voice said:

"Beulah, I want you to come down to my study and make my tea. Do you feel strong enough?"

"Yes, sir." She rose at once and followed him, resolved to seem cheerful.

The study was an oblong room, and on one side bookshelves rose almost to the ceiling. The opposite wall, between the windows, was covered with paintings, and several statues stood in the recesses near the chimney. Over the low marble mantelpiece hung a full-length portrait, shrouded with black crape, and underneath was an exquisitely chased silver case, containing a small Swiss clock. A beautiful *terra cotta* vase of antique shape stood on the hearth, filled with choice and fragrant flowers, and near the window sat an elegant rosewood melodeon. A circular table occupied the middle of the room, and here the evening meal was already arranged. Beulah glanced timidly around as her conductor seated her beside the urn, and seeing only cups for two persons, asked hesitatingly:

"Shall I make your tea now?"

"Yes, and remember, Beulah, I shall expect you to make it every evening at this hour. Breakfast and dinner I take with my sister and Pauline in the dining-room, but my evenings are always spent here. There, make another cup for yourself."

A long silence ensued. Doctor Hartwell seemed lost in reverie, for he sat with his eyes fixed on the tablecloth, and his head resting on his hand. His features resumed their habitual expression of stern rigidity, and as Beulah looked at him she could scarcely believe that he was the same kind friend who had been so gentle and fatherly in his manner. Intuitively she felt then that she had to deal with a chaotic, passionate and moody nature, and as she marked the knitting of his brows, and the iron compression of his lips, her heart was haunted by grave forebodings. While she sat pondering his haughty, impenetrable appearance a servant entered.

"Sir, there is a messenger at the door."

His master started slightly, pushed away his cup and said:

"Is the buggy ready?"

"Yes, sir, waiting at the door."

"Very well, I am coming."

The windows opened down to the floor, and led into a vine-covered piazza. He stepped up to one and stood a moment, as if loth to quit his sanctum; then turning round, addressed Beulah:

"Ah, child, I had almost forgotten you. It is time you were asleep. Do you know the way back to your room?"

"I can find it," said she, rising from the table.

"Good night; let me see you at breakfast if you feel strong enough to join us."

He opened the door for her, and hurrying out, Beulah found her own room without difficulty. Walking up to Harriet, whom she saw waiting for her, she said in a grave, determined manner:

"You have been very kind to me since I came here, and I feel grateful to you, but I have not been accustomed to have some one always waiting on me, and in future I shall not want you. I can dress myself without any assistance, so you need not come to me night and morning."

"I am obeying master's orders. He said I was to 'tend to you," answered Harriet, wondering at the independent spirit evinced by the newcomer.

"I do not want any tending, so you may leave me, if you please."

"Haven't you been here long enough to find out that you might as well fight the waves of the sea as my master's will? Take care, child, how you begin to countermand his orders, for I tell you now there are some in this house who will soon make it a handle to turn you out into the world again. Mind what I say."

"Do you mean that I am not wanted here?"

"I mean, keep your eyes open." Harriet vanished in the dark passage, and Beulah locked the door, feeling that now she was indeed alone, and could freely indulge the grief that had so long sought to veil itself from curious eyes. Yet there was no disposition to cry. She sat down on the bed and mused on the strange freak of fortune which had so suddenly elevated the humble nurse into the possessor of that elegantly furnished apartment. There was no elation in the quiet wonder with which she surveyed the change in her position. She did not belong there, she had no claim on the master of the house, and she felt that she was trespassing on the rights of the beautiful Pauline. Rapidly plans for the future were written in firm resolve. She would thankfully remain under the roof that had so kindly sheltered her, until she could qualify herself to teach. She would ask Doctor Hartwell to give her an education, which, once obtained, would enable her to repay its price. To her proud nature there was something galling in the thought of dependence, and throwing herself on her knees for the first time in several weeks, she earnestly besought the God of orphans to guide and assist her.

CHAPTER IX.

"Do you wish her to commence school at once?"

"Not until her wardrobe has been replenished. I expect her clothes to be selected and made just as Pauline's are. Will you attend to this business, or shall I give directions to Harriet?"

"Certainly, Guy, I can easily arrange it. You intend to dress her just as I do Pauline?"

"As nearly as possible. Next week I wish her to begin school with Pauline, and Hansell will give her music lessons. Be so good as to see about her clothes immediately."

Dr. Hartwell drew on his gloves and left the room. His sister followed him to the door where his buggy awaited him.

"Guy, did you determine about that little affair for Pauline? She has so set her heart on it."

"Oh, do as you please, May, only I am—"

"Stop, Uncle Guy! Wait a minute: may I have a birthday party? May I?" Almost out of breath, Pauline ran up the steps; her long hair floating over her face, which exercise had flushed to crimson.

"You young tornado! Look how you have crushed that cluster of heliotrope, rushing over the flower-beds as if there were no walks." He pointed with the end of his whip to a drooping spray of purple blossoms.

"Yes; but there are plenty more. I say, may I?—may I?" She eagerly caught hold of his coat.

"How long before your birthday?"

"Just a week from to-day. Do, please, let me have a frolic!"

"Poor child! you look as if you needed some relaxation," said he, looking down into her radiant face, with an expression of mock compassion.

"Upon my word, Uncle Guy, it is awfully dull here. If it were not for Charon and Mazeppa I should be moped to death. Do, pray, don't look at me as if you were counting the hairs in my eyelashes. Come, say, yes: do, Uncle Guy."

"Take your hands off of my coat, and have as many parties as you like, provided you keep to your own side of the house. Don't come near my study with your Babel, and don't allow your company to demolish my flowers. Mind, not a soul is to enter the greenhouse. The parlors are at your service, but I will not have a regiment of wildcats tearing up and down my greenhouse and flower-garden; mind that." He stepped into his buggy.

"Bravo! I have won my wager, and got the party too! Hugh Cluis bet me a *papier-maché* writing-desk that you would not give me a party. When I send his invitation, I will write on the envelope 'The writing-desk is also expected.' Hey, shadow, where did you creep from?" She fixed her merry eyes on Beulah, who just then appeared on the terrace. Dr. Hartwell leaned from the buggy, and looked earnestly at the quiet little figure.

"Do you want anything, Beulah?"

"No, sir, I thought you had gone. May I open the gate for you?"

"Certainly, if you wish to do something for me." His pale features relaxed, and his whole face lighted up, like a sun-flushed cloud.

Beulah walked down the avenue, lined on either side with venerable poplars and cedars, and opened the large gate leading into the city. He checked his horse, and said:

"Thank you, my child; now how are you going to spend the day? Remember you commence with school duties next week, so make the best of your holiday."

"I have enough to occupy me to-day. Good-by, sir."

"Good-by, for an hour or so." He smiled kindly and drove on, while she walked slowly back to the house, wondering why smiles were such rare things in this world, when they cost so little, and yet are so very valuable to mourning hearts. Pauline sat on the steps with an open book in her hand. She looked up as Beulah approached, and exclaimed gaily:

"Aren't you glad I am to have my birthday frolic?"

"Yes, I am glad on your account," answered Beulah, gravely.

"Can you dance all the fancy dances? I don't like any so well as the mazourka."

"I do not dance at all."

"Don't dance! Why, I have danced ever since I was big enough to crawl! What have you been doing all your life, that you don't know how to dance?"

"My feet have had other work to do," replied her companion; and as the recollections of her early childhood flitted before her, the brow darkened.

"I suppose that is one reason you look so forlorn all the time. I will ask Uncle Guy to send you to the dancing school for—"

"Pauline, it is school-time, and you don't know one word of that Quackenbos; I would be ashamed to start from home as ignorant of my lessons as you are." Mrs. Chilton's head was projected from the parlor window, and the rebuke was delivered in no very gentle tone.

"Oh, I don't mind it at all: I have got used to it," answered the daughter, tossing up the book as she spoke.

"Get ready for school this minute."

Pauline scampered into the house for her bonnet and satchel; and fixing her eyes upon Beulah, Mrs. Chilton asked sternly:

"What are you doing out there? What did you follow my brother to the gate for? Answer me!"

"I merely opened the gate for him," replied the girl, looking steadily up at the searching eyes.

"There was a servant with him to do that. In future don't make yourself so conspicuous. You must keep away from the flower-beds too. The doctor wishes no one prowling about them; he gave particular directions that no one should go there in his absence."

They eyed each other an instant; then drawing up her slender form to its utmost height, Beulah replied proudly:

"Be assured, madam, I shall not trespass on forbidden ground!"

"Very well." The lace curtains swept back to their place—the fair face was withdrawn.

"She hates me!" thought Beulah, walking on to her own room, "she hates me, and certainly I do not love her. I shall like Pauline very much, but her mother and I never will get on smoothly. What freezing eyes she has, and what a disagreeable look there is about her mouth whenever she sees me. She wishes me to remember all the time that I am poor, and that she is the mistress of this elegant house. Ah, I am not likely to forget it!" The old smile of bitterness crossed her face.

The days passed swiftly. Beulah spent most of her time in her own room, for Dr. Hartwell was sometimes absent all day, and she longed to escape his sister's icy espionage. When he was at home, and not engaged in his study, his manner was always kind and considerate; but she fancied he was colder and graver, and often his stern abstraction kept her silent when they were together. Monday was the birthday, and on Monday morning she expected to start to school. Madam St. Cymon's was the fashionable institution of the city, and thither, with Pauline, she was destined. Beulah rose early, dressed herself carefully, and after reading a chapter in her Bible, and asking God's special guidance through the day, descended to the breakfast-room. Dr. Hartwell sat reading a newspaper; he did not look up, and she quietly seated herself unobserved. Presently Mrs. Chilton entered and walked up to her brother.

"Good morning, Guy. Are there no tidings of that vessel yet? I hear the Grahams are terribly anxious about it. Cornelia said her father was unable to sleep."

"No news yet, but, May, be sure you do not let—"

"Was it the Morning Star? Is he lost?"

Beulah stood crouching at his side, with her hands extended pleadingly, and her white face convulsed.

"My child, do not look so wretched; the vessel that Eugene sailed in was disabled in a storm, and has not yet reached the place of destination. But there are numerous ways of accounting for the detention, and you must hope and believe that all is well, until you know the contrary." He drew her to his side, and stroked her head compassionately.

"I knew it would be so," said she, in a strangely subdued, passionless tone.

"What do you mean, child?"

"Death and trouble come on everything I love."

"Perhaps at this very moment Eugene may be writing you an account of his voyage. I believe that we shall soon hear of his safe arrival. You need not dive down into my eyes in that way. I do believe it, for the vessel was seen after the storm, and though far out of the right track, there is good reason to suppose she has put into some port to be repaired."

Beulah clasped her hands over her eyes, as if to shut out some horrid phantom, and while her heart seemed dying on the rack, she resolved not to despair till the certainty came.

"Time enough when there is no hope; I will not go out to meet sorrow." With a sudden, inexplicable revulsion of feeling she sank on her knees, and there beside her protector, vehemently prayed Almighty God to guard and guide the tempest-tossed loved one. If her eyes had rested on the face of Deity, and she had felt his presence, her petition could not have been more importunately preferred. For a few moments Dr. Hartwell regarded her curiously; then his brow darkened, his lips curled sneeringly, and a mocking smile passed over his face. Mrs. Chilton smiled, too, but there was a peculiar gleam in her eyes, and an uplifting of her brows which denoted anything but pleasurable emotions. She moved away, and sat down at the head of the table. Dr. Hartwell put his hand on the shoulder of the kneeling girl, and asked, rather abruptly:

"Beulah, do you believe that the God you pray to hears you?"

"I do. He has promised to answer prayer."

"Then, get up and be satisfied, and eat your breakfast. You have asked Him to save and protect Eugene, and, according to the Bible, He will certainly do it; so, no more tears. If you believe in your God, what are you looking so wretched about?" There was something in all this that startled Beulah, and she looked up at him. His chilly smile pained her, and she rose quickly, while again and again his words rang in her ear. Yet, what was there so strange about this application of faith? True, the Bible declared that "whatsoever ye ask, believing, that ye shall receive," she had often prayed for blessings, and often been denied. Was it because she had not had the requisite faith, which should have satisfied her? Yet God knew that she had trusted Him. With innate quickness of perception, she detected the tissued veil of irony, which the doctor had wrapped about his attempted consolation, and she looked at him so intently, so piercingly, that he hastily turned away and seated himself at the table. Just then, Pauline bounded into the room exclaiming:

"Fourteen to-day! Only three more years of school, and then I shall step out a brilliant young lady, the—"

"There; be quiet; sit down. I would almost as soon select a small whirlwind for a companion. Can't you learn to enter a room without blustering like a March wind, or a Texas norther?" asked her uncle.

"Have you all seen a ghost? You look as solemn as grave-diggers. What ails you, Beulah? Come along to breakfast. How nicely you look in your new clothes." Her eyes ran over the face and form of the orphan.

"Pauline, hush! and eat your breakfast. You annoy your uncle," said her mother, severely.

"Oh, do, for gracious sake, let me talk! I feel sometimes as if I should suffocate. Everything about this house is so demure, and silent, and solemn, and Quakerish, and hatefully prim. If ever I have a house of my own, I mean to paste in great letters over the doors and windows, '*Laughing and talking freely allowed!*' This is my birthday, and I think I might stay at home. Mother, don't forget to have the ends of my sash fringed, and the tops of my gloves trimmed." Draining her small china cup, she sprang up from the table, but paused beside Beulah.

"By the bye, what are you going to wear to-night, Beulah?"

"I shall not go into the parlors at all," answered the latter.

"Why not?" said Dr. Hartwell, looking suddenly up. He met the sad, suffering expression of the gray eyes, and bit his lip with vexation. She saw that he understood her feelings, and made no reply.

"I shall not like it, if you don't come to my party," said Pauline, slowly; and as she spoke she took one of the orphan's hands.

"You are very kind, Pauline, but I do not wish to see strangers."

"But, you never will know anybody if you make such a nun of yourself. Uncle Guy, tell her she must come down into the parlors to-night."

"Not unless she wishes to do so. But, Pauline, I am very glad that you have shown her you desire her presence." He put his hand on her curly head, and looked with more than usual affection at the bright, honest face.

"Beulah, you must get ready for school. Come down as soon as you can. Pauline will be waiting for you." Mrs. Chilton spoke in the calm, sweet tone peculiar to her and her brother, but to Beulah there was something repulsive in that even voice, and she hurried from the sound of it. Kneeling beside her bed, she again implored the Father to restore Eugene to her, and crushing her grief and apprehension down into her heart, she resolved to veil it from strangers. As she walked on by Pauline's side, only the excessive paleness of her face, and drooping of her eyelashes, betokened her suffering.

Entering school is always a disagreeable ordeal, and to a sensitive nature such as Beulah's, it was torturing. Madam St. Cymon was a good-natured, kind, little body, and received her with a warmth and cordiality which made amends in some degree for the battery of eyes she was forced to encounter.

"Ah, yes! the doctor called to see me about you—wants you to take the Latin course. For the present, my dear, you will sit with Miss Sanders. Clara, take this young lady with you."

The girl addressed looked at least sixteen years of age, and rising promptly she came forward and led Beulah to a seat at her desk, which was constructed for two persons. The touch of her fingers sent a thrill through Beulah's frame, and she looked at her very earnestly.

Clara Sanders was not a beauty in the ordinary acceptation of the term, but there was an expression of angelic sweetness and purity in her countenance which fascinated the orphan. She remarked the scrutiny of the young stranger, and smiling good-humoredly said, as she leaned over and arranged the desk:

"I am glad to have you with me, and dare say we shall get on very nicely together. You look ill."

"I have been ill recently and have not yet regained my strength. Can you tell me where I can find some water? I feel rather faint."

Her companion brought her a glass of water. She drank it eagerly, and as Clara resumed her seat, said in a low voice:

"Oh, thank you. You are very kind."

"Not at all. If you feel worse you must let me know." She turned to her books and soon forgot the presence of the newcomer.

The latter watched her, and noticed now that she was dressed in deep mourning; was she too an orphan, and had this circumstance rendered her so kindly sympathetic? The sweet, gentle face, with its soft, brown eyes, chained her attention, and in the shaping of the mouth there was something very like Lilly's. Soon Clara left her for recitation, and then she turned to the new books which madam had sent to her desk. Thus passed the morning, and she started when the recess bell rang its summons through the long room. Bustle, chatter, and confusion ensued. Pauline called to her to come into the lunch-room, and touched her little basket as she spoke, but Beulah shook her head and kept her seat. Clara also remained.

"Pauline is calling you," said she gently.

"Yes, I hear; but I do not want anything." And Beulah rested her head on her hands.

"Don't you feel better than you did this morning?"

"Oh, I am well enough in body; a little weak, that is all."

"You look quite tired; suppose you lean your head against me and take a short nap?"

"You are very good indeed, but I am not at all sleepy."

Clara was engaged in drawing, and looking on, Beulah became interested in the progress of the sketch. Suddenly a hand was placed over the paper, and a tall, handsome girl, with black eyes and sallow complexion, exclaimed sharply:

"For heaven's sake, Clara Sanders, do you expect to swim into the next world on a piece of drawing-paper? Come over to my seat and work out that eighth problem for me. I have puzzled over it all the morning, and can't get it right."

"I can show you here quite as well." Taking out her Euclid, she found and explained the obstinate problem.

"Thank you. I cannot endure mathematics, but father is bent upon my being 'thorough," as he calls it. I think it is all thorough nonsense. Now with you it is very different, you expect to be a teacher, and of course will have to acquire all these branches; but for my part I see no use in it. I shall be rejoiced when this dull school-work is over."

"Don't say that, Cornelia, I think our schooldays are the happiest, and feel sad when I remember that mine are numbered."

Here the bell announced recess over, and Cornelia moved away to her seat. A trembling hand sought Clara's arm.

"Is that Cornelia Graham?"

"Yes; is she not very handsome?"

Beulah made no answer, she only remembered that this girl was Eugene's adopted sister, and looking after the tall, queenly form, she longed to follow her, and ask all the particulars of the storm. Thus ended the first dreaded day at school, and on reaching home, Beulah threw herself on her bed with a low wailing cry. The long pent sorrow must have vent, and she sobbed until weariness sank her into a heavy sleep.

Far out into a billowy sea, strewed with wrecks, and hideous with the ghastly, upturned faces of floating corpses, she and Eugene were drifting—now clinging to each other—now tossed asunder by howling waves. Then came a glimmering sail on the wide waste of waters; a little boat neared them, and Lilly leaned over the side and held out tiny, dimpled hands to lift them in. They were climbing out of their watery graves, and Lilly's long, fair curls already touched their cheeks, when a strong arm snatched Lilly back, and struck them down into the roaring gulf, and above the white faces of the drifting dead, stood Mrs. Grayson, sailing away with Lilly struggling in her arms. Eugene was sinking and Beulah could not reach him; he held up his arms imploringly toward her, and called upon her to save him, and then his head with its wealth of silken, brown locks disappeared. She ceased to struggle; she welcomed drowning now that he had gone to rest among coral temples. She sank down—down. The rigid corpses were no longer visible. She was in an emerald palace, and myriads of rosy shells paved the floors. At last she found Eugene reposing on a coral bank, and playing with pearls; she hastened to join him, and was just taking his hand when a horrible phantom, seizing him in its arms, bore him away, and looking in its face she saw that it was Mrs. Chilton. With a wild scream of terror, Beulah awoke. She was lying across the foot of the bed, and both hands were thrown up, grasping the post convulsively. The room was dark, save where the moonlight crept through the curtains and fell slantingly on the picture of Hope and the Pilgrims, and by that dim light she saw a tall form standing near her.

"Were you dreaming, Beulah, that you shrieked so wildly?"

The doctor lifted her up, and leaned her head against his shoulder.

"Oh, Dr. Hartwell! I have had a horrible, horrible dream." She shuddered, and clung to him tightly, as if dreading it might still prove a reality.

"Poor child. Come with me, and I will try to exorcise this evil spirit which haunts even your slumbers."

Keeping her hand in his, he led her down to his study, and seated her on a couch drawn near the window. The confused sound of many voices, and the tread of dancing feet, keeping time to a band of music, came indistinctly from the parlors. Dr. Hartwell closed the door, to shut out the unwelcome sounds, and seating himself before the melodeon, poured a flood of soothing, plaintive melody upon the air. Beulah sat entranced, while he played on and on, as if unconscious of her presence. Her whole being was inexpressibly thrilled; and, forgetting her frightful vision, her enraptured soul hovered on the very confines of fabled elysium. Sliding from the couch, upon her knees, she remained with her clasped hands pressed over her heart, only conscious of her trembling delight. Once or twice before she had felt thus, in watching a gorgeous sunset in the old pine grove; and now, as the musician seemed to play upon her heartstrings, calling thence unearthly tones, the tears rolled swiftly over her face. Images of divine beauty filled her soul, and nobler aspirations than she had ever known, took possession of her. Soon the tears ceased, the face became calm, singularly calm; then lighted with an expression which nothing earthly could have kindled. It was the look of one whose spirit, escaping from gross bondage, soared into realms divine, and proclaimed itself God-born. Dr. Hartwell was watching her countenance, and, as the expression of indescribable joy and triumph flashed over it, he involuntarily paused. She waited till the last deep echoing tone died away, and then approaching him, as he still sat before the instrument, she laid her hand on his knee, and said slowly:

"Oh! thank you, I can bear anything now."

"Can you explain to me how the music strengthened you? Try, will you?"

She mused for some moments, and answered thoughtfully:

"First, it made me forget the pain of my dream; then it caused me to think of the wonderful power which created music; and then, from remembering the infinite love and wisdom of the Creator, who has given man the power to call out this music, I thought how very noble man was, and what he was capable of doing; and, at last, I was glad because God has given me some of these powers; and, though I am ugly, and have been afflicted in losing my dear loved ones, yet I was made for God's glory in some way, and am yet to be shown the work he has laid out for me to do. Oh! sir, I can't explain it all to you, but I do know that God will prove to me that '*He doeth all things well.*' "

She looked gravely up into the face beside her, and sought to read its baffling characters. He had leaned his elbow on his melodeon, and his wax-like fingers were thrust through his hair. His brow was smooth, and his mouth at rest, but the dark eyes, with their melancholy splendor, looked down at her moodily. They met her gaze steadily, and then she saw into the misty depths, and a shudder crept over her, as she fell on her knees, and said, shiveringly:

"Oh, sir, can it be?"

He put his hand on her head, and asked, quietly:

"Can what be, child?"

"Have you no God?"

His face grew whiter than was his wont. A scowl of bitterness settled on it, and the eyes burned with an almost unearthly brilliance, as he rose and walked away. For some time he stood before the window, with his arms folded; and, laying her head on the stool of the melodeon, Beulah knelt just as he left her. It has been said, "Who can refute a sneer?" Rather ask, who can compute its ruinous effects. To that kneeling figure came the thought, "If he, surrounded by wealth, and friends, and blessings, cannot believe in God, what cause have I, poor, wretched and lonely, to have faith in Him?" The bare suggestion of the doubt stamped it on her memory, yet she shrank with horror from the idea, and an eager, voiceless prayer ascended from her heart, that she might be shielded from such temptations in future. Dr. Hartwell touched her, and said, in his usual low, musical tones:

"It is time you were asleep. Do not indulge in any more horrible dreams, if you please. Good night, Beulah. Whenever you feel that you would like to have some music, do not hesitate to ask me for it."

He held open the door for her to pass out. She longed to ask him what he lived for, if eternity had no joys for him; but, looking in his pale face, she saw from the lips and eyes that he would not suffer any questioning, and, awed by the expression of his countenance, she said "good night," and hurried away. The merry hum of childish voices again fell on her ear, and as she ascended the steps a bevy of white-clad girls emerged from a room near her, and walked on just below her. Pauline's party was at its height. Beulah looked down on the fairy gossamer robes, and gaily tripping girls, and then hastened to her own room, while the thought presented itself:

"Why are things divided so unequally in this world? Why do some have all of joy, and some only sorrow's brimming cup to drain?" But the sweet voice of Faith answered, "*What I do, thou knowest not now, but thou shalt know hereafter,*" and, trusting the promise, she was content to wait.

CHAPTER X.

"Cornelia Graham, I want to know why you did not come to my party? You might at least have honored me with an excuse." Such was Pauline's salutation, the following day, when the girls gathered in groups about the schoolroom.

"Why, Pauline, I did send an excuse, but it was addressed to your mother, and probably she forgot to mention it. You must acquit me of any such rudeness."

"Well, but why didn't you come? We had a glorious time. I have half a mind not to tell you what I heard said of you, but I believe you may have it second-hand. Fred Vincent was as grum as a preacher, all the evening, and when I asked him what on earth made him so surly and owlish, he said, 'it was too provoking you would not come, for no one else could dance the Schottisch to his liking.' Now there was a sweet specimen of manners for you! You had better teach your beau politeness."

Cornelia was leaning listlessly against Clara's desk, and Beulah fancied she looked very sad and abstracted. She colored at the jest, and answered contemptuously:

"He is no beau of mine, let me tell you, and as for manners, I commend him to your merciful tuition."

"But what was your excuse?" persisted Pauline.

"I should think you might conjecture, that I felt no inclination to go to parties and dance, when you know that we are all so anxious about my brother."

"Oh, I did not think of that!" cried the heedless girl, and quite as heedlessly she continued:

"I want to see that brother of yours. Uncle Guy says he is the handsomest boy in the city, and promises to make something extraordinary. Is he so very handsome?"

"Yes," the proud lip trembled.

"I heard Anne Vernon say she liked him better than all her other beaux, and that is great praise, coming from her queenship," said Emily Wood, who stood near.

Cornelia's eyes dilated angrily, as she answered with curling lips:

"Eugene one of her beaux! It is no such thing."

"You need not look so insulted. I suppose if the matter is such a delicate one with you, Anne will withdraw her claim," sneered Emily, happy in the opportunity afforded of wounding the haughty spirit, whom all feared, and few sympathized with.

Cornelia was about to retort, but madam's voice prevented, as leaning from the platform opposite, she held out a note, and said,

"Miss Graham, a servant has just brought this for you."

The girl's face flushed and paled alternately, as she received the note, and broke the seal with trembling fingers. Glancing over the contents, her countenance became irradiated, and she exclaimed joyfully:

"Good news! the Morning Star has arrived at Amsterdam. Eugene is safe in Germany."

Beulah's head went down on her desk, and just audible were the words,

"My Father in Heaven, I thank thee!"

Only Clara and Cornelia heard the broken accents, and they looked curiously at the bowed figure, quivering with joy.

"Ah! I understand; this is the Asylum Beulah, I have often heard him speak of. I had almost forgotten the circumstance. You knew him very well, I suppose?" said Cornelia, addressing herself to the orphan, and crumpling the note between her fingers, while her eyes ran with haughty scrutiny over the dress and features before her.

"Yes, I knew him very well." Beulah felt the blood come into her cheeks, and she ill-brooked the cold, searching look bent upon her.

"You are the same girl that he asked my father to send to the public school. How came you here?"

A pair of dark gray eyes met Cornelia's gaze, and seemed to answer defiantly, "What is it to you?"

"Has Dr. Hartwell adopted you? Pauline said so, but she is so heedless, that I scarcely believed her, particularly when it seemed so very improbable."

"Hush, Cornelia! Why, you need Pauline's tuition about as much as Fred Vincent, I am disposed to think. Don't be so inquisitive, it pains her," remonstrated Clara, laying her arm around Beulah's shoulder as she spoke.

"Nonsense! She is not so fastidious, I will warrant. At least, she might answer civil questions."

"I always do," said Beulah.

Cornelia smiled derisively, and turned off, with the parting taunt:

"It is a mystery to me what Eugene can see in such a homely, unpolished specimen. He pities her, I suppose."

Clara felt a long shiver creep over the slight form, and saw the ashen hue that settled on her face, as if some painful wound had been inflicted. Stooping down, she whispered:

"Don't let it trouble you. Cornelia is hasty, but she is generous, too, and will repent her rudeness. She did not intend to pain you; it is only her abrupt way of expressing herself."

Beulah raised her head, and putting back the locks of hair that had fallen over her brow, replied coldly:

"It is nothing new; I am accustomed to such treatment. Only professing to love Eugene, I did not expect her to insult one whom he had commissioned her to assist, or at least sympathize with."

"Remember, Beulah, she is an only child, and her father's idol, and perhaps—"

"The very blessings that surround her should teach her to feel for the unfortunate and unprotected," interrupted the orphan.

"You will find that prosperity rarely has such an effect upon the heart of its favorite," answered Clara, musingly.

"An unnecessary piece of information. I discovered that pleasant truth some time since," said Beulah, bitterly.

"I don't know, Beulah; you are an instance to the contrary. Do not call yourself unfortunate, so long as Doctor Hartwell is your friend. Ah! you little dream how blessed you are."

Her voice took the deep tone of intense feeling, and a faint glow tinged her cheek.

"Yes, he is very kind, very good," replied the other, more gently.

"Kind! good! is that all you can say of him?" The soft brown eyes kindled with unwonted enthusiasm.

"What more can I say of him, than that he is good?" returned the orphan, eagerly, while the conversation in the study, the preceding day, rushed to her recollection.

Clara looked at her earnestly for a moment, and then averting her head, answered evasively.

"Pardon me; I have no right to dictate the terms in which you should mention your benefactor." Beulah's intuitions were remarkably quick, and she asked, slowly:

"Do you know him well?"

"Yes; oh, yes! very well indeed. Why do you ask?"

"And you like him very much?"

"Very much."

She saw the gentle face now, and saw that some sorrow had called tears to the eyes, and sent the blood coldly back to her heart.

"No one can like him as I do. You don't know how very kind he has been to me—me, the miserable, lonely orphan," murmured Beulah, as his smile and tones recurred to her.

"Yes, I can imagine, because I know his noble heart; and, therefore, child, I say you cannot realize how privileged you are."

The discussion was cut short by a call to recitation, and too calmly happy in the knowledge of Eugene's safety, to ponder her companion's manner, Beulah sank into a reverie, in which Eugene, and Heidelberg, and long letters, mingled pleasingly. Later in the day, as she and Pauline were descending the steps, the door of the primary department of the school opened, and a little girl, clad in deep black, started up the same flight of steps. Seeing the two above, she leaned against the wall, waiting for them to pass. Beulah stood still, and the satchel she carried fell unheeded from her hand, while a thrilling cry broke from the little girl's lips; and springing up the steps, she threw herself into Beulah's arms.

"Dear Beulah! I have found you at last!" She covered the thin face with passionate kisses; then heavy sobs escaped her, and the two wept bitterly together.

"Beulah, I did love her very much; I did not forget what I promised you. She used to put her arms around my neck every night, and go to sleep close to me; and whenever she thought about you and cried, she always put her head in my lap. Indeed I did love her."

"I believe you, Claudy," poor Beulah groaned in her anguish.

"They did not tell me she was dead; they said she was sick in another room! Oh, Beulah! why didn't you come to see us? Why didn't you come? When she was first taken sick, she called for you all the time; and the evening they moved me into the next room, she was asking for you. 'I want my sister Beulah! I want my Beulah!' was the last thing I heard her say; and when I cried for you, too, mamma said we were both crazy with fever. Oh!"—she paused and sobbed convulsively. Beulah raised her head, and while the tears dried in her flashing eyes, said fiercely:

"Claudy, I did go to see you! On my knees, at Mrs. Grayson's front door, I prayed her to let me see you! She refused, and ordered me to come there no more! She would not suffer my sister to know that I was waiting there on my knees to see her dear, angel face. That was long before you were taken sick. She did not even send me word that Lilly was ill; I knew nothing of it, till my darling was cold in her little shroud! Oh, Claudy! Claudy!"

She covered her face with her hands and tried to stifle the wail that crossed her lips. Claudia endeavored to soothe her, by winding her arms about her and kissing her repeatedly. Pauline had looked wonderingly on, during this painful reunion; and now drawing nearer, she said, with more gentleness than was her custom:

"Don't grieve so, Beulah. Wipe your eyes and come home; those girls yonder are staring at you."

"What business is it of yours?" began Claudia; but Beulah's sensitive nature shrank from observation, and rising hastily, she took Claudia to her bosom, kissed her and turned away.

"Oh, Beulah! shan't I see you again?" cried the latter, with streaming eyes.

"Claudia, your mamma would not be willing."

"I don't care what she thinks. Please, come to see me—please, do! Beulah, you don't love me now, because Lilly is dead! Oh, I could not keep her—God took her!"

"Yes, I do love you Claudy—more than ever; but you must come to see me. I cannot go to that house again. I can't see your mamma Grayson. Come and see me, darling!"

She drew her bonnet over her face and hurried out.

"Where do you live? I will come and see you!" cried Claudia running after the retreating form.

"She lives at Doctor Hartwell's—that large, brick house, out on the edge of town; everybody knows the place."

Pauline turned back to give this piece of information, and then hastened on to join Beulah. She longed to inquire into all the particulars of the orphan's early life; but the pale, fixed face gave no encouragement to question, and they walked on in perfect silence until they reached the gate at the end of the avenue. Then Pauline asked, energetically:

"Is that little one any kin to you?"

"No; I have no kin in this world," answered Beulah drearily.

Pauline shrugged her shoulders, and made no further attempt to elicit confidence. On entering the house, they encountered the doctor, who was crossing the hall. He stopped, and said:

"I have glad tidings for you, Beulah. The Morning Star arrived safely at Amsterdam, and by this time, Eugene is at Heidelberg."

Beulah stood very near him, and answered tremblingly:

"Yes, sir, I heard it at school."

He perceived that something was amiss, and untying her bonnet, looked searchingly at the sorrow-stained face. She shut her eyes, and leaned her head against him.

"What is the matter, my child? I thought you would be very happy in hearing of Eugene's safety."

She was unable to reply just then; and Pauline, who stood swinging her satchel to and fro, volunteered an explanation.

"Uncle Guy, she is curious, that is all. As we were leaving school, she met a little girl on the steps, and they flew at each other, and cried, and kissed, and—you never saw anything like it! I thought the child must be a very dear relation; but she says she has no kin. I don't see the use of crying her eyes out, particularly when the little one is nothing to her."

Her uncle's countenance resumed its habitual severity and taking Beulah's hand, he led her into that quietest of all quiet places, his study. Seating himself, and drawing her to his side, he said:

"Was it meeting Claudia that distressed you so much? That child is very warmly attached to you. She raved about you constantly during her illness. So did Lilly. I did not understand the relationship then, or I should have interfered, and carried you to her. I called to see Mr. and Mrs. Grayson last week, to remove the difficulties in the way of your intercourse with Claudia, but they were not at home. I will arrange matters so that you may be with Claudia as often as possible. You have been wronged, child, I know; but try to bury it; it is all past now." He softly smoothed back her hair as he spoke.

"No, sir; it never will be past; it will always be burning here in my heart."

"I thought you professed to believe in the Bible."

She looked up instantly, and answered:

"I do, sir. I do."

"Then your belief is perfectly worthless; for the Bible charges you to 'forgive and love your enemies,' and here you are trying to fan your hate into an everlasting flame."

She saw the scornful curl of his lips, and sinking down beside him, she laid her head on his knee, and said hastily:

"I know it is wrong, sinful, to feel toward Mrs. Grayson as I do. Yes, sir; the Bible tells me it is very sinful; but I have been so miserable, I could not help hating her. But I will try to do so no more. I will ask God to help me forgive her." His face flushed even to his temples, and then the blood receded, leaving it like sculptured marble. Unable or unwilling to answer, he put his hands on her head, softly, reverently, as though he touched something ethereal. He little dreamed, even then, that suffering heart was uplifted to the Throne of Grace, praying the Father that she might so live and govern herself, that *he* might come to believe the Bible, which her clear insight too surely told her he despised.

Oh! protean temptation. Even as she knelt, with her protector's hands resting on her brow, ubiquitous evil suggested the thought: "Is he not kinder, and better, than any one you ever knew? Has not Mrs. Grayson a pew in the most fashionable church? Did not Eugene tell you he saw her there, regularly, every Sunday? Professing Christianity, she injured you; rejecting it, he has guarded and most generously aided you. 'By their fruits ye shall judge.' " Very dimly all this passed through her mind. She was perplexed and troubled at the confused ideas veiling her trust.

"Beulah, I have an engagement, and must leave you. Stay here if you like, or do as you please with yourself. I shall not be home to tea, so good night." She looked pained, but remained silent. He smiled, and drawing out his watch, said gaily:

"I verily believe you miss me when I leave you. Go, put on your other bonnet, and come down to the front door; I have nearly an hour yet, I see, and will give you a short ride. Hurry, child; I don't like to wait."

She was soon seated beside him in the buggy, and Mazeppa's swift feet had borne them some distance from home ere either spoke. The road ran near the bay, and white elegant residences lined one side, the other was bounded by a wide expanse of water, rippling, sparkling, glowing in the evening sunlight. Small sail boats, with their gleaming canvas, dotted the blue bosom of the bay; and the balmy breeze, fresh from the gulf, fluttered the bright pennons that floated from their masts. Beulah was watching the snowy wall of foam, piled on either side of the prow of a schooner, and thinking how very beautiful it was, when the bugged stopped suddenly, and Dr. Hartwell addressed a gentleman on horseback:

"Percy, you may expect me; I am coming as I promised."

"I was about to remind you of your engagement. But, Guy, whom have you there?"

"My protégée I told you of. Beulah, this is Mr. Lockhart." The rider reined his horse near her side, and leaning forward as he raised his hat, their eyes met. Both started visibly, and extending his hand, Mr. Lockhart said eagerly:

"Ah, my little forest friend! I am truly glad to find you again."

She shook hands very quietly, but an expression of pleasure stole over her face. Her guardian observed it, and asked:

"Pray, Percy, what do you know of her?"

"That she sings very charmingly," answered his friend, smiling at Beulah.

"He saw me once when I was at the Asylum," said she. "And was singing part of the *régime* there?"

"No, Guy; she was wandering about the piney woods, near the Asylum, with two beautiful elves, when I chanced to meet her. She was singing at the time. Beulah, I am glad to find you out again; and in future, when I pay the doctor long visits, I shall expect you to appear for my entertainment. Look to it, Guy, that she is present. But I am fatigued with my unusual exercise, and must return home. Good-by, Beulah; shake hands. I am going immediately to my room, Guy; so come as soon as you can." He rode slowly on, while Dr. Hartwell shook the reins, and Mazeppa sprang down the road again. Beulah had remarked a great alteration in Mr. Lockhart's appearance; he was much paler, and bore traces of recent and severe illness. His genial manner and friendly words had interested her, and looking up at her guardian, she said, timidly:

"Is he ill, sir?"

"He has been, and is yet quite feeble. Do you like him?"

"I know nothing of him, except that he spoke to me one evening some months ago. Does he live here, sir?"

"No; he has a plantation on the river, but is here on a visit occasionally. Much of his life has been spent in Europe, and thither he goes again very soon."

The sun had set. The bay seemed a vast sheet of fire, as the crimson clouds cast their shifting shadows on its bosom; and forgetting everything else, Beulah leaned out of the buggy, and said almost unconsciously:

"How beautiful! how very beautiful!" Her lips were parted; her eyes clear, and sparkling with delight. Dr. Hartwell sighed, and turning from the bay road, approached his home. Beulah longed to speak to him of what was pressing on her heart, but glancing at his countenance to see whether it was an auspicious time, she was deterred by the sombre sternness which overshadowed it, and before she could summon courage to speak, they stopped at the front gate:

"Jump out, and go home; I have not time to drive in."

She got out of the buggy, and looking up at him as he rose to adjust some part of the harness, said bravely:

"I am very much obliged to you for my ride. I have not had such a pleasure for years. I thank you very much."

"All very unnecessary, child. I am glad you enjoyed it."

He seated himself, and gathered up the reins, without looking at her; but she put her hand on top of the wheel, and said in an apologetic tone:

"Excuse me, sir; but may I wait in your study till you come home? I want to ask you something." Her face flushed, and her voice trembled with embarrassment.

"It may be late before I come home to-night. Can't you tell me now what you want? I can wait."

"Thank you, sir; to-morrow will do as well, I suppose. I will not detain you." She opened the gate and entered the yard. Dr. Hartwell looked after her an instant, and called out, as he drove on:

"Do as you like Beulah, about waiting for me; of course the study is free to you at all times."

The walk, or rather carriage-road, leading up to the house was bordered by stately poplars and cedars, whose branches interlaced overhead, and formed a perfect arch. Beulah looked up at the dark-green depths among the cedars, and walked on with a feeling of contentment, nay, almost of happiness, which was a stranger to her heart. In front of the house, and in the center of a grassy circle, was a marble basin, from which a fountain ascended. She sat down on the edge of the reservoir, and taking off her bonnet, gave unrestrained license to her wandering thoughts. Wherever her eyes turned, verdure, flowers, statuary met her gaze; the air was laden with the spicy fragrance of jasmins, and the low, musical babble of the fountain had something very soothing in its sound. With her keen appreciation of beauty, there was nothing needed to enhance her enjoyment; and she ceased to remember her sorrows. Before long, however, she was startled by the sight of several elegantly dressed ladies, emerging from the house; at the same instant, a handsome carriage, which she had not previously observed, drove from a turn in the walk and drew up to the door to receive them. Mrs. Chilton stood on the steps, exchanging smiles and polite nothings, and as one of the party requested permission to break a sprig of geranium growing near, she gracefully offered to collect a bouquet, adding, as she severed some elegant clusters of heliotrope and jasmin:

"Guy takes inordinate pride in his *parterre,* arranges and overlooks all the flowers himself. I often tell him I am jealous of my beautiful rivals; they monopolize his leisure so completely."

"Nonsense! we know to our cost, that you of all others need fear rivalry from no quarter. There: don't break any more. What superb taste the doctor has! This lovely spot comes nearer my ideal of European elegance than any place I know at the South. I suppose the fascination of his home makes him such a recluse! Why doesn't he visit more? He neglects us shamefully! He is such a favorite in society too; only I believe everybody is rather afraid of him. I shall make a most desperate effort to charm him, so soon as an opportunity offers. Don't tell him I said so, though, 'fore-warned, fore-armed.' " All this was very volubly uttered by a dashing, showy young lady, dressed in the extreme of fashion, and bearing unmistakable marks of belonging to *beau monde.* She extended a hand cased in white kid, for the flowers, and looked steadily at the lady of the house as she spoke.

"I shall not betray your designs, Miss Julia. Guy is a great lover of the beautiful, and I am not aware than anywhere in the book of fate is written the decree that he shall not marry again. Take care, you are tearing your lace point on that rose-bush: let me disengage it." She stooped to rescue the cobweb wrapping, and looking about her, Miss Julia exclaimed:

"Is that you, Pauline? Come and kiss me! Why, you look as unsociable as your uncle, sitting there all alone!"

She extended her hand before Beulah, who, as may be supposed, made no attempt to approach her. Mrs. Chilton smiled, and, clasping the bracelet on her arm, discovered to her visitor the mistake.

"Pauline is not at home. That is a little beggarly orphan Guy took it into his head to feed and clothe, till some opportunity offered of placing her in a respectable home. I have teased him unmercifully about this display of taste;

asked him what rank he assigned her in his catalogue of beautiful treasures." She laughed as if much amused.

"Oh, that reminds me that I heard some of the schoolgirls say that the doctor had adopted an orphan. I thought I would ask you about it. Mother here declared that she knew it could not be so, but I told her he was so very odd, there was no accounting for his notions. So he has not adopted her."

"Pshaw! of course not! She was a wretched little object of charity, and Guy brought her here to keep her from starving. He picked her up at the hospital, I believe."

"I knew it must be a mistake. Come, Julia, remember you are going out to-night, and it is quite late. Do come very soon, my dear Mrs. Chilton." Mrs. Vincent, Miss Julia, and their companions entered the carriage, and were soon out of sight. Beulah still sat at the fountain. She would gladly have retreated on the appearance of the strangers, but could not effect an escape without attracting the attention she so earnestly desired to be spared, and therefore kept her seat. Every word of the conversation which had been carried on in anything but a subdued tone, reached her, and though the head was unbowed as if she had heard nothing, her face was dyed with shame. Her heart throbbed violently, and as the words, "beggarly orphan," "wretched object of charity," fell on her ears, it seemed as if a fierce fire-bath had received her. As the carriage disappeared, Mrs. Chilton approached her, and stung to desperation by the merciless taunts, she instantly rose and confronted her. Never had she seen the widow look so beautiful, and for a moment they eyed each other.

"What are you doing here, after having been told to keep out of sight?—answer me!" She spoke with the inflexible sternness of a mistress to an offending servant.

"Madam, I am not the miserable beggar you represented me a moment since; nor will I answer questions addressed in any such tone of authority and contempt."

"Indeed! well, then, my angelic martyr, how do you propose to help yourself?" answered Mrs. Chilton, laughing, with undisguised scorn.

"Doctor Hartwell brought me to his house, of his own accord; you know that I was scarcely conscious when I came into it. He has been very kind to me—has offered to adopt me. This you know perfectly well. But I am not in danger of starvation, away from this house. You know that instead of having been picked up at the hospital, I was earning my living, humble though it was, as a servant. He offered to adopt me, because he saw that I was very unhappy; not because I needed food, or clothes, as you asserted just now, and as you knew was untrue. Madam, I have known, ever since my recovery, that you hated me, and I scorn to accept bounty, nay, even a shelter, where I am so unwelcome. I have never dreamed of occupying the place you covet for Pauline. I intended to accept Doctor Hartwell's kindness, so far as receiving an education, which would enable me to support myself less laboriously; but, madam, I will relieve you of my hated presence. I can live without any assistance from your family. The despised and ridiculed orphan will not remain to annoy you. Oh, you might have effected your purpose with less cruelty! You could have told me kindly that you did not want me here, and I would not have wondered at it. But to crush me publicly, as you have done"—wounded pride stifled the trembling accents.

Mrs. Chilton bit her lip. She had not expected this expression of proud independence; and seeing that she had gone too far, pondered the best method of rectifying the mischief with as little compromise of personal dignity as possible. Ultimately to eject her, she had intended from the first; but perfectly conscious that her brother would accept no explanation or palliation of the girl's departure at this juncture and that she and Pauline would soon follow her from the house, she felt that her own interest demanded the orphan's presence for a season. Nearly blinded by tears of indignation, and mortification, Beulah turned from her, but the delicate white hand arrested her and pressed heavily on her shoulder. She drew herself up, and tried to shake off the hold, but firm as iron was the grasp of the snowy fingers, and calm and cold as an Arctic night was the tone which said:

"Pshaw! girl, are you mad? You have sense enough to know that you are one too many in this house, but if you only desire to be educated, as you profess, why, I am perfectly willing that you should remain here. The idea of your growing up as my brother's heiress and adopted child was too preposterous to be entertained, and you can see the absurdity yourself; but so long as you understand matters properly, and merely desire to receive educational advantages, of course you can and will remain. I do not wish this to go any further, and, as a sensible girl, you will not mention it. As a friend, however, I would suggest that you should avoid putting yourself in the way of observation." As she concluded, she quietly brushed off a small spider, which was creeping over Beulah's sleeve.

"Don't trouble yourself, madam; I am not at all afraid of poisonous things; I have become accustomed to them."

Smiling bitterly, she stooped to pick up her new bonnet, which had fallen on the grass at her feet, and fixing her eyes defiantly on the handsome face before her, said, resolutely:

"No! contemptible as you think me, beggarly and wretched as you please to term me, I have too much self-respect to stay a day longer, where I have been so grossly, so needlessly insulted. You need not seek to detain me. Take your hand off my arm: I am going now; the sooner the better. I understand, madam, your brother will not countenance your cruelty, and you are ashamed for him to know what, in his absence, you were not ashamed to do. I scorn to retaliate! He shall not learn from me why I left so suddenly. Tell him what you choose."

Mrs. Chilton was very pale, and her lips were compressed till they grew purple. Clinching her hand, she said under her breath:

"You artful little wretch. Am I to be thwarted by such a mere child? You shall not quit the house. Go to your room, and don't make a fool of yourself. In future I shall not concern myself about you, if you take root at the front door. Go in, and let matters stand. I promise you I will not interfere again, no matter what you do. Do you hear me?"

"No. You have neither the power to detain, nor to expel me. I shall leave here immediately, and you need not attempt to coerce me; for, if you do, I will acquaint Doctor Hartwell with the whole affair, as soon as he comes, or when I see him. I am going for my clothes; not those you so reluctantly had made, but the old garments I wore when I worked for my bread." She shook off the detaining hand, and went up to her room. Harriet had already lighted her lamp, and as she entered the door, the rays fell brightly on the picture she had learned to love so well. Now she looked at it through scalding tears, and, to her excited fancy, the smile seemed to have faded from the lips of Hope, and the valley looked more dreary, and the pilgrims more desolate and miserable. She turned from it, and taking off the clothes she wore, dressed herself in the humble apparel of former days. The old trunk was scarcely worth keeping, save as a relic; and folding up the clothes and books into as small a bundle as possible, she took it in her arms, and descended the steps. She wished very much to tell Harriet good-by, and thank her for her unvarying kindness; and now, on the eve of her departure, she remembered the words whispered during her illness, and the offer of assistance when she "got into trouble," as Harriet phrased it; but dreading to meet Mrs. Chilton again, she hurried down the hall, and left the house. The friendly stars looked kindly down upon the orphan, as she crossed the common, and proceeded toward the Asylum, and raising her eyes to the jewelled dome, the solemn beauty of the night hushed the wild tumult in her heart, and she seemed to hear the words pronounced from the skyey depths: "*Lo, I am with you always, even unto the end.*" Gradually, the results of the step she had taken obtruded themselves before her, and with a keen pang of pain and grief, came the thought, "what will Dr. Hartwell think of me?" All his kindness during the time she had passed beneath his roof, his genial tones, his soft, caressing touch on her head, his rare, but gentle smile, his constant care for her comfort and happiness, all rushed like lightning over her mind, and made the hot tears gush over her face. Mrs. Chilton would, of course, offer some plausible solution of her sudden departure. He would think her ungrateful, and grow indifferent to her welfare or fate. Yet hope whispered, "he will suspect the truth; he must know his sister's nature; he will not blame me." But all this was in the cloudy realm of conjecture, and the stern realities of her position weighed heavily on her heart. Through Dr. Hartwell, who called to explain her sudden disappearance, Mrs. Martin had sent her the eighteen dollars due for three months' service, and this little sum was all that she possessed. As she walked on, pondering the many difficulties which attended the darling project of educating herself thoroughly, the lights of the Asylum greeted her, and it was with a painful sense of desolation that she mounted the steps, and stood upon the threshold where she and Lily had so often sat, in years gone by. Mrs. Williams met her at the door, wondering what unusual occurrence induced a visitor at this unseasonable hour. The hall lamp shone on her kind, but anxious face, and as Beulah looked at her remembered care and love caused a feeling of suffocation, and with an exclamation of joy, she threw her arms around her. Astonished at a greeting so unexpected, the matron glanced hurriedly at the face pressed against her bosom, and recognizing her quondam charge, folded her tenderly to her heart.

"Beulah, dear child, I am so glad to see you!" As she kissed her white cheeks, Beulah felt the tears dropping upon them.

"Come into my room, dear, and take off your bonnet." She led her to the quiet little room, and took the bundle, and the antiquated bonnet, which Pauline declared "Mrs. Noah had worn all through the forty days' shower."

"Mrs. Williams, can I stay here with you until I can get a place somewhere? The managers will not object, will they?"

"No, dear, I suppose not. But, Beulah, I thought you had been adopted, just after Lilly died, by Doctor Hartwell? Here I have been, ever since I heard it from some of the managers, thinking how lucky it was for you, and feeling so thankful to God, for remembering his orphans. Child, what has happened? Tell me freely, Beulah."

With her head on the matron's shoulder, she imparted enough of what had transpired to explain her leaving her adopted home. Mrs. Williams shook her head, and said, sadly:

"You have been too hasty, child. It was Dr. Hartwell's house; he had taken you to it, and without consulting, and telling him, you should not have left it. If you felt that you could not live there in peace, with his sister, it was your duty to have told him so, and then decided as to what course you would take. Don't be hurt, child, if I tell you you are too proud. Poverty and pride make a bitter lot in this world; and take care you don't let your high spirit ruin your prospects. I don't mean to say, dear, that you ought to bear insult and oppression, but I do think you owed it to the doctor's kindness to have waited until his return, before you quitted his house."

"Oh, you do not know him! If he knew all that Mrs. Chilton said and did, he would turn her and Pauline out of the house immediately. They are poor, and, but for him, could not live without toil. I have no right to cause their ruin. She is his sister, and has a claim on him. I have none. She expects Pauline to inherit his fortune, and could not bear to think of his adopting me. I don't wonder at that so much. But she need not have been so cruel, so insulting. I don't want his money, or his house, or his elegant furniture. I only want an education, and his advice, and his kind care for a few years. I like Pauline very much indeed. She never treated me at all unkindly; and I could not bear to bring misfortune on her, she is so happy."

"That is neither here nor there. He will not hear the truth, of course; and even if he did, he will not suppose you were actuated by any such Christian motives, to shield his sister's meanness. You ought to have seen him first."

"Well, it is all over now, and I see I must help myself. I want to go to the public school, where the tuition is free; but how can I support myself in the meantime? Eighteen dollars would not board me long, and besides, I shall have to buy clothes." She looked up, much perplexed, in the matron's anxious face. The latter was silent a moment, and then said:

"Why, the public school closes in a few weeks; the next session will not begin before autumn, and what could you do until then? No, I will just inform Dr. Hartwell of the truth of the whole matter. I think it is due him, and—"

"Indeed you must not! I promised Mrs. Chilton that I would not implicate her, and your doing it would amount to the same thing. I would not be the means of driving Pauline out of her uncle's house, for all the gold in California."

"Silly child. What on earth possessed you to promise any such thing?"

"I wanted her to see that I was honest in what I said. She knew that I could, by divulging the whole affair, turn her out of the house (for Dr. Hartwell's disposition is a secret to no one who has lived in his home), and I wished to show her that I told the truth in saying I only wanted to be educated for a teacher."

"Suppose the doctor comes here, and asks you about the matter?"

"I shall tell him that I prefer not being dependent on any one. But he will not come. He does not know where I am." Yet the dread that he would, filled her mind with new anxieties.

"Well, well, it is no use to fret over what can't be undone. I wish I could help you, but I don't see any chance just now."

"Could not I get some plain sewing? Perhaps the managers would give me work?"

"Ah, Beulah, it would soon kill you, to have to sew for your living."

"No, no, I can bear more than you think," answered the girl, with a dreary smile.

"Yes, your spirit can endure more than your body. Your father died with consumption, child; but don't fret about it any more to night. Come, get some supper, and then go to sleep. You will stay in my room, with me, dear, till something can be done to assist you."

"Mrs. Williams, you must promise me that you never will speak of what I have told you, regarding that conversation with Mrs. Chilton."

"I promise you, dear, I never will mention it, since you prefer keeping the matter secret."

"What will Dr. Hartwell think of me?" was the recurring thought, that would not be banished; and, unable to sleep, Beulah tossed restlessly on her pillow all night, dreading lest he should despise her for her seeming ingratitude.

CHAPTER XI.

For perhaps two hours after Beulah's departure, Mrs. Chilton wandered up and down the parlors, revolving numerous schemes, explanatory of her unexpected exodus. Completely nonplussed, for the first time in her life, she sincerely rued the expression of dislike and contempt which had driven the orphan from her adopted home; and, unable to decide on the most plausible solution to be offered her brother, she paced restlessly to and fro. Engrossed by no particularly felicitous reflections, she failed to notice Mazeppa's quick tramp, and remained in ignorance of the doctor's return, until he entered the room, and stood beside her. His manner was hurried, his thoughts evidently preoccupied, as he said:

"May, I am going into the country to be absent all of to-morrow, and possibly longer. There is some surgical work to be performed for a careless hunter, and I must start immediately. I want you to see that a room is prepared for Percy Lockhart. He is very feeble, and I have invited him to come and stay with me while he is in the city. He rode out this evening, and is worse from the fatigue. I shall expect you to see that everything is provided for him that an invalid could desire. Can I depend upon you?"

"Certainly; I will exert myself to render his stay here pleasant; make yourself easy on that score." It was very evident that the cloud was rapidly lifting from her heart and prospects; but she veiled the sparkle in her eye, and unsuspicious of anything amiss, her brother left the room. Walking up to one of the mirrors, which extended from floor to ceiling, she surveyed herself carefully, and a triumphant smile parted her lips.

"Percy Lockhart is vulnerable as well as other people, and I have yet to see the man whose heart will proudly withstand the allurements of flattery, provided the homage is delicately and gracefully offered. Thank heaven! years have touched me lightly, and there was more truth than she relished in what Julia Vincent said about my beauty!"

This self-complacent soliloquy was cut short by the appearance of her brother, who carried a case of surgical instruments in his hand.

"May, tell Beulah I am sorry I did not see her. I would go up and wake her, but have not time. She wished to ask me something. Tell her, if it is anything of importance, to do just as she likes; I will see about it when I come home. Be sure you tell her. Good night; take care of Percy." He turned away, but she exclaimed:

"She is not here, Guy. She asked me this evening if she might spend the night at the Asylum. She thought you would not object, and certainly I had no authority to prevent her. Indeed the parlor was full of company, and I told her she might go if she wished. I suppose she will be back early in the morning."

His face darkened instantly, and she felt that he was searching her with his piercing eyes.

"All this sounds extremely improbable to me. If she is not at home again at breakfast, take the carriage and go after her. Mind, May! I will sift the whole matter when I come back." He hurried off, and she breathed freely once more. Dr. Hartwell sprang into his buggy, to which a fresh horse had been attached, and dismissing Hal, whose weight would only have retarded his progress, he drove rapidly off. The gate had been left open for him, and he was passing through, when arrested by Harriet's well-known voice.

"Stop, master! Stop a minute!"

"What do you want? I can't stop!" cried he impatiently.

"Are you going after that poor, motherless child?"

"No. But what the devil is to pay here; I shall get at the truth now. Where is Beulah? talk fast."

"She is at the Asylum to-night, sir. I followed and watched the poor little thing. Master, if you don't listen to me, if you please, sir, you will never get at the truth, for that child won't tell it. I heard her promise Miss May she would not. You would be ready to fight if you knew all I know."

"Why did Beulah leave here this evening?"

"Because Miss May abused and insulted her; told her before some ladies that she was a 'miserable beggar' that you picked up at the hospital, and that you thought it was charity to feed and clothe her till she was big enough to work. The ladies were in the front yard, and the child happened to be sitting by the fountain; she had just come from riding. I was sewing at one of the windows up-stairs, sir, and heard every word. When the folks were gone, Miss May walks up to her and asks her what she is doing where anybody could see her? Oh, master! if you could have seen that child's looks. She fairly seemed to rise off her feet, and her face was as white as a corpse. She said she had wanted an education; that she knew you had been very kind; but she never dreamed of taking Miss Pauline's place in your house. She said she would not stay where she was unwelcome; that she was not starving when you took her home; that she knew you were kind and good; but that she *scorned*—them were the very words, master—she scorned to stay a day longer where she had been so insulted! Oh, she was in a towering rage; she trembled all over, and Miss May began to be scared, for she knew you would not suffer such doings, and she tried to pacify her and make up the quarrel by telling her she might stay and have an education, if that was all she wanted. But the girl would not hear to anything she said, and told her she need not be frightened, that she wouldn't go to you with the fuss; she would not tell you why she left your house. She went to her room and she got every rag of her old clothes, and left the house with the tears raining out of her eyes. Oh, master, it's a crying shame! If you had only been here to hear that child talk to Miss May. Good Lord, how her big eyes did blaze when she told her she could earn a living!"

By the pale moonlight she could see that her master's face was rigid as steel; but his voice was even calmer than usual, when he asked:

"Are you sure she is now at the Asylum?"

"Yes, sir; sure."

"Very well; she is safe then for the present. Does any one know that you heard the conversation?"

"Not a soul, sir, except yourself."

"Keep the matter perfectly quiet till I come home. I shall be away a day, or perhaps longer; meantime see that Beulah does not get out of your sight. Do you understand me?"

"Yes sir—I do."

The buggy rolled swiftly on, and Harriet returned to the house by a circuitous route, surmising that "Miss May's" eyes might detect her movements.

The same night, Clara Sanders sat on the doorstep of her humble cottage home. The moonlight crept through the clustering honeysuckle and silvered the piazza floor with grotesque fret-work, while it bathed lovingly the sad face of the girlish watcher. Her chin rested in her palms, and the soft eyes were bent anxiously on the countenance of her infirm and aged companion.

"Grandpa, don't look so troubled. I am very sorry, too, about the diploma; but if I am not to have it, why, there is no use in worrying about it. Madame St. Cymon is willing to employ me as I am, and certainly I should feel grateful for her preference, when there are several applicants for the place. She told me this evening that she thought I would find no difficulty in performing what would be required of me."

This was uttered in a cheerful tone, which might have succeeded very well, had the sorrowful face been veiled.

"Ah, Clara, you don't dream of the burden you are taking upon yourself! The position of assistant teacher, in an establishment like Madame St. Cymon's, is one that you are by nature totally unfitted for. Child, it will gall your spirit; it will be unendurable." The old man sighed heavily.

"Still, I have been educated with an eye to teaching, and though I am now to occupy a very subordinate place, the trials will not be augmented. On the whole, I do not know but it is best as it is. Do not try to discourage me. It is all I can do, and I am determined I will not despond about what can't be helped."

"My dear child, I did not mean to depress you. But you are so young to bow your neck to such a yoke! How old are you?" He turned round to look at her.

"Only sixteen and a few months. Life is before me yet, an untrodden plain. Who knows but this narrow path of duty may lead to a calm, sweet resting-place for us both? I was thinking just now of that passage from your favorite Wallenstein: '*My soul's secure! In the night only, Friedland's stars can beam.*' The darkness has come down upon us, grandpa; let us wait patiently for the uprising of stars. I am not afraid of the night."

There was silence for some moments; then the old man rose, and, putting back the white locks which had fallen over his face, asked in a subdued tone:

"When will you commence your work?"

"To-morrow, sir."

"God bless you, Clara, and give you strength, as he sees you have need." He kissed her fondly, and withdrew to his own room. She sat for some time looking vacantly at the mosaic of light and shade on the floor before her, and striving to divest her mind of the haunting thought that she was the victim of some unyielding necessity, whose decree had gone forth, and might not be annulled. In early childhood her home had been one of splendid affluence; but reverses came thick and fast, as misfortunes ever do, and, ere she could realize the swift transition, penury claimed her family among its crowding legions. Discouraged and embittered, her father made the wine-cup the sepulchre of care, and in a few months found a deeper and far more quiet grave. His mercantile embarrassments had dragged his father-in-law to ruin; and, too aged to toil up the steep again, the latter resigned himself to spending the remainder of his days in obscurity, and perhaps want. To Clara's gifted mother, he looked for aid and comfort in the clouded evening of life, and with unceasing energy she toiled to shield her father and her child from actual labor. Thoroughly acquainted with music and drawing, her days were spent in giving lessons in those branches which had been acquired with reference to personal enjoyment alone, and the silent hours of the night often passed in stitching the garments of those who had flocked to her costly entertainments in days gone by. When Clara was about thirteen years of age, a distant relative chancing to see her, kindly proposed to contribute the sum requisite for affording her every educational advantage. The offer was gratefully accepted by the devoted mother, and Clara was placed at Madame St. Cymon's, where more than ordinary attention could be bestowed on the languages.

The noble woman, whose heart had bled incessantly over the misery, ruin, and degradation of her husband, sank slowly under the intolerable burden of sorrows, and a few weeks previous to the evening of which I write, folded her weary hands and went home to rest. In the springtime of girlhood, Clara felt herself transformed into a woman. Standing beside her mother's tomb, supporting her grandfather's tottering form, she shuddered in anticipating the dreary future that beckoned her on; and now as if there were not troubles enough already to disquiet her, the annual amount advanced toward her school expenses was suddenly withdrawn. The cousin, residing in a distant State, wrote that pecuniary troubles had assailed him, and prevented all further assistance. In one more year she would have finished the prescribed course and graduated honorably; and more than all, she would have obtained a diploma, which might have been an "open sesame" to any post she aspired to. Thus frustrated in her plans, she gladly accepted the position of assistant teacher in the primary department, which, having become vacant by the dismissal of the incumbent, madam kindly tendered her. The salary was limited, of course, but nothing else presented itself, and quitting the desk, where she had so often pored over her text-books, she prepared to grapple with the trials which thickly beset the path of a young woman thrown upon her own resources for maintenance. Clara was naturally amiable, unselfish, and trusting. She was no intellectual prodigy, yet her mind was clear and forcible, her judgment matured, and, above all, her pure heart warm and loving. Notwithstanding the stern realities that marked her path, there was a vein of romance in her nature which, unfortunately, attained more than healthful development, and while it often bore her into the utopian realms of fancy, it was still impotent to modify, in any degree, the social difficulties with which she was forced to contend. Ah, there is a touching beauty in the radiant uplook of a girl just crossing the limits of youth, and commencing her journey through the chequered sphere of womanhood! It is all dew-sparkle and morning glory to her ardent, buoyant spirit, as she presses forward exulting in blissful anticipations. But the withering heat of the conflict of life creeps on; the dewdrops exhale, the garlands of hope, shattered and dead, strew the path, and too often, ere noontide, the clear brow and sweet smile are exchanged for the weary look of one longing for the evening rest, the twilight, the night. Oh, may the good God give His sleep early unto these many!

There was a dawning light in Clara's eyes, which showed that, though as yet a mere girl in years, she had waked to the consciousness of emotions which belong to womanhood. She was pretty, and of course she knew it, for I am skeptical of those characters who grow up to mature beauty, all unsuspicious of the fatal dower, and are some day startled by a discovery of their possessions. She knew, too, that female loveliness was an all-potent spell, and depressing as were the circumstances of her life and situation, she felt that a brighter lot might be hers, without any very remarkable or seemingly inconsistent course of events.

CHAPTER XII.

"Harriet, bring me a cup of strong coffee."

Dr. Hartwell had returned late in the afternoon of the second day, and travel-worn and weary, threw himself down on the sofa in his study. There was a pale severity in his face, which told that his reflections during his brief absence had been far from pleasant, and as he swept back the hair from his forehead, and laid his head on the cushion, the whole countenance bespoke the bitterness of a proud, but miserable man. He remained for some time, with closed eyes, and when the coffee was served, drank it without comment. Harriet busied herself about the room, doing various unnecessary things, and wondering why her master did not inquire concerning home affairs; finally, having exhausted every pretext for lingering, she coughed very spasmodically once or twice, and putting her hand on the knob of the door, said deferentially—

"Do you want anything else, sir? The bath-room is all ready."

"Has my sister been to the Asylum?"

"No, sir."

"Go and arrange Beulah's room."

She retired; and springing up, he paced the floor, striving to master the emotion which so unwontedly agitated him. His lips writhed, and the thin nostril expanded, but he paused before the melodeon, sat down and played several pieces, and gradually the swollen veins on his brow lost their corded appearance, and the mouth resumed its habitual compression. Then, with an exterior as calm as the repose of death, he took his hat, and went toward the parlor. Mr. Lockhart was reclining on one of the sofas, Pauline sat on an ottoman near him, looking over a book of prints, and Mrs. Chilton, tastefully attired, occupied the piano-stool. Witching strains of music greeted her brother, as he stopped at the door and looked in. In the mirror opposite she saw his image reflected, and for an instant her heart beat rapidly, but the delicate fingers flew over the keys as skilfully as before, and only the firm setting of the teeth betokened the coming struggle. He entered, and walking up to the invalid, said cordially:

"How are you, Percy? better, I hope." While one hand clasped his friend's, the other was laid with brotherly freedom on the sick man's head.

"Of course I am. There was no malady in Eden, was there? Verily, Guy, in your delightful home I am growing well again."

"Ah! so much for not possessing Ithuriel's spear. I am glad to find you free from fever."

"Howd'y-do, uncle! Don't you see me?" said Pauline, reaching up her hand.

"It is always hard to find you, Pauline, you are such a demure, silent little body," said he, shaking her hand kindly.

"Welcome, Guy! I expected you yesterday; what detained you so long?"

Mrs. Chilton approached with outstretched hand, and at the same time offered her lips for a kiss.

He availed himself of neither, but fixing his eyes intently on hers, said as sweetly as if he had been soothing a fretful child:

"Necessity of course; but now that I have come, I shall make amends, I promise you, for the delay. Percy, has she taken good care of you?"

"She is an admirable nurse; I can never requite the debt she has imposed. Is not my convalescence sufficient proof of her superior skill?" Mr. Lockhart raised himself, and leaning on his elbow, suffered his eyes to rest admiringly on the graceful form and faultless features beside him.

"Are you really so much better?" said Dr. Hartwell, gnawing his lip.

"Indeed I am! Why are you so incredulous? Have you so little confidence in your own prescriptions?"

"Confidence! I had little enough when given, immeasurably less now. But we will talk of all this after a while. I have some matters to arrange, and will be with you at tea. May, I wish to see you."

"Well, Guy, what is it?" without moving an inch, she looked up at him.

"Come to my study," answered her brother, quietly.

"And leave your patient to amuse himself? Really, Guy, you exercise the rites of hospitality so rarely, that you forget the ordinary requirements. Apropos, your little protégée has not returned. It seems she did not fancy living here, and prefers staying at the Asylum. I would not trouble myself about her, if I were you. Some people cannot appreciate kindness, you know." She uttered this piece of counsel, with perfect *sang-froid,* and met her brother's eye as innocently as Pauline would have done.

"I am thoroughly acquainted with her objections to this place, and determined to remove them so completely, that she cannot refuse to return."

A gray pallor crept over his sister's face, but she replied with her usual equanimity.

"You have seen her, then? I thought you had hurried back to your sick friend here, without pausing by the way."

"No! I have not seen her, and you are aware, her voluntary promise would seal her lips, even if I had." He smiled contemptuously, as he saw her puzzled look, and continued: "Percy will excuse you for a few moments, come with me. Pauline, entertain this gentleman in our absence."

She took his offered arm, and they proceeded to the study in silence.

"Sit down." Dr. Hartwell pushed a chair toward her, and stood looking her fully in the face. She did not shrink, and asked unconcernedly:

"Well, Guy, to what does all this preamble lead?"

"May, is the doctrine of future punishments laid down as orthodox in that elegantly gilded prayer-book you take with you in your weekly pilgrimages to church?"

"Come, come, Guy; if you have no respect for religion, yourself, don't scoff at its observances in my presence. It is very unkind, and I will not allow it." She rose, with an air of offended dignity.

"Scoff! you wrong me. Why, verily, your religion is too formidable to suffer the thought. I tell you, sister mine, your creed is a terrible one in my eyes." He looked at her with a smile of withering scorn.

She grew restless under his impaling gaze, and he continued mockingly:

"From such creeds! such practice! Good Lord deliver us!"

She turned to go, but his hand fell heavily on her shoulder.

"I am acquainted with all that passed between Beulah and yourself the evening she left my house. I was cognizant of the whole truth before I left the city."

"Artful wretch! She is as false as contemptible!" muttered the sister, through set teeth.

"Take care! I do not too hastily apply your own individual standard of action to others. She does not dream that I am acquainted with the truth, though doubtless she wonders that, knowing you so well, I should not suspect it."

"Ah, guided by your favorite Mephistopheles, you wrapped the mantle of invisibility about you, and heard it all. Eh?"

"No; Mephistopheles is not ubiquitous, and I left him at home here, it seems, when I took that child to ride. It is difficult for me to believe you are my sister! very difficult! It is the most humiliating thought that could possibly be suggested to me. May, I very nearly decided to send you and Pauline out into the world without a dime!—without a cent!—just as I found you, and I may do so yet—"

"You dare not! You dare not! You swore a solemn oath to the dying that you would always provide for us! I am not afraid of your breaking your vow!" cried Mrs. Chilton, leaning heavily against the table to support herself.

"You give me credit for too much nicety. I tell you I would break my oath to-morrow, nay to-night; for your duplicity cancels it, but for that orphan you hate so cordially. She would never return if you and Pauline suffered for the past; for her sake and hers only, I will still assist, support you, for have her here I will! if it costs me life and fortune! I would send you off to the plantation, but there are no educational advantages there for Pauline; and therefore, if Beulah returns, I have resolved to buy and give you a separate home, wherever you may prefer. Stay here, you cannot and shall not!"

"And what construction will the world place on your taking a young girl into your house at the time that I leave it? Guy, with what marvelous foresight you are endowed!" said she, laughing sardonically.

"I shall take measures to prevent any improper construction! Mrs. Watson, the widow of one of my oldest and best friends, has been left in destitute circumstances, and I shall immediately offer her a home here, to take charge of my household, and look after Beulah when I am absent. She is an estimable woman past fifty years of age, and her character is so irreproachable, that her presence here will obviate the objection you have urged. You will decide to-night where you wish to fix your future residence, and let me know to-morrow. I shall not give you longer time for a decision. Meantime, when Beulah returns you will not allude to the matter. At your peril, May! I have borne much from you, but by all that I prize, I swear, I will make you suffer severely if you dare to interfere again. Do not imagine that I am ignorant of your schemes! I tell you now, I would gladly see Percy Lockhart lowered into the grave, rather than know that you have succeeded in blinding him! Oh, his noble nature would loath you, could he see you as you are. There, go! or I shall forget that I am talking to a woman: much less a woman claiming to by *my sister!* Go go!" He put up his hands as if unwilling to look at her, and leaving the room, descended to the front door. A large family-carriage, drawn by two horses, stood in readiness, and seating himself within it, he ordered the coachman to drive to the Asylum. Mrs. Williams met him at the entrance, and despite her assumed composure, felt nervous and uncomfortable, for his scrutinizing look disconcerted her.

"Madam, you are the matron of this institution, I presume. I want to see Beulah Benton."

"Sir, she saw your carriage, and desired me to say to you that though she was very grateful for your kindness, she did not wish to burden you, and preferred remaining here until she could find some position which would enable her to support herself. She begs you will not insist upon seeing her; she does not wish to see you."

"Where is she? I shall not leave the house until I do see her."

She saw from his countenance that it was useless to contend. There was an unbending look of resolve which said plainly, "Tell me where to find her, or I shall search for her at once." Secretly pleased at the prospects of reconciliation, the matron no longer hesitated, and pointing to the staircase, said:

"She is in the first right-hand room."

He mounted the steps, opened the door, and entered. Beulah was standing by the window; she had recognized his step, and knew that he was in the room, but felt as if she would not meet his eye for the universe. Yet there was in her heart an intense longing to see him again. During the two past days she had missed his kind manner and grave watchfulness, and now, if she had dared to yield to the impulse that prompted, she would have sprung to meet him, and caught his hand to her lips. He approached, and stood looking at the drooped face; then his soft, cool touch was on her head, and he said in his peculiar low musical tones.

"Proud little spirit, come home and be happy."

She shook her head, saying resolutely:

"I cannot: I have no home. I could not be happy in your house."

"You can be in future. Beulah, I know the whole truth of this matter; how I discovered it is no concern of yours—you have not broken your promise. Now mark me, I make your return to my house the condition of my sister's pardon. I am not trifling! If you persist in leaving me, I tell you solemnly I will send her and Pauline out into the world to work for their daily bread, as you want to do! If you will come back, I will given them a comfortable home of their own wherever they may prefer to live, and see that they are always well cared for. But they shall not remain in my house whether you come or not. I am in earnest! Look at me; you know I never say what I do not mean. I want you to come back; I ask you to come with me now. I am lonely; my home is dark and desolate, come, my child, come!" He held her hands in his, and drew her gently toward him. She looked eagerly into his face, and as she noted the stern sadness that marred its noble beauty, the words of his sister flashed upon her memory: He had been married! Was it the loss of his wife that had so darkened his elegant home?—That gave such austerity to the comparatively youthful face? She gazed into the deep eyes till she grew dizzy, and answered indistinctly:

"I have no claim on you—will not be the means of parting you and your sister. You have Pauline, make her your child."

"Henceforth my sister and myself are parted, whether you will it or not, whether you come back or otherwise. Once for all, if you would serve her, come, for on this condition only will I provide for her. Pauline does not suit me; you do. I can make you a friend, in some sort a companion. Beulah, you want to come to me; I see it in your eyes; but I see too that you want conditions; what are they?"

"Will you always treat Pauline just as kindly as if you had never taken me to your house?"

"Except having a separate home, she shall never know any difference. I promise you this. What else?"

"Will you let me go to the public school instead of Madame St. Cymon's?"

"Why, pray?"

"Because the tuition is free."

"And you are too proud to accept any aid from me?"

"No, sir; I want your counsel and guidance, and I want to be with you to show you that I do thank you for all your goodness; but I want to cost you as little as possible."

"You do not expect to depend on me always, then?" said he, smiling despite himself.

"No, sir; only till I am able to teach. If you are willing to do this, I shall be glad to go back, very glad; but not unless you are." She looked as firm as her guardian.

"Better stipulate also that you are to wear nothing more expensive than bit calico." He seemed much amused.

"Indeed, sir, I am not jesting at all. If you will take care of me while I am educating myself, I shall be very grateful to you; but I am not going to be adopted."

"Very well. Then I will try to take care of you. I have signed your treaty; are you ready to come home."

"Yes, sir; glad to come." Her fingers closed confidingly over his, and they joined Mrs. Williams in the hall below. A brief explanation from Beulah sufficed for the rejoicing matron, and soon she was borne rapidly from the Asylum. Dr. Hartwell was silent until they reached home, and Beulah was going to her own room, when he asked, suddenly:

"What was it that you wished to ask me about the evening of the ride?"

"That I might go to the public school."

"What put that into your head?"

"As a dependent orphan, I am insulted at Madame St. Cymon's."

"By whom?" His eyes flashed.

"No matter now, sir."

"By whom? I ask you."

"Not by Pauline. She would scorn to be guilty of anything so ungenerous."

"You do not mean to answer my question, then?"

"No, sir; do not ask me to do so, for I cannot."

"Very well. Get ready for tea. Mr. Lockhart is here. One word more. You need fear no further interference from any one."

He walked on, and glad to be released, Beulah hastened to her own room, with a strange feeling of joy on entering it again. Harriet welcomed her warmly, and without alluding to her absence, assisted in braiding the heavy masses of hair, which required arranging. Half an hour after, Dr. Hartwell knocked at the door, and conducted her down-stairs. Mrs. Chilton rose and extended her hand, with an amicable expression of countenance, for which Beulah was not prepared. She could not bring herself to accept the hand, but her salutation was gravely polite.

"Good evening, Mrs. Chilton."

Mr. Lockhart made room for her on the sofa; and quietly ensconced in one corner, she sat for some time so engaged in listening to the general conversation, that the bitter recollection of by-gone trials was entirely banished. Dr. Hartwell and his friend were talking of Europe, and the latter, after recounting much of interest in connection with his former visits, said earnestly:

"Go with me this time, Guy; one tour cannot have satiated you. It will be double—nay, triple, enjoyment, to have you along. It is, and always has been, a mystery to me, why you should persist in practising. You do not need the pecuniary aid; your income would enable you to live just as you pleased. Life is short at best: why not glean all of pleasure that travel affords to a nature like yours? Your sister was telling me that in a few days she goes North to place Pauline at some celebrated school, and without her you will be desolate. Come, let's to Europe together; what do you say?"

Dr. Hartwell received this intimation of his sister's plans without the slightest token of surprise, and smiled sarcastically as he replied:

"Percy, I shall answer you in the words of a favorite author of the day. He says 'it is for want of self culture that the superstition of traveling, whose idols are Italy, England, Egypt, retains its fascination for all educated Americans. He who travels to be amused, or to get somewhat which he does not carry, travels away from himself, and grows old, even in youth, among old things. In Thebes, in Palmyra, his will and mind have become old and dilapidated as they. He carries ruins to ruins. Traveling is a fool's paradise. At home I dream that at Naples, at Rome, I can be intoxicated with beauty, and lose my sadness. I pack my trunk, embark, and finally wake up in Naples, and there beside me, is the stern fact, the sad, self, unrelenting, identical, that I fled from. I affect to be intoxicated with sights, and suggestions, but I am not. My giant goes with me wherever I go.' Percy, I endeavored to drown my giant in the Mediterranean; to bury it forever beneath the green waters of Lago Maggiore; to hurl it from solemn, icy, Alpine heights; to dodge it in museums of art; but, as Emerson says, it clung to me with unerring allegiance, and I came home. And now, daily, and yearly, I repeat the hopeless experiment in my round of professional duties. Yes, May and Pauline are going away, but I shall have Beulah to look after, and I fancy time will not drag its wheels through coming years. How soon do you think of leaving America. I have some commissions for you when you start."

"I hope I shall be able to go North within a fortnight, and after a short visit to Newport or Saratoga, sail for Havre. What do you want from the great storehouse of art, sculpture and paintings, cameos and prints?"

"I will furnish you with a catalogue. Do you go through Germany, or only flaunt, butterfly-like, under the sunny skies of the Levant?"

"I have, as yet, no settled plans; but probably before I return, shall explore Egypt, Syria, and Arabia. Do you want anything from the dying world? From Dendera, Carnac, or that city of rock, lonely, silent, awful Petra?"

"Not I. The flavor of Sodom is too prevalent. But there are a few localities that I shall ask you to sketch for me." Subsequently, Mr. Lockhart requested Beulah to sing her forest song for him again. The blood surged quickly into her face, and, not without confusion, she begged him to excuse her. He insisted, and tried to draw her from her seat, but sinking further back into the corner, she assured him she could not; she never sang, except when alone. Dr. Hartwell smiled, and, looking at her curiously, said:

"I never heard her even attempt to sing. Beulah, why will you not try to oblige him?"

"Oh, sir! my songs are all connected with sorrows. I could not sing them now; indeed I could not." And as the memory of Lilly, hushed by her lullaby, rose vividly before her, she put her hands over her eyes and wept quietly.

"When you come home from your Oriental jaunt, she will be able to comply with your request. Meantime, Percy, come into the study; I want a cigar and game of chess."

Beulah quitted the parlor at the same time, and was mounting the steps, when she heard Mr. Lockhart ask: "Guy, what are you going to do with that solemn-looking child?"

"Going to try to show her that the world is not altogether made up of brutes." She heard no more, but long after she laid her head upon her pillow, pondered on the kind fate which gave her so considerate, so generous a guardian; and, in the depths of her gratitude, she vowed to show him that she reverenced and honored him.

CHAPTER XIII.

Three years passed swiftly, unmarked by any incidents of interest, and one dreary night in December, Beulah sat in Dr. Hartwell's study, wondering what detained him so much later than usual. The lamp stood on the tea-table, and the urn awaited the master's return. The room, with its books, statues, paintings, and melodeon, was unaltered, but time had materially changed the appearance of the orphan. She had grown tall, and the mazarine blue merino dress fitted the slender form with scrupulous exactness. The luxuriant black hair was combed straight back from the face, and wound into a circular knot, which covered the entire back of the head, and gave a classical outline to the whole. The eyelashes were longer and darker, the complexion had lost its sickly hue, and though there was no bloom on the cheeks, they were clear and white. I have spoken before of that singular conformation of the massive brow, and now the style in which she wore her hair fully exposed the outline. The large gray eyes had lost their look of bitterness, but more than ever they were grave, earnest, restless, and searching; indexing a stormy soul. The whole countenance betokened that rare combination of mental endowments, that habitual train of deep, concentrated thought, mingled with somewhat of dark passion, which characterizes the eagerly-inquiring mind that struggles to lift itself far above common utilitarian themes. The placid element was as wanting in her physiognomy as in her character, and even the lines of that mouth gave evidence of strength and restlessness, rather than peace. Before her lay a book on geometry, and, engrossed by study, she was unobservant of Dr. Hartwell's entrance. Walking up to the grate, he warmed his fingers, and then, with his hands behind him, stood still on the rug, regarding his protégée attentively. He looked precisely as he had done more than three years before, when he waited at Mrs. Martin's, watching little Johnny and his nurse. The colorless face seemed as if chiseled out of ivory, and stern gravity, blended with bitterness, was enthroned on the lofty, unfurrowed brow. He looked at the girl intently, as he would have watched a patient to whom he had administered a dubious medicine, and felt some curiosity concerning the result.

"Beulah, put up your book and make the tea, will you?"

She started up, and seating herself before the urn, said, joyfully:

"Good evening! I did not know you had come home. You look cold, sir."

"Yes, it is deucedly cold; and, to mend the matter, Mazeppa must needs slip on the ice in the gutter, and lame himself. Knew, too, I should want him again to-night." He drew a chair to the table and received his tea from her hand, for it was one of his whims to dismiss Mrs. Watson and the servants at this meal, and have only Beulah present.

"Who is so ill as to require a second visit to-night?"

She very rarely asked anything relative to his professional engagements, but saw that he was more than usually interested.

"Why, that quiet, little Quaker friend of yours, Clara Sanders, will probably lose her grandfather this time. He had a second paralytic stroke to-day, and I doubt whether he survives till morning."

"Are any of Clara's friends with her?" asked Beulah quickly.

"Some two or three of the neighbors. What now?" he continued as she rose from the table.

"I am going to get ready and go with you when you return."

"Nonsense! The weather is too disagreeable; and besides, you can do no good; the old man is unconscious. Don't think of it."

"But I must think of it, and what is more, you must carry me, if you please. I shall not mind the cold, and I know Clara would rather have me with her, even though I could render no assistance. Will you carry me? I shall thank you very much." She stood on the threshold.

"And if I will not carry you?" he answered questioningly.

"Then, sir, though sorry to disobey you, I shall be forced to walk there."

"So I supposed. You may get ready."

"Thank you." She hurried off to wrap up for the ride, and acquaint Mrs. Watson with the cause of her temporary absence. On reentering the study she found the doctor lying on the sofa, with one hand over his eyes; without removing it he tossed a letter to her, saying:

"There is a letter from Heidelberg. I had almost forgotten it. You will have time to read it; the buggy is not ready." He moved his fingers slightly, so as to see her distinctly, while she tore off the envelope and perused it. At first she looked pleased; then the black eyebrows met over the nose, and as she refolded it, there was a very decided curl in the compressed upper lip. She put it into her pocket without comment.

"Eugene is well, I suppose?" said the doctor, still shading his eyes.

"Yes, sir, quite well."

"Does he seem to be improving his advantages?"

"I should judge not, from the tone of this letter."

"What does it indicate?"

"That he thinks of settling down into mercantile life on his return; as if he needed to go to Germany to learn to keep books." She spoke hastily and with much chagrin.

"And why not? Germany is par excellence the land of book-making, and book-reading; why not of book-keeping?"

"German proficiency is not the question, sir."

Dr. Hartwell smiled, and passing his fingers through his hair, replied:

"You intend to annihilate that plebeian project of his, then?"

"His own will must govern him, sir; over that I have no power."

"Still you will use your influence in favor of a learned profession?"

"Yes, sir, if I have any."

"Take care your ambitious pride does not ruin you both! There is the buggy. Be so good as to give me my fur gauntlets out of the drawer of my desk. That will do, come."

The ride was rather silent. Beulah spoke several times, but was answered in a manner which informed her that her guardian was in a gloomy mood, and did not choose to talk. He was to her as inexplicable as ever. She felt that the barrier which divided them, instead of melting away with long and intimate acquaintance, had strengthened and grown impenetrable. Kind but taciturn, she knew little of his opinions on any of the great questions which began to agitate her own mind. For rather more than three years they had spent their evenings together; she in studying, he in reading or writing. Of his past life she knew absolutely nothing, for no unguarded allusion to it ever escaped his lips. As long as she had lived in his house he had never mentioned his wife's name, and but for his sister's words she would have been utterly ignorant of his marriage. Whether the omission was studied, or merely the result of abstraction, she could only surmise. Once, when sitting around the fire, a piece of crape fell upon the hearth from the shrouded portrait. He stooped down, picked it up, and without glancing at the picture, threw the fragment into the grate. She longed to see the covered face, but dared not unfasten the sable folds, which had grown rusty with age. Sometimes she fancied her presence annoyed him; but if she absented herself at all during the evening, he invariably inquired the cause. He had most scrupulously avoided all reference to matters of faith; she had endeavored several times to direct the conversation to religious topics, but he adroitly eluded her efforts, and abstained from any such discussion; and though on Sabbath she generally accompanied Mrs. Watson to church, he never alluded to it. Occasionally, when more than ordinarily fatigued by the labors of the day, he had permitted her to read aloud to him from some of his favorite volumes, and these brief glimpses had given her an intense longing to pursue the same paths of investigation. She revered and admired him; nay, she loved him; but it was more earnest gratitude than genuine affection. Love casteth out fear, and most certainly she feared him. She had entered her seventeenth year, and feeling that she was no longer a child, her pride sometimes rebelled at the calm, commanding manner he maintained toward her.

They found Clara kneeling beside her insensible grandfather, while two or three middle-aged ladies sat near the hearth, talking in under tones. Beulah put her arms tenderly around her friend ere she was aware of her presence, and the cry of blended woe and gladness, with which Clara threw herself on Beulah's bosom, told her how well-timed that presence was. Three years of teaching and care had worn the slight young form, and given a troubled, strained, weary look to the fair face. Thin, pale, and tearful, she clung to Beulah, and asked, in broken accents, what would become of her when the aged sleeper was no more.

"Our good God remains to you, Clara. I was a shorn lamb, and He tempered the winds for me. I was very miserable, but He did not forsake me."

Clara looked at the tall form of the physician, and while her eyes rested upon him with a species of fascination she murmured:

"Yes, you have been blessed indeed! You have him. He guards and cares for your happiness, but I, oh I am alone!"

"You told me he had promised to be your friend. Rest assured he will prove himself such," answered Beulah, watching Clara's countenance as she spoke.

"Yes, I know; but—" She paused, and averted her head, for just then he drew near, and said gravely:

"Beulah, take Miss Clara to her own room, and persuade her to rest. I shall remain probably all night; at least until some change takes place."

"Don't send me away," pleaded Clara mournfully.

"Go, Beulah, it is for her own good." She saw that he was unrelenting, and complied without opposition. In the seclusion of her room she indulged in a passionate burst of grief, and thinking it was best thus vented, Beulah paced up and down the floor, listening now to the convulsive sobs, and now to the rain which pelted the window-panes. She was two years younger than her companion, yet felt that she was immeasurably stronger. Often during their acquaintance, a painful suspicion had crossed her mind; as often she had banished it, but now it haunted her with a pertinacity which she could not subdue. While her feet trod the chamber floor, memory trod the chambers of the past, and gathered up every link which could strengthen the chain of evidence. Gradually dim conjecture became sad conviction, and she was conscious of a degree of pain and sorrow for which she could not readily account. If Clara loved Dr. Hartwell, why should it grieve her? Her step grew nervously rapid, and the eyes settled upon the carpet with a fixedness of which she was unconscious. Suppose he was double her age, if Clara loved him notwithstanding, what business was it of hers? Besides, no one would dream of the actual disparity in years, for he was a very handsome man, and certainly did not look more than ten years older. True, Clara was not very intellectual, and he was particularly fond of literary pursuits; but had not she heard him say that it was a singular fact in anthropology, that men selected their opposites for wives? She did not believe her guardian ever thought of Clara save when in her presence. But how did she know anything about his thoughts and fancies, his likes and dislikes! He had never even spoken of his marriage—was it probable that the subject of a second love would have escaped him? All this passed rapidly in her mind, and when Clara called her to sit down on the couch beside her, she started as from a painful dream. While her friend talked sadly of the future, Beulah analyzed her features, and came to the conclusion that it would be a very easy matter to love her; the face was so sweet and gentle, the manner so graceful, the tone so musical and winning. Absorbed in thought, neither noticed the lapse of time. Midnight passed; two o'clock came; and then at three, a knock startled the watchers. Clara sprang to the door; Dr. Hartwell pointed to the sick room, and said gently:

"He has ceased to suffer. He is at rest."

She looked at him vacantly, an instant, and whispered, under her breath: "He is not dead?"

He did not reply, and with a frightened expression, she glided into the chamber of death, calling piteously on the sleeper to come back and shield her. Beulah would have followed, but the doctor detained her.

"Not yet, child. Not yet."

As if unconscious of the act, he passed his arm around her shoulders, and drew her close to him. She looked up in astonishment, but his eyes were fixed on the kneeling figure in the room opposite, and she saw that, just then, he was thinking of anything else than her presence.

"Are you going home now, sir?"

"Yes, but you must stay with that poor girl yonder. Can't you prevail on her to come and spend a few days with you?"

"I rather think not," answered Beulah, resolved not to try.

"You look pale, my child. Watching is not good for you. It is a long time since you have seen death. Strange that people will not see it as it is. Passing strange."

"What do you mean?" said she, striving to interpret the smile that wreathed his lips.

"You will not believe if I tell you. '*Life is but the germ of Death, and Death the development of a higher Life.*' "

"Higher in the sense of heavenly immortality?"

"You may call it heavenly if you choose. Stay here till the funeral is over, and I will send for you. Are you worn out, child?" He had withdrawn his arm, and now looked anxiously at her colorless face.

"No, sir."

"Then why are you so very pale?"

"Did you ever see me, sir, when I was anything else?"

"I have seen you look less ghostly. Good-by." He left the house without even shaking hands.

The day which succeeded was very gloomy, and after the funeral rites had been performed, and the second day looked in, Beulah's heart rejoiced at the prospect of returning home. Clara shrank from the thought of being left alone, the little cottage was so desolate. She would give it up now, of course, and find a cheap boarding-house; but the furniture must be rubbed, and sent down to an auction room, and she dreaded the separation from all the objects which linked her with the past.

"Clara, I have been commissioned to invite you to spend several days with me, until you can select a boarding-house. Dr. Hartwell will be glad to have you come."

"Did he say so?" asked the mourner, shading her face with her hand.

"He told me I must bring you home with me," answered Beulah.

"Oh, how good, how noble he is! Beulah, you are lucky, lucky indeed." She dropped her head on her arms.

"Clara, I believe there is less difference in our positions than you seem to imagine. We are both orphans, and in about a year I too shall be a teacher. Dr. Hartwell is my guardian and protector, but he will be a kind friend to you also."

"Beulah, you are mad to dream of leaving him, and turning teacher! I am older than you, and have traveled over the very track that you are so eager to set out upon. Oh, take my advice; stay where you are! Would you leave summer sunshine for the icebergs of Arctic night? Silly girl, appreciate your good fortune."

"Can it be possible, Clara, that you are fainting so soon? Where are all your firm resolves? If it is your duty, what matter the difficulties?" She looked down, pityingly, on her companion, as in olden time one of the atheletæ might have done upon a drooping comrade.

"Necessity knows no conditions, Beulah. I have no alternative but to labor in that horrible treadmill round, day after day. You are more fortunate; can have a home of elegance, luxury and—"

"And dependence! Would you be willing to change places with me, and indolently wait for others to maintain you?" interrupted Beulah, looking keenly at the wan, yet lovely face before her.

"Ah, gladly, if I had been selected as you were. Once, I too felt hopeful and joyous; but now life is dreary, almost a burden. Be warned, Beulah, don't suffer your haughty spirit to make you reject the offered home that may be yours."

There was a strong approach to contempt in the expression with which Beulah regarded her, as the last words were uttered, and she answered coldly:

"You are less a woman that I thought you, if you would be willing to live on the bounty of others when a little activity would enable you to support yourself."

"Ah, Beulah! it is not only the bread you eat, or the clothes that you wear; it is sympathy and kindness, love and watchfulness. It is this that a woman wants. Oh, was her heart made, think you, to be filled with grammars and geographies, and copy books? Can the feeling that you are independent and doing your duty, satisfy the longing for other idols? Oh! Duty is an icy shadow. It will freeze you. It cannot fill the heart's sanctuary. Woman was intended as a pet plant, to be guarded and cherished; isolated and uncared for, she droops, languishes and dies." Ah! the dew-sparkle had exhaled, and the morning glory had vanished; the noontide heat of the conflict was creeping on, and she was sinking down, impotent to continue the struggle.

"Clara Sanders, I don't believe one word of all this languishing nonsense. As to my being nothing more nor less than a sickly geranium, I know better. If you have concluded that you belong to that dependent family of plants, I pity you sincerely and beg that you will not put me in any such category. Duty may be a cold shadow to you, but it is a vast volcanic agency, constantly impelling me to action. What was my will given to me for, if to remain passive and suffer others to minister to its needs? Don't talk to me about woman's clinging, dependent nature. You are opening your lips to repeat that senseless simile of oaks and vines; I don't want to hear it; there are no creeping tendencies about me. You can wind, and lean, and hang on somebody else if you like; but I feel more like one of those old pine-trees yonder. I can stand up. Very slim, if you will, but straight and high. Stand by myself: battle with wind and rain, and tempest roar; be swayed and bent, perhaps, in the storm, but stand unaided, nevertheless. I feel humbled when I hear a woman bemoaning the weakness of her sex, instead of showing that she has a soul and mind of her own, inferior to none."

"All that sounds very heroic in the pages of a novel, but the reality is quite another matter. A tame, joyless, hopeless time you will have if you scorn good fortune, as you threaten, and go into the world to support yourself," answered Clara, impatiently.

"I would rather struggle with her for a crust than hang on her garments asking a palace. I don't know what has come over you. You are strangely changed," cried Beulah, pressing her hands on her friend's shoulders.

"The same change will come over you when you endure what I have. With all your boasted strength, you are but a woman; have a woman's heart, and one day will be unable to hush its hungry cries."

"Then I will crush it; so help me Heaven!" answered Beulah.

"No! sorrow will do that time enough; no suicidal effort will be necessary." For the first time Beulah marked an expression of bitterness in the usually gentle, quiet countenance. She was pained more than she chose to evince, and seeing Dr. Hartwell's carriage at the door, prepared to return home.

"Tell him that I am very grateful for his kind offer; that his friendly remembrance is dear to a bereaved orphan. Ah, Beulah! I have know him from my childhood, and he has always been a friend as well as a physician. During my mother's long illness, he watched her carefully and constantly, and when we tendered him the usual recompense for his services, he refused all remuneration, declaring he had only been a friend. He knew we were poor, and could ill afford any expense. Oh, do you wonder that I—. Are you going immediately? Come often when I get to a boarding-house. Do, Beulah! I am so desolate; so desolate." She bowed her head on Beulah's shoulder, and wept unrestrainedly.

"Yes, I will come as often as I can; and, Clara, do try to cheer up. I can't bear to see you sink down in this way." She kissed the tearful face, and hurried away.

It was Saturday, and retiring to her own room, she answered Eugene's brief letter. Long before, she had seen with painful anxiety, that he wrote more and more rarely, and while his communications clearly conveyed the impression that he fancied they were essential to her happiness, the protective tenderness of early years gave place to a certain commanding, yet condescending tone. Intuitively perceiving, yet unable to analyze this gradual revolution of feeling, Beulah was sometimes tempted to cut short the correspondence. But her long and ardent attachment drowned the whispers of wounded pride, and hallowed memories of his boyish love ever prevented an expression of the pain and wonder with which she beheld the alteration in his character. Unwilling to accuse him of the weakness, which prompted much of his arrogance and egotism, her heart framed various excuses for his seeming coldness. At first she had written often, and without reference to ordinary epistolary debts, but now she regularly waited (and that for some time) for the arrival of his letters; not from a diminution of affection, so much as from true womanly delicacy, lest she should obtrude herself too frequently upon his notice. More than once she had been troubled by a dawning consciousness of her own superiority, but accustomed for years to look up to him as a sort of infallible guide, she would not admit the suggestion, and tried to keep alive the admiring respect, with which she had been wont to defer to his judgment. He seemed to consider his dogmatic dictation both acceptable and necessary, and it was this assumed mastery, unaccompanied with manifestations of former tenderness, which irritated and aroused her pride. With the brush of youthful imagination she had painted him as the future statesman—gifted, popular, and revered; and while visions of his fame and glory flitted before her the promise of sharing all with her was by no means the least fascinating feature in her fancy picture. Of late, however, he had ceased to speak of the choice of a profession, and mentioned vaguely Mr. Graham's wish that he should acquaint himself thoroughly with French, German, and Spanish, in order to facilitate the correspondence of the firm with foreign houses. She felt that once embarked on the sea of mercantile life, he would have little leisure or inclination to pursue the paths which she hoped to travel by his side, and, on this occasion, her letter was longer and more earnest than usual, urging his adherence to the original choice of the law, and using every forcible argument she could adduce. Finally, the reply was sealed and directed, and she went down to the study to place it in the marble receiver which stood on her guardian's desk. Hal, who accompanied the doctor in his round of visits, always took their letters to the post-office, and punctually deposited all directed to them in the vase. To her surprise she found no fire in the grate. The blinds were drawn closely, and in placing her letter on the desk, she noticed several addressed to the doctor, and evidently unopened. They must have arrived the day before, and while she wondered at the aspect of the room, Harriet entered.

"Miss Beulah, do you know how long the master expects to be gone? I thought, maybe, you could tell when you came home, for Mrs. Watson does not seem to know any more than I do."

"Gone! What do you mean?"

"Don't you know he has gone up the river to the plantation? Why, I packed his valise at daylight yesterday, and he left in the early morning boat. He has not been to the plantation since just before you came here. Hal says he heard him tell Dr. Asbury to take charge of his patients, that his overseer had to be looked after. He told me he was going to the plantation, and I would have asked him when he was coming back, but he was in one of his unsatisfactory ways; looked just like his mouth had been dipped in hot sealing-wax, so I held my tongue."

Beulah bit her lips with annoyance, but sat down before the melodeon, and said as unconcernedly as possible:

"I did not know he had left the city, and of course have no idea when he will be back. Harriet, please make me a fire here, or call Hal to do it."

"There is a good fire in the dining-room; better go in there and sit with Mrs. Watson. She is busy seeding raisins for mince-meat and fruit-cake."

"No, I would rather stay here."

"Then I will kindle you a fire right away."

Harriet moved about the room with cheerful alacrity. She had always seemed to consider herself Beulah's special guardian and friend, and gave continual proof of the strength of her affection. Evidently she desired to talk about her master, but Beulah's face gave her no encouragement to proceed. She made several efforts to renew the conversation, but they were not seconded, and she withdrew, muttering to herself:

"She is learning all his ways. He does hate to talk any more than he can help, and she is patterning after him just as fast as she can. They don't seem to know what the Lord gave them tongues for."

Beulah practised perseveringly for some time, and then drawing a chair near the fire, sat down and leaned her head on her hand. She missed her guardian—wanted to see him—felt surprised at his sudden departure, and mortified that he had not thought her of sufficient consequence to bid adieu to, and be apprised of his intended trip. He treated her precisely as he did when she first entered the house; seemed to consider her a mere child, whereas she knew she was no longer such. He never alluded to her plan of teaching, and when she chanced to mention it, he offered no comment, looked indifferent or abstracted. Though invariably kind, and sometimes humorous, there was an impenetrable reserve respecting himself, his past and future, which was never laid aside. When not engaged with his flowers or music, he was deep in some favorite volume, and, outside of these sources of enjoyment, seemed to derive no real pleasure. Occasionally he had visitors, but these were generally strangers, often persons residing at a distance, and Beulah knew nothing of them. Several times he had attended concerts and lectures, but she had never accompanied him; and frequently, when sitting by his side, felt as if a glacier lay between them. After Mrs. Chilton's departure for New York, where she and Pauline were boarding, no ladies ever came to the house, except a few of middle age, who called now and then to see Mrs. Watson, and, utterly isolated from society, Beulah was conscious of entire ignorance of all that passed in polite circles. Twice Claudia had called, but unable to forget the past sufficiently to enter Mrs. Grayson's house, there intercourse had ended with Claudia's visits. Mrs. Watson was a kind-hearted and most excellent woman, who made an admirable housekeeper, but possessed few of the qualifications requisite to render her an agreeable companion. With an ambitious nature, and an eager thirst for knowledge, Beulah had improved her advantages as only those do who have felt the need of them. While she acquired, with unusual ease and rapidity, the branches of learning taught at school, she had availed herself of the extensive and select library, to which she had free access, and history, biography, travels, essays and novels had been perused with singular avidity. Dr. Hartwell, without restricting her reading, suggested the propriety of incorporating more of the poetic element in her course. The hint was timely, and induced an acquaintance with the great bards of England and Germany, although her taste led her to select works of another character. Her secluded life favored habits of study, and at an age when girls are generally just beginning to traverse the fields of literature, she had progressed so far as to explore some of the footpaths which entice contemplative minds from the beaten track. With earlier cultivation and superiority of years, Eugene had essayed to direct her reading; but now, in point of advancement, she felt that she was in the van. Dr. Hartwell had told her, whenever she was puzzled, to come to him for explanation, and his clear analysis taught her how immeasurably superior he was, even to those instructors whose profession it was to elucidate mysteries. Accustomed to seek companionship in books, she did not, upon the present occasion, long reflect on her guardian's sudden departure, but took from the shelves a volume of Poe which contained her mark. The parting rays of the winter sun grew fainter; the dull, somber light of the vanishing day made the room dim, and it was only by means of the red glare from the glowing grate that she deciphered the print. Finally the lamp was brought in, and shed a mellow radiance over the dusky apartment. The volume was finished and dropped upon her lap. The spell of this incomparable sorcerer was upon her imagination; the sluggish, lurid tarn of Usher; the pale, gigantic water lilies, nodding their ghastly, everlasting heads over the dreary Zäire; the shrouding shadow of Helusion; the ashen skies, and sere, crisped leaves in the ghoul-haunted woodland of Weir, hard by the dim lake of Auber—all lay with grim distinctness before her; and from the red bars of the grate, the wild, lustrous, appalling eyes of Ligeia looked out at her, while the unearthly tones of Morella whispered from every corner of the room. She rose and replaced the book on the shelf, striving to shake off the dismal hold which all this phantasmagoria had taken on her fancy. Her eyes chanced to fall upon a bust of Athene which surmounted her guardian's desk, and immediately the mournful refrain of the Raven, solemn and dirge-like, floated through the air, enhancing the spectral element which enveloped her. She retreated to the parlor, and running her fingers over the keys of the piano, endeavored by playing some of her favorite airs, to divest her mind of the dreary, unearthly images which haunted it. The attempt was futile, and there in the dark, cold parlor, she leaned her head against the piano, and gave herself up to the guidance of one who, like the "Ancient Mariner," holds his listener fascinated and breathless. Once her guardian had warned her not to study Poe too closely, but the book was often in his own hand, and yielding to the matchless ease and rapidity of his diction, she found herself wandering in a wilderness of baffling suggestions. Under the drapery of "William Wilson," of "Morella" and "Ligeia," she caught tantalizing glimpses of recondite psychological truths and processes, which dimly hovered over her own consciousness, but ever eluded the grasp of analysis. While his unique imagery filled her mind with wondering delight, she shrank appalled from the mutilated fragments which he presented to her as truths, on the point of his glittering scalpel of logic. With the eagerness of a child clutching at its own shadows in a glassy lake, and thereby destroying it, she had read that anomalous prose poem "Eureka." The quaint humor of that "bottled letter" first arrested her attention, and, once launched on the sea of Cosmogonies, she was amazed at the seemingly infallible reasoning, which, at the conclusion, coolly informed her that she was her own God. Mystified, shocked, and yet admiring, she had gone to Dr. Hartwell for a solution of the difficulty. False she felt the whole icy tissue to be, yet could not detect the adroitly disguised sophisms. Instead of assisting her, as usual, he took the book from her, smiled and put it away, saying, indifferently:

"You must not play with such sharp tools just yet. Go and practise your music lesson."

She was too deeply interested to be put off so quietly, and constantly pondered this singular production, which confirmed in some degree a fancy of her own concerning the preexistence of the soul. Only on the hypothesis of an anterior life could she explain some of the mental phenomena which puzzled her. Heedless of her guardian's warning she had striven to comprehend the philosophy of this methodical madman, and now felt bewildered and restless. This study of Poe was the portal through which she entered the vast Pantheon of Speculation.

CHAPTER XIV.

A week later, at the close of a dull winter day, Beulah sat as usual in the study. The large parlors and dining-room had a desolate look at all times, and of the whole house, only the study seemed genial. Busily occupied during the day, it was not until evening that she realized her guardian's absence. No tidings of him had been received, and she began to wonder at his prolonged stay. She felt very lonely without him, and though generally taciturn, she missed him from the hearth, missed the tall form, and the sad, stern face. Another Saturday had come, and all day she had been with Clara in her new home, trying to cheer the mourner, and dash away the gloom that seemed settling down upon her spirits. At dusk, she returned home, spent an hour at the piano, and now walked up and down the study, rapt in thought. The room had a cozy, comfortable aspect; the fire burned brightly; the lamplight silvered the paintings and statues; and on the rug before the grate lay a huge black dog of the St. Bernard order, his shaggy head thrust between his paws. The large, intelligent eyes followed Beulah as she paced to and fro, and seemed mutely to question her restlessness. His earnest scrutiny attracted her notice, and she held out her hand, saying musingly:

"Poor Charon; you too miss your master. Charon, King of Shadows, when will he come?"

The great black eyes gazed intently into hers, and seemed to echo, "when will he come?" He lifted his grim head, snuffed the air, listened, and sullenly dropped his face on his paws again. Beulah threw herself on the rug, and laid her head on his thick neck; he gave a quick, short bark of satisfaction, and very soon both girl and dog were fast asleep. A quarter of an hour glided by, and then Beulah was suddenly roused by a violent motion of her pillow. Charon sprang up, and leaped frantically across the room. The comb which confined her hair had fallen out, and gathering up the jetty folds which swept over her shoulders, she looked around. Dr. Hartwell was closing the door.

"Down, Charon; you ebon scamp! Down, you keeper of Styx!" He forced down the paws from his shoulders, and patted the shaggy head, while his eyes rested affectionately on the delighted countenance of his sable favorite. As he threw down his gloves, his eyes fell on Beulah, who had hastily risen from the rug, and he held out his hand, saying:

"Ah! Charon waked you rudely. How are you?"

"Very well, thank you, sir. I am so glad you have come home, so glad." She took his cold hand between both hers, rubbed it vigorously, and looked up joyfully in his face. She thought he was paler and more haggard than she had ever seen him; his hair clustered in disorder about his forehead; his whole aspect was weary and wretched. He suffered her to keep his hand in her warm tight clasp, and asked kindly:

"Are you well, Beulah? Your face is flushed, and you feel feverish."

"Perfectly well. But you are as cold as an Esquimaux hunter. Come to the fire." She drew his arm-chair, with its candle-stand and book-board, close to the hearth, and put his warm velvet slippers before him. She forgot her wounded pride; forgot that he had left without even bidding her good-by; and only remembered that he had come home again, that he was sitting there in the study, and she would be lonely no more. Silently leaning back in the chair, he closed his eyes with a sigh of relief. She felt as if she would like very much to smooth off the curling hair that lay thick and damp on his white, gleaming brow, but dared not. She stood watching him for a moment, and said considerately:

"Will you have your tea now? Charon and I had our supper long ago."

"No, child; I only want to rest."

Beulah fancied he spoke impatiently. Had she been too officious in welcoming him to his own home? She bit her lip with proud vexation, and taking her geometry, left him. As she reached the door, the doctor called to her:

"Beulah, you need not go away. This is a better fire than the one in your own room." But she was wounded, and did not choose to stay.

"I can study better in my own room. Good night, sir."

"Why, child, this is Saturday night. No lessons until Monday."

She was not particularly mollified by the reiteration of the word "child," and answered, coldly:

"There are hard lessons for every day we live."

"Well, be good enough to hand me the letters that have arrived during my absence."

She emptied the letter receiver, and placed several communications in his hand. He pointed to a chair near the fire, and said quietly:

"Sit down, my child; sit down."

Too proud to discover how much she was piqued by his coldness, she took the seat and commenced studying. But lines and angles swam confusedly before her, and, shutting the book, she sat looking into the fire. While her eyes roamed into the deep, glowing crevices of the coals, a letter was hurled into the fiery mass, and in an instant blazed and shriveled to ashes. She looked up in surprise, and started at the expression of her guardian's face. Its Antonoüs-like beauty had vanished; the pale lips writhed, displaying the faultless teeth; the thin nostrils were expanded, and the eyes burned with fierce anger. The avalanche was upheaved by hidden volcanic fires, and he exclaimed, with scornful emphasis:

"Idiot! blind lunatic! In his dotage!"

There was something so marvelous in this excited, angry manifestation, that Beulah, who had never before seen him other than phlegmatic, looked at him with curious wonder. His clenched hand rested on the arm of the chair, and he continued, sarcastically:

"Oh, a precious pair of idiots! They will have a glorious life. Such harmony, such congeniality! Such incomparable sweetness on her part, such equable spirits on his! Not the surpassing repose of a windless tropic night can approach to the divine serenity of their future. Ha! by the Furies! he will have an enviable companion; a matchless Griselda!" Laughing scornfully, he started up and strode across the floor. As Beulah caught the withering expression which sat on every feature, she shuddered involuntarily. Could she bear to incur his contempt? He approached her, and she felt as though her very soul shrank from him; his glowing eyes seemed to burn her face, as he paused and said ironically:

"Can't you participate in my joy? I have a new brother-in-law. Congratulate me on my sister's marriage. Such desperate good news can come but rarely in a life-time."

"Whom has she married, sir?" asked Beulah, shrinking from the iron grasp on her shoulder.

"Percy Lockhart, of course. He will rue his madness. I warned him. Now let him seek apples in the orchards of Sodom! Let him lay his parched lips to the treacherous waves of the Dead Sea! Oh, I pity the fool! I tried to save him, but he would seal his own doom. Let him pay the usurious school-fee of experience."

"Perhaps your sister's love for him will—"

"Oh, you young, ignorant lamb! You poor, little unfledged birdling! I suppose you fancy she is really attached to him. Do you, indeed? About as much as that pillar of salt in the plain of Sodom was attached to the memory of Lot. About as much as this peerless Niobe of mine is attached to me." He struck the marble statue as he spoke.

"Then, how could she marry him?" asked Beulah naïvely.

"Ha! ha! I will present you to the Smithsonian Institute as the last embodiment of effete theories. Who exhumed you, patron saint of archaism, from the charnel-house of centuries?" He looked down at her with an expression of intolerable bitterness and scorn. Her habitually pale face flushed to crimson as she answered with sparkling eyes:

"Not the hands of Diogenes, encumbered with his tub!"

He smiled grimly.

"Know the world as I do, child, and tubs and palaces will be alike to you. Feel the pulse of humanity, and you will—"

"Heaven preserve me from looking on life through your spectacles!" cried she impetuously, stung by the contemptuous smile which curled his lips.

"Amen." Taking his hands from her shoulders, he threw himself back into his chair. There was silence for some minutes, and Beulah said:

"I thought Mr. Lockhart was in Syria?"

"Oh, no; he wants a companion in his jaunt to the Holy Land. How devoutly May will kneel on Olivet and Moriah! What pious tears will stain her lovely cheek as she stands in the hall of Pilate, and calls to mind all the thirty years' history! Oh! Percy is cruel to subject her tender soul to such torturing associations. Beulah, go and play something; no matter what. Anything to hush my cursing mood. Go, child." He turned away his face to hide its bitterness, and, seating herself at the melodeon, Beulah played a German air, of which he was very fond. At the conclusion, he merely said:

"Sing."

A plaintive prelude followed the command, and she sang. No description could do justice to the magnificent voice, as it swelled deep and full in its organ-like tones; now thrillingly low in its wailing melody, and now ringing clear and sweet as silver bells. There were soft, rippling notes, that seemed to echo from the deeps of her soul, and voice its immensity. It was wonderful what compass there was, what rare sweetness and purity too. It was a natural gift, like that conferred on birds. Art could not produce it, but practise and scientific culture had improved and perfected it. For three years the best teachers had instructed her, and she felt that now she was mistress of a spell which, once invoked, might easily exorcise the evil spirit which had taken possession of her guardian. She sang several of his favorite songs, then closed the melodeon, and went back to the fire. Dr. Hartwell's face lay against the purple velvet lining of the chair, and the dark surface gave out the contour with bold distinctness. His eyes were closed, and as Beulah watched him, she thought, "How inflexible he looks, how like a marble image. The mouth seems as if the sculptor's chisel had just carved it; so stern, so stony. Ah! he is not scornful now; he looks only sad, uncomplaining, but very miserable. What has steeled his heart, and made him so unrelenting, so haughty? What can have isolated him so completely? Nature lavished on him every gift which could render him the charm of social circles, yet he lives in the seclusion of his own heart, independent of sympathy, contemptuous of the world he was sent to improve and bless." These reflections were interrupted by his opening his eyes, and saying, in his ordinary calm tone:

"Thank you, Beulah. Did you finish that opera I spoke of some time since?"

"Yes, sir."

"You found it difficult?"

"Not so difficult as your description led me to imagine."

"Were you lonely while I was away?"

"Yes, sir."

"Why did not Clara come and stay with you?"

"She was engaged in changing her home; has removed to Mrs. Hoyt's boarding-house."

"When did you see her last? How does she bear the blow?"

"I was with her to-day. She is desponding, and seems to grow more so daily."

She wondered very much whether he suspected the preference which she felt sure Clara entertained for him; and as the subject recurred to her, she looked troubled.

"What is the matter?" he asked, accustomed to reading her expressive face.

"Nothing that can be remedied, sir."

"How do you know that? Suppose you let me be the judge."

"You could not judge of it, sir; and besides, it is no concern of mine."

A frigid smile fled over his face, and for some time he appeared lost in thought. His companion was thinking too; wondering how Clara could cope with such a nature as his; wondering why people always selected persons totally unsuited to them; and fancying that if Clara only knew her guardian's character as well as she did, the gentle girl would shrink in dread from his unbending will, his habitual, moody taciturnity. He was generous and unselfish, but also as unyielding as the Rock of Gibraltar. There was nothing pleasurable in this train of thought, and taking up a book she soon ceased to think of the motionless figure opposite. No sooner were her eyes once fastened on her book, than his rested searchingly on her face. At first she read without much manifestation of interest, regularly and slowly passing her hand over the black head which Charon had laid on her lap. After a while the lips parted eagerly, the leaves were turned quickly, and the touches on Charon's head ceased. Her long, black lashes could not veil the expression of enthusiastic pleasure. Another page fluttered over, a flush stole across her brow; and as she closed the volume, her whole face was irradiated.

"What are you reading?" asked Dr. Hartwell, when she seemed to sink into a reverie.

"Analects from Richter."

"De Quincey's?"

"Yes, sir."

"Once that marvelous 'Dream upon the Universe' fascinated me as completely as it now does you."

Memories of earlier days clustered about him, parting the somber clouds with their rosy fingers. His features began to soften.

"Sir, can you read it now without feeling your soul kindle?"

"Yes, child: it has lost its interest for me. I read it as indifferently as I do one of my medical books. So will you one day."

"Never! It shall be a guide-book to my soul, telling of the pathway arched with galaxies and paved with suns, through which that soul shall pass in triumph to its final rest!"

"And who shall remain in that 'illimitable dungeon of pure, pure darkness, which imprisons creation? That dead sea of nothing, in whose unfathomable zone of blackness the jewel of the glittering universe is set, and buried forever?' Child, is not that, too, a dwelling-place?" He passed his fingers through his hair, sweeping it all back from his ample forehead. Beulah opened the book, and read aloud:

"Immediately my eyes were opened, and I saw, as it were, an interminable sea of light; all spaces between all heavens were filled with happiest light, for the deserts and wastes of the creation were now filled with the sea of light, and in this sea the suns floated like ash-gray blossoms, and the planets like black grains of seed. Then my heart comprehended that immortality dwelled in the spaces between the worlds, and *Death only among the worlds;* and the murky planets I perceived were but cradles for the infant spirits of the universe of light! In the Zaarahs of the creation I saw, I heard, I felt—the glittering, the echoing, the breathing of life and creative power!"

She closed the volume, and while her lips trembled with deep feeling, added earnestly:

"Oh, sir, it makes me long, like Jean Paul, 'for some narrow cell or quiet oratory in this metropolitan cathedral of the universe.' It is an infinite conception and painting of infinity, which my soul endeavors to grasp, but wearies in thinking of!"

Dr. Hartwell smiled, and pointing to a row of books, said with some eagerness:

"I will test your love of Jean Paul. Give me that large volume in crimson binding on the second shelf. No—further on; that is it."

He turned over the leaves for a few minutes, and with a finger still on the page, put it into her hand, saying:

"Begin here at 'I went through the worlds,' and read down to 'when I awoke.' "

She sat down and read. He put his hand carelessly over his eyes, and watched her curiously through his fingers. It was evident that she soon became intensely interested. He could see the fierce throbbing of a vein in her throat, and the tight clutching of her fingers. Her eyebrows met in the wrinkling forehead, and the lips were compressed severely. Gradually the flush faded from her cheek, an expression of pain and horror swept over her stormy face, and rising hastily, she exclaimed:

"False! false! 'That everlasting storm which no one guides tells me in thunder tones that there is a home of rest in the presence of the infinite father! Oh, chance does not roam, like a destroying angel, through that 'snow-powder of stars!' The love of our God is over all his works as a mantle! Though you should 'take the wings of the morning and dwell in the uttermost parts of the sea,' lo! He is there! The sorrowing children of the universe are not orphans! Neither did Richter believe it; well might he declare that with this sketch he would 'terrify himself' and vanquish the specter of Atheism! Oh, sir! the dear God stretches his arm about each and all of us! 'When the sorrow-laden lays himself, with a galled back, into the earth, to sleep till a fairer morning,' it is not true that 'he awakens in a stormy chaos, in an everlasting midnight!' It is not true! He goes home to his loved dead, and spends a blissful eternity in the kingdom of Jehovah, where death is no more, 'where the wicked cease from troubling, and the weary are at rest!' "

She laid the volume on his knee, and tears which would not be restrained, rolled swiftly over her cheeks.

He looked at her mournfully, and took her hand in his.

"My child, do you believe all this as heartily as you did when a little girl? Is your faith in your religion unshaken?"

He felt her fingers close over his spasmodically, as she hastily replied:

"Of course, of course! What could shake a faith which years should strengthen?"

But the shiver which crept through her frame denied her assertion, and with a keen pang, he saw the footprints of the Destroyer. She must not know, however, that he doubted her words, and with an effort, he said:

"I am glad, Beulah; and if you would continue to believe, don't read my books promiscuously. There are many on those shelves yonder which I would advise you never to open. Be warned in time, my child."

She snatched her hand from his, and answered proudly:

"Sir, think you I could be satisfied with a creed which I could not bear to have investigated? If I abstained from reading your books, dreading lest my faith be shaken, then I could no longer confide in that faith. Christianity has triumphed over the subtleties of infidelity for eighteen hundred years; what have I to fear?"

"Beulah, do you want to be just what I am? Without belief in any creed! hopeless of eternity as of life! Do you want to be like me? If not, keep your hands off of my books! Good night; it is time for you to be asleep."

He motioned her away, and too much pained to reply, she silently withdrew.

CHAPTER XV.

The day had been clear, though cold, and late in the afternoon, Beulah wrapped a shawl about her, and ran out into the front yard for a walk. The rippling tones of the fountain were hushed; the shrubs were bare, and, outside the greenhouse not a flower was to be seen. Even the hardy chrysanthemums were brown and shriveled. Here vegetation slumbered in the grave of winter. The hedges were green, and occasional clumps of cassina bent their branches beneath the weight of coral fruitage. Tall poplars lifted their leafless arms helplessly toward the sky, and threw grotesque shadows on the ground beneath, while the wintry wind chanted a mournful dirge through the somber foliage of the aged, solemn cedars. Noisy flocks of robins fluttered among the trees, eating the ripe, red yupon berries, and now and then, parties of pigeons circled round and round the house, Charon lay on the doorstep, blinking at the setting sun, with his sage face dropped on his paws. Afar off was heard the hum of the city; but here all was quiet and peaceful. Beulah looked over the beds, lately so brilliant and fragrant in their wealth of floral beauty; at the bare gray poplars, whose musical rustling had so often hushed her to sleep in cloudless summer nights, and an expression of serious thoughtfulness settled on her face. Many months before, she had watched the opening spring in this same garden. Had seen young leaves and delicate blossoms bud out from naked stems, had noted their rich luxuriance as the summer heat came on—their mature beauty; and when the first breath of autumn sighed through the land, she saw them flush and decline, and gradually die and rustle down to their graves. Now, where green boughs and perfumed petals had gaily looked up in the sunlight, all was desolate. The piercing northern wind seemed to whisper as it passed, "Life is but the germ of death, and death the development of a higher life." Was the cycle eternal then? Were the beautiful ephemera she had loved so dearly gone down into the night of death, but for a season, to be born again, in some distant springtime, mature, and return, as before, to the charnel-house? Were the three score and ten years of human life analogous? Life, too, had its springtime, its summer of maturity, its autumnal decline, and its wintry night of death. Were the cold sleepers in the neighboring cemetery waiting, like those dead flowers, for the tireless processes of nature, whereby their dust was to be reanimated, remolded, lighted with a soul, and set forward for another journey of three score and ten years of life and labor? Men lived and died; their ashes enriched mother Earth, new creations sprang, phoenix-like, from the sepulcher of the old. Another generation trod life's path in the dim footprints of their predecessors, and that, too, vanished in the appointed process, mingling dust with dust, that Protean matter might hold the even tenor of its way, in accordance with the oracular decrees of Isis. Was it true that, since the original Genesis, "nothing had been gained, and nothing lost?" Was earth, indeed, a monstrous Kronos? If so, was not she as old as creation? To how many other souls had her body given shelter? How was her identity to be maintained? True, she had read that identity was housed in "consciousness," not bones and muscles? But could there be consciousness without bones and muscles? She drew her shawl closely around her, and looked up at the cloudless sea of azure. The sun had sunk below the horizon; the birds had all gone to rest; Charon had sought the study rug; even the distant hum of the city was no longer heard. "The silver sparks of stars were rising on the altar of the east, and falling down in the red sea of the west." Beulah was chilled; there were cold thoughts in her mind—icy specters in her heart; and she quickened her pace up and down the avenue, dusky beneath the ancient gloomy cedars. One idea haunted her: aside from revelation, what proof had she that unlike those moldering flowers, her spirit should never die? No trace was to be found of the myriads of souls who had preceded her. Where were the countless hosts? Were life and death balanced? was her own soul chiliads old, forgetting its former existences, save as dim, undefinable reminiscences, flashed fitfully upon it? If so, was it a progression? How did she know that her soul had not entered her body fresh from the release of the hangman, instead of coming down on angel wings from its starry home, as she had loved to think? A passage which she had read many weeks before flashed upon her mind: "Upon the dead mother, in peace and utter gloom, are reposing the dead children. After a time, uprises the everlasting sun; and the mother starts up at the summons of the heavenly dawn, with a resurrection of her ancient bloom. And her children?—Yes, but they must wait awhile!" This resurrection was springtime, beckoning dormant beauty from the icy arms of winter; how long must the children wait for the uprising of the morning star of eternity? From childhood these unvoiced queries had perplexed her mind, and, strengthening with her growth, now cried out peremptorily for answers. With shuddering dread, she strove to stifle the spirit which, once thoroughly awakened, threatened to explore every nook and cranny of mystery. She longed to talk freely with her guardian, regarding many of the suggestions which puzzled her, but shrank instinctively from broaching such topics. Now in her need, the sublime words of Job came to her: "Oh, that my words were now written! oh, that they were printed in a book; for I know that my Redeemer liveth, and that he shall stand at the latter day upon the earth: and though worms destroy this body, yet in my flesh shall I see God." Handel's "Messiah" had invested this passage with resistless grandeur, and leaving the cold, dreary garden, she sat down before the melodeon and sang a portion of the Oratorio. The sublime strains seemed to bear her worshipping soul up to the presence chamber of Deity, and exultingly she repeated the concluding words:

"For now is Christ risen from the dead;
The first-fruits of them that sleep."

The triumph of faith shone in her kindled eyes, though glittering drops fell on the ivory keys, and the whole countenance bespoke a heart resting in the love of the Father. While her fingers still rolled waves of melody through the room, Dr. Hartwell entered, with a parcel in one hand and a magnificent cluster of greenhouse flowers in the other. He laid the latter before Beulah, and said:

"I want you to go with me to-night to hear Sontag. The concert commences at eight o'clock, and you have no time to spare. Here are some flowers for your hair; arrange it as you have it now; and here, also, a pair of white gloves. When you are ready, come down and make my tea."

"Thank you sir, for remembering me so kindly, and supplying all my wants so—"

"Beulah, there are tears on your lashes. What is the matter?" interrupted the doctor, pointing to the drops which had fallen on the rosewood frame of the melodeon.

"Is it not enough to bring tears to my eyes when I think of all your kindness?" She hurried away without suffering him to urge the matter.

The prospect of hearing Sontag gave her exquisite pleasure and she dressed with trembling eagerness, while Harriet leaned on the bureau and wondered what would happen next. Except to attend church and visit Clara and Mrs. Williams, Beulah had never gone out before; and the very seclusion in which she lived, rendered this occasion one of interest and importance. As she took her cloak and ran down-stairs, the young heart throbbed violently. Would her fastidious guardian be satisfied with her appearance? She felt the blood gush over her face as she entered the room; but he did not look at her, continued to read the newspaper he held, and said, from behind the extended sheet:

"I will join you directly."

She poured out the tea with an unsteady hand. Dr. Hartwell took his silently; and as both rose from the table, handed her a paper, saying:

"The carriage is not quite ready, yet. There is a program."

As she glanced over it, he scanned her closely, and an expression of satisfaction settled on his features. She wore a dark blue silk (one he had given her some weeks before), which exquisitely fitted her slender, graceful figure, and was relieved by a lace collar, fastened with a handsome cameo pin, also his gift. The glossy black hair was brushed straight back from the face, in accordance with the prevailing style, and wound into a knot at the back of the head. On either side of this knot she wore a superb white camellia, which contrasted well with the raven hair. Her face was pale, but the expression was one of eager expectation. As the carriage rattled up to the door, he put his hand on her shoulder and said:

"You look very well to-night, my child. Those white japonicas become you." She breathed freely once more.

At the door of the concert hall he gave her his arm, and while the pressure of the crowd detained them a moment at the entrance, she clung to him with a feeling of dependence utterly new to her. The din of voices, the dazzling glare of the gaslights bewildered her, and she walked on mechanically, till the doctor entered his seat, and placed her beside him. The brilliant chandeliers shone down on elegant dresses, glittering diamonds, and beautiful women, and looking forward, Beulah was reminded of the glowing descriptions in the "Arabian Nights." She observed that many curious eyes were bent upon her, and ere she had been seated five minutes, more than one lorgnette was leveled at her. Everybody knew Dr. Hartwell, and she saw him constantly returning the bows of recognition which assailed him from the ladies in their vicinity. Presently, he leaned his head on his hand, and she could not forbear smiling at the ineffectual attempts made to arrest his attention. The hall was crowded, and as the seats filled to their utmost capacity, she was pressed against her guardian. He looked down at her and whispered:

"Very democratic. Eh, Beulah?"

She smiled, and was about to reply, when her attention was attracted by a party which just then took their places in front of her. It consisted of an elderly gentleman and two ladies, one of whom Beulah instantly recognized as Cornelia Graham. She was now a noble-looking, rather than beautiful woman; and the incipient pride, so apparent in girlhood, had matured into almost repulsive *hauteur*. She was very richly dressed, and her brilliant black eyes wandered indifferently over the room, as though such assemblages had lost their novelty and interest for her. Chancing to look back, she perceived Dr. Hartwell, bowed, and said with a smile:

"Pray, do not think me obstinate; I had no wish to come, but father insisted."

"I am glad you feel well enough to be here," was his careless reply.

Cornelia's eyes fell upon the quiet figure at his side, and as Beulah met her steady gaze, she felt something of her old dislike warming in her eyes. They had never met since the morning of Cornelia's contemptuous treatment, at Madam St. Cymon's; and now, to Beulah's utter astonishment, she deliberately turned round, put out her white-gloved hand, over the back of the seat, and said energetically:

"How are you, Beulah? You have altered so materially that I scarcely knew you."

Beulah's nature was generous; she was glad to forget old injuries, and as their hands met in a friendly clasp, she answered.

"You have changed but little."

"And that for the worse, as people have a pleasant way of telling me. Beulah, I want to know honestly, if my rudeness caused you to leave madam's school?"

"That was not my only reason," replied Beulah, very candidly.

At this moment a burst of applause greeted the appearance of the cantatrice, and all conversation was suspended. Beulah listened to the warbling of the queen of song with a thrill of delight. Passionately fond of music, she appreciated the brilliant execution, and entrancing melody, as probably very few in that crowded house could have done. With some of the pieces selected she was familiar, and others she had long desired to hear. She was unconscious of the steady look with which her guardian watched her, as with parted lips, she leaned eagerly forward to catch every note. When Sontag left the stage, and the hum of conversation was heard once more, Beulah looked up, with a long sigh of delight, and murmured:

"Oh, sir! isn't she a glorious woman?"

"Miss Graham is speaking to you," said he, coolly.

She raised her head, and saw the young lady's eyes riveted on her countenance.

"Beulah, when did you hear from Eugene?"

"About three weeks since, I believe."

"We leave, for Europe, day-after-to-morrow; shall, perhaps, go directly to Heidelberg. Have you any commissions, any messages?" Under the mask of seeming indifference, she watched Beulah intently, as, shrinking from the cold, searching eyes, the latter replied:

"Thank you, I have neither to trouble you with."

Again the prima-donna appeared on the stage, and again Beulah forgot everything but the witching strains. In the midst of one of the songs, she felt her guardian start violently; and the hand which rested on his knee, was clinched spasmodically. She looked at him; the wonted pale face was flushed to the edge of his hair; the blue veins stood out hard and corded on his brow; and the eyes, like burning stars, were fixed on some object not very remote, while he gnawed his lip, as if unconscious of what he did. Following the direction of his gaze, she saw that it was fastened on a gentleman, who sat at some little distance from them. The position he occupied rendered his countenance visible, and a glance sufficed to show her that the features were handsome, the expression sinister, malignant and cunning. His entire appearance was foreign, and conveyed the idea of reckless dissipation. Evidently, he came there, not for the music, but to scan the crowd, and his fierce eyes roamed over the audience with a daring impudence, which disgusted her. Suddenly they rested on her own face, wandered to Dr. Hartwell's and lingering there a full moment, with a look of defiant hatred, returned to her, causing her to shudder at the intensity and freedom of his gaze. She drew herself up proudly, and, with an air of haughty contempt, fixed her attention on the stage. But the spell of enchantment was broken; she could hear the deep, irregular breathing of her guardian, and knew, from the way in which he stared down on the floor, that he could with difficulty remain quietly in his place. She was glad when the concert ended, and the mass of heads began to move toward the door. With a species of curiosity that she could not repress, she glanced at the stranger; their eyes met, as before, and his smile of triumphant scorn made her cling closer to her guardian's arm, and take care not to look in that direction again. She felt inexpressibly relieved when, hurried on by the crowd in the rear, they emerged from the heated room into a long dim passage leading to the street. They were surrounded on all sides by chattering groups, and while the light was too faint to distinguish faces, these words fell on her ear with painful distinctness: "I suppose that was Dr. Hartwell's protégée he had with him. He is a great curiosity. Think of a man of his age and appearance settling down as if he were sixty years old, and adopting a beggarly orphan. She is not at all pretty. What can have possessed him?"

"No, not pretty, exactly; but there is something odd in her appearance. Her brow is magnificent, and I should judge she was intellectual. She is as colorless as a ghost. No accounting for Hartwell; ten to one he will marry her. I have heard it surmised that he was educating her for a wife—" Here the party who were in advance vanished, and as he approached the carriage, Dr. Hartwell said, coolly:

"Another specimen of democracy."

Beulah felt as if a lava tide surged madly in her veins, and as the carriage rolled homeward, she covered her face with her hands. Wounded pride, indignation and contempt, struggled violently in her heart. For some moments there was silence; then her guardian drew her hands from her face, held them firmly in his, and leaning forward, said gravely:

"Beulah, malice and envy love lofty marks. Learn, as I have done, to look down with scorn from the summit of indifference upon the feeble darts aimed from the pits beneath you. My child, don't suffer the senseless gossip of the shallow crowd to wound you."

She endeavored to withdraw her hands, but his unyielding grasp prevented her.

"Beulah, you must conquer your morbid sensitiveness, if you would have your life other than a dreary burden."

"Oh, sir! you are not invulnerable to these wounds; how, then, can I, an orphan girl, receive them with indifference?" She spoke passionately, and drooped her burning face till it touched his arm.

"Ah! you observed my agitation to-night. But for a vow made to my dying mother, that villain's blood had long since removed all grounds of emotion. Six years ago, he fled from me, and his unexpected reappearance to-night excited me more than I had fancied it was possible for anything to do." His voice was as low, calm and musical as though he were reading aloud to her some poetic tale of injuries; and in the same even quiet tone, he added:

"It is well. All have a Nemesis."

"Not on earth, sir."

"Wait till you have lived as long as I, and you will think with me. Beulah, be careful how you write to Eugene of Cornelia Graham; better not mention her name at all. If she lives to come home again, you will understand me."

"Is not her health good?" asked Beulah, in surprise.

"Far from it. She has a disease of the heart, which may end her existence any moment. I doubt whether she ever returns to America. Mind, I do not wish you to speak of this to any one. Good night. If you are up in time in the morning, I wish you would be so good as to cut some of the choicest flowers in the greenhouse, and arrange a handsome bouquet, before breakfast. I want to take it to one of my patients, an old friend of my mother."

They were at home, and only pausing at the door of Mrs. Watson's room to tell the good woman the "music was charming," Beulah hastened to her own apartment. Throwing herself into a chair, she recalled the incidents of the evening, and her cheeks burned painfully, as her position in the eyes of the world was forced upon her recollection. Tears of mortification rolled over her hot face, and her heart throbbed almost to suffocation. She sank upon her knees, and tried to pray, but sobs choked her utterance; and leaning her head against the bed, she wept bitterly.

Ah! is there not pain, and sorrow, and evil enough, in this fallen world of ours, that meddling gossips must needs poison the few pure springs of enjoyment and peace? Not the hatred of the Theban brothers could more thoroughly accomplish this fiendish design, than the whisper of detraction, the sneer of malice, or the fatal innuendo of envious, low-bred tattlers. Human life is shielded by the bulwark of legal provisions, and most earthly possessions are similarly protected; but there are assassins whom the judicial arm cannot reach, who infest society in countless hordes, and while their work of ruin and misery goes ever on, there is for the unhappy victims no redress. The holy precepts, O, Christ! alone can antidote this universal evil.

Beulah calmed the storm that raged in her heart, and as she took the flowers from her hair, said resolutely:

"Before long I shall occupy a position where there will be nothing to envy, and then, possibly, I may escape the gossiping rack. Eugene may think me a fool, if he likes; but support myself I will, if it costs me my life. What difference should it make to him, so long as I prefer it? One more year of study, and I shall be qualified for any situation; then I can breathe freely. May God shield me from all harm!"

CHAPTER XVI.

That year of study rolled swiftly away; another winter came and passed! another spring hung its verdant drapery over earth, and now ardent summer reigned once more. It was near the noon of a starry July night that Beulah sat in her own room beside her writing-desk. A manuscript lay before her, yet damp with ink, and as she traced the concluding words, and threw down her pen, a triumphant smile flashed over her face. To-morrow the session of the public school would close, with an examination of its pupils; to-morrow she would graduate, and deliver the valedictory to the graduating class. She had just finished copying her address, and placing it carefully in the desk, rose and leaned against the window, that the cool night air might fan her fevered brow. The hot blood beat heavily in her temples, and fled with arrowy swiftness through her veins. Continued mental excitement, like another Shylock, peremptorily exacted its debt, and as she looked out on the solemn beauty of the night, instead of soothing, it seemed to mock her restlessness. Dr. Hartwell had been absent since noon, but now she detected the whir of wheels in the direction of the carriage-house, and knew that he was in the study. She heard him throw open the shutters, and speak to Charon, and gathering up her hair, which hung loosely about her shoulders, she confined it with a comb, and glided noiselessly down the steps. The lamplight gleamed through the open door, and pausing on the threshold, she asked;

"May I come in for a few minutes, or are you too much fatigued to talk?"

"Beulah, I positively forbade your sitting up this late. It is midnight, child; go to bed." He held some papers, and spoke without even glancing toward her.

"Yes, I know; but I want to ask you something before I sleep."

"Well, what is it?" Still he did not look up from his papers.

"Will you attend the exercises to-morrow?"

"Is it a matter of consequence whether I do or not?"

"To me, sir, it certainly is."

"Child, I shall not have leisure."

"Be honest, and say that you have not sufficient interest," cried she, passionately.

He smiled, and answered passively:

"Good night, Beulah. You should have been asleep long ago." Her lips quivered, and she lingered, loth to leave him in so unfriendly a mood. Suddenly he raised his head, looked at her steadily, and said:

"Have you sent in your name as an applicant for a situation?"

"I have."

"Good night." His tone was stern, and she immediately retreated. Unable to sleep, she passed the remaining hours of the short night in pacing the floor, or watching the clockwork of stars point to the coming dawn. Though not quite eighteen, her face was prematurely grave and thoughtful, and its restless, unsatisfied expression plainly discovered a perturbed state of mind and heart. The time had come when she must go out into the world, and depend only upon herself; and though she was anxious to commence the work she had assigned herself, she shrank from the thought of quitting her guardian's home and thus losing the only companionship she really prized. He had not sought to dissuade her; had appeared perfectly indifferent to her plans, and this unconcern had wounded her deeply. To-morrow would decide her election as teacher, and as the committee would be present at her examination (which was to be more than usually minute in view of her application), she looked forward impatiently to this occasion. Morning dawned, and she hailed it gladly; breakfast came, and she took hers alone; the doctor had already gone out for the day. This was not an unusual occurrence, yet this morning she noted it particularly. At ten o'clock the Academy was crowded with visitors, and the commissioners and teachers were formidably arrayed on the platform raised for this purpose. The examination began; Greek and Latin classes were carefully questioned, and called on to parse and scan to a tiresome extent; then came mathematical demonstrations. Every conceivable variety of lines and angles adorned the black-boards; and next in succession were classes in rhetoric and natural history. There was a tediousness in the examinations incident to such occasions, and as repeated inquiries were propounded, Beulah rejoiced at the prospect of release. Finally the commissioners declared themselves quite satisfied with the proficiency attained, and the graduating class read the compositions for the day. At length, at a signal from the superintendent of the department, Beulah ascended the platform, and surrounded by men signalized by scholarship and venerable from age, she began her address. She wore a white mull muslin, and her glossy black hair was arranged with the severe simplicity which characterized her style of dress. Her face was well-nigh as colorless as the paper she held, and her voice faltered with the first few sentences.

The theme was "Female Heroism," and as she sought among the dusky annals of the past for instances in confirmation of her predicate, that female intellect was capable of the most exalted attainments, and that the elements of her character would enable woman to cope successfully with difficulties of every class, her voice grew clear, firm and deep. Quitting the fertile fields of history, she painted the trials which hedge woman's path, and with unerring skill defined her peculiar sphere, her true position. The reasoning was singularly forcible, the imagery glowing and gorgeous, and occasional passages of exquisite pathos drew tears from her fascinated audience; while more than once, a beautiful burst of enthusiasm was received with flattering applause. Instead of flushing, her face grew paler, and the large eyes were full of lambent light, which seemed to flash out from her soul. In conclusion, she bade adieu to the honored halls where her feet had sought the paths of knowledge; paid a just and grateful tribute to the Institution of Public Schools, and to the Commissioners through whose agency she had been enabled to enjoy so many privileges; and turning to her fellow-graduates, touchingly reminded them of the happy past, and warned of the shrouded future. Crumpling the paper in one hand, she extended the other toward her companions and in thrilling accents conjured them in any and every emergency, to prove themselves true women of America—ornaments of the social circle, angel guardians of the sacred hearthstone, ministering spirits where suffering and want demanded succor. Women qualified to assist in a council of statesmen, if dire necessity ever required it; while, in whatever positions they might be placed, their examples should remain imperishable monuments of true female heroism. As the last words passed her lips she glanced swiftly over the sea of heads, and perceived her guardian leaning with folded arms against a pillar, while his luminous eyes were fastened on her face. A flash of joy irradiated her countenance, and bending her head amid the applause of the assembly, she returned to her seat. She felt that her triumph was complete; the whispered, yet audible inquiries regarding her name, the admiring, curious glances directed toward her, were not necessary to assure her of success; and when, immediately after the diplomas were distributed, she rose and received hers with the calm look of one who has toiled long for some meed, and puts forth her hand for what she is conscious of having deserved. The crowd slowly dispersed, and beckoned forward once more, Beulah confronted the august committee whose prerogative it was to elect teachers. A certificate was handed her, and the chairman informed her of her election to a vacant post in the Intermediate Department. The salary was six hundred dollars, to be paid monthly, and her duties would commence with the opening of the next session, after two months' vacation. In addition, he congratulated her warmly on the success of her valedictory effort, and suggested the propriety of cultivating talents which might achieve for her an enviable distinction. She bowed in silence, and turned away to collect her books. Her guardian approached, and said in a low voice:

"Put on your bonnet, and come down to the side gate. It is too warm for you to walk home."

Without waiting for her answer, he descended the steps, and she was soon seated beside him in the buggy. The short ride was silent, and on reaching home, Beulah would have gone immediately to her room, but the doctor called her into the study, and as he rang the bell, said gently:

"You look very much exhausted; rest here, while I order a glass of wine."

It was speedily brought, and having iced it, he held it to her white lips. She drank the contents, and her head sank on the sofa cushions. The fever of excitement was over, a feeling of lassitude stole over her, and she soon lost all consciousness in a heavy sleep. The sun was just setting as she awakened from her slumber, and sitting up, she soon recalled the events of the day. The evening breeze, laden with perfume, stole in refreshingly through the blinds, and as the sunset pageant faded, and darkness crept on, she remained on the sofa, pondering her future course. The lamp and her guardian made their appearance at the same moment, and throwing himself down in one corner of the sofa, the latter asked:

"How are you since your nap? A trifle less ghastly, I see."

"Much better, thank you, sir. My head is quite clear again."

"Clear enough to make out a foreign letter?" He took one from his pocket and put it in her hand.

An anxious look flitted across her face, and she glanced rapidly over the contents, then crumpled the sheet nervously in her fingers.

"What is the matter now?"

"He is coming home. They will all be here in November."

She spoke as if bitterly chagrined and disappointed.

"Most people would consider that joyful news," said the doctor, quietly.

"What! after spending more than five years (one of them in traveling), to come back without having acquired a profession, and settle down into a mere walking ledger! To have princely advantages at his command, and yet throw them madly to the winds, and be content to plod along the road of mercantile life, without one spark of ambition, when his mental endowments would justify his aspiring to the most exalted political stations in the land."

Her voice trembled from intensity of feeling.

"Take care how you disparage mercantile pursuits; some of the most masterly minds of the age were nurtured in the midst of ledgers."

"And I honor and reverence all such far more than their colleagues, whose wisdom was culled in classic academic halls, for the former, struggling amid adverse circumstances, made good their claim to an exalted place in the temple of Fame. But necessity forced them to purely mercantile pursuits. Eugene's case is by no means analogous; situated as he is, he could be just what he chose. I honor all men who do their duty nobly and truly in the positions fate has assigned them; but, sir, you know there are some more richly endowed than others, some whom nature seems to have destined for arduous diplomatic posts; whose privilege it is to guide the helm of state, and achieve distinction as men of genius. To such the call will be imperative; America needs such men. Heaven only knows where they are to rise from, when the call is made! I do not mean to disparage mercantile pursuits; they afford constant opportunities for the exercise and display of keenness and clearness of intellect, but do not require the peculiar gifts so essential in statesmen. Indolence is unpardonable in any avocation, and I would be commended to the industrious, energetic merchant, in preference to superficial, so-called, 'professional men.' But Eugene had rare educational advantages, and I expected him to improve them, and be something more than ordinary. He expected it, five years ago. What infatuation possesses him latterly, I cannot imagine."

Dr. Hartwell smiled, and said very quietly: "Has it ever occurred to you that you might have over-estimated Eugene's abilities?"

"Sir, you entertained a flattering opinion of them when he left here." She could animadvert upon his fickleness, but did not choose that others should enjoy the same privilege.

"I by no means considered him an embryo Webster or Calhoun; never looked on him as an intellectual prodigy. He had a good mind, a handsome face, and frank, gentlemanly manners which, in the aggregate, impressed me favorably." Beulah bit her lips, and stooped to pat Charon's head. There was silence for some moments, and then the doctor asked:

"Does he mention Cornelia's health?"

"Only once, incidentally. I judge from the sentence, that she is rather feeble. There is a good deal of unimportant chat about a lady they have met in Florence. She is the daughter of a Louisiana planter; very beautiful and fascinating; is a niece of Mrs. Graham's, and will spend part of next winter with the Grahams."

"What is her name?"

"Antoinette Dupres."

Beulah was caressing Charon, and did not observe the purplish glow which bathed the doctor's face at the mention of the name. She only saw that he rose abruptly, and walked to the window, where he stood until tea was brought in. As they concluded the meal, and left the table, he held out his hand.

"Beulah, I congratulate you on your signal success to-day. Your valedictory made me proud of my protégée." She had put her hand in his, and looked up in his face, but the cloudy splendor of the eyes was more than she could bear, and drooping her head a little, she answered:

"Thank you."

"You have vacation for two months?"

"Yes, sir, and then my duties commence. Here is the certificate of my election." She offered it for inspection, but without noticing it, he continued:

"Beulah, I think you owe me something for taking care of you, as you phrased it long ago, at the Asylum. Do you admit the debt?"

"Most gratefully, sir! I admit that I can never liquidate it; I can repay you only with the most earnest gratitude." Large tears hung upon her lashes, and with an uncontrollable impulse, she raised his hand to her lips.

"I am about to test the sincerity of your gratitude. I doubt it."

She trembled, and looked at him uneasily. He laid his hand on her shoulder, and said, slowly:

"Relinquish the idea of teaching. Let me present you to society as my adopted child. Thus you can requite the debt."

"I cannot! I cannot!" cried Beulah, firmly, though tears gushed over her cheeks.

"Cannot? cannot?" repeated the doctor, pressing heavily upon her shoulders.

"Will not, then!" said she, proudly.

They looked at each other steadily. A withering smile of scorn and bitterness distorted his Apollo-like features, and he pushed her from him, saying, in the deep, concentrated tone of intense disappointment:

"I might have known it. I might have expected it; for fate has always decreed me just such returns."

Leaning against the sculptured Niobe, which stood near, Beulah exclaimed, in a voice of great anguish:

"Oh, Dr. Hartwell! do not make me repent the day I entered this house. God knows I am grateful, very grateful for your unparalleled kindness. Oh, that it were in my power to prove to you my gratitude! Do not upbraid me. you knew that I came here only to be educated. Even then I could not bear the thought of always imposing on your generosity; and every day that passed strengthened this impatience of dependence. Through your kindness, it is now in my power to maintain myself, and after the opening of next session, I cannot remain any longer the recipient of your bounty. Oh, sir, do not charge me with ingratitude! It is more than I can bear; more than I can bear!"

"Mark me, Beulah! Your pride will wreck you; wreck your happiness, your peace of mind. Already its iron hand is crushing your young heart. Beware, lest, in yielding to its decrees, you become the hopeless being a similar course has rendered me. Beware! But why should I warn you? Have not my prophecies ever proved Cassandran? Leave me."

"No, I will not leave you in anger." She drew near him, and took his hand in both hers. The fingers were cold and white as marble, rigid and inflexible as steel.

"My guardian, would you have me take a step (through fear of your displeasure), which would render my life a burden? Will you urge me to remain, when I tell you I cannot be happy here? I think not."

"Urge you to remain? By the Furies, no. I urge you to go! Yes, go! I no longer want you here. Your presence would irritate me beyond measure. But listen to me: I am going to New York on business; had intended taking you with me; but since you are so stubbornly proud, I can consent to leave you.

I shall start to-morrow evening—rather earlier than I expected—and shall not return before September, perhaps even later. What your plans are, I shall not inquire, but it is my request that you remain in this house, under Mrs. Watson's care, until your school duties commence; then you will, I suppose, remove elsewhere. I also request, particularly, that you will not hesitate to use the contents of a purse, which I shall leave on my desk for you. Remember that in coming years, when trials assail you, if you need a friend, I will still assist you. You will leave me now, if you please, as I have some letters to write." He motioned her away, and, unable to frame any reply, she left the room.

Though utterly miserable, now that her guardian seemed so completely estranged, her proud nature rebelled at his stern dismissal, and a feeling of reckless defiance speedily dried the tears on her cheek. That he should look down upon her with scornful indifference, stung her almost to desperation, and she resolved, instead of weeping, to meet and part with him as coldly as his contemptuous treatment justified. Weary in mind and body, she fell asleep, and soon forgot all her plans and sorrows. The sun was high in the heavens when Harriet waked her, and starting up, she asked:

"What time is it? How came I to sleep so late?"

"It is eight o'clock. Master ate breakfast an hour ago. Look here, child; what is to pay? Master is going off to the North, to be gone till October. He sat up all night, writing, and giving orders about things on the place, 'specially the green house, and the flower seeds to be saved in the front yard. He has not been in such a way since seven years ago. What is in the wind now? What ails him?" Harriet sat with her elbows on her knees, and her wrinkled face resting in the palms of her hands. She looked puzzled and discontented.

"He told me last night that he expected to leave home this evening; that he was going to New York on business." Beulah affected indifference; but the searching eyes of the old woman were fixed on her, and as she turned away, Harriet exclaimed:

"Going this evening! Why, child, he has gone. Told us all good-by, from Mrs. Watson down to Charon. Said his trunk must be sent down to the wharf at three o'clock; that he would not have time to come home again. There, good gracious! you are as white as a sheet; I will fetch you some wine." She hurried out, and Beulah sank into a chair, stunned by the intelligence.

When Harriet proffered a glass of cordial, she declined it, and said composedly:

"I will come, after a while, and take my breakfast. There is no accounting for your master's movements. I would as soon engage to keep up with a comet. There, let go my dress; I am going into the study for a while." She went slowly down the steps, and locking the door of the study to prevent intrusion, looked around the room. There was an air of confusion, as though books and chairs had been hastily moved about. On the floor lay numerous shreds of crape, and glancing up, she saw, with surprise, that the portrait had been closely wrapped in a sheet, and suspended with the face to the wall. Instantly, an uncontrollable desire seized her to look at that face. She had always supposed it to be his wife's likeness, and longed to gaze upon the feature of one whose name her husband had never mentioned. The mantel was low, and standing on a chair, she endeavored to catch the cord which supported the frame; but it hung too high. She stood on the marble mantel, and stretched her hands eagerly up; but though her fingers touched the cord she could not disengage it from the hook, and with a sensation of keen disappointment, she was forced to abandon the attempt. A note on the desk attracted her attention; it was directed to her, and contained only a few words:

> "Accompanying this is a purse containing a hundred dollars. In any emergency which the future may present, do not hesitate to call on
>
> "YOUR GUARDIAN."

She laid her head down on his desk, and sobbed bitterly. For the first time she realized that he had, indeed, gone—gone without one word of adieu: one look of kindness or reconciliation. Her tortured heart whispered: "Write him a note; ask him to come home; tell him you will not leave his house." But pride answered: "He is a tyrant; don't be grieved at his indifference; he is nothing to you; go to work boldly, and repay the money you have cost him." Once more, as in former years, a feeling of desolation crept over her. She had rejected her guardian's request, and isolated herself from sympathy; for who would assist and sympathize with her mental difficulties as he had done? The tears froze in her eyes, and she sat for some time looking at the crumpled note. Gradually, an expression of proud defiance settled on her features; she took the purse, walked up to her room, and put on her bonnet and mantle. Descending to the breakfast-room, she drank a cup of coffee, and telling Mrs. Watson she would be absent an hour or two, left the house, and proceeded to Madam St. Cymon's. She asked to see Miss Sanders, and after waiting a few minutes in the parlor, Clara made her appearance. She looked wan and weary, but greeted her friend with a gentle smile.

"I heard of your triumph yesterday, Beulah, and most sincerely congratulate you."

"I am in no mood for congratulations just now. Clara, did not you tell me, a few days since, that the music teacher of this establishment was ill, and that Madam St. Cymon was anxious to procure another?"

"Yes, I have no idea she will ever be well again. If strong enough, she is going back to her family in Philadelphia, next week. Why do you ask?"

"I want to get the situation, and wish you would say to madam that I have called to see her about it. I will wait here till you speak to her."

"Beulah, are you mad? Dr. Hartwell will never consent to your teaching music," cried Clara, with astonishment written on every feature.

"Dr. Hartwell is not my master, Clara Sanders! Will you speak to madam, or shall I have to do it?"

"Certainly, I will speak to her. But oh, Beulah! are you wild enough to leave your present home for such a life?"

"I have been elected a teacher in the public schools, but shall have nothing to do until the first of October. In the meantime I intend to give music lessons. If madam will employ me for two months, she may be able to procure a professor by the opening of the next term. And further, if I can make this arrangement, I am coming immediately to board with Mrs. Hoyt. Now speak to madam for me, will you?"

"One moment more. Does the doctor know of all this?"

"He knows that I intend to teach in the public school. He goes to New York this afternoon."

Clara looked at her mournfully, and said, with sad emphasis:

"Oh, Beulah! you may live to rue your rashness."

To Madam St. Cymon the proposal was singularly opportune, and hastening to meet the applicant, she expressed much pleasure at seeing Miss Benton again. She was very anxious to procure a teacher for the young ladies boarding with her, and for her own daughters, and the limited engagement would suit very well. She desired, however, to hear Miss Benton perform. Beulah took off her gloves, and played several very difficult pieces, with the ease which only constant practise and skilful training can confer. Madam declared herself more than satisfied with her proficiency, and requested her to commence her instructions on the following day. She had given the former teacher six hundred dollars a year, and would allow Miss Benton eighty dollars for the two months. Beulah was agreeably surprised at the ample remuneration, and having arranged the hours of her attendance at the school, she took leave of the principal. Clara called to her as she reached the street;

and assuming a gaiety which, just then, was very foreign to her real feelings, Beulah answered:

"It is all arranged. I shall take tea with you in my new home, provided Mrs. Hoyt can give me a room." She kissed her hand, and hurried away. Mrs. Hoyt found no difficulty in providing a room; and, to Beulah's great joy, managed to have a vacant one adjoining Clara's. She was a gentle, warm-hearted woman; and as Beulah examined the apartment, and inquired the terms, she hesitated, and said:

"My terms are thirty dollars a month; but you are poor, I judge, and being Miss Clara's friend, I will only charge you twenty-five."

"I do not wish you to make any deductions in my favor. I will take the room at thirty dollars," answered Beulah, rather haughtily.

"Very well. When will you want it?"

"Immediately. Be kind enough to have it in readiness for me; I shall come this afternoon. Could you give me some window-curtains? I should like it better, if you could do so without much inconvenience."

"Oh, certainly! they were taken down yesterday to be washed. Everything shall be in order for you."

It was too warm to walk home again, and Beulah called a carriage. The driver had not proceeded far, when a press of vehicles forced him to pause a few minutes. They happened to stand near the post-office and as Beulah glanced at the eager crowd collected in front, she started violently on perceiving her guardian. He stood on the corner, talking to a gentleman of venerable aspect, and she saw that he looked harassed. She was powerfully impelled to beckon him to her, and at least obtain a friendly adieu, but again pride prevailed. He had deliberately left her, without saying good-by, and she would not force herself on his notice. Even as she dropped her veil to avoid observation, the carriage rolled on, and she was soon at Dr. Hartwell's door. Unwilling to reflect on the steps she had taken, she busied herself in packing her clothes and books. On every side were tokens of her guardian's constant interest and remembrance; pictures, vases, and all the elegant appendages of a writing-desk. At length the last book was stowed away, and nothing else remained to engage her. The beautiful little Nuremberg clock on the mantel struck two, and looking up, she saw the solemn face of Harriet, who was standing in the door. Her steady, wondering gaze, disconcerted Beulah, despite her assumed indifference.

"What is the meaning of all this commotion? Hal says you ordered the carriage to be ready at five o'clock to take you away from here. Oh, child!

what are things coming to? What will master say? What won't he say? What are you quitting this house for, where you have been treated as well as if it belonged to you? What ails you?"

"Nothing. I have always intended to leave here as soon as I was able to support myself. I can do so now, very easily, and am going to board. Your master knows I intend to teach."

"But he has no idea that you are going to leave here before he comes home, for he gave us all express orders to see that you had just what you wanted. Oh, he will be in a tearing rage when he hears of it! Don't anger him, child! Do, pray, for mercy's sake, don't anger him! He never forgets anything! When he once sets his head, he is worse than David on the Philistines! If he is willing to support you, it is his own lookout. He is able, and his money is his own. His kin won't get it. He and his brother don't speak; and as for Miss May! they never did get along in peace, even before he was married. So, if he chooses to give some of his fortune to you, it is nobody's business but his own; and you are mighty simple, I can tell you, if you don't stay here and take it."

"That will do, Harriet. I do not wish any more advice. I don't want your master's fortune, even if I had the offer of it! I am determined to make my own living: so just say no more about it."

"Take care, child. Remember, '*Pride goeth before a fall.*' "

"What do you mean?" cried Beulah, angrily.

"I mean that the day is coming, when you will be glad enough to come back and let my master take care of you! That's what I mean. And see if it doesn't come to pass. But he will not do it then; I tell you now he won't. There is no forgiving spirit about him; he is as fierce, and bears malice as long as a Camanche Injun! It is no business of mine though. I have said my say: and I will be bound you will go your own gait. You are just about as hard-headed as he is himself. Anybody would almost believe you belonged to the Hartwell family. Every soul of them is alike in the matter of temper; only Miss Pauline has something of her pa's disposition. I suppose, now her ma is married again, she will want to come back to her uncle; should not wonder if he 'dopted her, since you have got the bit between your teeth."

"I hope he will," answered Beulah. She ill brooked Harriet's plain speech, but remembrances of past affection checked the severe rebuke which more than once rose to her lips.

"We shall see; we shall see!" and Harriet walked off with anything but a placid expression of countenance, while Beulah sought Mrs. Watson to explain her sudden departure, and acquaint her with her plans for the summer. The housekeeper endeavored most earnestly to dissuade her from taking the contemplated step, assuring her that the doctor would be grieved and displeased; but her arguments produced no effect, and with tears of regret, she bade her farewell.

The sun was setting when Beulah took possession of her room at Mrs. Hoyt's house. The furniture was very plain, and the want of several articles vividly recalled the luxurious home she had abandoned. She unpacked and arranged her clothes, and piled her books on a small table, which was the only substitute for her beautiful desk and elegant rosewood bookcase. She had gathered a superb bouquet of flowers, as she crossed the front yard, and in lieu of her Sèvres vases, placed them in a dim-looking tumbler, which stood on the tall, narrow mantelpiece. He room was in the third story, with two windows, one opening to the south, and one to the west. It grew dark by the time she had arranged the furniture, and too weary to think of going down to tea, she unbound her hair, and took a seat beside the window. The prospect was extended; below her were countless lamps, marking the principal streets; and, in the distance, the dark cloud of masts, told that river and bay might be distinctly seen by daylight. The quiet stars looked dim through the dusty atmosphere, and the noise of numerous vehicles rattling by, produced a confused impression, such as she had never before received at this usually calm twilight season. The events of the day passed in a swift review, and a mighty barrier seemed to have sprung up (as by some foul spell) between her guardian and herself. What an immeasurable gulf now yawned to separate them. Could it be possible that the friendly relations of years were thus suddenly and irrevocably annulled? Would he relinquish all interest in one whom he had so long watched over and directed? Did he intend that they should be completely estranged henceforth? For the first time since Lilly's death, she felt herself thrown upon the world. Alone and unaided, she was essaying to carve her own fortune from the huge quarries, where thousands were diligently laboring. An undefinable feeling of desolation crept into her heart; but she struggled desperately against it, and asked, in proud defiance of her own nature:

"Am I not sufficient unto myself? Leaning only on myself, what more should I want? Nothing! His sympathy is utterly unnecessary."

A knock at the door startled her, and in answer to her "come in" Clara Sanders entered. She walked slowly, and seating herself beside Beulah, said, in a gentle, but weary tone:

"How do you like your room? I am so glad it opens into mine."

"Quite as well as I expected. The view from this window must be very fine. There is the tea-bell, I suppose. Are you not going down? I am too much fatigued to move."

"No; I never want supper, and generally spend the evenings in my room. It is drearily monotonous here. Nothing to vary the routine for me, except my afternoon walk, and recently the warm weather has debarred me even from that. You are a great walker, I believe, and I look forward to many pleasant rambles with you, when I feel stronger, and autumn comes. Beulah, how long does Dr. Hartwell expect to remain in the North? He told me, some time ago, that he was a delegate to the Medical Convention."

"I believe it is rather uncertain; but probably he will not return before October."

"Indeed! That is a long time for a physician to absent himself."

Just then an organ-grinder paused on the pavement beneath the window, and began a beautiful air from "Sonnambula." It was a favorite song of Beulah's, and as the melancholy tones swelled on the night air, they recalled many happy hours spent in the quiet study beside the melodeon. She leaned out of the window till the last echo died away, and as the musician shouldered his instrument and trudged off, she said, abruptly:

"Is there not a piano in the house!"

"Yes, just such a one as you might expect to find in a boarding-house, where unruly children are thrumming upon it from morning till night. It was once a fine instrument, but now is capable of excruciating discords. You will miss your grand piano."

"I must have something in my own room to practise on. Perhaps I can hire a melodeon or piano for a moderate sum; I will try to-morrow."

"The Grahams are coming home soon, I hear. One of the principal upholsterers boards here, and he mentioned this morning at breakfast that he had received a letter from Mr. Graham, directing him to attend to the unpacking of an entirely new set of furniture. Everything will be on a grand scale. I suppose Eugene returns with them?"

"Yes, they will all arrive in November."

"It must be a delightful anticipation for you."

"Why so, pray?"

"Why? Because you and Eugene are such old friends."

"Oh, yes; as far as Eugene is concerned, of course it is a very pleasant anticipation."

"He is identified with the Grahams."

"Not necessarily," answered Beulah, coldly.

A sad smile flitted over Clara's sweet face, as she rose and kissed her friend's brow, saying gently:

"Good night, dear. I have a headache, and must try to sleep it off. Since you have determined to battle with difficulties, I am very glad to have you here with me. I earnestly hope that success may crown your efforts, and the sunshine of happiness dispel for you the shadows that have fallen thick about my pathway. You have been rash, Beulah, and short-sighted; but I trust that all will prove for the best. Good night."

She glided away, and locking the door, Beulah returned to her seat, and laid her head wearily down on the window-sill. What a Hermes is thought! Like a vanishing dream fled the consciousness of surrounding objects, and she was with Eugene. Now, in the earlier years of his absence, she was in Heidelberg, listening to the evening chimes; and rambling with him through the heart of the Odenwald. Then they explored the Hartz, climbed the Brocken, and there among the clouds, discussed the adventures of Faust, and his kinsman, Manfred. Anon, the arrival of the Grahams disturbed the quiet of Eugene's life, and far away from the picturesque haunts of Heidelberg students, he wandered with them over Italy, Switzerland, and France. Engrossed by these companions, he no longer found time to commune with her, and when occasionally he penned a short letter, it was hurried, constrained, and unsatisfactory. One topic had become stereotyped; he never failed to discourage the idea of teaching; urged most earnestly the folly of such a step, and dwelt upon the numerous advantages of social position arising from a residence under her guardian's roof. We have seen that from the hour of Lilly's departure from the Asylum, Beulah's affections, hopes, pride, all centered in Eugene. There had long existed a tacit compact, which led her to consider her future indissolubly linked with his; and his parting words seemed to seal this compact as holy and binding, when he declared, "I mean of course to take care of you myself, when I come home, for you know you belong to me." His letters for many months retained the tone of dictatorship, but the tenderness seemed all to have melted away. He wrote as if with a heart preoccupied by weightier matters, and now Beulah could no longer conceal from herself the painful fact that the man was far different from the boy. After five years' absence, he was coming back a man; engrossed by other thoughts and feelings than those which had prompted him in days gone by. With the tenacious hope of youth she still trusted that she might have misjudged him; he could never be other than noble and generous; she would silence her forebodings, and wait till his return. She wished beyond all expression to see him once more, and the prospect of a speedy reunion often made her heart throb painfully. That he would reproach her for her obstinate resolution of teaching, she was prepared to expect; but strong in the consciousness of duty, she committed herself to the care of a merciful God, and soon slept as soundly as though under Dr. Hartwell's roof.

CHAPTER XVII.

Sometimes, after sitting for five consecutive hours at the piano, guiding the clumsy fingers of tyros, and listening to a tiresome round of scales and exercises, Beulah felt exhausted, mentally and physically, and feared that she had miserably overrated her powers of endurance. The long, warm days of August dragged heavily by, and each night she felt grateful that the summer was one day nearer its grave. One afternoon, she proposed to Clara to extend their walk to the home of her guardian, and as she readily assented, they left the noise and crowd of the city, and soon found themselves on the common.

"This is my birthday," said Beulah, as they passed a clump of pines, and caught a glimpse of the white gate beyond.

"Ah! how old are you?"

"Eighteen—but I feel much older."

She opened the gate, and as they leisurely ascended the avenue of aged cedars, Beulah felt once more as if she were going home. A fierce bark greeted her, and the next moment Charon rushed to meet her; placing his huge paws on her shoulders, and whining and barking joyfully. He bounded before her to the steps, and laid down contentedly on the piazza. Harriet's turbaned head appeared at the entrance, and a smile of welcome lighted up her ebon face, as she shook Beulah's hand.

Mrs. Watson was absent, and after a few questions, Beulah entered the study, saying:

"I want some books, Harriet; and Miss Sanders wishes to see the paintings."

Ah! every chair and book-shelf greeted her like dear friends, and she bent down over some volumes to hide the tears that sprang into her eyes. The only really happy portion of her life had been passed here; every article in the room was dear from association, and though only a month had elapsed since her departure, those bygone years seemed far, far off, among the mist of very distant recollections. Thick and fast fell the hot drops, until her eyes were blinded, and she could no longer distinguish the print they were riveted on. The memory of kind smiles haunted her, and kinder tones seemed borne to her from every corner of the apartment. Clara was eagerly examining the paintings, and neither of the girls observed Harriet's entrance, until she asked:

"Do you know that the yellow fever has broke out here?"

"Oh, you are mistaken! It can't be possible!" cried Clara, turning pale.

"I tell you, it is a fact. There are six cases now at the hospital; Hal was there this morning. I have lived here a good many years, and from the signs, I think we are going to have dreadfully sickly times. You young ladies had better keep out of the sun; first thing you know, you will have it."

"Who told you there was yellow fever at the hospital?"

"Dr. Asbury said so; and what is more, Hal has had it himself, and nursed people who had it; and he says it is the worst sort of yellow fever."

"I am not afraid of it," said Beulah, looking up for the first time.

"I am dreadfully afraid of it," answered Clara, with a nervous shudder.

"Then you had better leave town as quick as possible, for folks who are easily scared always catch it soonest."

"Nonsense!" cried Beulah, noting the deepening pallor of Clara's face.

"Oh, I will warrant, if everybody else—every man, woman, and child in the city—takes it, you won't! Miss Beulah, I should like to know what you are afraid of!" muttered Harriet, scanning the orphan's countenance, and adding, in a louder tone: "Have you heard anything from master?"

"No." Beulah bit her lips to conceal her emotion.

"Hal hears from him. He was in New York when he wrote the last letter." She took a malicious pleasure in thus torturing her visitor; and, determined not to gratify her by any manifestation of interest or curiosity, Beulah took up a couple of volumes and turned to the door, saying:

"Come, Clara, we must each have a bouquet. Harriet, where are the flower-scissors? Dr. Hartwell never objected to my carefully cutting even his choicest flowers. There! Clara, listen to the cool rippling of the fountain. How I have longed to hear its silvery murmur once more!"

They went out into the front yard. Clara wandered about the flower-beds, gathering blossoms which were scattered in lavish profusion on all sides; and leaning over the marble basin, Beulah bathed her brow in the crystal waters. There was bewitching beauty and serenity in the scene before her, and as Charon nestled his great head against her hand, she found it very difficult to realize the fact that she had left this lovely retreat for the small room at Mrs. Hoyt's boarding-house. It was not her habit, however, to indulge in repinings and though her ardent appreciation of beauty rendered the place incalculably dear to her, she resolutely gathered a cluster of flowers, bade adieu to Harriet, and descended the avenue. Charon walked soberly beside her, now and then looking up, as if to inquire the meaning of her long absence, and wonder at her sudden departure. At the gate she patted him affectionately on the head, and passed out; he made no attempt to follow her, but barked violently, and then laid down at the gate, whining mournfully.

"Poor Charon! I wish I might have him," said she, sadly.

"I dare say the doctor would give him to you," answered Clara, very simply.

"I would just as soon think of asking him for his own head," replied Beulah.

"It is a mystery to me, Beulah, how you can feel so coldly toward Dr. Hartwell."

"I should very much like to know what you mean by that?" said Beulah, involuntarily crushing the flowers she held.

"Why, you speak of him just as you would of anybody else."

"Well?"

"You seem to be afraid of him."

"To a certain extent, I am; and so is everybody else who knows him intimately."

"This fear is unjust to him."

"How so, pray?"

"Because he is too noble to do aught to inspire it."

"Certainly he is feared, nevertheless, by all who know him well."

"It seems to me that, situated as you have been, you would almost worship him!"

"I am not addicted to worshiping anything but God!" answered Beulah, shortly.

"You are an odd compound, Beulah. Sometimes I think you must be utterly heartless!"

"Thank you."

"Don't be hurt. But you are so cold, so freezing; you chill me."

"Do I? Dr. Hartwell (your Delphic oracle it seems), says I am as fierce as a tropical tornado."

"I do not understand how you can bear to give up such an enchanting home, and go to hard work, as if you were driven to it from necessity."

"Do not go over all that beaten track again, if you please. It is not my home! I can be just as happy, nay happier, in my little room."

"I doubt it," said Clara, pertinaciously.

Stopping suddenly, and fixing her eyes steadily on her companion, Beulah hastily asked:

"Clara Sanders, why should you care if my guardian and I are separated?"

A burning blush dyed cheek and brow, as Clara drooped her head, and answered:

"Because he is my friend also, and I know that your departure will grieve him."

"You over-estimate my worth, and his interest. He is a man who lives in a world of his own and needs no society, save such as is afforded in his tasteful and elegant home. He loves books, flowers, music, paintings, and his dog! He is a stern man, and shares his griefs and joys with no one. All this I have told you before."

There was a long silence, broken at last by an exclamation from Beulah:

"Oh! how beautiful! how silent! how solemn! Look down the long dim aisles. It is an oratory where my soul comes to worship! Presently the breeze will rush up from the gulf, and sweep the green organ, and a melancholy chant will swell through these gilded shrines in comparison with these grand forest temples, where the dome is the bending vault of God's blue, and the columns are these everlasting pines!" She pointed to a thick clump of pines sloping down to a ravine.

The setting sun threw long quivering rays through the clustering boughs, and the broken beams, piercing the gloom beyond, showed the long aisles as in a "cathedral light."

As Clara looked down the dim glade, and then watched Beulah's parted lips and sparkling eyes, as she stood bending forward with rapturous delight written on every feature, she thought that she had indeed misjudged her in using the epithets "freezing and heartless."

"You are enthusiastic," said she gently.

"How can I help it? I love the grand and beautiful too well to offer a tribute of silent admiration. Oh, my homage is that of a whole heart!"

They reached home in the gloaming, and each retired to her own room.

For a mere trifle Beulah had procured the use of a melodeon, and now, after placing the drooping flowers in water, she sat down before the instrument and poured out the joy of her soul in song. Sad memories no longer floated like corpses on the sea of the past; grim forebodings crouched among the mists of the future, and she sang song after song, exulting in the gladness of her heart. An analysis of these occasional hours of delight was as impossible as their creation. Sometimes she was conscious of their approach, while gazing up at the starry islets in the boundless lake of azure sky; or when a gorgeous sunset pageant was passing away; sometimes from hearing a solemn chant in church, or a witching strain from a favorite opera. Sometimes from viewing dim old pictures; sometimes from reading a sublime passage in some old English or German author. It was a serene elevation of feeling; an unbounded peace; a chastened joyousness, which she was rarely able to analyze, but which isolated her for a time from all surrounding circumstances. How long she sang on the present occasion she knew not, and only paused on hearing a heavy sob behind her. Turning round, she saw Clara sitting near, with her face in her hands. Kneeling beside her, Beulah wound her arms around her, and asked earnestly:

"What troubles you, my friend? May I not know?"

Clara dropped her head on Beulah's shoulder, and answered hesitatingly:

"The tones of your voice always sadden me. They are like organ-notes, solemn and awful! Yes, awful, and yet very sweet—sweeter than any music I ever heard. Your singing fascinates me, yet, strange as it may seem, it very often makes me weep. There is an unearthliness, a spirituality that affects me singularly."

"I am glad that is all. I was afraid you were distressed about something. Here, take my rocking-chair; I am going to read, and if you like, you may have the benefit of my book."

"Beulah, do put away your books for one night, and let us have a quiet time. Don't study now. Come sit here, and talk to me."

"Flatterer, do you pretend that you prefer my chattering to the wonderful words of a man who 'talked like an angel?' You must listen to the tale of that 'Ancient Mariner with glittering eyes.'"

"Spare me that horrible ghostly story of vessels freighted with staring corpses! Ugh! it curdled the blood in my veins once, and I shut the book in disgust. Don't begin it now, for heaven's sake!"

"Why, Clara? It is the most thrilling poem in the English language. Each reperusal fascinates me more and more. It requires a dozen readings to initiate you fully into its weird supernatural realms."

"Yes; and it is precisely for that reason that I don't choose to hear it. There is quite enough of the grim and hideous in reality, without hunting it up in the pages of fiction. When I read, I desire to relax my mind, not put it on the rack, as your favorite books invariably do. Absolutely, Beulah, after listening to some of your pet authors, I feel as if I had been standing on my head. You need not look so coolly incredulous; it is a positive fact. As for that 'Ancient Mariner' you are so fond of, I am disposed to take the author's own opinion of it, as expressed in those lines addressed to himself."

"I suppose, then, you fancy 'Christabel' as little as the other, seeing that it is a tale of witchcraft. How would you relish that grand anthem to nature's God, written in the vale of Chamouni?"

"I never read it," answered Clara, very quietly.

"What? Never read 'Sibylline Leaves?' Why, I will wager my head that you have parsed from them a thousand times! Never read that magnificent hymn before sunrise, in the midst of glaciers and snow-crowned, cloud-piercing peaks? Listen, then; and if you don't feel like falling upon your knees, you have not a spark of poetry in your soul!"

She drew the lamp close to her, and read aloud. Her finely modulated voice was peculiarly adapted to the task, and her expressive countenance faithfully depicted the contending emotions which filled her mind as she read. Clara listened with pleased interest, and when the short poem was concluded said:

"Thank you; it is beautiful. I have often seen extracts from it. Still, there is a description of Mont Blanc in 'Manfred' which I believe I like quite as well."

"What? That witch fragment?"

"Yes."

"I don't understand 'Manfred.' Here and there are passages in cipher. I read and catch a glimpse of hidden meaning; I read again, and it vanishes in mist. It seems to me a poem of symbols, dimly adumbrating truths, which my clouded intellect clutches at in vain. I have a sort of shadowy belief that 'Astarte,' as in its ancient mythological significance, symbolizes nature. There is a dusky veil of mystery shrouding her, which favors my idea of her, as representing the universe. Manfred, with daring hand, tore away that 'Veil of Isis,' which no mortal had ever pierced before, and, maddened by the mockery of the stony features, paid the penalty of his sacrilegious rashness, and fled from the temple, striving to shake off the curse. My guardian has a curious print of 'Astarte' taken from some European Byronic gallery. I have studied it, until almost it seemed to move and speak to me. She is clad in the ghostly drapery of the tomb, just as invoked by Nemesis, with trailing tresses, closed eyes, and folded hands. The features are dim, spectral, yet marvelously beautiful. Almost one might think the eyelids quivered, there is such an air of waking dreaminess. That this is a false and inadequate conception of Byron's 'Astarte,' I feel assured, and trust that I shall yet find the key to this enigma. It interests me greatly, and by some inexplicable process, whenever I sit pondering the mystery of Astarte, that wonderful creation in Shirley presents itself. Astarte becomes in a trice that 'woman-Titan,' Nature, kneeling before the red hills of the west, at her evening prayers. I see her prostrate on the great steps of her altar, praying for a fair night, for mariners at sea, for lambs in moors, and unfledged birds in woods. Her robe of blue air spreads to the outskirts of the heath. A veil, white as an avalanche, sweeps from her head to her feet, and arabesques of lightning flame on its borders. I see her zone, purple, like the horizon; through its blush shines the star of evening. Her forehead has the expanse of a cloud, and is paler than the early moon, risen long before dark gathers. She reclines on the ridge of Stillbro'-Moor, her mighty hands are joined beneath it. So kneeling, face to face 'Nature speaks with God.' Oh! I would give twenty years of my life to have painted that Titan's portrait. I would rather have been the author of this, than have wielded the scepter of Zenobia, in the palmiest days of Palmyra!"

She spoke rapidly, and with white lips that quivered. Clara looked at her wonderingly, and said, hesitatingly:

"I don't understand the half of what you have been saying. It sounds to me very much as if you had stumbled into a lumber-room of queer ideas; snatched up a handful, all on different subjects, and woven them into a speech as incongruous as Joseph's variegated coat." There was no reply. Beulah's hands were clasped on the table before her, and she leaned forward with eyes fixed steadily on the floor. Clara waited a moment, and then continued:

"I never noticed any of the mysteries of 'Manfred,' that seem to trouble you so much. I enjoy the fine passages, and never think of the hidden meanings, as you call them; whereas it seems you are always plunging about in the dark, hunting you know not what. I am content to glide on the surface, and—"

"And live in the midst of foam and bubbles!" cried Beulah, with a gesture of impatience.

"Better that, than grope among subterranean caverns, black and icy, as you are forever doing. You are even getting a weird, unearthly look. Sometimes, when I come in, and find you, book in hand, with that far-off expression in your eyes, I really dislike to speak to you. There is no more color in your face and hands, than in that wall yonder. You will dig your grave among books, if you don't take care. There is such a thing as studying too much. Your mind is perpetually at work; all day you are thinking, thinking, thinking; and at night, since the warm weather has made me open the door between our rooms, I hear you talking earnestly and rapidly in your sleep. Last week I came in on tip-toe, and stood a few minutes beside your bed. The moon shone in through the window, and though you were fast asleep, I saw that you tossed your hands restlessly; while I stood there, you spoke aloud, in an incoherent manner, of the 'Dream Fugue,' and 'Vision of sudden Death,' and now and then you frowned, and sighed heavily, as if you were in pain. Music is a relaxation to most people, but it seems to put your thoughts on the rack. You will wear yourself out prematurely, if you don't quit this constant studying."

She rose to go, and, glancing up at her, Beulah answered, musingly:

"We are very unlike. The things that I love, you shrink from as dull and tiresome. I live in a different world. Books are to me what family, and friends, and society, are to other people. It may be that the isolation of my life necessitates this. Doubtless you often find me abstracted. Are you going so soon? I had hoped we should spend a profitable evening, but it has slipped away, and I have done nothing. Good night." She rose and gave the customary good-night kiss, and as Clara retired to her own room, Beulah turned up the wick of her lamp, and resumed her book. The gorgeous mazes of Coleridge no longer imprisoned her fancy; it wandered mid the silence, and desolation, and sand rivulets of the Thebaid desert; through the date groves of the lonely Laura; through the museums of Alexandria. Over the cool, crystal depths of "Hypatia," her thirsty spirit hung eagerly. In Philammon's intellectual nature she found a startling resemblance to her own. Like him, she had entered a forbidden temple, and learned to question; and the same "insatiable craving to know the mysteries of learning," was impelling her, with irresistible force, out into the world of philosophic inquiry. Hours fled on unnoted; with nervous haste the leaves were turned. The town clock struck three. As she finished the book, and laid it on the table, she bowed her head upon her hands. She was bewildered. Was Kingsley his own Raphael-Aben-Ezra? or did he heartily believe in the Christianity of which he had given so hideous a portraiture? Her brain whirled, yet there was a great dissatisfaction. She could not contentedly go back to the Laura with

Philammon; "Hypatia" was not sufficiently explicit. She was dissatisfied; there was more than this Alexandrian ecstasy, to which Hypatia was driven; but where, and how should she find it? Who would guide her? Was not her guardian, in many respects, as skeptical as Raphael himself? Dare she enter, alone and unaided, this Cretan maze of investigation, where all the wonderful lore of the gifted Hypatia had availed nothing? What was her intellect given her for, if not to be thus employed? Her head ached with the intensity of thought, and as she laid it on her pillow and closed her eyes, day looked out over the eastern sky.

The ensuing week was one of anxious apprehension to all within the city. Harriet's words seemed prophetic; there was every intimation of a sickly season. Yellow fever had made its appearance in several sections of the town, in its most malignant type. The Board of Health devised various schemes for arresting the advancing evil. The streets were powdered with lime, and huge fires of tar kept constantly burning, yet daily, hourly, the fatality increased; and as colossal ruin strode on, the terrified citizens fled in all directions. In ten days the epidemic began to make fearful havoc; all classes and ages were assailed indiscriminately. Whole families were stricken down in a day, and not one member spared to aid the others. The exodus was only limited by impossibility; all who could, abandoned their homes, and sought safety in flight. These were the fortunate minority; and, as if resolved to wreak its fury on the remainder, the contagion spread into every quarter of the city. Not even physicians were spared; and those who escaped, trembled in anticipation of the fell stroke. Many doubted that it was yellow fever, and conjectured that the veritable plague had crossed the ocean. Of all Mrs. Hoyt's boarders, but half-a-dozen determined to hazard remaining in the infected region; these were Beulah, Clara, and four gentlemen. Gladly would Clara have fled to a place of safety, had it been in her power; but there was no one to accompany or watch over her, and as she was forced to witness the horrors of the season, a sort of despair seemed to nerve her trembling frame. Mrs. Watson had been among the first to leave the city. Madam St. Cymon had disbanded her school; and as only her three daughters continued to take music lessons, Beulah had ample leisure to contemplate the distressing scenes which surrounded her. At noon, one September day, she stood at the open window of her room. The air was intensely hot; the drooping leaves of the China-trees were motionless; there was not a breath of wind stirring, and the sable plumes of the hearses were still as their burdens. The brazen, glittering sky, seemed a huge glowing furnace, breathing out only scorching heat. Beulah leaned out of the window, and wiping away the heavy drops that stood on her brow, looked down the almost deserted street. Many of the stores were closed; whilom busy haunts were silent; and very few persons were visible, save the drivers of two hearses, and of a cart filled with coffins. The church bells tolled unceasingly, and the desolation, the horror, was indescribable, as the sable wings of the destroyer hung over the doomed city. Out of her ten fellow-graduates, four slept in the cemetery. The night before, she had watched beside another, and at dawn, saw the limbs stiffen, and the eyes grow sightless. Among her former schoolmates, the contagion had been particularly fatal, and, fearless of danger, she had nursed two of them. As she stood fanning herself Clara entered hurriedly, and sinking into a chair, exclaimed, in accents of terror:

"It has come! as I knew it would! Two of Mrs. Hoyt's children have been taken, and, I believe, one of the waiters also! Merciful God! what will become of me?" Her teeth chattered, and she trembled from head to foot.

"Don't be alarmed, Clara! Your excessive terror is your greatest danger. If you would escape, you must keep as quiet as possible."

She poured out a glass of water, and made her drink it; then asked;

"Can Mrs. Hoyt get medical aid?"

"No; she has sent for every doctor in town, and not one has come."

"Then I will go down and assist her." Beulah turned toward the door, but Clara caught her dress, and said hoarsely:

"Are you mad, thus continually to put your life in jeopardy? Are you shod with immortality, that you thrust yourself into the very path of destruction?"

"I am not afraid of the fever, and therefore think I shall not take it. As long as I am able to be up, I shall do all that I can to relieve the sick. Remember, Clara, nurses are not to be had now for any sum." She glided down the steps, and found the terrified mother wringing her hands helplessly over the stricken ones. The children were crying on the bed, and with the energy which the danger demanded, Beulah speedily ordered the mustard baths, and administered the remedies she had seen prescribed on previous occasions. The fever rose rapidly, and undaunted by thoughts of personal danger, she took her place beside the bed. It was past midnight when Dr. Asbury came; exhausted and haggard from unremitting toil and vigils, he looked several years older than when she had last seen him. He started on perceiving her perilous post, and said anxiously:

"Oh, you are rash! very rash! What would Hartwell say? What will he think when he comes?"

"Comes! Surely you have not urged him to come back now!" said she, grasping his arm convulsively.

"Certainly. I telegraphed to him to come home by express. You need not look so troubled; he has had this Egyptian plague, will run no risk, and even if he should, will return as soon as possible."

"Are you sure that he has had the fever?"

"Yes, sure. I nursed him myself, the summer after he came from Europe, and thought he would die. That was the last sickly season we have had for years, but this caps the climax of all I ever saw or heard of in America. Thank God, my wife and children are far away; and, free from apprehension on their account, I can do my duty."

All this was said in an undertone, and after advising everything that could possibly be done, he left the rom, beckoning Beulah after him. She followed, and he said earnestly:

"Child, I tremble for you. Why did you leave Hartwell's house, and incur all this peril? Beulah, though it is nobly unselfish in you to devote yourself to the sick, as you are doing, it may cost you your life—nay, most probably it will."

"I have thought of it all, sir, and determined to do my duty."

"Then God preserve you. Those children have been taken violently; watch them closely; good nursing is worth all the apothecary shops. You need not send for me any more; I am out constantly; whenver I can I will come; meantime, depend only on the nursing. Should you be taken yourself, let me know at once; do not fail. A word more—keep yourself well stimulated."

He hurried away, and she returned to the sick-room, to speculate on the probability of soon meeting her guardian. Who can tell how dreary were the days and nights that followed? Mrs. Hoyt took the fever, and mother and children moaned together. On the morning of the fourth day, the eldest child, a girl of eight years, died, with Beulah's hand grasped in hers. Happily, the mother was unconscious, and the little corpse was borne into an adjoining room. Beulah shrank from the task which she felt, for the first time in her life, called on to perform. She could nurse the living, but dreaded the thought of shrouding the dead. Still, there was no one else to do it, and she bravely conquered her repugnance, and clad the young sleeper for the tomb. The gentlemen boarders, who had luckily escaped, arranged the mournful particulars of the burial; and after severing a sunny lock of hair for the mother, should she live, Beulah saw the cold form borne out to its last resting-place. Another gloomy day passed slowly, and she was rewarded by the convalescence of the remaining sick child. Mrs. Hoyt still hung upon the confines of eternity; and Beulah, who had not closed her eyes for many nights, was leaning over the bed, counting the rushing pulse; when a rapid step caused her to look up, and falling forward in her arms, Clara cried:

"Save me! save me! The chill is on me now!"

It was too true; and as Beulah assisted her to her room, and carefully bathed her feet, her heart was heavy with dire dread lest Clara's horror of the disease should augment its ravages. Dr. Asbury was summoned with all haste, but as usual seemed an age in coming, and when at last he came, could only prescribe what had already been done. It was pitiable to watch the agonized expression of Clara's sweet face, as she looked from the countenance of the physician to that of her friend, striving to discover their opinion of her case.

"Doctor, you must send Hal to me. He can nurse Mrs. Hoyt and little Willie while I watch Clara. I can't possibly take care of all three, though Willie is a great deal better. Can you send him at once? He is a good nurse."

"Yes, he has been nursing poor Tom Hamil, but he died about an hour ago, and Hal is released. I look for Hartwell hourly. You do keep up amazingly! Bless you, Beulah!" Wringing her hand, he descended the stairs.

Reentering the room, Beulah sat down beside Clara, and taking one burning hand in her cool palms, pressed it softly, saying, in an encouraging tone:

"I feel so much relieved about Willie, he is a great deal better; and I think Mrs. Hoyt's fever is abating. You were not taken so severely as Willie, and if you will go to sleep quietly, I believe you will only have a light attack."

"Did those down-stairs have black-vomit?" asked Clara, shudderingly.

"Lizzie had it; the others did not. Try not to think about it. Go to sleep."

"What was that the doctor said about Dr. Hartwell! I could not hear very well, you talked so low. Ah! tell me, Beulah."

"Only that he is coming home soon—that was all. Don't talk any more."

Clara closed her eyes, but tears stole from beneath the lashes, and coursed rapidly down her glowing cheeks. The lips moved in prayer, and her fingers closed tightly over those of her companion. Beulah felt that her continued vigils and exertions were exhausting her. Her limbs trembled when she walked, and there was a dull pain in her head, which she could not banish. Her appetite had long since forsaken her, and it was only by the exertion of a determined will that she forced herself to eat. She was warmly attached to

Clara, and the dread of losing this friend caused her to suffer keenly. Occasionally she stole away to see the other sufferers, fearing that when Mrs. Hoyt discovered Lizzie's death, the painful intelligence would seal her own fate. It was late at night. She had just returned from one of these hasty visits, and finding that Hal was as attentive as any one could be, she threw herself, weary and anxious, into an armchair beside Clara's bed. The crimson face was turned toward her, the parched lips parted, the panting breath, labored and irregular. The victim was delirious; the hazel eyes, inflamed and vacant, rested on Beulah's countenance, and she murmured:

"He will never know! Oh, no! how should he? The grave will soon shut me in, and I shall see him no more—no more!" She shuddered and turned away.

Beulah leaned her head against the bed, and as a tear slid down upon her hand, she thought and said with bitter sorrow:

"I would rather see her the victim of death, than have her drag out an aimless, cheerless existence, rendered joyless by this hopeless attachment!"

She wondered whether Dr. Hartwell suspected this love. He was remarkably quick-sighted, and men, as well as women, were very vain and wont to give even undue weight to every circumstance which flattered their self-love. She had long seen this partiality; would not the object of it be quite as penetrating? Clara was very pretty; nay, at times she was beautiful. If conscious of her attachment, could he ever suffer himself to be influenced by it? No; impossible! There were utter antagonisms of taste and temperament which rendered it very certain that she would not suit him for a companion. Yet she was very lovable. Beulah walked softly across the room and leaned out of the window. An awful stillness brooded over the scourged city.

> "The moving moon went up the sky,
> And nowhere did abide;
> Softly she was going up,
> And a star or two beside."

The soft beams struggled to pierce the murky air, dense with smoke from the burning pitch. There was no tread on the pavement, all was solemn as Death, who held such mad revel in the crowded graveyards. Through the shroud of smoke she could see the rippling waters of the bay, as the faint southern breeze swept its surface. It was a desolation realizing all the horrors of the "Masque of the Red Death," and as she thought of the mourning hearts in that silent city, of Clara's danger and her own, Beulah repeated, sadly, those solemn lines:

> "Like clouds that rake the mountain summit,
> Or waves that own no curbing hand,
> How fast has brother followed brother,
> From sunshine to the sunless land!"

Clasping her hands, she added, earnestly:

"I thank thee, my Father! that the Atlantic rolls between Eugene and this 'besom of destruction.'"

A touch on her shoulder caused her to look around, and her eyes rested on her guardian. She started, but did not speak, and held out her hand. He looked at her, long and searchingly; his lip trembled, and instead of taking her offered hand, he passed his arm around her, and drew her to his bosom. She looked up with surprise; and bending his haughty head, he kissed her pale brow, for the first time. She felt then that she would like to throw her arms round his neck, and tell him how very glad she was to see him again—how unhappy his sudden departure had made her; but a feeling she could not pause to analyze, prevented her from following the dictates of her heart; and holding her off, so as to scan her countenance, Dr. Hartwell said:

"How worn and haggard you look! Oh, child! your rash obstinacy has tortured me beyond expression."

"I have but done my duty. It has been a horrible time. I am glad you have come. You will not let Clara die."

"Sit down child. You are trembling from exhaustion."

He drew up a chair for her, and taking her wrist in his hand, said, as he examined the slow pulse:

"Was Clara taken violently? How is she?"

"She is delirious, and so much alarmed at her danger that I feel very uneasy about her. Come and see her; perhaps she will know you." She led the way to the bedside; but there was no recognition in the wild, restless eyes, and as she tossed from side to side, her incoherent muttering made Beulah dread lest she should discover to its object the adoring love which filled her pure heart. She told her guardian what had been prescribed. He offered no suggestion as to the treatment, but gave a potion which she informed him was due. As Clara swallowed the draught, she looked at him, and said eagerly:

"Has he come? Did he say he would see me and save me? Did Dr. Hartwell send me this?"

"She raves," said Beulah, hastily.

A shadow fell upon his face, and stooping over the pillow, he answered, very gently:

"Yes, he has come to save you. He is here."

She smiled, and seemed satisfied for a moment, then moaned, and muttered on indistinctly.

"He knows it all? Oh, poor, poor Clara!" thought Beulah, shading her face, to prevent his reading what passed in her mind.

"How long have you been sitting up, Beulah?"

She told him.

"It is no wonder you look as if years had suddenly passed over your head! You have a room here, I believe. Go to it, and go to sleep; I will not leave Clara."

It was astonishing how his presence removed the dread weight of responsibility from her heart. Not until this moment had she felt as if she could possibly sleep.

"I will sleep now, so as to be refreshed for to-morrow and to-morrow night. Here is a couch; I will sleep here, and if Clara grows worse you must wake me." She crossed the room, threw herself on the couch, and laid her aching head on her arm. Dr. Hartwell placed a pillow under her head; once more his fingers sought her wrist; once more his lips touched her forehead, and as he returned to watch beside Clara, and listen to her ravings, Beulah sank into a heavy, dreamless sleep of exhaustion.

CHAPTER XVIII.

She was awakened by the cool pattering of raindrops, which beat through the shutters and fell upon her face. She sprang up with a thrill of delight, and looked out. A leaden sky lowered over the city, and as the torrents came down in whitening sheets the thunder rolled continuously overhead, and trailing wreaths of smoke from the dying fires, drooped like banners over the roofs of the houses. Not the shower which gathered and fell around sea-girt Carmel was more gratefully received.

"Thank God! it rains!" cried Beulah, and turning toward Clara, she saw with pain that the sufferer was all unconscious of the tardy blessing. She kissed the hot, dry brow; but no token of recognition greeted her anxious gaze. The fever was at its height; the delicate features were strangely sharpened and distorted. Save the sound of her labored breathing the room was silent, and sinking on her knees, Beulah prayed earnestly that the gentle sufferer might be spared. As she rose, her guardian entered, and she started at the haggard, wasted, harassed look of the noble face, which she had not observed before. He bent down and coaxed Clara to take a spoonful of medicine, and Beulah asked, earnestly:

"Have you been ill, sir?"

"No."

He did not even glance at her. The affectionate cordiality of the hour of meeting had utterly vanished. He looked as cold, stern, and impenetrable as some half-buried sphinx of the desert.

"Have you seen the others this morning?" said she, making a strong effort to conceal the chagrin this revulsion of feeling occasioned.

"Yes; Mrs. Hoyt will get well."

"Does she know of her child's death?"

"Yes."

"You are not going, surely?" she continued, as he took his hat and glanced at his watch.

"I am needed elsewhere. Only nursing can now avail here. You know very well what is requisite. Either Dr. Asbury or I will be here again to-night, to sit up with this gentle girl."

"You neither of you come to sit up with her. I will do that myself. I shall not sleep another moment until I know that she is better."

"Very well." He left the room immediately.

"How he cases his volcanic nature in ice," thought Beulah, sinking into the armchair. "Last night he seemed so kind, so cordial, so much my friend and guardian! To-day there is a mighty barrier, as though he stood on some towering crag, and talked to me across an infinite gulf! Well, well, even an Arctic night passes away; and I can afford to wait till his humor changes."

For many hours the rain fell unceasingly, but towards sunset the pall of clouds was scourged on by a brisk western breeze, and the clear canopy of heaven, no longer fiery as for days past, but cool and blue, bent serenely over the wet earth. The slanting rays of the swiftly sinking sun flashed through dripping boughs, creating myriads of diamond sprays; and over the sparkling waters of the bay sprang a brilliant bow, arching superbly along the eastern horizon, where a bank of clouds still lay. Verily, it seemed a new covenant, that the destroying demon should no longer desolate the beautiful city, and to many an anxious, foreboding heart that glorious rainbow gave back hope and faith. A cool, quiet twilight followed. Beulah knew that hearses still bore the dead to their silent chambers; she could hear the rumbling, the melancholy, solemn sound of the wheels; but firm trust reigned in her heart, and with Clara's hand in hers, she felt an intuitive assurance that the loved one would not yet be summoned from her earthly field of action. The sick in the other part of the house were much better, and though one of the gentlemen boarders had been taken since morning, she lighted the lamp and stole about the room with a calmer, happier spirit than she had known for many days. She fancied that her charge breathed more easily, and the wild stare of the inflamed eyes were concealed under the long lashes which lay on the cheeks. The sufferer slept, and the watcher augured favorably. About nine o'clock she heard steps on the stairs, and soon after Doctors Asbury and Hartwell entered together. There was little to be told, and less to be advised, and while the latter attentively examined the pulse, and looked down at the altered countenance, stamped with the signet of the dread disease the former took Beulah's hand in both his, and said kindly:

"How do you do, my little heroine? By Nebros! you are worth your weight in medical treatises. How are you, little one?"

"Quite well, thank you, sir, and I dare say I am much more able to sit up with the sick than you, who have had no respite whatever. Don't stand up, when you must be so weary; take this easy-chair." Holding his hand firmly, she drew him down to it. There had always been a fatherly tenderness in his manner toward her, when visiting at her guardian's, and she regarded him with reverence and affection. Though often blunt, he never chilled nor repelled her, as his partner so often did, and now she stood beside him, still holding one of his hands. He smoothed back the gray hair from his furrowed brow, and with a twinkle in his blue eye, said:

"How much will you take for your services? I want to engage you to teach my madcap daughters a little quiet bravery and uncomplaining endurance."

"I have none of the Shylock in my composition; only give me a few kind words and I shall be satisfied. Now, once for all, Dr. Asbury, if you treat me to any more bare-faced flattery of this sort, I nurse no more of your patients."

Dr. Hartwell here directed his partner's attention to Clara, and thoroughly provoked at the pertinacity with which he avoided noticing her, she seized the brief opportunity to visit Mrs. Hoyt and little Willie. The mother welcomed her with a silent grasp of the hand and gush of tears. But this was no time for acknowledgments, and Beulah strove by a few encouraging remarks, to cheer the bereaved parent and interest Willie, who, like all other children under such circumstances, had grown fretful. She shook up their pillows, iced a fresh pitcher of water for them, and promising to run down and see them often, now that Hal was forced to give his attention to the last victim, she noiselessly stole back to Clara's room. Dr. Hartwell was walking up and down the floor, and his companion sat just as she had left him. He rose as she entered, and putting on his hat, said kindly:

"Are you able to sit up with Miss Sanders to-night? If not say so candidly."

"I am able, and determined to do so."

"Very well. After to-morrow it will not be needed."

"What do you mean?" cried Beulah, clutching his arm.

"Don't look so savage, child. She will either be convalescent, or beyond all aid. I hope and believe the former. Watch her closely till I see you again. Good night, dear child." He stepped to the door; and with a slight inclination of his head, Dr. Hartwell followed him.

It was a vigil Beulah never forgot. The night seemed interminable, as if the car of time were driven backward, and she longed inexpressibly for the dawning of day. Four o'clock came at last; silence brooded over the town; the western breeze had sung itself to rest, and there was a solemn hush, as though all nature stood still, to witness the struggle between dusky Azrael and a human soul. Clara slept. The distant stars looked down encouragingly from their homes of blue, and once more the lonely orphan bent her knee in supplication before the throne of Jehovah. But a cloud seemed hovering between her heart and the presence-chamber of Deity. In vain she prayed, and tried to believe that life would be spared in answer to her petitions. Faith died in her soul, and she sat with her eyes riveted upon the face of her friend. The flush of consuming fever paled, the pulse was slow and feeble, and by the gray light of day, Beulah saw that the face was strangely changed. For several hours longer she maintained her watch; still the doctor did not come, and while she sat with Clara's fingers clasped in hers, the brown eyes opened, and looked dreamily at her. She leaned over, and kissing the wan cheek, asked, eagerly:

"How do you feel, darling?"

"Perfectly weak and helpless. How long have I been sick?"

"Only a few days. You are a great deal better now." She tenderly smoothed the silky hair that clustered in disorder round the face. Clara seemed perplexed; she thought for a moment, and said, feebly:

"Have I been very ill?"

"Well—yes. You have been right sick. Had some fever, but it has left you."

Clara mused again. Memory came back slowly, and at length she asked:

"Did they all die?"

"Did who die?"

"All those down-stairs." She shuddered violently.

"Oh, no! Mrs. Hoyt and Willie are almost well. Try to go to sleep again, Clara."

Several minutes glided by; the eyes closed, and clasping Beulah's fingers lightly, she asked again:

"Have I had any physician?"

"Yes. I thought it would do no harm to have Dr. Asbury see you," answered Beulah, carelessly. She saw an expression of disappointment pass sadly over the girl's countenance; and thinking it might be as well to satisfy her at once, she continued, as if speaking on indifferent topics:

"Dr. Hartwell came home since you were taken sick, and called to see you two or three times."

A faint glow tinged the sallow cheek, and while a tremor crept over her lips, she said, almost inaudibly:

"When will he come again?"

"Before long, I dare say. Indeed, there is his step now. Dr. Asbury is with him."

She had not time to say more, for they came in immediately, and with a species of pity she noted the smile of pleasure which curved Clara's mouth, as her guardian bent down and spoke to her. While he took her thin hand, and fixed his eyes on her face, Dr. Asbury looked over his shoulder, and said bluntly:

"Hurrah for you! All right again, as I thought you would be! Does your head ache at all this morning? Feel like eating half-a-dozen partridges?"

"She is not deaf," said Dr. Hartwell, rather shortly.

"I am not so sure of that; she has been to all my questions lately. I must see about Carter, below. Beulah, child, you look the worse for your apprenticeship to our profession."

"So do you, sir," said she, smiling, as her eyes wandered over his grim visage.

"You may well say that, child. I snatched about two hours' sleep this morning, and when I woke I felt very much like Coleridge's unlucky sailor:

"'I moved, and could not feel my limbs;
"'I was so light—almost,
I thought that I had died in sleep,
And was a blessed ghost.'"

He hurried away to another part of the house, and Beulah went into her own apartment to arrange her hair, which she felt must need attention sadly.

Looking into the glass, she could not forbear smiling at the face which looked back at her, it was so thin and ghastly; even the lips were colorless, and the large eyes sunken. She unbound her hair, and had only shaken it fully out, when a knock at her door called her from the glass. She tossed her hair all back, and it hung like an inky veil almost to the floor, as she opened the door and confronted her guardian.

"Here is some medicine, which must be mixed in a tumbler of water. I want a tablespoonful given every hour, unless Clara is alseep. Keep everything quiet."

"Is that all?" said Beulah, coolly.

"That is all." He walked off, and she brushed and twisted up her hair, wondering how long he meant to keep up that freezing manner. It accorded very well with his treatment before his departure for the North, and she sighed as she recalled the brief hour of cordiality which followed his return. She began to perceive that this was the way they were to meet in future; she had displeased him, and he intended that she should feel it. Tears gathered in her eyes, but she drove them scornfully back, and exclaimed indignantly:

"He wants to rule me with a rod of iron, because I am indebted to him for an education and support for several years. As I hope for a peaceful rest hereafter, I will repay him every cent he has expended for music, drawing and clothing! I will economize until every picayune is returned."

The purse had not been touched, and hastily counting the contents, to see that all the bills were there, she relocked the drawer, and returned to the sick-room with anything but a calm face. Clara seemed to be asleep, and picking up a book, Beulah began to read. A sick-room is always monotonous and dreary, and long confinement had rendered Beulah restless and uncomfortable. Her limbs ached—so did her head, and continued loss of sleep made her nervous to an unusual degree. She longed to open her melodeon and play; this would have quieted her, but of course was not to be thought of, with four invalids in the house, and death on almost every square in the city. She was no longer unhappy about Clara, for there was little doubt that, with care, she would soon be well, and thus drearily the hours wore on. Finally, Clara evinced a disposition to talk. Her nurse discouraged it, with exceedingly brief replies; intimating that she would improve her condition by going to sleep. Toward evening, Clara seemed much refreshed by a long nap, and took some food which had been prepared for her.

"The sickness is abating, is it not, Beulah?"

"Yes, very perceptibly; but more from lack of fresh victims than anything else. I hope we shall have a white frost soon."

"It has been very horrible! I shudder when I think of it," said Clara.

"Then don't think of it," answered her companion.

"Oh! how can I help it? I did not expect to live through it. I was sure I should die when that chill came on. You have saved me, dear Beulah!" Tears glistened in her soft eyes.

"No; God saved you."

"Through your instrumentality," replied Clara, raising her friend's hand to her lips.

"Don't talk any more; the doctor expressly enjoined quiet for you."

"I am glad to owe my recovery to him also. How noble and good he is—how superior to everybody else!" murmured the sick girl.

Beulah's lips became singularly compact, but she offered no comment. She walked up and down the room, although so worn out that she could scarcely keep herself erect. When the doctor came, she escaped unobserved to her room, hastily put on her bonnet, and ran down the steps for a short walk. It was perfect Elysium to get out once more under the pure sky and breathe the air, as it swept over the bay, cool, sweet and invigorating. The streets were still quiet, but hearses and carts, filled with coffins, no longer greeted her on every side, and she walked for several squares. The sun went down, and too weary to extend her ramble, she slowly retraced her steps. The buggy no longer stood at the door, and after seeing Mrs. Hoyt and trying to chat pleasantly, she crept back to Clara.

"Where have you been?" asked the latter.

"To get a breath of fresh air, and see the sun set."

"Dr. Hartwell asked for you. I did not know what had become of you."

"How do you feel to-night?" said Beulah, laying her hand softly on Clara's forehead.

"Better, but very weak. You have no idea how feeble I am. Beulah, I want to know whether—"

"You were told to keep quiet, so don't ask any questions, for I will not answer one."

"You are not to sit up to-night: the doctor said I would not require it."

"Let the doctor go back to the North, and theorize in his medical conventions! I shall sleep here by your bed, on this couch. If you feel worse, call me. Now, good-night; and don't open your lips again." She drew the couch close to the bed, and shading the lamp, threw her weary frame down to rest; ere long, she slept. The pestilential storm had spent its fury. Daily the number of deaths diminished; gradually the pall of silence and desolation which had hung over the city vanished. The streets resumed their usual busy aspect, and the hum of life went forward once more. At length, fugitive families ventured home again; and though bands of crape, grim badges of bereavement, met the eye on all sides, all rejoiced that Death had removed his court; that his hideous carnival was over. Clara regained her strength very slowly;

and when well enough to quit her room, walked with the slow, uncertain step of feebleness. On the last day of October, she entered Beulah's apartment, and languidly approached the table, where the latter was engaged in drawing.

"Always at work! Beulah, you give yourself no rest. Day and night, you are constantly busy."

Apparently, this remark fell on deaf ears; for, without replying, Beulah lifted her drawing, looked at it intently, turned it round once or twice, and then resumed her crayon.

"What a hideous countenance! Who is it?" continued Clara.

"Mors."

"She is horrible! Where did you ever see anything like it?"

"During the height of the epidemic, I fell asleep for a few seconds, and dreamed that Mors was sweeping down, with extended arms, to snatch you. By the clock, I had not slept quite two minutes, yet the countenance of Mors was indelibly stamped on my memory, and now I am transferring it to paper. You are mistaken; it is terrible, but not hideous!" Beulah laid aside her pencil, and leaning her elbows on the table, sat, with her face in her hands, gazing upon the drawing. It represented the head and shoulders of a winged female; the countenance was inflexible, grim, and cadaverous. The large, lurid eyes, had an owlish stare; and the outspread pinions, black as night, made the wan face yet more livid by contrast. The extended hands were like those of a skeleton.

"What strange fancies you have. It makes the blood curdle in my veins, to look at that awful countenance," said Clara, shudderingly.

"I cannot draw it as I saw it in my dream! Cannot do justice to my ideal Mors!" answered Beulah, in a discontented tone, as she took up the crayon, and retouched the poppies which clustered in the sable locks.

"For heaven's sake, do not attempt to render it any more horrible! Put it away, and finish this lovely Greek face. Oh, how I envy you your talent for music and drawing! Nature gifted you rarely!"

"No! she merely gave me an intense love of beauty, which constantly impels me to embody, in melody or coloring, the glorious images, which the contemplation of beauty creates in my soul. Alas! I am not a genius. If I were, I might hope to achieve an immortal renown. Gladly would I pay its painful and dangerous price!" She placed the drawing of Mors in her portfolio, and began to touch lightly an unfinished head of Sappho.

"Ah, Clara! how connoisseurs would carp at this portrait of the 'Lesbian Muse.' My guardian, for one, would sneer superbly."

"Why, pray? It is perfectly beautiful."

"Because, forsooth, it is no low-browed, swarthy Greek. I have a penchant for high, broad, expansive foreheads, which are antagonistic to all the ancient models of beauty. Low foreheads characterize the antique; but who can fancy 'violet-crowned, immortal Sappho.

—'With that gloriole
Of ebon hair, on calmed brows,'

other than I have drawn her!" She held up the paper, and smiled triumphantly.

In truth, it was a face of rare loveliness; of oval outline, with delicate, yet noble features, whose expression seemed the reflex of the divine afflatus. The uplifted eyes beamed with the radiance of inspiration; the full, ripe lips, were just parted; the curling hair clustered, with childlike simplicity, round the classic head; and the exquisitely formed hands clasped a lyre.

"Beulah, don't you think the eyes are most too wild?" suggested Clara, timidly.

"What? for a poetess? Remember poesy hath madness in it," answered Beulah, still looking earnestly at her drawing.

"Madness? What do you mean?"

"Just what I say. I believe poetry to be the highest and purest phase of insanity. Those finely-strung, curiously nervous natures, that you always find coupled with poetic endowments, are characterized by a remarkable activity of the mental organs; and this continued excitement, and premature development of the brain, results in a disease which, under this aspect, the world offers premiums for. Though I enjoy a fine poem as much as anybody, I believe, in nine cases out of ten, it is the spasmodic vent of a highly nervous system, overstrained, diseased. Yes, diseased! If it does not result in the frantic madness of Lamb, or the final imbecility of Southey, it is manifested in various other forms, such as the morbid melancholy of Cowper, the bitter misanthropy of Pope, the abnormal moodiness and misery of Byron, the unsound and dangerous theories of Shelley, and the strange, fragmentary nature of Coleridge."

"Oh, Beulah! what a humiliating theory! The poet placed on an ignominious level with the nervous hypochondriac! You are the very last person I should suppose guilty of entertaining such a degraded estimate of human powers," interposed Clara, energetically.

"I know it is customary to rave about Muses, and Parnassus, and Helicon, and to throw the charitable mantle of 'poetic idiosyncrasies' over all those dark spots on poetic disks. All conceivable and inconceivable eccentricities are pardoned, as the usual concomitants of genius; but looking into the home lives of many of the most distinguished poets, I have been painfully impressed with the truth of my very unpoetic theory. Common sense has arraigned before her august tribunal some of the so-called 'geniuses' of past ages, and the critical verdict is, that much of the famous 'fine frenzy,' was *bona fide* frenzy of a sadder nature."

"Do you think that Sappho's frenzy was established by the Leucadian leap?"

"You confound the poetess with a Sappho, who lived later, and threw herself into the sea from the promontory of Leucate. Doubtless she too had 'poetic idiosyncrasies;' but her spotless life, and I believe natural death, afford no indication of an unsound intellect. It is rather immaterial, however, to—" Beulah paused abruptly, as a servant entered and approached the table, saying:

"Miss Clara, Dr. Hartwell is in the parlor, and wishes to see you."

"To see me!" repeated Clara, in surprise, while a rosy tinge stole into her wan face; "to see me? No! It must be you, Beulah."

"He said Miss Sanders," persisted the servant, and Clara left the room.

Beulah looked after her, with an expression of some surprise; then continued penciling the chords of Sappho's lyre. A few minutes elapsed, and Clara returned with flushed cheeks, and a smile of trembling joyousness.

"Beulah, do pin my mantle on straight. I am in such a hurry. Only think how kind Dr. Hartwell is; he has come to take me out to ride; says I look too pale, and he thinks a ride will benefit me. That will do, thank you."

She turned away, but Beulah rose, and called out:

"Come back here, and get my velvet mantle. It is quite cool, and it will be a marvelous piece of management to ride out for your health, and come home with a cold. What! no gloves either! Upon my word, your thoughts must be traveling over the bridge Shinevad."

"Sure enough; I had forgotten my gloves; I will get them as I go down. Good-by." With the mantle on her arm, she hurried away.

Beulah laid aside her drawing materials, and prepared for her customary evening walk. Her countenance was clouded, her lip unsteady. Her guardian's studied coldness and avoidance pained her, but it was not this which saddened her now. She felt that Clara was staking the happiness of her life on the dim hope that her attachment would be returned. She pitied the delusion, and dreaded the awakening to a true insight into his nature; to a consciousness of the utter uncongeniality which, she fancied, barred all thought of such a union. As she walked on, these reflections gave place to others entirely removed from Clara and her guardian; and on reaching the grove of pines, opposite the Asylum, where she had so often wandered in days gone by, she paced slowly up and down the "arched aisles," as she was wont to term them. It was a genuine October afternoon, cool and sunny. The delicious haze of Indian summer wrapped every distant object in its soft, purple veil; the dim vistas of the forest ended in misty depths; the very air, in its dreamy languor, resembled the atmosphere which surrounded

"The mild-eyed, melancholy lotus-eaters"

of the far East. Through the openings, pale, golden poplars shook down their dying leaves and here and there along the ravine, crimson maples gleamed against the background of dark green pines. In every direction, bright-colored leaves, painted with "autumnal hectic," strewed the bier of the declining year. Beulah sat down on a tuft of moss, and gathered clusters of golden-rod and purple and white asters. She loved these wild wood-flowers much more than gaudy exotics or rare hot-house plants. They linked her with the days of her childhood, and now each graceful spray of goldenrod seemed a wand of memory calling up bygone joys, griefs and fancies. Ah, what a hallowing glory invests our past, beckoning us back to the hunts of the olden time! The paths our childish feet trod seem all angel-guarded and thornless; the songs we sang then sweep the harp of memory, making magical melody: the words carelessly spoken, now breathe a solemn, mysterious import; and faces that early went down to the tomb, smile on us still with unchanged tenderness. Aye, the past, the long past is all fairy-land. Where our little feet were bruised, we now see only springing flowers; where childish lips drank from some Marah, verdure and garlands woo us back. Over the rustling leaves a tiny form glided to Beulah's side; a pure infantine face with golden curls looked up at her, and a lisping voice of unearthly sweetness whispered in the autumn air. Here she had often brought Lilly, and filled her baby fingers with asters and golden-rod; and gathered bright scarlet leaves to please her childish fancy. Bitter waves had broken over her head since then; shadows had gathered about her heart. Oh, how far off were the early years! How changed she was; how different life and the world seemed to her now! The flowery meadows were behind her, with the vestibule of girlhood, and now she was a woman, with no ties to link her with any human being; alone, and dependent only on herself. Verily, she might have exclaimed in the mournful words of Lamb:

"All, all are gone, the old familiar faces."

She sat looking at the wild-flowers in her hand; a sad, dreamy light filled the clear gray eyes, and now and then her brow was plowed by some troubled thought. The countenance told of a mind perplexed and questioning. The "cloud no bigger than a man's hand," had crept up from the horizon of faith, and now darkened her sky; but she would not see the gathering gloom; shut her eyes resolutely to the coming storm. As the cool October wind stirred the leaves at her feet, and the scarlet and gold cloud-flakes faded in the west, she rose and walked slowly homeward. She was too deeply pondering her speculative doubts to notice Dr. Hartwell's buggy whirling along the street; did not see his head extended, and his cold, searching glance; and of course he believed the blindness intentional, and credited it to pique or anger. On reaching home, she endeavored by singing a favorite hymn to divert the current of her thoughts, but the shadows were growing tenacious, and would not be banished so easily. "If a man die shall he live again?" seemed echoing on the autumn wind. She took up her Bible and read several chapters, which she fancied would uncloud her mind; but in vain. Restlessly she began to pace the floor; the lamplight gleamed on a pale, troubled face. After a time the door opened, and Clara came in. She took a seat without speaking, for she had learned to read Beulah's countenance, and saw at a glance that she was abstracted and in no mood for conversation. When the tea-bell rang, Beulah stopped suddenly in the middle of the room.

"What is the matter?" asked Clara.

"I feel as if I needed a cup of coffee, that is all. Will you join me?"

"No; and if you take it you will not be able to close your eyes."

"Did you have a pleasant ride?" said Beulah, laying her hand on her companion's shoulder, and looking gravely down into the sweet face, which wore an expression she had never seen there before.

"Oh, I shall never forget it! never!" murmured Clara.

"I am glad you enjoyed it; very glad. I wish the color would come back to your cheeks. Riding is better for you now than walking." She stooped down and pressed her lips to the warm cheek as she spoke.

"Did you walk this evening, after I left you?"

"Yes."

"What makes you look so grave?"

"A great many causes—you among the number."

"What have I done?"

"You are not so strong as I should like to see you. You have a sort of spiritual look that I don't at all fancy."

"I dare say I shall soon be well again." This was said with an effort, and a sigh quickly followed.

Beulah rang the bell for a cup of coffee, and taking down a book, drew her chair near the lamp.

"What! studying already?" cried Clara, impatiently.

"And why not? Life is short at best, and rarely allows time to master all departments of knowledge. Why should I not seize every spare moment?"

"Oh, Beulah! though you are so much younger, you awe me. I told your guardian to-day that you were studying yourself into a mere shadow. He smiled, and said you were too wilful to be advised. You talk to me about not looking well! You never have had any color, and lately you have grown very thin and hollow-eyed. I asked the doctor if he did not think you were looking ill, and he said that you had changed very much since the summer. Beulah, for my sake, please don't pore over your books so incessantly." She took Beulah's hand, gently, in both hers.

"Want of color is as constitutional with me as the shape of my nose. I have always been pale, and study has no connection with it. Make yourself perfectly easy on my account."

"You are very wilful, as your guardian says," cried Clara, impatiently.

"Yes, that is like my sallow complexion—constitutional," answered Beulah, laughing, and opening a volume of Carlyle as she spoke.

"Oh, Beulah, I don't know what will become of you!" Tears sprang into Clara's eyes.

"Do not be at all uneasy, my dear, dove-eyed Clara. I can take care of myself."

CHAPTER XIX.

It was the middle of November, and absentees, who had spent their summer at the North, were all at home again. Among these were Mrs. Asbury and her two daughters; and only a few days after their return, they called to see Beulah. She found them polished, cultivated, and agreeable; and when, at parting, the mother kindly pressed her hand, and cordially invited her to visit them often and sociably, she felt irresistibly drawn toward her, and promised to do so. Ere long, there came a friendly note, requesting her to spend the evening with them; and thus, before she had known them many weeks, Beulah found herself established on the familiar footing of an old friend. Universally esteemed and respected, Dr. Asbury's society was sought by the most refined circle of the city, and his house was a favorite resort for the intellectual men and women of the community. Occupying an enviable position in his profession, he still found leisure to devote much of his attention to strictly literary topics, and the honest frankness and cordiality of his manners, blended with the instructive tone of his conversation, rendered him a general favorite. Mrs. Asbury merited the elevated position which she so ably filled, as the wife of such a man. While due attention was given to the education and rearing of her daughters, she admirably discharged the claims of society, and by a consistent adherence to the principles of the religion she professed, checked by every means within her power the frivolous excesses and dangerous extremes which prevailed throughout the fashionable circles in which she moved. Zealously, yet unostentatiously, she exerted herself in behalf of the various charitable institutions, organized to ameliorate the sufferings of the poor in their midst; and while, as a Christian, she conformed to the outward observances of her church, she faithfully inculcated and practised at home the pure precepts of a religion whose effects should be the proper regulation of the heart, and charity toward the world. Her parlors were not the favorite rendezvous where gossips met to retail slander. Refined, dignified, gentle, and hospitable, she was a woman too rarely, alas! met with, in so-called fashionable circles. Her husband's reputation secured them the acquaintance of all distinguished strangers, and made their house a great center of attraction. Beulah fully enjoyed and appreciated the friendship thus tendered her, and soon looked upon Dr. Asbury and his noble wife as counselors, to whom in any emergency she could unhesitatingly apply. They based their position in society on their own worth; not the extrinsic appendages of wealth and fashion, and readily acknowledged the claims of all who (however humble their abode or avocation) proved themselves worthy of respect and esteem. In their intercourse with the young teacher, there was an utter absence of that contemptible supercilious condescension which always characterizes an ignorant and *parvenu* aristocracy. They treated her as an equal in intrinsic worth, and prized her as a friend. Helen Asbury was older than Beulah, and Georgia somewhat younger. They were sweet-tempered, gay girls, lacking their parent's intellectual traits, but sufficiently well-informed and cultivated to constitute them agreeable companions. Of their father's extensive library, they expressed themselves rather afraid, and frequently bantered Beulah about the grave books she often selected from it. Beulah found her school duties far less irksome than she had expected, for she loved children, and soon became interested in the individual members of her classes. From eight o'clock until three she was closely occupied; then the labors of the day were over, and she spent her evenings much as she had been wont, ere the opening of the session. Thus, November glided quickly away, and the first of December greeted her, ere she dreamed of its approach. The Grahams had not returned, though daily expected; and notwithstanding two months had elapsed without Eugene's writing, she looked forward with intense pleasure to his expected arrival. There was one source of constant pain for her in Dr. Hartwell's continued and complete estrangement. Except a cold, formal bow, in passing, there was no intercourse whatever; and she sorrowed bitterly over this seeming indifference in one to whom she owed so much and was so warmly attached. Remotely connected with this cause of disquiet, was the painful change in Clara. Like a lily suddenly transplanted to some arid spot, she had seemed to droop, since the week of her ride. Gentle, but hopeless and depressed, she went, day after day, to her duties at Madam St. Cymon's school, and returned at night wearied, silent and wan.

Her step grew more feeble, her face thinner, and paler. Often Beulah gave up her music and books, and devoted the evenings to entertaining and interesting her; but there was a constraint and reserve about her which could not be removed.

One evening, on returning from a walk with Helen Asbury, Beulah ran into her friend's room with a cluster of flowers. Clara sat by the fire, with a piece of needle-work in her hand; she looked listless and sad. Beulah threw the bright golden and crimson chrysanthemums in her lap, and stooping down, kissed her warmly, saying:

"How is your troublesome head? Here is a flowery cure for you."

"My head does not ache quite so badly. Where did you find these beautiful chrysanthemums?" answered Clara, languidly.

"I stopped to get a piece of music from Georgia, and Helen cut them for me. Oh, what blessed things flowers are! They have been well styled, 'God's undertones of encouragement to the children of earth.'"

She was standing on the hearth, warming her fingers. Clara looked up at the dark, clear eyes and delicate fixed lips before her, and sighed involuntarily. Beulah knelt on the carpet, and throwing one arm around her companion, said, earnestly:

"My dear Clara, what saddens you to-night? Can't you tell me?"

A hasty knock at the door gave no time for an answer. A servant looked in.

"Is Miss Beulah Benton here? There is a gentleman in the parlor to see her; here is the card."

Beulah still knelt on the floor, and held out her hand indifferently. The card was given, and she sprang up with a cry of joy.

"Oh, it is Eugene!"

At the door of the parlor she paused, and pressed her hand tightly to her bounding heart. A tall form stood before the grate, and a glance discovered to her a dark moustache and heavy beard; still it must be Eugene, and extending her arms unconsciously, she exclaimed:

"Eugene! Eugene! have you come at last?"

He started, looked up, and hastened toward her. Her arms suddenly dropped to her side, and only their hands met in a firm, tight clasp. For a moment, they gazed at each other in silence, each noting the changes which time had wrought. Then he said, slowly:

"I should not have known you, Beulah. You have altered surprisingly." His eyes wandered wonderingly over her features. She was pale and breathless; her lips trembled violently, and there was a strange gleam in her large, eager eyes. She did not reply, but stood looking up intently into his handsome face. Then she shivered; the long, black lashes drooped; her white fingers relaxed their clasp of his, and she sat down on the sofa near. Ah! her womanly intuitions, infallible as Ithuriel's spear, told her that he was no longer the Eugene she had loved so devotedly. An iron hand seemed to clutch her heart, and again a shudder crept over her, as he seated himself beside her, saying:

"I am very much pained to find you here. I am just from Dr. Hartwell's, where I expected to see you."

He paused, for something about her face rather disconcerted him, and he took her hand again in his.

"How could you expect to find me there, after reading my last letter?"

"I still hoped that your good sense would prevent your taking such an extraordinary step."

She smiled, icily, and answered:

"Is it so extraordinary, then, that I should desire to maintain my self-respect?"

"It would not have been compromised by remaining where you were."

"I should scorn myself were I willing to live idly on the bounty of one upon whom I have no claim."

"You are morbidly fastidious, Beulah."

Her eyes flashed, and snatching her hand from his, she asked with curling lips: "Eugene, if I prefer to teach for a support, why should you object?"

"Simply because you are unnecessarily lowering yourself in the estimation of the community. You will find that the circle, which a residence under Dr. Hartwell's roof gave you the *entrée* of, will look down with contempt upon a subordinate teacher in a public school—"

"Then, thank Heaven, I am forever shut out from that circle! Is my merit to be gauged by the cost of my clothes, or the number of fashionable parties I attend, think you?"

"Assuredly, Beulah, the things you value so lightly are the standards of worth and gentility in the community you live in, as you will unfortunately find."

She looked at him steadily, with grief, and scorn, and wonder in her deep, searching eyes, as she exclaimed:

"Oh, Eugene! what has changed you so, since the bygone years, when, in the Asylum, we talked of the future? of laboring, conquering, and earning homes for ourselves! Oh, has the foul atmosphere of foreign lands extinguished *all* your self-respect? Do you come back sordid and sycophantic, and the slave of opinions you would once have utterly detested? Have you narrowed your soul, and bowed down before the miserable standard which every genuine, manly spirit must loathe? Oh! has it come to this? Has it come to this?" Her voice was broken, and bitter, scalding tears of shame and grief gushed over her cheeks.

"This fierce recrimination and unmerited tirade is not exactly the welcome I was prepared to expect," returned Eugene, haughtily; and rising he took his hat from the table. She rose also, but made no effort to detain him, and leaned her head against the mantelpiece. He watched her a moment, then approached, and put his hand on her shoulder:

"Beulah, as a man, I see the world and its relations in a far different light from that in which I viewed it while a boy."

"It is utterly superfluous to tell me so!" replied Beulah, bitterly.

"I grapple with realities now, and am forced to admit the expediency of prudent policy. You refuse to see things in their actual existence, and prefer toying with romantic dreams. Beulah, I have awakened from these since we parted."

She put up her hand deprecatingly, and answered:

"Then let me dream on! let me dream on!"

"Beulah, I have been sadly mistaken in my estimate of your character. I could not have believed there was so much fierce obstinacy, so much stubborn pride, in your nature."

She instantly lifted her head, and their eyes met. Other days came back to both; early confidence, mutual love and dependence. For a moment his nobler impulses prevailed, and with an unsteady lip, he passed his arm quickly around her. But she drew coldly back and said:

"It seems we are mutually disappointed in each other. I regret that the discharge of my duty should so far conflict with your opinions and standard of propriety, as to alienate us so completely as it seems likely to do. All my life I have looked to you for guidance and counsel; but to-night you have shaken my trust, and henceforth I must depend upon my own heart to support me in my work. Oh, Eugene! friend of my childhood! beware, lest you sink yourself in your own estimation! Oh, for days, and months, and years, I have pictured the hour of your return, little dreaming that it would prove one of the saddest of my life! I have always looked up to you. Oh, Eugene!

Eugene! you are not what you were! Do not! oh, do not make me pity you! That would kill me!" She covered her face with her hands, and shuddered convulsively.

"I am not so changed as you think me," returned Eugene, proudly.

"Then, in early years, I was miserably deceived in your character. For the sake of wealth, and what the world calls 'position,' you have sold yourself. In lieu of his gold and influence, Mr. Graham has your will, your conscience. Ah, Eugene! how can you bear to be a mere tool in his hands?"

"Beulah, your language, your insinuations are unpardonable! By Heaven, no one but yourself might utter them, and not even you can do so with impunity! If you choose to suffer your foolish pride and childish whims to debar you from the enviable position in society, which Dr. Hartwell would gladly confer on you, why you have only yourself to censure. But my situation in Mr. Graham's family has long been established. He has ever regarded me as his son, treated me as such, and as such I feel bound to be guided by him in my choice of a profession. Beulah, I have loved you well, but such another exhibition of scorn and bitterness will indeed alienate us. Since you have set aside my views and counsel, in the matter of teaching, I shall not again refer to it, I promise you. I have no longer the wish to control your actions, even had I the power. But remember, since the hour you stood beside your father's grave, leaning on me, I have been constantly your friend. My expostulations were for what I considered your good. Beulah, I am still, to you, the Eugene of other days. It will be your own fault if the sanctity of our friendship is not maintained."

"It shall not be my fault, Eugene." She hastily held out her hand. He clasped it in his, and, as if dismissing the topics which had proved so stormy, drew her to a seat, and said, composedly:

"Come, tell me what you have been doing with yourself these long five years, which have changed you so. I have heard already of your heroism in nursing the sick, during the late awful season of pestilence and death."

For an hour they talked on indifferent themes, each feeling that the other was veiling the true impulses of the heart, and finally Eugene rose to go.

"How is Cornelia's health now?" asked Beulah, as they stood up before the fire.

"About the same. She never complains, but does not look like herself. Apropos! she intrusted a note to me, for you, which I had quite forgotten. Here it is. Miss Dupres is with her for the winter; at least a part of it.

Cornelia will come and see you in a day or two, she requested me to say; and I do hope, Beulah, that you will visit her often; she has taken a great fancy to you."

"How long since?" answered Beulah, with an incredulous smile.

"Since she met you at a concert, I believe. By the way, we are very musical at our house, and promise ourselves some delightful evenings this winter. You must hear Antoinette Dupres sing; she is equal to the best prima-donna of Italy. Do you practise much?"

"Yes."

"Well, I must go. When shall I see you again?"

"Whenever you feel disposed to come; and I hope that will be often. Eugene, you were a poor correspondent; see that you prove a better visitor."

"Yes, I will. I have a thousand things to say, but scarcely know where to commence. You are always at home in the evenings, I suppose?"

"Yes, except occasionally when I am with the Asburys."

"Do you see much of them?"

"Yes, a good deal."

"I am glad to hear it; they move in the very first circle. Now, Beulah, don't be offended if I ask what is the matter with Dr. Hartwell? How did you displease him?"

"Just as I displeased you; by deciding to teach. Eugene, it pains me very much that he should treat me as he does, but it is utterly out of my power to rectify the evil."

"He told me that he knew nothing of your movements or plans. I wish, for your sake, you could be reconciled."

"We will be some day. I must wait patiently," said she, with a sigh.

"Beulah, I don't like that troubled look about your mouth. What is the matter? Can I in any way remove it? Is it connected with me, even remotely? My dear Beulah, do not shrink from me."

"Nothing is the matter that you can rectify," said she, gravely.

"Something is the matter, then, which I may not know?"

"Yes."

"And you will not trust me?"

"It is not a question of trust, Eugene."

"You think I cannot help you?"

"You cannot help me, I am sure."

"Well, I will see you again to-morrow; till then good-by." They shook hands, and she went back to her own room. Cornelia's note contained an invitation to spend the next evening with them; she would call as soon as possible. She put it aside, and throwing her arms on the mantelpiece, bowed her head upon them. This, then, was the hour which, for five years, she had anticipated as an occasion of unmixed delight. She was not weeping; no, the eyes were dry, and the lips firmly fixed. She was thinking of the handsome face which a little while before was beside her; thinking, with keen agony, of footprints there, which she had never dreamed of seeing; they were very slight, yet unmistakable—the fell signet of dissipation. Above all, she read it in the eyes, which once looked so fearlessly into hers. She knew he did not imagine, for an instant, that she suspected it; and of all the bitter cups which eighteen years had proffered, this was by far the blackest. It was like a hideous dream, and she groaned, and passed her hand over her brow, as if to sweep it all away. Poor Beulah! the idol of her girlhood fell from its pedestal, and lay in crumbling ruins at her feet. In this hour of reunion, she saw clearly into her own heart; she did not love him, save as a friend, as a brother. She was forced to perceive her own superiority; could she love a man whom she did not revere? Verily, she felt now that she did not love Eugene. There was a feeling of contempt for his weakness, yet she could not bear to see him other than she had hoped. How utterly he had disappointed her? Could it be possible that he had fallen so low as to dissipate habitually? This she would not believe; he was still too noble for such a disgraceful course. She felt a soft touch on her shoulder, and raised her sad, tearless face. Clara, with her ethereal, spiritual countenance, stood on the hearth: "Do I disturb you?" said she, timidly.

"No; I am glad you came. I was listening to cold, bitter, bitter thoughts. Sit down, Clara; you look fatigued."

"Oh, Beulah! I am weary in body and spirit; I have no energy; my very existence is a burden to me."

"Clara, it is weak to talk so. Rouse yourself, and fulfill the destiny for which you were created."

"I have no destiny, but that of loneliness and misery."

"Our situations are similar, yet I never repine as you do."

"You have not the same cause. You are self-reliant; need no society to conduce to your happiness; your heart is bound up in your books."

"Where yours had better have been," answered Beulah. She walked across the floor several times, then said impressively, as she threw her arm round Clara's waist:

"Crush it; crush it; if you crush your heart in the effort."

A moan escaped Clara's lips, and she hid her face against her friend's shoulder.

"I have known it since the night of your grandfather's death. If you want to be happy and useful, crush it out of your heart."

"I have tried, and cannot."

"Oh! but you can. I tell you there is nothing a woman cannot do, provided she puts on the armor of duty, and unsheathes the sword of a strong, unbending will. Of course, you can do it, if you will."

"Wait till you feel as I do, Beulah, and it will not seem so light a task."

"That will never happen. If I live till the next geological period, I never shall love anybody as insanely as you love. Why, Clara, don't you see that you are wrecking your happiness? What strange infatuation has seized you?"

"I know now that it is perfectly hopeless," said Clara calmly.

"You might have known it from the first."

"No; it is but recently that the barrier has risen."

"What barrier?" asked Beulah, curiously.

"For Heaven's sake, Beulah, do not mock me! You know too well what separates us."

"Yes; utter uncongeniality."

Clara raised her head, looked into the honest face before her, and answered:

"If that were all, I could yet hope to merit his love; but you know that is not so. You know that he has no love to bestow."

Beulah's face seemed instantly steeled. A grayish hue crept over it; and drawing her slender form to its full height, she replied, with haughty coldness:

"What do you mean? I can only conjecture."

"Beulah, you know he loves you!" cried Clara, with a strangely quiet smile.

"Clara Sanders, never say that again as long as you live, for there is not the shadow of truth in it."

"Ah, I would not believe it till it was forced upon me. The heart bars itself a long time to painful truths! I have looked at you, and wondered whether you could be ignorant of what I saw so clearly. I believe you are honest in what you say. I know that you are; but it is nevertheless true. I saw it the evening I went to ride. He loves you, whether you see it or not. And, moreover, the world has begun to join your names. I have heard more than once, that he educated you with the intention of marrying you; and recently it has been rumored that the marriage would take place very soon. Do not be hurt with me, Beulah! I think it is right that you should know all this."

"It is utterly false from beginning to end! He never had such a thought! never! never!" cried Beulah, striking her clenched hand heavily on the table.

"Why, then, was he so anxious to prevent your teaching?"

"Because he is generous and kind, and fancied it was a life of hardship, which I could escape by accepting his offer to adopt me. Your supposition is perfectly ridiculous. He is double my age. A stern, taciturn man; what could possibly attract him to one whom he looks upon as a mere child? And moreover, he is a worshipper of beauty! Now, it is an indisputable fact that I am anything but a beauty! Oh, the idea is absurd beyond all degree. Never mention it to me again. I tell you solemnly, Clara, your jealous fancy has run away with your common sense."

A sad, incredulous smile flitted over Clara's face, but she made no reply.

"Clara, rouse yourself from this weak dream. Oh, where is your pride—your womanly pride—your self-respect? Is your life to be aimless and dreary because of an unrequited attachment? Shake it off! Rise above it! Destroy it! Oh, it makes the blood tingle in my veins to think of your wasting your energies and hopes in love for one who is so utterly indifferent to you. Much as I love you, Clara, had I the power to make you his wife to-morrow, I would rather see you borne to your grave. You know nothing of his fitful, moody nature; his tyrannical will. You could not be happy with him; you would see how utterly unsuited you are."

"Are you acquainted with the circumstances of his early life, and ill-fated marriage?" asked Clara, in a low, passionless tone.

"No; he never alluded to his marriage in any way. Long as I lived in his house there was no mention of his wife's name, and I should never have known of his marriage but from his sister."

"It was a most unhappy marriage," said Clara, musingly.

"So I conjectured from his studious avoidance of all allusion to it."

"His wife was very, very beautiful; I saw her once when I was a child," continued Clara.

"Of course she must have been for he could not love one who was not."

"She lived but a few months; yet even in that short time they had become utterly estranged, and she died of a broken heart. There is some mystery connected with it; they were separated."

"Separated!" cried Beulah, in amazement.

"Yes, separated; she died in New Orleans, I believe."

"And yet you profess to love him! A man who broke his wife's heart," said Beulah, with a touch of scorn.

"No; you do his noble nature injustice. He is incapable of such a course. Even a censorious world acquitted him of unkindness."

"And heaped contumely on the unhappy victim, eh?" rejoined Beulah.

"Her conduct was not irreproachable, it has been whispered."

"Aye, whispered by slanderous tongues! Not openly avowed, to admit of denial and refutation! I wonder the curse of Gomorrah does not descend on this gossiping libellous community."

"No one seems to know anything definite about the affair, though I have often heard it commented upon and wondered over."

"Clara, let it be buried henceforth. Neither you nor I have any right to discuss and censure what neither of us know anything about. Dr. Hartwell has been my best and truest friend. I love and honor him; his faults are his own, and only his Maker has the right to balance his actions. Once for all, let the subject drop." Beulah compressed her lips with an expression which her companion very well understood. Soon after the latter withdrew, and leaning her arms on the table near her, Beulah sank into a reverie which was far from pleasant. Dismissing the unsatisfactory theme of her guardian's idiosyncrasies, her thoughts immediately reverted to Eugene, and the revolution which five years had effected in his character.

In the afternoon of the following day, she was engaged with her drawing, when a succession of quick raps at her door forced an impatient "come in" from her lips. The door opened, and she rose involuntarily as the queenly form of Cornelia Graham stood before her. With a slow, stately tread she approached and extending her hand, said unconcernedly:

"I have waived ceremony, you see, and come up to your room."

"How are you?" said Beulah, as they shook hands, and seated themselves.

"Just as usual. How did you contrive to escape the plague?"

"By resolving not to have it, I believe."

"You have a wan, sickly look, I think."

"So have you, I am sure. I hoped that you would come home strong and well." Beulah noted, with a feeling of compassion, the thin, hollow cheeks, and sunken, yet burning eyes before her. Cornelia bit her lip, and asked haughtily:

"Who told you that I was not well?"

"Your countenance would tell me, if I had never heard it from others," replied Beulah, with an instantaneous recollection of her guardian's warning.

"Did you receive my note yesterday?"

"Yes. I am obliged by your invitation, but cannot accept it."

"So I supposed, and, therefore, came to make sure of you. You are too proud to come until all the family call upon you, eh?"

"No: only people who consider themselves inferior are on the watch for slights, and scrupulously exact the minutest requirements of etiquette. On the plane of equality these barriers melt away."

As Beulah spoke, she looked steadily into the searching, black eyes, which seemed striving to read her soul. An expression of pleasure lighted the sallow face, and the haughty lines about the beautiful mouth melted into a half smile.

"Then you have not forgiven my rudeness during early school-days?"

"I had nothing to forgive. I had forgotten the affair, until you spoke."

"Then, why will you not come?"

"For reasons which would not be removed by a recapitulation."

"And you positively will not come?"

"Not this evening. Another time, I certainly will come, with pleasure."

"Say to-morrow, then."

"To-morrow I shall be engaged."

"Where? Excuse my pertinacity."

"At Dr. Asbury's: I have promised to practise some duets with Helen."

"Do you play well, Beulah? Are you a good musician?"

"Yes."

Cornelia mused a moment, and then said, slowly, as if watching the effect of her question:

"You have seen Eugene, of course?"

"Yes."

"He has changed very much in his appearance, has he not?"

"More than I was prepared to expect."

"He is to be a merchant, like my father."

"So he wrote me."

"You endeavored to dissuade him from complying with my father's wishes, did you not?"

"Yes, most earnestly," answered Beulah, gravely.

"Beulah Benton, I like you! You are honest indeed. At last I find one who is." With a sudden impulse, she laid her white jeweled hand on Beulah's.

"Is honesty, or rather candor, so very rare, Cornelia?"

"Come out from your 'loop-hole of retreat,' into the world, and you can easily answer your own question."

"You seem to have looked on human nature through misanthropic lenses."

"Yes, I bought a pair of spectacles, for which I paid a most exorbitant price; but they were labeled 'experience!'" She smiled frigidly.

"You do not seem to have enjoyed your tour particularly."

"Yes, I did; but one is glad to rest sometimes. I may yet prove a second Bayard Taylor, notwithstanding. I should like you for a companion. You would not sicken me with stereotyped nonsense."

Her delicate fingers folded themselves about Beulah's, who could not bring herself to withdraw her hand.

"And sure enough, you would not be adopted? Do you mean to adhere to your determination, and maintain yourself by teaching?"

"I do."

"And I admire you for it! Beulah, you must get over your dislike to me."

"I do not dislike you, Cornelia."

"Thank you for your negative preference," returned Cornelia, rather amused at her companion's straightforward manner. Then, with a sudden contraction of her brow, she added:

"I am not so bearish as they give me credit for."

"I never heard you called so."

"Ah? that is because you do not enter the enchanted circle of 'our clique.' During morning calls I am flatterd, cajoled, and fawned upon. The carriages are not out of hearing before my friends and admirers, like hungry harpies, pounce upon my character, manners, and appearance, with most laudable zest and activity. Wait till you have been initiated into my coterie of fashionable friends! Why, the battle of Marengo was a farce, in comparison with the havoc they can effect in the space of a morning among the characters of their select visiting list! What a precious age of backbiting we city belles live in." She spoke with an air of intolerable scorn.

"As a prominent member of this circle, why do you not attempt to rectify this spreading evil? You might effect lasting good."

"I am no Hercules, to turn the Peneus of reform through the Augean realms of society," answered Cornelia, with an impatient gesture; and rising, she drew on her glove. Beulah looked up at her, and pitied the joyless, cynical nature, which gave an almost repulsively austere expression to the regular, faultless features.

"Beulah, will you come on Saturday morning, and spend an hour or so with me?"

"No; I have a music lesson to give; but if you will be at home in the afternoon, I will come with pleasure."

"I shall expect you, then. You were drawing when I came in; are you fond of it?" As she spoke she took up a piece which was nearly completed.

"Yes, but you will find my sketches very crude."

"Who taught you to draw?"

"I have had several teachers. All rather indifferent, however."

"Where did you see a St. Cecilia? There is too much breadth of brow here," continued Cornelia, with a curious glance at the young teacher.

"Yes; I deviated from the original intentionally. I copied it from a collection of heads which Georgia Asbury brought from the North."

"I have a number of choice paintings, which I selected in Europe. Any that you may fancy are at your service for models."

"Thank you. I shall be glad to avail myself of the privilege."

"Good-by. You will come Saturday?"

"Yes; if nothing occurs to prevent, I will come in the afternoon." Beulah pressed her offered hand, and saw her descend the steps with a feeling of pity, which she could not exactly analyze. Passing by the window, she glanced down, and paused to look at an elegant carriage standing before the door. The day was cold, but the top was thrown back, and on one of the cushions sat, or rather reclined, a richly dressed, and very beautiful girl. As Beulah leaned out to examine the lovely stranger more closely, Cornelia appeared. The driver opened the low door and as Cornelia stepped in, the young lady, who was Miss Dupres, of course, ejaculated rather peevishly:

"You stayed an age."

"Drive down the Bay-road, Wilson," was Cornelia's reply, and as she folded her rich cloak about her, the carriage was whirled away.

Beulah went back to the fire, warmed her fingers, and resumed her drawing; thinking that she would not willingly change places with the petted child of wealth and luxury.

CHAPTER XX.

It was a dreary Saturday afternoon, but Beulah wrapped a warm shawl about her, and set out to pay the promised visit. The air was damp and raw, and leaden, marbled clouds hung low in the sky. Mr. Graham's house was situated in the fashionable part of the city, near Mr. Grayson's residence, and as Beulah passed the crouching lions, she quickened her steps, to escape the painful reminiscences which they recalled. In answer to her ring, the servant ushered her into the parlors furnished with almost oriental magnificence, and was retiring, when she gave her name.

"You are Miss Benton, then. I have orders to show you up at once to Miss Cornelia's room. She has seen no visitors to-day. This way, miss, if you please."

He led the way, up an easy, spiral flight of steps, to the door of a room, which he threw open. Cornelia was sitting in a large cushioned chair by the fire, with a *papier-mâché* writing-desk beside her, covered with letters. There was a bright fire in the grate, and the ruddy haze, together with the reflection from the crimson damask curtains, gave a dim, luxurious aspect to the chamber, which in every respect betokened the fastidious taste of a petted invalid. Clad in a dark silk *robe-de-chambre,* with her cheek pressed against the blue velvet lining of the chair, Cornelia's face wore a sickly, sallow hue, which was rendered more palpable by her black, glittering eyes and jetty hair. She eagerly held out her hand, and smile of sincere pleasure parted the lips, which a paroxysm of pain seemed to have just compressed.

"It is such a gloomy day, I feared you would not come. Take off your bonnet and shawl."

"It is not so gloomy out as you imagine," said Beulah.

"What? not, with dull clouds, and a stiff, raw, northeaster? I looked out of the window a while since, and this bay looked just as I have seen the North Sea, gray and cold. Why don't you take off your bonnet?"

"Because I can only sit with you a short time," answered Beulah, resisting the attempt made to take her shawl.

"Why, can't you spend the evening?" said Cornelia frowning.

"I promised not to remain more than an hour."

"Promised whom?"

"Clara Sanders. She is sick; unable to leave her room, and is lonely when I am away."

"My case is analogous; so I will put myself on the charity list for once. I have not been down-stairs for two days."

"But you have everything to interest you even here," returned Beulah, glancing around at the numerous paintings and engravings which were suspended on all sides, while ivory, marble, and bronze statuettes were scattered in profusion about the room. Cornelia followed her glance, and asked, with a joyless smile:

"Do you suppose these bits of stone and canvas satisfy me?"

"Certainly. 'A thing of beauty should be a joy forever.' With all these, and your library, surely you are never lonely."

"Pshaw! they tire me immensely. Sometimes, the cramped positions, and unwinking eyes of that 'holy family' there over the chimneypiece, make me perfectly nervous."

"You must be morbidly sensitive at such times."

"Why? do you never feel restless and dissatisfied, without any adequate reason?"

"No, never."

"And yet, you have few sources of pleasure," said Cornelia, in a musing tone, as her eyes wandered over her visitor's plain attire.

"No! my sources of enjoyment are as varied and extended as the universe."

"I should like you to map them. Shut up all day with a parcel of rude stupid children, and released only to be caged again in a small room in a second-rate boarding house. Really, I should fancy they were limited indeed."

"No, I enjoy my brisk walk to school, in the morning; the children are neither so dull, nor so bearish as you seem to imagine. I am attached to many of them, and do not feel the day to be very long. At three, I hurry home, get my dinner, practise, and draw, or sew, till the shadows begin to dim my eyes, then I walk until the lamps are lighted, find numberless things to interest me, even in a winter's walk, and go back to my room, refreshed and eager to get to my books. Once seated with them, what portion of the earth is there that I may not visit, from the crystal Arctic temples of Odin and Thor, to the groves of Abyssina? In this age of travel, and cheap books, I can sit in my room in the third story, and by my lamplight, see all, and immeasurably more, than you, who have been traveling for eighteen months. Wherever I go, I find sources of enjoyment; even the pictures in bookstores give me pleasure, and contribute food for thought; and when, as now, I am surrounded by all that wealth can collect, I admire and enjoy the beauty, and elegance, as much as if I owned it all. So you see, that my enjoyments are as varied as the universe itself."

"Eureka!" murmured Cornelia, eyeing her companion curiously, "Eureka! you shall have the tallest case in the British Museum, or Barnum's, just as your national antipathies may incline you."

"What impresses you as so singular in my mode of life?" asked Beulah, rather dryly.

"Your philosophic contentment, which I believe you are too candid to counterfeit. Your easy solution of that great human riddle, given the world, to find happiness. The Athenian and Alexandrian schools dwindle into nothingness. Commend me to your 'categories,' O, Queen of Philosophy." She withdrew her searching eyes, and fixed them moodily on the fire, twirling the tassel of her robe as she mused.

"You are most egregiously mistaken, Cornelia, if you have been led to suppose, from what I said a moment since, that I am never troubled about anything. I merely referred to enjoyments derived from various sources, open alike to rich and poor. There are Marahs hidden in every path; no matter whether the draught is taken in jeweled goblets or unpolished gourds."

"Sometimes, then, you are 'blued' most dismally, like the balance of unphilosophic men and women, eh?"

"Occasionally my mind is very much perplexed and disturbed; not exactly 'blued' as you express it, but dimmed, clouded."

"What clouds it? will you tell me?" said Cornelia, eagerly.

"The struggle to see that, which I suppose it never was intended I should see."

"I don't understand you," said Cornelia, knitting her brows.

"Nor would you, even were I to particularize."

"Perhaps I am not so very obtuse as you fancy."

"At any rate, I shall not enter into detail," answered Beulah, smiling quietly at the effect of her words.

"Do you ever weary of your books?" Cornelia leaned forward, and bent a long searching look on her guest's countenance as she spoke.

"Not of my books; but sometimes, nay, frequently, of the thoughts they excite."

"A distinction without a difference," said the invalid, coldly.

"A true distinction nevertheless," maintained Beulah.

" Be good enough to explain it then."

"For instance, I read Carlyle for hours, without the slightest sensation of weariness. Midnight forces me to lay the book reluctantly aside, and then the myriad conjectures and inquiries which I am conscious of, as arising from those same pages, weary me beyond all degrees of endurance."

"And these conjectures cloud your mind?" said Cornelia, with a half smile breaking over her face.

"I did not say so, I merely gave it as an illustration of what you professed not to understand."

"I see your citadel of reserve and mistrust cannot be carried by storm," answered Cornelia, petulantly.

Before Beulah could reply, a servant entered, and addressed Cornelia.

"Your mother wants to show your Paris hat and veil, and handsomest point-lace set, to Mrs. Vincent, and Miss Julia says can't she run up and see you a minute?"

A sneering smile accompanied the contemptuous answer, which was delivered in no particularly gentle manner.

"This is the second time those 'particular friends' of ours have called to inspect my winter outfit. Take down my entire wardrobe to them: dresses, bonnets, mantles, laces, handkerchiefs, ribbons, shawls—nay, gloves and slippers, for there is a 'new style' of catch on one, and of bows and buckles on the other. Do you hear me, Mary? don't leave a rag of my French finery behind. Let the examination be sufficiently complete this time. Don't forget the Indian shawl and the opera cloak and hood, nor that ornamental comb, named after the last popular danseuse; and tell Miss Julia she will please excuse me—another time I will try to see her. Say I am engaged."

Some moments elapsed, during which Mary opened and shut a number of drawers and boxes, and finally disappeared, staggering beneath a load of silks, velvets and laces. As the door closed behind her, Cornelia smoothed her brow, and said, apologetically:

"Doubtless, it seems a mere trifle of accommodation to display all that mass of finery to their eagerly curious eyes; but I assure you, that though I have not been at home quite a week, those things have vacated their places at least twenty times for inspection; and this ridiculous mania for the 'latest style' disgusts me beyond measure. I tell you, the majority of the women in this town think of nothing else. I have not yet looked over my wardrobe myself. Mother selected it in Paris, and I did not trouble myself to examine it when it was unpacked."

Beulah smiled, but offered no comment. Cornelia suddenly sank back in her chair, and said hastily:

"Give me that vial on the bureau! Quick! quick!"

Beulah sprang up and handed her the vial, which she put to her lips. She was ghastly pale, her features writhed, and heavy drops glistened on her brow, corrugated by severe pain.

"Can I do anything for you, Cornelia? Shall I call your mother?"

"No. You may fan me, if you will." She moaned and closed her eyes.

Beulah seized a fan, and did as requested, now and then wiping away the moisture which gathered around her lips and forehead. Gradually, the paroxysm passed off, and opening her eyes, she said, wearily:

"That will do, thank you. Now pour out a glass of water from the pitcher yonder."

Beulah handed her the draught, saying with surprise:

"Sitting wrapped up by a fire, and drinking ice-water!"

"Yes, I use ice-water the year round. Please touch the bell-rope, will you?"

As Beulah resumed her seat, Cornelia added, with a forced laugh:

"You look as if you pitied me."

"I do most sincerely. Do you suffer in this way often?"

"Yes—no—well, when I am prudent, I don't." Then turning to the servant, who stood at the door, she continued: "John, go to Dr. Hartwell's office (not his house, mind you), and leave word that he must come here before night. Do you understand?—shut the door—stop! send up some coal."

"She drew her chair closer to the fire, and extending her slippered feet on the marble hearth, said:

"I have suffered more during the last three days than in six months before. Last night I did not close my eyes—and Dr. Hartwell must prepare me some medicine. What is the matter with Clara Sanders? She looks like an alabaster image!"

"She has never recovered entirely from that attack of yellow fever; and a day or two ago, she took cold, and has had constant fever since. I suppose she will see the doctor while I am here. I feel anxious about her."

"She looks ethereal, as if refined for a translation to heaven," continued Cornelia, musingly; then suddenly lifting her head she listened an instant, and exclaimed, angrily: "It is very strange that I am not to have an hour's peace and enjoyment with you, without—"

The door opened, and a graceful form and lovely face approached the fireplace. "Miss Benton, suffer me to introduce my cousin, Miss Dupres," said Cornelia, very coldly.

The young lady just inclined her head, and proceeded to scan Beulah's countenance and dress, with a degree of cool impertinence which was absolutely amusing. Evidently, however, Cornelia saw nothing amusing in this ill-bred stare, for she pushed a light chair impatiently toward her, saying: "Sit down, Antoinette!"

She threw herself into the seat, with a sort of languid grace, and said, in the most musical of voices:

"Why would you not see Julia Vincent? She was so much disappointed."

"Simply and solely because I did not choose to see her. Be good enough to move your chair to one side, if you please," snapped Cornelia.

"That was very unkind in you, considering she is so fond of you. We are all to spend the evening with her next week; you, and your brother, and I. A mere 'sociable,' she says." She had been admiringly inspecting her small hands, loaded with diamonds; and now turning round, she again freely scrutinized Beulah, who had been silently contemplating her beautiful oval profile and silky auburn curls. Certainly, Antoinette Dupres was beautiful, but it was such a beauty as one sees in wax dolls—blank, soulless, expressionless, if I may except the predominating expression of self-satisfaction. Beulah's quiet dignity failed to repel the continued stare fixed upon her, and gathering up the folds of her shawl, she rose.

"Don't go," said Cornelia, earnestly.

"I must; Clara is alone, and I promised to return soon."

"When will you come again?" Cornelia took her hand, and pressed it warmly.

"I do not know. I hope you will be better soon."

"Eugene will be disappointed: he expects you to spend the evening with us. What shall I tell him?"

"Nothing."

"I will come and see you, the very first day I can get out of this prison-house of mine. Meantime, if I send for you, will you come and sit with me?"

"That depends upon circumstances. If you are sick and lonely, I certainly will. Good-by."

"Good-by, Beulah." The haughty heiress drew the orphan's face down to hers, and kissed her cordially. Not a little surprised by this unexpected demonstration of affection in one so cold and stately, Beulah bowed distantly to the cousin, who returned the salutation still more distantly, and hastening down the steps, was glad to find herself once more under the dome of sky, gray and rainy though it was. The wind sighed and sobbed through the streets, and a few cold drops fell, as she approached Mrs. Hoyt's. Quickening her steps, she ran in by a side entrance and was soon at Clara's room. The door stood open, and with bonnet and shawl in her hand, she entered, little prepared to meet her guardian, for she had absented herself, with the hope of avoiding him. He was sitting by a table, preparing some medicine, and looked up involuntarily as she came in. His eyes lighted instantly, but he merely said:

"Good evening, Beulah."

The tone was less icy than on previous occasions, and crossing the room at once, she stood beside him, and held out her hand.

"How are you, sir?"

He did not take the hand, but looked at her keenly, and said:

"You are an admirable nurse, to go off and leave your sick friend."

Beulah threw down her bonnet and shawl, and retreating to the hearth, began to warm her fingers, as she replied, with indifference:

"I have just left another of your patients. Cornelia Graham has been worse than usual for a day or two. Clara, I will put away my out-door wrappings, and be with you presently." She retired to her own room, and leaning against the windows, where the rain was now pattering drearily, she murmured faintly.

"Will he always treat me so! Have I lost my friend forever? Once he was so different; so kind, even in his sternness!" A tear hung upon her lash and fell on her hand; she brushed it hastily away, and stood thinking over his alienation, so painful and unnatural, when she heard her guardian close Clara's door, and walk across the hall, to the head of the stairs. She waited awhile, until she thought he had reached his buggy, and slowly proceeded to Clara's room. Her eyes were fixed on the floor, and her hand was already on the bolt of the door, when a deep voice startled her.

"Beulah!"

She looked up at him proudly. Resentment had usurped the place of grief. But she could not bear the earnest eyes that looked into hers with such misty splendor; and provoked at her own emotion, she asked, coldly:

"What do you want, sir?"

He did not answer at once, but stood observing her closely. She felt the hot blood rush into her unusually cold, pale face, and, despite her efforts to seem perfectly indifferent, her eyelids and lips would tremble. His hands rested lightly on her shoulder, and he spoke very gently:

"Child, have you been ill? You look wretchedly. What ails you, Beulah?"

"Nothing, sir."

"That will not answer. Tell me, child, tell me!"

"I tell you I am as well as usual," cried she, impatiently, yet her voice faltered. She was struggling desperately with her own heart. The return of his old manner, the winning tones of his voice, affected her more than she was willing he should see. ,

"Beulah, you used to be truthful and candid."

"I am so still," she returned, stoutly, though tears began to gather in her eyes.

"No, child, already the world has changed you."

A shadow fell over his face, and the sad eyes were like clouded stars.

"You know better, sir! I am just what I always was! It is you who are so changed! Once you were my friend; my guardian! Once you were kind, and guided me; but now you are stern, and bitter, and tyrannical!" She spoke passionately, and tears, which she bravely tried to force back, rolled swiftly down her cheeks. His light touch on her shoulder tightened, until it seemed a hand of steel, and with an expression which she never forgot, even in after years, he answered:

"Tyrannical! Not to you, child!"

"Yes, sir, tyrannical! cruelly tyrannical! Because I dared to think and act for myself, you have cast me off—utterly! You try to see how cold and distant you can be; and show me that you don't care whether I live or die, so long as I choose to be independent of you. I did not believe that you could ever be so ungenerous!" She looked up at him with swimming eyes. He smiled down into her tearful face, and asked:

"Why did you defy me, child?"

"I did not, sir, until you treated me worse than the servants! Worse than you did Charon even."

"How?"

"How, indeed! You left me in your own house without one word of good-by, when you expected to be absent an indefinite time. Did you suppose that I would remain there an hour after such treatment?"

He smiled again, and said in the low winning tone which she had always found so difficult to resist.

"Come back, my child. Come back to me!"

"Never, sir! Never!" answered she, resolutely.

A stony hue settled on his face; the lips seemed instantly frozen, and removing his hand from her shoulder, he said as if talking to a perfect stranger: "See that Clara Sanders needs nothing; she is far from being well."

He left her, but her heart conquered for an instant, and she sprang down two steps, and caught his hand. Pressing her face against his arm, she exclaimed brokenly:

"Oh, sir! do not cast me off entirely! My friend, my guardian indeed, I have not deserved this!"

He laid his hand on her bowed head, and said calmly:

"Fierce, proud spirit! Ah! it will take long years of trial and suffering to tame you. Go, Beulah! You have cast yourself off. It was no wish, no work of mine."

He lifted her head from his arm, gently unclasped her fingers, and walked away. Beulah dried the tears on her cheek, and composing herself by a great effort, returned to Clara. The latter still sat in an easy-chair, and leaned back with closed eyes. Beulah made no effort to attract her attention, and sat down noiselessly to reflect upon her guardian's words, and the separation which, she now clearly saw, he intended should be final. There, in the gathering gloom of twilight, sat Clara Sanders, nerving her heart for the dreary future: solemnly and silently burying the cherished hopes that had irised her path, and now looking steadily forward to coming years, she said to her drooping spirit, "be strong, and bear this sorrow. I will conquer my own heart." How is it, that when the human soul is called to pass through a fierce ordeal, and numbing despair seizes the faculties and energies in her sepulchral grasp, how is it, that superhuman strength is often suddenly infused into the sinking spirit? There is a mysterious yet resistless power given, which winds up, and set again in motion, that marvelous bit of mechanism, the human will; that curiously intricate combination of wheels; that main-spring of action, which has baffled the ingenuity of philosophers, and remains yet undiscovered, behind the cloudy shrine of the unknown. Now, there are times when this human clock well-nigh runs down; when it seems that volition is dead; when the past is all gilded, the future all shrouded and the soul grows passive, hoping nothing, fearing nothing. Yet when the slowly-swinging pendulum seems about to rest, even then an unseen hand touches the secret spring; and as the curiously folded coil quivers on again, the resuscitated will is lifted triumphantly back to its throne. This new-born power is from God. But, ye wise ones of earth, tell us how, and by whom, is the key applied? Are ministering angels (our white-robed idols, our loved dead) ordained to keep watch over the machinery of the will, and attend to the winding up? Or is this infusion of strength, whereby to continue its operations, a sudden tightening of those invisible cords, which bind the All-Father to the spirits he has created? Truly, there is no Œdipus for this vexing riddle. Many luckless theories have been devoured by the Sphinx; when will metaphysicians solve it? One tells us vaguely enough, "who knows the mysteries of will, with its vigor? Man doth not yield him to the angels, not unto death, utterly, save only through the weakness of his feeble will." This pretty bubble of a "latent strength" has vanished; the power is from God; but who shall unfold the process? Clara felt that this precious help was given in her hour of need; and looking up undauntedly to the clouds that darkened the sky, said to her hopeless heart: "I will live to do my duty, and God's work on earth: I will go bravely forward in my path of labor, strewing flowers and sunshine. If God needs a lonely, chastened spirit to do his behests, oh! shall I murmur and die because I am chosen? What are the rushing, howling waves of life, in comparison with the calm, shoreless ocean of all eternity?"

The lamp was brought in, and the fire renewed, and the two friends sat by the hearth, silent, quiet. Clara's face had a sweet, serene look; Beulah's was composed, so far as rigidity of features betokened; yet the firm curve of her full upper lip might have indexed somewhat of the confusion which reigned in her mind. Once, a great, burning light flashed out from her eyes, then the lashes drooped a little, and veiled the storm. After a time, Clara lifted her eyes, and said gently:

"Will you read to me, Beulah?"

"Gladly, gladly; what shall it be?" She sprang up eagerly.

"Anything hopeful and strengthening. Anything but your study-book of philosophy and metaphysics. Anything but those, Beulah."

"And why not those?" asked the girl, quickly.

"Because they always confuse and darken me."

"You do not understand them, perhaps?"

"I understand them sufficiently to know that they are not what I need."

"What do you need, Clara?"

"The calm content and courage to do my duty through life. I want to be patient and useful."

The gray eyes rested searchingly on the sweet face, and then with a contracted brow Beulah stepped to the window and looked out. The night was gusty, dark and rainy; heavy drops pattered briskly down the panes. She turned away, and standing on the hearth, with her hands behind her, slowly repeated the beautiful lines, beginning:

"The day is done, and the darkness
  Falls from the wings of night,
As a feather is wafted downward
  From an eagle in his flight."

Her voice was low and musical, and as she concluded the short poem which seemed so singularly suited to Clara's wishes, the latter said earnestly:

"Yes, yes, Beulah,

"'Such songs have power to quiet
  The restless pulse of care,
And come like the benediction
  That follows after prayer.'

Let us obey the poet's injunction, and realize the closing lines:

"'And the night shall be filled with music,
  And the cares that infest the day,
Shall fold their tents, like the Arabs,
  And as silently steal away.'"

Still Beulah stood on the hearth, with a dreamy abstraction looking out from her eyes, and when she spoke there was a touch of impatience in her tone:

"Why try to escape it all, Clara? If those 'grand old masters,' those 'bards sublime,' who tell in trumpet-tones of 'life's endless toil and endeavor,' speak to you through my loved books, why should you 'long for rest?'"

"An unfledged birdling cannot mount to the dizzy eyries of the eagle," answered Clara, meekly.

"One grows strong only by struggling with difficulties. Strong swimmers are such from fierce buffetings with hungry waves. Come out of your warm nest of inertia! Strengthen your wings by battling with storm and wind!" Her brow bent as she spoke.

"Beulah, what sustains you would starve me."

"Something has come over you, Clara."

"Yes; a great trust in God's wisdom and mercy has stolen into my heart. I no longer look despondingly into my future."

"Why? Because you fancy that future will be very short and painless? Ah, Clara, is this trust, when the end comes, and there is no more work to do?"

"You are mistaken; I do not see death beckoning me home. Oh, I have not earned a home yet! I look forward to years of labor, profit, and peace. To-day I found some lines in the morning paper. Nay, don't curl your lips with a sneer at what you call 'newspaper poetry.' Listen to the words that come like a message from the spirit-land to my murmuring heart." Her voice was low and unsteady, as she read:

"'Two hands upon the breast, and labor's done:
Two pale feet crossed in rest, the race is won.
Two eyes with coin-weights shut, all tears cease;
Two lips where grief is mute, and wrath at peace.
So pray we oftentimes, mourning our lot;
God, in his kindness, answereth not!'

Such, Beulah, I felt had been my unvoiced prayer; but now:

"'Two hands to work addressed; aye, for his praise,
Two feet that never rest; walking his ways;
Two eyes that look above, still through all tears;
Two lips that breathe but love; never more fears.
So we cry afterward, low at our knees,
Pardon those erring cries! Father, hear these!'

Oh, Beulah, such is now my prayer."

As Beulah stood near the lamp, strange shadows fell on her brow; shadows from the long, curling lashes. After a brief silence, she asked, earnestly:

"Are your prayers answered, Clara? Does God hear you?"

"Yes; oh yes!"

"Wherefore?"

"Because Christ died!"

"Is your faith in Christ so firm? Does it never waver?"

"Never; even in my most desponding moments."

Beulah looked at her keenly; and asked, with something like a shiver:

"Did it never occur to you to doubt the plan of redemption, as taught by divines; as laid down in the New Testament?"

"No, never. I want to die before such a doubt occurs to me. Oh, what would my life be without that plan? What would a fallen, sin-cursed world be without a Jesus?"

"But why curse a race in order to necessitate a Saviour?"

Clara looked in astonishment at the pale, fixed features before her. A frightened expression came over her own countenance, a look of shuddering horror; and putting up her wasted hands, as if to ward off some grim phantom, she cried:

"Oh, Beulah! what is this? You are not an infidel?"

Her companion was silent a moment; then said, emphatically:

"Dr. Hartwell does not believe the religion you hold so dear." Clara covered her face with her hands, and answered, brokenly:

"Beulah, I have envied you; because I fancied that your superior intellect won you the love which I was weak enough to expect, and need. But if it has brought you both to doubt the Bible, I thank God that the fatal gift was withheld from me. Have your books and studies brought you to this? Beulah! Beulah! throw them into the fire, and come back to trust in Christ." She held out her hand imploringly; but with a singularly cold smile, her friend replied:

"You must go to sleep. Your fever is rising. Don't talk any more to-night; I will not hear you."

An hour after, Clara slept soundly, and Beulah sat in her own room bending over a book. Midnight study had long since become a habitual thing; nay, two and three o'clock frequently found her beside the waning lamp. Was it any marvel that, as Dr. Hartwell expressed it, she "looked wretchedly." From her earliest childhood she had been possessed by an active spirit of inquiry, which constantly impelled her to investigate, and as far as possible to explain the mysteries which surrounded her on every side. With her growth grew this haunting spirit, which asked continually: "What am I?

Whence did I come? And whither am I bound? What is life? What is death? Am I my own mistress, or am I but a tool in the hands of my Maker? What constitutes the difference between my mind and my body? Is there any difference? If spirit must needs have body to incase it, and body must have a spirit to animate it, may they not be identical?" With these primeval foundation questions began her speculative career. In the solitude of her own soul she struggled bravely and earnestly to answer those "dread questions, which, like swords of flaming fire, tokens of imprisonment, encompass man on earth." Of course, mystery triumphed. Panting for the truth, she pored over her Bible, supposing that here, at least, all clouds would melt away; but here, too, some inexplicable passages confronted her. Physically, morally, and mentally, she found the world warring. To reconcile these antagonisms with the conditions and requirements of Holy Writ, she now most faithfully set to work. Ah, proudly-aspiring soul! How many earnest thinkers had essayed the same mighty task, and died under the intolerable burden? Unluckily for her, there was no one to direct or assist her. She scrupulously endeavored to conceal her doubts and questions from her guardian. Poor child! she fancied she concealed them so effectually from his knowledge; while he silently noted the march of skepticism in her nature. There were dim, puzzling passages of Scripture, which she studied on her knees; now trying to comprehend them, and now beseeching the Source of all knowledge to enlighten her. But, as has happened to numberless others, there was seemingly no assistance given. The clouds grew denser and darker, and like the "cry of strong swimmers in their agony," her prayers had gone up to the Throne of Grace. Sometimes she was tempted to go to the minister of the church, where she sat Sunday after Sunday, and beg him to explain the mysteries to her. But the pompous austerity of his manners repelled her whenever she thought of broaching the subject, and gradually she saw that she must work out her own problems. Thus, from week to week, and month to month, she toiled on, with a slowly dying faith, constantly clambering over obstacles which seemed to stand between her trust and revelation. It was no longer study for the sake of erudition; these riddles involved all that she prized in Time and Eternity, and she grasped books of every description with the eagerness of a famishing nature. What dire chance threw into her hands such works as Emerson's, Carlyle's and Goethe's? Like the waves of the clear, sunny sea, they only increased her thirst to madness. Her burning lips were ever at these fountains; and in her reckless eagerness, she plunged into the gulf of German speculation. Here she believed that she had indeed found the "true processes," and with renewed zest, continued the work of questioning. At this stage of the conflict, the pestilential scourge was laid upon the city, and she paused from her metaphysical toil to close glazed eyes and shroud soulless clay. In the awful hush of those hours of watching, she looked calmly for some solution, and longed for the unquestioning faith of early years. But these influences passed without aiding her in the least, and with rekindled ardor, she went back to her false prophets. In addition, ethnology beckoned her on to conclusions apparently antagonistic to the revealed system, and the stony face of geology seemed radiant with characters of light, which she might decipher and find some security in. From Dr. Asbury's extensive collection, she snatched treatise after treatise. The sages of geology talked of the pre-Adamic eras, and of man's ending the slowly forged chain, of which the radiata form the lowest link; and then she was told that in those pre-Adamic ages, Palæontologists find no trace whatever of that golden time, when the vast animal creation lived in harmony, and bloodshed was unknown; ergo, man's fall in Eden had no agency in bringing death into the world; ergo, that chapter in Genesis need puzzle her no more.

Finally, she learned that she was the crowning intelligence in the vast progression; that she would ultimately become part of the Deity. "The long ascending line, from dead matter to man, had been a progress Godwards, and the next advance would unite creation and Creator in one person." With all her aspirations, she had never dreamed of such a future as was here promised her. To-night she was closely following that most anomalous of all guides, "Herr Teufelsdrockh." Urged on by the same "unrest," she was stumbling along dim, devious paths, while from every side whispers came to her: "Nature is one, she is your mother, and divine: she is God! The 'living garment of God.'" Through the "everlasting No," and the "everlasting Yea," she groped her way, darkly, tremblingly, waiting for the daystar of Truth to dawn; but at last, when she fancied she saw the first rays silvering the night, and looked up hopefully, it proved one of many ignes-fatui, which had flashed across her path, and she saw that it was Goethe, uplifted as the prophet of the genuine religion. The book fell from her nerveless fingers; she closed her eyes, and groaned. It was all "confusion, worse confounded." She could not for her life have told what she believed, much less, what she did not believe. The landmarks of earlier years were swept away; the beacon light of Calvary had sunk below her horizon. A howling chaos seemed about to ingulf her. At that moment she would gladly have sought assistance from her guardian; but how could she approach him after their last interview? The friendly face and cordial kindness of Dr. Asbury flashed upon her memory, and she resolved to confide her doubts and difficulties to him, hoping to obtain, from his clear and matured judgment, some clew which might enable her to emerge from the labyrinth that involved her. She knelt, and tried to pray. To what did she, on bended knees, send up passionate supplications? To nature? to heroes? These were the new deities. She could not pray; all grew dark; she pressed her hands to her throbbing brain, striving to clear away the mists. "Sartor" had effectually blindfolded her, and she threw herself down to sleep with a shivering dread, as of a young child separated from its mother, and wailing in some starless desert.

CHAPTER XXI.

It was Christmas eve; cold, cloudy, and damp. The store windows were gay with every conceivable and inconceivable device for attracting attention. Parents, nurses, and porters hurried along with mysterious looking bundles, and important countenances. Crowds of curious, merry children thronged the sidewalks; here a thinly clad, meager boy, looked, with longing eyes and empty pockets, at pyramids of fruit and sweetmeats; and there a richly dressed group chattered like blackbirds, and occasionally fired a pack of crackers, to the infinite dismay of horses and drivers. Little chaps just out of frocks rushed about, with their round rosy faces hid under grotesque masks; and shouts of laughter, and the squeak of penny trumpets, and mutter of miniature drums, swelled to a continuous din, which would have been quite respectable even on the plain of Shinar. The annual jubilee had come, and young and old seemed determined to celebrate it with due zeal. From her window Beulah looked down on the merry groups, and involuntarily contrasted the bustling, crowded streets, with the silence and desolation which had reigned over the same thoroughfares only a few months before. One brief year ago, childish voices prattled of Santa Claus and gift stockings, and little feet pattered along these same pavements, with tiny hands full of toys. Fond parents, too, had gone eagerly in and out of these gay shops, hunting presents for their darlings. Where were they? children and parents? Ah! a cold, silent band of sleepers in yonder necropolis, where solemn cedars were chanting an everlasting dirge. Death's harvest time was in all seasons; when would her own throbbing pulses be stilled, and her questioning tones hushed? Might not the summons be on that very wintry blast, which rushed over her hot brow? And if it should be so? Beulah pressed her face closer to the window, and thought it was too inconceivable that she also should die. She knew it was the common birthright, the one unchanging heritage of all humanity; yet long vistas of life opened before her, and though, like a pall, the shadow of a tomb hung over the end, it was very distant, very dim.

"What makes you look so solemn?" asked Clara, who had been busily engaged in dressing a doll for one of Mrs. Hoyt's children.

"Because I feel solemn, I suppose."

Clara came up, and passing her arm around Beulah's shoulder, gazed down into the noisy street. She still wore mourning, and the alabaster clearness of her complexion contrasted vividly with the black bombazine dress. Though thin and pale, there was an indescribable expression of peace on the sweet face; a calm, clear light of contentment in the mild brown eyes. The holy serenity of the countenance was rendered more apparent by the restless, stormy visage of her companion. Every passing cloud of perplexed thought cast its shadow over Beulah's face, and on this occasion she looked more than usually grave.

"Ah! how merry I used to be on Christmas eve. Indeed, I can remember having been half wild with excitement. Yet now it all seems like a flitting dream." Clara spoke musingly, yet without sadness.

"Time has laid his wonder-working touch upon you," answered Beulah.

"How is it, Beulah, that you never speak of your childhood?"

"Because it was

"'All dark and barren as a rainy sea.'"

"But you never talk about your parents?"

"I love my father's memory. Ah! it is enshrined in my heart's holiest sanctuary. He was a noble, loving man, and my affection for him bordered on idolatry."

"And your mother?"

"I knew little of her. She died before I was old enough to remember much about her." Her face was full of bitter recollections; her eyes seemed wandering through some storehouse of sorrows. Clara feared her friend, much as she loved her, and since the partial discovery of her skepticism, she had rather shunned her society. Now she watched the heavy brow, and deep, piercing eyes, uneasily, and gently withdrawing her arm, she glided out of the room. The tide of life still swelled through the streets, and forcibly casting the load of painful reminiscences from her, Beulah kept her eyes on the merry faces, and listened to the gay, careless prattle of the excited children. The stately rustle of brocaded silk caused her to look up, and Cornelia Graham greeted her with:

"I have come to take you home with me for the holidays."

"I can't go."

"Why not? You cling to this dark garret of yours as if it possessed all the charms of Vaucluse."

"Diogenes loved his tub, you know," said Beulah, quietly.

"An analogous case, truly. But jesting aside, you must come, Beulah. Eugene expects you; so do my parents; and, above all, I want you. Come." Cornelia laid her hand on the girl's shoulder as she spoke.

"You have been ill again," said Beulah, examining the sallow face.

"Not ill, but I shall be soon, I know. One of my old attacks is coming on; I feel it; and Beulah, to be honest, which I can with you (without casting pearls before swine), that very circumstance makes me want you. I dined out today, and have just left the fashionable crowd to come and ask you to spend the holidays with me. The house will be gay. Antoinette intends to have a set of tableaux, but it is probable I shall be confined to my room. Will you give your time to a cross invalid, for such I certainly am? I would be stretched upon St. Lawrence's gridiron before I could be brought to say as much to anybody else. I am not accustomed to ask favors, Beulah; it has been my habit to grant them. Nevertheless, I want you, and am not too proud to come after you. Will you come?"

"Yes, if I may remain with you, altogether."

"Thank you. Come, get ready, quick! Give me a fan." Sinking into a chair, she wiped away the cold drops which had collected about her brow.

"Cornelia, I have only one day's leisure. School begins again day-after-to-morrow."

"Well, well; one day, then. Be quick."

In a few moments, Beulah was ready; and after informing Clara and Mrs. Hoyt of her intended absence, the two entered Mr. Graham's elegant carriage. The gas was now lighted, and the spirited horses dashed along, through streets brilliantly illuminated and thronged with happy people.

"What a Babel! About equal to Constantinople, and its dog-orchestra," muttered Cornelia, as the driver paused to allow one of the military companies to pass. The martial music, together with the hubbub which otherwise prevailed, alarmed the horses, and they plunged violently. The driver endeavored to back out into an alley, but in the attempt the carriage was whirled round, the coachman jerked over the dashboard into the gutter, and the frightened animals dashed at furious speed down the main street. Luckily the top was thrown back, making the carriage open, and springing forward to the post so unceremoniously vacated by the driver, Beulah snatched the reins, which were just within her reach. Curb the rushing horses, she did not hope to do, but by cautious energy, succeeded in turning them sufficiently aside to avoid coming in collision with several other carriages. The street was full of vehicles, and though, as may well be imagined, there was every effort made to give the track, the carriage rushed against the bright yellow wheels of a light buggy in which two young men were trying to manage a fast trotter. There was a terrible smash of wheels, the young gentlemen were suddenly landed in the mud, and their emancipated steed galloped on, with the wreck of the buggy at his heels. Men, women, and children gathered on the corners to witness the dénoûement. Drays, carts, and wagons were seized with a simultaneous stampede, which soon cleared the middle of the street, and uninjured by the collision, our carriage flew on. Cornelia sat on the back seat, ghastly pale, and motionless, expecting every minute to be hurled out, while Beulah stood up in front, reins in hand, trying to guide the maddened horses. Her bonnet fell off; the motion loosened her comb, and down came her long, heavy hair, in black, blinding folds. She shook it all back from her face, and soon saw that this reckless game of dodging vehicles could not last much longer. Right ahead, at the end of the street, was the wharf, crowded with cotton bales, barrels, and a variety of freight; just beyond was the river. A number of gentlemen stood on a neighboring corner, and with one impulse they rushed forward with extended arms. On sprang the horses, almost upon them; eager hands grasped at the bits.

"Stand back—all of you! You might as well catch at the winds!" shouted Beulah, and with one last effort, she threw her whole weight on the reins, and turned the horses into a cross street. The wheels struck the curbstone, the carriage tilted, rocked, fell back again, and on they went for three squares more, when the horses stopped short before the livery-stable where they were kept. Embossed with foam, and panting like stags at bay, they were seized by a dozen hands.

"By all the gods of Greece! you have had a flying trip of it!" cried Dr. Asbury, with one foot on the carriage step, and both hands extended, while his gray hair hung in confusion about his face. He had followed them for at least half-a-dozen blocks, and was pale with anxiety.

"See about Cornelia," said Beulah, seating herself for the first time, and twisting up the veil of hair which swept round her form.

"Cornelia has fainted! Halloo, there! some water! quick!" said the doctor, stepping into the carriage, and attempting to lift the motionless figure. But Cornelia opened her eyes, and answered unsteadily.

"No! carry me home! Dr. Asbury, take me home!"

The brilliant eyes closed, a sort of spasm distorted her features, and she sank back once more, rigid and seemingly lifeless. Dr. Asbury took the reins firmly in his hands, seated himself, and speaking gently to the trembling horses, started homeward. They plunged violently at first, but he used the whip unsparingly, and in a few moments they trotted briskly along. Mrs. Graham and her niece had not yet reached home, but Mr. Graham met the carriage at the door, with considerable agitation and alarm in his usually phlegmatic countenance. As Cornelia's colorless face met his view, he threw up his hands, staggered back, and exclaimed: "My God! is she dead? I knew it would end this way, some day!"

"Nonsense, Graham! She is frightened out of her wits—that is all! These Yankee horses of yours have been playing the very deuce. Clear the way there, all of you!"

Lifting Cornelia in his strong arms, Dr. Asbury carried her up to her own room, and placed her on a sofa. Having known her from childhood, and treated her so often in similar attacks, he immediately administered some medicine, and ere long had the satisfaction of seeing the rigid aspect leave her face. She sat up, and without a word, began to take off her kid gloves, which fitted tightly. Suddenly looking up at her father, who was anxiously regarding her, she said, abruptly:

"There are no more like her—she kept me from making a simpleton of myself."

"Whom do you mean, my dear?"

"Whom? whom? why, Beulah Benton, of course! Where is she? Come out of that corner, you quaint, solemn statue!" She held out her hand, and a warm, glad smile broke over her pallid face, as Beulah approached her.

"You certainly created a very decided sensation. Beulah made quite a passable Medea, with her inky hair trailing over the back of the seat, and her little hands grasping the reins with desperate energy. By Phœbus! you turned that corner at the bank, like an electric bolt. Shake hands, Beulah! After this, you will do in any emergency." The doctor looked at her with an expression of paternal pride and affection.

"I feel very grateful to you," began Mr. Graham; but Beulah cut short his acknowledgments, by saying hastily:

"Sir, I did nothing at all; Dr. Asbury is resolved to make a heroine of me, that is all. You owe me nothing."

At this moment the coachman limped into the room with garments dabbled with mud, and inquired anxiously whether the young ladies were hurt.

"No, you son of Pluto; not hurt at all, thanks to your careful driving," answered the doctor, putting his hands in his pockets, and eyeing the discomfited coachman humorously.

"Were you hurt by your fall?" asked Beulah.

"Considerably bumped, and thumped, but not much hurt, thank you, miss. I was awfully scared when I rose out of that choking gutter, and saw you standing up, and the horses flying, like ole Satan himself was after them. I am marvelous glad nothing was hurt. And now, master, sir, I want you to go to the mayor and have this 'ere fire-cracker-business stopped. A parcel of rascally boys set a match to a whole pack, and flung 'em right under Andrew Jackson's feet! Of course I couldn't manage him after that. I 'clare to gracious! it's a sin and a shame, the way the boys in this town do carry on Christmas times, and indeed every other time!" Wilson hobbled out, grumbling audibly.

"Beulah, you must come and spend Christmas at my house. The girls and my wife were talking about it to-day, and concluded to send the carriage for you early in the morning." The doctor drew on his gloves as he spoke.

"They may spare themselves the trouble, sir; she spends it with me," answered Cornelia.

"With you! After such a frolic as you two indulged in this evening, you ought not to be trusted together. If I had not been so anxious about you, I could have laughed heartily at the doleful countenances of those two young gents, as they picked themselves up out of the mud. Such rueful plight as their lemon-colored gloves were in! I will send Hartwell to see you to-morrow, Cornelia. A merry Christmas to you all, in spite of your Mazeppa episode." His good-humored countenance vanished.

"There comes Antoinette ejaculating up the steps. Father, tell her I do not want to see her, or anybody else. Don't let her come in here," cried Cornelia, with a nervous start, as voices were heard in the passage.

Mr. Graham, who felt a certain awe of his willful child, notwithstanding his equable temper, immediately withdrew. His wife hastened into the room, and with trembling lips touched her daughter's cheeck and brow, exclaiming:

"Oh, my child, what a narrow escape! It is horrible to think of—horrible!"

"Not at all, mother, seeing that nothing was hurt in the least. I was sick, any way, as I told you. Don't you see Beulah sitting there?"

Mrs. Graham welcomed her guest cordially.

"You have a great deal of presence of mind, I believe, Miss Beulah? You are fortunate."

"I thanked my stars that Antoinette was not in the carriage, for most certainly she would have made matters worse, by screaming like an idiot, and jumping out. Beulah taught me common sense," answered Cornelia, unclasping a bracelet, and tossing a handful of jewelry across the room to her dressing-table.

"You underrate yourself, my dear," said her mother, a little proudly.

"Not at all. Humility, genuine or feigned, is not one of our family traits. Mother, will you send up tea for us? We want a quiet time; at least I do, and Beulah will stay with me."

"But, my love, it is selfish to exclude the balance of the family. Why not come down to the sitting-room, where we can all be together?" pleaded the mother.

"Because I prefer staying just where I am. Beulah, put down that window, will you? Mary must think that I have been converted into a Polar bear; and mother, have some coal brought up. If there is any truth in the metempsychosis of the Orient, I certainly was a palm-tree or a rhinoceros in the last stage of my existence." She shivered, and wrapped a heavy shawl up to her very chin.

"May I come in?" asked Eugene at the door.

"No, go and sing duets with Netta, and amuse yourself down-stairs," said she, shortly, while a frown darkened her face.

Nevertheless he came in, shook hands with Beulah, and leaning over the back of Cornelia's chair, asked tenderly:

"How is my sister? I heard on the street that you were injured."

"Oh, I suppose the whole city will be bemoaning my tragic fate. I am not at all hurt, Eugene."

"You have had one of those attacks, though, I see from your face. Has it passed off entirely?"

"No; and I want to be quiet. Beulah is going to read me to sleep after a while. You may go down, now."

"Beulah, you will be with us to-morrow, I suppose?"

"Yes."

"I am sorry I am obliged to dine out; I shall be at home, however, most of the day. I called the other evening, but you were not at home."

"Yes; I was sorry I did not see you," said Beulah, looking steadily at his flushed face and sparkling eyes.

"Dine out, Eugene! For what, I should like to know?" cried Cornelia, raising herself in her chair, and fixing her eyes impatiently upon him.

"Henderson and Millbank are both here, you know, and I could not refuse to join them in a Christmas dinner."

"Then, why did you not invite them to dine at your own house?" Her voice was angry; her glance searching.

"The party was made up before I knew anything about it. They will all be here in the evening."

"I doubt it!" said she, sneeringly. The flush deepened on his cheek, and he bit his lip; then turning suddenly to Beulah, he said, as he suffered his eyes to wander over her plain, fawn-colored merino dress:

"You have not yet heard Netta sing, I believe!"

"No."

"Where is she, Cornelia?"

"I have no idea."

"I hope my sister will be well enough to take part in the tableaux to-morrow evening." Taking her beautifully molded hand, he looked at her anxiously. Her piercing, black eyes were riveted on his countenance, as she answered:

"I don't know, Eugene; I have long since abandoned the hope of ever being well again. Perhaps I may be able to get down to the parlors. There is Antoinette in the passage. Good night." She motioned him away. He kissed her tenderly, shook hands a second time with Beulah, and left the room. Cornelia bowed her head on her palms; and though her features were concealed, Beulah thought she moaned, as if in pain.

"Cornelia, are you ill again? What can I do for you?"

The feeble woman lifted her haggard face, and answered:

"What can you do? That remains to be seen. Something must be done. Beulah, I may die at any hour, and you must save him."

"What do you mean?" Beulah's heart throbbed painfully, as she asked this simple question.

"You know very well what I mean! Oh, Beulah! Beulah! it bows my proud spirit into the dust!" Again she averted her head; there was a short silence. Beulah leaned her face on her hand, and then Cornelia continued:

"Did you detect it when he first came home?"

"Yes."

"Oh, it is like a hideous nightmare! I cannot realize that Eugene, so noble, so pure, so refined, could ever have gone to the excesses he has been guilty of. He left home all that he should be; but five years abroad have strangely changed him. My parents will not see it; my mother says 'all young men are wild at first'; and my father shuts his eyes to his altered habits. Eugene constantly drinks too much. I have never see him intoxicated. I don't know that he has been, since he joined us in Italy, but I dread, continually, lest his miserable associates lead him further astray. I had hoped that, in leaving his companions at the university, he had left temptation too; but the associates he has found here are even worse. I hope I shall be quiet in my grave, before I see him drunk! It would kill me, I verily believe, to know that he had so utterly degraded himself." She shaded her face with her hands, and Beulah replied, hastily:

"He surely cannot fall so low! Eugene will never reel home, an unconscious drunkard! Oh, no, it is impossible! impossible! The stars in heaven will fall first!"

"Do you believe what you say?"

"I hope it; and hope engenders faith," answered Beulah.

A bitter smile curled Cornelia's lips, and sinking back in her chair, she continued:

"Where excessive drinking is not considered a disgrace, young men indulge, without a thought of the consequences. Instead of excluding them from genteel circles, their dissipation is smoothed over, or unnoticed; and it has become so prevalent in this city that of all the gentlemen whom I meet in so-called fashionable society, there are very few who abstain from the wine-cup. I have seen them at parties, staggering through a quadrille, or talking the most disgusting nonsense to girls, who have long since ceased to regard dissipation as a stigma upon the names and characters of their friends. I tell you, the dissipation of the young men here is sickening to think of. Since I came home, I have been constantly reminded of it; and oh, Eugene is following in their disgraceful steps! Beulah, if the wives and mothers, and sisters, did their duty, all this might be remedied. If they carefully and constantly strove to shield their sons and brothers from temptation, they might preserve them from the fatal habit, which, once confirmed, it is almost impossible to eradicate. But alas! they smile as sweetly upon the reckless, intoxicated beaux as if they were what men should be. I fancied that I could readily redeem Eugene from his dangerous lapses, but my efforts are rendered useless by the temptations which assail him from every quarter. He shuns me; hourly the barriers between us strengthen. Beulah, I look to you. He loves you, and your influence might prevail, if properly directed. You must save him! You must!"

"I have not the influence you ascirbe to me," answered Beulah.

"Do not say so! do not say so! Are you not to be his wife one day?" She stood up, and heavy drops glistened on her pale forehead.

"His wife! Cornelia Graham, are you mad?" cried Beulah, lifting her head proudly, and eyeing her companion with unfeigned astonishment, while her eyes burned ominously.

"He told me that he expected to marry you; that it had always been a settled thing. Beulah, you have not broken the engagement—surely you have not?" She grasped Beulah's arm convulsively.

"No positive engagement ever existed. While we were children, we often spoke of our future as one, but of late, neither of us have alluded to the subject. We are only friends, linked by memories of early years. Nay, since his return, we have almost become strangers."

"Then I have been miserably deceived. Not two months since, he told me that he looked upon you as his future wife. What has alienated you? Beulah Benton, do you not love him?"

"Love him! No!"

"You loved him once—hush! don't deny it! I know that you did. You loved him during his absence, and you must love him still. Beulah, you do love him!"

"I have a true sisterly affection for him; but as for the love which you allude to, I tell you, Cornelia, I have not one particle!"

"Then he is lost!" Sinking back in her chair, Cornelia groaned aloud.

"Why Eugene should have made such an impression on your mind, I cannot conjecture. He has grown perfectly indifferent to me; and even if he had not, we could never be more than friends. Boyish fancies have all passed away. He is a man now—still my friend, I believe; but no longer what he once was to me. Cornelia, I, too, see his growing tendency to dissipation, with a degree of painful apprehension, which I do not hesitate to avow. Though cordial enough when we meet, I know and feel that he carefully avoids me. Consequently, I have no opportunity to exert what little influence I may possess. I looked at his flushed face, just now, and my thoughts flew back to the golden days of his boyhood, when he was all that a noble, pure, generous nature could make him. I would ten thousand times rather know that he was sleeping by my little sister's side in the graveyard, than see him disgrace himself!" Her voice faltered, and she dropped her head to conceal the anguish which convulsed her features.

"Beulah, if he loves you still, you will not reject him?" cried Cornelia, eagerly.

"He does not love me."

"Why will you evade me? Suppose that he does?"

"Then I tell you solemnly, not all Christendom could induce me to marry him!"

"But to save him, Beulah! to save him!" replied Cornelia, clasping her hands entreatingly.

"If a man's innate self-respect will not save him from habitual disgusting intoxication, all the female influence in the universe would not avail. Man's will, like woman's, is stronger than his affection, and once subjugated by vice, all external influence will be futile. If Eugene once sinks so low, neither you, nor I nor his wife—had he one—could reclaim him."

"He has deceived me! Fool that I was, not to probe the mask!" Cornelia started up, and paced the floor with uncontrollable agitation.

"Take care how you accuse him rashly! I am not prepared to believe that he could act dishonorably toward any one—I will not believe it."

"Oh! you, too, will get your eyes open in due time. Ha! it is all as clear as daylight! And I, with my boasted penetration!—it maddens me!" Her eyes glittered like polished steel.

"Explain yourself; Eugene is above suspicion!" cried Beulah, with pale, fluttering lips.

"Explain myself! Then understand that my honorable brother professed to love you, and pretended that he expected to marry you, simply and solely to blind me, in order to conceal the truth. I taxed him with a preference for Antoinette Dupres, which I fancied his manner evinced. He denied it, most earnestly, protesting that he felt bound to you. Now do you understand?" Her lips were white, and writhed with scorn.

"Still you may misjudge him," returned Beulah, haughtily.

"No, no! My mother has seen it all along. But, fool that I was, I believed his words! Now, Beulah, if he marries Antoinette, you will be amply revenged, or my name is not Cornelia Graham!" She laughed bitterly, and dropping some medicine from a vial, swallowed the potion, and resumed her walk up and down the floor.

"Revenged! What is it to me, that he should marry your cousin? If he loves her, it is no business of mine, and certainly you have no right to object. You are miserably deceived if you imagine that his marriage would cause me an instant's regret. Think you I could love a man whom I knew to be my inferior? Indeed, you know little of my nature." She spoke with curling lips and a proud smile.

"You place an exalted estimate upon yourself," returned Cornelia.

They looked at each other half-defiantly, for a moment; then the heiress bowed her head, and said, in low broken tones:

"Oh, Beulah, Beulah! child of poverty! would I could change places with you!"

"You are weak, Cornelia," answered Beulah, gravely.

"In some respects, perhaps, I am; but you are bold to tell me so."

"Genuine friendship ignores all hesitancy in speaking the truth. You sought me: I am very candid—perhaps blunt. If my honesty does not suit you, it is an easy matter to discontinue our intercourse. The whole matter rests with you."

"You wish me to understand that you do not need my society—my patronage?"

"Patronage implies dependence, which, in this instance, does not exist. An earnest, self-reliant woman, cannot be patronized, in the sense in which you employ the term." She could not forbear smiling. The thought of being under patronage was, to her, supremely ridiculous.

"You do not want my friendship, then?"

"I doubt whether you have any to bestow. You seem to have no love for anything," replied Beulah, coldly.

"Oh! you wrong me," cried Cornelia, passionately.

"If I do, it is your own fault. I only judge you from what you have shown of your nature."

"Remember, I have been an invalid all my life."

"I am not likely to forget it in your presence; but, Cornelia, your whole being seems embittered."

"Yes, and you will be just like me when you have lived as long as I have. Wait till you have seen something of the world."

"Sit down, Cornelia: you tremble from head to foot." She drew a chair close to the hearth, and the sufferer sank into it, as if completely exhausted. For some time neither spoke. Beulah stood with her hands on the back of the chair, wishing herself back in her quiet little room. After a while, Cornelia said slowly:

"If you only knew Antoinette as well as I do, you could ill brook the thought of her ever being Eugene's wife."

"He is the best judge of what will promote his happiness."

"No; he is blinded, infatuated. Her pretty face veils her miserable, contemptible defects of character. She is utterly unworthy of him."

"If she loves him sincerely, she will—"

"Don't talk of what you do not understand. She is too selfish to love anything or anybody but herself. Mark me, whether I live to see it or not, if he marries her, he will despise her in less than six months, and curse himself for his blind folly. Oh, what a precious farce it will prove!" She laughed sneeringly.

"Cornelia, you are not able to bear this excitement. For the present, let Eugene and his future rest, and try to compose yourself. You are so nervous, you can scarcely sit still."

The colorless face, with its gleaming eyes, was suddently lifted; and throwing her arms round Beulah's neck, Cornelia rested her proud head on the orphan's shoulder.

"Be my friend while I live. Oh, give me some of your calm contentment, some of your strength!"

"I am your friend, Cornelia; I will always be such; but every soul must be sufficient for itself. Do not look to me; lean upon your own nature; it will suffice for all its needs."

With the young teacher, pity was almost synonymous with contempt; and as she looked at the joyless face of her companion, she could not avoid thinking her miserably weak.

CHAPTER XXII.

Christmas day was sunny and beautiful. The bending sky was as deeply blue as that which hung over Bethlehem eighteen hundred years before; God's coloring had not faded. Happy children prattled as joyously as did the little Jew boys who clustered curiously about the manger, to gaze upon the holy babe, the sleeping Jesus. Human nature had not altered one whit beneath the iron wheel of Time. Is there a man so sunk in infamy, or steeped in misanthropy, that he has not, at some period of his life, exclaimed, in view of earth's fadeless beauty:

> "This world is very lovely. O my God!
> I thank Thee that I live."

Alas, for the besotted soul, who cannot bend the knee of humble adoration before nature's altar, where sacrifices are offered to the Jehovah, pavilioned in invisibility. There is an ardent love of nature, as far removed from gross materialism or subtle pantheism on the one hand, as from stupid inappreciation on the other. There is such a thing as looking "through nature up to nature's God," notwithstanding the frightened denials of those who, shocked at the growing materialism of the age, would fain persuade this generation to walk blindfold through the superb temple a loving God has placed us in. While every sane and earnest mind must turn, disgusted and humiliated, from the senseless rant, which resolves all divinity into materialistic elements, it may safely be proclaimed that genuine æsthetics is a mighty channel, through which the love and adoration of Almighty God enters the human soul. It were an insult to the Creator to reject the influence which even the physical world exerts on contemplative natures. From bald, hoary mountains, and somber, solemn forests; from thundering waves, and wayside violets; from gorgeous sunset clouds, from quiet stars, and whispering winds, come unmistakable voices, hymning of the Eternal God: the God of Moses, of Isaac, and of Jacob. Extremes meet in every age, and in every department. Because one false philosophy would deify the universe, startled opponents tells us to close our ears to these musical utterances, and shut our eyes to glorious nature, God's handiwork. Oh! why has humanity so fierce a hatred of medium paths?

Ragged boys and barefooted girls tripped gaily along the streets, merry and uncomplaining; and surrounded by velvet, silver and marble, by every superfluity of luxury, Cornelia Graham, with a bitter heart and hopeless soul, shivered in her easy-chair before a glowing fire. The Christmas sunlight crept in through the heavy crimson curtains, and made gorgeous fret-work on the walls, but its cheering radiance mocked the sickly pallor of the invalid, and as Beulah retreated to the window and peeped into the street, she felt an intense longing to get out under the blue sky once more. Mr. and Mrs. Graham, and Antoinette, sat round the hearth, discussing the tableaux for the evening, while, with her cheek upon her hand, Cornelia listlessly fingered a diamond necklace which her father had just given her. The blazing jewels slipped through her pale fingers all unnoticed, and she looked up abstractedly when Mr. Graham touched her, and repeated his question for the third time:

"My child, won't you come down to the sitting-room?"

"No, sir; I am better here."

"But you will be so lonely."

"Not with Beulah."

"But, of course, Miss Benton will desire to see the tableaux. You would not keep her from them?" remonstrated her father.

"Thank you, Mr. Graham, I prefer remaining with Cornelia," answered Beulah, who had no wish to mingle in the crowd which, she understood from the conversation, would assemble that evening in the parlors. The trio round the hearth looked at each other, and evidently thought she manifested very heathenish taste. Cornelia smiled, and leaned back with an expression of pleasure which very rarely lighted her face.

"Your are shockingly selfish and exacting," said Antoinette, curling her long ringlets over her pretty fingers, and looking very bewitching. Her cousin eyed her in silence, and not particularly relishing her daughter's keen look, Mrs. Graham rose, kissed her forehead, and said, gently:

"My love, the Vincents, and Thorntons, and Hendersons all sent to inquire after you this morning. Netta and I must go down now, and prepare for our tableaux. I leave you in good hands; Miss Benton is considered an admirable nurse, I believe."

"Mother, where is Eugene?"

"I really do not know. Do you, Mr. Graham?"

"He has gone to the hotel to see some of his old Heidelberg friends," answered Netta, examining Beulah's plain merino dress very minutely as she spoke.

"When he comes home, be good enough to tell him that I wish to see him."

"Very well, my dear." Mrs. Graham left the room, followed by her husband and niece. For some time, Cornelia sat just as they left her; the diamond necklace slipped down, and lay a glittering heap on the carpet, and the delicate waxen hands drooped listlessly over the arms of the chair. Her profile was toward Beulah, who stood looking at the regular beautiful features, and wondering how (with so many elements of happiness in her home) she could seem so discontented. She was thinking, too, that there was a certain amount of truth in that persecuted and ignored dictum, "A man only sees that which he brings with him the power of seeing," when Cornelia raised herself, and turning her head to look for her companion, said, slowly:

"Where are you? Do you believe in the Emersonian 'law of compensation,' rigid and inevitable as fate? I say, Beulah, do you believe it?"

"Yes, I believe it."

"Hand me the volume there on the table. His exposition of 'the absolute balance of Give and Take, the doctrine that everything has its price,' is the grandest triumph of his genius. For an hour this sentence has been ringing in my ears: 'in the nature of the soul is the compensation for the inequalities of condition.' We are samples of the truth of this. Ah, Beulah, I have paid a heavy, heavy price! You are destitute of one, it is true, but exempt from the other. Yet, mark you, this law of 'compensation' pertains solely to earth and its denizens; the very existence and operation of the law precludes the necessity, and I may say the possibility of that future state, designed, as theologians argue, for rewards and punishments." She watched her visitor very closely:

"Of course it nullifies the belief in future adjustments, for he says emphatically, 'Justice is not postponed. A perfect equity adjusts its balance in all parts of life.' 'What will you have? Pay for it, and take it. Nothing venture, nothing have.' There is no obscurity whatever in that remarkable essay on compensation." Beulah took up one of the volumes, and turned the pages carelessly.

"But all this would shock a Christian."

"And deservedly; for Emerson's works, collectively and individually, are aimed at the doctrines of Christianity. There is a grim, terrible fatalism scowling on his pages, which might well frighten the reader who clasped the Bible to his heart."

"Yet you accept his 'compensation.' Are you prepared to receive his deistic system?" Cornelia leaned forward, and spoke eagerly. Beulah smiled.

"Why strive to cloak the truth? I should not term his fragmentary system 'deistic.' He knows not yet what he believes. There are singular antagonisms existing among even his pet theories."

"I have not found any," replied Cornelia, with a gesture of impatience.

"Then you have not studied his works as closely as I have done. In one place, he tells you he feels 'the eternity of man, the identity of his thought,' that Plato's truth, and Pindar's fire, belong as much to him, as to the ancient Greeks, and on the opposite page, if I remember aright, he says, 'Rare extravagant spirits come by us at intervals, who disclose to us new facts in nature. I see that men of God have, from time to time, walked among men, and made their commission felt in the heart and soul of the commonest hearer. Hence evidently the tripod, the priest, the priestess, inspired by the divine afflatus.' Thus at one moment he finds no 'antiquity in the worships of Moses, of Zoroaster, of Menu, or Socrates, they are as much his as theirs,' and at another, clearly asserts that spirits do come into the world to discover to us new truths. At some points we are told that the cycles of time reproduce all things; at others, this theory is denied. Again in 'Self-Reliance,' he says, 'Trust thyself; insist on yourself; obey thy heart, and thou shalt reproduce the fore-world again.' All this was very comforting to me, Cornelia; self-reliance was the great secret of success and happiness; but I chanced to read the 'Over-Soul' soon after, and lo! these words: 'I am constrained every moment to acknowledge a higher origin for events than the will I call mine.' This was directly antagonistic to the entire spirit of 'self-reliance,' but I read on, and soon found the last sentence utterly nullified by one which declared positively 'that the Highest dwells with man; the sources of nature are in his own mind.' Sometimes we are informed that our souls are self-existing, and all powerful; an incarnation of the divine and universal, and before we fairly digest this tremendous statement, he coolly asserts that there is above all, an 'over-soul,' whose inevitable decrees upset our plans, and 'overpower private will.' Cognizant of these palpable contradictions, Emerson boldly avows and defends them, by declaring that 'A foolish consistency is the hobgoblin of little minds. With consistency, a great soul has simply nothing to do. Speak what you think now in hard words; and to-morrow speak what to-morrow thinks in hard words again, though it contradict everything you said to-day. Why should you keep your head over your shoulder? Why drag about this corpse of your memory, lest you contradict somewhat you have stated in this or that public place? Suppose you should contradict yourself?' His writings are, to me, like heaps of broken glass, beautiful in the individual crystal, sparkling, and often dazzling, but gather them up, and try to fit them into a whole, and the jagged edges refuse to unite. Certainly, Cornelia, you are not an Emersonian." Her deep, quiet eyes looked full into those of the invalid.

"Yes, I am. I believe in that fatalism which he shrouds under the gauze of an 'Over-Soul,' replied Cornelia, impressively.

"Then you are a fair sample of the fallacy of his system, if the disjointed bits of logic deserve the name."

"How so?"

"He continually exhorts to a happy, contented, and uncomplaining frame of mind; tells you sternly, that 'Discontent is the want of self-reliance; it is infirmity of will.'"

"You are disposed to be severe," muttered Cornelia, with an angry flash.

"What? because I expect his professed disciple to obey his injunctions?"

"Do you then conform so irreproachably to your own creed? Pray what is it?"

"I have no creed. I am honestly and anxiously hunting one. For a long time I thought that I had found a sound one in Emerson. But a careful study of his writings taught me that of all Pyrrhonists he is the prince. Can a creedless soul aid me in my search? verily no. He exclaims, 'To fill the hour—that is happiness; to fill the hour, and leave no crevice for repentance or an approval. We live amid surfaces, and the true art of life, is to skate well on them.' Now this sort of oyster existence does not suit me, Cornelia Graham, nor will it suit you."

"You do him injustice. He has a creed (true it is pantheistic), which he steadfastly adheres to under all circumstances."

"Oh! has he, indeed? Then he flatly contradicts you when he says, 'But lest I should mislead any, when I have my own head, and obey my whims, let me remind the reader that I am only an experimenter. Do not set the least value on what I do, or the least discredit on what I do not, as if I pretended to settle anything as true or false. I unsettle all things. No facts are to me sacred; none are profane. I simply experiment, an endless seeker, with no past at my back.' To my fancy that savors strongly of nihilism, as regards creeds."

"There is no such passage in Emerson," cried Cornelia, stamping one foot, unconsciously, on her blazing necklace.

"Yes, the passage is, word for word, as I quoted it, and you will find it in 'Circles.'"

"I have read 'Circles' several times, and do not remember it. At all events, it does not sound like Emerson."

"For that matter, his own individual circle of ideas is so much like St. Augustine's 'Circle, of which the center is everywhere and the circumference nowhere,' that I am not prepared to say what may or may not be found within it. You will ultimately think with me, that, though an earnest and profound thinker, your master is no Memnon, waking only before the sunlight of truth. His utterances are dim and contradictory." She replaced the book on the table, and taking up a small basket, resumed her sewing.

"But, Beulah, did you not accept his 'Law of Compensation?'"

"I believe its operations are correct as regards mere social position; wealth, penury, even the endowments of genius. But further than this, I do not accept it. I want to believe that my soul is immortal. Emerson's 'Duration of the attributes of the Soul' does not satisfy me. I desire something more than an immutability, or continued existence hereafter, in the form of an abstract idea of truth, justice, love or humility."

Cornelia looked at her steadily, and after a pause, said, with indescribable bitterness and despair:

"If our past and present shadows the future, I hope that my last sleep may be unbroken and eternal."

Beulah raised her head, and glanced searchingly at her companion; then silently went on with her work.

"I understand your honest face. You think I have no cause to talk so. You see me surrounded by wealth; petted, indulged in every whim, and you fancy that I am a very enviable woman; but—"

"There you entirely mistake me," interrupted Beulah, with a cold smile.

"You think that I ought to be very happy and contented, and useful in the sphere in which I move; and regard me, I know, as a weak hypochondriac. Beulah, physicians told me, long ago, that I lived upon the very brink of the grave, that I might die at any moment, without warning. My grandmother and one of my uncles died suddenly with this disease of the heart, and the shadow of death seems continually around me; it will not be dispelled—it haunts me forever. 'Boast not thyself of to-morrow,' said the preacher; but I cannot even boast of to-day, or this hour. The world knows nothing of this; it has been carefully concealed by my parents; but I know it! and, Beulah, I feel as did that miserable, doomed prisoner of Poe's 'Pit and Pendulum,' who saw the pendulum, slowly but surely, sweeping down upon him. My life has been a great unfulfilled promise. With what are generally considered elements of happiness in my home, I have always been solitary and unsatisfied. Conscious of my feeble tenure on life, I early set out to anchor myself in a calm faith, which would secure me a happy lot in eternity. My nature was strongly religious, and I longed to find hope and consolation in some of our churches. My parents always had a pew in the fashionable church in this city. You need not smile—I speak advisedly when I say 'fashionable' church; for assuredly, fashion has crept into religion also, nowadays. From my childhood, I was regularly dressed, and taken to church; but I soon began to question the sincerity of the pastor, and the consistency of the members. Sunday after Sunday, I saw them in their pews, and week after week, listened to their gossiping, slanderous chit-chat. Prominent members busied themselves about charitable associations, and headed subscription lists, and all the while set examples of frivolity, heartlessness, and what is softly termed 'fashionable excesses,' which shocked my ideas of Christian propriety, and disgusted me with the mockery their lives presented. I watched the minister in his social relations, and instead of reverencing him as a meek and holy man of God, I could not forbear looking with utter contempt upon his pompous, self-sufficient demeanor toward the mass of his flock; while to the most opulent and influential members he bowed down, with a servile, fawning sycophancy, absolutely disgusting. I attended various churches, listening to sermons, and watching the conduct of the prominent professing Christians of each. Many gave most liberally to so-called religious causes and institutions, and made amends by heavily draining the purses of widows and orphans. Some affected an ascetical simplicity of dress, and yet hugged their purses where their Bibles should have been. It was all Mammon worship; some grossly palpable, some adroitly cloaked under solemn faces and severe observance of the outward ceremonials. The clergy, as a class, I found strangely unlike what I had expected: instead of earnest zeal for the promotion of Christianity, I saw that the majority were bent only on the aggrandizement of their particular denomination. Verily, I thought in my heart, 'Is all this bickering the result of their religion? How these churches do hate each other!' According to each, salvation could only be found in their special tenets—within the pale of their peculiar organization; and yet, all professed to draw their doctrines from the same book: and, Beulah, the end of my search was, that I scorned all creeds and churches, and began to find a faith outside of a revelation which gave rise to so much narrow-minded bigotry—so much pharisaism and delusion. Those who call themselves ministers of the Christian religion should look well to their commissions, and beware how they go out into the world, unless the seal of Jesus be indeed upon their brows. They offer themselves as the Pharos of the people, but, ah! they sometimes wreck immortal souls by their unpardonable inconsistencies. For the last two years I have been groping my way after some system upon which I could rest the little time I have to live. Oh, I am heart-sick and despairing!"

"What? already! Take courage, Cornelia; there is truth somewhere," answered Beulah, with kindling eyes.

"Where, where? Ah! that echo mocks you, turn which way you will. I sit like Raphael-Aben-Ezra—at the 'Bottom of the Abyss,' but unlike him, I am no Democritus to jest over my position. I am too miserable to laugh, and my grim Emersonian fatalism gives me precious little comfort, though it is about the only thing that I do firmly believe in."

She stooped to pick up her necklace, shook it in the glow of the fire until a shower of rainbow hues flashed out, and holding it up, asked contemptuously:

"What do you suppose this piece of extravagance cost?"

"I have no idea."

"Why, fifteen hundred dollars—that is all! Oh, what is the blaze of diamonds to a soul like mine, shrouded in despairing darkness, and hovering upon the very confines of eternity, if there be any!" She threw the costly gift on the table, and wearily closed her eyes.

"You have become discouraged too soon, Cornelia. Your very anxiety to discover truth evinces its existence, for Nature always supplies the wants she creates!"

"You will tell me that this truth is to be found down in the depths of my own soul; for no more than logic, has it ever been discovered 'parceled and labeled.' But how do I know that all truth is not merely subjective? Ages ago, skepticism intrenched itself in an impregnable fortress: 'There is no criterion of truth.' How do I know that my 'truth,' 'good,' and 'beautiful' are absolutely so? My reason is no infallible plummet to sound the sea of phenomena and touch noumena. I tell you, Beulah, it is all—"

A hasty rap at the door cut short this discussion, and as Eugene entered, the cloud on Cornelia's brow instantly lifted. His gay Christmas greeting, and sunny, handsome face, diverted her mind, and as her hand rested on his arm, her countenance evinced a degree of intense love, such as Beulah had supposed her incapable of feeling.

"It is very selfish, sister mine, to keep Beulah so constantly beside you, when we all want to see something of her."

"Was I ever anything else but selfish?"

"But I thought you prided yourself on requiring no society?"

"So I do, as regards society in general; but Beulah is an exception."

"You intend to come down to-night, do you not?"

"Not if I can avoid it. Eugene, take Beulah into the parlor, and ask Antoinette to sing. Afterward make Beulah sing, also, and be sure to leave all the doors open, so that I can hear. Mind, you must not detain her long."

Beulah would have demurred, but at this moment she saw Dr. Hartwell's buggy approaching the house. Her heart seemed to spring to her lips, and feeling that after their last unsatisfactory interview, she was in no mood to meet him, she quickly descended the steps, so blinded by haste that she failed to perceive the hand Eugene extended to assist her. The door-bell uttered a sharp peal as they reached the hall, and she had just time to escape into the parlor when the doctor was ushered in.

"What is the matter?" asked Eugene, observing the nervous flutter of her lips.

"Ask Miss Dupres to sing, will you?"

He looked at her curiously an instant, then turned away and persuaded the little beauty to sing.

She took her seat, and ran her jeweled fingers over the pearl keys with an air which very clearly denoted her opinion of her musical proficiency.

"Well, sir, what will you have?"

"That favorite morceau from *'Linda.'*"

"You have never heard it, I suppose," said she, glancing over her shoulder at the young teacher.

"Yes, I have heard it," answered Beulah, who could with difficulty repress a smile.

Antoinette half shrugged her shoulders, as if she thought the statement questionable, and began the song. Beulah listened attentively; she was conscious of feeling more than ordinary interest in this performance, and almost held her breath as the clear, silvery voice caroled through the most intricate passages. Antoinette had been thoroughly trained, and certainly her voice was remarkably sweet and flexible; but as she concluded the piece, and fixed her eyes complacently on Beulah, the latter lifted her head, in proud consciousness of superiority.

"Sing me something else," said she.

Antoinette bit her lips, and answered ungraciously.

"No; I shall have to sing to-night, and can't wear myself out."

"Now, Beulah, I shall hear you. I have sought an opportunity ever since I returned." Eugene spoke rather carelessly.

"Do you really wish to hear me, Eugene?"

"Of course I do," said he, with some surprise.

"And so do I," added Mrs. Graham, leaning against the piano, and exchanging glances with Antoinette.

Beulah looked up, and asked quietly:

"Eugene, shall I sing you a ballad? One of those simple old tunes we used to love so well in days gone by."

"No, no. Something operatic," cried Antoinette, without giving him an opportunity to reply.

"Well, then, Miss Dupres, select something."

"Can't you favor us with *'Casta-Diva'?*" returned the beauty, with something very like a sneer.

Beulah's eyes gave a momentary flash, but by a powerful effort she curbed her anger, and commenced the song.

It was amusing to mark the expression of utter astonishment which gradually overspread Antoinette's face, as the magnificent voice of her despised rival swelled in waves of entrancing melody through the lofty rooms. Eugene looked quite as much amazed. Beulah felt her triumph, and heartily enjoyed it. There was a sparkle in her eye, and a proud smile on her lip, which she did not attempt to conceal. As she rose from the piano, Eugene caught her hand, and said eagerly:

"I never dreamed of your possessing such a voice. It is superb—perfectly magnificent! Why did not you tell me of it before?"

"You heard it long ago, in the olden time," said she, withdrawing her hand and looking steadily at him.

"Ah, but it has improved incredibly. You were all untutored then."

"It is the culture, then, not the voice itself? Eh, Eugene?"

"It is both. Who taught you?"

"I had several teachers, but owe what excellence I may possess to my guardian. He aided me more than all the instruction books that ever were compiled."

"You must come and practise with the musical people who meet here very frequently," said Mrs. Graham.

"Thank you, madam; I have other engagements which will prevent my doing so."

"Nonsense, Beulah, we have claims on you. I certainly have," answered Eugene.

"Have you? I was not aware of the fact."

There was a patronizing manner in all this which she felt no disposition to submit to.

"Most assuredly I have, Beulah, and mean to maintain them."

She perfectly understood the haughty expression of his countenance, and, moving toward the door, replied coldly:

"Another time, Eugene, we will discuss them."

"Where are you going?" inquired Mrs. Graham, rather stiffly.

"To Cornelia. The doctor came down a few minutes since."

She did not pause to hear what followed, but ran up the steps, longing to get out of a house where she plainly perceived her presence was by no means desired. Cornelia sat with her head drooped on her thin hand, and without looking up, said, more gently than was her custom:

"Why did you hurry back so soon?"

"Because the parlor was not particularly attractive."

There came the first good-humored laugh which Beulah had ever heard from Cornelia's lips as the latter replied:

"What friends you and old growling Diogenes would have been. Pray, how did my cousin receive your performance?"

"Very much as if she wished me amid the ruins of Persepolis, where I certainly shall be before I inflict anything more upon her. Cornelia, do not ask or expect me to come here again, for I will not; of course, it is quite as palpable to you as to me that I am no favorite with your parents, and something still less with your cousin. Consequently, you need not expect to see me here again."

"Do not say so, Beulah; you must, you shall come, and I will see that no one dares interfere with my wishes. As for Antoinette, she is simply a vain idiot; you might just as well be told the truth, for doubtless you will see it for yourself; she is my mother's niece, an only child, and possessed of considerable wealth. I suppose it is rather natural that my parents should fondle the idea of her being Eugene's wife. They do not see how utterly unsuited they are. Eugene will, of course, inherit the fortune which I once imagined I should have the pleasure of squandering. My father and mother dread lest Eugene should return to his 'boyish fancy' (as you are pleased to term it), and look on you with jealous eyes. Oh! Mammon is the God of this generation. But, Beulah, you must not allow all this miserable maneuvering to keep you from me. If you do, I will very soon succeed in making this home of mine very unpleasant for Antoinette Dupres. When I am dead, she can wheedle my family as successfully as they choose to permit; but while I do live, she shall forbear. Poor, contemptible human nature! verily, I rejoice sometimes when I remember that I shall not be burdened with any of it long." An angry spot burned on each pallid cheek, and the beautiful mouth curled scornfully.

"Do not excite yourself so unnecessarily, Cornelia. What you may or may not think of your relatives is no concern of mine. You have a carriage always at your command, and when you desire to see a real friend, you can visit me. Let this suffice for this subject. Suppose we have a game of chess or backgammon? What do you say?"

She wheeled a light table toward the hearth, but the invalid motioned it away, and answered moodily:

"I am in no humor for games. Sit down and tell me about your leaving Dr. Hartwell's protection."

"I have nothing to tell."

"He is a singular being?"

Receiving no answer, she added impatiently:

"Don't you think so?"

"I do, in the sense of great superiority."

"The world is not so flattering in its estimate."

"No, for slander loves a lofty mark."

"Beulah Benton, do you mean that for me?"

"Not unless you feel that it applies to you particularly."

"If he is so faultless and unequaled, pray, why did not you remain in his house?"

"I am not in the habit of accounting to any one for my motives or my actions." She lifted her slender form haughtily.

"In which case, the public has a habit of supplying both."

"Then accept its fabrications."

"You need not be so fierce. I like Dr. Hartwell quite as well as you do, I dare say; but probably I know more of his history."

"It is all immaterial to me. Drop the subject, if you please, and let me read to you. I believe I came here for quiet companionship, not recrimination and cross-questioning."

"Beulah, the world says you are to marry your guardian. I do not ask from impertinent curiosity, but sincere friendship—is it true?"

"About as true as your notion of my marriage with Eugene. No; scarcely so plausible."

"Our families were connected, you know."

"No, I neither know, nor wish to know. He never alluded to his wife, or his history, and I have just now no desire to hear anything about the matter. He is the best friend I ever had; I want to honor and reverence him always; and, of course, the world's version of his domestic affairs does him injustice. So be good enough to say no more about him."

"Very well. On hearing your voice from the parlor, he left a small parcel, which he requested me to give you. He laid it on the table, I believe; yes, there it is. Now read 'Egmont' to me, if you please."

Cornelia crossed the room, threw herself on a couch, and settled her pillow comfortably. Beulah took the parcel, which was carefully sealed, and wondered what it contained. It was heavy, and felt hard. They had parted in anger; what could it possibly be? Cornelia's black eyes were on her countenance. She put the package in her pocket, seated herself by the couch, and commenced "Egmont."

It was with a feeling of indescribable relief that the orphan awoke, at dawn the following morning, and dressed by the gray twilight. She had fallen asleep the night before amid the hum of voices, of laughter and of dancing feet. Sounds of gaiety from the merry party below had found their way to the chamber of the heiress, and when Beulah left her at midnight she was still wakeful and restless. The young teacher could not wait for the late breakfast of the luxurious Grahams, and just as the first level ray of sunshine flashed up from the east she tied on her bonnet, and noiselessly entered Cornelia's room. The heavy curtains kept it close and dark, and on the hearth a taper burned with pale, sickly light. Cornelia slept soundly; but her breathing was heavy and irregular, and the face wore a scowl, as if some severe pain had distorted it. The ivory-like arms were thrown up over the head, and large drops glistened on the wan brow. Beulah stood beside the bed a few minutes; the apartment was furnished with almost oriental splendor; but how all this satin, and rosewood, and silver and marble, mocked the restless, suffering sleeper? Beulah felt tears of compassion weighing down her lashes as she watched the haggard countenance of this petted child of fortune; but unwilling to rouse her, she silently stole down the steps. The hall was dark; the smell of gas almost stifling. Of course, the servants followed the example of their owners, and as no one appeared she unlocked the street door and walked homeward with a sensation of pleasurable relief, which impressed itself very legibly on her face. The sky was cloudless; the early risen sun looked over the earth in dazzling radiance; and the cold, pure, wintry air, made the blood tingle in Beulah's veins. A great unspeakable joy filled her soul; the uplifted eyes beamed with gladness; her brave, hopeful spirit, looked into the future with unquestioning trust; and as the image of her unhappy friend flitted across her mind, she exclaimed:

"This world is full of beauty, like other worlds above;
And if we did our duty, it might be full of love."

She ran up to her room, threw open the blinds, looped back the curtains, and drew that mysterious package from her pocket. She was very curious to see the contents, and broke the seal with trembling fingers. The outer wrappings fell off, and disclosed an oblong, *papier-mâché* case. It opened with a spring, and revealed to her a beautiful watch and chain, bearing her name in delicate tracery. A folded slip of paper lay on the crimson velvet lining of the box, and recognizing the characters, she hastily read this brief sentence:

"Wear it constantly, Beulah, to remind you that, in adversity, you still have

"A GUARDIAN."

Tears gushed unrestrained, as she looked at the beautiful gift. Not for an instant did she dream of accepting it, and she shrank shudderingly from widening the breach which already existed, by a refusal. Locking up the slip of paper in her work-box, she returned the watch to its case, and carefully retied the parcel. Long before, she had wrapped the purse in paper, and prevailed on Clara to give it to the doctor. He had received it without comment, but she could not return the watch in the same way, for Clara was now able to attend regularly to her school duties, and it was very uncertain when she would see him. Yet she felt comforted, for this gift assured her, that however coldly he chose to treat her when they met, he had not thrown her off entirely. With all her independence, she could not bear the thought of his utter alienation; and the consciousness of his remaining interest thrilled her heart with gladness.

CHAPTER XXIII.

One Saturday morning, some days subsequent to her visit to the Grahams, Beulah set off for the business part of the city. She was closely veiled, and carried under her shawl a thick roll of neatly written paper. A publishing house was the place of her destination; and as she was ushered into a small back room, to await the leisure of the gentleman she wished to see, she could not forbear smiling at the novelty of her position, and the audacity of the attempt she was about to make. There she sat, in the editor's sanctum, trying to quiet the tumultuous beating of her heart. Presently, a tall, spare man, with thin, cadaverous visage, entered, bowed, took a chair, and eyed her with a "what-do-you-want" sort of expression. His grizzled hair was cut short, and stood up like bristles, and his keen blue eyes were by no means promising, in their cold glitter. Beulah threw off her veil, and said, with rather an unsteady voice:

"You are the editor of the magazine published here, I believe?"

He bowed again, leaned back in his chair, and crossed his hands at the back of his head.

"I came to offer you an article for the magazine." She threw down the roll of paper on a chair.

"Ah!—hem!—will you favor me with your name?"

"Beulah Benton, sir. One altogether unknown to fame."

He contracted his eyes, coughed, and said, constrainedly:

"Are you a subscriber?"

"I am."

"What is the character of your manuscript?" He took it up as he spoke, and glanced over the pages.

"You can determine that from a perusal. If the sketch suits you, I should like to become a regular contributor."

A gleam of sunshine strayed over the countenance, and the editor answered, very benignly:

"If the article meets with our approbation, we shall be very happy to afford you a medium of publication in our journal. Can we depend on your punctuality?"

"I think so. What are your terms?"

"Terms, madam? I supposed that your contribution was gratuitous," said he, very loftily.

"Then you are most egregiously mistaken! What do you imagine induces me to write?"

"Why, desire for fame, I suppose."

"Fame is rather unsatisfactory fare. I am poor, sir, and write to aid me in maintaining myself."

"Are you dependent solely on your own exertions, madam?"

"Yes."

"I am sorry I cannot aid you; but nowadays, there are plenty of authors, who write merely as a pastime and we have as many contributions as we can well look over."

"I am to understand, then, that the magazine is supported altogether by gratuitous contributions?" said Beulah, unable to repress a smile.

"Why you see, authorship has become a sort of luxury," was the hesitating reply.

"I think the last number of your magazine contained, among other articles in the 'editor's drawer,' an earnest appeal to southern authors to come to the rescue of southern periodicals?"

"True, madam: southern intellect seems steeped in a lethargy, from which we are most faithfully endeavoring to arouse it."

"The article to which I allude, also animadverted severely upon the practise of southern authors patronizing northern publishing establishments?"

"Most certainly, it treated the subject stingently." He moved uneasily.

"I believe the subscription is the same as that of the northern periodicals?"

A very cold bow was the only answer.

"I happen to know that northern magazines are not composed of gratuitous contributions; and it is no mystery why southern authors are driven to northern publishers. Southern periodicals are mediums only for those of elegant leisure, who can afford to write without remuneration. With the same subscription price, you cannot pay for your articles. It is no marvel that, under such circumstances, we have no southern literature. Unluckily, I belong to the numerous class who have to look away from home for remuneration. Sir, I will not trouble you with my manuscript." Rising, she held out her hand for it; but the keen eyes had fallen upon a paragraph which seemed to interest the editor, and knitting his brows, he said, reluctantly:

"We have not been in the habit of paying for our articles, but I will look over this, and perhaps you can make it worth our while to pay you. The fact is, madam, we have more trash sent us than we can find room for; but if you can contribute anything of weight, why, it will make a difference of course. I did not recognize you at first, but I now remember that I heard your valedictory to the graduating class of the public schools. If we should conclude to pay you for regular contributions, we wish nothing said about it."

"Very well. If you like the manuscript, and decide to pay me, you can address me a note through the post-office. Should I write for the magazine, I particularly desire not to be known." She lowered her veil, and most politely he bowed her out. She was accustomed to spend a portion of each Saturday in practising duets with Georgia Asbury, and thither she now directed her steps. Unluckily, the parlor was full of visitors, and without seeing any of the family, she walked back into the music room. Here she felt perfectly at home, and closing the door, forgot everything but her music. Taking no heed of the lapse of time, she played piece after piece, until startled by the clear tones of the doctor's voice. She looked up, and saw him standing in the door which opened into the library, taking off his great-coat.

"Why, Beulah, that room is cold as a Texas norther. What on earth are you doing there without a fire? Come in here, child, and warm your frozen digits. Where are those two harum-scarum specimens of mine?"

"I believe they are still entertaining company, sir. The parlor was full when I came, and they know nothing of my being here." She sat down by the bright fire, and held her stiff fingers toward the glowing coals.

"Yes, confound their dear rattlepates; that is about the sum-total of their cogitations." He drew up his chair, put his feet on the fender of the grate, and lighting his cigar, added:

"Is my spouse also in the parlor?"

"I suppose so, sir."

"Time was, Beulah, when Saturday was the great day of preparation for all housekeepers. Bless my soul! My mother would just about as soon have thought of anticipating the discovery of the open Polar Sea, by a trip thither, as going out to visit on Saturday. Why, from my boyhood, Saturday has been synonymous with scouring, window-washing, pastry-baking, stocking-darning, and numerous other venerable customs, which this age is rapidly dispensing with. My wife had a lingering reverence for the duties of the day, and tried to excuse herself, but I suppose those pretty wax dolls of mine have coaxed her into 'receiving,' as they call it. Beulah, my wife is an exception, but the mass of married women nowaday, instead of being thorough housewives (as nature intended they should), are delicate, do-nothing, know-nothing, fine ladies. They have no duties. 'O tempora, O mores!'" He paused to relight his cigar, and just then Georgia came in, dressed very richly. He tossed the taper into the grate, and exclaimed, as she threw her arms around his neck and kissed him:

"You pretty imp; what is to pay now? Here Beulah has been sitting, nobody knows how long, in that frigid zone you call your music-room. What are you rigged out in all that finery for?"

"We are going to dine out to-day, father. Beulah will excuse me, I know."

"Indeed! Dine where?"

"Mrs. Delmont came round this morning to invite us to dine with some of her young friends from New Orleans."

"Well, I shan't go, that is all."

"Oh, you are not expected, sir," laughed Georgia, brushing the gray locks from his ample forehead.

"Not expected, eh? Does your lady mother contemplate leaving me to discuss my dinner in doleful solitude?"

"No, mother has gone with Mrs. Rallston to see about some poor starving family in the suburbs. She will be back soon, I dare say. Mrs. Delmont has sent her carriage, and Helen is waiting for me; so I must go. Beulah, I am very sorry we have been cut out of our practising. Don't go home; stay with mother to-day, and when I come back we will have a glorious time. Can't you now? There's a darling."

"Oh, you wheedling, hypocritical madcap, take yourself off! Of course Beulah will try to endure the stupid talk of a poor old man, whose daughters are too fashionable to look after him, and whose wife is so extremely charitable that she forgets it 'begins at home.' Clear out, you trial of paternal patience!" He kissed her rosy lips, and she hurried away, protesting that she would prefer remaining at home.

"Beulah, I gave Hartwell that parcel you intrusted to me. He looked just as if I had plunged him into a snow-bank, but said nothing."

"Thank you, sir."

"Oh, don't thank me for playing go-between. I don't relish any such work. It is very evident that you two have quarreled. I would about as soon consult that poker as ask Hartwell what is to pay. Now, child, what *is* the matter?"

"Nothing new, sir. He has never forgiven me for turning teacher."

"Forgiven! Bless me, he is as spiteful as a Pequod."

"Begging your pardon, Dr. Asbury, he is no such thing," cried Beulah, impetuously.

"Just what I might have expected. I am to understand, then, that you can abuse my partner sufficiently without any vituperative assistance from me?" He brushed the ashes from his cigar, and looked at her quizzically.

"Sir, it pains me to hear him spoken of so lightly."

"Lightly! Upon my word I thought Indianic malice was rather a heavy charge. However, I can succeed better if you will allow—"

"Don't jest, sir. Please say no more about him."

His face became instantly grave, and he answered earnestly:

"Beulah, as a sincere friend, I would advise you not to alienate Hartwell. There are very few such men: I do not know his equal. He is interested in your welfare and happiness, and is the best friend you ever had or ever will have."

"I know it, and prize his friendship above all others."

"Then, why did you return that watch? If he wished you to wear it, why should you refuse? Mark me, he said nothing about it to me, but I saw the watch, with your name engraved on the case, at the jewelry store where I bought one just like it for Georgia. I surmised it was that same watch, when you intrusted the package to me."

"I was already greatly indebted to him, and did not wish to increase the obligation."

"My child, under the circumstances, you were too fastidious. He was very much annoyed; though, as I told you before, he made no allusion to the subject."

"Yes; I knew he would be, and I am very sorry, but could not think of accepting it."

"Oh, you are well matched, upon my word."

"What do you mean?"

"That you are both as proud as Lucifer, and as savage as heathens. Child, I don't see what is to become of you."

"Every soul is the star of its own destiny," answered Beulah.

"Well, very sorry destinies the majority make, I can tell you. Have you seen Mrs. Lockhart and Pauline?"

"No. I was not aware that they were in the city."

"Lockhart's health is miserable. They are all at Hartwell's for a few weeks, I believe. Pauline has grown up a perfect Di Vernon beauty."

"I should like very much to see her. She is a generous, noble-souled girl."

"Yes, I rather think she is. Hartwell said the other day that Pauline was anxious to see you; and since I think of it, I believe he asked me to tell you of her arrival. Now I will wager my head that you intend to wait until she calls formally, which it is your place to do."

"Then, sir, expect immediate decapitation, for I shall go out to see her this very afternoon," replied Beulah.

"That is right, my dear child."

"Dr. Asbury, if you will not think me troublesome, I should like to tell you of some things that perplex me very much," said she, hesitatingly.

"I shall be glad to hear whatever you have to say, and if I can possibly help you, rest assured I will. What perplexes you?"

"A great many things, sir. Of late, I have read several works that have unsettled my former faith, and indeed confused and darkened my mind most miserably, and I thought you might aid me in my search after truth."

He threw his cigar into the fire, and while an expression of sorrow clouded his face, said, very gravely:

"Beulah, I am afraid I am one of the last persons to whom you should apply for assistance. Do the perplexities to which you allude involve religious questions?"

"Yes, sir, almost entirely."

"I am too unsettled myself to presume to direct others."

Beulah looked up, in unfeigned astonishment.

"You certainly are not what is termed skeptical?"

"Most sincerely do I wish that I was not."

There was a short silence, broken by Beulah's saying, slowly and sorrowfully:

"You cannot aid me, then!"

"I am afraid not. When a young man, I was thoroughly skeptical in my religious views (if I may be said to have had any). At the time of my marriage I was an infidel, and such the world still calls me. If I am not now, it is because my wife's unpretending consistent piety has taught me to revere the precepts of a revelation which I long ago rejected. Her pure religion makes me respect Christianity, which once I sneered at. I am forced to acknowledge the happy results of her faith, and I may yet be brought to yield up old prejudices and confess its divine origin. I am no Atheist, thank God! never have been. But I tell you candidly, my doubts concerning the Bible make me an unsafe guide for a mind like yours. For some time I have marked the course of your reading, by the books I missed from my shelves, and have feared just what has happened. On one point my experience may be of value to you. What is comprised under the head of philosophical research will never aid or satisfy you. I am an old man, Beulah, and have studied philosophic works for many years; but, take my word for it, the mass of them are sheer humbug. From the beginning of the world, philosophers have been investigating the countless mysteries which present themselves to every earnest mind; but the arcana are as inscrutable now as ever. I do not wish to discourage you, Beulah; nor do I desire to underrate human capabilities, but, in all candor, this kind of study does not pay. It has not repaid me—it has not satisfied Hartwell, who went deeper into metaphysics than any one I know, and who now has less belief of any sort than any one I ever wish to know. I would not advise you to prosecute this branch of study. I am content to acknowledge that of many things I know nothing, and never can be any wiser; but Guy Hartwell is too proud to admit his incapacity to grapple with some of these mysteries. Beulah, my wife is one of the happiest spirits I ever knew: she is a consistent Christian. When we were married, I watched her very closely; I tell you, child, I hope very much that I should find some glaring incongruity in her conduct which would have sanctioned my skepticism. I was continually on the lookout for defects of character that might cast contempt on the religion she professed. I did not expect her to prove so pure-hearted, unselfish, humble, and genuinely pious as I found her. I do most sincerely revere such religion as hers. Ah! if it were not so rare, I should never have been so skeptical. She has taught me that the precepts of the Bible do regulate the heart and purify the life; and to you, child, I will say, candidly, 'almost she has persuaded me to be a Christian.' Whatever of—"

He said no more, for at this moment the door opened, and Mrs. Asbury entered. She welcomed Beulah with a cordial sincerity, singularly soothing to the orphan's heart, and keeping her hand in a tight clasp, asked several questions, which her husband cut short by drawing her to his side.

"Where have you been straying to, madam?"

"Where you must stray to, sir, just as soon as you start out this evening on your round of visits."

She softly smoothed back his hair and kissed his forehead. She was a noble-looking woman, with a tranquil countenance that betokened a serene, cloudless soul; and as she stood beside her husband, his eyes rested on her face with an expression bordering on adoration. Beulah could not avoid wondering why such women were so very rare, and the thought presented itself with painful force, "if Cornelia Graham and I had had such mothers, we might both have been happier and better." Probably something of what crossed her mind crept into her countenance, for the doctor asked, laughingly:

"In the name of Venus! what are you screwing up your lips, and looking so ugly about?"

"I suppose one reason is, that I must go home." She rose, with a suppressed sigh.

"I am disposed to think it much more probable that you were envying me my wife. Come, confess."

"I was wishing that I had such a mother."

With some sudden impulse she threw her arms round Mrs. Asbury's neck, and hid her face on her shoulder.

"Then let me be your mother, my dear child," said she, pressing the girl affectionately to her heart, and kissing her pale cheek.

"Are you troubled about anything, my dear?" continued Mrs. Asbury, surprised at this manifestation of feeling in one usually so cold and reserved.

"An orphan heart mourns its dead idols," answered Beulah, raising her head, and withdrawing from the kind arm that encircled her. Mrs. Asbury interpreted a quick glance from her husband, and did not press the matter further; but at parting, she accompanied Beulah to the front door, and earnestly assured her that if she could in any way advise or assist her she would consider it both a privilege and a pleasure to do so. Returning to the library, she laid her soft hand on her husband's arm, and said anxiously:

"George, what is the matter with her?"

"She is distressed, or rather perplexed about her religious doubts, I inferred from what she said just before you came in. She has drifted out into a troubled sea of philosophy, I am inclined to think, and not satisfied with what she has found, is now irresolute as to the proper course. Poor child, she is terribly in earnest about the matter." He sighed heavily.

His wife watched him eagerly.

"What did you tell her?"

"Not to come to me; that it would be a perfect exemplification of 'the blind leading the blind;' and when she learned my own state of uncertainty, she seemed to think so herself."

"An expression of acute pain passed over her features, but banishing it as speedily as possible, she answered very gently:

"Take care, my husband, lest by recapitulating your doubts, you strengthen hers."

"Alice, I told her the whole truth. She is not a nature to be put off with half-way statements. Hartwell is an avowed infidel, and she knows it; yet I do not believe his views have weighed with her against received systems of faith. My dear Alice, this spirit of skepticism is scattered far and wide over the land; I meet with it often where I least expect it. It broods like a hideous nightmare over this age, and Beulah must pass through the same ordeal which is testing the intellectual portion of every community. But—there is that eternal door-bell. Let us have dinner, Alice, I must go out early this afternoon."

He took down a pair of scales, and began to weigh some medicine. His wife wisely forbore to renew the discussion, and ringing the bell for dinner, interested him with an account of her visit to a poor family, who required his immediate attention.

With a heart unwontedly heavy, Beulah prepared to call upon Pauline, later in the afternoon of the same day. It was not companionship she needed, for this was supplied by books, and the sensation of loneliness was one with which she had not yet been made acquainted; but she wanted a strong, healthy, cultivated intellect to dash away the mists that were wreathing about her own mind. Already, the lofty, imposing structure of self-reliance began to rock to its very foundations. She was nearly ready for her walk, when Mrs. Hoyt came in.

"Miss Beulah, there is a lady in the parlor waiting to see you."

"Is it Miss Graham?"

"No. She is a stranger, and gave no name."

Beulah descended to the parlor in rather an ungracious mood. As she entered, a lady sprang to meet her, with both hands extended. She was superbly beautiful, with a complexion of dazzling whiteness, and clear, radiant, violet eyes, over which arched delicately penciled brows. The Grecian mouth and chin were faultlessly chiseled; the whole face was one of rare loveliness.

"You don't know me! For shame, Beulah, to forget old friends."

"Oh, Pauline, is it you? I am very glad to see you."

"Don't say that for politeness' sake! Here I have been for ten days and you have not stirred a foot to see me."

"I didn't know you were in town till this morning, and just as you came I was putting on my bonnet to go and see you."

"Are you telling the truth?"

"Yes; positively I am."

"Well, I am glad you felt disposed to see me. After my uncle, you and Charon are all I cared anything about meeting here. Bless your dear, solemn, gray eyes! how often I have wanted to see you."

The impulsive girl threw her arms round Beulah's neck, and kissed her repeatedly.

"Be quiet, and let me look at you. Oh, Pauline, how beautiful you have grown!" cried Beulah, who could not forbear expressing the admiration she felt.

"Yes; the artists in Florence raved considerably about my beauty. I can't tell you the number of times I sat for my portrait. It is very pleasant to be pretty; I enjoy it amazingly," said she, with all the candor which had characterized her in childhood; and with a vigorous squeeze of Beulah's hand, she continued:

"I was astonished when I came, and found that you had left Uncle Guy, and were teaching little ragged, dirty children their A, B, Cs. What possessed you to do such a silly thing?"

"Duty, my dear Pauline."

"Oh, for heaven's sake, don't begin about duty. Ernest—" She paused, a rich glow swept over her face, and shaking back her curls, she added:

"You must quit all this. I say you must!"

"I see you are quite as reckless and scatter-brained as ever," answered Beulah, smiling at her authoritative tone.

"No, I positively am not the fool Uncle Guy used to think me. I have more sense than people give me credit for, though I dare say I shall find you very skeptical on the subject. Beulah, I know very well why you took it into your wise head to be a teacher. You were unwilling to usurp what you considered my place in Uncle Guy's home and heart. You need not straighten yourself in that ungraceful way. I know perfectly well it is the truth; but I am no poor, suffering, needy innocent, that you should look after. I am well provided for, and don't intend to take one cent of Uncle Guy's money, so you might just as well have the benefit of it. I know, too, that you and ma did not exactly adore each other. I understand all about that old skirmishing. But things have changed very much, Beulah; so you must quit this horrid nonsense about working, and being independent."

"How you do rattle on, about things you don't comprehend," laughed Beulah.

"Come, don't set me down for a simpleton! I tell you I am in earnest! You must come back to Uncle Guy!"

"Pauline, it is worse than useless to talk of this matter. I decided long ago as to what I ought to do, and certainly shall not change my opinion now. Tell me what you saw in Europe."

"Why, has not Eugene told you all you wish to know? Apropos! I saw him at a party last night, playing the devoted to that little beauty, Netta Dupres. We were all in Paris at the same time. I don't fancy her; she is too insufferably vain and affected. It is my opinion that she is flirting with Eugene, which must be quite agreeable to you. Oh, I tell you, Beulah, I could easily put her mind, heart and soul, in my thimble!"

"I did not ask your estimate of Miss Dupres. I want to know something of your European tour. I see Eugene very rarely."

"Oh! of course we went to see all the sights, and very stupid it was. Mr. Lockhart scolded continually about my want of taste and appreciation, because I did not utter all the interjections of delight and astonishment over old tumble-down ruins, and genuine 'master-pieces' of art, as he called them. Upon my word, I have been tired almost to death, when he and ma descanted by the hour on the 'inimitable, and transcendent, and entrancing' beauties and glories of old pictures that were actually so black with age that they looked like daubs of tar, and I could not tell whether the figures were men or women, archangels or cow-drivers. Some things I did enjoy; such as the Alps, and the Mediterranean, and St. Peter's, and Westminster Abbey, and some of the German cathedrals. But as to keeping my finger on the guide-book, and committing all the ecstasy to memory, to spout out just at the exact moment, when I saw nothing to deserve it, why that is all fudge. I tell you there is nothing in all Europe equal to our Niagara! I was heartily glad to come home, though I enjoyed some things amazingly."

"How is Mr. Lockhart's health?"

"Very poor, I am sorry to say. He looks so thin and pale, I often tell him he would make quite as good a pictured saint as any we saw abroad."

"How long will you remain here?"

"Till Uncle Guy thinks Mr. Lockhart is well enough to go to his plantation, I suppose."

"What makes you so restless, Pauline? Why don't you sit still?" asked Beulah, observing that her visitor twisted about as if uncomfortable.

"Because I want to tell you something, and really do not know how to begin," said she, laughing and blushing.

"I cannot imagine what should disconcert you, Pauline."

"Thank you. Truly, that is a flattering tribute to my sensibility. Beulah, can't you guess what I have to tell you?"

"Certainly not. But why should you hesitate to disclose it?"

"Simply because your tremendous gray eyes have such an owlish way of looking people out of countenance. Now don't look quite through me, and I will pluck up my courage and confess. Beulah—I am going to be married soon." She hid her crimsoned cheeks behind her hands.

"Married? impossible!" cried Beulah.

"But I tell you I am! Here is my engagement ring. Now, the most astonishing part of the whole affair is, that my intended sovereign is a minister! A preacher, as solemn as Job!"

"You a minister's wife, Pauline? Oh, child, you are jesting!" said Beulah, with an incredulous smile.

"No! absurd as it may seem, it is nevertheless true. I am to be married in March. Ma says I am a fool; Mr. Lockhart encourages and supports me; and Uncle Guy laughs heartily every time the affair is alluded to. At first, before we went to Europe, there was violent opposition from my mother, but she found I was in earnest, and now it is all settled for March. Uncle Guy knows Ernest Mortimor, and esteems him very highly, but thinks that I am the last woman in the United States who ought to be a minister's wife. I believe he told Ernest as much, but of course he did not believe him."

"Where does Mr. Mortimor reside?"

"In Georgia; has charge of a church there. He had a sister at the same school I attended in New York; and during a visit to her, he says he met his evil-angel in me. He is about five years my senior; but he is here now, and you will have an opportunity of forming your own opinion of him."

"How long have you known him?"

"About two years. I am rather afraid of him, to tell you the honest truth. He is so grave, and has such rigid notions, that I wonder very much what ever induced his holiness to fancy such a heedless piece of womanhood, as he is obliged to know I am; for I never put on any humility or sanctity. What do you think, Beulah? Uncle Guy coolly told me, this morning, in Ernest's presence, that he was only charmed by my pretty face, and that if I did not learn some common sense, he would very soon repent his choice. Oh, the doleful warnings I have been favored with! But you shall all see that I am worthy of Mr. Mortimor's love."

Her beautiful face was radiant with hope, yet in the violet eyes there lurked unshed tears.

"I am very glad that you are so happy, Pauline; and if you will, I am very sure you can make yourself all that Mr. Mortimor could desire."

"I am resolved I will. Yesterday he talked to me very seriously about the duties which he said would devolve on me. I tried to laugh him out of his sober mood, but he would talk about 'pastoral relations,' and what would be expected of a pastor's wife, until I was ready to cry with vexation. Ernest is not dependent on his salary; his father is considered wealthy, I believe, which fact reconciles ma in some degree. To-morrow he will preach in Dr. Hew's church, and you must go to hear him. I have never yet heard him preach, and am rather anxious to know what sort of sermons I am to listen to for the remainder of my life." She looked at her watch, and rose.

"I shall certainly go to hear him," answered Beulah.

"Of course you will, and after service you must go home and spend the day with me. Ma begs that you will not refuse to dine with her; and as you are engaged all the week, Uncle Guy expects you also; that is, he told me to insist on your coming, but thought you would probably decline. Will you come? Do say yes."

"I don't know yet. I will see you at church."

Thus they parted.

CHAPTER XXIV.

On Sabbath morning, Beulah sat beside the window, with her folded hands resting on her lap. The day was cloudless and serene; the sky of that intense melting blue which characterizes our clime. From every quarter of the city brazen muezzins called worshippers to the temple, and bands of neatly clad, happy children thronged the streets, on their way to Sabbath school. Save these, and the pealing bells, a hush pervaded all things, as though nature were indeed "at her prayers." Blessed be the hallowed influences which every sunny Sabbath morn exerts! Blessed be the holy tones, which at least once a week call every erring child back to its Infinite Father! For some time Beulah had absented herself from church, for she found that instead of profiting by sermons, she came home to criticise and question. But early associations are strangely tenacious, and as she watched the children trooping to the house of God, there rushed to her mind memories of other years, when the orphan bands from the Asylum regularly took their places in the Sabbath school. The hymns she sang then rang again in her ears; long-forgotten passages of Scripture, repeated then, seemed learned but yesterday. How often had the venerable superintendent knelt and invoked special guidance for the afflicted band from the God of orphans? Now she felt doubly orphaned. In her intellectual pride, she frequently asserted that she was "the star of her own destiny;" but this morning childish memories prattled of the Star of Bethlehem, before which she once bent the knee of adoration. Had it set forever amid clouds of superstition, sin and infidelity? Glittering spires pointed to the bending heavens, and answered: "It burns on forever, 'brighter and brighter unto the perfect day!'" With a dull weight on her heart, she took down her Bible and opened indifferently at the bookmark. It proved the thirty-eighth chapter of Job and she read on and on, until the bells warned her it was the hour of morning service. She walked to church, not humbled and prepared to receive the holy teachings of revelation, but with a defiant feeling in her heart, which she did not attempt or care to analyze. She was not accustomed to attend Dr. Hew's church, but the sexton conducted her to a pew, and as she seated herself, the solemn notes of the organ swelled through the vaulted aisles. The choir sang a magnificent anthem from Haydn's "Creation," and then only the deep, thundering peal of the organ fell on the dim, cool air. Beulah could bear no more; as she lowered her veil, bitter tears gushed over her troubled face. Just then, she longed to fall on her knees before the altar and renew the vows of her childhood; but this impulse very soon died away, and while the pews on every side rapidly filled, she watched impatiently for the appearance of the minister. Immediately in front of her sat Mr. and Mrs. Graham and Antoinette Dupres. Beulah was pondering the absence of Cornelia and Eugene, when a full, manly voice fell on her ear, and looking up she saw Mr. Mortimor standing in the pulpit. He looked older than Pauline's description had prepared her to expect, and the first impression was one of disappointment. But the longer she watched the grave, quiet face the more attractive it became. Certainly he was a handsome man, and, judging from the contour of head and features, an intellectual one. There was an absolute repose in the countenance, which might have passed with casual observers for inertia, indifference; but to the practised physiognomist it expressed the perfect peace of a mind and heart completely harmonious. The voice was remarkably clear and well modulated. His text was selected from the first and last chapters of Ecclesiastes, and consisted of these verses:

"For in much wisdom is much grief; and he that increaseth knowledge, increaseth sorrow."

"And further, by these, my son, be admonished; of making many books there is no end, and much study is a weariness of the flesh. Let us hear the conclusion of the whole matter. Fear God, and keep his commandments, for this is the whole duty of man."

To the discourse which followed Beulah listened with the deepest interest. She followed the speaker over the desert of ancient oriental systems, which he rapidly analyzed, and held up as empty shells; lifting the veil of soufism, he glanced at the mystical creed of Algazzali; and in an epitomized account of the Grecian schools of philosophy, depicted the wild vagaries into which many had wandered, and the unsatisfactory results to which all had attained. Not content with these instances of the insufficiency and mocking nature of human wisdom and learning, he adverted to the destructive tendency of the Helvetian and D'Holbach systems, and after a brief discussion of their ruinous tenets, dilated, with some erudition, upon the conflicting and dangerous theories propounded by Germany. Then came the contemplation of Christianity, from its rise among the fishermen of Galilee to its present summit of power. For eighteen hundred years it had been assaulted by infidelity, yet each century saw it advancing—a conquering colossus. Throughout the sermon, the idea was maintained that human reason was utterly inadequate to discover to man his destiny, that human learning was a great cheat, and that only from the pages of Holy Writ could genuine wisdom be acquired. Men were to be as little children in order to be taught the truths of immortality. Certainly, the reasoning was clear and forcible, the philosophic allusions seemed very apropos, and the language was elegant and impassioned. The closing hymn was sung; the organ hushed its worshipping tones; the benediction was pronounced; the congregation dispersed.

As Beulah descended the steps, she found Pauline and Mrs. Lockhart waiting at the carriage for her. The latter greeted her with quite a show of cordiality; but the orphan shrank back from the offered kiss, and merely touched the extended hand. She had not forgotten the taunts and unkindness of other days; and though not vindictive, she could not feign oblivion of the past, nor assume a friendly manner foreign to her. She took her seat in the carriage, and found it rather difficult to withdraw her fascinated eyes from Pauline's lovely face. She knew what was expected of her, however; and said, as they drove rapidly homeward:

"Mr. Mortimor seems to be a man of more than ordinary erudition."

"Did you like his sermon? Do you like him?" asked Pauline, eagerly.

"I like him very much, indeed; but do not like his sermon at all," answered Beulah, bluntly.

"I am sure everybody seemed to be delighted with it," said Mrs. Lockhart.

"Doubtless the majority of his congregation were; and I was very much interested, though I do not accept his views. His delivery is remarkably impressive, and his voice is better adapted to the pulpit than any I have ever listened to." She strove to say everything favorable which, in candor, she could.

"Still you did not like his sermon?" said Pauline, gravely.

"I cannot accept his conclusions."

"I like the discourse particularly, Pauline. I wish Percy could have heard it," said Mrs. Lockhart.

The daughter took no notice whatever of this considerate speech, and sat quite still, looking more serious than Beulah had ever seen her. Conversation flagged, despite the young teacher's efforts, and she was heartily glad when the carriage entered the avenue. Her heart swelled as she caught sight of the noble old cedars, whose venerable heads seemed to bow in welcome, while the drooping branches held out their arms, as if to embrace her. Each tree was familiar; even the bright coral yupon clusters were like dear friends greeting her after a long absence. She had never realized until now how much she loved this home of her early childhood, and large drops dimmed her eyes as she passed along the walks where she had so often wandered. The carriage approached the house, and she saw her quondam guardian standing before the door. He was bareheaded, and the sunshine fell like a halo upon his brown, clustering hair, threading it with gold. He held, in one hand, a small basket of grain, from which he fed a flock of hungry pigeons. On every side they gathered about him—blue and white, brown and mottled—some fluttering down from the roof of the house; two or three, quite tame, perched on his arm, eating from the basket; and one, of uncommon beauty, sat on his shoulder, cooing softly. By his side stood Charon, looking gravely on, as if he, wise soul, thought this familiarity signally impudent. It was a singularly quiet, peaceful scene, which indelibly daguerreotyped itself on Beulah's memory. As the carriage whirled round the circle, and drew up at the door, the startled flock wheeled off; and brushing the grain from his hands, Dr. Hartwell advanced to assist his sister. Pauline sprang out first, exclaiming:

"You abominable heathen! Why didn't you come to church? Even Dr. Asbury was out."

"Guy, you missed an admirable sermon," chimed in Mrs. Lockhart.

He was disengaging the fringe of Pauline's shawl, which caught the button of his coat, and looking up as his sister spoke, his eyes met Beulah's anxious gaze. She had wondered very much how he would receive her. His countenance expressed neither surprise nor pleasure; he merely held out his hand to assist her, saying, in his usual grave manner:

"I am glad to see you, Beulah."

She looked up in his face for some trace of the old kindness, but the rare, fascinating smile and protective tenderness had utterly vanished. He returned her look with a calmly indifferent glance, which pained her more than any amount of sternness could have done. She snatched her hand from his, and, missing the carriage-step, would have fallen, but he caught and placed her safely on the ground, saying coolly:

"Take care; you are awkward."

She followed Pauline up the steps, wishing herself at home in her little room. But her companion's gay chat diverted her mind, and she only remembered how very beautiful was the face she looked on.

They stood together before a mirror, smoothing their hair, and Beulah could not avoid contrasting the images reflected. One was prematurely grave and thoughtful in its expression—the other radiant with happy hopes. Pauline surmised what was passing in her friend's mind, and said merrily:

"For shame, Beulah! to envy me my poor estate of good looks! Why, I am all nose and eyes, curls, red lips and cheeks; but you have an additional amount of brains to balance my gifts. Once I heard Uncle Guy say that you had more intellect than all the other women and children in the town! Come, Mr. Lockhart wants to see you very much."

She ran down the steps as heedlessly as in her childhood, and Beulah followed her more leisurely. In the study they found the remainder of the party; Mr. Lockhart was wrapt in a heavy dressing-gown, and reclined on the sofa. He welcomed Beulah, very warmly, keeping her hand in his, and making her sit down near him. He was emaciated, and a hacking cough prevented his taking any active part in the conversation. One glance at his sad face sufficed to show her that his days on earth were numbered, and the expression with which he regarded his wife told all the painful tale of an unhappy marriage. She was discussing the sermon, and declaring herself highly gratified at the impression which Mr. Mortimor had evidently made on his large and fashionable congregation. Dr. Hartwell stood on the hearth, listening in silence to his sister's remarks. The Atlantic might have rolled between them, for any interest he evinced in the subject. Pauline was restless and excited; finally she crossed the room, stood close to her uncle, and carelessly fingering his watch chain, said earnestly: "Uncle Guy, what did Ernest mean, this morning, by a 'Fourieristic-phalanx?'"

"A land where learned men are captivated by blue eyes and rosy lips," answered the doctor, looking down into her sparkling face.

As they stood together, Beulah remarked how very much Pauline resembled him. True, he was pale, and she was a very Hebe, but the dazzling transparency of the complexion was the same; the silky nut-brown hair the same, and the classical chiseling of mouth and nose identical. Her eyes were "deeply, darkly," matchlessly blue, and his were hazel; her features were quivering with youthful joyousness and enthusiasm, his might have been carved in ivory, they seemed so inflexible, still they were alike. Pauline did not exactly relish the tone of his reply and said hastily:

"Uncle Guy, I wish you would not treat me as if I were an idiot; or what is not much better, a two-year-old child! How am I ever to learn any sense?"

"Indeed, I have no idea," said he, passing his soft hand over her glossy curls.

"You are very provoking! Do you want Ernest to think me a fool?"

"Have you waked to a consciousness of that danger?"

"Yes, and I want you to teach me something. Come, tell me what that thing is I asked you about."

"Tell you what?"

"Why, what a—a 'Fourieristic-phalanx' is?" said she, earnestly.

Beulah could not avoid smiling, and wondered how he managed to look so very serious as he replied:

"I know very little about the tactics of Fourieristic phalanxes, but believe a phalange is a community or association of about eighteen hundred persons, who were supposed or intended to practise the Fourieristic doctrines. In fine, a phalange is a sort of French Utopia."

"And where is that, sir?" asked Pauline, innocently, without taking her eyes from his face.

"Utopia is situated in No-country, and its chief city is on the banks of the river Waterless."

"Oh, Uncle Guy! how can you quiz me so unmercifully, when I ask you to explain things to me?"

"Why, Pauline, I am answering your questions correctly. Sir Thomas More professed to describe Utopia, which means No-place, and mentions a river Waterless. Don't look so desperately lofty. I will show you the book if you are so incorrigibly stupid." He passed his arm around her as he spoke, and kept her close beside him.

"Mr. Lockhart, is he telling the truth?" cried she, incredulously.

"Certainly he is," answered her stepfather, smiling.

"Oh, I don't believe either of you! You two think that I am simple enough to believe any absurdity you choose to tell me. Beulah, what is Utopia?"

"Just what your uncle told you. More used Greek words which signified nothing, in order to veil the satire."

"Oh, a satire! Now, what is the reason you could not say it was a satire, you wiseacre?"

"Because I gave you credit for some penetration, and at least common sense."

"Both of which I have proved myself devoid of, I suppose? Thank you."

She threw her arms around his neck, kissed him once or twice, and laughingly added: "Come, now, Uncle Guy, tell me what these 'phalanxes,' as you call them, have to do with Ernest's text?"

"I really cannot inform you. There is the dinner-bell." Unclasping her arms, he led the way to the dining-room.

Later in the afternoon Mr. Lockhart retired to his own room; his wife fell asleep on the sofa, and Beulah and Pauline sat at the parlor window discussing the various occurrences of their long separation. Pauline talked of her future—how bright it was; how very much she and Ernest loved each other, and how busy she would be when she had a home of her own. She supposed she would be obliged to give up dancing; she had an indistinct idea that preachers' wives were not in the habit of indulging in any such amusements, and as for the theater and opera, she rather doubted whether either were to be found in the inland town where she was to reside. Uncle Guy wished to furnish the parsonage, and, among other things, had ordered an elegant piano for her; she intended to practise a great deal, because Ernest was so fond of music. Uncle Guy had a hateful habit for lecturing her about "domestic affairs," but she imagined the cook would understand her own business; and if Mr. Mortimor supposed she was going to play housemaid, why she would very soon undeceive him. Beulah was much amused at the child-like simplicity with which she discussed her future, and began to think the whole affair rather ludicrous, when Pauline started, and exclaimed, as the blood dyed her cheeks:

"There is Ernest coming up the walk!"

He came in, and greeted her with gentle gravity. He was a dignified, fine-looking man, with polished manners and perfect self-possession. There was no trace of austerity in his countenance, and nothing in his conversation betokening a desire to impress strangers with his ministerial dignity. He was highly cultivated in all his tastes, agreeable, and in fine, a Christian gentleman. Pauline seemed to consider his remarks oracular, and Beulah could not forbear contrasting her quietness in his presence with the wild, frolicsome recklessness which characterized her manner on other occasions. She wondered what singular freak induced this staid, learned clergyman to select a companion so absolutely antagonistic in every element of character. But a glance at Pauline's perfectly beautiful face explained the mystery. How could any one help loving her, she was so radiant and so winning in her unaffected artlessness. Beulah conjectured that they might, perhaps, entertain each other without her assistance, and soon left them for the greenhouse, which was connected with the parlors by a glass door. Followed by Charon, who had remained beside her all day, she walked slowly between the rows of plants, many of which were laden with flowers. Brilliant clusters of scarlet geranium, pale, fragrant heliotropes, and camellias of every hue surrounded her. Two or three canary birds, in richly ornate cages, chirped and twittered continually, and for a moment she forgot the changes that had taken place since the days when she sought this favorite greenhouse to study her text-books. Near her stood an antique china vase containing a rare creeper, now full of beautiful, star-shaped lilac flowers. Many months before, her guardian had given her this root, and she had planted it in this same vase; now the long, graceful wreaths were looped carefully back, and tied to a slender stake. She bent over the fragrant blossoms, with a heart brimful of memories, and tears dropped thick and fast on the delicate petals. Charon gave a short bark of satisfaction, and raising her head she saw Dr. Hartwell at the opposite end of the greenhouse. He was clipping the withered flowers from a luxuriant white japonica, the same that once furnished ornaments for her hair. Evidently, he was rather surprised to see her there, but continued clipping the faded blossoms, and whistled to his dog. Charon acknowledged the invitation by another bark, but nestled his great head against Beulah, and stood quite still, while she passed her hand caressingly over him. She fancied a smile crosssed her guardian's lips, but when he turned toward her, there was no trace of it, and he merely said:

"Where is Pauline?"

"In the parlor, with Mr. Mortimor."

"Here are the scissors; cut as many flowers as you like."

He held out the scissors, but she shook her head, and answered, hastily:

"Thank you, I do not want any."

He looked at her searchingly, and observing unshed tears in her eyes said, in a kinder tone than he had yet employed:

"Beulah, what *do* you want?"

"Something that I almost despair of obtaining."

"Child, you are wasting your strength and energies in a fruitless undertaking. Already you have grown thin, and hollow-eyed; your accustomed contented, cheerful spirit, is deserting you. Your self-appointed task is a hopeless one; utterly hopeless!"

"I will not believe it," said she, firmly.

"Very well; some day you will be convinced that you are not infallible." He smiled grimly, and busied himself with his flowers.

"Sir, you could help me, if you would." She clasped her hands over his arm, and fixed her eyes on his countenance, with all the confidence and dependence of other days.

"Did I ever refuse you anything you asked?" said he, looking down at the little hands on his arm, and at the pale, anxious face, with its deep, troubled eyes.

"No! and it is precisely for that reason that I ask assistance from you now."

"I suppose you are reduced to the last necessity. What has become of your pride, Beulah?"

"It is all here, in my heart, sir! thundering to me to walk out and leave you, since you are so unlike yourself."

He looked stern and indescribably sad. She glanced up an instant at his fascinating eyes, and then laying her head down on his arm, as she used to do in childhood, said, resolutely:

"Oh, sir! you must aid me. Whom have I to advise me but you?"

"My advice has about as much weight with you as Charon's would, could he utter it. I am an admirable counselor, only so long as my opinions harmonize with the dictates of your own will. How am I to aid you? I went, at twelve o'clock last night, to see a dying man, and passing along the street, saw a light burning from your window. Two hours later, as I returned, it glimmered there still. Why were you up? Beulah, what is the matter with you? Has your last treatise on the 'Origin of Ideas' run away with those of its author, and landed you both in a region of vagaries? Remember, I warned you."

"Something worse, sir."

"Perhaps German metaphysics have stranded you on the bleak, bald cliffs of Pyrrhonism?"

"Sir, it seems to me there is a great deal of unmerited odium laid upon the innocent shoulders of German metaphysics. People declaim against the science of metaphysics, as if it were the disease itself, whereas it is the remedy. Metaphysics do not originate the trouble; their very existence proves the priority of the disease which they attempt to relieve—"

"Decidedly a homeopathic remedy," interrupted her guardian, smiling.

"But, sir, the questions which disturb my mind are older than my acquaintance with so-called philosophic works. They have troubled me from my childhood."

"Nevertheless, I warned you not to explore my library," said he, with a touch of sorrow in his voice.

"How, then, can you habitually read books which you are unwilling to put into my hands?"

"To me all creeds and systems are alike null. With you, Beulah, it was once very different."

"Once! yes, once!" She shuddered at the wild waste into which she had strayed.

"What are the questions that have so long disturbed you?"

"Questions, sir, which, all my life, have been printed on evening sun-flushed clouds, on rosy sea shells, on pale, sweet, delicate blossoms, and which I have unavailingly sought to answer for myself. There are mysteries in physics, morals and metaphysics that have wooed me on to an investigation; but the further I wander, deeper grows the darkness. Alone, and unaided, I have been forced to brave these doubts; I have studied, and read, and thought. Cloudy symbolisms mock me on every side; and the more earnestly I strive to overtake truth, the tighter grow my gyves. Now, sir, you are much older; you have scaled the dizzy heights of science, and carefully explored the mines of philosophy; and if human learning will avail, then you can help me. It is impossible for you to have lived and studied so long, without arriving at some conclusion relative to these vexing questions of this and every other age. I want to know whether I have ever lived before; whether there is not an anterior life of my soul of which I get occasional glimpses, and the memory of which haunts and disquiets me. This doubt has not been engendered by casual allusions to Plato's 'reminiscence theory;' before I knew there was such a doctrine in existence I have sat by your study fire, pondering some strange coincidences, for which I could not account. It seemed an indistinct outgoing into the far past; a dim recollection of scenes and ideas, older than the aggregate of my birthdays: now a flickering light, then all darkness; no clew; all shrouded in the mystery of voiceless ages. I tried to explain these psychological phenomena by the theory of association of ideas, but they eluded an analysis; there was no chain along which memory can pass. They were like *ignes fatui,* flashing up from dank caverns, and dying out while I looked upon them. As I grew older, I found strange confirmation in those curious passages of Coleridge and Wordsworth,* and continually I propound to my soul these questions: 'If you are immortal, and will exist through endless ages, have you not existed from the beginning of time? Immortality knows neither commencement nor ending. If so, whither

*Coleridge's "Sonnet on the birth of a son." Wordsworth's "Ode—Intimations of Immortality."

shall I go, when this material frame-work is dissolved, to make other frame-works, to a final rest? or shall the I, the me, the soul, lose its former identity? Am I a minute constituent of the all-diffused, all-pervading Spirit, a breath of the Infinite Essence, one day to be divested of my individuality? or is God an awful, gigantic, immutable, isolated Personality? If so, what medium of communication is afforded? Can the spiritual commune with matter? Can the material take cognizance of the purely spiritual and divine?' Oh, sir! I know that you do not accept the holy men of Galilee as His deputed oracles. Tell me where you find surer prophets! Only show me the truth—the eternal truth and I would give my life for it? Sir, how can you smile at such questions as these; questions involving the soul's destiny? One might fancy you a second Parrhasius."

She drew back a step or two, and regarded him anxiously, nay, pleadingly, as though he held the key to the Temple of Truth, and would not suffer her to pass the portal. A sarcastic smile lighted his Apollo-like face, as he answered:

"There is more truth in your metaphor than you imagined; *à la* Parrhasius, I do see you, a tortured Prometheus, chained by links of your own forging to the Caucasus of Atheism. But listen to—"

"No, no; not that! not Atheism! God save me from that deepest, blackest gulf!" She shuddered, and covered her face with her hands.

"Beulah, you alone must settle these questions with your own soul; my solutions would not satisfy you. For thousands of years they have been propounded, and yet no answer comes down on the 'cloudy wings of centuries.' Each must solve to suit his or her peculiar conformation of mind. My child, if I could aid you, I would gladly do so; but I am no Swedenborg, to whom the arcana of the universe have been revealed."

"Still, after a fashion, you have solved these problems; may I not know what your faith is?" said she, earnestly.

"Child, I have no faith! I know that I exist; that a beautiful universe surrounds me, and I am conscious of a multitude of conflicting emotions; but, like Launcelot Smith, I doubt whether I am 'to pick and choose myself out of myself.' Further than this, I would assure you of nothing. I stand on the everlasting basis of all skepticism, 'there is no criterion of truth!' All must be but subjectively, relatively true."

"Sir, this may be so as regards psychological abstractions; but can you be contented with this utter negation of the grand problems of ontology?"

"A profound philosophic writer of the age intimates that the various psychological systems which have so long vexed the world are but veiled ontologic speculations. What matters the machinery of ideas, but as enabling philosophy to cope successfully with ontology? Philosophy is a huge wheel, which has been revolving for ages; early metaphysicians hung their finely-spun webs on its spokes, and metaphysicians of the nineteenth century gaze upon and renew the same pretty theories as the wheel revolves. The history of philosophy shows but a reproduction of old systems and methods of inquiry. Beulah, no mine of ontologic truth has been discovered. Conscious of this, our seers tell us there is nothing now but 'electicism!' Ontology is old as human nature, yet the stone of Sisyphus continues to roll back upon the laboring few who strive to impel it upward. Oh, child, do you not see how matters stand? Why, how can the finite soul cope with Infinite Being? This is one form—the other, if we can take cognizance of the Eternal and Self-Existing Being, underlying all phenomena, why, then, we are part and parcel of that Infinity. Pantheism or utter skepticism—there is no retreat."

"I don't want to believe that, sir. I will not believe it. What was my reason given to me for? Was this spirit of inquiry after truth only awakened in my soul to mock me with a sense of my nothingness? Why did my Maker imbue me with an insatiable thirst for knowledge? Knowledge of the deep things of philosophy, the hidden wonders of the universe, the awful mysteries of the shadowy spirit realm? Oh, there are analogies pervading all departments! There is physical hunger to goad to exertions which will satisfy its demands, and most tonics are bitter; so, bitter struggles develop and strengthen the soul, even as hard study invigorates the mind, and numerous sorrows chasten the heart. There is truth for the earnest seeker somewhere—somewhere! If I live a thousand years, I will toil after it till I find it. If, as you believe, death is annihilation, then will I make the most of my soul while I have it. Oh, sir, what is life for? Merely to eat and drink, to sleep and to be clothed! Is it to be only a constant effort to keep soul and body together? If I thought so, I would rather go back to nothingness this day—this hour! No, no. My name bids me press on; there is a land of Beulah somewhere for my troubled spirit. Oh, I will go back to my humble home, and study on, unguided, unassisted even as I have begun. I cannot rest on your rock of negation."

She could not control her trembling voice, and tears of bitter disappointment fell over her pale, fixed features. A melancholy smile parted Dr. Hartwell's lips, and smoothing the bands of rippling hair which lay on her white brow, he answered in his own thrilling, musical accents:

"Child, you are wasting your energies in vain endeavors to build up walls of foam, that—"

"Sir, I am no longer a child! I am a woman, and—"

"Yes, my little Beulah, and your woman's heart will not be satisfied long with these dim abstractions, which now you chase so eagerly. Mark me, there surely comes a time when you will loathe the bare name of metaphysics. You are making a very hot-bed of your intellect, while your heart is daily becoming a dreary desert. Take care, lest the starvation be so complete, that eventually you will be unable to reclaim it. Dialectics answer very well in collegiate halls, but will not content you. Remember 'Argemone.'"

"She is a miserable libel on woman's nature and intellect. I scorn the attempted parallel!" answered Beulah, indignantly.

"Very well; mark me though, your intellectual pride will yet wreck your happiness."

He walked out of the greenhouse, whistling to Charon, who bounded after him. Beulah saw from the slanting sunlight that the afternoon was far advanced, and feeling in no mood to listen to Pauline's nonsense, she found her bonnet and shawl, and repaired to the parlor to say good-by to the happy pair, who seemed unconscious of her long absence. As she left the house, the window of the study was thrown open, and Dr. Hartwell called out, carelessly:

"Wait, and let me order the carriage."

"No, thank you."

"I am going into town directly, and can take you home in the buggy."

"I will not trouble you; I prefer walking. Good-by."

He bowed coldly, and she hurried away, glad to reach the gate, and feel that she was once more free from his searching glance, and beyond the sound of his reserved, chilling tones. As she walked on, groups of happy parents and children were seen in every direction, taking their quiet Sabbath ramble through the suburbs; and as joyous voices and innocent laughter fell upon the still air, she remembered with keen sorrow that she had no ties, no kindred, no companions. Lilly's cherub face looked out at her from the somber frame of the past, and Eugene's early friendship seemed now a taunting specter. In her warm, loving heart were unfathomable depths of intense tenderness; was it the wise providence of God which sealed these wells of affection, or was it a grim, merciless fate which snatched her idols from her, one by one, and left her heart desolate? Such an inquiry darted through her mind, but she put it resolutely aside, and consoled herself much after this fashion: "Why should I question the circumstances of my life? If the God of Moses guards his creation, all things are well. If not, life is a lottery, and though I have drawn blanks thus far, the future may contain a prize, and for me that prize may be the truth my soul pants after. I have no right to complain; the very loneliness of my position fits me peculiarly for the work I have to do. I will labor, and be content." The cloud passed swiftly from her countenance, and she looked up to the quiet sky with a brave, hopeful heart.

CHAPTER XXV.

Among the number of gentlemen whom Beulah occasionally met at Dr. Asbury's house, were two whose frequent visits and general demeanor induced the impression that they were more than ordinarily interested in the sisters. Frederick Vincent evinced a marked preference for Georgia, while Horace Maxwell was conspicuously attentive to Helen. The former was wealthy, handsome, indolent, and self-indulgent; the latter rather superior, as to business habits, which a limited purse peremptorily demanded. Doubtless both would have passed as men of medium capacity, but certainly as nothing more. If fine, they were fair samples, perfect types of the numerous class of fashionable young men who throng all large cities. Good-looking, vain, impudent, heartless, frivolous, and dissipated; adepts at the gaming-table and pistol gallery, ciphers in an intelligent, refined assembly. They smoked the choicest cigars, drank the most costly wines, drove the fastest horses, and were indispensable at champagne and oyster suppers. They danced and swore, visited and drank, with reckless indifference to every purer and nobler aim. Notwithstanding manners of incorrigible effrontery which characterized their clique, the ladies always received them with marked expressions of pleasure, and the entrée of the "first circle" was certainly theirs. Dr. Asbury knew comparatively little of the young men who visited so constantly at his house, but of the two under discussion he chanced to know that they were by no means models of sobriety, having met them late one night as they supported each other's tottering forms homeward, after a card and wine party, which ended rather disastrously for both. He openly avowed his discontent at the intimacy their frequent visits induced, and wondered how his daughters could patiently indulge in the heartless chit-chat which alone could entertain them. But he was a fond, almost doting father, and seemed to take it for granted that they were mere dancing acquaintances, whose society must be endured. Mrs. Asbury was not so blind, and discovered, with keen sorrow and dismay, that Georgia was far more partial to Vincent than she had dreamed possible. The mother's heart ached with dread, lest her child's affections were really enlisted, and without her husband's knowledge she passed many hours of bitter reflection, as to the best course she should pursue to arrest Vincent's intimacy at the house. Only a woman knows woman's heart, and she felt that Georgia's destiny would be decided by the measures she now employed. Ridicule, invective, and even remonstrance, she knew would only augment her interest in one whom she considered unjustly dealt with. She was thoroughly acquainted with the obstinacy which formed the stamen of Georgia's character, and very cautiously the maternal guidance must be given. She began by gravely regretting the familiar footing Mr. Vincent had acquired in her family, and urged upon Georgia and Helen the propriety of discouraging attentions that justified the world in joining their names. This had very little effect. She was conscious that because of his wealth, Vincent was courted and flattered by the most select and fashionable of her circle of acquaintances, and knew, alas! that he was not more astray than the majority of the class of young men to which he belonged. With a keen pang, she saw that her child shrank from her, evaded her kind questions, and seemed to plunge into the festivities of the season with unwonted zest. From their birth, she had trained her daughters to confide unreservedly in her, and now to perceive the youngest avoiding her caresses, or hurrying away from her anxious glance, was bitter indeed. How her pure-hearted darling could tolerate the reckless, frivolous being, in whose society she seemed so well satisfied, was a painful mystery; but the startling reality looked her in the face and she resolved, at every hazard, to save her from the misery which was in store for Fred Vincent's wife. Beulah's quick eye readily discerned the state of affairs relative to Georgia and Vincent, and she could with difficulty restrain an expression of the digust a knowledge of his character inspired. He was a brother of the Miss Vincent she had once seen at Dr. Hartwell's, and probably this circumstance increased her dislike. Vincent barely recognized her when they chanced to meet, and of all his antipathies, hatred of Beulah predominated. He was perfectly aware that she despised his weaknesses and detested his immoralities; and while he shrank from the steadfast gray eyes, calm but contemptuous, he hated her heartily.

Cornelia Graham seemed for a time to have rallied all her strength, and attended parties and kept her place at the opera, with a regularity which argued a complete recovery. Antoinette Dupres was admired and flattered; the season was unusually gay. What if Death had so lately held his awful assize in the city? Bereaved families wrapped their sable garments about lonely hearts, and wept over the countless mounds in the cemetery; but the wine-cup and song and dance went their accustomed rounds in fashionable quarters, and drink, dress and be merry appeared the all-absorbing thought. Into this gaiety Eugene Graham eagerly plunged; night after night was spent in one continued whirl; day by day he wandered further astray, and ere long his visits to Beulah ceased entirely. Antoinette thoroughly understood the game she had to play, and easily and rapidly he fell into the snare. To win her seemed his only wish, and not even Cornelia's keenly searching eyes could check his admiration and devotion. January had gone; February drew near its close; Beulah had not seen Eugene for many days, and felt more than usually anxious concerning him, for little intercourse now existed between Cornelia and herself. One evening, however, as she stood before a glass and arranged her hair with more than ordinary care, she felt that she would soon have an opportunity of judging whether reports were true. If he indeed rushed along the highway to ruin, one glance would discover to her the fact. Dr. Asbury wished to give Pauline Chilton a party, and his own and Mrs. Asbury's kind persuasions induced the orphan to consent to attend. The evening had arrived; she put on her simple Swiss muslin dress, without a wish for anything more costly, and entered the carriage her friends had sent to convey her to the house. The guests rapidly assembled; soon the rooms were thronged with merry people, whose moving to and fro prevented regular conversation. The brilliant chandeliers flashed down on rich silks and satins, gossamer fabrics, and diamonds which blazed dazzlingly. Pauline was superbly beautiful. Excitement lighted her eyes, and flushed her cheeks, until all paused to gaze at her transcendent loveliness. It was generally known that ere many days her marriage would take place, and people looked at her in her marvelous, queenly beauty, and wondered what infatuation induced her to give her hand to a minister, when she, of all others present, seemed made to move in the gay scene where she reigned supreme. From a quiet seat near the window Beulah watched her airy, graceful form glide through the quadrille, and feared that in future years she would sigh for the gaieties which in her destined lot would be withheld from her. She tried to fancy the dazzling beauty metamorphosed into the staid clergyman's wife, divested of satin and diamonds, and visiting the squalid and suffering portion of her husband's flock. But the contrast was too glaring, and she turned her head to watch for Eugene's appearance. Before long she saw him cross the room with Antoinette on his arm. The quadrille had ended, and, as at the request of one of the guests, the band played a brilliant mazurka, numerous couples took their places on the floor. Beulah had never seen the mazurka danced in public; she knew that neither Helen nor Georgia ever danced the so-called "fancy dances," and was not a little surprised when the gentlemen encircled the waists of their partners and whirled away. Her eyes followed Eugene's tall form, as the circuit of the parlors was rapidly made, and he approached the corner where she sat. He held his lovely partner close to his heart, and her head drooped very contentedly on his shoulder. He was talking to her as they danced, and his lips nearly touched her glowing cheek. On they came, so close to Beulah that Antoinette's gauzy dress floated against her, and as the music quickened, faster flew the dancers. Beulah looked on with a sensation of disgust, which might have been easily read in her countenance; verily she blushed for her degraded sex, and, sick of the scene, left the window and retreated to the library, where the more sedate portion of the guests were discussing various topics. Here were Mr. and Mrs. Grayson; Claudia was North, at school. Beulah found a seat near Mrs. Asbury, and endeavored to banish the painful recollections which Mrs. Grayson's face recalled. They had not met since the memorable day when the orphan first found a guardian, and she felt that there was still an unconquerable aversion in her heart, which caused it to throb heavily. She thought the time tediously long, and when at last the signal for supper was given, felt relieved. As usual, there was rushing and squeezing into the supper-room, and waiting until the hall was comparatively deserted she ran up to the dressing-room for her shawl, tired of the crowd and anxious to get home again. She remembered that she had dropped her fan behind one of the sofas in the parlor, and as all were at supper, fancied she could obtain it unobserved, and entered the room for that purpose. A gentleman stood by the fire, but without noticing him she pushed the sofa aside, secured her fan, and was turning away, when a well known voice startled her.

"Beulah, where are you going?"

"Home, sir."

"What! so soon tired?"

"Yes, heartily tired," said she, wrapping her shawl about her.

"Have you spoken to Eugene to-night?"

"No."

Her guardian looked at her very intently, as if striving to read her soul, and said slowly:

"Child, he and Antoinette are sitting in the front parlor. I happened to overhear a remark as I passed them. He is an accepted lover; they are engaged."

A quick shiver ran over Beulah's frame, and a dark frown furrowed her pale brow, as she answered:

"I feared as much."

"Why should you fear, child? She is a beautiful heiress, and he loves her," returned Dr. Hartwell, without taking his eyes from her face.

"No; he thinks he loves her, but it is not so. He is fascinated by her beauty, but I fear the day will come when, discovering her true character, he will mourn his infatuation. I know his nature, and I know, too, that she cannot make him happy." She turned away, but he walked on with her to the carriage, handed her in, and said "good night" as coldly as usual. Meantime, the rattle of plates, jingle of forks and spoons, in the supper-room would have rendered all conversation impossible, had not the elevation of voices kept pace with the noise and confusion. At one end of the table, Cornelia Graham stood talking to a distinguished foreigner, who was spending a few days in the city. He was a handsome man, with fine colloquial powers, and seemed much interested in a discussion which he and Cornelia carried on, relative to the society of American cities as compared with European. A temporary lull in the hum of voices allowed Cornelia to hear a remark made by a gentleman quite near her.

"Miss Laura, who did you say that young lady was that Mrs. Asbury introduced me to? The one with such magnificent hair and teeth?"

His companion was no other than Laura Martin, whose mother, having built an elegant house, and given several large parties, was now a "fashionable," *par excellence*. Laura elevated her nose very perceptibly, and answered:

"Oh, a mere nobody! Beulah Benton. I can't imagine how she contrived to be invited here. She is a teacher in the public school, I believe, but that is not the worst. She used to hire herself out as a servant. Indeed, it is a fact, she was my little brother's nurse some years ago. I think 'ma hired her for six dollars a month." She laughed affectedly, and allowed her escort to fill her plate with creams.

Cornelia grew white with anger, and the stranger asked, with a smile, if he should consider this a sample of the society she boasted of. Turning abruptly to Laura, she replied, with undisguised contempt:

"The Fates forbid, Mr. Falconer, that you should judge American society from some of the specimens you may see here to-night. Misfortune placed Miss Benton, at an early age, in an orphan asylum, and while quite young, she left it to earn a support. Mrs. Martin (this young lady's mother), hired her as a nurse; but she soon left this position, qualified herself to teach, and now, with a fine intellect thoroughly cultivated, is the pride of all who can appreciate true nobility of soul, and, of course, an object of envy and detraction to her inferiors, especially to some of our fashionable *parvenus,* whose self-interest prompts them to make money alone the standard of worth, and who are in the habit of determining the gentility of different persons by what they have, not what they are." Her scornful glance rested witheringly on Laura's face, and, mortified and enraged, the latter took her companion's arm, and moved away.

"I have some desire to become acquainted with one who could deserve such eulogy from you," answered the foreigner, somewhat amused at the course the conversation had taken, and quite satisfied that Americans were accustomed to correct false impressions in rather an abrupt manner.

"I will present her to you with great pleasure. She is not here; we must search for her." She took his arm, and they looked for Beulah from room to room; finally, Dr. Hartwell informed Cornelia that she had gone home, and tired, and out of humor, the latter excused herself, and prepared to follow her friend's example. Her father was deep in a game of whist, her mother unwilling to return home so soon, and Eugene and Antoinette—where were they? Dr. Hartwell saw her perplexed expression, and asked:

"Whom are you looking for?"

"Eugene."

"He is with your cousin on the west gallery. I will conduct you to them, if you wish it." He offered his arm, and noticed the scowl that instantly darkened her face. Unconsciously, her fingers grasped his arm tightly, and she walked on with a lowering brow. As they approached the end of the gallery, Cornelia saw that the two she sought stood earnestly conversing. Eugene's arm passed round Antoinette's waist. Dr. Hartwell watched his companion closely; the light from the window gleamed over her face, and showed it gray and rigid. Her white lips curled as she muttered:

"Let us take nother turn before I speak to them."

"Surely, you are not surprised?"

"Oh no! I am not blind."

"It was an unlucky chance that threw your cousin in his path," said the doctor, composedly.

"Oh, it is merely another link in the chain of fatality which binds my family to misfortune. She has all the family traits of the Labords, and you know what they are," cried Cornelia.

He compressed his lips, and a lightning glance shot out from his eyes, but he stilled the rising tempest, and replied coldly:

"Why, then, did you not warn him?"

"Warn him! So I did. But I might as well grasp at the stars yonder as hope to influence him in this infatuation."

Once more they approached the happy pair, and leaning forward, Cornelia said, hoarsely:

"Eugene, my father is engaged; come home with me."

He looked up, and answered carelessly: "Oh, you are leaving too early; can't you entertain yourself a little longer?"

"No, sir."

Her freezing tone startled him, and for the first time he noticed the haggard face, with its expression of angry scorn. Her eyes were fixed on Antoinette, who only smiled, and looked triumphantly defiant.

"Are you ill, Cornelia? Of course, I will take you home if you really desire it. Doctor, I must consign Miss Dupres to your care till I return."

Eugene by no means relished the expression of his sister's countenance. She bade Dr. Hartwell adieu, passed her arm through her brother's, and they proceeded to their carriage. The ride was short and silent. On reaching home, Eugene conducted Cornelia into the house, and was about to return, when she said, imperiously:

"A word with you before you go."

She entered the sitting-room, threw her wrappings on a chair, and began to divest herself of bracelets and necklace. Eugene lighted a cigar, and stood waiting to hear what she might choose to communicate. Fastening her brilliant black eyes on his face, she said, sneeringly:

"Eugene Graham, did you learn dissimulation in the halls of Heidelberg?"

"What do you mean, Cornelia?"

"Where did you learn to deceive one who believed you pure and truthful as an archangel? Answer me that." Her whole face was a glare of burning scorn.

"Insulting insinuations are unworthy of you, and beneath my notice," he proudly replied.

"Well, then, take the more insulting truth! What crawling serpent of temptation induced you to tell me you expected to marry Beulah? No evasion! I will not be put off! Why did you deceive me with a falsehood I was too stupidly trusting to discover until recently?"

"When I told you so, I expected to marry Beulah; not so much because I loved her, but because I supposed that she rather considered me bound to her by early ties. I discovered, however, that her happiness was not dependent on me, and therefore abandoned the idea."

"And my peerless cousin is to be your bride, eh?"

"Yes, she has promised me her hand at an early day."

"No doubt. You don't deserve anything better. Beulah scorns you; I see it in her eyes. Marry you! You! Oh, Eugene, she is too far superior to you. You are blind now; but the day will surely come when your charmer will, with her own hand, tear the veil from your eyes, and you will curse your folly. It is of no use to tell you that she is false, heartless, utterly unprincipled; you will not believe it, of course, till you find out her miserable defects yourself. I might thunder warnings in your ears from now till doomsday, and you would not heed me. But whether I live to see it or not, you will bitterly rue your infatuation. You will blush for the name which, as your wife, Antoinette will disgrace. Now leave me."

She pointed to the door, and too much incensed to reply, he quitted the room with a suppressed oath, slamming the door behind him. Cornelia went up to her own apartment, and, without ringing for her maid, took off her elegant dress she wore, and threw her dressing-gown round her. The diamond hairpins glowed like coals of fire in her black braids, mocking the gray, bloodless face, and look of wretchedness. She took out the jewels, laid them on her lap, and suffered the locks of hair to fall upon her shoulders. Then great hot tears rolled over her face; heavy sobs convulsed her frame, and bowing down her head, the haughty heiress wept passionately. Eugene was the only being she really loved; for years her hopes and pride had centered in him. Now, down the long vista of coming time, she looked and saw him staggering on to ruin and disgrace. She knew her own life would at best be short, and felt that now it had lost its only interest, and she was ready to sink to her last rest rather than witness his future career. This was the first time she had wept since the days of early childhood; but she calmed the fearful struggle in her heart, and, toward dawn, fell asleep, with a repulsive sneer on her lips. The ensuing day she was forced to listen to the complacent comment of her parents who were well pleased with the alliance. Antoinette was to return home immediately, the marriage would take place in June, and they were all to spend the summer at the North; after which it was suggested that the young couple should reside with Mr. Graham. Cornelia was standing apart when her mother made this proposition, and turning sharply toward the members of her family, the daughter exclaimed:

"Never! You all know that this match is utterly odious to me. Let Eugene have a house of his own; I have no mind to have Antoinette longer in my home. Nay, father; it will not be for a great while. When I am gone they can come; I rather think I shall not long be in their way. While I do live, let me be quiet, will you?"

Her burning, yet sunken eyes ran over the group.

Eugene sprang up, and left the room; Antoinette put her embroidered handkerchief to dry eyes; Mrs. Graham looked distressed; and her husband wiped his spectacles. But the mist was in his eyes, and presently large drops fell over his cheeks as he looked at the face and form of his only child.

Cornelia saw his emotion; the great flood-gate of her heart seemed suddenly lifted. She passed her white fingers over his gray hair, and murmured brokenly:

"My father—my father! I have been a care and a sorrow to you all my life; I am very wayward and exacting, but bear with your poor child; my days are numbered. Father, when my proud head lies low in the silent grave, then give others my place."

He took her in his arms, and kissed her hollow cheek, saying tenderly:

"My darling, you break my heart. Have you ever been denied a wish? What is there that I can do to make you happy?"

"Give Eugene a house of his own, and let me be at peace in my home. Will you do this for me?"

"Yes."

"Thank you, my father."

Disengaging his clasping arm, she left them.

A few days after the party at her house, Mrs. Asbury returned home from a visit to the Asylum (of which she had recently been elected a manager). In passing the parlor door, she heard suppressed voices, looked in, and perceiving Mr. Vincent seated near Georgia, retired, without speaking, to her own room. Securing the door, she sank on her knees, and besought an all-wise God to direct and aid her in her course of duty. The time had arrived when she must hazard everything to save her child from an ill-fated marriage; and though the mother's heart bled, she was firm in her resolve. When Mr. Vincent took leave, and Georgia had returned to her room, Mrs. Asbury sought her. She found her moody and disposed to evade her questions. Passing her arm round her, she said, very gently:

"My dear child, let there be perfect confidence between us. Am I not more interested in your happiness than any one else? My child, what has estranged you of late?"

Georgia made no reply.

"What, but my love for you, and anxiety for your happiness, could induce me to object to your receiving Mr. Vincent's attentions?"

"You are prejudiced against him, and always were!"

"I judge the young man only from his conduct. You know—you are obliged to know, that he is recklessly dissipated, selfish and immoral."

"He is no worse than other young men. I know very few who are not quite as wild as he is. Beside, he has promised to sign the temperance pledge, if I will marry him."

"My child, you pain me beyond expression. Does the depravity which prevails here sanction Vincent's dissipation? Oh, Georgia, has association deprived you of horror of vice? Can you be satisfied because others are quite as degraded? He does not mean what he promises, it is merely to deceive you. His intemperate habits are too confirmed to be remedied now; he began early, at college, and has constantly grown worse."

"You are prejudiced," persisted Georgia, unable to restrain her tears.

"If I am, it is because of his profligacy! Can you possibly be attached to such a man?"

Georgia sobbed, and cried heartily. Her good sense told her that her mother was right, but it was difficult to relinquish the hope of reforming him. As gently as possible, Mrs. Asbury dwelt upon his utter worthlessness, and the misery and wretchedness which would surely ensue from such a union. With streaming eyes she implored her to banish the thought, assuring her she would sooner see her in her grave, than the wife of a drunkard. And now the care of years was to be rewarded; her firm, but gentle reasoning prevailed. Georgia had always reverenced her mother; she knew she was invariably guided by principle; and now, as she listened to her earnest entreaties, all her obstinacy melted away; throwing herself into her mother's arms, she begged her to forgive the pain and anxiety she had caused her. Mrs. Asbury pressed her to her heart, and silently thanked God for the success of her remonstrances. Of all this, Dr. Asbury knew nothing. When Mr. Vincent called, the following day, Georgia very decidedly rejected him. Understanding from her manner, that she meant what she said, he became violently enraged; swore, with a solemn oath, that he would make her repent her trifling, took his hat, and left the house. This sufficed to remove any lingering tenderness from Georgia's heart; and from that hour, Fred Vincent darkened the home circle no more.

CHAPTER XXVI.

Pauline's wedding-day dawned clear and bright, meet for the happy event it was to chronicle. The ceremony was to be performed in church, at an early hour, to enable the newly married pair to leave on the morning boat, and the building was crowded with the numerous friends assembled to witness the rites. The minister stood within the altar, and after some slight delay, Mr. Mortimor led Pauline down the aisle. Dr. Hartwell and Mrs. Lockhart stood near the altar. Mr. Lockhart's indisposition prevented his attendance. Satin, blond and diamonds were discarded; Pauline was dressed in a gray traveling habit, and wore a plain drab traveling bonnet.

It was a holy, touching bridal. The morning sunshine, stealing through the lofty, arched windows, fell on her pure brow with dazzling radiance, and lent many a golden wave to the silky, clustering curls. Pauline was marvelously beautiful; the violet eyes were dewy with emotion, and her ripe, coral lips wreathed with a smile of trembling joyousness. Perchance a cursory observer might have fancied Mr. Mortimor's countenance too grave and thoughtful for such an occasion; but though the mouth was at rest, and the dark, earnest eyes sparkled not, there was a light of grateful, chastened gladness shed over the quiet features. Only a few words were uttered by the clergyman, and Pauline, the wild, wayward, careless, high-spirited girl, stood there a wife. She grew deadly pale, and looked up with a feeling of awe to him who was now, for all time, the master of her destiny. The vows yet upon her lips bound her irrevocably to his side, and imposed on her, as a solemn duty, the necessity of bearing all trials for herself; of smoothing away home cares from his path; and, when her own heart was troubled, of putting by the sorrow and bitterness, and ever welcoming his coming with a word of kindness, or a smile of joy. A wife! She must be brave enough to wrestle with difficulties for herself, instead of wearying him with all the tedious details of domestic trials, and yet turn to him for counsel and sympathy in matters of serious import. No longer a mere self-willed girl, consulting only her own wishes and tastes, she had given another the right to guide and control her; and now realizing, for the first time, the importance of the step she had taken, she trembled in anticipation of the trouble her wayward, obstinate will would cause her. But with her wonted, buoyant spirit, she turned from all unpleasant reflections, and received the congratulations of her friends with subdued gaiety. Beulah stood at some distance, watching the April face, checkered with smiles and tears; and looking with prophetic dread into the future she saw how little genuine happiness could result from a union of natures so entirely uncongenial. To her the nuptial rites were more awfully solemn than those of death; for how infinitely preferable was a quiet resting-place in the shadow of mourning cedars to the life-long agony of an unhappy union. She looked up at her quondam guardian as he stood, grave and silent, regarding his niece with sadly anxious eyes; and as she noted the stern inflexibility of his sculptured mouth, she thought that he stood there a marble monument, recording the misery of an ill-assorted marriage. But it was schooltime, and she approached to say "good-by," as the bridal pair took their seats in the carriage. Pauline seemed much troubled at bidding her adieu; she wept silently a minute, then throwing her arms around Beulah's neck, whispered pleadingly:

"Won't you go back to Uncle Guy? Won't you let him adopt you? Do, please. See how grim and pale he looks. Won't you?"

"No. He has ceased to care about my welfare; he is not distressed about me, I assure you. Good-by. Write to me often."

"Yes, I will; and in vacation, Ernest says you are to come up and spend at least a month with us. Do you hear?"

The carriage was whirled away, and Beulah walked on to her schoolroom, with a dim foreboding that when she again met the beautiful, warm-hearted girl, sunshine might be banished from her face. Days, weeks and months passed by. How systematic industry speeds the wheels of time. Beulah had little leisure, and this was employed with the most rigid economy. School duties occupied her until late in the day; then she gave, every afternoon, a couple of music lessons, and it was not until night that she felt herself free. The editor of the magazine found that her articles were worth remuneration, and consequently a monthly contribution had to be copied, and sent in at stated intervals. Thus engaged, spring glided into summer, and once more a June sun beamed on the city. One Saturday she accompanied Clara to a jewelry store to make some trifling purchase, and saw Eugene Graham leaning over the counter, looking at some sets of pearl and diamonds. He did not perceive her immediately, and she had an opportunity of scanning his countenance unobserved. Her lip trembled as she noticed the flushed face and inflamed eyes, and saw that the hand which held a bracelet, was very unsteady. He looked up, started and greeted her with evident embarrassment. She waited until Clara had completed her purchase, and then said, quietly:

"Eugene, are you going away without coming to see me?"

"Why, no; I had intended calling yesterday, but was prevented, and I am obliged to leave this afternoon. By the way, help me to select between these two pearl sets. I suppose you can imagine their destination?"

It was the first time he had alluded to his marriage, and she answered with an arch smile:

"Oh, yes! I dare say I might guess very accurately. It would not require Yankee ingenuity."

She examined the jewels, and after giving an opinion as to their superiority, turned to go, saying:

"I want to see you a few moments before you leave the city. I am going home immediately, and any time during the day when you can call will answer."

He looked curious, glanced at his watch, pondered an instant, and promised to call in an hour.

She bowed and returned home, with an almost intolerable weight on her heart. She sat with her face buried in her hands, collecting her thoughts, and when summoned to meet Eugene, went down with a firm heart, but trembling frame. It was more than probable that she would be misconstrued and wounded, but she determined to hazard all, knowing how pure were the motives that actuated her. He seemed restless and ill at ease, yet curious withal, and after some trifling commonplace remarks, Beulah seated herself on the sofa, beside him, and said:

"Eugene, why have you shunned me so pertinaciously since your return from Europe?"

"I have not shunned you, Beulah; you are mistaken. I have been engaged, and therefore could visit but little."

"Do not imagine that any such excuses blind me to the truth," said she, with an impatient gesture.

"What do you mean?" he answered, unable to bear the earnest, troubled look of the searching eyes.

"Oh, Eugene! be honest—be honest! Say at once you shunned me lest I should mark your altered habits in your altered face. But I know it all, notwithstanding. It is no secret that Eugene Graham has more than once lent his presence to midnight carousals over the wine-cup. Once you were an example of temperance and rectitude, but vice is fashionable, and patronized in this city, and your associates soon dragged you down from your proud height to their degraded level. The circle in which you move were not shocked at your fall. Ladies accustomed to hear of drunken revels ceased to attach disgrace to them, and you were welcomed and smiled upon as though you were all a man should be. Oh, Eugene! I understand why you have carefully shunned one who has an unconquerable horror of that degradation into which you have fallen. I am your friend, your best and most disinterested friend. What do your fashionable acquaintances care that your moral character is impugned and your fair name tarnished? Your dissipation keeps their brothers and lovers in countenance; your once noble, unsullied nature would shame their depravity. Do you remember one bright, moonlight night, about six years ago, when we sat in Mrs. Williams' room, at the Asylum, and talked of our future? Then, with a soul full of pure aspirations you said: 'Beulah, I have written "Excelsior" on my banner, and I intend, like that noble youth, to press forward over every obstacle, mounting at every step, until I too stand on the highest pinnacle and plant my banner where its glorious motto shall float over the world!' 'Excelsior!' Ah, my brother, that banner trails in the dust! Alpine heights tower far behind you, dim in the distance, and now with another motto—'Lower still'—you are rushing down to an awful gulf. Oh, Eugene! do you intend to go on to utter ruin? Do you intend to wreck happiness, health, and character in the sea of reckless dissipation? Do you intend to spend your days in disgusting intoxication? I would you had a mother, whose prayers might save you, or a father, whose gray hairs you dared not dishonor, or a sister to win you back from ruin. Oh, that you and I had never, never left the sheltering walls of the Asylum!"

She wept bitterly, and more moved than he chose to appear, Eugene shaded his face with his fingers. Beulah placed her hand on his shoulder, and continued, falteringly:

"Eugene, I am not afraid to tell you the unvarnished truth. You may get angry, and think it is no business of mine to counsel you, who are older and master of your own fate; but when we were children I talked to you freely, and why should I not now? True friendship strengthens with years, and shall I hesitate to speak to you of what gives me so much pain? In a very few days you are to be married; Eugene, if the wine-cup is dearer to you than your beautiful bride, what prospect of happiness have either of you? I had hoped her influence would deter you from it, at least during her visit here; but if not then, how can her presence avail in future? Oh, for heaven's sake! for Antoinette's, for your own, quit the ranks of ruin you are in, and come back to temperance and honor. You are bowing down Cornelia's proud head in humiliation and sorrow. Oh, Eugene, have mercy on yourself!"

He tried to look haughty and insulted, but it would not answer. Her pale face, full of earnest, tearful entreaty, touched his heart, not altogether indurated by profligate associations. He knew she had not given an exaggerated account; he had imagined that she would not hear of his revels, but certainly she told only the truth. Yet he resolved not to admit the charge, and shaking off her hand, answered proudly:

"If I am the degraded character you flatteringly pronounce me, it should certainly render my society anything but agreeable to your fastidious taste. I shall not soon forget your unmerited insults." He rose as he spoke.

"You are angry now, Eugene, because I have held up your own portrait for your inspection. You are piqued because I tell you the truth. But when all this has subsided, and you think the matter calmly over, you will be forced to acknowledge that only the purest friendship could prompt me to remonstrate with you on your ruinous career. Of course, if you choose, you can soon wreck yourself; you are your own master, but the infatuation will recoil upon you. Your disgrace and ruin will not affect me, save that, as your friend, I should mourn your fall. Ah, Eugene, I have risked your displeasure—I have proved my friendship!"

He took his hat and turned toward the door, but she placed herself before it, and holding out both hands, exclaimed sorrowfully:

"Do not let us part in anger. I am an orphan without relatives or protectors, and from early years you have been a kind brother. At least, let us part as friends. I know that in future we shall be completely alienated, but your friend Beulah will always rejoice to hear of your welfare and happiness; and if her warning words, kindly meant, have no effect, and she hears, with keen regret, of your final ruin, she at least will feel that she honestly and anxiously *did all in her power to save you.* Good-by. Shake hands, Eugene, and bear with you to the altar my sincere wishes for your happiness."

She held out her hands entreatingly, but he took no notice of the movement, and hurrying by left the house. For a moment Beulah bowed her head and sobbed; then she brushed the tears from her cheek, and the black brows met in a heavy frown. True, she had not expected much else, yet she felt bitterly grieved, and it was many months ere she ceased to remember the pain of this interview; notwithstanding the contempt, she could not avoid feeling for his weakness.

The Grahams all accompanied Eugene, and after the marriage, went North for the summer. A handsome house was erected near Mr. Graham's residence, and in the fall the young people were to take possession of it. Mr. Lockhart rallied sufficiently to be removed to his home "up the country," and, save Dr. Asbury's family, Beulah saw no one but Clara and her pupils. With July came the close of the session, and the young teacher was free again. One afternoon she put on her bonnet and walked to a distant section of the town to inquire after Kate Ellison (one of her assistant teachers), who, she happened to hear, was quite ill. She found her even worse than she had expected, and on offering her services to watch over the sick girl was anxiously requested to remain with her during the night. She despatched a message to Mrs. Hoyt, cheerfully laid aside her bonnet, and took a seat near the sufferer, while the infirm mother retired to rest. The family were very poor, and almost entirely dependent on Kate's salary for a support. The house was small and comfortless; the scanty furniture of the plainest kind. About dusk, Beulah left her charge in a sound sleep, and cautiously opening the blinds, seated herself on the window sill. The solitary candle on the table gave but a dim light, and she sat for a long time looking out into the street and up at the quiet, clear sky. A buggy drew up beneath the window—she supposed it was the family physician. Mrs. Ellison had not mentioned his coming, but of course it must be a physician, and sure enough there was a knock at the door. She straightened one or two chairs, picked up some articles of clothing scattered about the floor, and opened the door.

She knew not what doctor Mrs. Ellison employed, and as her guardian entered she drew back with a start of surprise. She had not seen him since the morning of Pauline's marriage, five months before, and then he had not noticed her. Now he stopped suddenly, looked at her a moment, and said, as if much chagrined:

"What are you doing here, Beulah?"

"Nursing Kate, sir. Don't talk so loud; she is asleep," answered Beulah, rather frigidly.

She did not look at him, but knew his eyes were on her face, and presently he said:

"You are always where you ought not to be. That girl has typhus fever, and, ten to one, you will take it. In the name of common sense! why don't you let people take care of their own sick, and stay at home instead of hunting up cases like a professed nurse? I suppose the first confirmed case of smallpox you hear of you will hasten to offer your services. You don't intend to spend the night here, it is to be hoped?"

"Her mother has been sitting up so constantly that she is completely exhausted, and somebody must assist in nursing Kate. I did not know that she had any contagious disease, but if she has, I suppose I might as well run the risk as anybody else. It is but common humanity to aid the family."

"Oh! if you choose to risk your life, it is your own affair. Do not imagine for an instant that I expected my advice to weigh an iota with you."

He walked off to Kate, felt her pulse, and without waking her proceeded to replenish the glass of medicine on the table. Beulah was in no mood to obtrude herself on his attention; she went to the window, and stood with her back to him. She could not tamely bear his taunting manner, yet felt that it was out of her power to retort, for she still reverenced him. She was surprised when he came up to her and said abruptly:

"To-day I read an article in 'T——'s Magazine,' called the 'Inner Life,' by 'Delta.'"

A deep crimson dyed her pale face an instant, and her lips curled ominously, as she replied, in a would-be indifferent tone:

"Well, sir?"

"It is not well, at all. It is very ill. It is most miserable!"

"Well! what do I care for the article in 'T——'s Magazine?'" These words were jerked out, as it were, with something like a sneer.

"You care more than you will ever be brought to confess. Have you read this precious 'Inner Life?'"

"Oh, yes!"

"Have you any idea who the author is?"

"Yes, sir, I know the author; but if it had been intended or desired that the public should know also the article would never have appeared over a fictitious signature."

This "Inner Life," which she had written for the last number of the magazine, was an allegory, in which she boldly attempted to disprove the truth of the fact Tennyson has so inimitably embodied in "The Palace of Art," namely, that love of beauty, and intellectual culture cannot satisfy the God-given aspirations of the soul. Her guardian fully comprehended the dawning, and as yet unacknowledged dread which prompted this article, and hastily laying his hand on her shoulder, he said:

"Ah, proud girl! you are struggling desperately with your heart. You, too, have reared a 'palace' on dreary, almost inaccessible crags; and because already you begin to weary of your isolation, you would fain hurl invectives at Tennyson, who explores your mansion, 'so royal, rich and wide,' and discovers the grim specters that dwell with you! You were very miserable when you wrote that sketch; you are not equal to what you have undertaken. Child, this year of trial and loneliness has left its impress on your face. Are you not yet willing to give up the struggle?"

The moon had risen, and as its light shone on her countenance, he saw a fierce blaze in her eyes he had never noticed there before. She shook off his light touch, and answered:

"No! I will never give up!"

He smiled, and left her.

She remained with her sick friend until sunrise the next morning, and ere she left the house, was rewarded by the assurance that she was better. In a few days Kate was decidedly convalescent. Beulah did not take typhus fever.

CHAPTER XXVII.

The day was sullen, stormy and dark. Gray, leaden clouds were scourged through the sky by a howling southeastern gale, and the lashed waters of the bay broke along the shore with a solemn, continued boom. The rain fell drearily, and sheet lightning, pale and constant, gave a ghastly hue to the scudding clouds. It was one of those lengthened storms which, during the month of August, are so prevalent along the gulf coast. Clara Sanders sat near a window, bending over a piece of needlework, while with her hands clasped behind her, Beulah walked up and down the floor. Their countenances contrasted vividly; Clara's sweet, placid face, with drooped eyelids and Madonna-like serenity; the soft, auburn hair curled about her cheeks, and the delicate lips in peaceful rest. And Beulah!—how shall I adequately paint the gloom and restlessness written in her stormy countenance? To tell you that her brow was bent and lowering, that her lips were now unsteady, and now tightly compressed, and that her eyes were full of troubled shadows, would convey but a faint impression of the anxious discontent which seemed to have taken entire possession of her. Clara glanced at her, sighed, and went on with her work; she knew perfectly well she was in no humor for conversation. The rain increased until it fell in torrents, and the hoarse thunder muttered a dismal accompaniment. It grew too dark to see the stitches; Clara put by her work, and folding her hands on her lap, sat looking out into the storm, listening to the roar of the rushing wind as it bowed the tree-tops and uplifted the white-capped billows of the bay. Beulah paused beside the window, and said abruptly:

"It is typical of the individual, social, moral, and intellectual life. Look which way you will, you find antagonistic elements fiercely warring. There is a broken cog somewhere in the machinery of this plunging globe of ours. Everything organic, and inorganic, bears testimony to a miserable derangement. There is not a department of earth where harmony reigns. True, the stars are serene, and move in their everlasting orbits with fixed precision, but they are not of earth; here there is nothing definite, nothing certain. The seasons are regular, but they are determined by other worlds. Verily, the contest is still fiercely waged between Ormuzd and Ahriman, and the last has the best of it so far. The three thousand years of Ahriman seem dawning."

She resumed her walk, and looking after her anxiously Clara answered:

"But remember, the 'Zend-Avesta' promises that Ormuzd shall finally conquer, and reign supreme. In this happy kingdom, I love to trace the resemblance to the millennium which was shown St. John on lonely Patmos."

"It is small comfort to anticipate a time of blessedness for future generations. What benefit is steam or telegraph to the molding mummies of the catacombs? I want to know what good the millennium will do you and me, when our dust is mingled with mother earth, in some silent necropolis?"

"Oh, Beulah! what ails you to-day? You look so gloomy and wretched. It seems to me you have changed sadly of late. I knew that a life of labor, such as you voluntarily assumed, would chasten your spirit, but I did not expect this utter revolution of your nature so soon. Oh, have done with skepticism!"

"Faith in creeds is not to be put on and laid aside at will, like a garment. Granted that these same doctrines of Zoroaster are faint adumbrations of the Hebrew creed, the Gordian knot is by no means loosed. That prologue in Faust horrified you yesterday; yet, upon my word, I don't see why; for very evidently it is taken from Job, and Faust is but an ideal Job, tempted in more subtle manner than by the loss of flocks, houses and children. You believe that Satan was allowed to do his utmost to ruin Job, and Mephistopheles certainly set out on the same fiendish mission. Mephistopheles is not the defiant demon of Milton, but a powerful prince in the service of God. You need not shudder; I am giving no partial account, I merely repeat the opinion of many on this subject. It is all the same to me. Evil exists: that is the grim fact. As to its origin, I would about as soon set off to search for the city Asgard."

"Still, I would not give my faith for all your learning and philosophy. See what it has brought you to," answered Clara, sorrowfully.

"Your faith! what does it teach you of this evil principle?" retorted Beulah, impatiently.

"At least, more than all speculation has taught you. You admit that of its origin you know nothing; the Bible tells me, that time was when earth was sinless, and man holy, and that death and sin entered the world by man's transgression—"

"Which I don't believe," interrupted Beulah.

"So you might sit there and stop your ears, and close your eyes, and assert that this was a sunny, serene day. Your reception or rejection of the Biblical record by no means affects its authenticity. My faith teaches that the evil you so bitterly deprecate is not eternal; shall finally be crushed, and the harmony you crave, pervade all realms. Why an All-wise, and All-powerful God, suffers evil to exist, is not for his finite creatures to determine. It is one of many mysteries which it is as utterly useless to bother over as to weave ropes of sand."

She gathered up her sewing materials, put them in her basket, and retired to her own room. Beulah felt relieved when the door closed behind her, and taking up Theodore Parker's "Discourses," began to read. Poor famishing soul! what chaff she eagerly devoured. In her anxious haste, she paused not to perceive that the attempted refutations of Christianity contained objections more gross and incomprehensible than the doctrine assailed. Long before she had arrived at the conclusion that ethical and theological truth must be firmly established on psychological foundations, hence she plunged into metaphysics, studying treatise after treatise, and system after system. To her grievous disappointment, however, the psychology of each seemed different, nay opposed. She set out believing her "consciousness" the infallible criterion of truth; this she fancied philosophy taught, at least professed to teach; but instead of unanimity among metaphysicians, she found fierce denunciation of predecessors, ingenious refutations of principles, which they had evolved from rigid analysis of the facts of consciousness and an intolerant dogmatism which astonished and confused her. One extolled Locke as an oracle of wisdom; another ridiculed the shallowness of his investigations and the absurdity of his doctrines; while a third, showed conclusively, that Locke's assailant knew nothing at all of what he wrote, and maintained that he alone could set matters right. She studied Locke for herself. Either he was right, and all the others were wrong, or else there was no truth in any. Another philosopher professed to ground some points of his faith on certain principles of Descartes; the very next work she read proclaimed that Descartes never held any such principles, that the writer had altogether mistaken his views; whereupon up started another who informed her that nobody knew what

Descartes really did believe on the subject under discussion; that it was a mooted question among his disciples. This was rather discouraging, but, nothing daunted, she bought, borrowed and read on.

Brown's descent upon Reid greatly interested her; true, there were very many things she could not assent to, yet the arguments seemed plausible enough, when lo! a metaphysical giant rescues Reid; tells her that Brown was an ignoramus; utterly misunderstood the theory he set himself to criticise, and was a wretched bungler; after which he proceeds to show that although Brown had not acumen enough to perceive it, Reid had himself fallen into grave errors, and culpable obscurity. Who was right, or who was wrong, she could not for her life decide. It would have been farcical, indeed, had she not been so anxiously in earnest. Beginning to distrust herself, and with a dawning dread lest, after all, psychology would prove an incompetent guide, she put by the philosophies themselves and betook herself to histories of philosophy, fancying that here all bitter invective would be laid aside, and stern impartiality prevail. Here the evil she fled from increased fourfold. One historian of philosophy (who was a great favorite of her guardian) having lost all confidence in the subjects he treated, set himself to work to show the fallacy of all systems, from Anaximander to Cousin. She found the historians of philosophy as much at variance as the philosophers themselves, and looked with dismay into the dim land of vagaries, into which metaphysics had drawn the brightest minds of the past. Then her guardian's favorite quotation recurred to her with painful significance: "There is no criterion of truth; all is merely subjective truth." It was the old skeptical palladium, ancient as metaphysics. She began to despair of the truth in this direction; but it certainly existed somewhere. She commenced the study of Cousin with trembling eagerness; if at all, she would surely find in a harmonious "Eclecticism" the absolute truth she had chased through so many metaphysical doublings; "Eclecticism" would cull for her the results of all search and reasoning. For a time, she believed she had indeed found a resting-place; his "true" satisfied her; his "beautiful" fascinated her; but when she came to examine his "Theodicea," and trace its results, she shrank back appalled. She was not yet prepared to embrace his subtle pantheism. Thus far had her sincere inquiries and efforts brought her. It was no wonder her hopeful nature grew bitter and cynical; no wonder her brow was bent with puzzled thought, and her pale face haggard and joyless. Sick of systems, she began to search her own soul; did the very thing of all others best calculated to harass her mind and fill it with inexplicable mysteries. She constituted her own reason the sole judge;

and then, dubious of the verdict, arraigned reason itself. Now began the desperate struggle. Alone and unaided, she wrestled with some of the grimmest doubts that can assail a human soul. The very prevalence of her own doubts augmented the difficulty. On every side she saw the footprints of skepticism; in history, essays, novels, poems, and reviews. Still, her indomitable will maintained the conflict. Her hopes, aims, energies, all centered in this momentous struggle. She studied over these world-problems until her eyes grew dim, and the veins on her brow swelled like cords. Often gray dawn looked in upon her, still sitting before her desk, with a sickly, waning lamp-light gleaming over her pallid face. And to-day, as she looked out on the flying clouds and listened to the mournful wail of the rushing gale she seemed to stand upon the verge of a yawning chaos. What did she believe? She knew not. Old faiths had crumbled away; she stood in a dreary waste, strewn with the wreck of creeds and systems; a silent desolation! And with Richter's Christ she exclaimed: "Oh! how is each so solitary in this wide grave of the All? I am alone with myself. Oh, Father! oh, Father, where is thy infinite bosom, that I might rest on it?" A belief in something she must have; it was an absolute necessity of the soul. There was no scoffing tendency in her skepticism; she could not jest over the solemn issues involved, and stood wondering which way she should next journey after this "pearl of great price." It was well for her that garlands of rhetoric and glittering logic lay over the pitfalls before her; for there were unsounded abysses, darker than any she had yet endeavored to fathom. Clara came back, and softly laid her hand on her friend's arm.

"Please put up your book, and sing something for me, won't you?"

Beulah looked at the serene countenance, so full of resignation, and answered, gloomily:

"What! are you, too, tired of listening to this storm-anthem nature has treated us to for the last two days? It seems to me the very universe, animate and inanimate, is indulging in an uncontrollable fit of the 'blues.' One would almost think the dead-march was being played up and down the aisles of creation."

She pressed her hands to her hot brow, as if to wipe away the cobwebs that dimmed her vision, and raising the lid of the piano, ran her fingers over the keys.

"Sing me something hopeful and heart-cheering," said Clara.

"I have no songs of that description."

"Yes you have: 'Look Aloft,' and the 'Psalm of Life.'"

"No, no. I could not sing either now," replied Beulah, averting her face.

"Why not now? They are the excelsior strains of struggling pilgrims. They were written for the dark hours of life."

"They are a mockery to me. Ask me for anything else," said she, compressing her lips.

Clara leaned her arm on the piano, and looking sadly at her companion, said, as if with a painful effort:

"Beulah, in a little while we shall be separated, and only the All-Father knows whether we shall meet on earth again. My application for that situation as governess, up the country, brought me an answer to-day. I am to go very soon."

Beulah made no reply, and Clara continued, sorrowfully:

"It is very painful to leave my few remaining friends, and go among perfect strangers, but it is best that I should." She leaned her head on her hand and wept.

"Why is it best?"

"Because here I am constantly reminded of other days, and other hopes, now lying dead on my heart. But we will not speak of this. Of all my ties here, my love for you is now the strongest. Oh, Beulah, our friendship has been sacred, and I dread the loneliness which will be my portion when hundreds of miles lay between us! The links that bind orphan hearts like ours are more lasting than all others."

"I shall be left entirely alone, if you accept this situation. You have long been my only companion. Don't leave me, Clara," murmured Beulah, while her lips writhed and quivered.

"You will have the Asburys still, and they are sincere friends."

"Yes, friends, but not companions. What congeniality is there between those girls and myself? None. My isolation will be complete when you leave me!"

"Beulah, will you let me say what is in my heart?"

"Say it freely, my brown-eyed darling."

"Well then, Beulah; give it up; give it up. It will only bow down your heart with untold cares and sorrows."

"Give up what?"

"This combat with loneliness and poverty."

"I am not lonely," answered Beulah, with a wintry smile.

"Oh, Beulah! yes, you are; wretchedly lonely. I have been but a poor companion for you; intellectually, you are far beyond me, and there has been little congeniality in our tastes and pursuits. I have always known this; and

I know, too, that you never will be a happy woman until you have a companion equal in intellect, who understands and sympathizes with you. Ah, Beulah! with all your stubborn pride, and will, and mental endowments, you have a woman's heart; and crush its impulses as you may, it will yet assert its sway. As I told you long ago, grammars, and geographies, and duty, could not fill the void in my heart; and believe me, neither will metaphysics and philosophy, and literature, satisfy you. Suppose you do attain celebrity as a writer. Can the plaudits of strangers bring back to your solitary hearth the loved dead, or cheer you in your hours of gloom? I too am an orphan; I speak of what I can appreciate. You are mistaken, Beulah, in thinking you can dispense with sympathy. You are not sufficient for yourself, as you have so proudly maintained. God has created us for companionship; it is a necessity of human nature."

"Then why are you and I orphaned for all time?" asked Beulah, coldly.

"The sablest clouds of sorrow have silver linings. Perhaps that you and I might turn more continually to the God of orphans. Beulah, God has not flooded earth with eternal sunlight. He knew that shadows were needed to chasten the spirits of his children, and teach them to look to him for the renewal of all blessings. But shadows are fleeting, and every season of gloom has its morning star. Oh, I thank God that his own hand arranged the *chiaroscuro* of earth!" She spoke earnestly; the expression of her eyes told that her thoughts had traveled into the dim, weird land of futurity. Beulah offered no comment, but the gloom deepened on her brow, and her white fingers crept restlessly over the piano keys. After a moment's silence, Clara continued:

"I would not regret our separation so much if I left you in the possession of Christian faith; armed with a perfect trust in the religion of Jesus Christ. Oh, Beulah, it makes my heart ache when I think of you, struggling so fiercely in the grasp of infidelity! Many times have I seen the light shining beneath your door, long after midnight, and wept over the conflict in which I knew you were engaged; and only God knows how often I have mingled your name in my prayers, entreating Him to direct you in your search, to guide you safely through the paths of skepticism, and place your weary feet upon the 'rock of ages.' Oh, Beulah, do not make my prayers vain by your continued questioning! Come back to Christ, and the Bible." Tears glided down her cheeks as she passed her arm round her friend, and dropped her head on her shoulder. Beulah's eyelids trembled an instant, but there was no moisture in the gray depths, as she answered:

"Thank you, Clara, for your interest. I am glad you have this faith you would fain lead me to. Not for worlds would I unsettle it, even if I could. You are comforted in your religion, and it is a priceless blessing to you. But I am sincere, even in my skepticism. I am honest; and God, if he sees my heart, sees that I am. I may be an infidel, as you call me, but, if so, I am an honest one; and if the Bible is all true, as you believe, God will judge my heart. But I shall not always be skeptical; I shall find the truth yet. I know it is a tedious journey I have set out on, and it may be my life will be spent in the search, but what of that, if at last I attain the goal? What if I only live to reach it? What will my life be to me without it?"

"And can you contentedly contemplate your future, passed as this last year has been?" cried Clara.

"Perhaps 'contentedly' is scarcely the right term. I shall not murmur, no matter how dreary the circumstances of my life may be, provided I succeed at last," replied Beulah, resolutely.

"Oh, Beulah, you make my heart ache!"

"Then try not to think of or care for me."

"There is another heart, dear Beulah, a heart sad, but noble, that you are causing bitter anguish. Are you utterly indifferent to this also?"

"All of the last exists merely in your imagination. We will say no more about it, if you please."

She immediately began a brilliant overture, and Clara retreated to the window. With night the roar of the tempest increased; the rain fell with a dull, uninterrupted patter, the gale swept furiously on, and the heaving, foaming waters of the bay gleamed luridly beneath the sheet-lightning. Clara stood looking out, and before long Beulah joined her; then the former said, suddenly:

"Do you remember, that about six years ago, a storm like this tossed the Morning Star far from its destined track, and for many days it was unheard of? Do you remember, too, that it held one you loved; and that in an agony of dread lest he should find a grave among coral beds you bowed your knee in prayer to Almighty God, imploring him to calm the tempest, hush the gale, and save him who was so dear to you? Ah, Beulah, you distrusted human pilots then."

As Beulah made no reply, she fancied she was pondering her words. But memory had flown back to the hour when she knelt in prayer for Eugene, and she thought she could far better have borne his death then, in the glorious springtime of his youth, than know that he had fallen from his noble height. Then she could have mourned his loss, and cherished his memory ever after; now she could only pity and despise his folly. What was that early shipwreck she so much dreaded, in comparison with the sea of vice, whose every wave tossed him helplessly on to ruin. He had left her, an earnest believer in religion; he came back scoffing at everything sacred. This much she had learned from Cornelia. Was there an intimate connection between the revolutions in his nature? Misled by her silence, Clara said, eagerly:

"You were happy in that early faith. Oh, Beulah, you will never find another so holy, so comforting!"

Beulah frowned, and looked up impatiently.

"Clara, I am not to be persuaded into anything. Leave me to myself. You are kind, but mistaken."

"If I have said too much, forgive me; I was actuated by sincere affection, and pity for your state of mind."

"I am not an object of pity by any means," replied Beulah, very coldly.

Clara was unfortunate in her expressions; she seemed to think so, and turned away; but, conscious of having spoken hastily, Beulah caught her hand, and exclaimed frankly:

"Do not be hurt with me; I did not intend to wound you. Forgive me, Clara. Don't go. When are you to leave for your new home?"

"Day after to-morrow. Mr. Arlington seems anxious that I should come immediately. He has three children; a son and two daughters. I hope they are amiable; I dread lest they prove unruly and spoiled. If so, woe to their governess."

"Does Mr. Arlington reside in the village to which you directed your letter?"

"No; he resides on his plantation, several miles from the village. The prospect of being in the country is the only redeeming feature in the arrangement. I hope my health will be permanently restored by the change; but of the success of my plan only time can decide."

"And when shall we meet again?" said Beulah, slowly.

"Perhaps, henceforth, our paths diverge widely. We may meet no more on earth; but dear Beulah, there is a 'peaceful shore, where billows never beat nor tempests roar,' where assuredly we shall spend an eternity together if we keep the faith here. Oh, if I thought our parting now was for all time, I should mourn bitterly, very bitterly; but I will not believe it. The arms of our God support you. I shall always pray that he will guide and save you." She leaned forward, kissed Beulah's forehead, and left the room.

CHAPTER XXVIII.

One afternoon in October, the indisposition of one of her music pupils released Beulah earlier than usual, and she determined to seize this opportunity and visit the Asylum. Of the walk across the common she never wearied; the grass had grown brown, and, save the deep, changeless green of the ancient pines, only the hectic coloring of the dying year met her eye. The day was cool and windy, and the common presented a scene of boisterous confusion, which she paused to contemplate. A number of boys had collected to play their favorite games; balls flew in every direction, and merry shouts rang cheerily through the air. She looked on a few moments at their careless, happy sports, and resumed her walk, feeling that their joyousness was certainly contagious, she was so much lighter-hearted from having watched their beaming faces and listened to their ringing laughter.

As she drew near the Asylum gate memory began to pass its fingers over her heart; but here, too, sounds of gladness met her. The orphans were assembled on the lawn in front of the building, chatting as cheerfully as though they were all members of one family. The little ones trundled hoops and chased each other up and down the graveled walks; some of the boys tossed their balls, and a few of the larger girls were tying up chrysanthemums to slender stakes. They were dressed alike; all looked contented, neat and happy, and their rosy faces presented a noble tribute to the efficacy and untold blessings of the institution. To many of them Beulah was well known; she threw off her bonnet and shawl, and assisted the girls in their work among the flowers, while the little ones gathered around her, lisping their childish welcome and coaxing her to join to their innocent games. The stately China trees, where, in years gone by, Lilly and Claudy had watched the chirping robins, were again clad in their rich, golden livery; and as Beulah looked up at the red brick walls that had sheltered her head in the early days of orphanage, it seemed but yesterday that she trod these walks and listened to the wintry wind sighing through these same loved trees. The children told her that their matron had been sick and was not yet quite well, and needing no pilot, Beulah went through the house in search of her. She found her at last in the store-room, giving out materials for the evening meal, and had an opportunity of observing the change which had taken place in the last few months. She was pale and thin, and her sharpened features wore a depressed, weary expression; but, turning round, she perceived Beulah, and a glad smile broke instantly over her countenance as she clasped the girl's hand in both hers.

"Dear child, I have looked for you a long time. I did not think you would wait so many weeks. Come in and sit down."

"I did not know you had been sick until I came and heard the children speak of it. You should have sent me word. I see you have not entirely recovered."

"No, I am quite feeble yet; but in time, I hope I shall be well again. Ah, Beulah, I have wanted to see you so much! so much! Child, it seems to me I shall never get used to being separated from you."

Beulah sat on the sofa near her, and the matron's withered hands were passed caressingly over the glossy bands of hair which lay on the orphan's white temples.

"I love to come here occasionally; it does me good; but not too often; that would be painful, you know."

Beulah spoke in a subdued voice, while memory painted the evening when Eugene had sought her in this apartment, and wiped away her tears for Lilly's absence. Her features twitched as she thought of the bitter changes that rolling years work, and she sighed unconsciously. The matron's hands were still smoothing her hair, and presently she said, with an anxious, scrutinizing look:

"Have you been sick since you were here last?"

"No. What makes you imagine such a thing?"

"Dear child, I do not imagine; I know you look worn and ill. Why, Beulah, hold up your hand; there, see how transparent it is! Almost like wax! Something ails you, child; that I know well enough."

"No, I assure you, I am not ill. Sometimes, of late, I have been troubled with the old headaches you used to cure, when I was a child; but, on the whole, I am well."

"Beulah, they tell me Eugene is married," said the kind-hearted woman, with another look at the quiet face beside her.

"Yes, he was married nearly five months ago." A tremor passed over her lips as she spoke.

"Did you see his wife?"

"Yes; she is a very pretty woman. I may say a beautiful woman; but she does not suit him. At least, I am afraid she will not."

"Ah, I knew as much! I thought as much!" cried Mrs. Williams.

"Why?" asked Beulah, wonderingly.

"Oh, money cloaks all faults, child. I knew he did not marry her for love!"

Beulah started a little, and said hastily:

"You do him injustice—great injustice! Eugene was charmed by her beauty, not her fortune."

"Oh, heiresses are always beautiful and charming in the eyes of the world! Beulah, do you know that I watched for Eugene for days and weeks and months, after his return from Europe? I wanted to see him—oh, so much! I loved you both as though you were my own children. I was so proud of that boy! I had raised him from a crawling infant, and never dreamed that he would forget me. But he did not come. I have not seen him since he left, six years ago, for Germany. Oh, the boy has pained me—pained me! I loved him so much!"

Beulah's brow clouded heavily as she said:

"It is better so—better that you should not see him. He is not what he was when he quitted us."

"It is true, then, that he drinks—that he is wild and dissipated? I heard it once, but would not believe it. Oh, it can't be that Eugene drinks?"

"Yes, he drinks—not to stupid intoxication, but too freely for his health and character. He does not look like himself now."

Mrs. Williams bowed down her head, and wept bitterly, while Beulah, continued, sorrowfully:

"His adoption was his ruin. Had he remained dependent on his individual exertions, he would have grown up an honor to himself and his friends. But Mr. Graham is considered very wealthy, and Eugene weakly desisted from the honest labor which was his duty. His fashionable associates have ruined him. In Europe he learned to drink, and here his companions dragged him constantly into scenes of dissipation. But I do not despair of him yet. It may be long before he awakens from this infatuation, but I trust he will yet reform. I cannot bear to think of him as a confirmed drunkard! Oh, no! no! I may be wrong, but I still hope that his nobler nature will conquer."

"God help the boy! I have prayed for him for years, and I shall pray for him still, though he has forgotten me."

She sobbed, and covered her face with her apron. A joyless smile flitted over Beulah's fixed, grave features as she said, encouragingly:

"He will come to see you when he returns from the North. He has not forgotten you—that is impossible. Like me, he owes you too much."

"I shall leave here, very soon," said Mrs. Williams, wiping her eyes.

"Leave the Asylum! for what?"

"I am getting old, child, and my health is none of the best. The duties are very heavy here, and I am not willing to occupy the position unless I could discharge all the duties faithfully. I have sent in my resignation to the managers, and as soon as they succeed in getting another matron I shall leave the Asylum. I am sorry to be obliged to go; I have been here so long that I am very much attached to the place and the children. But I am not able to do what I have done, and I know it is right that I should give up the position."

"What are you going to do?"

"I have means enough to live plainly the remainder of my life. I intend to rent or buy a small house, and settle down, and be quiet. I feel now as if I should like to spend my days in peace."

"Do you intend to live alone?"

"Yes, child; except a servant, I suppose I shall be quite alone. But you will come to see me often, and perhaps Eugene will remember me, some day, when he is in trouble."

"No, I shall not come to see you at all! I mean to come and live with you—that is, if I may?" cried Beulah, springing up and laying her hand on the matron's.

"God bless you, dear child, how glad I shall be!" She wound her arms round the slender form, and laughed through her tears.

Beulah gently put back the gray locks that had fallen from the border of her cap, and said hopefully:

"I am sick of boarding—sick of town! Let us get a nice little house, where

I can walk in and out to my school. Have you selected any particular place?"

"No. I have looked at two or three, but none suited me exactly. Now you can help me. I am so thankful you are going to be with me. Will you come as soon as I can be released here?"

"Yes, just as soon as you are ready for me; and I think I know a house for rent which will just suit us. Now, I want it understood that I am to pay the rent."

"Oh, no. child! I won't hear to it, for I am—"

"Very well, then; I will stay where I am."

"Oh Beulah! you are not in earnest?"

"Yes, I am; so say no more about it. I will come on no other condition. I will see the owner of the house, ascertain what I can obtain it for, and send you word. Then you can look at it and decide."

"I am quite willing to trust it to you, child; only I can't bear the thought of your paying the rent for it. But we can arrange that afterward."

"No, you must be perfectly satisfied with the house. I will go by this evening and find out about it, so as to let you know at once. Have you any idea when the 'board' will procure another matron?"

"They have advertised, and several persons applied, I believe, but they were not exactly pleased with the applicants. I suppose, however, that in a few days they will find a substitute for me."

"Well, be sure you get a good servant, and now I must go."

She put on her bonnet and shawl with unwonted haste, and ran down the steps. In her frequent walks, she had noticed two cottages in course of erection, not very far from the pine grove in front of the Asylum, and now crossing the common she directed her steps toward them. The lots were small and belonged to Dr. Asbury, who said he would build a couple of cottages for poor families to rent at cheap rates. As Beulah approached the houses she saw the doctor's buggy standing near the door, and thinking it a good omen, quickened her steps. Each building contained only three rooms and a hall, with a gallery, or rather portico in front. They were genuine *cottages orné,* built after Downing's plans, and presented a tasteful, inviting appearance. The windows were arched and the woodwork elaborately carved. Beulah pushed open the freshly painted gate, ran up the steps, and into the hall. The carpenters were still at work in the kitchen, and as she conjectured, here she found her friend, giving some final directions. She looked round the snug little kitchen, and walking up to Dr. Asbury, who stood with his back to the door, she shook his hand, with a cheerful salutation.

"Halloo, Beulah! where did you drop from? Glad to see you; glad to see you. How came you prying into my new houses? Answer me that! Did you see my spouse as you came through the hall?"

"No, I will go back and hunt for her—"

"You need not; there she comes down the steps of the house. She would insist on seeing about some shelves for this precious kitchen; thinks I am bound to put pantries, and closets, and shelves all over the house for my future tenants. I suppose before the first poor family take possession, I shall be expected to fill the closet with table-linen and cutlery, and the larder with sugar, flour, and wax candles. Look here, Mrs. Asbury, how many more shelves is this kitchen to have?"

"It is well she has a conscience, sir, since nature denied you one," answered Beulah, whom Mrs. Asbury received very affectionately.

"Conscience! Bless my soul! she has none, as regards my unlucky purse. Positively, she wanted to know, just now, if I would not have that little patch of ground between the house and the paling laid off into beds; and if I would not plant a few rose-bushes and vines, for the first rascally set of children to tear up by the roots, just as soon as their parents moved in. There's conscience for you with a vengeance."

"And what did you say, sir?"

"What did I say? Why just what every other meek husband says to appeals which 'wont cost much, you know.' Of course I had no opinion of my own. Madam, here, is infallible; so I am put down for maybe a hundred dollars more. You need not have asked the result, you true daughter of Eve; every one of you understand wheedling. Those two mischieveous imps of mine are almost as great adepts as their mother. Hey, Beulah, no whispering there! You look as wise as an owl. What am I to do next? Paper the walls and fresco the ceilings? Out with it."

"I want to ask, sir, how much rent your conscience will allow you to demand for this pigeon-box of a house?"

"Well, I had an idea of asking two hundred dollars for it. Cheap enough at that. You may have it for two hundred," said he, with a good-humored nod toward Beulah.

"Very well, I will take it at that, provided Mrs. Williams likes it as well as I do. In a day or two I will determine."

"In the name of common sense, Beulah, what freak is this?" said the doctor, looking at her with astonishment.

"I am going to live with the matron of the Asylum, whom you know very well. I think this house will suit us exactly, and the rent suits my purse far better than a larger building would. I am tired of boarding. I want a little home of my own, where, when the labors of school are over, I can feel at ease. The walk, twice a day, will benefit me, I feel assured. You need not look so dismal and perplexed, I will make a capital tenant. Your door-facings shan't be pencil-marked; your windows shan't be broken, nor your gate swung off its hinges. As for those flowers you are so anxious to plant, and that patch of ground you are so much interested in, it shall blossom like the plain of Sharon."

He looked at her wistfully; took off his spectacles, wiped them with the end of his coat, and said, dubiously:

"What does Hartwell think of this project?"

"I have not consulted him."

"The plain English of which is, that whether he approves or condemns, you are determined to carry out this new plan? Take care, Beulah; remember the old adage about 'cutting off your nose to spite your face.'"

"Rather mal apropos, Dr. Asbury," said she indifferently.

"I am an old man, Beulah, and know something of life and the world."

"Nay, George: why dissuade her from this plan? If she prefers this quiet little home to the confinement and bustle of a boarding-house, if she thinks she would be happier here with Mrs. Williams than in the heart of the city why should not she come? Suffer her to judge for herself. I am disposed to applaud her choice," interrupted Mrs. Asbury.

"Alice, do you suppose she will be satisfied to bury herself out here, with an infirm old woman for a companion? Here she must have an early breakfast; trudge through rain and cold into town; teach stupid little brats till evening; then listen to others equally stupid thrum over music lessons, and at last, tired out, drag herself back here about dark, when it is too late to see whether her garden is a cotton patch or a peach orchard! Will you please to tell me what enjoyment there is for one of her temperament in such a tread-mill existence?"

"Your picture is all shadow, George; and even if it were not, she is the best judge of what will promote her happiness. Do not discourage her. Ah, humble as the place is, I know how her heart aches for a spot she can call 'home.' These three rooms will be a haven of rest for her when the day is done. My dear Beulah, I trust you may be very happy here, or wherever you decide to live; you deserve to be."

"Thank you, madam, for your friendly sympathy. I am glad you approve my design."

"Well, well; if you soon weary of this freak you can easily give up the house, that is all. Now, Beulah, if you determine to take it, rest assured I will gladly make any additions or alterations you may suggest. I dare say I shall like you for a tenant. But see here, Mrs. Asbury, I have patients to look after. Please to remember that I am a professional character, consequently can call no moment my own. What! another row of shelves round that side? This building houses for rent is a ruinous speculation! Come, it is too late now to go over the rooms again; tomorrow will do as well. Beulah, are you going to play cook, too?"

"No, indeed! Mrs. Williams will find us a servant. Good-by. I will decide about the house as soon as possible."

The following day she dispatched a note to the matron, with information concerning the house; and at the close of the week all arrangements were completed, so that they might take possession as soon as a new matron was secured. Thus the last of October glided swiftly away, and one cold, clear day in November, Beulah was notified that Mrs. Williams was comfortably settled in the new home. She went to school as usual, and when the recitations were ended started out with a glad heart and springing step. In half an hour she reached the little white gate, and found Mrs. Williams waiting there to welcome her. Everything was new and neat; the tastefully selected carpets were not tapistry, but cheap ingrain; the snowy curtains were of plain dimity, with rose-colored borders, and the tea-table held instead of costly Sèvres, simple white china, with a band of gilt. A bright fire crackled and glowed in the chimney, and as Beulah stood on the hearth, and glanced round the comfortable little room, which was to be both parlor and dining-room, she felt her heart thrill with delight, and exclaimed:

"This is home! at last I feel that I have a home of my own. Not the Rothschilds, in their palaces, are so happy as I!"

For years she had been a wanderer, with no hearthstone, and now for the first time since her father's death she was at home. Not the home of adoption; nor the cheerless room of a boarding-house, but the humble home which labor and rigid economy had earned for her. Her heart bounded with joy; an unwonted glow suffused her cheeks, and her parted lips trembled. The evening passed quickly, and when she retired to her own room she was surprised to find a handsome rosewood bookcase and desk occupying one corner. She opened the glass doors and saw her books carefully arranged on the shelves. Could her guardian have sent it? No, since her refusal of the watch, she felt sure he would not have offered it. A small note lay on the shelf and recognizing the delicate handwriting, she read the lines, containing these words:

"BEULAH: Accept the accompanying case and desk as a slight testimony of the affection of

"Your sincere friend,
"ALICE ASBURY."

Tears sprang into her eyes as she opened the desk and discovered an elegant pen and pencil, and every convenience connected with writing. Turning away she saw beside the fire a large, deep easy-chair, cushioned with purple morocco, and knew it was exactly like one she had often seen in Dr. Asbury's library. On the back was pinned a narrow slip of paper, and she read, in the doctor's scrawling, quaint writing:

"Child, don't be too proud to use it."

She was not; throwing herself into the luxurious chair, she broke the seal of a letter received that day from Pauline Mortimor. Once before, soon after her marriage, a few lines of gay greeting had come, and then many months had elapsed. As she unfolded the sheet she saw, with sorrow, that in several places, it was blotted with tears; and the contents, written in a paroxysm of passion, disclosed a state of wretchedness which Beulah little suspected. Pauline's impulsive, fitful nature, was clearly indexed in the letter, and after a brief apology for her long silence she wrote as follows:

"Oh, Beulah, I am so miserable; so very, very wretched! Beulah, Ernest does not love me! You will scarcely believe me. Oh, I hardly know how to believe it myself! Uncle Guy was right; I do not suit Ernest; but I loved him so very, very dearly; and thought him so devoted to me. Fool that I was! my eyes are opened at last. Beulah, it nearly drives me wild, to think that I am bound to him for life, an unloved wife. Not a year has passed since our marriage, yet already he has tired of my 'pretty face.' Oh, Beulah, if I could only come to you, and put my arms round your neck, and lay my poor weary head down on your shoulder, then I could tell you all—"

Here several sentences were illegible from tears, and she could only read what followed.

"Since yesterday morning, Ernest has not spoken to me. While I write he is sitting in the next room reading, as cold, indifferent and calm as if I were not perfectly wretched. He is tyrannical; and because I do not humor all his whims, and have some will of my own, he treats me with insulting indifference. He is angry now, because I resented some of his father's impertinent speeches about my dress. This is not the first, nor the second time that we have quarreled. He has an old maid sister, who is forever meddling about my affairs, and sneering at my domestic arrangements; and because I finally told her I believed I was mistress of my own house, Ernest has never forgiven me. Ellen (the sister I loved, and went to school with) has married, and moved to a distant part of the State. The other members of his family are bigoted, proud and parsimonious, and they have chiefly made the breach between us. Oh, Beulah, if I could only undo the past, and be Pauline Chilton once more! Oh, if I could be free and happy again! But there is no prospect of that. I am his wife, as he told me yesterday, and suppose I must drag out a miserable existence. Yet I will not be trampled on by his family! His sister spends much of her time with us; reads to Ernest; talks to him about things that she glories in telling me I don't understand the first word of. Beulah, I was anxious to study, and make myself a companion for him, but try as I may Lucy contrives always to fret and thwart me. Two days ago she nearly drove me beside myself with her sneers and allusions to my great mental inferiority to Ernest (as if I were not often enough painfully reminded of the fact without any of her assistance!). I know I should not have said it, but I was too angry to think of propriety, and told her that her presence in my home was very disagreeable. Oh, if you could have seen her insulting smile, as she answered, that her 'noble brother needed her, and she felt it a duty to remain with him.' Beulah, I love my husband; I would do anything on earth to make him happy, if we were left to ourselves, but as to submitting to Lucy's arrogance and sneers, I will not! Ernest requires me to apologize to his father and sister, and I told him I would not! I would die first! He does not love me, or he would shield me from such trials. He thinks his sister is perfection, and I tell you I do absolutely detest her. Now, Beulah, there is no one else to whom I would mention my unhappiness. Mother does not suspect it, and never shall, even when she visits me. Uncle Guy predicted it, and I would not have him know it for the universe. But I can trust you; I feel that you will sympathize with me, and I want you to counsel me. Oh, tell me what I ought to do to rid myself of this tormenting sister-in-law and father-in-law, and I may say, all Ernest's kin. Sometimes, when I think of the future, I absolutely shudder; for if matters go on this way much longer I shall learn to hate my husband too. He knew my disposition before he married me and has no right to treat me as he does. If it were only Ernest I could bring myself to 'obey' him, for I love him very devotedly; but as to being dictated to by all his relatives, I never will! Beulah, burn this blurred letter, don't let anyone know how drearily I am situated. I am too proud to have my misery published. To know that people pitied me, would kill me. I never can be happy again, but perhaps you can help me to be less miserable. Do write to me! Oh, how I wish you could come to me! I charge you, Beulah, don't let Uncle Guy know that I am not happy. Good-by. Oh, if ever you marry, be sure your husband has no old maid sisters and no officious kin! I am crying so, that I can barely see the lines. Good-by, dear Beulah.

"PAULINE."

Beulah leaned forward and dropped the letter into the glowing mass of coals. It shriveled, blazed and vanished, and with a heavy sigh she sat pondering the painful contents. What advice could she possibly give that would remedy the trouble? She was aware that the young wife must indeed have been "very wretched," before she could consent to disclose her domestic feuds to another. Under happier auspices, she felt that Pauline would have made a devoted, gentle wife, but feared it was now too late to mold her character in conformity with her husband's wishes. "So much for a union of uncongenial natures," thought Beulah, as she prepared to answer the unlucky letter. As guardedly as possible, she alluded to Mr. Mortimor and his family, and urged Pauline to talk to her husband gently, but firmly, and assure him that the continued interference of his family was unendurable. If her remonstrances proved futile, to do what she considered due to herself as mistress of her own establishment, and try not to notice the annoyances of others. Beulah felt and acknowledged her inability to advise the young wife in the difficult position in which she was placed, and closed by assuring her that only her own good sense, guided by sincere love for her husband, could rightly direct her course. She was warmly attached to Pauline, and it was with a troubled heart that she addressed her reply.

CHAPTER XXIX.

The Grahams were all at home again, and Eugene and his bride had been for several weeks fairly settled in their elegant new house. Beulah had seen none of the family since their return, for her time was nearly all occupied, and as soon as released from school she gladly hurried out to her little home. One evening, as she left the Academy, Mr. Graham's spirited horses dashed up to the gate and the coachman handed her a note. It was from Mrs. Graham.

"Miss Benton:

"Cornelia is quite indisposed, and begs that you will call and see her this afternoon. As it threatens rain, I send the carriage.

"S. Graham."

Beulah crumpled the note between her fingers and hesitated. The coachman perceived her irresolution, and hastened to say:

"You needn't be afraid of the horses, miss. Miss Nett' rides so much they are tamed down."

"I am not at all afraid of the horses. Has Cornelia been sick since her return from the North?"

"Why, miss, she came home worse than ever. She has not been downstairs since. She is sick all the time now."

Beulah hesitated no longer. Mrs. Graham met her at the door, and greeted her more cordially than she had done on any previous occasion. She looked anxious and weary, and said, as she led the way to her daughter's apartment:

"We are quite uneasy about Cornelia; you will find her sadly altered." She ushered Beulah into the room, then immediately withdrew.

Cornelia was propped up by cushions and pillows in her easy-chair; her head was thrown back, and her gaze appeared to be riveted on a painting which hung opposite. Beulah stood beside her a moment, unnoticed, and saw with painful surprise the ravages which disease had made in the once beautiful face and queenly form. The black, shining hair was cut short and clustered in thick wavy locks about the wan brow, now corrugated as by some spasm of pain. The cheeks were hollow and ghastly pale; the eyes sunken, but unnaturally large and brilliant; and the colorless lips compressed as though to bear habitual suffering. Her wasted hands, grasping the arms of the chair, might have served as a model for a statue of death, so thin, pale, almost transparent. Beulah softly touched one of them, and said:

"Cornelia, you wished to see me."

The invalid looked at her intently, and smiled.

"I thought you would come. Ah, Beulah, do you recognize this wreck as your former friend?"

"I was not prepared to find you so changed; for until this afternoon I was not aware your trip had been so fruitless. Do you suffer much?"

"Suffer! Yes, almost all the time; but it is not the bodily torture that troubles me so much—I could bear that in silence. It is my mind, Beulah; my mind."

She pointed to a chair; Beulah drew it near her, and Cornelia continued:

"I thought I should die suddenly, but it is to be otherwise. The torture is slow, lingering. I shall never leave this house again except to go to my final home. Beulah, I have wanted to see you very much; I thought you would hear of my illness and come. How calm and pale you are. Give me your hand. Ah, cool and pleasant; mine parched with fever. And you have a little home of your own, I hear. How have things gone with you since we parted? Are you happy?"

"My little home is pleasant, and my wants are few," replied Beulah.

"Have you seen Eugene recently?"

"Not since his marriage."

A bitter laugh escaped Cornelia's lips, as she writhed an instant, and then said:

"I knew how it would be. I shall not live to see the end, but you will. Ha! Beulah, already he has discovered his mistake. I did not expect it so soon; I fancied Antoinette had more policy. She has dropped the mask. He sees himself wedded to a woman completely devoid of truth; he knows her now as she is: as I tried to show him she was, before it was too late; and

Beulah, as I expected, he has grown reckless—desperate. Ah, if you could have witnessed a scene at the St. Nicholas, in New York, not long since, you would have wept over him. He found his bride heartless; saw that she preferred the society of other gentlemen to his; that she lived only for the adulation of the crowd; and one evening, on coming home to the hotel, found she had gone to the opera with a party she knew he detested. Beulah, it sickens me when I think of his fierce railings, and anguish, and scorn. He drank in mad defiance, and when she returned, greeted her with imprecations that would have bowed any other woman in utter humiliation into the dust. She laughed derisively, told him he might amuse himself as he chose, she would not heed his wishes as regarded her own movements. Luckily, my parents knew nothing of it; they little suspected, nor do they now know, why I was taken so alarmingly ill before dawn. I am glad I am to go so soon. I could not endure to witness his misery and disgrace."

She closed here eyes and groaned.

"What induced her to marry him?" asked Beulah.

"Only her own false heart knows. But I have always believed she was chiefly influenced by a desire to escape from the strict discipline to which her father subjected her at home. Her mother was anything but a model of propriety; and her mother's sister, who was Dr. Hartwell's wife, was not more exemplary. My uncle endeavored to curb Antoinette's dangerous fondness for display and dissipation, and she fancied that, as Eugene's wife, she could freely plunge into gaieties which were sparingly allowed her at home. I know she does not love Eugene; she never did; and, assuredly, his future is dark enough. I believe, if she could reform him, she would not; his excesses sanction, or at least in some degree palliate, hers. Oh, Beulah, I see no hope for him!"

"Have you talked to him kindly, Cornelia? Have you faithfully exerted your influence to check him in his route to ruin?"

"Talked to him? Ay; entreated, remonstrated, upbraided, used every argument at my command. But I might as well talk to the winds, and hope to hush their fury. I shall not stay to see his end; I shall soon be silent and beyond all suffering; death is welcome, very welcome."

Her breathing was quick and difficult, and two crimson spots burned on her sallow cheeks. Her whole face told of years of bitterness, and a grim defiance of death, which sent a shudder through Beulah, as she listened to the panting breath. Cornelia saturated her handkerchief with some delicate perfume from a crystal vase, and passing it over her face, continued:

"They tell me it is time I should be confirmed; talk vaguely of seeing preachers, and taking the sacrament, and preparing myself, as if I could be frightened into religion and the church. My mother seems just to have waked up to a knowledge of my spiritual condition, as she calls it. Ah, Beulah, it is all dark before me; black, black as midnight! I am going down to an eternal night; down to annihilation. Yes, Beulah, soon I shall descend into what Schiller's Moor calls the 'nameless yonder.' Before long I shall have done with mystery; shall be sunk into unbroken rest." A ghastly smile parted her lips as she spoke.

"Cornelia, do you fear death?"

"No, not exactly. I am glad I am so soon to be rid of my vexed, joyless life; but you know it is all a dark mystery; and sometimes, when I recollect how I felt in my childhood, I shrink from the final dissolution. I have no hopes of a blissful future, such as cheer some people in their last hour. Of what comes after death, I know and believe nothing. Occasionally I shiver at the thought of annihilation; but if, after all, Revelation is true, I have something worse than annihilation to fear. You know the history of my skepticism; it is the history of hundreds in this age. The inconsistencies of professing Christians disgusted me. Perhaps I was wrong to reject the doctrines, because of their abuse; but it is too late now for me to consider that. I narrowly watched the conduct of some of the members of the various churches, and, as I live, Beulah, I have never seen but one who practised the precepts of Christ. I concluded she would have been just what she was without religious aids. One of my mother's intimate friends was an ostentatious, pharisaical Christian; gave alms, headed charity lists, was remarkably punctual in her attendance at church, and apparently very devout; yet I accidentally found out that she treated a poor seamstress (whom she hired for a paltry sum), in a manner that shocked my ideas of consistency, of common humanity. That girl was miserably poor, and had aged parents and brothers and sisters dependent on her exertions; but her Christian employer paid her the lowest possible price and trampled on her feelings as though she had been a brute. Oh, the hollowness of the religion I saw practised! I sneered at everything connected with churches, and heard no more sermons, which seemed only to make hypocrites and pharisees of the congregation. I have never known but one exception. Mrs. Asbury is a consistent Christian. I have watched her, under various circumstances; I have tempted her, in divers ways, to test her; and to-day, skeptic as I am, I admire and revere that noble woman. If all Christians set an example as pure and bright as hers there were less infidelity and atheism in the land. If I had known even half a dozen such I might have had a faith to cheer me in the hour of my struggle. She used to talk gently to me in days past, but I would not heed her. She often comes to see me now; and though I do not believe the words of comfort that fall from her lips, still they soothe me; and I love to have her sit near me, that I may look at her sweet, holy face, so full of winning purity. Beulah, a year ago we talked of these things; I was then, as now, hopeless of creeds, of truth, but you were sure you would find the truth. I looked at you eagerly when you came in, knowing I could read the result in your countenance. Ah, there is no peace written there! Where is your truth? Show it to me?"

She twined her thin, hot fingers round Beulah's cold hand, and spoke in a weary tone. The orphan's features twitched an instant, and her old troubled look came back, as she said:

"I wish I could help you, Cornelia. It must be terrible, indeed, to stand on the brink of the grave and have no belief in anything. I would give more than I possess to be able to assist you, but I cannot; I have no truth to offer you; I have yet discovered nothing for myself. I am not so sanguine as I was a year ago, but I still hope that I shall succeed."

"You will not; you will not. It is all mocking mystery, and no more than the aggregated generations of the past can you find any solution."

Cornelia shook her head, and leaned back in her chair.

"Philosophy promises one," replied Beulah, resolutely.

"Philosophy? take care; that hidden rock stranded me. Listen to me: philosophy, or, what is nowaday its synonym, metaphysical systems, are worse than useless. They will make you doubt your own individual existence, if that be possible. I am older than you; I am a sample of the efficacy of such systems. Oh, the so-called philosophers of this century and the last are crowned-heads of humbugry! Adepts in the famous art of

———"'Wrapping nonsense round,
With pomp and darkness, till it seems profound.'

They mock earnest, inquiring minds with their refined infinitesimal, homœopathic 'developments' of deity; metaphysical wolves in Socratic cloaks. Oh, they have much to answer for! 'Spring of philosophy!' ha! ha! they have made a frog-pond of it, in which to launch their flimsy, painted toy-barks. Have done with them, Beulah, or you will be miserably duped."

"Have you lost faith in Emerson and Theodore Parker?" asked Beulah.

"Yes, lost faith in everything and everybody, except Mrs. Asbury. Emerson's atheistic fatalism is enough to unhinge human reason; he is a great, and I believe an honest thinker, and of his genius I have the profoundest admiration. An intellectual Titan, he wages a desperate war with received creeds, and rising on the ruins of systems, struggles to scale the battlements of truth. As for Parker, a careful perusal of his works was enough to disgust me. But no more of this, Beulah—so long as you have found nothing to rest upon. I had hoped much from your earnest search, but since it has been futile let the subject drop. Give me that glass of medicine. Dr. Hartwell was here, just before you came; he is morose and haggard; what ails him?"

"I really don't know. I have not seen him for several months—not since August, I believe."

"So I supposed, as I questioned him about you; and he seemed ignorant of your movements. Beulah, does not life look dreary and tedious when you anticipate years of labor and care? Teaching is not child's sport; are you not already weary in spirit?"

"No, I am not weary; neither does life seem joyless. I know that I shall have to labor for a support, but necessity always supplies strength. I have many, very many sources of happiness, and look forward, hopefully, to a life of usefulness."

"Do you intend to teach all your days? Are you going to weary out your life over primers and slates?"

"Perhaps so. I know not how else I shall more easily earn a subsistence."

"I trust you will marry, and be exempted from that dull, tedious routine," said Cornelia, watching her countenance.

Beulah made a gesture of impatience.

"That is a mode of exemption so extremely remote that I never consider it. I do not find teaching so disagreeable as you imagine, and dare say, at fifty (if I live that long), I shall be in a schoolroom. Remember the trite line—

"'I dreamed and thought that life was beauty:
I woke, and found that life was duty.'

Labor, mental and physical, is the heritage of humanity, and happiness is inseparably bound up with the discharge of duty. It is a divine decree that all should work, and a compliance with that decree insures a proper development of the moral, intellectual and physical nature."

"You are brave, Beulah, and have more of hope in your nature than I. For twenty-three years I have been a petted child, but life has given me little enjoyment. Often have I asked why was I created? for what am I destined? I have been like a gilded bubble, tossed about by every breath! Oh, Beulah! often, in the desolation of my heart, I have recalled that grim passage of Pollok's and thought that verily I was that

———"'Atom which God
Had made superfluously, and needed not
To build creation with; but back again
To nothing threw, and left it in the void,
With everlasting sense, that once it was!'

My life has not been useful, it has been but joyless, and clouded with the shadow of death from my childhood."

Her voice was broken, and tears trickled over her emaciated face. She put up her thin hand and brushed them away, as if ashamed of her emotion.

"Sometimes I think if I could only live, and be strong, I would make myself useful in the world—would try to be less selfish and exacting; but all regrets are vain, and the indulged child of luxury must take her place in the pale realms of death along with the poverty-stricken and laboring. Beulah, I was in pain last night, and could not sleep, and for hours I seemed to hear the words of that horrible vision: 'And he saw how world after world shook off its glimmering souls upon the sea of Death, as a water-bubble scatters swimming lights on the waves.' Oh! my mind is clouded and my heart hopeless; it is dismal to stand alone as I do, and confront the final issue, without belief in anything. Sometimes, when the paroxysms are severe and prolonged, I grow impatient of the tedious delay, and would spring, open-armed, to meet Death, the deliverer."

Beulah was deeply moved, and answered, with a faltering voice and trembling lip:

"I wish I could comfort and cheer you, but I cannot—I cannot! If the hand of disease placed me to-day on the brink beside you, I should be as hopeless as you. Oh, Cornelia! it makes my heart ache to look at you now, and I would give my life to be able to stand where you do, with a calm trust in the God of Israel; but—"

"Then, be warned by my example. In many respects we resemble each other; our pursuits have been similar. Beulah, do not follow me to the end! Take my word for it, all is dark and grim."

She sank back, too much exhausted to continue the conversation, and Beulah rose to go.

"Can't you stay with me?" said the feeble girl.

"No, my companionship is no benefit to you now. If I could help you, I would not leave you at all."

She pressed her lips to the forehead furrowed by suffering, and hastened away.

It was dusk when she reached home, and passing the dining-room, where the tea-table awaited her arrival, she sought her own apartment. A cheerful fire blazed in welcome, but just now all things were somber to her vision, and she threw herself into a chair and covered her face with her hands. Like a haunting specter, Cornelia's haggard countenance pursued her, and a dull foreboding pointed to a coming season when she, too, would quit earth in hopeless uncertainty. She thought of her guardian and his skeptical misanthropy. He had explored every by-path of speculation, and after years of study and investigation had given up in despair and settled down into a refined pantheism. Could she hope to succeed better? Was her intellect so vastly superior to those who for thousands of years had puzzled by midnight lamps over these identical questions of origin and destiny? What was the speculation of all ages, from Thales to Comte, to the dying girl she had just left? Poor Beulah! for the first time her courage forsook her, and bitter tears gushed over her white cheeks. There was no stony bitterness in her face, but an uplifting shadow that mutely revealed the unnumbered hours of strife and desolation which were slowly bowing that brave heart to the dust. She shuddered, as now, in self-communion, she felt that atheism, grim and murderous, stood at the entrance of her soul, and threw its benumbing shadow into the inmost recesses. Unbelief hung its murky vapors about her heart, curtaining it from the sunshine of God's smile. It was not difficult to trace her gradual progress, if so she might term her unsatisfactory journey. Rejecting literal revelation, she was perplexed to draw the exact line of demarkation between myths and realities; then followed doubts as to the necessity, and finally, as to the probability and possibility of an external, verbal revelation. A revealed code, or system, was antagonistic to the doctrines of rationalism; her own consciousness must furnish the necessary data. But how far was "individualism" allowable? And here the hydra of speculation reared its horrid head; if consciousness alone furnished truth, it was but true for her, true according to the formation of her mind, but not absolutely true. Admit the supremacy of the individual reason, and she could not deny "that the individual mind is the generating principle of all human knowledge; that the soul of man is like the silkworm, which weaves its universe out of its own being; that the whole mass of knowledge to which we can ever attain lies potentially within us from the beginning; that all truth is nothing more than a self-development."

She became entangled in the finely spun webs of ontology, and knew not what she believed. Her guardian's words rang in her ears like a knell. "You must accept either utter skepticism, or absolute, consistent pantheism."

A volume, which she had been reading the night before lay on the table, and she opened it at the following passage:

"Every being is sufficient to itself; that is, every being is, in and by itself, infinite: has its God, its highest conceivable being, in itself. The object of any subject is nothing else than the subject's own nature taken objectively. Such as are a man's thoughts and dispositions, such is his God! Consciousness of God, is self-consciousness; by his God, you know the man, and by the man, his God: the two are identical! Religion is merely the consciousness which a man has of his own, not limited, but infinite nature; it is an early form of self-knowledge. God is the objective nature of the understanding."

Thus much Feuerbach offered her. She put down the book and leaned her head wearily on her hands. A light touch on her arm caused her to glance up, and Mrs. Williams' anxious face looked down at her.

"What is the matter with you, Beulah? Are you sick?"

"No, I am as well as usual." She hastily averted her head.

"But something troubles you, child!"

"Yes, a great many things trouble me; but I am used to troubles, you know, and can cope with them unaided."

"Won't you tell me what they are, Beulah?"

"You cannot help me, or I would. One cause of sorrow, however, is the approaching death of a friend, whom I shall miss and mourn. Cornelia Graham cannot live much longer. I saw her this evening, and found her sadly altered."

"She is young to die," said the matron, with a sigh.

"Yes, only twenty-three."

"Perhaps her death will be the means of reclaiming my poor boy."

Beulah shook her head, and Mrs. Williams added:

"She has lived only for this world and its pleasures. Is she afraid of the world to come? Can she die peacefully?"

"She will die calmly, but not hopefully. She does not believe in Christianity."

She felt that the matron was searching her countenance, and was not surprised when she said, falteringly:

"Neither do you believe in it. Oh, Beulah! I have known it since you came to reside under the same roof with me, and I have wept and prayed over you almost as much as over Eugene. When Sabbath after Sabbath passed, and you absented yourself from church, I knew something was wrong. Beulah, who has taught you infidelity? Oh, it would have been better that you too had followed Lilly, in the early days when you were pure in heart! Much as I love you, I would rather weep over your grave than know you had lived to forget God."

Beulah made no reply, and passing her hands tenderly over the girl's head, she continued:

"When you came to me, a little child, I taught you your morning and evening prayers. Oh, Beulah! Beulah! now you lay down to sleep without a thought of prayer. My child, what is to become of you?"

"I don't know. But do not be distressed about me; I am trying to do my duty just as conscientiously as though I went to church."

"Don't deceive yourself, dear child. If you cease to pray and read your Bible how are you to know what your duty is? How are you to keep yourself 'pure and unspotted from the world?' Beulah, a man without religion is to pitied; but, oh! a Godless woman is a horror above all things. It is no marvel you look so anxious and hollow-eyed. You have forsaken the 'ways of pleasantness, and the paths of peace.'"

"I am responsible to no one for my opinions."

"Yes, you are; responsible to God, for he has given truth to the world, and when you shut your eyes and willingly walk in darkness, he will judge you accordingly. If you had lived in an Indian jungle, out of hearing of Gospel truth, then God would not have expected anything but idolatry from you; but you live in a Christian land; in the land of bibles, and 'to whom much is given, much will be expected.' The people of this generation are running after new doctrines, and overtake much error. Beulah, since I have seen you, sitting up, nearly all night, poring over books that rail at Jesus and his doctrines, I have repented the hour I first suggested your educating yourself to teach. If this is what all your learning has brought you to, it would have been better if you had been put out to learn millinery or mantua-making. Oh, my child, you have been my greatest pride, but now you are a grief to me!"

She took Beulah's hand in hers, and pressed her lips to it, while the tears fell thick and fast. The orphan was not unmoved; her lashes were heavy with unshed drops, but she said nothing.

"Beulah, I am fifty-five years old; I have seen a great deal of the world, and I tell you, I have never yet known a happy man or woman, who did not reverence God and religion. I can see that you are not happy; child, you never will be, so long as you wander away from God. I pray for you, but you must also pray for yourself. May God help you, my dear child."

She left her, knowing her nature too well to hope to convince her of her error.

Beulah remained for some time in the same position, with her eyes fixed on the fire, and her forehead ploughed by torturing thought. The striking of the clock roused her from her reverie, and drawing a chair near her desk she took up her pen to complete an article due the next day at the magazine office. Ah, how little the readers dreamed of the heavy heart that put aside its troubles to labor for their amusement. To-night she did not succeed as well as usual; her manuscript was blurred, and forced to copy the greater part of it the clock struck three before she laid her weary head on her pillow.

CHAPTER XXX.

Mr. Graham sat by his daughter's bed, with his elbow resting on her pillow, and his head drooped on his hand. It was noon, and sunshine sparkled out of doors, but here the heavy curtains swept across the windows and cast a lurid light over the sick-room. His heart ached as he looked upon the wreck of his once brilliant and beautiful child, and he shaded his face to conceal the tears which stole down his furrowed cheeks. The restless sufferer threw up her arms over the pillow, and turning toward him said in a voice sharpened by disease:

"Has mother gone? I want to say something to you."

"We are alone, my child; speak to me freely."

"There are a few things I wish to have arranged, and my time is short. You have never refused me any gratification I desired, and I know you will grant my last request. Father, if I were a bride to-day, what would be my portion of the estate? How much would you give me?"

"I would give every cent I possess to purchase you a life of happiness."

"You do not understand me. I have always been considered an heiress, and I want to know how much I would be entitled to, if I should live? Of course Eugene has an equal share; how much is it?"

"About eighty thousand dollars apiece, I suppose, leaving as much for your mother. Why do you ask, my daughter?"

"Eighty thousand dollars. How much good might be done with it, if judiciously distributed and invested? Father, I shall not live to squander it in frivolous amusements, or superfluous luxuries. Are you willing that I should dispose of a portion of it before my death?"

"Yes, Cornelia, if it will afford you any gratification. My poor afflicted child: how can I deny you anything you choose to ask!"

She put up one arm around his neck, and drawing his head close to her, said earnestly:

"I only wish to use a part of it. Father, I want to leave Beulah about five thousand dollars. That sum will enable her to live more comfortably, and labor less, and I should like to feel before I die that I had been the means of assisting her. Will you invest that amount in stocks for her or pay the money into her own hands? Will you see that it is arranged so that she will certainly receive it, no matter what happens?"

"Yes, I promise you that she shall have five thousand dollars to dispose of as she thinks proper."

"She is proud, and will not receive it willingly; but you must arrange it so that she will be benefited by it. Father, can you do this for me?"

"Yes, without difficulty, I think."

"Let it be kept secret, will you?"

"Rest assured it shall have no unnecessary publicity."

"See that it is conveyed to her so securely that no quibbles of law can wrest it from her at any future day, for none of us knows what may happen."

"I promise you she shall have it, if I live twelve hours longer."

"Then, I want five thousand more given to the Orphan Asylum. Give it in your own name. You only have the right to give. Don't have my name mentioned in the matter. Will you promise me this, also?"

"Yes, it shall all be done. Is there anything else?"

"Thank you, that is all as regards money matters. Raise my pillow a little; there, that will do. Father, can't you do something to save Eugene? You must see now how reckless he is growing."

"Recently I have expostulated with him, and he seemed disposed to reform his habits; acknowledged that his associations had been injurious, and regretted the excesses into which he had been led. He has been rather wild since he came from college, but I think, now he is married, he will sober down. That is one reason why I encouraged his marrying so early. Intemperance is his only fault, and I trust his good sense will soon lead him to correct it." A smothered sigh concluded the sentence.

"Father, Antoinette is not the woman to reform him. Don't trust to her influence; if you do, Eugene will be ruined. Watch over him closely yourself; try to win him away from the haunts of dissipation; I tell you now his wife will never do it. She has duped you and my mother as to her character, but you will find that she is as utterly heartless as her own mother was. I always opposed the match, because I probed her mask of dissimulation, and knew Eugene could not be happy with her. But the mistake is irretrievable, and it only remains for you to watch him the more carefully. Lift me, father, I can't breathe easily. There is the doctor on the steps; I am too tired to talk any more to-day."

* * * * * *

One week later, as Beulah was spending her Sabbath evening in her own apartment, she was summoned to see her friend for the last time. It was twilight when she reached Mr. Graham's house and glided noiselessly up the thickly-carpeted stairway. The bells were all muffled, and a solemn stillness reigned over the mansion. She left her bonnet and shawl in the hall, and softly entered the chamber unannounced. Unable to breathe in a horizontal position, Cornelia was bolstered up in her easy-chair. Her mother sat near her, with her face hid on her husband's bosom. Dr. Hartwell leaned against the mantel, and Eugene stood on the hearth opposite him, with his head bowed down on his hands. Cornelia drew her breath in quick gasps, and cold drops glistened on her pallid face. Her sunken eyes wandered over the group, and when Beulah drew near she extended her hands eagerly, while a shadowy smile passed swiftly over her sharpened features.

"Beulah, come close to me—close." She grasped her hands tightly, and Beulah knelt at the side of her chair.

"Beulah, in a little while I shall be at rest. You will rejoice to see me free from pain, won't you? I have suffered for so many months and years. But death is about to release me forever. Beulah, is it forever—is it forever? Am I going down into an eternal sleep, on a marble couch, where grass and flowers will wave over me, and the sun shine down on me? Yes, it must be so. Who has ever waked from this last dreamless slumber? Abel was the first to fall asleep, and since then, who has wakened? No one. Earth is full of pale sleepers; and I am soon to join the silent band."

There was a flickering light in her eyes, like the flame of a candle low in its socket, and her panting breath was painful to listen to.

"Cornelia, they say Jesus of Nazareth slept, and woke again; if so, you will—"

"Ha, but you don't believe that, Beulah. They say, they say! Yes, but I never believed them before, and I don't want to believe them now. I will not believe it. It is too late to tell me that now. Beulah, I shall know very soon; the veil of mystery is being lifted. Oh, Beulah, I am glad I am going; glad I shall soon have no more sorrow and pain; but it is all dark, dark! You know what I mean. Don't live as I have, believing nothing. No matter what your creed may be, hold fast, have firm faith in it. It is because I believe in nothing, that I am so clouded now. Oh, it is such a dark, dark, lonely way! If I had a friend to go with me, I should not shrink back, but oh, Beulah, I am so solitary. It seems to me I am going out into a great starless midnight." She shivered, and her cold fingers clutched Beulah's convulsively.

"Calm yourself, Cornelia. If Christianity is true, God will see that you were honest in your skepticism and judge you leniently. If not, then death is annihilation, and you have nothing to dread; you will sink into quiet oblivion of all your griefs."

"Annihilation! then I shall see you all no more! Oh, why was I ever created, to love others, and then be torn away forever and go back to senseless dust? I never have been happy; I have always had aspirations after purer, higher enjoyments than earth could afford me, and must they be lost in dead clay? Oh, Beulah, can you give me no comfort but this? Is this the sum of all your study, as well as mine? Ah, it is vain, useless; man can find out nothing. We are all blind; groping our way through mysterious paths, and now I am going into the last—the great mystery!"

She shook her head, with a bitter smile, and closed her eyes as if to shut out some hideous specter. Dr. Hartwell gave her a spoonful of some powerful medicine, and stood watching her face, distorted by the difficulty of breathing. A long silence ensued, broken only by the sobs of the parents. Cornelia leaned back, with closed eyes, and now and then her lips moved, but nothing intelligible escaped them. It was surprising how she seemed to rally sometimes and breathe with perfect ease; then the paroxysms would come on more violent than ever. Beulah knelt on the floor, with her forehead resting on the arm of the chair and her hands still grasped in the firm hold of the dying girl. Time seemed to stand still, to watch the issue, for moments were long as hours to the few friends of the sufferer. Beulah felt as if her heart were leaden, and a band of burning iron seemed drawn about her brow. Was this painful parting to be indeed eternal? Was there no future home for the dead of this world? Should the bands of love and friendship, thus rudely severed, be renewed no more? Was there no land where the broken links might be gathered up again? What did philosophy say of these grim hours of struggle and separation? Nothing—absolutely nothing! Was she to see her sister no more? Was a moldering mass of dust all that remained of the darling dead—the beautiful angel, Lily, whom she had so idolized? Oh! was life, then, a great mockery, and the soul, with its noble aims and impulses, but a delicate machine of matter? Her brain was in a wild, maddening whirl; she could not weep; her eyes were dry and burning. Cornelia moved an instant, and murmured, audibly:

"'For here we have no continuing city, but seek one to come.' Ah! what is its name? that 'continuing city!' Necropolis?" Again she remained, for some time speechless.

Dr. Hartwell softly wiped away the glistening drops on her brow, and opening her eyes, she looked up at him intently. It was an imploring gaze, which mutely said: "Can't you help me?" He leaned over, and answered it, sadly enough:

"Courage, Cornelia! It will very soon be over now. The worst is past, my friend."

"Yes, I know. There is a chill creeping over me. Where is Eugene?"

He came and stood near her; his face full of anguish, which could not vent itself in tears. Her features became convulsed as she looked at him: a wailing cry broke from her lips; and extending her arms toward him, she said, sobbingly:

"Shall I see you no more—no more? Oh, Eugene, my brother, my pride, my dearest hope! whom I have loved better than my own life, are we now parted forever—forever!"

He laid her head on his bosom, and endeavored to soothe her; but clinging to him, she said huskily:

"Eugene, with my last breath I implore you; forsake your intemperate companions. Shun them and their haunts. Let me die, feeling that at least my dying prayer will save you! Oh when I am gone; when I am silent in the graveyard, remember how the thought of your intemperance tortured me! Remember how I remonstrated, and entreated you not to ruin yourself! Remember that I loved you above everything on earth; and that, in my last hour, I prayed you to save yourself! Oh, Eugene, for my sake! for my sake! quit the wine cup, and leave drunkenness for others more degraded! —Promise me!—Where are you?—Oh, it is all cold and dark!—I can't see you!—Eugene, promise, promise!—Eugene!—"

Her eyes were riveted on his, and her lips moved for some seconds; then the clasping arms gradually relaxed; the gasps ceased. Eugene felt a long shudder creep over the limbs, a deep, heavy sigh passed her lips, and Cornelia Graham's soul was with its God.

Ah! after twenty-three years of hope and fear, struggling and questioning, what an exit. Eugene lifted the attenuated form, and placed it on the bed; then threw himself into her vacant chair, and sobbed like a broken-hearted child. Mr. Graham took his wife from the room; and after some moments Dr. Hartwell touched the kneeling figure, with the face still pressed against the chair Eugene now occupied.

"Come, Beulah, she will want you no more."

She lifted a countenance so full of woe, that as he looked at her the moisture gathered in his eyes, and he put his hand tenderly on her head, saying:

"Come with me, Beulah."

"And this is death? Oh, my God, save me from such a death!"

She clasped her hands over her eyes, and shivered; then rising from her kneeling posture threw herself on a couch and buried her face in its cushions. That long night of self-communion was never forgotten.

* * * * * *

The day of the funeral was cold, dark and dismal. A January wind howled through the streets, and occasional drizzling showers enhanced the gloom. The parlors and sitting-room were draped, and on the marble slab of one of the tables stood the coffin, covered with a velvet pall. Once before, Beulah had entered a room similarly shrouded; and it seemed but yesterday that she stood beside Lilly's rigid form. She went in alone, and waited some moments near the coffin, striving to calm the wild tumult of conflicting sorrows in her oppressed heart, then lifted the covering and looked on the sleeper. Wan, waxen and silent. No longer the fitful sleep of disease nor the refreshing slumber of health, but the still iciness of ruthless death. The black locks were curled around the forehead and the beautiful hands folded peacefully over the heart that should throb no more with the anguish of earth. Death had smoothed the brow and put the trembling mouth at rest, and every feature was in repose. In life she had never looked so placidly peaceful.

"What availed all her inquiries, and longings, and defiant cries? She died, no nearer the truth than when she began. She died without hope and knowledge. Only death could unseal the mystery," thought Beulah, as she looked at the marble face, and recalled the bitterness of its life-long expression. Persons began to assemble; gradually the rooms filled. Beulah bent down and kissed the cold lips for the last time, and lowering her veil, retired to a dim corner. She was very miserable, but her eyes were tearless, and she sat, she knew not how long, unconscious of what passed around her. She heard the stifled sobs of the bereaved parents, as in a painful dream; and when the solemn silence was broken, she started, and saw a venerable man, a stranger, standing at the head of the coffin; and these words fell upon her ears like a message from another world:

"I am the resurrection and the life," saith the Lord; "and he that believeth in me, though he were dead, yet shall he live; and whosoever liveth and believeth in me shall never die!"

Cornelia had not believed; but was she utterly lost? Beulah asked herself this question, and shrank from the answer. She did not believe: would she die as Cornelia died, without comfort? Was there but one salvation? When the coffin was borne out, and the procession formed, she went on mechanically, and found herself seated in a carriage with Mrs. Asbury and her two daughters. She sank back in one corner, and the long line of carriages, extending for many squares, slowly wound through the steets. The wind wailed and sobbed, as if in sympathy, and the rain drizzled against the window glass. When the procession reached the cemetery, it was too wet to think of leaving the carriages, but Beulah could see the coffin borne from the hearse, and heard the subdued voice of the minister; and when the shrouded form of the only child was lowered into its final resting-place she groaned and hid her face in her hands. "Should they meet no more?" Hitherto Mrs. Asbury had forborne to address her, but now she passed her arm round the shuddering form, and said gently:

"My dear Beulah, do not look so hopelessly wretched. In the midst of life, we are in death; but God has given a promise to cheer us all in sad scenes like this. St. John was told to write, 'From henceforth, blessed are the dead who die in the Lord, for they rest from their labors.'"

"And do you think she is lost forever, because she did not believe? Do you? Can you?" cried Beulah, vehemently.

"Beulah, she had the Bible, which promises eternal life. If she entirely rejected it, she did so voluntarily and deliberately; but only God knows the heart—only her Maker can judge her. I trust that even in the last hour the mists rolled from her mind."

Beulah knew better, but said nothing; it was enough to have witnessed that darkened soul's last hour on earth. As the carriage stopped at her door, Mrs. Asbury said:

"My dear Beulah, stay with me to-night. I think I can help you to find what you are seeking so earnestly."

Beulah shrank back, and answered:

"No, no. No one can help me; I must help myself. Some other time I will come."

The rain fell heavily as she reached her own home, and she went to her room with a heaviness of heart almost unendurable. She sat down on the rug before the fire, and threw her arms up over a chair, as she was wont to do in childhood, and as she remembered that the winter rain now beat pitilessly on the grave of one who had never known privation, nor aught of grief that wealth could shield her from, she moaned bitterly. What lamp had philosophy hung in the sable chambers of the tomb? The soul was impotent to explain its origin—how, then, could it possibly read the riddle of final destiny? Psychologists had wrangled for ages over the question of 'ideas.' Were infants born with or without them? Did ideas arise or develop themselves independently of experience? The affirmation or denial of this proposition alone distinguished the numerous schools which had so long wrestled with psychology; and if this were insolvable, how could human intellect question further? Could it bridge the gulf of Death, and explore the shores of Eternity?

CHAPTER XXXI.

Time, "like a star, unhasting, yet unresting," moved on. The keen blasts of winter were gathered back in their northern storehouses, and the mild airs of spring floated dreamily beneath genial skies. The day had been cloudless and balmy, but now the long, level rays of sunshine, darting from the horizon, told it "was well-nigh done;" and Beulah sat on the steps of her cottage home and watched the dolphin-like death. The regal splendors of southern springtime were on every side; the bright, fresh green of the grassy common, with its long, velvety slopes, where the sunshine fell slantingly; the wild luxuriance of the Cherokee rose-hedges, with their graceful streamers gleaming with the snow-powder of blossoms; the waving of new-born foliage; the whir and chirping of birds, as they sought their leafy shelters; brilliant patches of verbena, like flakes of rainbow, in the neighboring gardens; and the faint, sweet odor of violet, jasmin, roses and honeysuckle, burdening the air. Beulah sat with her hands folded on her lap; an open book lay before her—a volume of Ruskin; but the eyes had wandered away from his gorgeous descriptions to another and still more entrancing volume—the glorious page of Nature; and as the swift southern twilight gathered she sat looking out, mute and motionless. The distant pine-tops sang their solemn, soothing lullaby, and a new moon sat royally in the soft violet sky. Around the columns of the little portico a luxuriant wisteria clambered, and long, purple blossoms, with their spicy fragrance, drooped almost on Beulah's head as she leaned it against the pillar. The face wore a weary, suffering look; the large, restless eyes were sadder than ever, and there were tokens of languor in every feature. A few months had strangely changed the countenance, once so hopeful and courageous in its uplifted expression. The wasted form bore evidence of physical suffering, and the slender fingers were like those of a marble statue. Yet she had never missed an hour in the schoolroom, nor omitted one iota of the usual routine of mental labor. Rigorously the tax was levied, no matter how the weary limbs ached, or how painfully the head throbbed; and now nature rebelled at the unremitted exaction, and clamored for a reprieve. Mrs. Williams had been confined to her room for many days, by an attack of rheumatism, and the time devoted to her was generally reclaimed from sleep. It was no mystery that she looked ill and spent. Now, as she sat watching the silver crescent glittering in the west, her thoughts wandered to Clara Sanders, and the last letter received from her telling of a glorious day-star of hope which had risen in her cloudy sky. Mr. Arlington's brother had taught her that the dream of her girlhood was but a fleeting fancy, that she could love again more truly than before, and in the summer holidays she was to give him her hand and receive his name. Beulah rejoiced in her friend's happiness, but a dim foreboding arose, lest, as in Pauline's case, thorns should spring up in paths where now only blossoms were visible. Since that letter, so full of complaint and sorrow, no tidings had come from Pauline. Many months had elapsed, and Beulah wondered more and more at the prolonged silence. She had written several times, but received no answer, and imagination painted a wretched young wife in that distant parsonage. Early in spring she learned from Dr. Asbury that Mr. Lockhart had died at his plantation of consumption, and she conjectured that Mrs. Lockhart must be with her daughter. Beulah half-rose, then leaned back against the column, sighed involuntarily, and listened to that "still small voice of the level twilight behind purple hills." Mrs. Williams was asleep, but the tea-table waited for her, and in her own room, on her desk, lay an unfinished manuscript which was due the editor the next morning. She was rigidly punctual in handing in her contributions, cost her what it might; yet now she shrank from the task of copying and punctuating, and sat awhile longer, with the gentle southern breeze rippling over her hot brow. She no longer wrote incognito; by accident she was discovered as the authoress of several articles commented upon by other journals, and more than once her humble home had been visited by some of the leading *literati* of the place. Her successful career thus far inflamed the ambition which formed so powerful an element in her mental organization, and a longing desire for Fame took possession of her soul. Early and late she toiled; one article was scarcely in the hands of the compositor ere she was engaged upon another. She lived, as it were, in a perpetual brain-fever, and her physical frame suffered proportionably. The little gate opened and closed with a creaking sound, and hearing a step near her Beulah looked up and saw her guardian before her. The light from the dining-room fell on his face, and a glance showed her that, although it was pale and inflexible as ever, something of more than ordinary interest had induced this visit. He had never entered that gate before; and she sprang up, and held out both hands with an eager cry:

"Oh, sir, I am so glad to see you once more!"

He took her hands in his, and looked at her gravely; then made her sit down again on the step, and said:

"I suppose you would have died, before you could get your consent to send for me? It is well that you have somebody to look after you. How long have you had this fever?"

"Fever! Why, sir, I have no fever," she replied, with some surprise.

"Oh, child! are you trying to destroy yourself by your obstinancy? If so, like most other things you undertake, I suppose you will succeed."

He held her hands, and kept his finger on the quick bounding pulse. Beulah had not seen him since the night of Cornelia's death, some months before, and conjectured that Dr. Asbury had told him she was not looking well.

She could not bear the steady searching gaze of his luminous eyes, and moving restlessly, said:

"Sir, what induces you to suppose that I am sick? I have complained of indisposition to no one."

"Of course you have not, for people are to believe that you are a gutta-percha automaton."

She fancied his tone was slightly sneering; but his countenance wore the expression of anxious, protecting interest, which she had so prized in days past, and as her hands trembled in his clasp and his firm hold tightened she felt that it was useless to attempt to conceal the truth longer.

"I didn't know I was feverish, but for some time I have daily grown weaker; I tremble when I stand or walk, and am not able to sleep. That is all."

He smiled down at her earnest face and asked:

"Is that all, child? Is that all?"

"Yes, sir, all."

"And here you have been with a continued, wasting nervous fever, for you know not how many days, yet keep on your rounds of labors without cessation?"

He dropped her hands and folded his arms across his broad chest, keeping his eyes upon her.

"I am not at all ill; but I believe I need some medicine to strengthen me."

"Yes, child; you do, indeed, need a medicine, but it is one you will never take."

"Try me, sir," answered she, smiling.

"Try you? I might as well try to win an eagle from its lonely rocky home. Beulah, you need rest. Rest for mind, body and heart. But you will not take it; oh, no, of course you won't!"

He passed his hand over his brow, and swept back the glossy chestnut hair, as if it oppressed him.

"I would willingly take it, sir, if I could; but the summer vacation is still distant, and, besides, my engagements oblige me to exert myself. It is a necessity with me."

"Rather say sheer obstinacy," said he, sternly.

"You are severe, sir," replied Beulah, lifting her head haughtily.

"No, I only call things by their proper names."

"Very well; if you prefer it, then, obstinacy compels me just now to deny myself the rest you prescribe."

"Yes, rightly spoken; and it will soon compel you to a long rest, in the quiet place where Cornelia waits for you. You are a mere shadow now, and a few more months will complete your design. I have blamed myself more than once that I did not suffer you to die with Lilly, as you certainly would have done, had I not tended you so closely. Your death, then, would have saved me much care and sorrow and you many struggles."

There was a shadow on his face, and his voice had the deep musical tone which always made her heart thrill. Her eyelids drooped as she said, sadly:

"You are unjust. We meet rarely enough, heaven knows. Why do you invariably make these occasions seasons of upbraiding, of taunts, and sneers. Sir, I owe you my life, and more than my life, and never can I forget or cancel my obligations; but are you no longer my friend?"

His whole face lighted up; the firm mouth trembled.

"No, Beulah. I am no longer your friend."

She looked up at him, and a quiver crept across her lips. She had never seen that eager expression in his stern face before. His dark fascinating eyes were full of pleading tenderness, and as she drooped her head on her lap, she knew that Clara was right, that she was dearer to her guardian than any one else. A half smothered groan escaped her, and there was a short pause.

Dr. Hartwell put his hands gently on her bowed head and lifted the face. "Child, does it surprise you?"

She said nothing, and leaning her head against him, as she had often done years before, he passed his hand caressingly over the folds of hair, and added:

"You call me your guardian; make me such. I can no longer be only your friend; I must either be more or henceforth a stranger. My life has been full of sorrow and bitterness, but you can bring sunlight to my home and heart. You were too proud to be adopted. Once I asked you to be my child. Ah! I did not know my own heart then. Our separation during the yellow fever season first taught me how inexpressibly dear you were to me, how entirely you filled my heart. Now, I ask you to be my wife: to give yourself to me. Oh, Beulah, come back to my cheerless home! Rest your lonely heart, my proud darling."

"Impossible. Do not ask it. I cannot; I cannot;" cried Beulah, shuddering violently.

"Why not, my little Beulah?"

He clasped his arm around her, and drew her close to him while his head was bent so low that his brown hair touched her cheek.

"Oh, sir, I would rather die! I should be miserable as your wife. You do not love me, sir; you are lonely, and miss my presence in your house; but that is not love, and marriage would be a mockery. You would despise a wife who was such only from gratitude. Do not ask this of me; we would both be wretched. You pity my loneliness and poverty, and I reverence you; nay, more, I love you, sir, as my best friend; I love you as my protector. You are all I have on earth to look to for sympathy and guidance. You are all I have, but I cannot marry you; oh, no, no! a thousand times, no!" She shrank away from the touch of his lips on her brow, and an expression of hopeless suffering settled upon her face.

He withdrew his arm, and rose.

"Beulah, I have seen sun-lit bubbles gliding swiftly on the bosom of a clear brook, and casting golden shadows down upon the pebbly bed. Such a shadow you are now chasing; ah, child, the shadow of a gilded bubble! Panting and eager, you clutch at it; the bubble dances on, the shadow with it; and Beulah, you will never, never grasp it. Ambition such as yours, which aims at literary fame, is the deadliest foe to happiness. Man may content himself with the applause of the world, and the homage paid to his intellect; but woman's heart has holier idols. You are young, and impulsive, and aspiring, and Fame beckons you on, like the syren of antiquity; but the months and years will surely come when, with wasted energies and embittered heart, you are left to mourn your infatuation. I would save you from this, but you will drain the very dregs rather than forsake your tempting fiend, for such is ambition to the female heart. Yes, you will spend the springtime of your life chasing a painted specter, and go down to a premature grave, disappointed and miserable. Poor child, it needs no prophetic vision to predict your ill-starred career! Already the consuming fever has begun its march. In far distant lands, I shall have no tidings of you, but none will be needed. Perhaps, when I travel home to die, your feverish dream will have ended; or perchance, sinking to eternal rest in some palm grove of the far East, we shall meet no more. Since the day I took you in my arms from Lilly's coffin, you have been my only hope, my all. You little knew how precious you were to me, nor what keen suffering our estrangement cost me. Oh, child, I have loved you as only a strong, suffering, passionate heart could love its last idol! But I, too, chased a shadow. Experience should have taught me wisdom. Now, I am a gloomy, joyless man, weary of my home, and henceforth a wanderer. Asbury (if he lives) will be truly your friend, and to him I shall commit the legacy which, hitherto, you have refused to accept. Mr. Graham paid it into my hands, after his last unsatisfactory interview with you. The day may come when you will need it. I shall send you some medicine, which, for your own sake, you had better take immediately; but you will never grow stronger until you give yourself rest, relaxation, physically and mentally. Remember, when your health is broken, and all your hopes withered, remember I warned you, and would have saved you, and you would not." He stooped, and took his hat from the floor.

Beulah sat looking at him, stunned, bewildered, her tearless eyes strained and frightened in their expression. The transient illumination in his face had faded, like sunset tints, leaving dull, leaden clouds behind. His compressed lips were firm again, and the misty eyes became coldly glittering, as one sees stars brighten in a frosty air.

He put on his hat, and they looked at each other fixedly.

"You are not in earnest? you are not going to quit your home?" cried Beulah, in a broken, unsteady tone.

"Yes, going into the far East; to the ruined altars of Baalbec; to Meroc, to Tartary, India, China, and only fate knows where else. Perhaps find a cool Nebo in some Himalayan range. Going? Yes. Did you suppose I meant only to operate on your sympathies? I know you too well. What is it to you whether I live or die? whether my weary feet rest in an Indian jungle, or a sunny slope of the city cemetery? Yes, I am going very soon, and this is our last meeting. I shall not again disturb you in your ambitious pursuits. Ah, child—,"

"Oh, don't go! don't leave me! I beg, I implore you, not to leave me. Oh, I am so desolate! don't forsake me! I could not bear to know you were gone. Oh, don't leave me!" She sprang up, and throwing her arms round his neck, clung to him, trembling like a frightened child. But there was no relaxation of his pale, fixed features, as he coldly answered:

"Once resolved, I never waver. So surely as I live, I shall go. It might have been otherwise, but you decided it yourself. An hour ago you held my destiny in your hand; now it is fixed. I should have gone six years since, had I not indulged a lingering hope of happiness in your love. Child, don't shiver, and cling to me so. Oceans will soon roll between us, and, for a time, you will have no leisure to regret my absence. Henceforth we are strangers."

"No, that shall never be. You do not mean it; you know it is impossible. You know that I prize your friendship above every earthly thing. You know that I look up to you as to no one else. That I shall be miserable, oh, how miserable, if you leave me! Oh, sir, I have mourned over your coldness and indifference; don't cast me off! Don't go to distant lands, and leave me to struggle without aid or counsel in this selfish, unfriendly world! My heart dies within me, at the thought of your being where I shall not be able to see you. Oh, my guardian, don't forsake me!"

She pressed her face against his shoulder, and clasped her arms firmly round his neck.

"I am not your guardian, Beulah. You refused to make me such. You are a proud, ambitious woman, solicitous only to secure eminence as an authoress. I asked your heart; you have now none to give; but perhaps some day you will love me, as devotedly, nay, as madly as I have long loved you; for love like mine would wake affection even in a marble image; but *then,* rolling oceans and trackless deserts will divide us. And now, good-by. Make yourself a name; bind your aching brow with the chaplet of Fame, and see if ambition can fill your heart. Good-by, dear child."

Gently he drew her arms from his neck, and took her face in his soft palms. He looked at her a moment, sadly and earnestly, as if striving to fix her features in the frame of memory; then bent his head and pressed a long kiss on her lips. She put out her hands, he had gone, and sinking down on the step, she hid her face in her arms. A pall seemed suddenly thrown over the future, and the orphaned heart shrank back from the lonely path where only spectres were visible. Never before had she realized how dear he was to her, how large a share of her love he possessed, and now the prospect of a long, perhaps final separation, filled her with a shivering, horrible dread. We have seen that self-reliance was a powerful element of her character, and she had learned, from painful necessity, to depend as little as possible upon the sympathies of others; but in this hour of anguish, a sense of joyless isolation conquered; her proud soul bowed down beneath the weight of intolerable grief, and acknowledged itself not wholly independent of the love and presence of her guardian.

Beulah went back to her desk, and with tearless eyes began the allotted task of writing. The article was due, and must be finished; was there not a long, dark future in which to mourn? The sketch was designed to prove that woman's happiness was not necessarily dependent on marriage. That a single life might be more useful, more tranquil, more unselfish. Beulah had painted her heroine in glowing tints, and triumphantly proved her theory correct, while to female influence she awarded a sphere (exclusive of rostrums and all political arenas) wide as the universe, and high as heaven. Weary work it all seemed to her now; but she wrote on, and on, and finally the last page was copied and the last punctuation mark affixed. She wrapped up the manuscript, directed it to the editor, and then the pen fell from her nerveless fingers and her head went down, with a wailing cry, on the desk. There the morning sun flashed upon a white face, tear-stained and full of keen anguish. How her readers would have marveled at the sight? Ah, "Verily the heart knoweth its own bitterness."

CHAPTER XXXII.

One afternoon in the following week Mrs. Williams sat wrapped up in the hall, watching Beulah's movements in the yard at the rear of the house. The whitewashed paling was covered with luxuriant raspberry vines, and in one corner of the garden was a bed of strawberry plants. Over this bed Beulah was bending with a basket nearly filled with the ripe scarlet berries. Stooping close to the plants she saw only the fruit she was engaged in picking; and when the basket was quite full, she was suddenly startled by a merry laugh, and a pair of hands clasped over her eyes.

"Who blindfolds me?" said she.

"Guess, you solemn witch."

"Why, Georgia, of course."

The hands were removed, and Georgia Asbury's merry face greeted her.

"I am glad to see you, Georgia. Where is Helen?"

"Oh, gone to ride with one of her adorers, but I have brought somebody to see you who is worth the whole Asbury family. No less a personage than my famous cousin Reginald Lindsay, whom you have heard us speak of so often. Oh, how tempting those luscious berries are! Reginald and I intend to stay to tea, and father will perhaps come out in the carriage for us. Come, yonder is my cousin on the gallery looking at you and pretending to talk to Mrs. Williams. He has read your magazine sketches and is very anxious to see you. How nicely you look; only a little too statuish. Can't you get up a smile? That is better. Here, let me twine this cluster of wisteria in your hair; I stole it as I ran up the steps."

Beulah was clad in a pure white mull muslin, and wore a short black silk apron, confined at the waist by a heavy cord and tassel. Georgia fastened the purple blossoms in her silky hair, and they entered the house. Mr. Lindsay met them, and as his cousin introduced him, Beulah looked at him, and met the earnest gaze of a pair of deep blue eyes, which seemed to index a nature singularly tranquil. She greeted him quietly, and would have led the way to the front of the house, but Georgia threw herself down on the steps and exclaimed eagerly:

"Do let us stay here; the air is so deliciously sweet and cool. Cousin, there is a chair. Beulah, you and I will stem these berries at once, so that they may be ready for tea."

She took the basket, and soon their fingers were stained with the rosy juice of the fragrant fruit. All restraint vanished; the conversation was gay, and spiced now and then with repartees, which elicited Georgia's birdish laugh and banished for a time the weary, joyless expression of Beulah's countenance. The berries were finally arranged to suit Georgia's taste, and the party returned to the little parlor. Here Beulah was soon engaged by Mr. Lindsay in the discussion of some of the leading literary questions of the day. She forgot the great sorrow that brooded over her heart, a faint, pearly glow crept into her cheeks, and the mouth lost its expression of resolute endurance. She found Mr. Lindsay highly cultivated in his tastes, polished in his manners, and possessed of rare intellectual attainments, while the utter absence of egotism and pedantry impressed her with involuntary admiration. Extensive travel and long study had familiarized him with almost every branch of science and department of literature, and the ease and grace with which he imparted some information she desired respecting the European schools of arts contrasted favorably with the confused account Eugene had rendered of the same subject. She remarked a singular composure of countenance, voice, and even position, which seemed idiosyncratic, and was directly opposed to the stern rigidity and cynicism of her guardian. She shrank from the calm, steadfast gaze of his eyes, which looked into hers, with a deep yet gentle scrutiny, and resolved ere the close of the evening to sound him concerning some of the philosophic phases of the age. Had he escaped the upas taint of skepticism? An opportunity soon occurred to favor her wishes, for chancing to allude to his visit to Rydal Mount, while in the lake region of England, the transition to a discussion of the metaphysical tone of the "Excursion" was quite easy.

"You seemed disposed, like Howitt, to accord it the title of 'Bible of Quakerism,'" said Mr. Lindsay, in answer to a remark of hers concerning its tendency.

"It is a fertile theme of disputation, sir, and since critics are so divided in their verdicts, I may well be pardoned an opinion, which so many passages seem to sanction. If Quakerism is belief in 'immediate inspiration,' which you will scarcely deny, then throughout the 'Excursion' Wordsworth seems its apostle."

"No, he stands as a high-priest in the temple of nature, and calls mankind from scientific lore to offer their orisons there at his altar and receive passively the teachings of the material universe. Tells us,

> "'Our meddling intellect
> Misshapes the beauteous forms of things,'

and promises, in nature, an unerring guide and teacher of truth. In his lines on revisiting the Wye, he declares himself,

> ———"'Well pleased to recognize
> In nature, and the language of the sense,
> The anchor of my purest thoughts, the nurse,
> The guide, the guardian of my heart and soul,
> Of all my mortal being.'

Quakerism rejects all extraneous aids to a knowledge of God; a silent band of friends sit waiting for the direct inspiration, which alone can impart true light. Wordsworth made the senses, the appreciation of the beauty and sublimity of the universe, an avenue of light; while Quakerism, according to the doctrines of Fox and his early followers, is merely a form of mysticism, nearly allied to the 'ecstasy' of Plotinus. The Quaker silences his reason, his every faculty, and in utter passivity waits for the infusion of divine light into his mind; the mystic of Alexandria, as far as possible, divests his intellect of all personality, and becomes absored in the Infinite intelligence from which it emanated."

Beulah knitted her brows, and answered musingly:

"And here, then, extremes meet. To know God, we must be God. Mysticism and Pantheism link hands over the gulf which seemed to divide them."

"Miss Benton, is this view of the subject a novel one?" said he, looking at her very intently.

"No, a singular passage in the 'Biographia Literaria,' suggested it to me long ago. But unwelcome hints are rarely accepted, you know."

"Why unwelcome in this case?"

She looked at him, but made no reply, and none was needed. He understood why, and said quietly, yet impressively:

"It sets the seal of necessity upon Revelation. Not the mystical intuitions of the dreamers, who would fain teach of continued direct inspiration from God, even at the present time, but the revelation which began in Genesis and ended with John on Patmos. The very absurdities of philosophy are the most potent arguments in substantiating the claims of Christianity, Kant's theory, that we can know nothing beyond ourselves, gave the death-blow to philosophy. Mysticism contends that reason only darkens the mind, and consequently discarding all reasoning processes relies upon immediate revelation. But the extravagances of Swedenborg, and even of George Fox, prove the fallacy of the assumption of continued inspiration, and the only alternative is to rest upon the Christian Revelation, which has successfully defied all assaults."

There was an instantaneous flash of joy over Beulah's troubled face, and she said hastily:

"You have escaped the contagion, then? Such exemption is rare nowaday, for skepticism broods with sable wings over the age."

"It has always brooded where man essayed to lift the veil of Isis; to elucidate the arcana of the universe, to solve the unsolvable. Skepticism is the disease of minds, which Christian faith alone can render healthy."

The thrust showed she was not invulnerable, but before she could reply Georgia exclaimed:

"In the name of common sense, Reginald, what are you discoursing about so tiresomely? I suppose I am shamefully stupid, but I don't understand a word you two have been saying. When father and Beulah get on such dry, tedious subjects, I always set up an opposition at the piano, which in this instance I am forced to do, from sheer necessity."

She raised the lid of the piano, and rattled off a brilliant overture; then made Beulah join her in several instrumental duets. As the latter rose Mr. Lindsay said, somewhat abruptly:

"I believe you sing. My cousins have been extolling your voice, and I have some curiosity to hear you. Will you gratify me?"

"Certainly, if you desire it."

She could not refrain from smiling at the perfect nonchalance of his manner, and passing her fingers over the keys, sang a beautiful air from "Lucia." Her guest listened attentively, and when the song was ended approached the piano, and said, with some interest:

"I should prefer a simple ballad, if you will favor me with one."

"Something after the order of 'Lilly Dale,' Beulah; he hears nothing else in his country home," said Georgia, teasingly.

He smiled, but did not contradict her, and Beulah sang that exquisite ballad, "Why do Summer Roses Fade." It was one of her guardian's favorite airs, and now his image was associated with the strain. Ere the first verse was finished, a deep, rich, manly voice, which had sometimes echoed through the study, seemed again to join hers, and despite her efforts her own tones trembled.

Soon after, Beulah took her place at the tea-table in the center of the room, and conversation turned on the delights of country life.

"Reginald, how do you manage to amuse yourself in that little town of yours?" asked Georgia, drawing the bowl of strawberries near and helping him bountifully.

"I might answer, that I had passed the age when amusement was necessary, but I will not beg your question so completely. In the first place, I do not reside in town. My office is there, and during the day, when not absent at court, I am generally in my office; but evening always finds me at home. Once there, I have endless sources of amusement; my mother's flowers and birds, my farm affairs, my music, and my library, to say nothing of hunting and fishing. Remember, Georgia, that as a class, lawyers are not addicted to what you call amusements."

"But after living in Europe, and traveling so much, I should think that plantation would be horribly dull. Do you never suffer from *ennui,* cut off as you are from all society?"

"*Ennui* is a disease of which I am yet happily ignorant. But for my mother, I should feel the need of society; in a great measure, her presence supplies it. I shall tell you no more, cousin mine, since you and Helen are to spend a portion of your summer with us, and can judge for yourselves of the attractions of my country home."

"Are you residing near Mr. Arlington?" said Beulah.

"Quite near; his plantation adjoins mine. Is he a friend of yours?"

"No, but I have a friend living this year in his family. Miss Sanders is governess for his children. You probably know her."

"Yes, I see her occasionally. Report says she is soon to become the bride of Richard Arlington."

A slight smile curved his lips as he watched Beulah's countenance. She offered no comment, and he perceived that the *on dit* was new to her.

"Beulah, I suppose you have heard of Dr. Hartwell's intended journey to the East? What an oddity he is! Told me he contemplated renting a bungalow somewhere in heathendom, and turning either Brahmin or Parsee, he had not quite decided which. He has sold his beautiful place to the Farleys. The greenhouse plants he gave to mother, and all the statuary and paintings are to be sent to us until his return, which cannot be predicted with any certainty. Father frets a good deal over this freak, as he calls it, and says the doctor had much better stay at home and physic the sick. I thought it was a sudden whim, but he says he has contemplated the trip a long time. He is going immediately, I believe. It must be a trial to you," said the thoughtless girl.

"Yes, I cannot realize it yet," replied Beulah, struggling with herself for composure, and hastily setting down her tea-cup, which trembled violently. The shadows swept over her once more. Mr. Lindsay noticed her agitation and with delicate consideration forbore to look at her. Georgia continued, heedlessly:

"I wanted that melodeon that sits in his study, but though the remainder of the furniture is to be auctioned off he says he will not sell the melodeon, and requested my father to have it carefully locked up somewhere at home. I asked if I might not use it, and what do you suppose he said? That I might have his grand piano, if I would accept it, but that nobody was to touch his melodeon. I told him he ought to send the piano out to you, in his absence, but he looked cross, and said you would not use it if he did."

Poor Beulah; her lips quivered and her fingers clasped each other tightly, but she said nothing. Just then she heard Dr. Asbury's quick step in the hall, and to her infinite relief he entered, accompanied by Helen. She saw that though his manner was kind and bantering as usual, there was an anxious look on his benevolent face, and his heavy brows occasionally knitted. When he went into the adjoining room to see Mrs. Williams she understood his glance and followed him. He paused in the hall, and said, eagerly: "Has Hartwell been here lately?"

"Yes, he was here last week."

"Did he tell you of his whim about traveling East?"

"Yes, he told me."

"Beulah, take care what you are about! You are working mischief not easily rectified. Child, keep Guy at home!"

"He is master of his own movements, and you know his stubborn will. I would keep him here if I could, but I have no influence."

"All fiddlesticks! I know better! I am neither a bat nor a mole. Beulah, I warn you; I beg you, child, mind how you act. Once entirely estranged, all the steam in christendom could not force him back. Don't let him go; if you do, the game is up, I tell you now. You will repent your own work, if you do not take care. I told him he was a fool, to leave such a position as his, and go to dodging robbers in eastern deserts; whereupon he looked as bland and impenetrable as if I had compared him to Solomon. There, go back to your company, and mind what I say; don't let Guy go."

He left her; and though she exerted herself to entertain her guests, Mr. Lindsay saw that her mind was troubled and her heart oppressed. He endeavored to divert her thoughts, by introducing various topics; and she talked and smiled, and even played and sang, yet the unlifting cloud lay on her brow. The evening seemed strangely long, and she accompanied her visitors to the door with a sensation of relief. At parting, Mr. Lindsay took her hand, and said in a low voice:

"May I come whenever I am in your city?"

"Certainly, I shall be pleased to see you, when you have leisure," she replied, hurriedly.

"I shall avail myself of your permission, I assure you."

She had often heard Dr. Asbury speak, with fond pride, of this nephew; and as Eugene had also frequently mentioned him in his early letters from Heidelberg, she felt that he was scarcely a stranger in the ordinary acceptation of the term. To her his parting words seemed merely polite, commonplace forms; and with no thought of a future acquaintance she dismissed him from her mind, which was too painfully preoccupied to dwell upon the circumstances of his visit.

A few days passed, and on Saturday morning she sat in the dining-room finishing a large drawing upon which she had for months expended all her leisure moments. It was designed from a description in "Queen Mab," and she took up her crayon to give the final touch when heavy steps in the hall arrested her attention, and glancing toward the door she saw Hal, Dr. Hartwell's driver, with a wooden box on his shoulder and Charon by his side. The latter barked with delight, and sprang to meet the girl, who had hastily risen.

"How do you do, Miss Beulah? It is many a day since I have seen you, and you look the worse of wear too. Haven't been sick, have you?" said Hal, sliding the box down on the floor.

"Not exactly sick, but not so well as usual," she answered, passing her trembling hands over the dog's head.

"Well, I don't see, for my part, what is to become of us all, now master's gone—"

"Gone!" echoed Beulah.

"Why, to be sure. He started to the plantation yesterday, to set things all in order there, and then he is going straight on to New York. The house looks desolate enough, and I feel like I was about to dig my own grave. Just before he left he called me into the study and told me that as soon as he had gone I was to bring Charon over to you, and ask you to keep him and take care of him. He tried to unlock the collar on his neck, but somehow the key would not turn. Master looked dreadful sad when he patted poor Char's head and let the brute put his paws on his shoulders for the last time. Just as the boat pushed off he called to me to be sure to bring him to you; so here he is; and, Miss Beulah, the poor fellow seems to know something is wrong; he whined all night, and ran over the empty house this morning growling and snuffing. You are to keep him till master comes home; the Lord only knows when that will be. I tried to find out, but he looked for the world like one of them stone faces in the study, and gave me no satisfaction. Miss Beulah, Dr. Asbury was at the house just as I started, and he sent over this box to you. Told me to tell you that he had all the pictures moved to his house, but had not room to hang all, so he sent one over for you to take care of. Shall I take it out of the case?"

"Never mind, Hal, I can do that. Did your master leave no other message for me? was there no note?" She leaned heavily on a chair to support herself.

"None that I know of, except that you must be kind to Charon. I have no time to spare; Dr. Asbury needs me; so good-by, Miss Beulah. I will stop some day when I am passing and see how the dog comes on. I know he will be satisfied with you."

The faithful servant touched his hat and withdrew. The storm of grief could no longer be repressed, and sinking down on the floor Beulah clasped her arms round Charon's neck and hid her face in the soft curling hair, while her whole frame shook with convulsive sobs. She had not believed her guardian would leave without coming again, and had confidently expected him, and now he had gone. Perhaps forever; at best for many years. She might never see him again, and this thought was more than she could endure. The proud restraint she was wont to impose upon her feelings all vanished, and in her despairing sorrow she wept and moaned, as she had never done before, even when Lilly was taken from her. Charon crouched close to her, with a mute grief clearly written in his sober, sagacious countenance, and each clung to the other as to a last stay and solace. He was a powerful animal with huge limbs and a thick, shaggy covering, sable as midnight, without a speck of white about him. Around his neck was a silver chain, supporting a broad piece of plate, on which was engraved, in German letters the single word, "Hartwell." How long she sat there Beulah knew not, but a growl roused her, and she saw Mrs. Williams looking sorrowfully at her.

"My child, what makes you moan and weep so bitterly?"

"Oh, because I am so miserable; because I have lost my best friend; my only friend; my guardian. He has gone—gone! and I did not see him." With a stifled cry her face went down again.

The matron had never seen her so unnerved before, and wondered at the vehemence of her grief, but knew her nature too well to attempt consolation. Beulah lifted the box and retired to her room, followed by Charon. Securing the door, she put the case on the table and looked at it wistfully. Were her conjectures, her hopes correct? She raised the lid and unwrapped the frame, and there was the noble head of her guardian. She hung the portrait on a hook just above her desk, and then stood, with streaming eyes, looking up at it. It had been painted a few weeks after his marriage, and represented him in the full morning of manhood, ere his heart was embittered and his clear brow overshadowed. The artist had suffered a ray of sunshine to fall on the brown hair that rippled round his white temples with careless grace. There was no moustache to shade the sculptured lips, and they seemed about to part in one of those rare, fascinating smiles which Beulah had often watched for in vain. The matchless eyes looked down at her with brooding tenderness in their hazel depths, and now seemed to question her uncontrollable grief. Yet she had pained him; had in part caused his exile from the home of his youth, and added another sorrow to those which now veiled that peerless face in gloom. He had placed his happiness in her hands; and asked her to be his wife. She looked at the portrait, and shuddered and moaned. She loved him above all others; loved him as a child adores its father; but how could she, who had so reverenced him, consent to become his wife? Besides, she could not believe he loved her. He liked her; pitied her isolation and orphanage; felt the need of her society, and wanted her always in his home. But she could not realize that he, who so worshipped beauty, could possibly love her. It was all like a hideous dream which morning would dispel; but there was the reality, and there was Charon looking steadily up at the portrait he was at no loss to recognize.

"Oh, if I could have seen him once more. If he had parted with me in kindness, it would not be so intolerable. But to remember his stern, sad face, as last I saw it; oh, how can I bear it! To have it haunting me through life, like a horrible specter; no friendly words to cherish; no final message; all gloom and anger. Oh, how shall I bear it!" and she fell on Charon's neck and wept bitterly.

CHAPTER XXXIII.

In the early days of summer, Mr. and Mrs. Graham left the city for one of the fashionable watering-places on the Gulf, accompanied by Antoinette. Eugene remained, on some pretext of business, but promised to follow in a short time. The week subsequent to their departure saw a party of gentlemen assembled to dine in his house. The long afternoon wore away, still they sat round the table. The cloth had been removed, and only wine and cigars remained; bottle after bottle was emptied and finally decanters were in requisition. The servants shrugged their shoulders, and looked on with amused expectancy. The conversation grew loud and boisterous, now and then flavored with oaths; twilight came on—the shutters were closed—the magnificent chandelier lighted. Eugene seized a crystal ice bowl, and was about to extract a lump of ice when it fell from his fingers and shivered to atoms. A roar of laughter succeeded the exploit, and uncorking a fresh bottle of champagne he demanded a song. Already a few of the guests were leaning on the table stupefied, but several began the strain. It was a genuine Bacchanalian ode, and the deafening shout rose to the frescoed ceiling as the revellers leaned forward and touched their glasses. Touched, did I say; it were better written clashed. There was a ringing chorus as crystal met crystal; glittering fragments flew in every direction; down ran the foaming wine, thick with splintered glass, on the rosewood table. But the strain was kept up; fresh glasses were supplied; fresh bottles drained; the waiters looked on, wondered where all this would end, and pointed to the ruin of the costly service. The brilliant gaslight shone on a scene of recklessness pitiable indeed. All were young men, and, except Eugene, all unmarried; but they seemed familiar with such occasions. One or two, thoroughly intoxicated, lay with their heads on the table, unconscious of what passed; others struggled to sit upright, yet the shout was still raised from time to time.

"Fill up, and let us have that glorious song from 'Lucrezia Borgia.' Hey, Proctor!" cried Eugene.

"That is poor fun without Vincent. He sings it equal to Vestvali. Fill up there, Munroe, and shake up Cowdon. Come, begin, and ———"

He raised his glass with a disgusting oath, and was about to commence, when Munroe said, stammeringly:

"Where is Fred, anyhow? He is a devilish fine fellow for a frolic. I ———"

"Why, gone to the coast with Graham's pretty wife. He is all devotion. They waltz and ride, and in fine, he is her admirer *par excellence*. Stop your stupid stammering, and begin."

Eugene half rose at this insulting mention of his wife's name, but the song was now ringing around him, and sinking back, he, too, raised his unsteady voice. Again and again, the words were madly shouted; and then, dashing his empty glass against the marble mantel, Proctor swore he would not drink another drop. What a picture of degradation! Disordered hair, soiled clothes, flushed, burning cheeks, glaring eyes, and nerveless hands. Eugene attempted to rise, but fell back in his chair, tearing off his cravat, which seemed to suffocate him. Proctor, who was too thoroughly inured to such excesses to feel it as sensibly as the remainder of the party, laughed brutally, and kicking over a chair which stood in his way, grasped his host by the arm, and exclaimed:

"Come out of this confounded room; it is as hot as a furnace; and let us have a ride to cool us. Come, Munroe and Cowdon must look after the others. By Jove, Graham, old father Bacchus himself could not find fault with your cellar. Come."

Each took a cigar from the stand, and descended to the front door, where a light buggy was waiting the conclusion of the revel. It was a cloudless July night, and the full moon poured a flood of silver light over the silent earth. Proctor assisted Eugene into the buggy, and gathering up the reins seized the whip, gave a flourish and shout, and off sprang the spirited horse, which the groom could, with difficulty, hold until the riders were seated.

"Now, Graham, I will bet a couple of baskets of Heidsick that my royal Telegraph will make the first mile post in 2:30. What say you?"

"Done; 2:40 is the lowest."

"Phew! Telegraph, my jewel, show what manner of flesh you are made of. Now, then, out with your watch."

He shook the reins, and the horse rushed forward like an arrow. Before the mile post was reached, it became evident that Telegraph had taken the game entirely out of his master's hands. In vain the reins were tightened. Proctor leaned so far back that his hat fell off. Still the frantic horse sped on. The mile post flashed by, but Eugene could barely sit erect, much less note time. At this stage of the proceedings, the whir of wheels behind gave a new impetus to Telegraph's flying feet. They were near a point in the road where an alley led off at right angles, and thinking doubtless that it was time to retrace his steps, the horse dashed down the alley, heedless of Proctor's efforts to restrain him, and turning into a neighboring street, rushed back toward the city. Bareheaded, and with heavy drops of perspiration streaming from his face, Proctor cursed and jerked and drew the useless reins. On went Telegraph, making good his title, now swerving to this side of the road and now to that; but as he approached a mass of bricks which were piled on one side of the street, near the foundations of a new building, the moonlight flashed upon a piece of tin in the sand on the opposite side, and frightened by the glitter he plunged toward the bricks. The wheels struck, the buggy tilted, then came down again with a terrible jolt, and Eugene was thrown out on the pile. Proctor was jerked over the dashboard, dragged some distance, and finally left in the sand, while Telegraph ran on to the stable.

It was eleven o'clock, but Beulah was writing in her own room; and through the open window, heard the thundering tramp, the rattle among the bricks, Proctor's furious curses, and surmised that some accident had happened. She sprang to the window, saw the buggy just as it was wheeled on, and hoped nothing was hurt. But Charon, who slept on the portico, leaped over the paling, ran around the bricks, and barked alarmingly. She unlocked the door, saw that no one was passing, and opening the little gate looked out. Charon stood watching a prostrate form, and she fearlessly crossed the street and bent over the body. One arm was crushed beneath him; the other thrown up over the face. She recognized the watch chain, which was of a curious pattern; and for an instant all objects swam before her. She felt faint; her heart seemed to grow icy and numb; but with a great effort she moved the arm and looked on the face gleaming in the moonlight. Trembling like a weed in a wintry blast she knelt beside him. He was insensible, but not dead; though it was evident there must have been some severe contusion about the head. She saw that no time should be lost, and running into one of the neighboring houses, knocked violently. The noise of the horse and buggy had already aroused the inmates, and very soon the motionless form was borne into Beulah's little cottage and placed on a couch, while a messenger was dispatched for Dr. Asbury. Eugene remained just as they placed him; and kneeling beside him, Beulah held his cold hands in hers, and watched, in almost breathless anxiety, for some return of animation. She knew that he was intoxicated; that this, and this only, caused the accident; and tears of shame and commiseration trickled down her cheeks. Since their parting interview, previous to his marriage, they had met but once, and then in silence, beside Cornelia in her dying hour. It was little more than a year since she had risked his displeasure and remonstrated with him on his ruinous course; and that comparatively short period had wrought painful changes in his once noble, handsome face. She had hoped that Cornelia's dying prayer would save him; but now, alas, it was too apparent that the appeal had been futile. She knew not that his wife was absent, and determined to send for her as soon as possible. The long hour of waiting seemed an eternity, but, at last, Dr. Asbury came, and carefully examined the bruised limbs. Beulah grasped his arm.

"Oh! will he die?"

"I don't know, child; this arm is badly fractured, and I am afraid there is a severe injury on the back of the head. It won't do to move him home, so send Hal in from my buggy to help put him in bed. Have me some bandages at once, Beulah."

As they carried him into Mrs. Williams' room and prepared to set the fractured arm he groaned, and for a moment struggled, then relapsed into a heavy stupor. Dr. Asbury carefully straightened and bandaged the limb and washed the blood from his temples, where a gash had been inflicted in the fall.

"Will you go to his wife at once, sir, and inform her of his condition?" said Beulah, who stood by the blood-stained pillow, pale and anxious.

"Don't you know his wife is not here? She has gone for the summer. Wife did I say? she does not deserve the sacred name! If he had had a wife, he would never have come to this ruin and disgrace. It is nothing more than I expected when he married her. I could easily put her soul on the end of a lancet, and as for heart—she has none at all! She is a pretty flirt, fonder of admiration than of her husband. I will write by the earliest mail, informing Graham of the accident and its possible consequences, and perhaps respect for the opinion of the world may bring her home to him. Beulah, it is a difficult matter to believe that that drunken, stupid victim there is Eugene Graham, who promised to become an honor to his friends and his name.

Satan must have established the first distillery; the institution smacks of the infernal! Child, keep ice upon that head, will you, and see that as soon as possible he takes a spoonful of the medicine I mixed just now. I am afraid it will be many days before he leaves this house. If he lives, the only consolation is that it may be a lesson and warning to him. I will be back in an hour or so. As for Proctor, whom I met limping home, it would have been a blessing to the other young men of the city, and to society generally, if he had never crawled out of the sand where he was thrown."

A little while after the silence was broken by a heavy sob, and glancing up, Beulah perceived the matron standing near the bed gazing at the sleeper.

"Oh, that he should come to this! I would ten thousand times rather he had died in his unstained boyhood."

"If he lives, this accident may be his salvation."

"God grant it may—God grant it may!"

Falling on her knees the aged woman put up a prayer of passionate entreaty that Almighty God would spare his life and save him from a drunkard's fate.

"If I, too, could pray for him, it might save my aching heart," thought Beulah, as she listened to the imploring words of the matron.

And why not? Ah! murky vapors of unbelief shrouded the All Father from her wandering soul. Dawn looked in upon two sorrowing watchers beside that stupid slumberer and showed that the physician's fears were realized; a raging fever had set in, and this night was but the commencement of long and dreary vigils. About noon Beulah was crossing the hall with a bowl of ice in her hand when some one at the door pronounced her name, and Proctor approached her, accompanied by Cowdon. She had once met the former at Mr. Graham's, and having heard Cornelia regret the miserable influence he exerted over her brother, was prepared to receive him coldly.

"We have come to see Graham, madam," said he, shrinking from her sad, searching eyes, yet assuming an air of haughty indifference.

"You cannot see him, sir."

"But I tell you, I must! I shall remove him to his own house, where he can be properly attended to. Where is he?"

"The physician particularly urged the necessity of keeping everything quiet. He shall not be disturbed; but as he is unconscious, perhaps it will afford you some gratification to behold the ruin you have wrought. Gentlemen, here is your victim."

She opened the door and suffered them to stand on the threshold and look at the prostrate form, with the head enveloped in icy cloths and the face bloated and purplish from bruises and fever. Neither Proctor nor his companion could endure the smile of withering contempt which curled her lips as she pointed to the victim of their temptations and influence, and with a half-suppressed imprecation Proctor turned on his heel and left the house. Apparently this brief visit quite satisfied them, for it was not repeated. Days and nights of unremitted watching ensued; Eugene was wildly delirious, now singing snatches of drinking songs, and waving his hand as if to his guests; and now bitterly upbraiding his wife for her heartlessness and folly. The confinement of his fractured arm frenzied him; often he struggled violently to free himself, fancying that he was incarcerated in some horrid dungeon. On the morning of the fourth day after the accident a carriage stopped at the cottage gate, and, springing out, Mr. Graham hurried into the house. As he entered the sick-room and caught sight of the tossing sufferer a groan escaped him, and he covered his eyes an instant, as if to shut out the vision. Eugene imagined he saw one of the Heidelberg professors, and laughing immoderately began a rapid conversation in German. Mr. Graham could not conceal his emotion, and, fearing its effect on the excitable patient, Beulah beckoned him aside and warned him of the possible consequences. He grasped her hand and asked the particulars of the occurrence, which had been mentioned to him vaguely. She told him the account given by Eugene's servants of the night's revel and then the dénoûment in front of her door. In conclusion, she said, earnestly:

"Where is his wife! Why is she not here?"

"She seemed to think she could render no assistance; and fearing that all would be over before we could get here, preferred my coming at once and writing to her of his condition. Ah! she is miserably fitted for such scenes as you must have witnessed." And the gray-haired man sighed heavily.

"What! can she bear to commit her husband to other hands at such a crisis as this? How can she live away from his side, when every hour may be his last? Oh! is she indeed so utterly, utterly heartless, selfish, callous? Poor Eugene! better find release from such a union in death than go through life bound to a wife so unblushingly indifferent!"

Her face was one flash of scorn and indignation, and extending her hand toward the restless invalid she continued in a lower tone:

"She has deserted her sacred post; but a truer, better friend, one who has always loved him as a brother, will supply her place. All that a sister's care can do, assuredly he shall have."

"You are very kind, Miss Beulah; my family are under lasting obligations to you for your generous attentions to that poor boy of ours, and I—"

"No. You understand little of the nature of our friendship. We were orphan children, warmly attached to each other, before you took him to a home of wealth and lavish indulgence. Were he my own brother I could not feel more deeply interested in his welfare, and while he requires care and nursing I consider it my privilege to watch over and guard him. There is Dr. Asbury in the hall; he can tell you better than I of his probable recovery."

Ah, reader, is

—"Friendship but a name?
A charm that lulls to sleep,
A shade that follows wealth or fame,
And leaves the wretch to weep?"

Mr. Graham remained at the cottage, and having written to Antoinette of the imminent danger in which he found her husband, urged her to lose no time in joining him. Unluckily, he was ignorant of all the information which is so essential in the occupation of nursing. He was anxious to do everything in his power; but, like the majority of persons on such occasions, failed wretchedly in his attempts. Almost as restless and nervous as the sick man, he only increased the difficulties he would fain have remedied, and Beulah finally prevailed upon him to abandon his efforts and leave the room, where his constant movements annoyed and irritated the sufferer. Eugene recognized no one, but his eyes followed Beulah continually; and when his delirium was at its height only her voice and clasp of his hand could in any degree soothe him. In his ravings, she noticed two constantly conflicting emotions: a stern bitterness of feeling toward his wife, and an almost adoring fondness for his infant child. Of the latter, he talked incessantly, and vowed that she, at least, should love him. As the weary days crept by, Beulah started at every sound, fancying that the wife had certainly come; but hour after hour found only Mrs. Williams and the orphan guarding the deserted husband. Gradually the fever abated, and a death-like stupor succeeded. Mr. Graham stole about the house, like a haunting spirit, miserable and useless, and in the solemn stillness of midnight only Beulah sat by the pillow, where a head now rested motionless as that of a corpse. Mrs. Williams was asleep on a couch at the opposite end of the room, and in the dim, spectral light of the shaded lamp, the watcher and her charge looked unearthly. Faint from constant vigils, Beulah threw her arm on the bed and leaned her head upon it, keeping her eyes on the colorless face before her. Who that has watched over friends, hovering upon the borders of the spirit-land, needs to be told how dreary was the heart of the solitary nurse? And to those who have not thus suffered and endured no description would adequately portray the desolation and gloom.

The stars were waning when Eugene moved, threw up his hand over the pillow, and, after a moment, opened his eyes. Beulah leaned forward, and he looked at her fixedly, as if puzzled; then said, feebly:

"Beulah, is it you?"

A cry of joy rolled to her lips, but she hushed it, and answered tremblingly:

"Yes, Eugene, it is Beulah."

His eyes wandered about the room, and then rested again on her countenance, with a confused, perplexed expression.

"Am I at home? What is the matter?"

"Yes, Eugene, at home among your best friends. Don't talk any more; try to sleep again."

With a great joy in her heart, she extinguished the light, so that he could see nothing. After a few moments he said, slowly:

"Beulah, did I dream I saw you? Beulah!" She felt his hand put out, as if to feel for her.

"No, I am sitting by you, but will not talk to you now. You must keep quiet."

There was a short silence.

"But where am I? Not at home, I know."

She did not reply, and he repeated the question more earnestly.

"You are in my house, Eugene; let that satisfy you."

His fingers closed over hers tightly, and soon he slept.

The sun was high in the sky when he again unclosed his eyes and found Dr. Asbury feeling his pulse. His mind was still bewildered, and he looked around him, wonderingly.

"How do you feel, Graham?" said the doctor.

"Feel! as if I had been standing on my head. What is the matter with me, doctor? Have I been sick?"

"Well—yes; you have not been exactly well, and feel stupid after a long nap. Take a spoonful of this nectar I have prepared for you. No wry faces, man! It will clear your head?"

Eugene attempted to raise himself, but fell back exhausted, while, for the first time, he noticed his arm firmly incased in wood and bandages.

"What have you been doing to my arm? Why, I can't move it. I should—"

"Oh, don't trouble yourself, Graham; you injured it and I bound it up, that is all. When gentlemen amuse themselves with such gymnastic feats as you performed they must expect a little temporary inconvenience from crushed bones and overstrained muscles. Beulah, mind my directions about silence and quiet."

The doctor walked out to escape further questioning. Eugene looked at his useless, stiffened arm, and then at Beulah, saying anxiously:

"What is the matter with me?"

"You were thrown out of a buggy, and fractured your arm in the fall."

She thought it best to tell the truth at once.

Memory flew back to her deserted throne, and dimly the events of that evening's revel passed through his mind. A flush of shame rose to his temples, and turning his head toward the wall, he hid his face in the pillow. Then Beulah heard a deep, shuddering sigh, and a groan of remorseful agony. After a long silence, he said, in a tone of humiliation that drew tears to her eyes:

"How long have I been here?"

She told him the number of days, and he immediately asked:

"Have I been in any danger?"

"Yes, very great danger; but that has all passed now, and if you will only be composed and careful you will soon be strong again."

"I heard my father talking to you, who else is here?"

He looked at her with eager interest.

"No one else, except our kind matron. Mr. Graham came as soon as the letter reached him, and has not left the house since."

A look of indescribable sorrow and shame swept over his countenance, as he continued bitterly:

"And did Antoinette know all at once? Stop, Beulah, tell me the miserable truth. Did she know all, and still remain away?"

"She knew all that had been communicated to Mr. Graham, when he came; and he has written to her every day. He is now writing to inform her that you are better."

She shrank from giving the pain she was conscious her words inflicted.

"I deserve it all! Yes, ingratitude, indifference, and desertion! If I had died, she would have heard it unmoved. Oh, Cornelia, Cornelia, it is a fearful retribution; more bitter than death!" Averting his face, his whole frame trembled with ill-concealed emotion.

"Eugene, you must compose yourself. Remember you jeopardize your life by this sort of excitement."

"Why didn't you let me die? What have I to live for? A name disgraced, and a wife unloving and heartless! What has the future but wretchedness and shame?"

"Not unless you will it so. You should want to live to retrieve your character, to take an honorable position, which, hitherto, you have recklessly forfeited; to make the world respect you, your wife revere you, and your child feel that she may be proud of her father! Ah, Eugene, all this the future calls you to do."

He looked up at her as she stood beside him, pale, thin, and weary, and his feeble voice faltered, as he asked:

"Beulah, my best friend, my sister, do you quite despise me?"

She laid her hands softly on his, and stooping down pressed her lips to his forehead.

"Eugene, once I feared that you had fallen even below my pity; but now I believe you will redeem yourself. I hope that, thoroughly reformed, you will command the respect of all who know you, and realize the proud aspirations I once indulged for you. That you can do this I feel assured; that you will, I do most sincerely trust. I have not yet lost faith in you, Eugene. I hope still."

She left him to ponder in solitude the humiliating result of his course of dissipation.

CHAPTER XXXIV.

The hours of gradual convalescence were very trying to Beulah, now that the sense of danger no longer nerved her to almost superhuman endurance and exertion. Mr. Graham waited until his adopted son was able to sit up, and then returned to the watering-place, where his wife remained. Thus the entire charge of the invalid devolved on the tireless friends who had watched over him in the hour of peril. Beulah had endeavored to banish the sorrow that pressed so heavily on her heart, and to dispel the gloom and despondency which seemed to have taken possession of the deserted husband. She read, talked, sang to him, and constantly strove to cheer him, by painting a future in which the past was to be effectually canceled. Though well-nigh exhausted by incessant care and loss of sleep, she never complained of weariness, and always forced a smile of welcome to her lips when the invalid had his chair wheeled to her side, or tottered out into the dining-room to join her. One morning in August, she sat on the little gallery at the rear of the house, with a table before her, engaged in drawing some of the clusters of blue, white, and pink convolvulus which festooned the pillars and balustrade. Eugene sat near her, with his thin face leaned on his hand, his thoughts evidently far removed from flowers. His arm was still in a sling, and he looked emaciated and dejected. Mrs. Williams had been talking to him cheerfully about some money matters he had promised to arrange for her, so soon as he was well enough to go to his office; but, gathering up her working materials, the old lady went into the kitchen, and the two sat for some time in silence. One of his long-drawn sighs arrested Beulah's attention, and she said, kindly:

"What is the matter, brother mine? Are you tired of watching my clumsy fingers? Shall I finish that essay of Macaulay's you were so much interested in yesterday, or will you have another of Bryant's poems?" She laid down her pencil, quite ready to divert his mind by reading.

"No, do not quit your drawing; I should not enjoy even Macaulay to-day."

He threw his head back, and sighed again.

"Why, Eugene? Don't you feel as well as usual this morning? Remember your family will arrive to-day; you should be the happiest man living."

"Oh, Beulah! don't mock me. I cannot bear it. My life seems a hopeless blank."

"You ought not to talk so despondingly; you have everything to live for. Rouse your energies. Be indeed a man. Conquer this weak, repining spirit. Don't you remember the motto on the tombstone at St. Gilgen?

"'Look not mournfully on the past—it comes not back;
Enjoy the present—it is thine.
Go forth to meet the shadowy future,
With a manly heart, and without fear.'"

"You know little of what oppresses me. It is the knowledge of my—, of Antoinette's indifference, which makes the future so joyless, so desolate. Beulah, this has caused my ruin. When I stood by Cornelia's coffin, and recalled her last frantic appeal; when I looked down at her cold face, and remembered her devoted love for her unworthy brother, I vowed never to touch wine again; to absent myself from the associates who had led me to dissipation. Beulah, I was honest, and intended to reform from that hour. But Antoinette's avowed coldness, or, to call it by its proper name, heartless selfishness, and fondness for admiration, first disgusted, and then maddened me. I would have gladly spent my evenings quietly, in our elegant home, but she contrived to have it crowded with visitors, as soulless and frivolous as herself. I remonstrated, she was sneering, defiant, and unyielding, and assured me she would 'amuse' herself as she thought proper; I followed her example, and went back to the reckless companions, who continually beset my path. I was miserably deceived in Antoinette's character. She was very beautiful, and I was blind to her mental, nay, I may as well say it at once, her moral defects. I believed she was warmly attached to me, and I loved her most devotedly. But no sooner were we married, than I discovered my blind rashness. Cornelia warned me, but what man, fascinated by a beautiful girl, ever listened to counsels that opposed his heart? Antoinette is too intensely selfish to love anything, or anybody but herself; she does not even love her child. Strange as it may seem, she is too entirely engrossed by her weak fondness for display and admiration, even to caress her babe. Except at breakfast and dinner, we rarely meet, and then, unless company is present (which is generally the case), our intercourse is studiedly cold. Do you wonder that I am hopeless in view of a life, passed with such a companion? Oh, that I could blot out the last two years of my existence!"

He groaned, and shaded his face with his hands.

"But, Eugene, probably your reformation and altered course will win you your wife's love and reverence," suggested Beulah, anxious to offer some incentive to exertion.

"I know her nature too well to hope that. A woman who prefers to dance and ride with gentlemen, rather than remain in her luxurious home, with her babe and her duties, cannot be won from her moth-like life. No, no! I despair of happiness from her society and affection, and if at all, must derive it from other sources. My child is the one living blossom amidst all my withered hopes, she is the only treasure I have, except your friendship. She shall never blush for her father's degradation. Henceforth, though an unhappy man, I shall prove myself a temperate one. I cannot trust my child's education to Antoinette, she is unworthy the sacred charge; I must fit myself to form her character. Oh, Beulah, if I could make her such a woman as you are, then I could indeed bear my lot patiently! I named her Cornelia, but henceforth she shall be called Beulah also, in token of her father's gratitude to his truest friend."

"No, Eugene, call her not after me, lest some of my sorrows come upon her young head. Oh, no! name her not Beulah: let her be called Cornelia. I would not have her soul shrouded as mine has been." Beulah spoke vehemently, and laying her hand on his arm, she added:

"Eugene, to-day you will leave me, and go back to your own house, to your family; but before you go, I ask you; if not for your sake, for that of your child, to promise me solemnly, that you will never again touch intoxicating drinks of any kind. Oh, will you promise? Will you reform entirely?"

There was a brief pause, and he answered slowly:

"I promise, Beulah. Nay, my friend, I swear I will abstain in future. Ah, I will never disgrace my angel child! Never, so help me heaven!"

The sound of approaching steps interrupted the conversation, and expecting to see Antoinette and her infant, accompanied by Mr. and Mrs. Graham, Beulah looked up quickly, and perceived Mr. Lindsay.

"Does my advent startle you, that you look so pale and breathless?" said he, smiling, as he took her hand.

"I am certainly very much surprised to see you here, sir."

"And I am heartily glad you have come, Reginald," cried Eugene, returning his friend's tight clasp.

"I intended coming to nurse you, Graham, as soon as I heard of the accident, but my mother's illness prevented my leaving home. I need not ask about your arm, I see it still requires cautious handling; but how are you otherwise? Regaining your strength, I hope?"

"Yes, gradually. I am better than I deserve to be, Reginald."

"That remains to be proved in future, Graham. Come, get well as rapidly as possible; I have a plan to submit to you, the earliest day you are strong enough to discuss business topics. Miss Beulah, let me sharpen your pencil."

He took it from her, trimmed it carefully, and handed it back; then drew her portfolio near him, and glanced over the numerous unfinished sketches.

"I have several books, filled with European sketches, which, I think, might afford you some pleasure. They were taken by different persons; and some of the views on the Rhine, and particularly some along the southern shore of Spain, are unsurpassed by any I have seen. You may receive them some day, after I return."

"Thank you, I shall copy them with great pleasure."

"I see you are not as much of a pyrrhonist in art as in philosophy," said Mr. Lindsay, watching her countenance as she bent over her drawing.

"Who told you, sir, that I was one in any department?" She looked up suddenly, with flashing eyes.

"There is no need to be told. I can readily perceive it."

"Your penetration is at fault, then. Of all others, the charge of pyrrhonism is the last I merit."

He smiled, and said, quietly:

"What, then, is your esthetic creed, if I may inquire?"

"It is nearly allied to Cousin's."

"I thought you had abjured eclecticism; yet Cousin is its apostle. Once admit his theory of the beautiful, and you cannot reject his psychology and ethics; nay, his theodicea?"

"I do not desire to separate his system; as such I receive it."

Beulah compressed her lips firmly, and looked at her interrogator half defiantly.

"You deliberately shut your eyes, then, to the goal his philosophy sets before you?"

"No, I am nearing the goal, looking steadily toward it." She spoke hastily, and with an involuntary wrinkling of her brow.

"And that goal is pantheism; draped gorgeously, but pantheism still," answered Mr. Lindsay, with solemn emphasis.

"No; his whole psychology is opposed to pantheism!" cried Beulah, pushing aside her drawing materials, and meeting his eyes fixedly.

"You probably attach undue weight to his assertion that, although God passes into the universe, or therein manifests all the elements of his being, he is not 'exhausted in the act.' Now, granting, for the sake of argument, that God is not entirely absorbed in the universe, Cousin's pet doctrine of the 'Spontaneous Apperception of Absolute Truths,' clearly renders man a modification of God. Difference in degree, you know, implies sameness of kind; from this there is no escape. He says, 'the God of consciousness is not a solitary sovereign, banished beyond creation, upon the throne of a silent eternity, and an absolute existence, which resembles existence in no respect whatever. He is a God, at once true and real, substance and cause, one and many, eternity and time, essence and life, end and middle; at the summit of existence, and at its base, infinite and finite together; in a word, a Trinity; being at the same time, God, Nature and Humanity.' His separation of reason and reasoning, and the results of his boasted 'spontaneous apperception,' are very nearly allied to those of Schelling's 'Intellectual Intuition;' yet I suppose you would shrink from the 'absolute identity' of the latter?"

"You have not stated the question fairly, sir. He reiterates that the absolute belongs to none of us. We perceive truth, but do not create it!" retorted Beulah.

"You will perhaps remember his saying, explicitly, that we can comprehend the Absolute?"

"Yes, I recollect; and moreover, he declares that 'we are conducted to God by a ray of his own being.'"

"Can limited faculties comprehend the infinite and eternal creator?"

"We do not attain a knowledge of him through finite channels. Cousin contends that it is by means of relation to the absolute that we know God."

"Then, to know the absolute, or God, you must be the absolute: or in other words, God only can find God. This is the simple doctrine, when you unwind the veil he has cleverly hung over it. True, he denounces pantheism;

but here is pantheism of the eclectic patent, differing from that of other systems only in subtlety of expression, wherein Cousin certainly excels. One of the most profound philosophical writers of the age,* and one whose opinion on this point certainly merits careful consideration, has remarked, in an analysis of Cousin's system, 'with regard to his notion of Deity, we have already shown how closely this verges upon the principle of Pantheism. Even if we admit that it is not a doctrine, like that of Spinoza, which identifies God with the abstract idea of substance; or even like that of Hegel, which regards Deity as synonymous with the absolute law and process of the universe; if we admit, in fact, that the Deity of Cousin possesses a conscious personality, yet still it is one which contains in itself the infinite personality and consciousness of every subordinate mind. God is the ocean—we are but the waves; the ocean may be one individuality, and each wave another; but still they are essentially one and the same. We see not how Cousin's Theism can possibly be consistent with any idea of moral evil; neither do we see how, starting from such a dogma, he can ever vindicate and uphold his own theory of human liberty. On such theistic principles, all sin must be simply defect, and all defect must be absolutely fatuitous. Eclecticism was a beautiful, but frail levee, opposed to the swollen tide of skepticism, and as in every other crevasse, when swept away, it only caused the stream to rush on more madly."

He watched her closely as he spoke, and observed the quiver of her long, curling lashes; he saw, too, that she was resolved not to surrender, and waited for an explicit defence; but here Eugene interrupted:

"All this tweedle-dum and tweedle-dee reminds me of Heidelberg days, when a few of us roamed about the Odenwald, chopping off flowers with our canes and discussing philosophy. Rare jargon we made of it; talking of cosmothetic idealism, or hypothetical dualism, of noetic, and dianoetic principles, of hylozoism, and hypostatis, and demonstrating the most undemonstrable propositions by appeals to the law of contradiction, or of excluded middle. I fancied then that I was growing very learned—wondered whether Beulah here would be able to keep up with me, and really thought I understood what I discoursed about so logically."

"You can at least console yourself, Graham, by determining that

> "'You know what's what, and that's as high
> As metaphysic wit can fly.'

*J. D. Morell, Speculative Philosophy of Europe.

I imagine there are very few of us who would agree with some of our philosophers, that 'the pursuit of truth is far more important than the attainment thereof'—that philosophizing is more valuable than philosophy. To be conversant with the abstractions which, in the hands of some metaphysical giants, have rendered both mind and matter like abstractions, is a course of proceeding I should scarcely indorse; and the best antidote I remember just now to any such web-spinning proclivities is a persual of the three first lectures of Sidney Smith on 'Moral Philosophy.' In recapitulating the tenets of the schools, he says: 'The speculations of many of the ancients on the human understanding are so confused, and so purely hypothetical, that their greatest admirers are not agreed upon their meaning; and whenever we can procure a plain statement of their doctrines, all other modes of refuting them appear to be wholly superfluous.' Miss Beulah, I especially commend you to these humorous lectures." He bowed to her with easy grace.

"I have them, sir—have read them with great pleasure," said Beulah, smiling at his droll manner of mingled reserve and freedom.

"What an exalted estimate that same incorrigible Sidney must have placed upon the public taste of this republican land of ours? In one of his lectures on 'the beauty of form,' I remember he says: 'A chin ending in a very sharp angle would be a perfect deformity. A man whose chin terminated in a point would be under the immediate necessity of retiring to America—he would be such a perfect horror!' Decidedly flattering to our national type of beauty." As Eugene spoke his lips wore a smile more akin to those of his boyhood than any Beulah had seen since his return from Europe.

"Yes, that was to show the influence of custom, be it remembered; and in the same connection, he remarks, honestly enough, that he 'hardly knows what a Grecian face is; but thinks it very probable that if the elegant arts had been transmitted to us from the Chinese, instead of the Greeks, that singular piece of deformity—a Chinese nose—would have been held in high estimation.' It was merely association."

"Which I don't believe a word of," cried Beulah, appropriating the last as a lunge at her favorite absolutism. Rising, she placed her drawings in the portfolio, for the sun had crept round the corner of the gallery, and was shining in her face.

Mr. Lindsay smiled, without replying, and gave his arm to assist Eugene into the house. They were comfortably seated in the dining-room, and Beulah knew that the discussion was about to be renewed, when a carriage dashed up to the door. Eugene turned pale, and a sudden rigidity seized his features. Beulah gave her guest a quick, meaning glance, and retreated to the gallery, whither he instantly followed her, leaving Eugene to receive his wife without witnesses. Leaning against one of the pillars, Beulah unfastened a wreath of blue convolvulus which Mrs. Williams had twined in her hair an hour before. The delicate petals were withered, and with a suppressed sigh, she threw them away. Mr. Lindsay drew a letter from his pocket, and handed it to her saying briefly:

"I was commissioned to give you this, and knowing the contents, hope a favorable answer."

It was from Clara, urging her to come up the following week and officiate as bridesmaid at her wedding. She could return home with Helen and George Asbury. Beulah read the letter, smiled sadly, and put it in her pocket.

"Will you go?"

"No, sir."

"Why not? You need a change of air, and the trip would benefit you. You do not probably know how much you have altered in appearance since I saw you. My uncle is coming out to persuade you to go. Can't I succeed without his aid?"

"I could not leave home now. Eugene's illness had prevented my accomplishing some necessary work, and as I consign him to other hands to-day, I must make amends for my long indolence. Thank you for taking charge of my letter, but I cannot think of going."

He perceived that no amount of persuasion would avail, and for an instant a look of annoyance crossed his face. But his brow cleared as he said, with a smile:

"For a year I have watched for your articles, and the magazine is a constant companion of my desk. Sometimes I am tempted to criticise your sketches; perhaps I may do so yet, and that in no Boswell spirit either."

"Doubtless, sir, you would find them very vulnerable to criticism, which nowadays has become a synonym for faultfinding; at least this carping proclivity characterizes the class, who seem desirous only of earning reputation as literary Jeffreys. I am aware, sir, that I am very vulnerable."

"Suppose, then, that at the next month's literary assize (as you seem disposed to consider it), you find in some of the magazines a severe animadversion upon the spirit of your writings? Dare I do this, and still hope for your friendship?"

He watched her closely.

"Certainly, sir. I am not writing merely to see myself in print, nor wholly for remuneration in dollars and cents. I am earnestly searching for truth, and if in my articles you discover error and can correct it, I shall be glad to have you do so, provided you adopt the Catholic spirit, which should distinguish such undertakings. Now, if you merely intend to hold me up for ridicule, as thoroughly as possible, I prefer that you let me and my articles rest; but a calm, dispassionate criticism I should not shrink from. I write only what I believe, and if I am in error, I shall be glad to have it corrected."

"Miss Benton, may I venture to correct it without having recourse to the vehicle of public criticism? Will you permit me to discuss with you, here in your quiet home, those vital questions whose solution seems to engage your every thought?"

She drew back, and answered with a dreary sort of smile:

"I am afraid you would derive little pleasure, and I less profit from such disputation. I have learned from bitter experience that merely logical forms of argumentation do not satisfy the hungry soul. The rigid processes of Idealism annihilated the external world; and Hume proved that Mind was a like chimera; yet who was ever seriously converted by their incontrovertible reasoning? I have lost faith in ratiocination."

"Still you cling to opinions founded on its errors. Why not be consistent, and in rejecting its most potent ally, reject the conclusions of Rationalism also?"

"Because I must believe something. Faith in some creed is an absolute necessity of human nature."

"You distinguish faith, then, from intellectual belief?"

"No; I compound them; my faith is based on mental conviction," replied Beulah, perceiving whither he was leading her and resolved not to follow.

"And this conviction results from those same processes of ratiocination which you condemn as unworthy of credence, because subject to gross, sometimes ludicrous perversions?"

"I am unable to detect any such perversion or inaccuracy in the cautious course of reasoning which has assisted me to my present belief."

"Pardon me, but does this fact convince you of the infallibility of the course? Have you constituted your individual reason the sole judge?"

"Yes; there is no other left me."

"And your conclusions are true for you only, since the individual organism of your mind makes them so. To an intellect of a higher or lower grade these conclusions would be untenable, since the depressed or exalted reason judged them accordingly. You may cling to some doctrine as absolutely and necessarily true, yet to my mind it may seem a shallow delusion, like the vagaries of spirit-rappers."

"No; reasoning is often fallacious, but reason is divine; reasoning often clouds the truth, but reason, by spontaneous apperception, grasps truth," persisted Beulah, unhesitatingly.

"Then truth has as many phases, and as antagonistic, as there are individuals in the universe. All men are prophets; all are alike inspired; all alike worthy of trust and credence. Spontaneous reason has grasped a number of oddly conflicting doctrines, let me tell you, and the reconciliation of these would be an undertaking to which the dozen labors of Hercules seem a farce."

"The susperstition of various ages and nations are not valid arguments against the existence of universal and necessary principles."

"Why, then, have these principles produced no unanimity of faith? The history of the human race is the history of the rise of one philosophy and religion from the ashes of its predecessor. There is one universal belief in the necessity of religion, and this belief built altars in the dawn of time; but your spontaneous reason is perpetually changing the idols on these altars. The God of one man's reason will not satisfy that of his neighbor."

Before Beulah could reply, she heard Eugene calling her in the hall, and was hastening to meet him; but Mr. Lindsay caught her hand, and said: "You have not yet given me permission to intrude on your seclusion." She withdrew her hand instantly.

"When you have nothing else to occupy you, and wish to while away an hour in literary discussion, you will generally find me at home during vacation."

She walked on and joined Eugene in the hall. Antoinette stood in the door, and they merely exchanged bows, while Mr. Graham grasped her hand and earnestly thanked her for the many kindnesses she had rendered to his family. Beulah looked at the composed, beautiful face of the young wife, and then at the thin form of the husband, and said, hastily:

"You owe me no thanks, sir; the claims of true friendship are imperative. In removing to his own house I trust Eugene's improvement may not be retarded."

Antoinette tripped down the steps, and gathering the flounces of her costly dress, seated herself in the carriage. Mr. Graham bit his lip, colored, and after a cordial good-by, joined her. Eugene smiled bitterly, and turning to Beulah, took both her hands in his, saying, feelingly:

"Beulah, I leave your house a wiser, if not less miserable man. I am going to atone for the past; to prove to you that your faith in me is not altogether unmerited. If I am saved from ruin and disgrace, I owe it to you; and to you I shall look for sympathy and encouragement. To you, my best friend, I shall often come for sisterly aid, when clouds gather black and stormy over my miserable home. God bless you, Beulah! I have promised reformation, and will keep my promise sacred if it cost me my life."

He raised her hand to his lips, and linking his arm in Mr. Lindsay's, left the house and entered the carriage, while the latter mounted his horse and rode slowly away.

"You look weary, child. You must give yourself some rest now," said Mrs. Williams, wiping her eyes with the corner of her apron.

"Rest! Ah, yes; if I could find it," returned the girl, taking the comb from the back of her head, and shaking down the folds of hair, till it hung around her like a long mourning veil.

"Suppose you try to sleep some," suggested the matron.

"I have some work to do first," said she, drawing a long breath, and wiping the dust from her desk.

Mrs. Williams withdrew; and, clasping her hands over her forehead, Beulah stood looking up, with dim eyes, at the cloudless face that smiled down on her, until she almost fancied the lips parted to address her.

CHAPTER XXXV.

Mr. Lindsay's visits grew more frequent. At first Beulah wondered what brought him so often from his distant home to the city, and supposed it must be some legal business which engaged him; but gradually a different solution dawned upon her mind. She rejected it as the prompting of vanity, but again and again the supposition recurred. The imperturbable gravity and repose of his manner often disconcerted her. It was in vain that she resorted to sarcasm and irony, he was incorrigibly unruffled; in vain she was cold, repellent, haughty: his quiet smile remained unaltered. His superior, and thoroughly cultivated intellect, and the unaffected simplicity of his manner, characterized by singular candor, rendered him an unusually agreeable companion; but Beulah rebelled against the unobtrusive yet constant care with which she fancied he watched her. The seclusion of her life, and reserve of her nature, conspired to impart a degree of abruptness to her own manners; and to one who understood her character less than Reginald Lindsay, there was an unhesitating sincerity of expression, which might have been termed rudeness. The frequency of his visits attracted the attention of strangers; already the busy tongue of meddling gossip had connected their names; Dr. Asbury, too, bantered her unmercifully upon his nephew's constant pilgrimages to the city; and the result was, that Mr. Lindsay's receptions grew colder and less flattering continually. From the first, she had not encouraged his visits, and now she positively discouraged them, by every intimation which the rules of etiquette justified her in offering. Yet she respected, esteemed, and in many things admired him; and readily confessed to her own heart that his society often gave her pleasure.

One winter evening she sat alone by the dining-room fire, with a newspaper in her hand, reading a notice of the last number of the magazine, in which one of her sketches was roughly handled. Of course, she was no better pleased with the unflattering criticism than the majority of writers in such cases. She frowned, bit her lip, and wondered who could have written it. The review was communicated, and the paper had been sent to her by some unknown hand. Once more she read the article, and her brow cleared, while a smile broke over her face. She had recognized a particular *dictum,* and was no longer puzzled. Leaning her head on her palm, she sat looking into the fire, ruminating on the objections urged against her piece; it was the first time she had ever been unfavorably criticised, and this was sufficient food for thought.

Mr. Lindsay came in and stood near her unobserved. They had not met for several weeks, and she was not aware that he was in the city. Charon, who lay on the rug at her feet, growled, and she looked round.

"Good evening," said the visitor, extending his hand.

She did not accept it, but merely inclined her head, saying:

"Ah, how do you do, sir?"

He laid a package on the table, drew a chair near the hearth, without looking at her, and calling to Charon, patted his huge head kindly.

"What have you there, Miss Beulah? Merely a newspaper? it seems to interest you intensely. May I see it?"

"I am certainly very much obliged to you, sir, for the chivalrous spirit in which you indited your criticism. I was just pondering it when you entered."

She smiled as she spoke, and shook the paper at him.

"I thought I had feigned a style you would not recognize," he answered, quite unconcernedly.

"You succeeded admirably, with the exception of one pet phrase, which betrayed you. Next time, recollect that you are very partial to some peculiar expressions, with which I happen to be acquainted, and avoid their introduction."

"I rather think I shall not repeat the experiment; especially as my arguments seem to have failed signally in their design. Are you quite sure that you understand my review perfectly?"

He looked a little curious—she fancied disappointed—and she replied, laughingly:

"Oh, I think I do; it is not so very abstruse."

He leaned forward, took the paper from her, before she was aware of his intention, and threw it into the fire.

She looked surprised, and he offered his hand once more.

"Are we still friends? Will you shake hands with your reviewer?"

She unhesitatingly put her hand in his, and answered:

"Friendship is not a gossamer thread, to be severed by a stroke of the pen."

She endeavored to withdraw her fingers, but he held them firmly, while his blue eyes rested upon her with an expression she by no means liked. Her black brows met in a heavy frown, and her lips parted angrily; he saw it, and instantly released her hand.

"Miss Beulah, my uncle commissioned me to say to you that he received a letter to-day from Dr. Hartwell. It was written during his voyage down the Red Sea and contained a long farewell, as inland travel would afford no facilities for writing."

He noted the tight clasp in which her fingers locked each other, and the livid paleness of her lips and brow, as the long lashes drooped, and she sat silently listening. Charon laid his head on her knee, and looked up at her. There was a brief silence, and Mr. Lindsay added, slowly:

"My uncle fears he will never return; do you cherish the hope?"

"Yes, he will come back, if his life is spared. It may be many years, but he will come, he will come."

Their eyes met; there was a long, searching look from Mr. Lindsay; she did not shrink from the scrutiny. An expression of keen sorrow swept over his face, but he conquered his emotion, took the parcel he had brought, and unwrapping a book, said, in his usual quiet tone:

"When I saw you last, you were regretting your inability to procure Sir William Hamilton's 'Philosophy of the Conditioned,' and I have taken the liberty of bringing you my own copy. Read it at your leisure; I shall not need it again soon. I do not offer it as a system which will satisfy your mind, by solving all your problems; but I do most earnestly commend his 'Philosophy of the Conditioned' as the surest antidote to the abstractions in which your speculation has involved you. The most erudite scholar of the age, and one of the finest metaphysical minds the world has ever known, he expressly sums up his vast philosophic researches with the humble confession: 'There are two sorts of ignorances; we philosophize to escape ignorance, and the consummation of our philosophy is ignorance; we start from the one, we repose in the other; they are the goals from which, and to which, we tend; and the pursuit of knowledge is but a course between two ignorances, as human life is itself only a travelling from grave to grave. The highest reach of human science is the scientific recognition of human ignorance.' Like you,

Miss Beulah, I set out to discover some system where no mysteries existed; where I should only believe what I could clearly comprehend. Yes, said I, proudly; I will believe nothing that I cannot understand. I wandered on, until, like you, I stood in a wide waste, strewn with the wreck of beliefs. My pride asserted that my reason was the only and sufficient guide, and whither did it lead me? Into vagaries more inexplicable than aught I fled from in Revelation. It was easier to believe that, 'in the beginning, God created the heaven and the earth,' than that the glorious universe looked to chance as its sole architect, or that it was a huge lumbering machine of matter, grinding out laws. I saw that I was the victim of a miserable delusion, in supposing my finite faculties could successfully grapple with the mysteries of the universe. I found that to receive the attempted solutions of philosophy required more faith than Revelation, and my proud soul humbled itself, and rested in the Bible. My philosophic experience had taught me that if mankind were to have any knowledge of their origin, their destiny, their God, it must be revealed by that God, for man could never discover aught for himself. There are mysteries in the Bible which I cannot explain; but it bears incontrovertible marks of divine origin, and as such I receive it. I can sooner believe the Mosaic revelation, than the doctrine which tells you that you are part of God, and capable of penetrating to absolute truth. To quote the expressive language of an acute critic (whose well known latitudinarianism and disbelief in the verbal inspiration of scripture, give peculiar weight to his opinion on this subject), 'when the advocates of this natural, spontaneous inspiration, will come forth from their recesses of thought, and deliver prophecies as clear as those of the Hebrew seer; when they shall mold the elements of nature to their will; when they shall speak with the sublime authority of Jesus of Nazareth; and with the same infinite ease, rising beyond all the influence of time, place and circumstances, explain the past, and unfold the future; when they die for the truth they utter, and rise again, as witnesses to its divinity; then we may begin to place them on the elevation which they so thoughtlessly claim; but until they either prove these facts to be delusions, or give their parallel in themselves, the world may well laugh at their ambition, and trample their spurious inspiration beneath its feet.' There is an infinite, eternal, and loving God; I am a finite creature, unable to comprehend him, and knowing him only through his own revelation. This very revelation is insufficient for our aspiring souls, I grant; but it declares emphatically that here 'we see through a glass darkly.' Better this than the starless night in which you grope, without a promise of the dawn of eternity, where all mystery shall be explained. Are you not weary of fruitless, mocking speculation?" He looked at her anxiously.

She raised her colorless face, and said drearily, as she passed her hand over her forehead:

"Weary? Ah, yes; weary as the lonely mariner, tempest-tossed on some pathless ocean, without chart or compass. In my sky, even the star of hope is shrouded. Weary? Yes, in body and mind."

"Then, humble your proud intellect; confess your ignorance and inability, and rest in God and Christianity."

She made an impatient gesture, and, turning away, he walked up and down the floor. For some moments neither spoke; finally, he approached her, and continued:

"There is strange significance in the Mosaic record of the Fall. Longing for the fruits of knowledge, whereby the mysteries of God would be revealed, cost man Eden. The first pair ate, knowledge mocked them, and only the curse remained. That primeval curse of desiring to know all things descended to all posterity, and at this instant you exemplify its existence. Ah! you must humble your intellect, if you would have it exalted; must be willing to be guided along unknown paths by other light than that of reason, if you would be happy. Well might Sir William Hamilton exclaim: 'It is this powerful tendency of the most vigorous minds to transcend the sphere of our faculties, which makes a "learned ignorance" the most difficult acquirement, perhaps indeed the consummation of knowledge.'"

He sighed as he uttered these words; she said nothing; and, putting his hand gently upon hers, as they lay folded on the table beside her, he added, sadly:

"I had hoped that I could aid you, but I see my efforts are useless; you will not be guided nor influenced by others; are determined to wander on in ever-deepening night, solitary and restless! God help you, Beulah!"

A shudder ran over her, but she made no reply.

He took her cold hands in his.

"And now we part. Since the evening I first saw you with your basket of strawberries, I have cherished the hope that I might one day be more than a friend. You have constantly shown me that I was nothing more to you; I have seen it all along, but still I hoped; and notwithstanding your coldness, I shall continue to hope. My love is too entirely yours to be readily effaced. I can wait patiently. Beulah, you do not love me now; perhaps never can, but I shall at least cling to the hope. I shall not come again; shall not weary you with professions and attentions. I know your nature, and even had I the power, would not persuade you to give me your hand now. But time may change your feelings; on this frail tenure I rest my hopes. Meantime, should circumstances occur which demand the aid or counsel of devoted friendship, may I ask you to feel no hesitancy in claiming any assistance I can render? And, Beulah, at any instant, a line, a word can recall me. The separation will be very painful to me, but I cannot longer obtrude myself on your presence. If, as I earnestly hope, the hour, however distant, should come, when you desire to see me, oh, Beulah, how gladly will I hasten to you—"

"We can never be more than friends; never!" cried Beulah.

"You think so now, and perhaps I am doomed to disappointment; but, without your sanction, I shall hope it. Good-by." He pressed his lips to her hand, and walked away.

Beulah heard the closing of the little gate, and then, for the first time, his meaning flashed upon her mind. He believed she loved her guardian; fancied that long absence would obliterate his image from her heart, and that, finally, grown indifferent to one who might never return, she would give her love to him whose constancy merited it. Genuine delicacy of feeling prevented his expressing all this, but she was conscious now that only this induced his unexpected course toward herself. A burning flush suffused her face as she exclaimed:

"Oh! how unworthy I am of such love as his? how utterly undeserving!"

Soon after, opening the book he had brought at the place designated, she drew the lamp near her and began its perusal. Hour after hour glided away, and not until the last page was concluded did she lay it aside. The work contained very little that was new; the same trains of thought had passed through her mind more than once before; but here they were far more clearly and forcibly expressed.

She drew her chair to the window, threw up the sash, and looked out. It was wintry midnight, and the sky blazed with its undying watch-fires. This starry page was the first her childish intellect had puzzled over. She had, from early years, gazed up into the glittering temple of night, and asked: "Whence came yon silent words, floating in solemn grandeur along the blue, waveless ocean of space? Since the universe sprang phœnix-like from that dim chaos, which may have been but the charnel-house of dead worlds, those unfading lights have burned on, bright as when they sang together at the creation. And I have stretched out my arms helplessly to them, and prayed to hear just once their unceasing chant of praise to the Lord of Glory. Will they shine on forever? or are they indeed God's light-bearers, set to illumine the depths of space and blaze a path along which the soul may travel to its God? Will they one day flicker and go out?" To every thoughtful mind, these questions propound themselves, and Beulah especially had essayed to answer them. Science had named the starry hosts, and computed their movements with wonderful skill; but what could it teach her of their origin and destiny? Absolutely nothing. And how stood her investigations in the more occult departments of psychology and ontology? An honest seeker of truth, what had these years of inquiry and speculation accomplished? Let her answer as, with face bowed on her palms, her eyes roved over the midnight sky.

"Once I had some principles, some truths clearly defined, but now I know nothing distinctly, believe nothing. The more I read and study, the more obscure seem the questions I am toiling to answer. Is this increasing intricacy the reward of an earnestly inquiring mind? Is this to be the end of all my glorious aspirations? Have I come to this? 'Thus far, and no farther.' I have stumbled on these boundaries many times, and now must I rest here? Oh, is this my recompense? Can this be all? All!" Smothered sobs convulsed her frame.

She had long before rejected a "revealed code" as unnecessary; the next step was to decipher nature's symbols, and thus grasp God's hidden laws; but here the old trouble arose; how far was "individualism" allowable and safe? To reconcile the theories of rationalism, she felt, was indeed a herculean task, and she groped on into deeper night. Now and then, her horizon was bestarred, and, in her delight, she shouted Eureka! But when the telescope of her infallible reason was brought to bear upon the coldly glittering points, they flickered and went out. More than once, a flaming comet, of German manufacture, trailed in glory athwart her dazzled vision; but close observation resolved the gilded nebula, and the nucleus mocked her. Doubt engendered doubt; the death of one difficulty was the instant birth of another. Wave after wave of skepticism surged over her soul, until the image of a great personal God was swept from its altar. But atheism never yet usurped the sovereignty of the human mind; in all ages, moldering vestiges of protean deism confront the giant specter, and every nation under heaven has reared its fane to the "unknown God." Beulah had striven to enthrone in her desecrated soul, the huge, dim, shapeless phantom of pantheism, and had turned eagerly to the system of Spinoza. The heroic grandeur of the man's life and character had strangely fascinated her; but now, that idol of a "substance, whose two infinite attributes were extension and thought," mocked her; and she hurled it from its pedestal, and looked back wistfully to the pure faith of her childhood. A Godless world; a Godless woman. She took up the lamp, and retired to her own room. On all sides, books greeted her; here was the varied lore of dead centuries; here she had held communion with the great souls entombed in these dusty pages. Here, wrestling alone with those grim puzzles, she had read out the vexed and vexing questions, in this debating club of the moldering dead, and endeavored to make them solve them. These well-worn volumes, with close "marginalias," echoed her inquiries, but answered them not to her satisfaction. Was her life to be thus passed in feverish toil, and ended as by a leap out into a black shoreless abyss? Like a spent child, she threw her arms on the mantelpiece, and wept uncontrollably, murmuring:

"Oh, better die now, than live as I have lived, in perpetual strugglings! What is life worth without peace of mind, without hope; and what hope have I? Diamonded webs of sophistry can no longer entangle; like Noah's dove, my soul has fluttered among them, striving in vain for a sure hold to perch upon; but, unlike it, I have no ark to flee to. Weary and almost hopeless, I would fain believe that this world is indeed as a deluge, and in it there is no ark of refuge but the Bible. It is true, I did not see this souls' ark constructed; I know nothing of the machinery employed; and no more than Noah's dove, can I explore and fully understand its secret chambers; yet, all untutored, the exhausted bird sought safety in the incomprehensible, and was saved. As to the mysteries of revelation and inspiration, why, I meet mysteries, turn which way I will. Man, earth, time, eternity, God, are all inscrutable mysteries. My own soul is a mystery unto itself, and so long as I am impotent to fathom its depths, how shall I hope to unfold the secrets of the universe?"

She had rejected Christian theism, because she could not understand how God had created the universe out of nothing. True, "with God, all things are possible," but she could not understand this creation out of nothing, and therefore would not believe it. Yet (oh, inconsistency of human reasoning!) she had believed that the universe created laws: that matter gradually created mind. This was the inevitable result of pantheism, for according to geology, there was a primeval period, when neither vegetable nor animal life existed; when the earth was a huge mass of inorganic matter. Of two incomprehensibilities, which was the most plausible? To-night this question recurred to her mind with irresistible force, and as her eyes wandered over the volumes she had so long consulted, she exclaimed:

"Oh, philosophy! thou hast mocked my hungry soul; thy gilded fruits have crumbled to ashes in my grasp. In lieu of the holy faith of my girlhood, thou hast given me but dim, doubtful conjecture, cold metaphysical abstractions, intangible shadows, that flit along my path, and lure me on to deeper morasses. Oh, what is the shadow of death, in comparison with the starless night which has fallen upon me, even in the morning of my life! My God, save me! Give me light: of myself I can know nothing!"

Her proud intellect was humbled, and falling on her knees, for the first time in many months, a sobbing prayer went up to the throne of the living God; while the vast clockwork of stars looked in on a pale brow and lips, where heavy drops of moisture glistened.

CHAPTER XXXVI.

Four years had passed since Eugene Graham returned to his home, after his severe illness, and now, as he sits alone in his library, with a bundle of legal documents before him, it is not difficult to perceive that his promise has been held sacred. Through the suggestions of Mr. Lindsay, and the persuasions of Beulah, he had closely applied himself to the study of law, immediately after his recovery. Hopeless of happiness in his home, ambition became the ruling passion, and scourged him on to unceasing exertion. The aspirations of his boyhood revived; the memory of his humiliating course goaded him to cover the past with the garlands of fame; and consciousness of unusual talents assured him of final success. Mr. Graham no longer opposed the design, as formerly, but facilitated its execution to the utmost of his ability. Under these circumstances, it was not surprising that earnest application soon procured his admission to the bar. His efforts were redoubled, and, ere long, his eloquence obtained for him a connection with one of the most prominent members of the profession. The world wondered at this complete revolution; many doubted its continuance; but, step by step, he climbed the ladder to eminence, and merited the applause which the public lavished upon him. Success only inflamed his ambition, and it became evident he aimed at political renown. Nature had fitted him for the political arena, had endowed him with oratorical powers of no ordinary stamp; and though long dormant, they were not impaired by his inertia. It was fortunate for him that an exciting Presidential canvass afforded numerous opportunities for the development of these, and at its close he found himself possessed of an enviable reputation. To a certain extent, his wife was elated with his success; she was proud of his acknowledged talent, but her selfish nature was utterly incapable of the tenderness and sincere affection he demanded. Their alienation was complete. No bickerings disturbed the serene atmosphere of their home, because mutual indifference precluded the necessity. Mrs. Graham gave parties, and attended them; rode, danced, spent her summers at fashionable watering-places, and her winters in a round of folly and dissipation, while her husband pursued his profession, careless of her movements, and rarely in her company. In the lady's conduct, the circle in which she moved, saw nothing reprehensible. She dressed superbly, gave elegant entertainments, and was, *par excellence,* the leader of bon-ton. True, she was quite as much of a belle as any young lady in the city, and received the attentions and flattery of gentlemen as unreservedly, nay, delightedly, as though she had no neglected husband and child at home, who had claims upon her; but this sort of conjugal indifference was in vogue, and as she frowned down, or smiled up, some family laboriously toiling to reach her circle, her "clique" blindly followed her example, and humored her whims. As regarded her deportment toward her husband, one alteration was perceptible; she respected—almost feared him; shrank from his presence, and generally contrived to fill the house with company when she was, for short intervals, at home. He ceased to upbraid, or even remonstrate; his days were spent in the court-room, or his office, and his evenings in his library. She dressed as extravagantly as she chose; he made no comments, paid her accounts, and grew more taciturn and abstracted, day by day.

Oh, women! women! when will you sever the fetters which fashion, wealth and worldliness have bound about you, and prove yourselves worthy the noble mission for which you were created? How much longer will heartless, soulless wives, mothers, daughters, and sisters, waltz, moth-like, round the consuming flame of fashion; and by neglecting their duties, and deserting their sphere, drive their husbands, sons and brothers, out into the world, reckless and depraved, with callous hearts, irrevocably laid on the altars of Mammon? God help the women of America! Grant them the true womanly instincts which, in the dawn of our republic, made "home" the Eden, the acme of all human hopes and joys. Teach them that gilded saloons, with their accompanying allurements of French latitude in dress, and dancing, and the sans-souci manners and style of conversation, (which, in less degenerate times, would have branded with disgrace and infamy all who indulged it), teach them that all these tend to the depths of social evil; and oh, lead them back to the hearthstone, that holy-post, which too many, alas, have deserted! Eugene Graham's love and tenderness were all bestowed on his daughter, a beautiful child, not yet five years old; the sole companion of the hours spent at home, she became his idol.

It was one sunny afternoon that he finished copying some papers, necessary in a case to be defended the following day. The sunshine, stealing through the shutters, fell on his lofty brow, pale from continued study; his whole countenance bespoke a nature saddened, vexed, but resolute, and leaning forward, he touched the bell-rope. As he did so, there came quick footsteps pattering along the hall; the door was pushed open, and a little fairy form, with a head of rich auburn ringlets, peeped in cautiously, while a sweet, childish voice, asked eagerly:

"May I come now, father? Have you done writing? I won't make a noise; indeed I won't."

The gloom fled from his face, and he held out his arms to her, saying:

"I have done writing; you may come now, my darling."

She sprang into his lap, and threw her little, snowy arms about his neck, kissing him rapturously, and passing her fragile fingers through his hair. She resembled him closely, having the same classical contour, and large, soft, dark eyes. He returned her caresses with an expression of almost adoring fondness, stroking her curls with a light, gentle touch. The evening was warm and large drops stood on his forehead. She noticed it, and standing on his knee, took the corner of her tiny, embroidered apron, and wiped away the moisture, kissing the forehead as she did so. A servant looked in at the door.

"Did you ring, sir?"

"Yes; tell Philip I want my buggy."

"Oh, you are going to ride! Can I go? and will we go to see Aunt Beulah—will we?" She looked at him earnestly.

"Would you like to go there, Cornelia?"

"Oh, yes! I always like to go there. I love her, she is so good! Let's go to see her, won't you?"

"Yes, you shall go with me, my darling."

He bent down to kiss her coral lips, and just then Mrs. Graham swept into the room. She was attired in an elegant riding habit, of dark purple, while a velvet hat of the same color, with a long, drooping plume, shaded her face. Her hands were incased in delicate kid gauntlets, which fitted with perfect exactness. She was a beautiful woman, and the costume heightened her loveliness. She started slightly, on perceiving her husband, and said hastily:

"I thought you were at your office. Cornelia, what on earth have you done with my riding-whip? you mischievous little wretch! You lost it once before. Go find it. I am waiting for it. Go this instant!"

"I don't know where it is," returned the child, making no effort to leave her father's arms.

Eugene glanced up at his wife; his eyes wandered over her becoming and beautiful dress, then went back to the sunny face of his child.

An angry flush dyed Antoinette's cheeks, as she observed her daughter's indifference.

"Where is my whip, I say? Flora saw you with it yesterday, whipping that hobby-horse. I told you to keep your hands off of it, didn't I? If you don't go and find it quick, I'll box you soundly, you meddlesome little brat!"

"I haven't had it since you told me I shouldn't play with it. Flora tells a story," answered Cornelia, sobbing.

"You did have it!" cried the angry mother, shaking her hand threateningly.

"Did you see her with it?" asked Eugene, rising, with the child in his arms.

"I know she had it!"

"Did you see her with it, I asked you?"

"No, but Flora did, and that is all the same; besides, I—"

"Here is the whip, ma'am. I found it last week in the hall behind a chair, and put it in the cane stand. The last time you went to ride, you put it and your gloves on a chair in the hall, and went into the parlor to see some company. Flora picked up the gloves and carried them up-stairs, but didn't see the whip."

John, the dining-room servant handed her a small whip, with mother-of-pearl handle, inlaid with gold.

"It is no such thing!" cried Mrs. Graham, gathering up the folds of her habit, and coloring with vexation.

John shrugged his shoulders and retired, and his mistress sailed out to the front door, where her horse and her escort awaited her.

"Run and get your hat and cape, Cornelia; I see the buggy coming round the corner."

Eugene wiped away the tear-drops glittering on her rosy cheeks, and she sprang off to obey him; while in the interim, he sent for Flora, and gave her to understand that he would allow no repetition of the deception he had accidentally discovered. The maid retired, highly incensed, of course, and resolved to wreak vengeance on both John and Cornelia; and Eugene took his seat in the buggy in no particular amiable mood. They found Beulah in her little flower garden, pruning some luxuriant geraniums. She threw down her knife, and hastened to meet them, and all three sat down on the steps.

Four years had brought sorrow to that cottage home; had hushed the kind accents of the matron: stilled the true heart that throbbed so tenderly for her orphan charge, and had seen her laid to rest in a warm, grassy slope of the cemetery. She died peaceably three months before the day of which I write; died exhorting Eugene and Beulah so to pass the season of probation that they might be reunited beyond the grave. In life she had humbly exemplified the teachings of our Saviour, and her death was a triumphant attestation of the joy and hope which only the Christian religion can afford in the final hour.

To Beulah, this blow was peculiarly severe, and never had the sense of her orphanage been more painfully acute than when she returned from the funeral to her lonely home. But to sorrow her nature was inured; she had learned to bear grief, and only her mourning dress and subdued manner told how deeply she felt this trial. Now she took Cornelia in her arms and kissed her fondly, while the child returned her caresses with a warmth which proved how sincerely she loved her.

"May I have some flowers, auntie?" cried she, patting Beulah's pale cheek with her plump, dimpled hands.

"Yes, just as many as you can carry home. Go gather some."

She sprang off, and the two sat watching the flutter of her white dress among the flower-beds. She piled her little apron as full as possible, and came back panting and delighted. Beulah looked down at the beautiful beaming face, and twining one of the silky curls over her finger, said musingly:

"Eugene, she always reminds me of Lilly. Do you see the resemblance?"

"Not in her features; in size and gay heedlessness of manner, she is like Lilly, as I saw her last."

"Yes, Lilly's eyes were blue, and your child's are dark, like your own; but she never comes up and puts her arms round my neck, without recalling bygone years. I could shut my eyes, and fancy my lost darling was once more mine. Ah! how carefully memory gathers up the golden links of childhood, and weaves the chain that binds our hearts to the older time! Sometimes I think I am only dreaming, and shall wake to a happy reality. If I could have Lilly back, oh, what a sunshine it would shed over my heart and life! But this may not be; and I can only love Cornelia instead."

Her long, black lashes were weighed down, with unshed tears, and there was a touching sadness in her low voice. Cornelia stood by her side, busily engaged in dressing Beulah's hair with some of the roses and scarlet geranium she had gathered. She noticed the unusual melancholy written in the quiet face, and said impatiently:

"With all my flowers, you won't look gay! It must be this black dress. Don't wear such ugly, dark things: I wish you wouldn't. I want to see you look beautiful, like mother."

"Cornelia, go and break that cluster of yellow berries yonder," said her father; and when she had left them he turned to his companion and asked:

"Beulah, have you reflected on what I said the last time I saw you?"

"Yes, Eugene."

"With what result?"

"My former decision is only confirmed, the more I ponder the subject."

"You have seen nothing of Reginald, then? He was here, on some legal business, last week."

"No; he has been in the city several times during the last four years, but never comes here; and except that one letter, which I did not answer, I have heard nothing from him. I doubt whether we ever meet again."

"You are a strange woman! Such devotion as his would have won any other being. He is as much attached to you now as the day he first offered you his hand. Upon my word, your obstinacy provokes me. He is the noblest man I ever knew. Everything that I should suppose a woman of your nature would admire; and yet year after year you remain apparently as indifferent as ever."

"And it were a miserable return for such unmerited love to marry him merely from gratitude. I do admire him, but cannot marry him. I told him so four years ago."

"But why did you not at least answer his letter?"

"Because his acceptance was made the condition of an answer; a negative one was not expected, and I had no other to give."

"Pardon me, Beulah; but why do you not love him?"

"A strange question truly. My heart is not the tool of my will."

"Beulah, do you intend to spend your life solitary and joyless, cut off, as you are here, from society, and dependent on books and music for sympathy? Why will you not marry Reginald, and make his home happy?"

"Eugene, I have told you before that I could not accept him, and told you why. Let the subject drop; it is an unpleasant one to me. I am happier here than I could possibly be anywhere else. Think you I would marry merely for an elegant home and an intellectual companion? Never! I will live and die here in this little cottage, rather than quit it with such motives. You are mistaken in supposing that Mr. Lindsay is still attached to me. It has been nearly two years since he wrote that letter, and from Georgia I hear that the world believes he is soon to marry a lady residing somewhere near him. I think it more than probable the report is true, and hope most sincerely it may be so. Now, Eugene, don't mention the subject again, will you?"

"It is generally believed that he will be elected to Congress; next month will decide it. The chances are all in his favor," persisted Eugene.

"Yes; so I judged from the papers," said she, coolly, and then added: "And one day I hope to see you, or rather hear of you, in Washington by his side. I believe I shall be gratified; and oh, Eugene, what a proud moment it will be to me! How I shall rejoice in your merited eminence."

Her face kindled as she spoke, but the shadows deepened in his countenance, as he answered moodily:

"Perhaps I may; but fame and position cannot lighten a loaded heart, or kindle the sacred flame of love in a dreary home. When a man blindly wrecks his happiness on the threshold of life by a fatal marriage, no after exertion can atone or rectify the one mistake."

"Hush! she will hear you," said Beulah, pointing to the little girl, who was slowly approaching them.

A bitter smile parted his lips.

"She is my all; yet precious as she is to my sad heart, I would gladly lay her in her grave to-morrow, sooner than see her live to marry an uncongenial spirit, or know that her radiant face was clouded with sorrow, like mine. God grant that her father's wretched lot may warn her of the quicksands which nearly ingulfed him." He took the child in his arms, as if to shield her from some impending danger, and said, hurriedly:

"Are you ready to go home?"

"Is it so very late?"

"It is time we were going back, I think."

Beulah tied on the hat and cape, which had been thrown aside, and saw them ride away.

There, in the golden twilight, she mused on the changes time bore on its swift chariot. The gorgeous dreamings of her girlhood had faded like the summer clouds above her, to the somber hue of reality. From the hour when her father (a poor artist, toiling over canvas to feed his children) had, in dying accents, committed the two to God's care, she only remembered sorrow up to the time that Dr. Hartwell took her to his home. Her life there was the one bright oasis in her desert past. Then she left it a woman, and began the long struggle with poverty and trials over again. In addition, skepticism threw its icy shadow over her. She had toiled in the cavernous mines of metaphysics hopelessly; and finally returning to the holy religion of Jesus Christ, her weary spirit found rest. Ah, that rest which only the exhausted wanderer through the burning wastes of speculation can truly comprehend and appreciate. She had been ambitious, and labored to obtain distinction as a writer; and this, under various fictitious signatures, was hers. She still studied and wrote, but with another aim, now, than mere desire of literary fame; wrote to warn others of the snares in which she had so long been entangled, and to point young seekers after truth to the only sure fountain. She was very lonely, but not unhappy. Georgia and Helen were both happily married, and she saw them very rarely; but their parents were still her counsellors and friends. At Mrs. Williams' death, they had urged her to remove to their house, but she preferred remaining at the little cottage, at least until the expiration of the year. She still kept her place in the schoolroom; not now as assistant, but as principal in that department; and the increased salary rendered rigid economy and music lessons no longer necessary. Her intense love of beauty, whether found in nature or art, was a constant source of pleasure; books, music, painting, flowers, all contributed largely to her happiness. The grim puzzles of philosophy no longer perplexed her mind; sometimes they thrust themselves before her, threatening as the sphinx of old; but she knew that here they were insolvable; that at least her reason was no Œdipus, and a genuine philosophy induced her to put them aside; and anchoring her hopes of God and eternity in the religion of Christ, she drew from the beautiful world in which she lived much pure enjoyment. Once she had worshiped the universe; now she looked beyond the wonderful temple whose architecture, from its lowest foundations of rock to its starry dome of sky, proclaimed the God of revelation; and loving its beauty and grandeur, felt that it was but a home for a season, where the soul could be fitted for yet more perfect dwelling-places. Her face reflected the change which a calm reliance on God had wrought in her feelings. The restless, anxious expression had given place to quiet. The eyes had lost their strained, troubled look; the brow was unruffled, the face serene. Serene, reader, but not happy and sparkling as it might have been. All the shadows were not yet banished from her heart; there was one spectral form which thrust itself continually before her, and kept her cheek pale and rendered her lip at times unsteady. She had struggled bravely against this one remaining sorrow; but as time rolled on, its power and influence only increased. Even now, in this quiet hour, when a holy hush had fallen on all nature, and twilight wrapped its soft, purple veil around her, this haunting memory came to stir the depths of her heart. Charon walked slowly up the steps, and laying down at her feet, nestled his head against her. Then, fancy painted a dreary picture, which

"Seemed all dark and red—a tract of sand,—
And some one pacing there alone,
Who paced forever in a glimmering land,
Lit with a low, large moon."

It was the thought of a lonely man wandering without aim or goal in far-distant deserts; away from home and friends; joyless, hopeless—one who was dearer to her than all on earth beside; who had left her in anger, and upon whose loved face she might look no more. For three years no tidings had come of his wanderings; none knew his fate; and, perhaps, even then his proud head lay low beneath the palms of the Orient, or was pillowed on the coral crags of distant seas. This thought was one she was unable to endure; her features quivered, her hands grasped each other in a paroxysm of dread apprehension, and while a deep groan burst from her lips, she bowed her face on the head of his last charge, his parting gift. The consciousness of his unbelief tortured her. Even in eternity, they might meet no more; and this fear cost her hours of agony, such as no other trial had ever inflicted. From the moment of her return to the Bible and to prayer, this struggle began, and for three years she had knelt, morning and evening, and entreated Almighty God to shield and guide the wanderer; to scatter the mists of unbelief which shrouded his mind. Constantly her prayers went up, mingled with tears and sobs, and as weary months wore on, the petitions grew more impassioned. Her anxiety increased daily, and finally it became the one intense, absorbing wish of her heart to see her guardian again. His gloom, his bitterness, were all forgotten; she only remembered his unceasing care and kindness, his noble generosity, his brilliant smile, which was bestowed only on her. Pressing her face against Charon's head, she murmured pleadingly:

"O Father, protect him from suffering and death. Guide him safely home. Give me my guardian back. O Father, give me my wandering friend once more."

CHAPTER XXXVII.

"Fold that coat for me, my dear; there, give it to me, I believe there is room in this trunk for it."

Mrs. Asbury took one of her husband's coats from Beulah's hand and carefully packed it away.

"How long will you be absent, do you suppose?"

"Probably not longer than a month. The doctor thinks a few days at Saratoga will invigorate him. If you had consented to go, we had intended spending a week at Niagara. I am sorry you will not go, Beulah; you would enjoy the trip, and, moreover, the change would benefit you. Why do you so pertinaciously reject that legacy of Cornelia's. The money has been in my husband's hands for some years untouched, and Mr. Graham said, not long since, that you might just as well accept it, for he would never receive a cent of it in return. The original sum has been considerably augmented by judicious investments, and would place you above the necessity of labor, if you would accept it. Your refusal wounds Mr. Graham; he told me so last week. It was Cornelia's particular request that you should have that amount, and he is anxious to see you in possession of it. I told him of your suggestion, that he should add this legacy to the sum already given to the Asylum; but he vowed solemnly he would have nothing to do with it. If you chose to give it to the Asylum, you could do so of course, the money was yours; he never would touch a cent of it. Beulah, if you will not think me officious, I will say, candidly, that I think you ought to accept it. That is, use it, for the legacy has been left, whether you employ it or not."

Beulah looked grave and troubled, but made no reply.

Mrs. Asbury finished packing the trunk, locked it, and turning toward the door, said:

"I am going up-stairs to see about the furniture in that room which Georgia calls the 'Pitti Gallery.' Come with me, my dear."

She led the way, and Beulah followed, until they reached a large apartment in the third story, the door of which Mrs. Asbury unlocked. As they entered, Beulah started on seeing the statuary and paintings with which she was so familiar in former years; and in one corner of the room stood the melodeon, carefully covered. A quantity of tissue-paper lay on the floor and Mrs. Asbury began to cover the paintings by pinning the sheets together. Beulah took off her gloves and assisted; there was silence for some time, but on lifting a piece of drapery, Mrs. Asbury exposed the face of a portrait, which Beulah recognized from the peculiarity of the frame as the one that had hung over the mantel in her guardian's study. Paper and pins fell from her fingers, and drawing a deep breath, she gazed upon the face she had so long desired to see. She traced a slight resemblance to Antoinette in the faultless features; the countenance was surpassingly beautiful. It was a young, girlish face, sparkling with joyousness, bewitching in its wonderful loveliness. The eloquent eyes were strangely, almost wildly, brilliant, the full crimson lips possessed that rare outline one sees in old pictures, and the cheek, tinted like a sea-shell, rested on one delicate dimpled hand. Beulah looked and grew dizzy. This was his wife; this, the portrait he had kept shrouded so long and so carefully. How he must have worshiped that radiant young bride!

Mrs. Asbury noticed her emotion, and asked with some surprise:

"Did you never see this before?"

"No; it was always covered, and hung too high for me to lift the crape." Beulah's eyes were riveted on the canvas. Mrs. Asbury watched her a moment and said:

"It is an undetermined question in my mind whether beauty such as this is not a curse. In this instance assuredly it proved so, for it wrecked the happiness of both husband and wife. My dear child, do you know your guardian's history?"

"I know nothing of him, save that he is my best friend."

"When I first saw Guy Hartwell, he was one of the noblest men I ever met; commanding universal admiration and esteem. It was before his marriage. He was remarkably handsome, as you can readily imagine he must have been, and his manners possessed a singular fascination for all who came within the circle of his acquaintance. Even now, after the lapse of ten years, I remember his musical, ringing laugh; a laugh I have never heard since. His family were aristocratic and wealthy, and Guy was his mother's idol. She was a haughty, imperious woman, and her 'boy,' as she fondly termed him, was her pride. His only sister (Mrs. Chilton, or rather Mrs. Lockhart) was his senior, and he had a younger brother, Harry, who was extremely wild; ran away from home and spent most of his time at sea. Guy was naturally of a happy, genial temperament; fond of study; fond of art, flowers, poetry, everything that was noble and beautiful, that could minister to highly cultivated tastes. Mr. Chilton was unfortunate in his speculations; lost his fortune, and died soon after Pauline's birth, leaving his wife and child dependent on her mother and brother. May and the old lady often disagreed, and only Guy could harmonize their discords. During a visit to New Orleans, he accidentally met the original of this portrait; her family were almost destitute, but he aided them very liberally. She was very beautiful, and in an unlucky hour he determined to marry her. She was a mere child, and he placed her for a while at a school, where she enjoyed every educational advantage. He was completely fascinated; seemed to think only of Creola, and hastened the marriage. His mother and sister bitterly opposed the match, ridiculed his humble and portionless bride; but he persisted, and brought her here a beautiful, heedless girl. Guy built that house, and his mother and sister occupied one near him, which was burnt before you knew anything about them. Of course his wife went constantly into society, and before six months elapsed, poor Guy discovered that he had made a fatal mistake. She did not love him; had married him merely for the sake of an elegant home, and money to lavish as her childish whims dictated. Ah, Beulah! it makes my heart ache to think of the change this discovery wrought in Guy's nature. He was a proud man, naturally; but now he became repulsive, cold and austere. The revolution in his deportment and appearance was almost incredible. His wife was recklessly imprudent, and launched into the wildest excesses which society sanctioned. When he endeavored to restrain her, she rebelled, and without his knowledge carried on a flirtation with one whom she had known previous to her marriage. I believe she was innocent in her folly, and merely thoughtlessly fed her vanity with the adulation excited by her beauty. Poor child! she might have learned discretion, but unfortunately Mrs. Chilton had always detested her, and now watching her movements, she discovered Creola's clandestine meetings with the gentleman whom her husband had forbidden her to recognize as an acquaintance. Instead of exerting herself to rectify the difficulties in her brother's home, she apparently exulted in the possession of facts which allowed her to taunt him with his wife's imprudence and indifference. He denied the truth of her assertions; she dared him to watch her conduct, and obtained a note which enabled him to return home one day, at an unusually early hour, and meet the man he had denounced in his own parlor. Guy ordered him out of the house and without addressing his wife, rode back to see his patients; but that night he learned from her that before he ever met her, an engagement existed between herself and the man he so detested. He was poor, and her mother had persuaded her to marry Guy for his fortune. She seemed to grow frantic, cursed the hour of her marriage, professed sincere attachment to the other, and, I firmly believe, became insane from that moment. Then and there they parted. Creola returned to her mother, and died suddenly a few weeks after leaving her husband. They had been married but a year. I have always thought her mind diseased, and it was rumored that her mother died insane. Doubtless Guy's terrible rage drove her to desperation; though he certainly had cause to upbraid. I have often feared that he would meet the object of his hatred, and once, and only once afterward, that man came to the city. Why, I never knew, but my husband told me that he saw him at a concert here some years ago. Poor Guy! how he suffered; yet how silently he bore it; how completely he sheathed his heart of fire in icy vestments. He never alluded to the affair in the remotest manner; never saw her after that night. He was sitting in our library, waiting to see my husband, when he happened to open the letter announcing her death. I was the only person present, and noticed that a change passed over his countenance; I spoke to him, but he did not reply; I touched him, but he took no notice whatever, and sat for at least an hour without moving a muscle or uttering a word. Finally George came and spoke to him appealingly. He looked up and smiled. Oh, what a smile! May I never see such another; it will haunt me while I live! Without a word he folded the letter, replaced it in the envelope, and left us. Soon after his mother died, and he went immediately to Europe. He was absent two years, and came back so stern, so cynical, so unlike his former self, I scarcely knew him. Mrs. Chilton took charge of his house from the hour of his separation from Creola, but they were not congenial. He was vastly her superior, save in intellect, which none of the Hartwell family ever lacked. My husband is very much attached to Guy; thinks he has not an equal, yet mourns over the blight which fell upon him in the very morn of his glorious manhood. About a year after his return from Europe, he took you to his house as an adopted child. I wondered at it, for I knew how imbittered his whole soul had become. But the heart must have an idol; he was desolate and miserable, and took you home to have something to love and interest him. You never knew him in the prime of his being, for though comparatively young in years, he had grown prematurely old in feeling before you saw him. Poor Guy! may a merciful and loving God preserve him wherever he may be, and bring him to a knowledge of that religion which alone can comfort a nature like his; so noble, so gifted, yet so injured, so imbittered."

She brushed away the tears that stood on her cheeks, and looked sorrowfully at the portrait of the unfortunate young wife.

Beulah sat with her face partially averted, and her eyes shaded with her hand; once or twice her lips moved, and a shiver ran over her. She looked up and said abruptly:

"Leave the key of this room with me, will you? I should like to come here occasionally."

"Certainly, come as often as you choose; and here on this bunch is the key of the melodeon. Take it also; the instrument needs dusting, I dare say, for it has never been opened since Guy left, nearly five years ago. There, the clock struck two, and the boat leaves at four; there, too, is my husband's step. Come, my dear, we must go down. Take these keys until I return."

She gave them to her, and they descended to the dining-room, where the doctor awaited them.

"Beulah, what are you going to do with yourself next year? You must not think of living in that cottage alone. Since Mrs. Williams' death, you should abandon the thought of keeping house. It will not do, child, for you to live there by yourself." So said the doctor a short time before he bade her adieu.

"I don't know yet what I shall do. I am puzzled about a home."

"You need not be; come and live in my house, as I begged you to do long ago. Alice and I will be heartily glad to have you. Child, why should you hesitate?"

"I prefer a home of my own, if circumstances permitted it. You and Mrs. Asbury have been very kind in tendering me a home in your house, and I do most sincerely thank you both for your friendly interest, but I—"

"Oh, Beulah, I should be so very glad to have you always with me. My dear child, come."

Mrs. Asbury passed her arm affectionately around the girl's waist. Beulah looked at her with trembling lips and said hastily:

"Will you take me as a boarder?"

"I would rather take you as a friend—as a daughter."

"Not a bit of it Alice. She shall pay the highest possible board. Don't imagine, Miss Independence, that I expected for a moment to offer you a home gratis. Pay board? That you shall; always in advance, and candles, and fires, and the use of my library, and the benefit of my explanations, and conversation charged as 'extras,'" cried the doctor, shaking his fist at her.

"Then, sir, I engage rooms."

"Will you really come, my child?" asked Mrs. Asbury, kissing the orphan's pale cheek tenderly.

"Gladly, as a boarder, and very grateful for such a privilege."

"Beulah, on reflection, I think I can possibly take Charon for half price; though I must confess to numerous qualms of conscience at the bare suggestion of receiving such an 'infernal' character into my household."

"Thank you," said she, and saw them depart for Saratoga whither Georgia and Helen had preceded them. Several weeks elapsed without her receiving any tidings, and then a letter came giving her information of a severe illness which had attacked the doctor immediately after his arrival in New York. He was convalescing rapidly when his wife wrote, and in proof thereof, subjoined a postscript, in his scrawling hand and wonted bantering style. Beulah laughed over it, refolded the letter, and went into her little garden to gather a bouquet for one of her pupils who had recently been quite sick. She wore a white muslin apron over her black dress, and soon filled it with verbena, roses and geranium sprigs. Sitting down on the steps, she began to arrange them, and soon became absorbed in her occupation. Presently a shadow fell on the step; she glanced up, and the flowers dropped from her fingers, while an exclamation of surprise escaped her.

Mr. Lindsay held out his hand.

"After four years of absence, of separation, have you no word of welcome?"

She gave him both hands, and said, eagerly:

"Oh, yes, I am very glad to see you again; very glad that I have an opportunity of congratulating you on your signal success. I am heartily glad my friend is soon to enter Congressional halls. Accept my most sincere congratulations on your election."

A sudden flush rose to his temples, and clasping her hands tightly, he exclaimed, passionately:

"Oh, Beulah, your congratulations mock me. I come to offer you, once more, my hand, my heart, my honors, if I have any. I have waited patiently: no, not patiently, but still I have waited, for some token of remembrance from you, and could bear my suspense no longer. Will you share the position which has been accorded me recently? Will you give me this hand which I desire more intensely than the united honors of the universe beside? Beulah, has my devoted love won me your affection? Will you go with me to Washington?"

"I cannot; I cannot."

"Cannot? Oh, Beulah, I would make you a happy wife, if it cost me my life!"

"No. I could not be happy as your wife. It is utterly impossible. Mr. Lindsay, I told you long ago you could never be more than a friend."

"And have years wrought no change in your heart?"

"Years have strengthened my esteem, my sincere friendship; but more than this, all time cannot accomplish."

"Your heart is tenacious of its idol," he answered, moodily.

"It rebels, sir, now as formerly, at the thought of linking my destiny with that of one whom I never loved." Beulah spoke rapidly, her cheeks burned, and her eyes sparkled with displeasure.

He looked at her and sighed deeply, then threw down a letter saying:

"Ah, Beulah, I understood long ago why you could not love me; but I hoped years of absence would obliterate the memory that prevented my winning you. I made unusual exertions to discover some trace of your wandering guardian; have written constantly to my former banker in Paris to find some clue to his whereabouts. Through him I learn that your friend was last heard of at Canton, and the supposition is that he is no longer living. I do not wish to pain you, Beulah; but I would fain show you how frail a hope you cling to. Believe me, dear Beulah, I am not so selfish as to rejoice at his prolonged absence. No, no. Love, such as mine, prizes the happiness of its object above all other things. Were it in my power, I would restore him to you this moment. I had hoped you would learn to love me, but I erred in judging your nature. Henceforth, I will cast off this hope, and school myself to regard you as my friend only. I have, at least, deserved your friendship."

"And it is inalienably yours," cried she, very earnestly.

"In future, when toiling to discharge my duties, I may believe I have one sincere friend, who will rejoice at my success?"

"Of this you may well rest assured. It seems a poor return, Mr. Lindsay, for all you have tendered me; but it is the most I can give, the most an honest heart will allow me to offer. Truly, you may always claim my friendship and esteem, if it has any worth."

"I prize it far more than your hand, unaccompanied by your heart.

Henceforth, we will speak of the past no more; only let me be the friend an orphan may require. You are to live in my uncle's house, I believe; I am very glad you have decided to do so; this is not a proper home for you now. How do you contrive to exorcise loneliness?"

"I do not always succeed very well. My flowers are a great resource; I don't know how I should live without them. My books, too, serve to occupy my attention." She was making a great effort to seem cheerful, but he saw that her smile was forced; and with an assurance that he would see her again before he went to Washington, he shooks hands cordially, and left her. She tied her bouquet, and dispatched it to the sick child, with a few lines of kind remembrance; then took the letter, which Mr. Lindsay had thrown on the steps, and opened it, with trembling fingers:

"MR. R. LINDSAY,

"DEAR SIR: Yours of the 3d came to hand yesterday. As I wrote you before, I accidentally learned that Dr. Hartwell had been in Canton; but since that, have heard nothing from him, and have been unable to trace him further. Letters from Calcutta state that he left that city, more than a year since, for China. Should I obtain any news of him, rest assured it shall be immediately transmitted to you.

"Very respectfully,
"R.A. FIELDS."

She crumpled the sheet, and threw it from her; and if ever earnest, heart-spoken prayer availed, her sobbing cry to the God of travelers insured his safety.

CHAPTER XXXVIII.

One day there came a letter, postmarked from an inland town, where Beulah had no correspondent. The direction, however, was instantly recognized, and she broke the seal, hurriedly:

"What has become of you, Beulah? and what can have become of my two letters which were never answered? Concluding you never received them, I hazard a third attempt to reach you through the medium of letters. You will readily perceive that we have removed to a distant section of the State. Ernest was called to take charge of this parish, and we are delightfully located here, within a few minutes' walk of the church. Beulah, the storm which darkened over me, in the first year of my marriage, has swept by, and it is all sunshine, glorious sunshine, with me. You know my home was very unhappy for a time. My husband's family caused misunderstandings between us, influenced him against me, and made me very, very wretched. I could not tolerate Lucy's presence, with any degree of patience, yet she would remain in our house. How it would have ended only Heaven knows, had not my husband been suddenly taken very ill. It was on Sabbath morning. He was displeased with me, because of some of my disputes with his sister, and scarcely spoke to me before he went into the pulpit. Lucy and I sat together in the rector's pew, hating each other cordially; and when Ernest began the morning service, I noticed he looked pale and weary. Before it was concluded, he sank back exhausted, and was borne into the vestry-room, covered with blood. He had a severe hemorrhage from the throat, the physician said, but Ernest thinks it was from his lungs. I was sure he would die; and oh,

Beulah, what agony I endured as I sat beside him, and watched his ghastly face! But his illness was 'the blessing in disguise;' he forgot all our disgraceful bickerings, and was never satisfied unless I was with him. Lucy grumbled, and sneered, and looked sour; but I had my husband's heart again, and determined to keep it. As soon as he was strong enough, I told him how wretched I had been, and how sincerely I desired to make him happy, if Lucy would only not interfere. He saw that our domestic peace was dependent upon the change, and from that hour his sister ceased meddling with my affairs. What he said to her I never knew; but soon after his recovery, she returned to her parents, and I was left in peace. I began, in sober earnest, to be all my husband wished me; and read the books he liked (though it was a terrible bore at first); read to him; took part in all the societies connected with his church; and, in short, became quite a demure pastor's wife. Occasionally, my old fondness for fun would break out, to the horror of some of his antediluvian flock; but Ernest was very good, and bore patiently with me, and now I am as prim and precise as an old maid of sixty. At home I do as I like, that is, when Ernest likes it too. I sing, and play, and romp with the dogs and kittens; but the moment the door bell rings, lo, a demure matron receives her guests! Ernest's health is quite restored, and I am as happy as the day is long. You should see me working in my garden, and sometimes churning before breakfast, to give Ernest a fresh glass of buttermilk. I would not change places with an empress, I am so happy. My husband loves me better than everything else beside, and what more could I desire? Do come and see me; we would be so delighted to have you spend some time in our home. I am such a genuine rustic, you would scarcely recognize me. Just fancy me with an apron on, my sleeves rolled up, churning as fast as the dasher can fly, and singing at the top of my voice. Mother was perfectly shocked, when she first came to live with me, and vowed I should not make a 'drudge' of myself. Drudge, indeed, because I chose to do something, with my own hands, for my husband! I told her I would 'drudge,' as she called it, just as long as Ernest loved such things as I could prepare for him myself; and I read her those famous remarks of Lady Mary Montagu, in which all domestic pursuits, even cooking, is dignified as a labor of love; whereupon Ernest gave me a kiss, and mother declined any further argumentation on the subject. How some of my fashionable city friends would elevate their fastidious noses at seeing me, with my check aprons, picking strawberries, or arranging curds for tea!

Come and see me; do, Beulah; I am the very happiest woman extant, that is, I would be, if I could only know something of Uncle Guy. It is almost five years since he left home, and for a long, long time we have heard nothing from him. This is the only sorrow I have. Sometimes I fear he must have died in some distant land, yet will not believe it. I want to see him very much; my heart aches when I think about him. Dear Uncle Guy! next to my husband, I believe I love him best. Can't you tell me something of him? or do you know as little as his relatives? Ernest says he will walk into our house some day, without any intimation of his coming. Oh, I hope so! I endeavor to believe so! Do write to me. I often think of you, in your loneliness, and wish you were as happy as your friend,

"PAULINE."

Beulah laid the letter beside one received the previous day from Clara, and mused for some moments. They were both happily married, and she sincerely rejoiced over their fortunate lots, but Clara had once loved her guardian; how could she possibly forget him so entirely? Was love a mere whim of the hour, fostered by fortuitously favorable circumstances, but chilled and vanquished by absence, or obstacles? Could the heart demolish the idol it had once enshrined, and set up another image for worship? Was Time the conquering iconoclast? Why, then, did she suffer more acutely as each year rolled on? She had little leisure, however, for these reflections; the Asburys had returned, and the cottage had been rented by a family, who were anxious to take possession immediately. Such articles of furniture as were no longer needed had been sent to an auction-room, and she sat down in the empty dining-room, to see the last load removed. To-day she bade adieu to the cottage, and commenced boarding once more. Her heart was heavy, but her eyes were undimmed, and her grave, composed face, betokened little of the sorrow which oppressed her. Here she had spent five years in peaceful seclusion; here she had toiled and earned reputation as a writer; and here many hours of happiness had been passed among her flowers. The place was very dear to her; it was the only spot on the face of the wide world she had ever felt was her home. Home! if it consists of but a sanded floor, and unplastered walls, what a halo is shed upon its humble hearth! A palatial mansion, or sequestered cottage among wild forests, were alike sanctified by the name. Home! the heart's home! who shall compute its value? But Beulah must relinquish her retreat and find refuge in the home of others. Would this content her? Was she to be always homeless? True, she was to reside with loved and tried friends, yet she would be a homeless orphan still, without claims upon one living being. The grave had closed over the kind matron who had so warmly loved her, and she was without ties in the world. These thoughts passed through her mind, as she saw the last chair deposited on a furniture cart, and borne away. Charon looked up at her mournfully, as if to ask:

"Are we homeless? Where shall we wander?" She stroked his head, and went into the flower garden to gather a last bouquet from plants she had so carefully tended. An early frost had nipped the buds, but the chrysanthemums were in all their glory—crimson, white and orange. She broke some of the beautiful clusters, and with a long, lingering look, turned away. The black mourning veil was thrown back from a pale, calm face; and as she walked on, reflecting upon the future, which stretched dimly before her, she exclaimed:

"Why should I wish it otherwise? The arms of a merciful God will shield me, under all circumstances. My life was not given for a mere holiday. So I but do my duty faithfully, all will be well. Ah, truly, I can say:

"'Let *me,* then, be up and doing,
With a heart for any fate;
Still achieving, still pursuing,
Learn to labor, and to wait!'

Yes, learn to labor and to wait. The heart cries out fiercely for its recompense; is loth to wait. But I can conquer even this. I will be patient and hopeful. Duty is its own recompense."

Mrs. Asbury spared no exertion to make the orphan happy in her house. She treated her with the gentle frankness which characterized her deportment toward her daughters; and to identify her with her own family, often requested her to assist in her household plans. She thoroughly understood and appreciated Beulah's nature, and perfect confidence existed between them. It was no sooner known that Beulah was an inmate of the house, than many persons, curious to see one of whom rumor spoke so flatteringly, availed themselves of the circumstance to make her acquaintance. Almost unconsciously, she soon found herself the center of a circle of literary people, whom she had often heard of, but had never known previously. Gradually, her reserve melted away, and her fine colloquial powers developed themselves; but she wearied of the visitors—wearied even of the themes discussed, and having passed her life in seclusion, found in solitude a degree of enjoyment which society could not confer. Helen had married a planter, and resided at some distance from the city, but Georgia and her husband remained at home. Thus, imperceptibly, time wore on. Eugene often came and spent an hour with Beulah; and still more frequently, Cornelia was sent to while away an evening with her merry prattle. Very steadily, Eugene advanced in his profession; the applause of the world cheered him on, and an enviable reputation was his at last. Grasping ambition lured him, step by step; and it was evident that he aimed at a seat beside Reginald Lindsay. Rejoiced at his entire reformation, and proud of his success, Beulah constantly encouraged his aspirations. Antoinette was as gay and indifferent as ever, and Eugene divided his heart between his child and his ambition.

By a system of rigid economy in the disposal of her time, Beulah not only attended to her school duties, her music, and her books, but found leisure, after writing her magazine articles, to spend some time each day with the family under whose roof she resided. Dr. Asbury's health was rather feeble, and of late his eyes had grown so dim as to prevent his reading or writing. This misfortune was to a great extent counterbalanced by his wife's devoted attention, and often Beulah shared the duties of the library. One bright Sunday afternoon, she walked out to the cemetery, which she visited frequently. In one corner of a small lot, inclosed by a costly iron railing, stood a beautiful marble monument, erected by Mr. Grayson over Lilly's grave. It represented two angels bearing the child up to its God. Just opposite, in the next lot, was a splendid mausoleum of the finest white marble, bearing in gilt letters the name "CORNELIA GRAHAM, aged twenty-three." It was in the form of a temple, with slender fluted columns supporting the portico; and on the ornate capitals was inscribed in corresponding gilt characters, "*Silentio! Silentio!*" At the entrance stood two winged forms, crowned with wreaths of poppies; and a pair of beautiful vases held withered flowers. Beulah sat on the marble steps. Before her stretched aisles of tombstones; the sunshine sparkled on their polished surfaces, and was reflected as from countless mirrors. Myrtle and laurel trees waved gently in the icy north wind, and stately, solemn cedars kept guard in every inclosure. All was silent and still, save those funeral evergreen boughs, which stirred softly as if fearful of disturbing the pale sleepers around them. Human nature shrinks appalled from death and all that accompanies it; but in the deep repose, the sacred hush, which reigned over the silent city, there was for Beulah something inexpressibly soothing. In a neighboring lot she could see a simple white slab Eugene had erected over the remains of the friend of their childhood. Her labors ended, the matron slept near the forms of Lilly and Cornelia. Here winter rains fell unheeded, and here the balmy breath of summer brought bright blossoms and luxuriant verdure. Mocking-birds sang cheerfully in the sentinel cedars, and friends wandered slowly over the shelled walks, recalling the past. Here there was no gloom to affright the timid soul; all was serene and inviting. Why should the living shrink from a resting-place so hallowed and peaceful? And why should death be invested with fictitious horrors? A procession entered one of the gates, and wound along the carriage-road to a remote corner of the burying-ground. The slow, measured tread of the horses, the crush of wheels on the rocky track, and the smothered sobs of the mourners, all came in subdued tones to Beulah's ears. Then the train disappeared, and she was again in solitude. Looking up, her eyes rested on the words above her: "Silentio! silentio!" They were appropriate, indeed, upon the monument of her who had gone down into the tomb so hopelessly, so shudderingly. Years had passed since the only child had been laid here; yet the hour of release was as fresh in Beulah's memory as though she had seen the convulsed features but yesterday; and the words repeated that night seemed now to issue from the marble lips of the statues beside her: "For here we have no continuing city, but seek one to come." With her cheek on her hand, the orphan sat pondering the awful mystery which darkened the last hour of the young sleeper; and looking back over her own life, during the season when she "was without God and without hope," she saw that only unbelief had clothed death with terror. Once she stood on this same spot, and with trembling horror saw the coffin lowered. Had death touched her then, she would have shrunk appalled from the summons, but now it was otherwise.

"I am the resurrection and the life, saith the Lord; he that believeth in me, though he were dead, yet shall he live; and whosoever liveth and believeth in me, shall never die."

She believed; and while a beautiful world linked her to life, and duty called to constant and cheerful labor, death lost its hideous aspect. With a firm faith in the Gospel of Christ, she felt that earth with all its loveliness was but a probationary dwelling-place; and that death was an angel of God, summoning the laborers to their harvest-home. She had often asked what is the aim and end of life? One set of philosophers told her it was to be happy. Another exclaimed it was to learn to endure with fortitude all ills. But neither satisfied her; one promised too much, the other too little, and only in revelation was an answer found. Yet how few pause to ponder its significance.

With the majority, life is the all: the springtime, the holiday; and death the hated close of enjoyment. They forget that:

> "Not enjoyment, and not sorrow,
> Is our destined end or way;
> But to act, that each to-morrow,
> Find us further than to-day."

The path of Christianity is neither all sunshine nor all shadow, checkered certainly, but leading to a final abode of unimaginable bliss, and with the Bible to guide her, the orphan walked fearlessly on, discharging her duties, and looking unto God and his Christ to aid her. She sat on the steps of the sepulchre, watching the last rays of the setting sun gild the monumental shafts that pointed to heaven. Her grave face might have told the scrutinizing observer of years of grief and struggle; but it also betokened an earnest soul calmly trusting the wisdom and mercy of the All-Father. She sighed as she thought of the gifted but unhappy woman who slept near her, and rising, walked on to Lilly's tomb. Ten years had rolled their waves over her since that little form was placed here. She looked down at the simple epitaph: "He taketh his young lambs home." The cherub face seemed to beam upon her once more, and the sweet, birdlike tones of her childish voice still lingered in the secret cells of memory. She extended her arms, as if to clasp the form borne up by the angels, and said tremulously:

"Lilly, my sister, my white-robed darling, but a little while, and we shall meet where orphanage is unknown! 'He doeth all things well!' Ah, little sleeper, I can wait patiently for our reunion."

As she turned her steps homeward, a shadowy smile stole over her features, and the lines about her mouth resumed their wonted composure.

"Beulah, father has been asking for you," said Georgia, who met her on the staircase.

"I will go down to him immediately," was the cheerful answer, and putting away her bonnet and shawl, she went at once to the library. The doctor was leaning very far back in his favorite chair, and she saw at a glance he had fallen asleep.

Mrs. Asbury sat at a table, weighing out some medicine he had directed sent to a patient. She looked up as Beulah entered, smiled, and said in an undertone:

"My liege lord is indulging in a nap. Come to the fire, dear, you look cold."

She left the room with the medicine, and Beulah stood before the bright wood fire, and watched the ruddy light flashing grotesquely over the pictures on the wall. The gas had not yet been lighted; she crossed the room, and sat down before the window. A red glow still lingered in the west, and one by one, the stars came swiftly out. She took up a book she had been reading that morning, but it was too dim to see the letters, and she contented herself with looking out at the stars, brightening as the night deepened. "So should it be with faith," thought she, "and yet, as troubles come thick and fast, we are apt to despair." Mrs. Asbury came back and lighted the gas, but Beulah was too much absorbed to notice it. The doctor waked, and began to talk about the severity of the winter further north, and the suffering it produced among the poor. Presently he said:

"What has become of that child, Beulah—do you know, Alice?"

"Yes; there she is by the window. You were asleep when she came in."

He looked round and called to her.

"What are you thinking about, Beulah? You look as cold as an iceberg. Come to the fire. Warm hands and feet will aid your philosophizing wonderfully."

"I am not philosophizing, sir," she replied, without rising.

"I will wager my elegant new edition of Coleridge against your old one, that you are! Now, out with your cogitations, you incorrigible dreamer!"

"I have won your Coleridge. I was only thinking of that Talmudish tradition regarding Sandalphon, the angel of prayer."

"What of him?"

"Why, that he stands at the gate of heaven, listens to the sounds that ascend from earth, and gathering all the prayers and entreaties, as they are wafted from sorrowing humanity, they change to flowers in his hands, and the perfume is borne into the celestial city to God. Yesterday I read Longfellow's lines on this legend, and suppose my looking up at the stars recalled it to my mind. But Georgia told me you asked for me. Can I do anything for you, sir? Are there any prescriptions you wish written off?" She came and stood by his chair.

"No, thank you, child; but I should like to hear more of that book you were reading to me last night—that is, if it will not weary you, my child."

"Certainly not—here it is. I was waiting for you to ask me for more of it. Shall I begin now, or defer it till after tea?"

"Now, if you please."

Mrs. Asbury seated herself on an ottoman at her husband's feet, and threw her arm up over his knee; and opening "Butler's Analogy," Beulah began to read where she left off the previous day, in the chapter on "a future life."

With his hand resting on his wife's head, Dr. Asbury listened attentively. At the conclusion of the chapter, she turned to the dissertation on "personal identity," so nearly related to it, and read it slowly and impressively.

"It is remarkably clear and convincing," said the doctor, when she ceased.

"Yes; his argument, that death, instead of being an abnormal event, is as much a law of our nature as birth (because necessary to future development), and that as at maturity, we have perfections, of which we never dreamed in infancy, so death may put us in possession of new powers, by releasing us from the chrysalis state, is one which has peculiar significance to my mind. Had Cornelia Graham studied it, she would never have been tortured by the thought of that annihilation which she fancied awaited her. From childhood, this question of 'personal identity' has puzzled me; but it seems to me, this brief treatise of Butler is quite satisfactory. It should be a text book in all educational institutions; should be scattered far and wide through the land."

Here the solemn tones of the church bells told that the hour of evening service drew near. The doctor started, and said, abruptly:

"Bless me! Alice, are we to have no tea to-night?"

"Yes, the tea-bell rang some minutes ago, but Beulah had not quite finished her chapter, and I would not interrupt."

As they walked on to the dining-room, he said:

"You two are going to church, I suppose?"

"No, I shall remain with you," answered his wife, gently.

"You need not, my dear. I will go with you if you prefer it."

Beulah did not look up, but she knew that true-hearted wife was unspeakably happy; and understood why, during tea, she was so quiet, so unwontedly silent.

CHAPTER XXXIX.

"I wish Hartwell would come home, and attend to his business," muttered Dr. Asbury, some weeks later; and as he spoke, he drew his feet impatiently over the fender of the grate, looking discontented enough.

"He will come, sir; he will come," answered Beulah, who sat near him.

"How do you know that so well, child? Why do you suppose he will come?" asked the doctor, knitting his bushy gray eyebrows.

"Perhaps, because I wish it so very much; and hope and faith are nearly allied, you know; and perhaps more than this—because I have prayed so long for his return."

She sat with her hands folded, looking quietly into the glowing grate. The old man watched her a moment, as the firelight glared over her grave, composed face, and tears came suddenly into his eyes.

"When Harry Hartwell died (about eighteen months since) he left his share of the estate to Guy. It is one of the finest plantations in the State, and for the last three years the crops have been remarkably good. The cotton has been sold regularly, and the bulk of the money is still in the hands of the factor. Yesterday I happened to pass the old house, and rode in to see how things looked; positively, child, you would scarcely recognize the place. You know the Farleys only occupied it a few months; since that time it has been rented. Just now it is vacant, and such a deserted looking tenement I have not seen for many days. As far as I am concerned—"

Here a servant entered to inform the doctor that he was wanted immediately to see one of his patients. He kicked off his slippers, and got up, grumbling:

"A plague on Guy's peregrinating proclivities. I am getting too old to jump up every three seconds to keep somebody's baby from jerking itself into a spasm or suffocating with the croup. Hartwell ought to be here to take all this practice off my hands."

He put on his overcoat, and went out.

Beulah sat quite still for some minutes after his departure; then glancing at the clock, she started up suddenly.

"Where are you going, my dear?" said Mrs. Asbury, looking up from a letter she was writing to Helen.

"To walk."

"But Mr. Leonard is coming here this afternoon to see you; he requested me to tell you so."

"I don't want to see him."

"But, my dear, he has already called several times recently without seeing you."

"And if he had any penetration he might perceive that the avoidance was intended. I am tired of his frequent visits and endless harangues, and he might see it if he chose." She looked rather impatient.

Mrs. Asbury had sealed her letter, and approaching the rug where Beulah stood, she laid her soft hand on her shoulder, and said gently:

"My dear child, do not think me officious, or prompted by mere idle curiosity, if I ask, do you intend to reject him?"

"Why, ma'am, I have rejected him once, and still he forces his society upon me. As to staying at home to see him, I won't do it."

Mrs. Asbury seemed surprised, and said smilingly:

"Upon my word, Beulah, you seem fastidious, indeed. What possible objection could you find to Hugh Leonard? Why, my dear, he is the best match in the city."

"I would about as soon think of marrying the doctor's arm-chair, there."

Beulah went to her own room, and put on her bonnet and cloak. Charon very rarely attended her in her rambles; he had grown old, and was easily fatigued, but this afternoon she called to him, and they set out. It was a mild, sunny evening for winter, and she took the street leading to her guardian's old residence. A quick walk soon brought her into the suburbs, and ere long she stood before the entrance. The great central gate was chained, but the little side gate was completely broken from its hinges, and lay on the ground. Alas! this was but the beginning; as she entered, she saw, with dismay, that the yard was full of stray cattle. Cows, sheep, goats, browsed about undisturbed among the shrubbery, which her guardian had tended so carefully. She had not been here since he sold it, but even Charon saw that something was strangely amiss. He bounded off, and soon cleared the inclosure of the herd, which had become accustomed to grazing here. Beulah walked slowly up the avenue; the aged cedars whispered hoarsely above her as she passed, and the towering poplars, whose ceaseless silvery rustle had an indescribable charm for her in summers past, now tossed their bare boughs toward her in mute complaining of the desolation which surrounded them. The reckless indifference of tenants has deservedly grown into a proverb, and here Beulah beheld an exemplification of its truth. Of all the choice shrubbery which it had been the labor of years to collect and foster, not a particle remained. Roses, creepers, bulbs—all were destroyed, and only the trees and hedges were spared. The very outline of the beds was effaced in many places, and walking round the paved circle in front of the door, she paused abruptly at the desolation which greeted her. Here was the marble basin of the fountain half filled with rubbish, as though it had been converted into a receptacle for trash, and over the whole front of the house the dark glossy leaves of the creeping ivy clung in thick masses. She looked around on all sides, but only ruin and neglect confronted her. She remembered the last time she came here and recalled the beautiful Sunday morning when she saw her guardian standing by the fountain feeding his pigeons. Ah, how sadly changed! She burst into tears, and sat down on the steps. Charon ran about the yard for some time; then came back, looked up at the somber house, howled, and laid down at her feet. Where was the old master? Wandering among eastern pagodas, while his home became a retreat for owls.

"He has forgotten us, Charon! He has forgotten his two best friends—you and I—who love him so well! Oh Charon, he has forgotten us!" cried she, almost despairingly. Charon gave a melancholy groan of assent, and nestled closer to her. Five years had gone since he left his native land, and for once her faith was faint and wavering. But after some moments she looked up at the calm sky arching above her, and wiping away her tears, added, resignedly:

"But he will come! God will bring him home when he sees fit! I can wait! I can wait!"

Charon's great, gleaming black eyes met hers wistfully; he seemed dubious of his master's return. Beulah rose, and he obeyed the signal.

"Come, Charon, it is getting late; but we will come back some day, and live here."

It was dusk when she entered the library, and found Mrs. Asbury discussing the political questions of the day with her husband. She had just finished reading aloud one of Reginald's Congressional speeches, and advocated it warmly, while the doctor reprobated some portion of his course.

"You have had a long walk," said Mrs. Asbury, looking up as the orphan entered.

"And look, for the universe, as if you had been ghost-seeing," cried the doctor, wiping his spectacles.

"I would rather meet an army of ghosts than see what I have seen!" answered Beulah.

"Good heavens! In the name of wonder, what have you seen, child? A rattle-snake, or a screech-owl?"

He put his broad palms on his knees, and looked mockingly curious and startled.

"I have been out to see the old place, sir; found the gate broken down, the front yard full of cows, and everything going to destruction, except the trees and hedges. Sir, it makes me feel very sad. I can't bear to have things go on this way any longer. It must be rectified."

"Bless my soul, that is easier said than done! The place is a perfect owl-roost, there is no denying that; but it is no business of ours. If Farley, or his agent, suffers the property to go to ruin, it is his loss."

"But I love the place. I want to save it. Won't you buy it, Dr. Asbury?"

"Won't I buy it? Why, what on earth do you suppose I should do with it? I don't want to live in it; and as for any more investments in real estate, why just excuse me if you please! Insurance and repairs eat up all the profits, and I am plagued to death with petitions in the bargain."

"Then I must buy it myself!" said Beulah, resolutely.

"In the name of common sense, what will you do with it?"

"I don't know yet; keep it, I suppose, until he comes home again. How much do you suppose the Farleys ask for it?"

"I really cannot conjecture. But, child, you must not think of this. I will see the agent about it, and perhaps I may purchase it, to oblige you. I will not hear of your buying it. Guy certainly cannot contemplate heathenating much longer. There is that eternal door-bell again! Somebody that believes I am constructed of wire and guttapercha, I dare say."

He leaned back and watched the door very uneasily. A servant looked in.

"Mr. Leonard, to see Miss Beulah."

"Thank heaven it is nobody to see me!" The doctor settled himself comfortably, and laughed at the perturbed expression of Beulah's countenance.

"Ask him to excuse me this evening," said she, without rising.

"Nay, my dear; he was here this afternoon, and you had gone to walk. It would be rude not to see him. Go into the parlor; do, my dear; perhaps he will not detain you long," remonstrated Mrs. Asbury.

Beulah said nothing; she set her lips firmly, rose, and went to the parlor.

"I will wager my head he won't stay fifteen minutes after he gets a glimpse of her face. Hugh ought to have sense enough to see that she does not fancy him," said the doctor, laughing.

"I should very much like to see the man she would fancy," answered his wife, knitting away busily on a purse for some sewing society.

"Oh, Alice! do you wonder she does not like Hugh Leonard? He is a 'catch,' as far as position and money and a certain sort of talent, and is very clever and upright, I know; but he does not suit Beulah. If she would not marry Reginald, of course she won't marry Hugh."

"Jangle," went the door-bell once more, and this time the doctor was forced to leave his chair and slippers.

The winter had been very gay, and without doubt the belle of the season was Claudia Grayson. She had grown up a brilliant, imperious beauty. Petted most injudiciously by Mr. and Mrs. Grayson, the best elements of her character, instead of being fostered and developed, were smothered beneath vanity and arrogance; and soon selfishness became the dominant characteristic. To those whom she considered her inferiors, she was supercilious and overbearing; while, even in her adopted home, she tyrannized over both servants and parents. Flattered and sought after in society, she was never happy unless the center of a gay circle. Ere long she discovered the heartlessness of her admirers; learned the malice and envy of the very people she visited most intimately; and once acquainted with their natures and habits, she found her greatest amusement in ridiculing those who did precisely the same thing the moment she left them. Beulah had never been able to conquer her feelings sufficiently to enter Mrs. Grayson's house; but she had met Claudia several times. The latter, when accompanied by any of her fashionable acquaintances, always shrank from recognizing her; and finally, thinking any allusion to former years and the Asylum a personal insult, she passed her without even a bow. The first time this occurred, Beulah was deeply wounded; she had loved Claudia very warmly, and her superciliousness was hard to bear. But the slight was repeated several times, and she learned to pity her weakness most sincerely.

"Ah!" thought she, "how much better it was that Lilly should die than live to grow up a heartless flirt, like Claudy! Much better, little sister! Much better!"

It was the morning after her walk to the old home of her guardian that Dr. Asbury threw down the paper on the breakfast-table, with an exclamation of horror.

"What is the matter, George?" cried his wife, while Beulah grew deadly pale, and clutched the paper; her mind, like "Hinda's"—

"Still singling *one* from all mankind."

"Matter! Why poor Grayson has committed suicide—shot himself last night, poor wretch! He has been speculating too freely, and lost every cent; and, worse than that, used money to do it that was not his. He made desperate throws and lost all; and the end of it was, that when his operations were discovered, he shot himself, leaving his family utterly destitute. I heard yesterday that they would not have a cent; but never dreamed of his being so weak as to kill himself. Miserable mistake!"

"What will become of Mrs. Grayson and Claudia?" asked Beulah, sorrowfully.

"I don't know, really. Mrs. Grayson has a brother living somewhere up the country; I suppose he will offer them a home such as he has. I pity her; she is a weak creature—weak, mind and body; and this reverse will come very near killing her."

For some days nothing was discussed but the "Grayson tragedy." It was well the unhappy man could not listen to the fierce maledictions of disappointed creditors and the slanders which were now heaped upon his name. Whatever his motives might have been, the world called his offenses by the darkest names, and angry creditors vowed every knife, fork and spoon should come under the hammer. The elegant house was sold—the furniture with it; and Mrs. Grayson and Claudia removed temporarily to a boarding-house. Not one of their fashionable intimates approached them—no, not one. When Claudia went one day to her mantuamaker, to have her mourning fitted, she met a couple of ladies who had formerly been constant visitors at the house and regular attendants at her parties. Unsuspectingly, she hastened to meet them, but, to her astonishment, instead of greeting her, in their usual fawning manner, they received her with a very cold bow, just touched the tips of her fingers, and, gathering up their robes, swept majestically from the room. Rage and mortification forced the tears into her eyes.

Mrs. Asbury had never admired Mrs. Grayson's character; she visited her formally about twice a year; but now, in this misfortune, she alone called to see her. When Claudia returned from the mantuamaker's she found Mrs. Asbury with her mother, and received from her hand a kind, friendly note from the girl she had so grossly insulted. Beulah was no flatterer; she wrote candidly and plainly; said she would have called at once, had she supposed her company would be acceptable. She would gladly come and see Claudia whenever she desired to see her, and hoped that the memory of other years would teach her the sincerity of her friendship. Claudia wept bitterly, as she read it, and vainly regretted the superciliousness which had alienated one she knew to be noble and trustworthy. She was naturally an impulsive creature, and without a moment's hesitation, dashed off an answer, all blurred with tears, begging Beulah to overlook her "foolishness," and come to see her.

Accordingly, after school, Beulah went to the house where they were boarding. Claudia met her rather awkwardly, but Beulah kissed her as if nothing had ever occurred to mar their intercourse; and after some desultory conversation asked her what they expected to do.

"Heaven only knows! starve, I suppose." She spoke gloomily, and folded her soft white hands over each other, as if the idea of work was something altogether foreign to her mind.

"But, Claudia, I reckon you hardly expect to starve," answered Beulah, who could not forbear smiling.

"Dear knows what is to become of us—I am sure I don't! Mamma has a brother living in some out-of-the-way place up the country. But he does not like me—thinks some of his own children ought to have been adopted in my place. Heaven knows I have made nothing by the operation, but a great disappointment, he need not be uneasy about the amount I am to get. But you see they don't want me, having an old spite at me, and mamma dislikes to ask them to take me; besides, I would almost as soon be buried at once as go to that farm, or plantation, or whatever it is. They have written to mamma to come, and she does not know what to do."

"You are a good musician, are you not?"

"No, not particularly; I never could endure to practise."

"Don't you draw and paint finely—I have heard that you did?"

"Yes, but what good will it do me now, I should like to know?" She twirled her little plump, jewelled fingers indolently.

"It might do you a great deal of good, if you chose. You might support yourself by giving lessons," said Beulah, decisively.

She up drew her shoulders, frowned and pouted without making any answer:

"Claudy, you do not wish to be dependent on a man who dislikes you?"

"Not if I can help myself!"

"And you certainly do not wish to be the means of preventing Mrs. Grayson from having a comfortable home with her brother?"

Claudia burst into tears; she did not love her mother, did not even respect her, she was so very weak and childish; yet the young orphan felt very desolate, and knew not what to do. Beulah took her hand, and said kindly:

"If you are willing to help yourself, dear Claudy, I will gladly do all I can to assist you. I think I can secure you a situation as teacher of drawing, and, until you can make something at it, I will pay your board; and you shall stay with me, if you like. You can think about it, and let me know as soon as you decide."

Claudia thanked her cordially, and returning home Beulah immediately imparted the plan to her friends. They thought it would scarcely succeed, Claudia had been so petted and spoiled. Beulah sat gazing into the fire for awhile; then, looking at the doctor, said abruptly:

"There is that Graham money, sir, doing nobody any good."

"That is just what I have been telling you for the last six years. I have invested it carefully, until it has almost doubled itself."

"It would make them very comfortable," continued she thoughtfully.

"Make them very comfortable?" repeated the doctor, throwing his cigar into the grate, and turning suddenly toward her.

"Yes, Claudia and Mrs. Grayson."

"Beulah Benton! are you going insane, I should like to know? Here you are, working hard every day of your life, and do you suppose I shall suffer you to give that legacy (nearly nine thousand dollars!) to support two broken-down fashionables in idleness? Who ever heard of such a piece of business since the world began? I will not consent to it! I tell you now, the money shall not leave my hands for any such purpose."

"I don't want it myself. I never shall touch a dollar of it for my own use," said she, resolutely.

"All very fine now. But wait till you get superannuated, or such a cripple with rheumatism that you can't hobble to that schoolhouse, which you seem to love better than your own soul. Wait till then, I say, and see whether some of this money will not be very acceptable."

"That time will never come, sir, never!" answered Beulah, laughing.

"Beulah Benton, you are a simpleton!" said he, looking affectionately at her from beneath his shaggy brows.

"I want that money, sir."

"You shall not have one cent of it. The idea of your playing Lady Bountiful to the Graysons! Pshaw! not a picayune shall you have."

"Oh, sir, it would make me so very happy to aid them. You cannot conceive how much pleasure it would afford me."

"Look here, child, all that sort of angelic disinterestedness sounds very well done up in a novel, but the reality is quite another matter. Mrs. Grayson treated you like a brute; and it is not to be expected that you will have any extraordinary degree of affection for her. Human nature is spiteful and unforgiving; and as for your piling coals of fire on her head to the amount of nine thousand dollars, that is being entirely too magnanimous!"

"I want to make Mrs. Grayson amends, sir. Once, when I was maddened by sorrow and pain, I said something which I always repented bitterly." As Beulah spoke, a cloud swept across her face.

"What was it, child? what did you say?"

"I cursed her! besought God to punish her severely for her unkindness to me. I hardly knew what I was saying; but even then it shocked me, and I prayed God to forgive my passion. I shudder when I remember it. I have forgiven her heartlessness long ago; and now, sir, I want you to give me that money. If it is mine at all, it is mine to employ as I choose."

"Cornelia did not leave the legacy to the Graysons."

"Were she living, she would commend the use I am about to make of it. Will you give me five thousand dollars of it?"

"Oh, Beulah, you are a queer compound! a strange being!"

"Will you give me five thousand dollars of that money to-morrow?" persisted Beulah, looking steadily at him.

"Yes, child, if you will have it so." His voice trembled, and he looked at the orphan with moist eyes.

Mrs. Asbury had taken no part in the conversation, but her earnest face attested her interest. Passing her arm around Beulah's waist, she hastily kissed her brow, and only said:

"God bless you, my dear, noble Beulah!"

"I do not see that I am at all magnanimous in giving away other people's money. If I had earned it by hard labor, and then given it to Claudy, there would have been some more show of generosity. Here come Georgia and her husband; you do not need me to read this evening, and I have work to do."

She extricated herself from Mrs. Asbury's clasping arm and retired to her own room. The following day, Claudia came to say that, as she knew not what else to do, she would gladly accept the position mentioned as teacher of drawing and painting. Mrs. Grayson's brother had come to take her home, but she was unwilling to be separated from Claudia. Beulah no longer hesitated, and the sum of five thousand dollars seemed to poor Claudia a fortune indeed. She could not understand how the girl, whom she and her mother had insulted, could possibly have the means of making them so comparatively comfortable. Beulah briefly explained the circumstances which had enabled her to assist them. The bulk of the money remained in Dr. Asbury's hands, and Claudia was to apply to him whenever she needed it. She and her mamma found a cheaper boarding-house, and Claudia's duties began at once. Mrs. Grayson was overwhelmed with shame when the particulars were made known to her, and tears of bitter mortification could not obliterate the memory of the hour when she cruelly denied the prayer of the poor orphan to whom she now owed the shelter above her head. Beulah did not see her for many weeks subsequent; she knew how painful such a meeting would be to the humbled woman, and while she constantly cheered and encouraged Claudia in her work, she studiously avoided Mrs. Grayson's presence.

Thus the winter passed; and once more the glories of a southern spring were scattered over the land. To the Asburys Beulah was warmly attached, and her residence with them was as pleasant as any home could possibly have been, which was not her own. They were all that friends could be to an orphan; still, she regretted her little cottage, and missed the home-feeling she had prized so highly. True, she had constant access to the greenhouse, and was rarely without her bouquet of choice flowers; but these could not compensate her for the loss of her own little garden. She struggled bravely with discontent; tried to look only on the sunshine in her path, and to be always cheerful. In this she partially succeeded; no matter how lonely and sad she felt, she hid it carefully, and the evenings in the library were never marred by words of repining or looks of sorrow. To the close observer, there were traces of grief in her countenance; and sometimes when she sat sewing while Mrs. Asbury read aloud, it was easy to see that her thoughts had wandered far from that little room. Time had changed her singularly since the old Asylum days. She was now a finely-formed, remarkably graceful woman, with a complexion of dazzling transparency. She was always pale, but the blue veins might be traced anywhere on her brow and temples; and the dark, gray eyes, with their long, jetty, curling lashes, possessed an indescribable charm, even for strangers. She had been an ugly child, but certainly she was a noble-looking, if not handsome woman. To all but the family with whom she resided, she was rather reserved; and while the world admired and eulogized her talents as a writer, she felt that, except Eugene, she had no friends beyond the threshold of the house she lived in. As weeks and months elapsed, and no news of her wandering guardian came, her hope began to pale. For weary years it had burned brightly, but constant disappointment was pressing heavily on her heart, and crushing out the holy spark. The heart-strings will bear rude shocks and sudden rough-handling, but the gradual tightening, the unremitted tension of long, tediously-rolling years, will in time accomplish what fierce assaults cannot. Continually she prayed for his return, but, despite her efforts, her faith grew fainter as each month crept by, and her smile became more constrained and joyless. She never spoke of her anxiety, never alluded to him, but pressed her hands over her aching heart and did her work silently—nay, cheerfully.

CHAPTER XL.

The day was dull, misty and gusty. All the morning there had been a driving southeasterly rain; but toward noon, there was a lull. The afternoon was heavy and threatening, while armies of dense clouds drifted before the wind. Dr. Asbury had not yet returned from his round of evening visits; Mrs. Asbury had gone to the Asylum to see a sick child, and Georgia was dining with her husband's mother. Beulah came home from school more than usually fatigued; one of the assistant teachers was indisposed, and she had done double work to relieve her. She sat before her desk, writing industriously on an article she had promised to complete before the end of the week. Her head ached; the lines grew dim, and she laid aside her manuscript and leaned her face on her palms. The beautiful lashes lay against her brow, for the eyes were raised to the portrait above her desk, and she gazed up at the faultless features with an expression of sad hopelessness. Years had not filled the void in her heart with other treasures. At this hour it ached with its own desolation, and extending her arms imploringly toward the picture she exclaimed sorrowfully:

"O my God, how long must I wait? Oh, how long!"

She opened the desk, and taking out a key, left her room, and slowly ascended to the third story. Charon crept up the steps after her. She unlocked the apartment which Mrs. Asbury had given into her charge some time before, and raising one of the windows, looped back the heavy blue curtains which gave a somber hue to all within. From this elevated position she could see the stormy, sullen waters of the bay breaking against the wharves, and hear their hoarse muttering as they rocked themselves to rest after the scourging of the tempest. Gray clouds hung low, and scudded northward;

everything looked dull and gloomy. She turned from the window and glanced around the room. It was at all times a painful pleasure to come here, and now, particularly the interior impressed her sadly. Here were the paintings and statues she had long been so familiar with, and here, too, the melodeon which at rare intervals she opened. The house was very quiet; not a sound came up from below; she raised the lid of the instrument, and played a plaintive prelude. Echoes, seven or eight years old, suddenly fell on her ears; she had not heard one note of this air since she left Dr. Hartwell's roof. It was a favorite song of his; a German hymn he had taught her, and now after seven years she sang it. It was a melancholy air, and as her trembling voice rolled through the house, she seemed to live the old days over again. But the words died away on her lips; she had over-estimated her strength; she could not sing it. The marble images around her, like ghosts of the past, looked mutely down at her grief. She could not weep; her eyes were dry, and there was an intolerable weight on her heart. Just before her stood the Niobe, rigid and woeful; she put her hands over her eyes, and drooped her face on the melodeon. Gloom and despair crouched at her side, their gaunt hands tugging at the anchor of hope. The wind rose and howled round the corners of the house; how fierce it might be on trackless seas, driving lonely barks down to ruin, and strewing the main with ghastly upturned faces. She shuddered and groaned. It was a dark hour of trial, and she struggled desperately with the phantoms that clustered about her. Then there came other sounds: Charon's shrill, frantic bark and whine of delight. For years she had not heard that peculiar bark, and started up in wonder. On the threshold stood a tall form, with a straw hat drawn down over the features, but Charon's paws were on the shoulders, and his whine of delight ceased not. He fell down at his master's feet and caressed them. Beulah looked an instant, and sprang into the doorway, holding out her arms, with a wild, joyful cry:

"Come at last! Oh, thank God! Come at last!" Her face was radiant, her eyes burned, her glowing lips parted.

Leaning against the door, with his arms crossed over his broad chest, Dr. Hartwell stood, silently regarding her. She came close to him, and her extended arms trembled, still he did not move, did not speak.

"Oh, I knew you would come; and, thank God, now you are here. Come home at last!"

She looked up at him so eagerly; but he said nothing. She stood an instant irresolute, then threw her arms around his neck, and laid her head on his bosom, clinging closely to him. He did not return the embrace, but looked down at the beaming face, and sighed; then he put his hand softly on her head, and smoothed the rippling hair. A brilliant smile broke over her features, as she felt the remembered touch of his fingers on her forehead, and she repeated in the low tones of deep gladness.

"I knew you would come; oh, sir, I knew you would come back to me!"

"How did you know it, child?" he said, for the first time.

Her heart leaped wildly at the sound of the loved voice she had so longed to hear, and she answered, tremblingly:

"Because for weary years I have prayed for your return. Oh, only God knows how fervently I prayed; and he has heard me."

She felt his strong frame quiver; he folded his arms about her, clasped her to his heart with a force that almost suffocated her, and bending his head kissed her passionately. Suddenly his arms relaxed their clasp; holding her off, he looked at her keenly, and said:

"Beulah Benton, do you belong to the tyrant Ambition, or do you belong to that tyrant, Guy Hartwell? Quick, child, decide."

"I have decided," said she. Her cheeks burned; her lashes drooped.

"Well!"

"Well, if I am to have a tyrant, I believe I prefer belonging to you?"

He frowned. She smiled and looked up at him.

"Beulah, I don't want a grateful wife. Do you understand me?"

"Yes, sir."

Just then his eyes rested on the portrait of Creola, which hung opposite. He drew back a step, and she saw the blood leave his lips, as he gazed upon it. Lifting his hand, he said sternly:

"Ah, what pale spectres that face calls up from the grim, gray ruins of memory! Doubtless you know my miserable history. I married her, thinking I had won her love. She soon undeceived me. We separated. I once asked you to be my wife, and you told me you would rather die. Child, years have not dealt lightly with me since then. I am no longer a young man. Look here." He threw off his hat, and passing his fingers through his curling hair, she saw, here and there, streaks of silver. He watched her as she noted it. She saw, too, how haggard he looked, now that the light fell full on his pale face. The splendid, dark eyes were unaltered, and as they looked down into hers, tears gathered on her lashes, her lips trembled, and throwing her arms again round his neck, she laid her face on his shoulder.

"Beulah, do you cling to me because you love me? or because you pity me? or because you are grateful to me for past love and kindness? Answer me, Beulah."

"Because you are my all."

"How long have I been your all?"

"Oh, longer than I knew myself!" was the evasive reply.

He tried to look at her, but she pressed her face close to his shoulder, and would not suffer it.

"Beulah?"

"Sir."

"Oh, don't 'sir' me, child? I want to know the truth, and you will not satisfy me."

"I have told you the truth."

"Have you learned that fame is an icy shadow? that gratified ambition cannot make you happy? Do you love me?"

"Yes."

"Better than teaching school, and writing learned articles."

"Rather better, I believe, sir."

"Beulah?"

"Well, sir."

"You have changed in many things, since we parted nearly six years ago?"

"Yes, I thank God, I am changed. My infidelity was a source of many sorrows; but the clouds have passed from my mind; I have found the truth in holy writ." Now she raised her head, and looked at him very earnestly.

"Child, does your faith make you happy?"

"Yes, the universe could not purchase it," she answered solemnly.

There was a brief silence. He put both hands on her shoulders, and stooping down, kissed her brow.

"And you prayed for me, Beulah?"

"Yes, evening and morning. Prayed that you might be shielded from all dangers, and brought safely home. And there was one other thing, which I prayed for not less fervently than for your return: that God would melt your hard, bitter heart, and give you a knowledge of the truth of the Christian religion. Oh, sir, I thought sometimes that possibly you might die in a far-off land, and then I should see you no more, in time or eternity! and oh, the thought nearly drove me wild! My guardian, my all, let me not have prayed in vain." She clasped his hand in hers, and looked up pleadingly into the loved face; and, for the first time in her life, she saw tears glistening in the burning eyes. He said nothing, however; took her face in his hands, and scanned it earnestly, as if reading all that had passed during his long absence. Presently he asked:

"So you would not marry Lindsay, and go to Congress. Why not?"

"Who told you anything about him?"

"No matter. Why did not you marry him?"

"Because I did not love him."

"He is a noble hearted, generous man."

"Yes, very; I do not know his superior."

"What?"

"I mean what I say," said she, firmly.

He smiled, one of his genial, irresistible smiles; and she smiled also, despite herself. "Give me your hand, Beulah?"

She did so very quietly.

"There—is it mine?"

"Yes, sir, if you want it."

"And may I claim it as soon as I choose?"

"Yes, sir."

She had never seen him look as he did then. His face kindled, as if in a broad flash of light; the eyes dazzled her, and she turned her face away, as he drew her once more to his bosom, and exclaimed:

"At last, then, after years of sorrow, and pain, and bitterness, I shall be happy in my own home; shall have a wife, a companion, who loves me for myself alone. Ah, Beulah, my idol, I will make you happy!"

The rain fell heavily, and it grew dark, for the night came rapidly down. There was a furious ringing of the library bell, the doctor had come home, and, as usual, wanted half a dozen things at once.

"Have you seen Dr. Asbury?"

"No. I came directly to the house; saw no one as I entered; and hearing the melodeon, followed the sound."

"What a joyful surprise it will be to him!" said Beulah, closing the window, and locking the melodeon. She led the way down the steps, followed by her guardian and Charon.

"Suppose you wait awhile in the music-room? It adjoins the library, and you can see and hear, without being seen," suggested she, with her hand on the bolt of the door. He assented, and stood near the threshold which connected the rooms, while Beulah went into the library. The gas burned brightly, and the doctor sat leaning far back in his arm-chair, with his feet on an ottoman. His wife stood near him, stroking the gray hair from his furrowed brow.

"Alice, I wish, dear, you would get me an iced lemonade, will you?"

"Let me make it for you," said Beulah, coming forward.

"Not you! At your peril, you touch it. You are over fond of the sour, miss. Alice knows exactly how to suit me."

"So you have turned homœopathist? take acids to—"

"None of your observations, if you please. Just be good enough to open the shutters, will you? It is as hot in this room, as if the equator ran between my feet and the wall. Charming weather, eh? And still more charming prospect, that I shall have to go out into it again before bed-time. One of my delectable patients has taken it into his head to treat his wife and children to a rare show, in the shape of a fit of mania-a-potu; and ten to one, I shall have to play spectator all night." He yawned as he spoke.

"You have an arduous time indeed," began Beulah; but he hastily put in:

"Oh, of all the poor devils, we pill-box gentry do have the hardest times! I am sick of patients; sick of physic; sick of the very sound of my own name."

"If my guardian were only here to relieve—"

"Confound your guardian! Don't mention him in my presence. He is a simpleton. He is what the Ettrick Shepherd calls a 'Sumph.' You have no guardian, I can tell you that. Before this, he has gone through all the transmigrations of 'Indur,' and the final metempsychosis, gave him to the world a Celestial. Yes, child, a Celestial. I fancy him at this instant, with two long plaits of hair trailing behind him, as, with all the sublime complacency of Celestials, he stalks majestically along, picking tea leaves. Confound your guardian. Mention his name to me again, at the peril of having your board raised."

"George, what is the matter with you?" asked his wife, smiling, as she handed him the lemonade he had desired.

"This prating young woman is, as usual, trying to discourse of—Alice, this is just right. Thank you, my dear." He drained the glass, and handed it back. Beulah stood, so that the light shone full on her face. He looked at her a moment, and exclaimed:

"Come here, child. What ails you? Why, bless my soul, Beulah, what is the matter? I never saw the blood in your face before; and your great solemn eyes seem to be dancing a jig. What ails you, child?" He grasped her hands eagerly.

"Nothing ails me; I am well—"

"I know better! Has Charon gone mad and bit you? Oho! by all the dead gods of Greece, Guy has come home. Where is he? Where is he?"

He sprang up, nearly knocking his wife down, and looked around the room. Dr. Hartwell emerged from the music-room and advanced to meet him.

"Oh, Guy! You heathen! you Philistine! you prodigal!"

He bounded over a chair, and locked his arms around the tall form, while his gray head dropped on his friend's shoulder. Beulah stole out quickly, and in the solitude of her own room, fell on her knees, and returned thanks to the God who hears and answers prayer.

CHAPTER XLI.

It was a sparkling August morning—one of those rare days, when all nature seems jubilant. The waters of the bay glittered like a sheet of molten silver; the soft southern breeze sang through the tree-tops and the cloudless sky wore that deep shade of pure blue, which is nowhere so beautiful as in our sunny South. Clad in a dress of spotless white, with her luxuriant hair braided, and twined with white flowers, Beulah stood beside her window, looking out into the street below. Her hands were clasped tightly over her heart, and on one slender finger blazed a costly diamond, the seal of her betrothal. She was very pale; now and then her lips quivered, and her lashes were wet with tears. Yet this was her marriage day. She had just risen from her knees, and her countenance told of a troubled heart. She loved her guardian above everything else; knew that, separated from him, life would be a dreary blank to her; yet, much as she loved him, she could not divest herself of a species of fear, of dread. The thought of being his wife filled her with vague apprehension. He had hastened the marriage; the old place had been thoroughly repaired and refurnished, and this morning she would go home a wife. She clasped her hands over her eyes; the future looked fearful. She knew the passionate, exacting nature of the man with whose destiny she was about to link her own, and she shrank back, as the image of Creola rose before her. The door opened, and Mrs. Asbury entered, accompanied by Dr. Hartwell. The orphan looked up, and leaned heavily against the window. Mrs. Asbury broke the silence.

"They are waiting for you, my dear. The minister came some moments ago. The clock has struck ten."

She handed her a pair of gloves from the table, and stood in the door, waiting for her. Beulah drew them on, and then, with a long breath, glanced at Dr. Hartwell. He looked restless, and she thought sterner, than she had seen him since his return. He was very pale and his lips were compressed firmly.

"You look frightened, Beulah. You tremble," said he, drawing her arm through his, and fixing his eyes searchingly on her face.

"Yes. Oh, yes. I believe I am frightened," she answered with a constrained smile.

She saw his brow darken, and his cheek flush, but he said no more, and led her down to the parlor, where the members of the family were assembled. Claudia and Eugene were also present. The minister met them in the center of the room; and there, in the solemn hush, a few questions were answered, a plain band of gold encircled her finger, and the deep tones of the clergyman pronounced her Guy Hartwell's wife. Eugene took her in his arms and kissed her tenderly, whispering:

"God bless you, dear sister and friend! I sincerely hope that your married life will prove happier than mine."

Their congratulations wearied her, and she was glad when the carriage came to bear her away. Bidding adieu to her friends she was handed into the carriage, and Dr. Hartwell took the seat beside her. The ride was short; neither spoke, and when the door was opened, and she entered the well-remembered house, she would gladly have retreated to the greenhouse, and sought solitude to collect her thoughts; but a hand caught hers, and she soon found herself seated on a sofa in the study. She felt that a pair of eyes were riveted on her face, and suddenly the blood surged into her white cheeks. Her hand lay clasped in his, and her head drooped lower, to avoid his searching gaze.

"Oh, Beulah! my wife! why are you afraid of me?"

The low, musical tones caused her heart to thrill strangely, she made a great effort, and lifted her head. She saw the expression of sorrow that clouded his face; saw his white brow wrinkle; and as her eyes fell on the silver threads scattered through his brown hair, there came an instant revolution of feeling; fear vanished; love reigned supreme. She threw her arms up about his neck, and exclaimed:

"I am not afraid of you now. May God bless my guardian! my husband!"

Reader, marriage is not the end of life; it is but the beginning of a new course of duties; but I cannot now follow Beulah. Henceforth, her history is bound up with another's. To save her husband from his unbelief is the labor of future years. She had learned to suffer, and to bear patiently; and though her path looks sunny, and her heart throbs with happy hopes, this one shadow lurks over her home and dims her joys. Weeks and months glided swiftly on. Dr. Hartwell's face lost its stern rigidity, and his smile became constantly genial. His wife was his idol; day by day, his love for her seemed more completely to revolutionize his nature. His cynicism melted insensibly away; his lips forgot their iron compression; now and then, his long-forgotten laugh rang through the house. Beulah was conscious of the power she wielded, and trembled lest she fail to employ it properly. One Sabbath afternoon, she sat in her room, with her cheek on her hand, absorbed in earnest thought. Her little Bible lay on her lap, and she was pondering the text she had heard that morning. Charon came and nestled his huge head against her. Presently she heard the quick tramp of hoofs and whir of wheels; and soon after her husband entered and sat down beside her.

"What are you thinking of?" said he, passing his hand over her head, carelessly.

"Thinking of my life—of the bygone years of struggle."

"They are past, and can trouble you no more. 'Let the dead past bury its dead!'"

"No, my past can never die. I ponder it often, and it does me good; strengthens me, by keeping me humble. I was just thinking of the dreary, desolate days and nights I passed, searching for a true philosophy, and going further astray with every effort. I was so proud of my intellect; put so much faith in my own powers; it was no wonder I was so benighted."

"Where is your old worship of genius?" asked her husband, watching her curiously.

"I have not lost it all. I hope I never shall. Human genius has accomplished a vast deal for man's temporal existence. The physical sciences have been wheeled forward in the march of mind, and man's earthly path gemmed with all that a merely sensual nature could desire. But looking aside from these channels, what has it effected for philosophy, that great burden, which constantly recalls the fabled labors of Sisyphus and the Danaides? Since the rising of Bethlehem's star in the cloudy sky of polytheism, what has human genius discovered of God, eternity, destiny? Metaphysicians build gorgeous cloud palaces, but the soul cannot dwell in their cold, misty atmosphere. Antiquarians wrangle and write; Egypt's moldering monuments are raked from their desert graves, and made the theme of scientific debate; but has all this learned disputation contributed one iota to clear the thorny way of strict morality? Put the Bible out of sight, and how much will human intellect discover concerning our origin—our ultimate destiny? In the morning of time, sages handled these vital questions, and died, not one step nearer the truth than when they began. Now, our philosophers struggle, earnestly and honestly, to make plain the same inscrutable mysteries. Yes, blot out the records of Moses, and we would grope in starless night; for notwithstanding the many priceless blessings it has discovered for man, the torch of science will never pierce and illumine the recesses over which Almighty God has hung his veil. Here we see, indeed, as 'through a glass, darkly.' Yet I believe the day is already dawning, when scientific data will not only cease to be antagonistic to scriptural accounts, but will deepen the impress of Divinity on the pages of holy writ; when 'the torch shall be taken out of the hand of the infidel, and set to burn in the temple of the living God;' when Science and Religion shall link hands. I revere the lonely thinkers to whom the world is indebted for its great inventions. I honor the tireless laborers who toil in laboratories; who sweep midnight skies, in search of new worlds; who upheave primeval rocks, hunting for footsteps of Deity; and I believe that every scientific fact will ultimately prove but another ramp, planted along the path which leads to a knowledge of Jehovah! Ah! it is indeed peculiarly the duty of Christians, 'to watch, with reverence and joy, the unveiling of the august brow of Nature, by the hand of Science; and to be ready to call mankind to a worship ever new!' Human thought subserves many useful, nay, noble ends; the Creator gave it, as a powerful instrument, to improve man's temporal condition; but oh, sir, I speak of what I know, when I say: alas, for that soul who forsakes the divine ark, and embarks on the gilded toys of man's invention, hoping to breast the billows of life, and be anchored safely in the harbor of eternal rest! The heathens, 'having no law, are a law unto themselves;' but for such as deliberately reject the given light, only bitter darkness remains. I know it; for I, too, once groped, wailing for help."

"Your religion is full of mystery," said her husband, gravely.

"Yes, of divine mystery. Truly, 'a God comprehended is no God at all!' Christianity is clear, as to rules of life and duty. There is no mystery left about the directions to man; yet there is a divine mystery infolding it, which tells of its divine origin, and promises a fuller revelation when man is fitted to receive it. If it were not so, we would call it man's invention. You turn from Revelation, because it contains some things you cannot comprehend; yet you plunge into a deeper, darker mystery, when you embrace the theory of an eternal, self-existing universe, having no intelligent creator, yet constantly creating intelligent beings. Sir, can you understand how matter creates mind?"

She had laid her Bible on his knee; her folded hands rested upon it, and her gray eyes, clear and earnest, looked up reverently into her husband's noble face. His soft hand wandered over her head, and he seemed pondering her words.

May God aid the wife in her holy work of love.